I0788781

ORDER OF
SCORPIONS

ORDER OF SCORPIONS

Copyright © 2022 by Ivy Asher

All rights reserved.

Edited by Polished Perfection
Cover by David Gardias at Best Selling Covers
Book Design and Typesetting: Enchanted Ink Publishing

ISBN: 978-1-959537-00-7 (Hardcover)

WWW.IVYASHER.COM

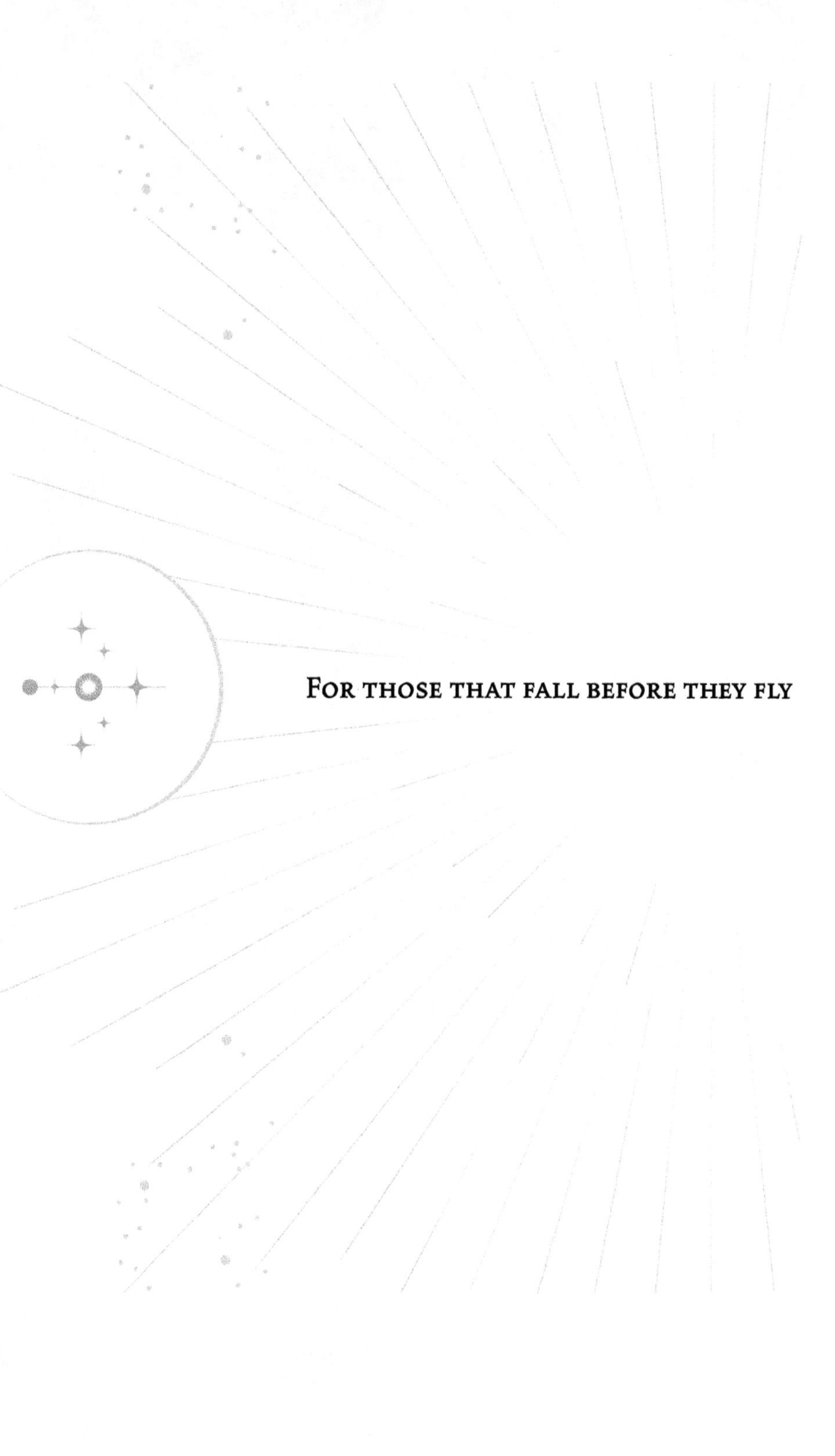

For those that fall before they fly

Order of Scorpions
IVY ASHER

1

LOUD CLANG OF METAL SLAMMING AGAINST metal jolts me awake. Stale air reeking of filthy bodies and unwashed chamber pots fills my lungs, and I gag at the offensive stench. Bitter cold settles deep in my bones, eliciting a shiver and igniting a flare of confusion.

Where am I?

The thought feels thick and hazy as it tumbles around in my mind. I try to open my eyes, but they're crusted shut. There's a twinge of pain from the pull of my eyelashes as I struggle to open my lids, and I rub at my eyes to clear them. My heart kicks up with worry as foreign, unwelcome sensations continue to assault my senses.

Something is very wrong.

I don't know what's happening or why my body aches as though it's been to war. I try to piece my chaotic confusion together, but it's as though I'm attempting to boil water with a fire that's all but gone out. I fight against the pounding in my head and the panic in my chest, and painfully I force my eyelids open. All I find for my struggle is endless layers of blackness all around me.

A quiet groan slips out of my mouth when I turn my head to better take in my inky surroundings. The slight movement invites the ache in my skull to spread down my neck and into my shoulders. Pain rolls through me like wind-pestered ripples over the surface of a glassy lake, and I pull in deep breaths of fetid air to try to fight the black spots that start to speckle my already dark vision.

Nausea roils in my belly, and I clench my fists, the movement a lethargic reaction to the misery coursing through me. My short nails scrape roughly against the frigid floor I'm sprawled across as the need to fight whoever has done this to me floats in my blood. Too bad everything about where I am or *why* is blank. It's as though someone hastily erased all the vital details of who I am, leaving only streaks of chalk and murky clouds of dust in their wake.

Barely suppressed sobs draw my attention somewhere to my left. My eyes struggle to adjust, to bring into focus what the surrounding blackness has wrapped in its cloying grip. I swallow down my trepidation, suddenly noticing the flavor of terror in my mouth as though it crawled inside, died, and has been rotting on my tongue for who knows how long. Bile tickles the back of my throat as my eyes finally sharpen in the drowning darkness all around me. I blink once against the onslaught of images, straining to catalog things as I take them in.

It isn't just the chilly stone underneath my battered limbs that's sapping my body of heat and comfort. There are metal bars surrounding me. Tall ominous rods embedded into a frosty stone floor and capped off by a baleful blackened metal top.

I'm in a cage.

A cage in part made of iron, and that realization triggers a jolt of panic and adrenaline—although I can't seem to remember why or how I recognize the danger in this metal. My body is clearly trying to tell me something, something it thinks I should know, but everything in my head is leaden and vacuous. Somehow, the parts of me I *need* in order to understand these reactions, are missing. Fear spikes even harder in my chest. My heart gallops like it's surging for first in a race. My body is responding in kind to my frantic emotions, but my thoughts are tripping all over themselves. My head is in last place with no hope of catching up to my body.

I squint into the darkness, seeing more cages. They line the walls of the room, some empty, their open maws ready and waiting to devour unsuspecting victims. Others are filled with helpless heaps like me. Once again I hear the hushed, terrified cadence of soft crying. I try to trace the shattered song to its source, but I can't tell where it's coming from.

Panic unfurls in my belly, and pain screams through my arms as I force myself up from the ground on shaky limbs. A silvery lock of hair falls into my face as I move. I freeze.

Staring at the unusual hue of the wisps, I wait for the color or texture to trigger some kind of recognition, any kind of cognizance in my addled, pockmarked mind. Nothing comes. I reach for a tuft, tugging at it gently, and feel the roots of the strands tighten against my scalp. It's definitely my hair.

Why do I feel so confused by that?

I sit up further, despite the warning twinge from my stiff and angry muscles. I rake long fingers through my tresses, pushing the dense strands out of my face. The ends tickle my lower back, but it's my hands that I've now pulled in front of me to stare at.

I don't know them.

Dread lodges in the base of my throat, thick and intrusive, as I run the pads of my fingers over the unfamiliar features of my face. Long lashes, straight nose, puffy lips, pointed ears, these are things I know, and yet...I don't. I'm not shocked by what I find at the tips of my fingers, but an image of what those parts create as a whole doesn't filter into my mind.

I don't know who I am.

Alarm-tinged certainty clings to that fact. I try to muddle through my memories, to look for anything that exists beyond waking up inside of this cage, but there's nothing there. My mind is black and barren, and all I find are questions and fear flying around inside of me like feathers on a violent rush of wind.

What's going on?

Faint shouting erupts somewhere outside of the room of cages, and a few of the others locked inside these iron bars release terrified squeaks of warning. Once again my body responds as though it knows exactly what they're afraid of. Adrenaline surges in my veins, helping to clear some of the cobwebs from my head and the ache from my limbs. Dismay tightens my muscles, and my heart starts to beat so loud and so fast that it's suddenly all I can hear. It's as though the blaring rhythm is trying to drown out the sounds of what's coming, trying to protect me from the horrors of what I'm going to encounter.

Instinct has me scurrying back in my cage, trying to get as far as I can from whatever is going on. A sizzling sting rips through my bare shoulders as they come in contact with the bars at my back. I yelp as I jerk away from the burning iron rods. The smell of scorched skin clings to the inside of my nose as I scramble to the middle of my cage. I reach behind me, hissing as my fingertips test the throbbing new injuries. It seems that my sleeveless shift protected my back at least, but I burned the backs of my shoulders and both arms. A helpless whimper slips from my lips as I huddle in the middle of my cage, eyeing the iron barriers as the yelling outside gets louder.

Iron hurts the fae.

Out of nowhere, my fear-laden mind provides this fact as though it's something I should know.

Fae.

Is that what I am? I wait expectantly as though the answer will pop up in my head just as unbidden and unexpected as the previous thought, but nothing comes. There's no sense of knowing or rightness at the notion of *fae*, only pain and panic.

The heavy tread of multiple feet reverberates somewhere outside the room of cages. I watch helplessly as other prisoners fold in on themselves as though they're trying to disappear into the darkness itself.

"What's happening?" I rasp, surprise moving through me at the discovery that I can use my voice for more than just whimpers and pained groans.

Before anyone can so much as wince in my direction, a large door at one end of the room slides open with a piercing screech. My eyes snap shut from the painful stab of light that slices into the room. I cover my head with my arms at the sound, my sensitive ears pounding from the abuse. No matter how much it makes me ache, I force myself to peek at the newcomers. I need answers, and I can't hide away from finding them, no matter how petrified I am.

"Which one is she in?" a snarling voice demands.

I can only make out dark, blurry silhouettes against the bright backlight. Two towering blobs and one much smaller and leaner dark visage.

"The far back kennel, Dorsin. The one away from the others," one of the big blobs grumbles, pique and displeasure layered in his obedient response.

"Bring her to my office like you were told to do from the beginning," the smaller silhouette, the one the other just called Dorsin, bellows. I automatically flinch from the exploding rage of the command.

An angry stomp of footfall starts and then quickly fades away as Dorsin's sliver of darkness grows smaller and smaller until it's swallowed up by the light of a long hallway. Then the two massive outlines step away from the light and begin to move through the room of cages. The brightness at their backs hides their features, but menace and fury pulse off the figures as they soundlessly make their way closer.

The smell of piss suddenly permeates the room. I look and see pools form around some of the other caged and huddled beings, their fear all at once stronger than their ability to hold their bladder. The direction the two mountainous males are moving in makes my stomach drop. Terror starts to choke me, and I fight the urge to close my eyes and pretend none of this is happening.

The light at the entrance only stretches so far, and as the hulking shadows close the distance, darkness works to paint the terrifying duo before slowly revealing their features. When the dark gray skin, slitted yellow eyes, and smashed facial features become apparent, the word *orc* screams in my head. I know that's what they are, just like I suddenly know they're members of the Night Court and native to the lava mines. Yet amidst all that certainty, there's still nothing but blankness when I scramble to search for anything that could explain who I am or what they want with me.

They reach for the front of my cage, and I hurry to get as far away from them as I can. Burning iron bars at my back once again immediately stop my retreat, and my pained shriek has one of the orcs humming in satisfaction as though my cry is its favorite sound in all of the realms.

"Please don't hurt me," I beg, my voice barely a croak, as a black key slides smoothly into the lock of my cage. With a flick of a thick wrist, the front of my enclosure swings open with a terrible weighted silence.

My gaze darts around, desperate for a path that leads to escape, or for help, but all that's there is the cool taunt of iron and the barbarous bulk of orc. Rounded claws tip the hulking hand that reaches for me, and dread slips out of my mouth on a mewl that quickly transforms to an anguished cry as he wraps his fist in my hair and yanks me brutally out of the cage. My hands shoot to the fist in my locks, leaving me defenseless to the palm that wraps around my throat. My tormented and horror-filled sounds are cut off when the orc tightens his grip on my neck and holds me in the air like I'm nothing more than a naughty *cria* in need of discipline.

Hot piss runs down my leg as I claw at the choking grip on my throat.

"Your fear is making me hard, little gash," a gravelly voice declares from behind me as the heat radiating off of him engulfs me.

The orc's thick armor-like skin presses against my back, and a sickeningly long, wet, and warm tongue moves up my cheek. He licks the tracks of tears spilling down one side of my face and then moves to lick the other side as the orc in front of me watches with lurid excitement. The iron burns on my shoulders turn agonizing against the inferno of the orc's skin, and black edges begin to frame my terrified, watery vision.

"Let me hear her, Ghat," the orc at my back commands, and the hand at my throat loosens as a large arm wraps around my waist to anchor me to one of the monster's bodies.

I wheeze and gasp, begging my lungs to fill and empty, over and over again, as pathetic whimpers pour out of me and fresh tears trail down my face.

"Please," I implore, the single angst-laced word all my damaged throat can manage before the hand tightens around my neck in warning.

"Begging for us already, is she, Eorn?" the orc at my front asks, his slitted yellow eyes raking over me with nauseating promises glowing in their depths.

He reaches for the urine-soaked hem of my shift, pulling it up with a jerk, and I explode into frenzied action. I fight and kick and scratch to get away, but the grip on my throat tightens until enclosing black threatens to take me and exhaustion weighs down every limb. My pitiful attempts to break away are useless, the orc's hold on me certain, and I try to embrace the anger surging through me and not give in to the helplessness that's now threatening to pull me under like an anchor.

They laugh as I impotently battle and try to keep their hands from my hips. The arm around my abdomen tightens as the orc in front of me, Ghat, bends over. His lips split into a vicious smile. Sharp teeth gleam at me before he juts out a thick black tongue. He licks a streak of piss from my thigh, loosening his hold on my neck as he laps up another and another. I'm horrified, and disgusted, and painfully aware that each lick is getting closer and closer to parts of me I would never offer freely to a beast like him. Hysteria and horror work to take over my every thought as I desperately gasp for air now that the orc's hold on my throat has loosened.

Ghat watches me, his salacious gaze never leaving mine as he licks the wet evidence of fear from my legs like he's savoring it. His eyes light up at the fright and alarm in mine, and he looks down at my piss-stained underwear and then up at me like he wants there to be no doubt where this is going.

"Come, brother, you know Dorsin doesn't like to be kept waiting. He's already all twisted up about this little prize," the orc at my back, Eorn, announces as he nuzzles my neck.

His breath reeks of rotten meat, and I try not to gag as another weak whimper crawls up my throat. Ghat growls irritably, but after another long revolting lick up my inner thigh, he straightens up. "Think he'll let us play with her later?" he asks.

"I don't think we'll get to come to this one's screams unless her people don't pay up. This was a big job though. I bet he gives us a couple of the others, lets us break them in before they're sold off," Eorn replies, a smile stretching across his horrible face.

I study the threatening gleam that grows in Ghat's eyes at his brother's words, then all of a sudden, his nails dig into my hip. I gasp in pain and ready myself to uselessly try to fight him off, but with a quick yank, he tears my underwear free from my body, laughing as he steps away from me. His hand drops from my throat, and he brings the crotch of the fabric he just tore from me to his mouth and starts to suck on it.

I don't know if I want to vomit with relief that he's no longer touching me or in revulsion at the fact that my soiled underwear is in the monster's mouth. Eorn laughs, the grating sound wrapping around me from behind just like his massive arm is. He snickers as though he just read my thoughts and finds my repugnance amusing. His brother did just lick urine from my skin as though it were petal wine, so I doubt I'm far off. Eorn drops me down his chest, and just when I think he's going to set me on my feet, he grinds against the bare cheeks of my ass. The leather of his pants does little to cover the feel of his hard prick against me, and I wail pitifully as I try to push out of his hold and away from the threat in his leathers.

"By the Kings, I hope they don't pay for you. I can tell you'd be so ripe and fun. Wouldn't you, little gash?" he asks as he and his brother start to move toward the brightly lit entrance.

Eorn takes every opportunity to continue to grind me against his dick with each step. He's so gargantuan that my toes dangle almost three feet from the floor. His arm around me is a steel band, and there's little I can do other than take what he's rubbing against me as he and his brother lead me out of the room of cages. I hurry to look at the others enclosed in the iron-barred cells, to search for anything that might spark recognition, but eyes are hidden and faces are buried deep in the protective embrace of shivering arms. I can only make out dark stringy hair and other beings who look like they're nothing more than a pile of rags and hopelessness.

"She would be fun," Ghat agrees. "You'd bleed all over my cock and scream nice and loud, wouldn't you, little gash?" he growls, leaning menacingly closer and then laughing when I shiver with abhorrence.

The clang of a door slides shut behind me, and I try to squint through the overwhelming brightness of the wide sandstone hallway we're now striding through. Nothing looks familiar. The orc's comments about "my people" don't conjure any flashes of memory. All I can focus on is trying to ignore the vile orc's length against my ass and the cold wetness of my shift as it clings to my upper thighs.

Ghat moves in front, checking the turns in the maze of halls and corridors as we go. Their steps are silent, which is surprising for two massive beings, and I get the impression that they don't want anyone to see us. I have no idea why that would be, but between the stifling terror clawing through my chest, my efforts to ignore the threat pressing against my backside with every step, and the fact that I'm being taken to someone worse than these two, the question of *why* they don't want someone seeing them doesn't rank high on my list of emergent worries.

Quicker than I realize, we arrive at a pair of plain white-oak double doors. Ghat bangs loudly three times, pauses, knocks once, waits a few more seconds, and then knocks one more time in some kind of code. The walls around me are large bricks of tan sandstone, and the floor is a thick slab of something else in the same color. There are no windows, but bright fairy light glows in hanging lanterns on the walls, illuminating the space as though it's midday.

The burns on my back throb, and the bruises that I know are forming around my neck and torso answer the call with their own pained pulse. I feel utterly depleted and afraid. I don't know if it's good or bad that the desolate wasteland that is my memory has no idea what's lying in wait on the other side of these doors. Unfortunately, I'm certain that scum like these orcs only bow to bigger, scarier things, and *that* hard understanding has my battered body shaking with frigid fear and my empty stomach churning with acrid consternation.

A low whine comes from Ghat at the door, and his yellow eyes are fixed on me again. He draws in a deep, slow inhale, his dark gray skin almost glimmering in the fairy light. His muscles look even bigger and more formidable than they did before. His leathers hug the tree trunks he has for legs and the vile member that's hard against his inner left thigh. Straps for more blades than I can count are built into the design of the orc's trousers. He's barefoot, his toenails black and long, and the awareness that they're not wearing any other armor or clothing on their upper halves trickles into my mind. It's as though they're comfortable here, like wherever we are is home.

I pull in a deep breath as a booming *enter* sounds off from the other side of the double doors. I don't smell any sulfur or ash, two scents that would definitely taint the air if we were in the lava mines. The atmosphere is dry and warm, or maybe that heat is coming from Eorn, the orc who's still grinding threateningly against me. His brother opens the door, and I'm rushed in behind him. The tall doors slam shut at our backs, the sound almost deafening in the silence of the vast quarters we enter.

My blood runs cold at the sight of a large bed piled with blankets and pillows in various lush and expensive fabrics. Immense hand-painted tapestries hang on the walls, scenes of rich greenery and beautiful flowers covering their surfaces.

The Dawn Court, my mind supplies, but why I know *that* and not my name is starting to feel more maddening than the orc dick now pressed into my back. My fearful gaze lands on a dark blond fae sitting behind a wide, elaborately carved desk. His fingers are steepled in front of him, and his bright blue eyes take in my every shiver. His gaze drops to the orc arm wrapped around my waist and the yellow wet spots on my crumpled shift. When he settles his perusing stare on my neck, his dark brown eyebrow twitches almost imperceptibly. Ever so slowly, his eyes rise to my lips, pause for the briefest of breaths, and then the fae's bright blue gaze finally settles on mine.

"You're as beautiful as she claimed, Auset. I'm so glad to *finally* meet you."

2

MY EARS PERK UP AT THE FAE'S USE OF A name, but they don't ring with any sense of keen recognition or remembrance.

Is that me...Auset?

He looks at me expectantly, but I keep my mouth shut and my forlorn voice silent. Muscle shifts under smooth bronze skin as the fae pushes out of a tall-backed chair that's equally as ornate and carefully crafted as the desk it's placed behind. He doesn't look as formidable as the orcs do, but commanding power pours off of him in waves as he rounds the desk and moves closer. There's no doubt in my being that I'm nothing but prey in a room full of predators. Eorn's arm around my middle tenses ever so slightly as the fae moves in front of me. The hard dick digging into my back softens, and instead of that making me feel better, alarm skitters over my flesh like hunting chirp ants.

The fae lifts a hand intent on caressing my tearstained cheek, but I jerk away from the uninvited touch. Anger and fear war inside of me for control. I hold my breath and wait for him to react to my slight, to punish me. Slowly his hand drops from where he was reaching for my face, and instead he picks up a lock of my long hair. He caresses the light strands, tugging softly when he reaches the end of the tangled length flowing through his fingers. I can see in this light that my hair isn't simply the silvery-blonde I thought it was in the darkness of the room of cages. No, I don't even know if silver or blonde are the right words for the moon-light-colored strands that aren't quite white or light gray, with the faintest kiss of the fairest blue. Somehow it's all of those things at different angles. A color I don't have a word for—although, with my memory issues, that's not all that surprising.

"Chain her," the fae suddenly orders, and my terrified eyes snap from my contemplative thoughts back to him.

His eyes are flat, emotionless, as the orcs immediately move me to the right corner and shackle me to an up-side-down-U anchor in the ground. The metal they fasten around my wrists and ankles isn't pure iron, so it doesn't burn, but there's enough of it in the cuffs for me to immediately feel the drain on my energy. Ghat tugs harshly on the long chain that attaches to my wrists, and I fall to my knees, unable to support my weight against the effects of the cuffs and the orc's cruelty.

The skin on my knees splits against the unforgiving grit of the floor, and Eorn drags his finger through the drops of blood speckling the ground beneath me, popping it in his mouth before he moves away. The bronze-skinned fae sits back in his chair, his attention now focused on the two orcs.

"Any issues?" he asks simply, but there's tension in the question.

"No, Dorsin, it's almost like they wanted her taken," Eorn jokes.

"Too easy," Ghat agrees with a rumbling laugh.

Their words don't have a calming effect on Dorsin. In fact, he almost looks more on edge with their declarations. "And why didn't you bring her straight to me?" he demands evenly, his eyes narrowing on the orcs.

"You told us not to be observed by anyone," Ghat grunts, annoyed. "Tilleo was running drills when we arrived back. We *had* to stash her until he was done. We figured you didn't want to cut your second in on what we're doing and what we're about to make off this," he adds, a touch of challenge in his tone.

The fae, Dorsin, doesn't say anything as he once again rises from his chair. This time, he strides to a long green antique buffet that has sets of tumblers and an array of liquor-filled crystal bottles decorating the top. My body reminds me of how thirsty it is as Dorsin grabs three glasses and pulls the stopper from a sparkling tall carafe. A deep crimson liquid fills each glass, and my teeth start to ache at the sight. It's an odd reaction. Then again, it's not like I know enough about myself one way or the other to know for sure.

For a moment, I think it's blood, as Dorsin places the stopper back in the carafe. However, the color of the liquid is too dark and the consistency looks too thin. Shockingly, my taste buds wake up just from the sight of whatever it is. I can't recall the taste of what's in those tumblers, just like I can't recall my name—or at least couldn't before Dorsin spoke it into existence. However, I keenly crave what's in the glasses all the same, and I suspect there's more to it than dehydration.

"Why am I here?" I ask, my voice rough and broken like it's more akin to grinding grains of sand than the voice of a girl with moonlight for hair.

The three males in the room all look at me, none of them bothering to answer the question as they greedily peruse my position on the ground.

"Why can't I remember anything? What did you do to me? If you tell me, maybe I can help somehow," I try again, but there's no power in my commands. I'm as weak and incapable as I was when trying to keep the orc from licking up my thighs. It would be laughable if it wasn't so bloody terrifying.

"Did you dose her with something?" Dorsin asks the orcs as he hands them their drinks.

"Only the hawx claw we discussed so she'd be out for the grab and transport."

Dorsin nods, his stare far away in thought as it scans over me. The word *please* is on the tip of my tongue, ready to spill out along with the other pleas crawling up my throat. I want to beg for them to *let me go, to not hurt me, to tell me what's going on*, but I swallow down the appeals. Like a dry pill, they scrape against my throat as they plummet uselessly back to my depths. I know it's pointless to beg. I can see it in the fae's calculating eyes. They've brought me here for a reason, for ransom it seems, and if the sum isn't to their liking, my future here is going to be filled with nothing but pain and petitions for it to stop. I need to find another way for this beast of a being to hear me...to care.

"A toast then," Dorsin declares, giving me his back as he raises his glass in the air. "To months of planning, days and hours of execution, and a lifetime of riches to come!"

He tosses the contents of the glass back with ease, and the orcs follow suit. The sound of crystal on wood is the only noise in the room as they set their tumblers on the desk.

"My brother and I deserve something to play with to-night—"

"Two somethings," Ghat interrupts, a strange sound coming from him like he's clearing his throat. His heavy brow furrows for a moment.

"Two somethings," Eorn corrects, his yellow eyes fixed on Dorsin. "Ones we can break...compliments of you, of course."

I cringe at the thought of what's being asked for. Will they be given some other girl from the room of cages? Or will they be allowed to pluck one from her life, like they've stolen me? My chains clink as I shift my weight slightly, and Eorn's hungry yellow eyes drop down to me, a slow smile splitting his flat leathery lips. Ghat makes a weird throat-clearing noise again, and with annoyance Eorn turns to him. I expect Ghat to ask for me or to propose some other term he feels as though his brother has forgotten to ask for. Instead, when he grabs for his throat, I see the confusion that flashes in both of the orcs' eyes.

A small, strangled wheeze escapes Ghat, like he's choking or having trouble filling his chest with air. I'm confused by what's wrong with him, and then a vicious snarl fills the room, making me yelp in response.

"What have you done?" Eorn bellows, as his brother drops heavily to the ground. Eorn takes a step toward Dorsin, and then his furious yellow eyes widen with rage and shock, and he grabs for his own throat. I track the orc's gaze as it moves from the fae to the empty glasses on the desk and back to Dorsin again. "You spineless traitor," he hisses as he takes another staggering step closer to Dorsin. "I'm… going…to…kill…you," he gasps, the threat falling flat to the floor just as he does.

Vibrations from the impact of the large orc's body buzz beneath my knees. I'm so taken aback by this shocking turn of events I don't even know what to think.

"Kill *me*?" Dorsin mocks with a humorless laugh. "Beat you to the punch there, you brainless sack of stench," he snaps, moving back to the other side of his desk where he settles gracefully into his fancy chair.

Why would he kill them? I wonder, adding the inane question to the pile of things I doubt I'll understand before someone probably kills me. I look back at the two orcs, one of them convulsing so hard I hear bones snapping. I silently hope my death isn't so painful. Movement in my periphery catches my attention, and fear erupts in my chest when I see Eorn slowly pulling himself closer. Angry yellow eyes are fixed on me as red foam gushes out of the irate orc's mouth.

I scramble back, the chains allowing me to move a few feet away until my body is pressed against the warm stone of a corner. I'm trapped and he's still slowly coming for me. I press back as much as I can, making myself as small as possible and ignoring the pain that climbs up my back from pressing my burns into the gritty slab behind me. I open my mouth to scream for help just as Eorn stops his steady progression and starts to convulse. I close my eyes against the sight of bright green blood as it starts to stream out of the orc's nose and eyes. I cover my ears with my hands to try to stop the sounds of a shattering skeleton from sinking deep inside of me and scarring whoever I am forever. I will my body to melt into the large brickwork at my back, knowing I'd be better off if it would simply swallow me whole and never spit me out again.

But nothing happens.

No one saves me from the sight feet away.

As quickly as it all started, it ends. The orc brothers go still. The room once again falls silent. The two hulking bodies start to melt like fresh snow in the desert. In one blink they're dead on the ground, and in the next blink all that remains is a thick cloudy green puddle, leather pants, and more blades than I can count soaking in the putrid fluorescent sludge.

I gag, pulling the neck of my ripped and dirty shift over my mouth and nose in an effort to block the smell that starts to plume from the puddles. Dorsin comes from around his desk and sprinkles a powder on the remains, creating an orange smoke that starts to billow and swell. The fae moves to the far wall and pushes a heavy tapestry out of the way. The fabric is secured by a hook in the stone, and then he unlatches the large window that the now pleated tapestry just revealed. Pushing it open, Dorsin twirls his hand, and a rush of air pushes into the room, gathers the orange smoke, and then promptly chases it out the window into the night.

Wide eyed, I watch it all. The air behaves as though it's an obedient herder and not a powerful wild element. Awareness settles like a fine mist in my mind. I've seen displays like this before. I recognize Dorsin's ability for what it is, though frustratingly, I can't put a name to it. I can't even recall when or where I've seen a powerful fae use a gift, but I know that I have.

Dorsin stands by the window, quietly watching something. Stars tease me over his shoulder, and I feel as though I can hear their celestial call, feel their encouragement to find a way out of these chains and far away from this place. The moonlight stretches toward me, its invisible caress a balm to my filthy fear-tracked skin and the wounds now marring my body. The back of my arms and shoulders starts to itch, the iron burns somehow healing. The chains attached to my wrists clang as I reach over my shoulder to feel for the wounds on my back. My fingertips find smooth undamaged skin, and my brow furrows with confusion.

"I allowed you to heal because it serves me," Dorsin declares, and my head snaps to where he's still standing by the open window, his cruel blue eyes now trained on me. "Your pain and broken body could serve me just as well. I want you to think about that while we...spend time together," he goes on, moving away from the window and closer to me.

I'm still pressed against the corner, the stone standing sentinel at my back. I drop my hands in front of me as though somehow they'll be useful if he attacks. *When* he attacks, I correct myself, because he will; I see it written all over his face.

"Your time with me doesn't have to be horrible. Do you understand that, Auset?"

My stomach starts to churn with renewed unease as he unhurriedly strides even closer. Panic pushes my heart faster, and my eyes prick with fear and frustration.

"I asked you a question, Auset, answer me," he snaps, and my spine goes rigid at his tone.

"Is...is that my name?" I stammer, instead of answering the threat he's pretending is a question.

He pauses mid-step, his dark brown eyebrow doing that small tic up that I observed earlier. "Don't play with me, girl," Dorsin warns. "You're old enough to have heard the horror stories about what I do to people who displease me. Don't think who your father is and what I want from him will spare you."

"Who is my father?" I demand, immediately cringing back when my steely command sparks an angry blaze in Dorsin's eyes. "I'm sorry," I rush to get out as he prowls toward me, menace etched in his features and his fists balled with promises of pain. "I'm not playing at anything. I swear, I don't know!"

He grabs the chains anchored to the metal embedded in the floor and yanks them hard. My limbs scream as I'm jerked away from the wall, and I fall forward at the murderous fae's feet. His hand is suddenly fisted in my hair, and he's pulling me up as I cry out and scramble to get my chained feet under me.

"I'm not being deceitful. I promise I'm not," I cry out as he brings his irate face even with mine.

He smells like early spring grass and fresh morning dew, and I struggle to fit the innocent scent of him with the look of rage he's wearing.

"Do I need to beat who you are and what your father owes me back into that useless mind of yours?" he roars, his eyes scanning my face for answers. "Should I fuck it into you instead?" he asks silkily, shaking me as though he expects an answer to come falling out. I whimper and try to push away from him, but his hold in my hair just makes it all hurt worse. "He's been hiding you away, hoping no one will notice, but he's forgotten how he got you in the first place," he snarls at me, spittle flinging from his lips and speckling my face. "I know what he needs from you...what he hopes your existence will give him," he hisses virulently. "He thinks he's so cunning. How many lords and heirs have crawled between these thighs and spilled their secrets alongside their seed?" he bellows at me, his other hand ripping my dirty, mangled shift from my body.

I scream, but he shoves the torn fabric into my mouth and throws me against the wall. I don't get my hands out in front of me fast enough, and I catch the rough wall with the side of my face. The impact disorients me as I crumble to the ground, unable to do anything as he starts to kick me. A hard boot connects with my stomach, ribs, arms, legs. He's screaming at me, but I can't hear what floats in the venom of his words over my own cries.

Pain explodes in my body as I try and fail to crawl into a protective position, but he just aims his rage at any newly exposed parts of me. I can't keep up, can't hold the hits off no matter how hard I try. I feel ribs break, and agony sweeps through me not only from Dorsin's attack but now it accompanies each move or gasped, desperate breath. My screams fade into pathetic mewls and whimpers, and all at once, I cease trying to stop what he's doing and instead...I embrace it.

Let me die and be done with all of this for good.

Just as I give in to that desire, Dorsin stops. I groan helplessly, blood dripping from my temple, my body now nothing more than bruises and abrasions. I get lost in the pain for a beat, and darkness begins to seep into my soul. When nothing happens for far too long, I risk looking up from my pitiful position on the cold stone floor. My eyes are filled with hate, and I'm all at once ready and eager to push this bastard and force him to give me the sweet release of death I find myself suddenly craving.

Shock ricochets through me when my battered and enraged gaze doesn't find a set of brutish blue eyes staring down at me with evil intensity. No. Instead, the gleam of fairy light on a sharp blade catches my eye. A blade that's being held to Dorsin's throat by a...skeleton. I blink, trying to clear the illusion from my gaze, but the bone-white fist gripping the handle of the dagger doesn't disappear. I can't make sense of what's happening until two other skeletal beings appear from behind Dorsin and move further into the room.

It's a glamour, I realize as I watch them stride confidently into the chamber. Sable leather encases strong legs, arms, and tapered torsos. Any skin not covered by armor or weapons appears inky and dark, that is, aside from the white of the bone correlating with the body part that's exposed. Skulls appear in place of male faces. Metacarpals and phalanges are all I can see of their hands. One of them turns, and I can count the vertebrae showing in place of his neck. Instead of empty sockets, I find onyx, emotionless eyes that are shrewdly studying their surroundings. Each of them has raven-black hair that's been pulled tight and knotted at the backs of their heads, and just like the orcs, none of them make the barest whisper of a sound as they move.

I snap my stunned gaze back to Dorsin, whose features are quickly morphing from shock into fury. He opens his mouth to say something, but the shining blade presses tighter against his throat, and Dorsin seems to think twice about whatever words are sitting on his tongue.

"Got it," a deep, no-nonsense voice declares, and before I can turn my head to identify what the stranger found, the blade at Dorsin's throat is drawn and hot blood sprays out of the wound.

Terror and repulsion detonate in my chest, and I twist away as Dorsin's life force showers me. I witness, with disconnected and deadened emotion, as the skeleton removes Dorsin's hand with a skilled chop of an ax, tossing it casually to one of his partners before letting the fae that was just attacking me drop dead to the floor with a heavy thunk.

The three glamoured beings don't even spare me a look as they make their way over to an empty expanse of wall, staring at it as though it's more than blank tan stone. I try to breathe through the fear coursing through me, terrified that my panicked gasps are creating so much noise that it'll be my throat they slit next. Without thinking about what I'm doing, I crawl over to the green puddle that was once an orc and pluck two long daggers from the sludge. The handles are slippery, and things I don't want to think about ooze through the seams of my fingers, but I tighten my grip all the same, not knowing what's going to happen next.

I will my newfound weapons to make me feel better, but I'm once again crouched in the corner, only this time I'm now naked, battered, splattered with blood, and there are three new threats standing on the other side of the room, staring at a wall. I hurt everywhere. I try and fail not to choke on fear as I watch what feels like a real-life game of Trumps unfold at my feet. However, instead of observing a card game where one higher suit trumps another, I'm watching monsters do it. Just when I think I know who and what to be afraid of, something new and even more dangerous is laid atop the deck.

The sound of stone scraping against stone catches my attention. Between the wide shoulders of the three skeletons, I see the large-bricked wall in front of them moving. Slowly, the rectangular stones fold in on themselves to reveal a small antechamber with rows and rows of shelves displaying things I can't make out. One of the skeletons disappears into the space and then quickly reappears, handing a small bag to one of his partners while tucking what looks like folded parchment into the inside of his tunic.

"Get everything?" the one with the small bag asks as he ties it to the waist of his pants.

"Everything we needed. I even left something to remember us by, not that anyone will be getting in there after tonight," the one with the parchment stuffed inside the front of his chest plate answers.

The skeletons move away from the open wall, and it immediately starts to brick itself back up. I stare mesmerized, or maybe I'm officially in shock, who's to say at this point of this horror-filled night?

"Want to do anything about her?" a cool voice asks, and I startle at the realization that one of the skeletons has silently moved closer and is looking down at me from only a few feet away.

I tighten my hold on the daggers, and I swear I see a tic of amusement move the corners of his lips. His mouth is made to look like the teeth of a skeleton's maw, but it doesn't stop me from making out the plush fullness under the glamour as well as his square jaw and defined cheekbones. Like a wraith appearing from shadow, another skeleton is suddenly by his side, observing me.

"She'll probably go to the flesh market if we do nothing," the first one points out.

"Not our problem," the third states as he moves toward the still open window.

"I can kill you if you'd like," the second offers, and it takes me a moment to realize he's talking to me. "You'd be better off dead than what this lot will do to you," he goes on, his black eyes hard and his tone even, factual.

"We need to go," the skeleton by the window calls out, a bite of irritation in his tone.

"Do you want me to kill you?" the other skeleton asks again, unhurried.

Do I?

I stare at him, uncertain. I was ready to die when Dorsin was kicking my bones in, but now...now with three monsters dead and two daggers in my hands, everything feels different, less desperate, less hopeless.

"Help me," I answer instead. "Take me with you," I plead, pushing up from my crouch in the corner. I cry out as my ribs object to the movement, my broken body forcing me back to the ground on my knees.

"You can't even walk, and if you could, we wouldn't be able to take you, little moonbeam. You're better off dead," the skeleton closest to me declares, and something about his calm assessment reignites my anger.

My eyes harden against his, and I say nothing as I pull my knives closer to my body in warning. Black eyes rake over me once, and then both skeletons near me move to meet their friend by the window.

"Suit yourself," one of them calls over his shoulder, not even bothering to look back at me, like I'm not even worthy of one last pitying glance.

Renewed panic starts to hammer at me as they move to leave, but what can I do? They'd rather see me dead than help me, and I don't truly *want* to die. It's one thing to think it amidst agony and defeat, when there's no way out and death is the only thing that will spare you more suffering. But as I sit among the slain, daggers in my hands, and the moon's healing call just on the other side of the skeletons now crawling out of the window...I want to survive.

I want to make anyone who would dare to hurt me again...pay.

Hot tears drip down my cheeks as the skeletons disappear out the window as stealthily as they arrived. Deep, cruel words echo in my mind as I move to Dorsin and search him for the key to my chains.

"You're better off dead."

That heartless statement is all I can hear as I cut Dorsin's tunic from his body and wrap the fabric around me, covering what I can with the soft silk. I try not to puke as I desperately search the orc goo for the keys to my freedom, but they must be in the desk, and my chains don't stretch that far. The soft touch of night caresses the bruises from my skin. The moonbeams that sneak in through the still open window painfully pop my bones back in place, healing the damage that Dorsin rained down on me. Sadly, the healing does little to restore my strength, and no matter how I try to wedge knives into the links of the chains or stab the locks on the cuffs, I can't get myself free.

I don't know how long I lay there, my cheek pressed against the cool floor, staring at Dorsin's dead eyes and the taunting open window. The sun is high in the sky when the first booming knock sounds at the white-oak doors. The skeleton's words loop through my mind in a jeering round, and I don't even stir when the demanding pounding comes again.

"You're better off dead."

Feet attached to leather-clad legs spill into the space before me. I don't flinch or have the wherewithal any longer to fear anything as I watch Dorsin's people take in the macabre scene. I'm as blank inside as my mind has been when trying to piece together the *why* of all this. Voices shout and argue, but I focus on nothing until a pair of pristine black boots step into my line of sight. I take in the freshly oiled surface of the footwear, stiffening when I spot a small skull pressed into the silver of the buckle that cinches the wearer's ankle.

What pain and horror will this pair bring me?

In a burst of speed I didn't know I was capable of, I lunge at the owner of the boots. Surprise flashes in his assessing gaze as he scrambles away. Just as I lift an orc dagger, a snarl of victory now climbing up my throat, my chains stop me, snapping me back and out of reach of the man I want to cut to ribbons. I stare at him, studying his face for the features that I earlier made out behind the skeletal glamour, but the aristocratic cheeks and the full lips are nowhere to be found in this fae's face.

His carob-hued eyes take me in, settling on the fae blood streaked and spattered over my skin, before moving to the orc remains now dried in my hair and stuck to my hands. He looks almost impressed for a moment before he shutters all readable emotion from his face.

"I'm Tilleo, Dorsin's second-in-command," he announces, jutting his chin in the direction of his dead former leader. "It seems as though you've been *busy* in here," he observes, his dark eyes raking down my gore-painted body.

Fighting back a shiver of revulsion at the dark gleam in his gaze, it dawns on me that he thinks *I* did all of this. I drop my gaze to the pools of blood, both green and red, all around me and then look back up at Tilleo. I don't correct his assumption. I can't tell if he's pleased with me or plotting how to make me suffer for what he thinks I've done. I wait for the fear to come, but I'm too empty for it to find purchase if it does decide to show up.

"Who are you?" he asks, tilting his head a little as though it will offer him recognition.

I debate whether to answer, but maybe he knows who I am. Maybe he holds the answers I desperately need. "Auset," I finally offer, clinging tightly to the only thing I know.

I watch him carefully, looking for any sign that my name means more to him than it currently does to me. His face is blank.

"You want me to put her with the others headed to market?" a thin, reedy fae asks.

Tilleo watches me for a moment and then another before a small smile spreads over his face. "No. No flesh market for this one. I think we can find a much better use for her...talents," he states, his eyes aglow with menace. "Put her with the other savages. Let's see what she can really do."

3

SIX YEARS LATER

I SIT BACK IN THE TEPID WATER, THE HARD EDGE OF the metal tub digging into my newly healed and now lash-free back. I daydream about the day that I can shove a sword through Master Vilde's chest. He whips me for looking at him and now whips me for not looking at him. There's no reasoning with the bastard, not that there's much reasoning with many of the animals that run this place. I weave the threadbare washrag between my fingers, getting lost in my bloodthirsty thoughts and the fluid movement of the cloth through the murky water of my bath before whispers lure me from my wandering fantasies.

"I want a place with the Vulpi, but the Wolves would be a good fit too," Paryn murmurs quietly to Sennet as she scrubs her arms with her own hole-pecked square of fabric.

"I don't care who claims me as long as it's not the Bruins," Linae declares, water sloshing over her metal tub as she turns to look at Paryn and Sennet, wanting to get in on the banter.

"You'll be claimed by no one if you keep chirping instead of scrubbing," Hord snaps from the doorway, and the bathing room is once again filled only by the sounds of frantic scrubbing and splashes of water.

I stand, the cloudy water sluicing off of me as I step out of the metal basin and wring my hair out. I can feel the buzz of excitement and nervousness floating in the atmosphere today against my skin, like static from an impending storm. I wish I knew how to feel about it all, but I don't. We've spent years preparing for this day, and it doesn't seem quite...real. I worry that any second now I'll startle awake and realize this is all some vivid dream. That everything I've been through, all the training and torture and fighting, isn't over, and I'm right back at the start of it all.

A sharp pain strikes through my palm, and I flinch and look down. I expect to find some forgotten wound the healers didn't notice, but all I see is calluses and lines. There's no cut or wound of any kind. I fist and unfist my hand against the phantom sting, a habit that will get me slapped if one of the masters catches me doing it. We're allowed no tics or coping mechanisms outside of what we carefully construct in our minds. Our bodies have been built to be smooth, strong, and unscarred thanks to the proficient healers Tilleo employs, and not because each of us hasn't been beaten within an inch of life and then brought back day after day. We've been poisoned, brutalized, trained, and honed, all in preparation of this...the Bidding. Today is the start of it all. The day when the finest members of the Orders of Assassins come to see which of us is worthy and which of us is only destined for the skin trade we've *mostly* been spared while coming up through the *ludere*.

I sigh, finger combing through my long hair in hopes it will free up some of the tangles and Wilik's braiding won't feel like the rending it usually resembles. Muffled grunting can be heard through the beige sandstone wall in front of me, which means the blade slaves in the male's bathing room are either brawling or fucking. It's impossible to say which. I learned long ago that there isn't much difference in the sounds made while in agony versus what comes out of our mouths in the throes of passion. Not that I know much about the passion side of things.

An occasional romp with a fellow blade slave barely scratches the itch let alone broaches anything resembling passion, at least not for me. I have heard some of the girls make each other scream just as loudly under the covers at night as they do in the ring with a sharp weapon and a deep cut. I know passion is possible. I've even been invited a couple of times to discover what all the fuss is about, but I don't get close to many of the slaves here. It's always a death sentence just waiting to be meted out, one way or another.

I stand in the bathing room, the stale, arid air working to dry me as I look around. I study the once white marble tiles at my feet, the snowy color now stained yellow by the sulfur in the water they pump in here for us to wash with. The sixteen metal tubs set in rows of four are rusted, the soap so acidic it eats through the tin the same way it'll eat through skin if left on for too long. It smells like mildew and anxious exhaustion in here, and as happy as I am to never see this room again after the Bidding is over, it's also all I've ever known. Something about that tugs at my gut in a way I never anticipated. It's not sadness or longing, but unease. I've spent a long time waiting to be free of this desert prison, but I can't help the worry that courses through me that what comes next might be worse.

I've never allowed myself to think about that before; there was no point when I didn't even know if I'd ever see this day. I've been careful about allowing my mind to wander down any path that leads too far into the future. But I can't seem to fend off morose thoughts today. Not when the possibility of *worse* is breathing down my neck like a handsy guard after a night of too much drinking.

Eight elite houses of killers will arrive at the ludere this afternoon. We'll wait on them hand and foot while also working to prove to them that we're worthy of their Order. Some are better than others. Some are more brutal and punishing, like the Order of Bruins. Others are more refined and sleek, like the Order of Vulpi. Every blade slave has a secret hope for where they'll end up, but hope is all it is, and in a place like this, hope can kill you faster than anything else.

I stride out of the bathing room, ignoring Hord when he slaps my ass as I pass him. The crack of his palm against my damp skin is loud, but I keep my head straight and my glare to myself. There's no point getting whipped twice in one day. He takes liberties, but he's not as bad as he could be. Enduring his attention quietly keeps me off the radar of the bigger predators, the ones who like a fight or a fair amount of screaming in order to enjoy themselves thoroughly.

I step into the adornment room, and Figg grunts at me and nods to the stool in front Wilik. I obey, silently sitting as Wilik starts to roughly comb through my damp hair. It's warm in here with only two small slivers of windows to allow any airflow. It's still early, and the sun hasn't been beating against the walls of the smaller room all day, allowing the thick humid air to still feel tolerable, but only just.

Wilik mans her usual corner with her chair—which she barely troubles herself to leave—and a stack of shelves attached to the wall next to her that she keeps her tools and products on. She forces all of us to sit on a wobbly stool that's far too small and then punishes us anytime it moves. Figg flutters about behind her long splinter-ridden table, pulling clothes and other things from the shelves and drawers behind her and arranging them in neat little stacks. The table is covered in piles of blue fabric and accessories, and Figg grumbles just as soon as my eyes land on the display.

"Don't want to hear no fuss about your togs tonight. I spent half the day scrubbing and mending what the masters picked out. So just keep your groans to yourself, or I'll have you whipped after the feast, and I won't call the healer until morning," Figg threatens, shaky fingers pushing wayward salt-and-pepper strands of hair from her sweaty, pink-cheeked face. She must be low on drink today—that's usually the key to her temper—or perhaps it's all the fuss over who's arriving and what they're here to do over the next handful of days.

A breeze picks up outside, stirring the folded piles of what looks like midnight blue silk, sprinkling sand on the shiny surfaces of the elegant fabric. I've never seen anything so rich and decadent, especially not something the masters would ever give us blade slaves, but I count eight stacks of fabric, and I know this is what we'll be draped in tonight. Wilik smacks me upside the head, and I immediately turn from the lush silky togs and look straight ahead like I know she wants me to. She tsks and grumbles her frustration over having to work through my thick tresses, but a direct order from the masters prevents her from shearing my head free of the menacing strands like she used to do when I first got here.

"I think I'll do something different...something special for tonight's festivities," Wilik declares, and I tense as she starts smoothing the front strands back. Her cruel, beady black eyes study me over her long hooked nose. Lips so thin they can barely be called lips at all twist up in a smile, and that's more threat than amusement seeping from the grim gray of her skin and features.

"There's no need to go through any trouble for me," I bite out, wincing at the desperate edge in my tone. "Fighting plaits have always been more than adequate," I go on, softening my voice and hoping I didn't just make this worse by sounding like I was trying to command her.

Wilik is quiet for a beat, and when she grabs a chunk of hair from the side of my head and starts to braid, I relax slightly.

"Nonsense," she coos at me spitefully. "You should look *extra* special tonight; all of the girls should. You've spent too much time as a raw diamond, Auset. It's time to shine you up, show the Orders what kind of stock the ludere breeds."

I close my eyes at her declaration and focus on my breathing. She's punishing me, setting me up in the worst way, and I want to use the comb in her hand to rip out her throat for it. Special is a problem here. Pretty is even worse. Too much of one, and the others will pick you off in order to increase their odds. Flaunting both could land any blade slave in a station worse than *hired sword*. I barely escaped the skin markets before. Tilleo thinking that I'd killed Dorsin was the only way I'd wedged my foot in the door of the ludere, and I've fought with *everything* I have to stay here ever since.

I've never alpha'd the pack. I've never fallen behind in the ranks either. I've worked to stay right in the middle. Not too good, but good enough to make it to the Bidding. Good enough to be bought by an Order...for a reasonable price. A price it won't take my entire life to pay back. A price that someday will be settled, after my hands have soaked too long in other fae's blood and there are more wrinkles on my face and pains in my limbs, I'll then be allowed to discover what freedom truly tastes like.

I dream of that day, savor what I think the flavor will be like on my tongue.

It's what gets me through every day in this sunbaked hellhole.

Someday I'll be free.

Wilik yanks my hair hard, and I hiss and tilt my head the way she wants. The nasty pixie could just use her words—by the stars, she has plenty to say about everything else around here—but no, she relishes the power she has over us while we're sitting on her stool. I'm going to kill her, or at least I like to imagine all the ways I can use her tools of torture against her while she does her best to rip the hair from my scalp. The plaiting we're forced to sit through every week is the only time I'm grateful for possessing so much hair. Otherwise, thanks to Wilik's rough treatment, I'd look patchy like Kin and Ency do. I want my price to be lower but not so low that I end up in a bad Order.

Wilik smooths the front of my hair back with some kind of cream I've never felt her use before and then wraps a thick braid from one side of my head over the top like a band. She grabs another thick braid from the other side of my head and crosses it over the opposite way before sewing it all in place. Once that's done, she begins to dry the long locks draped down my back with a brush that painfully twists and pulls as she magics everything into the shape that she wants.

A shiver crawls up my spine as Wilik works. She's only ever put in this much effort to make me look special one other time. Those memories rear up unexpectedly, forcing my heart to start pounding as sweat begins to bead on my brow. I close my eyes and think through this morning's drill instead, doing everything I can to push thoughts of that day as far from me as possible. I don't care how much this all calls to what happened before, I refuse to unlock that box and examine those scars no matter what.

Taria and Orit walk in, and Figg gives them the same threatening warning about the togs the masters have se-lected for us this evening as they wait their turn to suffer at Wilik's hands. A few more brutal yanks later, Wilik magics her stool out from under me, and I glare at her as I barely manage not to fall on my ass. You'd think she'd be more careful, surrounded by fae who've been taught how to kill without compunction, but she must be thirsty for death. Maybe when I'm finally sipping on freedom, I'll come give the pixie a mouthful of what she's clearly been craving all these years. Wilik smirks back at me, her dull dark eyes promising more pain the next time I'm at her mercy, but her days of battering this batch of blade slaves are numbered, and we both know it.

Orit snickers at something Taria says, and the petite huntress glares at her friend.

"They come for every Bidding for a reason," Taria defends, hurt gleaming in her bright brown eyes. Her skin is so dark it will never reveal a blush, but I suspect one invisibly heats her cheeks all the same.

"It's pure nonsense to even think it, Taria," Orit sneers. "The Scorpions come for the food, drinks, and the willing slits. Then they leave each Bidding with their Order intact exactly as it was when they arrived. Thinking you're going to be bid on by *them* is the most ridiculous thing I've ever heard."

Figg and Wilik both snort disdainfully, the sound a firm agreement with Orit's scathing words. Taria's eyes fall to her feet, her lips pursing for a beat as though she wants to argue, but she stays quiet and simmers in Orit's scorn.

"None of us have been to a Bidding before. Who's to say what will or won't happen?" I chime in, the defeat in Taria's eyes pulling at something in me.

"Sot told me exactly what happens," Orit jeers, as though getting on her knees for a guard who spills useless information down her throat as well as his seed places her above me in life.

I scoff but don't say any more as Figg limps out from behind the table, a blue dress clutched in her arthritic hands, the color so deep it looks as though it's been kissed by the night. Her small wings flutter at her back, the oddly frail looking appendages suddenly flapping hard to lift her round body in the air so she can fit the dress to me.

A flurry of giggles sound out from the bathing chamber, and more girls stumble into the already cramped space of the adornment room. Some of my fellow savages, as Tilleo likes to call us, look as though they've gotten into the stores of spirits that none of us are supposed to have access to. I know they're all simply excited for what's to come, for the promise of change and the chance to escape this place, but I find myself looking at each of them and wondering who won't make it. There were so many of us when I first came here. Now it's just down to eight of us females and eight males. I run my eyes over the faces of the other girls who I've fought against and trained with for the last six years. My feelings are mixed, just like they were in the bathing room. I'm happy to never see any of them again, and yet they're all I've ever really known. Them and this place.

In the past, some Orders have purchased multiple blade slaves from Tilleo, so I suppose it would be possible that I may end up somewhere with one of these girls or, more likely, one of the guys. However, I'm not sure if that thought reassures or troubles me. It could be nice to know someone wherever it is that I'm going. Then again, it's not as though there's any sense of loyalty between any of us in this fight for our survival. Why would it really matter if one of the many faces in my new life is one I happen to recognize?

Figg fusses with a metal belt, her short arms making it difficult to wrap it around my hips the way it's apparently supposed to be worn. I look down to see what the masters have ordered her to put us in, and I balk at the dress that's barely more than a couple long strips of fabric. The dark blue silk is soft against my skin, but there's not nearly enough of it. My wide worried eyes land on Figg's, and she glares a warning at me not to say a word.

Heat moves up my neck and into my cheeks as I survey the silky fabric that forms a V down my shoulders to barely cover my breasts. Below my navel, the two lines of fabric become one to cover my slit. In the back, the same V of dark blue fabric drops to the small of my back before it morphs into a single thin panel that covers the crack of my ass. Figg secures a metal belt that seems to be designed to help keep the front and back strips of silk from moving and revealing too much.

A small metal crest in the shape of a shield sits on top of my cunt, with thin chains of silver metal attaching it to the same crest that sits at the top curve of my ass in the back. The crest is Tilleo's, a fanged boar's head in front of two crossing swords. I don't know what it's supposed to mean, but it's marked into almost everything here at the ludere. I suspect we'd be wearing his mark too if it wasn't something that could identify us and lead potential enemies right back to him in the event that one of us was captured while out on a hunt.

The small chains are cold against the bare skin of my hips, and I'm all too aware that a strong breeze or quick twist of my body will expose parts of me that aren't on of-fer to any Order, regardless of what they might think they own. Some masters have encouraged us to offer all that we can to secure a place with an Order. Others have warned us that spreading our legs can work against us in the Bidding. Either way, I never took to the enticement training we were required to have here at the ludere. No matter how hard I was punished for it, I would not be convinced that my cunt ever needed to be involved in how I killed.

The other girls are quiet as they look over what they'll soon be draped in too. Taria shivers and Orit wraps an arm around her shoulders and pulls the small fae closer to her side. Solemnity blankets the adornment room as the truth of our circumstances chases away the excitement that was just sparkling in the air. The giggles fade to silence as Wilik starts to work on someone else, and Figg tugs the dress I'm wearing until it lies against me the way she wants. With a grunt, I'm dismissed, and I stride out of the room, making a concentrated effort not to open and close my fists as anger slowly bubbles in my stomach.

"Don't sit and crease yourself or lean against anything and dirty the dress either," Figg calls out after me. "March straight to the hashery and wait for your assignment. The caravans start arriving in the next few hours. I'll have you caned if there's a speck of sand on you," she threatens, and I huff with annoyance and wave her threats away.

The ludere is located somewhere in the Corozean des-ert; it's impossible not to have sand everywhere, especially when the wind charges in at night like a herd of wild sand stags. I don't know a life where I'm not covered in a layer of fine grit and sweat, or when Figg isn't threatening us to stay clean. Given everything that's happening tonight, she might follow through this time though. The Kings know, her patience is at an all-time low.

I walk slowly and awkwardly to the hashery. I feel too exposed in this getup, and I hate it. How am I supposed to fight in this? I keep checking to make sure everything is covered as I walk, despising the hot air that's touching too much of my skin. It snakes between my thighs as I walk, and I bristle at the lack of a barrier there. I try not to seethe too obviously. We're nude often here, either to fight off the oppressive heat at night or because the masters have or-dered us to train that way for the day. It's not the lack of clothing that's putting me on edge. It's being forced to feel even more vulnerable than we already are for the Orders. Like we really needed one more reminder that we're less than, that we're nothing.

Surviving this long in the ludere brings a certain level of understanding and expectation. We can be stripped down and know which guards or masters might push to take advantage. Time here reveals to all of us which of our fellow savages might ask to play under the cover of night, or worse, not ask. Life here is brutal, but there's a kind of safety in knowing where the threats lie. I've figured out a way to traverse the hazards, learning quickly who and what might come for me when I'm vulnerable. However, it won't be like that with the Orders.

We've all heard stories about this one and that, but none of us really know what's going to be coming through the outer doors in a couple of hours. Great houses of assas-sins are coming here. They're a combined threat to each other as well as us, and Tilleo wants us to bear the weight of all that while worrying if our cunts and tits are showing, which potentially could invite more trouble than any of us have ever deserved.

I suppose I should expect nothing less from a skin dealer. He sees us all in aurems, counting our worth and cost with every breath we take. I should be grateful I'm here instead of being sent off to some brothel or sold to a private, more nefarious collector, but gratitude isn't something I can muster much of these days.

My stomach growls, but I don't smell anything being made or prepared for us in the kitchens as I pass them. There's a flurry of activity and plenty being cooked and baked, but I know it's not for us—it smells too good. We never get anything that smells like that.

I wander into the hashery and find all of the male blade slaves waiting. They stand around wary and bored, having taken far less time to prepare for tonight's festivities than we girls have. I scan Leto, a desert-darkened force to be reckoned with and the only male I've ever given permission to touch me. He and all the others have freshly shorn heads and are wearing flowing salwar pants in the same deep blue silky fabric as my dress. A silver chain holds a pendant with Tilleo's crest between their defined pecs. They've been oiled up to accentuate the dips and mounds of their muscular, hardened frames. Each of them is lethal and capable, just like me and the seven other females who've made it this far.

Leto moves toward me like he always does when we train together. He jokes that I'm the sun his moon is always drawn to, which makes no sense with the way I look. Either way, I shut that kind of talk down whenever he starts it. The only thing I ever want to be to anyone is the last thing they see before they die. I watch him lithely stride closer, noticing that his flowy draped trousers hug his hips and his ankles, but the sides flap open, exposing his thick toned legs as he walks. It seems Tilleo has made the males just as accessible as he's made the rest of us.

Sparkling russet eyes run up my body before settling on mine, and Leto offers me his go-to sly smile that always makes me think he's up to something. "I guess Tilleo didn't want to give you many options for where to hide a blade," he teases, and I scoff.

"You know I don't need one if I really want to do some damage," I reply flatly, and his smile grows even wider.

"Meet me tonight on the roof? One last time before this place is nothing but a memory," he asks, his lips mere inches from my ear as his whisper dances over the skin of my neck.

My nipples harden in response, and I look around to ensure no guards are watching as I cross my arms over my chest to try to hide my body's reaction. Leto steps back, his own eyes scanning our surroundings in search of threats. He's the only slave I've let myself get close to in years. I'm not sure what it is about him that made me want to lower some of my walls, even though I know it's nothing but trouble, but time in this place is lonely. It wears on all of us, no matter how hard we fight it. It's not friendship, that's too dangerous. It's contact, a tenuous connection, and some days, that alone is the only tether to sanity.

"I'll try," I tell him quietly. "If I'm assigned to one of the tents though..." I trail off as he nods in understanding.

The palatial manor next to the ludere can accommodate many guests very comfortably. But we've been told that some Orders prefer more solitude than the manor provides. I'm not sure which ones don't play well with others, but according to some of the guards, the tents are just as cozy and luxurious as the main house is. They're still inside the walls of the stronghold, but they're placed out in the large expanse of empty sand between the manor and the ludere.

I've been inside the main residence once. I don't recall cozy luxury. All I remember is warm brown sandstone everywhere, blinding fairy lights, and fear. The masters told us that we'll be assigned to serve an Order while they're here. That's why they've gathered us in the hashery, to give us our assignments. If I'm tasked with serving someone in the tents, it could make sneaking off very complicated.

Leto gives me a nod and a wink before he backs away slowly, enfolding himself in the grouping of males like the ghost we've all been trained to be. Low chatter hums all around me, but any time any of us hears movement in our direction, we go silent. The masters don't like us talking to each other too much or doing anything else that could give the impression that the killers they're training might be looking to turn on them. We know better, and the crossbow-laden guards that walk the outer wall above us at all times guarantee that no one would get too far even if we did start to have *ideas*.

Slowly, the other females trickle in. We wait, all of us standing together but not too close, not too comfortable. I'm relieved more than I want to admit that Wilik has done something different and impressive with all of the female blade slaves' hair. She wasn't only singling me out for trouble like I initially thought. Each of us self-consciously tugs and tucks the scraps of fabric barely covering us as we wait. I watch many uncomfortable glances move around the room and a couple silent invitations being passed back and forth from slave to slave.

I sense the moment the atmosphere of the ludere changes, like my blood not only runs in *my* veins but in the drab floors and walls of this place too. A heavy severity ripples through the building, and I can taste an encroaching tang of fear. I straighten and tense right alongside all the savages in the room. My eyes stare straight ahead. My muscles lock. I pull in a deep breath and hold it. Tilleo is coming and that is never a good thing.

4

THE THUMP OF BOOTS AGAINST GRITTY SAND-stone drums in my ears like the warning it is. In my periphery, I see the guards who always precede Tilleo as they enter the room. Their sharp eyes sweep the space, searching for threats as they push aside two of the four long tables that we eat on in here. Sweat drips down my spine, and I curse myself for standing too close to a window and the rays of sun it's feeding into the room.

At least I didn't stand in front of it like Sennet did. If Tilleo takes too long, she'll need to see a healer for the burn her pale skin is guaranteed to get. Most of us have darkened and adapted to the punishing environment all around us, even me. The fair red-haired blade slave has a harder time of it though. It seems her skin is as stubborn as she is. It refuses to adapt and make things easier on her.

Magicked fans whir above us, the leafy blades circling so fast that they're a blur. The hot air they stir up plays with the silky fabric all of us have on, but each and every blade slave is as still as a statue while we wait for the man who condemned us to this life to grace us with his presence.

Carob-colored eyes shrewdly survey his crop of savages as Tilleo saunters into the hashery, decked out in an explosion of gems and jewel-toned silks. An extravagant swish fills his steps as he glides to the center of the room to pompously survey his property. The fans dare to disturb strands of his long, limp, dusty brown hair, and he smooths back the wayward locks with a hand that's the same color as the desert sand at high noon.

He pulls in a deep breath, the bejeweled vest he's wearing falling open to reveal the skin of his chest. Unlike the weapons he's honed us to be, his body is soft, the kind of soft that happens when everyone around you does everything that's hard. He's not round like Figg, but it's clear he's not missing any meals, and he's not dining on the same gruel we're expected to survive off of. His pants are the same style as the male blade slaves', a style favored by the desert dwellers of the Day Court, or so Figg likes to brag, as if she's ever left the walls of this place.

I see him, but I don't, because to look at him directly is an offense that will get you cut up and killed. I got away with it when I first met him, chained up and empty in Dorsin's office, but the next time my unknowing eyes met his, it took me weeks to heal from.

"Our guests will be here within the hour," he informs us, his crisp, brassy tone filling the room with ease and ringing authority. "You will greet them and follow them to their quarters where you will do anything and everything they require of you," he orders, his eyes moving across our stone-still line as he looks each of us over.

I can feel his gaze picking us apart, searching for flaws or anything that requires punishment. Each of us holds our breath as his gaze runs its course, knowing that any little thing at any moment could change our fate in his world just like it has for so many others.

"Linae, Kirid, and Ency, you're dismissed," he calls out indifferently as though the last two words spoken into this room didn't just end the aspirations and dreams of the three fae. I don't know what it is about them that displeased him, but just like that, their hopes of finding a place in an Order and escaping Tilleo's cruel clutches are over.

"No," Linae pleads, and my stomach drops at her idiocy.

I want to snap at her to shut up. She knows better. But I fight the urge, standing frozen in my stance of submission, because *I* know better. My mind silently whirs with thoughts of what they're going to do to her for daring to speak without permission. It's one thing to risk it with the guards or masters, but Tilleo is a whole other matter. Kirid and Ency stride out of the hashery noiselessly, accepting whatever fate now awaits them at Tilleo's fickle hands.

"Master, please, whatever you find wanting, I will fix it," Linae begs, and I hear the tears in her tone that I'm certain are now dripping down her face.

She might as well be hand delivering her death decree to the soulless fae in front of us. Unease simmers in my chest, but I try to rein in my judgment. If *I* had just been condemned to the skin market like she probably has, I might beg too. Truth stomps that thought from my mind like it's snuffing out a poisonous snake. I'd be distraught, yes, but I'd never be this stupid. Sure, death is better than a lifetime on your back and an unending train of unwanted cock between your thighs, but mouthing off to Tilleo won't get you death. Not right away at least. Not the quick and torture-free death that each of us desires to meet in the end. No, what Linea's doing will only bring pain. She'd have been better off walking out of here straight to the armory and slitting her own throat than what she's doing now.

"*You* will fix it?" Tilleo asks, his voice smooth and even, but to me it feels like the strands of a glass-tipped flogger against my back.

"Yes, master, I will do anything you desire. Please don't wash me from my place here. I'm your blade to command," she beseeches, her last words the only thing we're allowed to say when the masters give us orders.

"Jarwa, take *my blade* to the hot house. I'll be with her shortly," Tilleo commands, and the guard to his left grabs Linae and practically drags her from the room. Heat crawls over my skin as though *I've* been the one condemned to the brick enclosure that's more oven than room. I chase away the memories of punishments spent in that horrible place and watch as Linae looks on with hopeful eyes. I have no doubt that just like always, that hope will be her end.

Tension crawls over my scalp like scorch mites as we stand perfectly still, waiting, like the good slaves we are, for what Tilleo has yet to say. He doesn't hurry to get it over with, his eyes once again searching out disappointment as the tic in his jaw pulses. At first I think he's taking a moment to calm his temper, but the gleam in his eyes tells me he's more than likely thinking up punishments for Linae. If she's lucky, she'll be bitten by something poisonous and die before Tilleo finishes with us and moves on to her. Although with the immunities to poison the masters have forced us to build up over the years, there's probably not a viper, spider, or scorpion in the desert that could get the job done at this point.

"The time that you've been working toward is nearly upon us," Tilleo starts, gripping his hands behind his back as he begins to pace in front of us. "Soon you'll be observed by the realm's best hunters. They will study you while I push you and test you. Over the next five days, they will decide if you are worthy to bear their Order's name. I expect each and every one of you to represent me and this ludere accordingly. Not every crop of savages is worthy of a Bidding. You have earned it, but you're not free of me yet. Remember *that* over the next few days as you fight to secure a future that *I've* allowed to be possible. Remember what's at stake, and do not fail me," he practically snarls.

I defer the urge to tighten my hands into fists to relieve the tension now coursing through my body, and instead shout out in time with the others, "I am your blade to command."

Tilleo pulls in a deep breath and pauses his pacing. He reaches out an empty hand, and one of his guards hurries to place a scroll in it. Slowly, Tilleo unfurls the parchment, and his duplicitous eyes scan over what's written.

"Paryn and Kabit, you are with the Order of Wolves. Sennet and Taria, Order of Vulpi. Yotta and Taur, you'll be with the Order of Bruins," Tilleo commands, shouting out more assignments as my stomach clenches and I wait to hear my name. "Harsh and Auset, you're consigned to the Order of Scorpions. Kin and Zinnon, you will serve the Order of Crows."

My heart plummets in my chest, and Tilleo's voice falls to the background of my mind. The Order of Scorpions? Really? Worry finds a thorny perch in my chest, refusing to move when I try to brush it away. The Scorpions don't bid at these events. According to the house slaves, they come when requested, watch in silence, fuck the offerings occasionally, drink and talk mostly with their fellow Scorpions, and then leave. They never buy. The guards say they're stiff and haughty and look at everyone as though they're beneath them.

Tilleo assigning me to serve them while they're here for the Bidding isn't a vote of confidence. This isn't a good thing. I'll have to work even harder to catch the attention of the other Orders during our tests. Which means I won't be able to sit in the middle of the pack like I had planned. I'll have to show more of what I'm capable of, which, frustratingly, will have the potential to drive up my price.

Shit.

A fist flies for my face, and I battle every instinct that's been beaten into me *not* to block it. Knuckles crash into my cheek with a loud thwap, the momentum of the hit knocking me back. My years of training are the only thing that keep my feet under me so I don't go crashing to the floor.

Pain explodes in my cheek, but my body learned long ago not to respond to it like an untrained fae would. My eyes don't water. My mind doesn't reel with confusion. Anger does surge, but not at the guard, Crit, who's now standing in front of me leering. I'm pissed at myself. I got lost in my thoughts and dropped my guard, and what's worse is that Tilleo caught me doing it.

Bloody fuck.

I straighten up immediately, shoving the throbbing in my face to the back of my mind. I'm once again alert and focused. Crit stands in my space, his hardened leather armor brushing against my silk-covered breasts as he stares down at me, a cruel smile stretched across his face. He loves to put me in my place, and I can see in his dark gleaming eyes exactly what this is doing for him. If Tilleo wasn't here, Crit would grind the erection I know he has right now into me before searching for a secluded corner where he'd do his best to make me scream, and not in a good way. Crit isn't in the ludere often as he's part of Tilleo's personal guard, but when he's here, everyone knows to be careful and to steer clear of the shadows that he likes to lurk in.

Crit steps aside, and Tilleo moves to take his place looming over me. I stare at the pure gold crest resting on my master's chest and wait for him to wash me from the Bidding or punish me for not paying attention. He reaches out, and I steel myself against the flinch that wants to tick through me as he does. Slowly, he tucks a finger inside the dark blue silk at my neck, sliding it down my chest, over my nipple, and dropping even further until I feel his knuckle brushing past the muscles of my stomach. His trajectory only stops when it hits the top of the metal crest resting over my cunt.

I stop myself from holding my breath, forcing air in and out of my lungs evenly as I wait for what he'll do next. It feels like forever before Tilleo pulls his hand from my dress, reaching down and straightening the strip of fabric that hangs between my thighs to hammer home even harder that he can. His hand brushes against my smooth skin, pausing for a beat before he finally pulls away. It takes everything in me not to react to his unwanted touch. I want to recoil from it, but I know where that kind of reaction can lead. Some like the fight more than the fun. Besides, I already know that Tilleo likes to test me like this. It's a favorite game he likes to play, given my history here.

When enticement training was introduced to us, I'd refused. Master Lira threw a fit and punished me almost to death, but surprisingly, Tilleo stepped in and allowed me to reject this aspect of our instruction here. I was permitted to say *no* to learning how to seduce and entice and endure. I thought it was because Tilleo didn't want to waste what he'd invested in me up to that point. I was prepared to die rather than submit. I learned later what he had planned for me.

I shut down the alarm crawling up my throat as unwelcome memories break from their cage and try to swarm me. *I can handle this,* I tell myself. *So long as Tilleo doesn't push for more than just a feel of me, I can stand here and take it.* The flashbacks that haunt me won't pull me under if this is all he does. *But if he pushes,* my mind warns, *I know I'll do something stupid.* What Tilleo plans for Linae will look like a fun game compared to what he'll do to me for using what he's trained me to be against him, and I will.

I keep my breathing steady and paced, showing no outer signs of the inner turmoil that's rolling through me, as the room grows hotter and all eyes wait for what will happen next.

"I'm not sure where you went, Auset, but the rest of us are right here," Tilleo chides, as he pinches my chin. He tilts my face, taking in the pink skin and swelling that I can feel settling into my cheek and eye socket from the fist I just took. Crit's smile widens as he eyes the mark on my face. Not missing that reaction, Tilleo glares at the guard for a beat before returning his hard gaze to me. "Do you want your holes auctioned off instead of your abilities with a blade?" he threatens.

I say nothing, knowing he's still playing with me like a bored cat with a mouse.

"Speak," he orders, playing the game I've watched him play so many times with other slaves.

"No, master," I answer evenly, my heart hammering in my chest so hard I worry he can feel it.

"Should I make you a house whore, assign you to the barracks where you can let your mind wander all you want while they use up your tight gash and break this hard body?"

"No, master," I repeat, my stomach churning at the threat.

He leans closer, his lips skimming the lobe of my ear, and I tamp down on the repulsed shiver that wants to work its way up my spine and get me killed.

"I have high hopes for you, slave," he whispers so that only I can hear his declaration. "I've let you hold back. I've given you latitude with your training as a thank you for clearing my way of Dorsin, but my generosity ends here. Do you understand me?"

I swallow down my disquiet at his declaration. Tilleo can say he was doing me a kindness or in some odd way paying back a debt, but I know nothing could be further from the truth. I know this monster too well. He wants something from me, and he wants me to feel indebted, grateful, and eager to give him whatever it is.

"I am your blade to command," I whisper back to him submissively, my mind spinning with what he might demand of me.

"Good girl," he purrs, his carob-colored eyes glazed with greed as his hand skims down the exposed skin at my side. "There will be a time in the next couple of days when someone else from an Order will demand to play with you. He has a taste for rare beauties who have yet to be broken. He will single you out, get you alone, and when he does, you are to kill him. Am I clear?"

I stiffen at the command, unable to hide my shock. "Yes, master. I am your blade to command," I manage to answer evenly out of habit, despite every cell in my body revolting against what I've just been mandated to do.

I have no issue with the kill order, but the Bidding is supposed to be a sanctum, which means no Order members killing or threatening each other. No hunts. No sleight-of-hand. There is zero tolerance for any deceitful nonsense that violates the rules that ensure everyone's safety. To transgress the sanctum is a death wish. An Order member would earn a quick, easy end for doing so. A blade slave like me though...they'd rip me apart piece by piece for violating the safeties that have been put in place. They'd end me eventually for what Tilleo is ordering, but it would be nothing but brutal horror each and every second leading up to my last breath.

I want to scream, but I can't. I want to beg Tilleo to take it back, but I know there's no use. Just like with Ency, Kirid, and Linae, life as I know it is over with only a couple of casually muttered words. Tilleo is asking me to execute a member of an undisclosed Order for touching *me*, a blade slave. He's engineering my execution, and judging by the look on his face as he straightens in front of me, he has no intention of saving me from the fate he's damning me to. There will be no stepping in on his part and admitting he ordered the hit. No. He'll claim I'm defective and leave me to suffer and die for *him*, a malevolent master who's been setting me up for failure from the first moment he laid eyes on me.

"Go see a healer before this darkens any further," he orders with an impatient bark, gesturing to my face. Like the trained pet that I am, I immediately step around him, narrowly avoiding bumping shoulders with Crit, as I walk assuredly out of the hashery and head in the direction of the healer's wing.

My heart pounds and my thoughts race. Anger unfurls in my chest like a poisonous blooming flower as adrenaline takes root in my veins. There was a time these feelings would make me feel powerful, but I know better now, and it all just makes me feel worse. What good has getting pissed ever done for me? What power have I ever really found in anger and outrage? I *want* to rebel, to resist, but there's no fighting back here, there's no winning. All I've ever wanted was freedom, but it was never going to be mine. I saw the truth in Tilleo's face today. That bastard was never letting me leave this place. I've been a fucking fool, and now it's time to pay the price for it.

Robotically, I turn down the maze of arched hallways that encircle the large round training pits at the center of the ludere. My feet move of their own volition as the rest of me tries to come to terms with my imminent death and the joke my life has been up to this point. I thought I would get out. I would pay my debt back to the Order that purchased me, and one day have a life and a home that solely belonged to me. How stupid. I had hoped and dreamed despite knowing exactly where that would lead.

I could try to run, but I've seen too many others struck down by dozens of arrows only feet away from the ludere doors. They died nowhere even close to the gates that lead out of Tilleo's stronghold and into the oppressive and punishing desert beyond. If I can't run and I can't ignore the kill order, what does that even leave?

Death.

It all leads to death.

The only question now is by whose hands. Mine? Tilleo's? The guards? The Order's? I knew the reaper would find me eventually, but this is too soon.

By the time I step under the arch that leads into the healing chamber, an all-consuming numbness has taken hold and started to spread. A helpless sigh spills out of me at the cruel inevitability smothering my future like a blistering gust on the hottest desert day. I wait for a healer to notice me and fix whatever Crit did to my face, as a dreaded certainty settles in my soul.

Sometime in the next few days, I will die.

I fist my hands once before forcing my body to relax. There's no running from this; there's no winning against Tilleo. I will never know what freedom tastes like or figure out who I was before I was forced to become a savage. All the years of training. All the things I've done in the name of survival, only to die on these cursed specks of sand surrounded by the blood-soaked great wall that has caged me in for as long as I can remember.

I tell myself that death is better than being sold at the skin markets, but it does little to erase the sting of my bitter reality. I was raised in this hole of despair, and now, despite my every effort, I will die here never knowing anything different. Hope truly is a deadly viper, and at last its poison has finally come for me.

5

THE SOUL-JARRING TRUMPET OF THE GREAT bone horns stationed at the stronghold's entry fills the halls of the ludere. The sudden thunderous noise makes the healer attending to my cheek jump. I fight the immediate urge to run to join the assembly I'm supposed to be a part of as the healer finishes magically fixing my broken cheek and bruised face. The horns sound off again seconds later, announcing that the great doors are opening and that guests for the Bidding have finally arrived.

"Stop moving, pet. I am almost done, and then you can be off to watch the caravans roll through the gates," the healer chides, as though I'm some wiggly cria eager to be off and celebrating the arrival of a grand parade.

Fuck the Orders. Fuck this place.

"If you don't hurry, I'll be late to my post. Then I'll be back in here with far more than my cheek in need of healing," I grumble at the withered old man as anxiety picks up my heart and starts to sprint off with it.

While waiting for the healer to gather what he needed, I spent my time planning the best way to die. It's made my tongue more loose and cantankerous than I've ever dared before. Luckily, the healer seems more bothered by my injury than my impertinence.

The healer huffs with frustration at being rushed, but he knows I speak the truth. He increases his flow of magic into me, and I bite back my blood's reaction to it, willing away the sting that starts in my gums as the power fills me. I've forced my body to keep its secrets all this time, but the rush of magic and my current emotional state makes it harder to clamp down and shut off the way I *truly* want to respond to the pain.

"There, good as new, my pet," the healer announces, patting my shoulder and offering me a warm, yellow-toothed smile.

If only there were real kindness behind the gesture. I nod once, dismissing the empty show of compassion, and then I rush out of the healer's wing and race through the ludere toward the front gates. Hair the color of moonlight and deep blue fabric trail behind me as I sprint in the oppressive heat to where I'm supposed to be standing to greet the incoming guests. The sun is starting to dip, which, thankfully, will bring some relief as dusk steps in and begins its slow sensual dance with night. I fly through the main doors of the ludere, aiming for the now open gates that are built into the oppressive walls surrounding Tilleo's vast property.

Blade slaves run the sands between the ludere and the walls twice a day, but as I aim for the grand gates, instead of looping around the building like I usually do, there's a surprising current of exhilaration that zips through me. Maybe, if I time it right, I can ride the shadows and sneak out of the open gates. I immediately snort at my own ridiculousness. Better a quick death at the end of a blade than the slow burning death that awaits anyone trying to traverse the Corozean desert on foot. That's even if Tilleo didn't have me immediately hunted down and brought back before the elements could claim me. It wouldn't take him long to realize I was gone either. No, on a night like this, all the eyes out here are sharp and on alert.

Hurriedly, I close the distance between me and the gathering crowd. I entertained the thought of blowing this off and refusing to cooperate with anything Tilleo wants, but I'm still trying to figure out a plan, and the only way I can keep doing that is to play along until I can sort it all out. Spotting the other blade slaves amidst the assembling house slaves and guards, I wind my way in their direction.

I've never seen outside the ludere when the outer gates were open like they are now. Eyes all around me are on the lookout for the caravans as I weave through the tightening crowd. I, however, drink in the landscape beyond the cage of this place like it's a newfound oasis and I'm dying of thirst. All I see is dimming skies, rolling desert hills, and waving heat as far as the eye can see. In the distance, sand stags begin to slowly solidify. The large animals are certain to be pulling broad carriages filled with the members of the different Orders, and I rush to find my place amongst the lines of my fellow savages.

Tilleo has us standing on each side of the path the caravans will enter through. I spot a gap between Kin and Orit and hurry to fill it. Kin nods at me and then turns to watch her future slowly approach the wide open gates. I quickly straighten the panels of fabric I'm wearing, making sure that everything is covered and draped the way it's supposed to be. I adjust the metal belt at my hips, realigning Tilleo's crest over the apex of my thighs and the crack of my ass. A welcome breeze picks up the strands of my hair and invites them to dance around me. I rush to smooth them back, going still before my movements catch unwelcome eyes.

The bone horns bellow again, the deep sound reverberating through my body as the first set of sand stags glide lazily through the gates. I marvel at how the beasts move gracefully through the thick, hot sand. I've seen the herd that Tilleo owns before, but only from afar. Massive horns jut out from their heads, but they look more like odd antlers with the offshoots being large and flat. I study them, observing that the flat bits create shade that shrouds the front half of the sand stag's body. Their white coat is wiry and short, and golden sand plummets from it in tiny waterfalls with each step the animals take. They're twice the size of the biggest fae I've ever seen, and there's a majestic grace to their gait as they effortlessly pull the large carriage sleds behind them.

A sand stag trumpets a deep haunting sound, and I can practically hear the declaration that it's home and hungry in the robust call. Other stags behind bray in answer, and I wonder what it would be like to work as a team like they do.

Tilleo stands with a large contingent of guards and house slaves at the front of his massive desert manor. Layers of towering square sandstone peaks loom behind him as though the manor rose from the sand itself and formed solely because Tilleo decreed it. Rows of small rectangular windows are cut out from the collection of towers that somehow all come together to form one big building. I'm sure there are house slaves sneaking glances out of them to spy on what's going on down here.

Tilleo's astute gaze misses nothing as it slides from the convoy to us and back again. The first of the carriages stops in front of him. Slaves hurry to open the doors, and out step four stunning female fae dripping in jewels and dresses that are more extravagant than anything I could ever dream up. Tilleo kisses hands and smiles roguishly at them as they all greet each other like they're old friends. Taria and Sennet move closer, waiting to be called on as needed, and I connect that these women are from the Order of Vulpi, which Taria and Sennet are assigned to watch over while they're here for the Bidding.

Panic starts at the base of my throat as I suddenly realize I don't know how to identify who the Order of Scorpions are. I look over at Harsh and hope Tilleo told him while I was off having my face fixed and my future ruined. The masters explained that each of the Orders will be wearing some level of glamour during the entirety of the Bidding. They hide who they are from each other either by wearing a face that doesn't truly belong to them or cloaking themselves in the mascot of their Order, but I don't know how hard or easy it will be to tell who is who.

Trunks and cases are whisked away from the carriage by house slaves, and then another carriage is pulling up in front of Tilleo as the Order of Vulpi are escorted into the massive sandstone manor. Six huge males pour out of the doors of the next carriage. A snarling bear head is stitched on the back of the vests they wear over their tunics, marking them as the Order of Bruins. Orit shivers behind me, reminding me of the warning we received from one of the masters about the Bruins' brutal nature. Yotta and Taur, two male blade slaves, move closer to the Order. As they do, it dawns on me that Tilleo didn't assign a female blade slave to the Bruins' care, further supporting the Order's bad reputation when it comes to the female sex.

My mouth drops open before I quickly snap it shut when the next carriage presents three large fae that are half wolf, half man. They stand on two feet, wear suede trousers, and that's it as the rest of them is covered in thick, coarse fur that leads up to a wolf's head. I don't envy the Order of Wolves in this forsaken heat. Unsurprisingly, I watch as several house slaves immediately start fanning the three members as they greet Tilleo just as exuberantly as the other Orders have.

More carriages pull up and empty out, and I track Harsh closely for signs that our Order has arrived. Two carriages are left, and the sand stags stomp impatiently as they wait their turn to unload their cargo. I watch the curtained windows of the second to last carriage as it passes, wondering who's inside, but the fabric covering the windows is still, no one inside curious enough to push it aside and peek out.

Another light breeze moves through the open gates, cooling the sweat that's collecting at my nape. I want to wipe it away, but I have nowhere to wipe it other than the silk strips I'm wearing. I can picture Figg watching from the ludere and making a note to have me caned for daring to defile this ridiculous dress with my tainted perspiration. I silently beg the wind to blow a little harder, in desperate need of a little relief from the heat. Suddenly, Harsh moves toward the stopped carriage.

Trepidation makes my chest feel tight as I rush to fall into step with the male blade slave. The side door of the carriage opens, and I watch carefully, ready to take in the members of the Order Harsh and I are charged with serving, when my feet and my heart simultaneously stop. Tilleo bows to the three individuals that step gracefully down to meet him. His carob gaze fills with apprehension as he looks over the three glamoured skeletons.

Bloody bastards.

They're male, dressed in onyx suits that look far too regal for anything this deep in the desert. They stand stiffly, only their heads swiveling slightly as their black eyes scan their surroundings. I realize I'm standing and staring. All at once my survival instincts kick back in, restarting my brain and forcing my feet and legs back into motion. In a few strides, I catch up with where Harsh has stopped, waiting to be called on for any assistance.

Shock and fear pound through my pulse like war drums in the dead of night as I stare at the three skeletons exchanging stilted pleasantries with Tilleo. In all my time here at the ludere training for the Bidding, it never occurred to me that the three males who slit Dorsin's throat and then stole something from a hidden safe in his room were members of an Order. I feel utterly stupid in this moment for never having made that connection. I don't know why I thought I'd never see them again. I don't even know if these three are the same skeletons who appeared out of nowhere that night, but I fight back a tremor of apprehension all the same.

When I first arrived at this living nightmare, my memories of Dorsin and waking up in that cage haunted me. I expected they would always be memories I would battle against. All too soon though, new horrors shoved those old ones far from my mind. It wasn't long before I stopped bothering to work out how I ended up here altogether. What was the point? Trying to figure it out only whipped up taunting memories and too many questions that I could never answer. None of it did anything to change my position here as a blade slave. There was no escaping this place, and ultimately I needed to focus on surviving Tilleo, the masters, and the other savages.

Tilleo signals for me and Harsh to come closer, and one of the skeletons' black gazes lands on me. All at once, I can smell the potent rot of orcs' blood mixed with the tang of Dorsin's death. I feel the bite of boots against my ribs and hips as Dorsin kicked the last of the air and hope from my frail body. The ghost of an orc's tongue moves up my thigh as Harsh and I stride closer. Brutally, I shove those recollections from my mind. I work to focus on what's actually happening all around me, unwilling to give Tilleo any reason to take notice of me no matter how stunned and afraid I find myself right now.

Thankfully, my steps don't falter as a realization reaches up and slaps me across the face. Does Tilleo know? Does he know about the hunt the Order of Scorpions executed against his boss? Was *he* the one who purchased Dorsin's death? I quickly study Tilleo while he's not looking, and suddenly find myself questioning everything.

No. I reassure myself as Harsh and I stop near Tilleo, once again forgotten like the silent wraiths we were trained to be. Why would Tilleo have brought me here if he'd known who truly killed his master? Dorsin was supposed to be ransoming me to someone, so if Tilleo had known about that plan, he'd have picked up where Dorsin had left off before he'd mercilessly had his throat slit. I don't think Tilleo knew then. Which leads me to wonder if somehow he knows now?

Is that why I've been tasked with murdering one of the Order members attending this Bidding? Is it payback for unknowingly keeping the Order of Scorpions' secret?

Silently, I observe the three fae in their skeleton glamour. They're once again exchanging pleasantries with my master, and I begin to wonder which one of them I'm going to die for after I violate the sanctum and slit *their* throat. Tilleo has to be after revenge. Killing two birds with one stone is a favorite pastime of his.

"Follow my people to your tent. They'll set up baths for you and help you freshen up. There's time to rest before the celebrations start tonight," Tilleo tells them merrily, and it's all I can do not to clench my hands into fists at his friendly, easygoing tone.

What is wrong with me?

I want to slap sense back into myself. Normally, I'm more controlled than this. I don't slip. My thoughts don't wander. I don't get caught being off my game. I want to shake my head, force my frenzied thoughts to settle into the cold, calculating rock that I am, but I can't. It seems even *I* am not immune to the worries and distractions the Bidding brings. Neither can I run from the ghosts of my past I thought buried and long gone.

I watch the three skeletons as they nod and exchange temporary goodbyes with Tilleo. I wrap all of my distraction in a tight ball and stow it deep in my mind. The Bidding has started. I'm now surrounded by the best hired blades, one of which I'm supposed to kill. Now's not the time to get lost in questions and unsolvable mysteries. Now is the time to prove I'm not that frightened little girl who was found chained in a corner and surrounded by terror and death. Now is the time to show all of them the monster they created.

"I'm giving you two of my best," Tilleo informs the skeletons, gesturing over to where Harsh and I stand as still as the manor house at our backs. "Feel free to use them however suits you," he further instructs nonchalantly, and the representatives of the Order of Scorpions turn to look us over.

I breathe through the panic that hammers through me as I once again wonder if these are the fae from that night. Will they recognize me? Will I recognize them? I try to look past their glamour and fix on the features beneath the black and white painted across every inch of their exposed exteriors, but it's hard to focus. Their eyes slide down my body, and it feels as though it's their hands caressing over my skin instead of their pitch black gazes. Their onyx stares don't even bother to set upon Harsh before they turn to follow the house slaves now leading them to their tent.

Trunks of the Order's possessions are lifted high above the leading slaves' heads as we move away from Tilleo and the manor. I watch the Order of Scorpions' backs as we go. It's as though the skeletons *carve* a path instead of merely walking as they make their way through the sand to their lodgings. Harsh and I follow like we're water flowing through the ravine they leave behind in their wake. Power radiates off the trio like capes billowing in the desert wind. They're dark and dangerous and, for some reason, incredibly enticing.

Maybe it's the small part of me that's still hoping for answers about that night, but even if these three are the assassins that murdered Dorsin, they wouldn't know anything. They didn't want to help me then, and I doubt anything is different now. Harsh looks over at me like he's checking to see if I also feel the venom steeping in their power, but I keep my *good savage* mask in place and ignore his probing gaze. Internally I scoff at myself for shutting Harsh out. We're not exactly friendly, but it's more out of habit than anything else. I typically run on the side of too serious and cautious here, but really there's no point in reinforcing the protective barriers I usually have in place. I'm going to die before I ever see beyond these walls; maybe it's time to shake things up and live a little before I do.

The group approaches a gargantuan cream-colored tent that's been erected in the west quadrant of the stronghold. There's another matching structure in the south quadrant, but I don't look to see who's headed in its direction as the flaps of the enormous tent in front of me are pulled open by two guards who have been waiting for this very moment. House slaves pour into the mouth of the split-hide entryway, hurrying to place trunks and to find a home for everything the Order of Scorpions have brought with them. They stride into the tent like the honored guests they are, and the thick flaps drop closed behind me and Harsh as we follow closely behind.

We both take up position on either side of the entrance, and I try hard not to marvel at the luxuries revealed inside. Tall lamps containing bouncing fairy light softly illuminate the spacious interior. Lush carpets in all kinds of colors and patterns layer the ground as though it would be a sin for the skeletons to set foot on anything other than the softest of surfaces. Three inviting pallets are spaced out against the back wall of the tent. I suspect each of them is stuffed with the finest of feathers and padding. They certainly have the fluffiest blankets I've ever seen draped all over their surfaces, as well as piles of pillows arranged on top. I'm surprised Tilleo didn't add a flesh slave or two to each of the exquisite surfaces, their bodies spread enticingly in a special welcome I'd expect these fae would embrace wholeheartedly.

The temperature inside the tent is magical. I have to swallow down a moan of approval as we stand in the cool, crisp air, waiting to be ordered around. There are no fans in sight, and I can only guess what it would take to spell this space to remain so deliciously cold and comfortable. Slaves position trunks at the end of three pallets, while another goes to magically heat up the water sitting in the three separate gold baths to my right. She must be a conduit, and

I itch to ask her how her magic works as she hurries from one gilded tub to another. I keep my mouth shut, but the strange urge to rebel and do what I want feels warm as it settles just under my skin.

I've never fed the angry beast inside of me. Never allowed the fires of rage and frustration to be stoked too high. Tilleo and the masters would simply beat it out of anyone who dared to defy them. I've worked hard to deaden my recalcitrant urges over the years, but I find myself hesitant to continue the practice. What purpose does it serve to continue to bite my tongue and scour my every action ad nauseam? I've spent endless hours calculating what could make me a target, get me beaten, call too much attention or too little. What was the point of it all now?

I look around me at the audacious opulence slapping me across the face over and over again. Tilleo has all of this at his fingertips, and yet I've lived a life of starvation, stone surfaces, and brutality. I run my gaze over the three skeletons, who are examining their new quarters thoroughly, and I dare to wonder what makes *them* so deserving of all of this and not me? Are they not hired killers just like I've been honed to be? Were they blade slaves too at their genesis, or did death's calling find them some other way?

"You're dismissed," one of the skeletons commands, and I pull my thoughts and critical gaze back as the house slaves quickly bow and then scurry out of the flaps between me and Harsh. "Take the guards outside with you," he calls after the retreating slaves, and I debate if he means for me and Harsh to go too. Harsh doesn't move, so I don't either.

"I'm shattered. How long do we have to stay at this thing tonight before I can find a willing wet cunt and then the back of my eyelids?" one of the skeletons asks as he plops down into a hand-carved black maple chair.

There are three other magnificent works of art created solely for these males to set their delicate asses in. The gorgeous gleaming chairs surround a thick wood table made of the same precious wood, the cost of which could probably fund the ludere for a year...or five. I'm taken aback by the realization that I know what the table and chairs are made out of, let alone that they're extremely rare and coveted. I've never seen anything like it in my time as a blade slave, which means it must be something I know from my long forgotten life before.

Another skeleton snorts as he walks over to check the temperature of the water in one of the baths. "You snored almost the whole way out to this Kings' forsaken hovel. You have nothing to be shattered about, Ri—" The skeleton's all black eyes cautiously flick over to me and Harsh. "*Bones,*" he quickly corrects himself.

Bones's eyes follow the other skeleton's gaze back to where Harsh and I are standing inside the entryway, and a smile lifts one corner of his mouth. "I'm a growing boy, *Skull,*" he whines, over enunciating the other's fake name.

"Growing boys don't get to play with pretty cunts; they get to go to bed early and jerk off until their sheets grow hard enough to crack," the third skeleton points out as he removes his suit pieces and unties his black leather travel armor beneath.

Skull and Bones both chuckle lightly at that, and I even hear Harsh give a quiet snort of amusement.

"You're always the lame, wilted branch on the tree, Scorpius," Bones taunts the third skeleton as he rises from the end of the bed he's perched on and starts to pull off his own layers and hidden armor.

Bones pulls off his vambraces and then unties and removes his rerebraces and the attached shoulder pieces of his kit. Methodically he unbuckles the straps that fasten his black layered-leather breastplate and then shrugs it off too. I'm curious about his sure and swift movements as he disarms. I'd expect him to fumble without a servant to do the harder parts, but his fingers are deft and practiced, which means he does this on his own more often than not. Maybe this Order isn't as prissy as I thought they might be with servants waiting on their every whim to make life as convenient and cozy as possible.

Bones is sweaty under the layers of armor, and before I can look away, he pulls his coal-dyed tunic off and sighs with relief. The glamour paints his skin with shadow, only highlighting the shape of white bone where his actual bones should be. But I trace the grid of muscle on his abdomen, eyeing the lines of his hardened torso with a greed I have no business feeling. No. These three aren't like the flabby masters I've known.

There's nothing soft and complacent about the fae in front of me. He's raw, honed and sharpened bulk under smooth, unmarked skin. The glamour wants to trick me into seeing something else, but there's no missing the size of him or the way his muscles fill out his body despite the white bones and the pitch patches painted over his flesh. I lift my gaze to his defined pecs and see little black nipples that for some reason make me want to smile.

Skeletons don't have nipples; they need to work on their glamour.

Bones's chest begins to shake, and I look up to find his black eyes are fixed on me. A gleam of amusement lights up his onyx depths, and I hurry to look away, only to find the other two skeletons are watching me too.

"What's your name, cria?" Scorpius asks, and irritation flits through me at the condescending term.

Cria are babies of the herd animal fae have come to rely on for all kinds of things. We shear their coats and use them to make different fabrics and goods. Their meat is a staple in most fae diets—if you're not a blade slave, that is—and their bones are strong and used to forge useful weapons and tools. Cria can be a term of endearment spoken from a mother to her babe, but out of the skeleton's mouth, I know it's meant to make me feel small and useless.

"Slave," I reply, momentarily surprised by the cheek I've allowed to flow from my lips.

Scorpius's black gaze narrows slightly, and I hold my breath, waiting to see if he'll explode and punish me for my insolence.

Just like with the healer earlier, it appears my seditious thoughts have actually manifested and loosened the tight hold I should be maintaining over my lips and tongue. I tamp down my own shock as my mind screams at me in warning about just how stupid it is to mouth off to a member of an Order. The skeleton looks at me like my death might be even more imminent than Tilleo had planned, and for some reason, that doesn't have me shaking in my strips of silk like it might have before.

There's a part of me that welcomes the threat in his eyes while another piece of me promises I won't go easy. My blood doesn't run cold. Sweat doesn't bead my brow, and there's no hesitation weighing my muscles down as his eyes stay fixed on mine. All I can think is, if he's going to kill me, maybe sooner rather than later might not be such a bad thing, and I wonder how many of them I could take with me before I go.

6

UNEASE COILS AROUND ME, BUT IT'S HARSH'S, not my own. Instead, I'm more curious about what I might have just unleashed and strangely eager to see where this will lead. Scorpius glares at me as though he's mentally doing his best to light me on fire, and I quickly realize that I'm looking at him the exact same way. I know I should stop this. I need to check myself before I bite off more than I can chew. The only problem is I feel ravenous right now.

Laughter draws Scorpius's scowl. Skull stares at us both, a chuckle spilling from his lips and serving to lighten the building tension. "*Slave* is easy enough to remember," he points out, a smooth smile somehow brightening his skeletal features, while Bones watches on with amusement sparkling in his black eyes. Scorpius studies me like he's waiting for me to blush with embarrassment or apologize for my out-of-line and snappish response. I do neither, my unapologetic eyes meeting his blink for blink.

"Wash me, Slave," Scorpius orders, his ebony stare filled with challenge and his command designed to put me back under his thumb where he thinks I belong. His tone is deep, his order and authority absolute, and it speaks to a longing in me I didn't know existed until now.

Without missing a beat, I move toward a gold-plated tub, his long strides meeting me there. He reaches behind him and, in one smooth move, pulls off the black tunic that's sticking to the lines and curves of his body, dropping it on the ground, like the item of clothing means nothing to him. The disregard heats my blood even more, and I struggle not to allow any of it to settle my features into a glare.

As a blade slave, I'm only given annually two sets of training linens, two sets of underwear and wraps to bind my breasts, one form of ill-fitting training armor, and nothing else. Watching him brush aside something so easily, something that *I* would treasure, makes me want to slap him. Then again, he's about to be bathed by a blade slave in a golden tub with magically heated water, so what do I really expect? These fae aren't soft like my masters, but they're clearly just as pompous and entitled. They're hard on the outside, feeble and fussy on the inside, and I have zero respect for any of it.

Scorpius holds his arms out as though he's unable to unfasten his own pants, and Bones snickers at his fellow Order member's actions. I move closer, refusing to be intimidated, and reach for the laces that tuck away his cock. Before I begin to undo them, I notice several blades sheathed into the design of his black trousers, and I find myself reaching for them instead. He stiffens slightly. The movement is so minute I wouldn't have registered it if I weren't so close. I bite back the satisfied smile that wants to quirk my lips, and smoothly go to work disarming him. Arrogantly, I train my silver eyes on his sable stare as I pull knives and daggers from their sewn-in sheaths in his pants. I casually collect the blades in one hand as I go, moving deftly, as I instinctually find all of his hiding places without much effort.

His black eyes are filled with scorn, but there's intrigue floating around in that dark gaze too. All I need to do is look down at the laces of his pants for evidence that my unarming him this way is appreciated by his baser nature. I won't though. A smirk tilts his full lips as I slowly bend to pull the last blades from his calves, and I can practically see the filthy thoughts glowing freely in his gaze. He's doing it on purpose now. Trying to unsettle me. He's probing for a weakness.

I wonder for a split second if Tilleo warned them about my aversion to using my body in a way that I don't want. I decide quickly that it doesn't matter. My proximity to this arrogant Order member doesn't bother me. I don't feel threatened, only challenged, and I'm done handing my power over freely. If this Scorpion wants to play, then let's play. I sting too.

Harsh is suddenly next to me, his hands outstretched to take possession of the weapons gripped in my hand. I didn't see him move, and I don't know if I was too focused on the shape of Scorpius's face under the glamour to hear someone tell Harsh to relieve me of the collection in my palms or if Harsh is that stealthy. Carefully I hand them over while still nakedly studying the face under the skeleton mask.

"Careful, *Slave*," Scorpius taunts. "If I didn't know better, I'd think you were trying to remember me." I go still at his words.

Does *he* remember me from that night in Dorsin's room? Does he know that's *exactly* what I'm trying to do, to match his features and voice with that faded, dusty memory? He tilts his head at my stony reaction, and reality slams back into me. I hand off the last of the knives and decide I'm reading him wrong. He doesn't mean *remember* him from my past, he means I'm trying to remember what he looks like for the *future*. Knowing what he looks like could help to track him down. Little does he know, I'm going to kill one of them and then promptly have my head removed from my body, so getting called out for memorizing his features doesn't exactly pose the threat he thinks it does.

"My apologies, *master*," I offer, forcing my eyes to drop from his and doing my best to enact some semblance of humility and contrition.

I don't feel it, I'm just trying to throw him off. He thinks he has me pegged. He has nothing. I tap into my training and shut down. I've spent years perfecting a hardened, impenetrable exterior; time to put it to good use even if it no longer serves the purpose I thought it would. The vital protection provided by my walls and masks was nothing more than an illusion. It was never going to guide me to freedom like I thought it would. The truth of that stings, but as I shed my reservations and unchain parts of me I've locked away and hidden for so long, I find myself feeling slightly liberated as opposed to damned, which is oddly... unexpected.

"Mmmmm, *master* has a nice ring to it," Scorpius purrs at me.

I simply lift my unamused gaze back up to his and hold it for a beat before reaching for the ties of his pants. One by one, I begin to unlace his breeches like I haven't a care in the world. Skull and Bones both snicker at the *master* comment, but I don't pay them any mind as I peel Scorpius's leathers down his powerful thighs. I ignore the large cock that springs free entirely too close to my face as I bend down to pull the pants off of the skeleton's calves and feet.

The glamour works over the entirety of his body, now that all of him is exposed to my eyes. I try not to stare at the ink-soaked skin of the thick member at the apex of his thighs or at the dark sack hanging just below it. Even the hair dusting his base and crawling up to his belly button is as black as raven feathers.

I rise from the ground, embracing the confident predator that I am, and hand the trousers to Harsh, who's once again waiting with outstretched hands. Scorpius steps into the tub of warm water as I move to a side table that's been set up to hold different soaps, oils, and shampoos. I pick up a rag that just might be the softest thing I've ever felt and a glass bottle with the outline of a body etched into it. Blade slaves aren't supposed to be able to read, which means we're given pictures on things to help interpret contents. I was

surprised to find that I could read, several different languages in fact, but that's another set of secrets that will go
with me to the grave.

"So, Slave, tell me and my brothers why we should bid
on you," Scorpius orders as I turn back to him, soap and
washcloth in hand.

He hasn't dipped his body into the heated water like I
expected him to do. Instead, he's just standing there knee-
deep in the tub, his entire body on display, ready and waiting for me to scrub him clean. I grab a hammered gold
pitcher to use for rinsing, and when my eyes find Scorpius's
again, his soot-black gaze turns raptorial.

"Be sure to be very convincing, *Slave*, this might be your
only chance to impress us," he tells me, his cock twitching
at me like an excited pup at supper time.

I want to slap it down and laugh at his efforts to intimidate me. I've trained, bathed, and slept next to male blade
slaves my whole life. Yes, I refused the training that taught
me to fuck in order to kill, but that doesn't mean a large
dancing cock is going to fracture my delicate sensibilities.
Clearly, he has no idea what goes on under the roof of Tilleo's ludere.

I grab the base of Scorpius's cock like we're old acquaintances catching up after too much time has passed. I swear I
hear a gasp of surprise escape his lips before Bones's booming laugh covers it up. I use my grip on him to pull him
closer to the edge of the tub I'm standing outside of, and
then I release his member to wet the rag and apply soap to
it. I pour warm water over his body with the pitcher, and
then I start to methodically wash his body as though I've

trained my whole life to clean arrogant fae instead of assassinate them.

When I don't immediately speak up to answer the lude and thinly veiled question posed to me by this pompous prick, Harsh's assured voice fills the tent.

"I am at the top of this crop of blade slaves, masters. I wield swords as though they're an extension of my arms, killing with precision and great skill. I would serve the Order of Scorpions proudly, bringing great honor to you and your house. I am one of the best hunters this ludere has created, earning my rank through training and tests, not on my knees...or my back."

My silver gaze slices over to Harsh at his insinuation. Unable to help myself, my eyes narrow at the unfounded cheap shot he just took. He's correct in boasting about being one of the best here. Only Leto tops his skill and kill tally. What he doesn't know is that when I put in the effort, not even Leto matches me. Then again, only I know that. Guess it's good for Harsh that I always leashed my efforts.

I dismiss Harsh's insinuation, promising myself that I'll address his unfounded slight later, and focus back on the fae's body beneath my hands. Silence fills the tent again after Harsh's pitiful efforts to ingratiate himself. I want to scoff, but I choke it down. Begging these three to bid on any of us is a waste of breath from air-starved lungs. If they *are* the three from that night in Dorsin's office, they're as empty as the masters have trained us to be here at the ludere. If they're *not* the skeletons from my nightmares, then they're still members of the Order of Scorpions, a house that has never bid on a blade slave and more than likely never will.

All of this is a waste of time, and Tilleo has already guaranteed that I don't have much of that left.

Scorpius's muscles are unyielding beneath my touch as I circle soap over his skin. His glamour plays with my eyes, but my hands tell me the full story about just how deadly these Scorpions are when they want to be. They're playing with me and Harsh now, but just like their namesake, they could sting at any moment, and I have no doubt that a brush with them would be lethal.

My senses warn that there are too many eyes on me as I streak suds over Scorpius's abs. I reach behind him, spreading his cheeks so I can thoroughly scrub in between the globes of his ass. He suddenly jerks away from me, his heavy gaze narrowing at my efforts.

"My apologies, master, I thought I was to *wash* you?" I ask with faux confusion and a vapid tone.

Skull and Bones both cover their enjoyment at Scorpius's expense with well-placed bony hands over their mouths. While they hide their smirks, it does little to hide their titters, and I have to work hard to keep a grin from stretching across my own face at their unexpected giggles.

"I'm good there," Scorpius snaps, reclaiming the space in front of me from his retreat so I can finish with the rest of him.

As I start again, my thoughts wander to Leto. I begin to compare this fae's body with his. Maybe it's because Leto is the only other person I've had my hands on like this, but it's interesting to indulge in the differences between them. Either way, I quickly tabulate that Scorpius is taller and wider, but they both carry hard, unforgiving muscle under their smooth scar-free skin. It makes me wonder what the Order of Scorpions' training regime is like to keep them as fit as us blade slaves. Surprisingly, it also makes me wonder what this fae would feel like pumping into my slick heat. Would he be just as fast and eager as Leto, or has time and experience taught him that there's more to it all than the race to the finish? Or so I've heard Paryn claim a time or two.

"And what about you, Slave, are you the *cream* of the crop too? Why should we bid on you and bring you into the fold of the Order of Scorpions?" Skull asks as he strides past me, fully naked, and climbs into the gold bathtub behind me. I don't know when he stripped down, but I have the desire to get my hands on his body now too, if only to note the differences and allow my hands to see past his glamour of course.

I drop to my knees as I begin to wash Scorpius's corded thighs and calves, doing my best to give the three self-important assassins the show they've been nudging for. I'll never truly get on my knees for the reasons they want, but I can tell by the way Scorpius licks his skull-glamoured lips, that he'll at least spend some time tonight imagining me just like this.

Dream on, little bug.

I wrap my soapy hands around Scorpius's shaft and begin to squeeze and twist as I expertly *clean* him. I glance behind me at Skull, who's now leisurely sitting in the tub, his eyes hungrily taking in each twist and stroke of my hands like it's him I'm playing with and not his fellow skeleton in arms. There's a power to this that I didn't anticipate feeling. I've always enjoyed playing with Leto and allowing him to play with me, but this is different.

This feels more potent and heady. Even more surprising, I have to admit, I don't hate it. There's something to the vulnerability here, to the transference of power. Especially from fae like these three. They're killers. Life destroyers. I know I'm prey in their eyes, but being prey has never felt so intoxicating, so...promising. They're playing, but so am I, and it's yet to be determined who will come out on top.

I finally decide to answer Skull's question as I slowly work my hands up Scorpius's cock and then back down. I keep my tone even and unfazed, and I catch Scorpius's flash of irritation as I treat what I'm doing to him as no big deal and instead engage Skull in casual conversation.

"You won't choose me no matter what my record in the ludere boasts," I tell Skull, liking the smirk my answer coaxes from his lush lips.

"And why is that?" Bones asks huskily from where he's lying shirtless on his pallet.

Is he stroking himself?

The quick glance I just stole has me thinking yes, but I don't check to see if my suspicions are right. Instead, I release Scorpius's weeping cock, reach for the hammered gold pitcher, fill it, and methodically start to rinse him clean. I fix him with a defiant stare as I once again stand in front of him. I'm done with being batted around like the rodent they think I am. It's time to escape the cat's claws and call all of this nonsense a win. I fix my gaze back on Skull as he lounges in his own gold-plated bathtub.

How much food could I buy if just one of these things was melted down?

Skull's eager gaze tries to drink me in, but I hope he chokes on me.

"You won't choose me, because I'll be dead before the actual bidding even starts," I declare, dropping the pitcher into Scorpius's water with a loud splat.

The inside of the tent goes quiet, and I immediately question why I just said that. It's true, but based on their reaction, it could also open up a box of scorpions I don't really want to deal with. If one of them is my target—and it's very possible that they are—I shouldn't say anything that could give them the slightest inkling of what Tilleo has planned. Too bad I just can't find the will to care right now. Screw Tilleo, and screw these three. I quickly dismiss my doubt and turn to Skull and level him with a cynical stare.

"Would you like me to clean your dick next?" I ask emotionlessly.

His obsidian gaze grows dark. He's obviously unamused by the hint of disrespect layered in my query. "No, you're dismissed, *Slave*. Both of you, leave us," he commands, and I'm striding toward the tent's exit before he can rethink the aim of his anger and take it out on me like I deserve.

I push out into the heat of the newly born desert night, feeling like my throat is slowly trying to close in on itself. I press my palms to my neck as I hurry in the direction of the ludere.

What the hell just happened in there?

I stare down at the dusk-soaked sand as though it can tell me why I just behaved the way I did to one of the most revered houses of assassins in existence. Tilleo would cut out my tongue if he knew how I just spoke to the Order of Scorpions. He would torture me beyond comprehension, heal me, and then torture me again endlessly until not even madness could free me from the pain. And yet knowing all of that, I still can't find an ounce of anything inside of me that cares.

I've trained and worked and been brutalized and sold, just to have the purpose for it all torn away by Tilleo and his *high hopes* for me. It's all been for nothing. My life means nothing. And I want to make them pay for it, to pay me back for each healed mark on my skin, for each broken bone and scar on my soul. It's the least they can do after dashing my efforts when I was so close to escaping it all.

"What in the names of the Kings did you just do back there?" Harsh demands with a growl of outrage from behind me.

"Me?" I defend, irritated that he's even talking to me right now after what *he* pulled. "*You* threw *me* under the hooves to build yourself up, not the other way around," I snap at him over my shoulder, my strides lengthening even more to speedily carry me away from him.

Harsh makes the mistake of grabbing my arm to force me to stop so he can unload his indignation on me. In less time than it takes for me to exhale, Harsh is on his back, all the air fleeing his lungs, while I lean over him, the small pen knife that I palmed from Scorpius's trouser armory pressed against Harsh's throat. His dreary blue eyes widen with pure shock, and sick satisfaction washes through me for a moment before I scan my surroundings to confirm that no one is watching us.

The sun has already kissed the horizon goodnight, and luck is on my side as the ludere wraps me and Harsh in its cool shadow. The rooftop guards aren't patrolling this side right now, and far away, house slaves bustle around Tilleo's manor rushing here and there for who knows what. There's no one to even glance our way. I bring my face even with Harsh's, a cruel smile slipping over my plump lips.

"Touch me again without permission and I'll make sure that we're pitted against each other in the upcoming tests. I'll destroy you so wholly that Tilleo will have you bent over in a brothel before the sun even sets. Do you hear me?" I snarl at him, and his eyes narrow at me with rage before it sinks in that I'm not jesting or exaggerating in the slightest.

"I understand," he croaks breathlessly, and I push against his airway a little harder.

"Keep your mouth shut and your hands to yourself, and you'll end up with an Order just like you want. Don't test me, Harsh," I tell him venomously.

He surrenders, his nod jerky as his face starts to mottle and his lungs scream for air. I push off him, rising fluidly to my feet as he gasps desperate breaths and rubs at his throat.

"What happened to you?" he demands between coughs and wheezing breaths, his voice barely more than gravel.

I leave him there sprawled out in the sand, his question unanswered as I dart through the back entrance to the ludere. Quickly, I climb the narrow ridge of stairs that leads up to the second floor. The arched entryways that line the curved wall to my left are baleful and dark, but the halls and quarters that they lead to are thankfully quiet. The railing on my other side, the one that keeps us from accidentally falling down to the sand pits in the middle of the building, paints patterns on the gritty ground with the help of the moon.

I keep my shadow to myself, and my steps silent, as I make my way down the crescent-shaped corridor. My thoughts race as I search for a safe place to disappear for a while so I can try to get myself together again. Harsh's question echoes in my mind as I work to piece it all together. What happened to me is that they've finally stripped me of everything.

This is what happens when there's nothing more to live for, when there's nothing left to lose.

Out of nowhere, distant screams fill the air, and I can immediately tell they're coming from the far-off hot house. Someone has started in on Linae. I turn down the hall that leads to the bathing chambers, the adornment room, and ends in the sleeping chamber for the female blade slaves. I find my parchment-thin bed roll, laid under a thin cutout for a window, and plop down on it as Linae's screams serve to ground me. I think of what Figg would do to me if she saw me disrespecting the silk draped on me by lying on it, but I wave it away. It's nice not to care so much, not to have to worry about being a step ahead and having it all figured out. I put my hands behind my head and study the cracks in the flat ceiling above me.

I can do this. I can find an angle that gives me what I need before I die. Maybe freedom isn't just about where I live or paying off my purchasing price. Maybe it will have to be about finally embracing all that I am without fear or hesitation. I could take all that they've taught me, all that I *really* am, and use it to start chipping away at this place. Even if they kill me before I can do lasting damage, perhaps it could still be enough to help this shit hole crumble someday. I would have to be smart, work under the radar, but what better time to do that than at the Bidding when they all think they have us under their boot?

Yeah.

That feels right.

Now to figure out where to hit them so they don't feel it until it's too late.

7

SKULL

HAT IN THE KINGS' CROOKED DICKS WAS that?" Bones asks, completely awed as we all watch the tent flaps close behind the two blade slaves as they storm out of the tent.

"I...I don't even know," Scorpius surprisingly admits, looking down at his dick as though it has the answers we're all looking for.

I stare at my brother, not sure if I'm disturbed or delighted by how flummoxed the blade slave left him. He's normally so stoic and in control; it's fascinating to see him off-kilter and confused by whatever just happened.

"We've been attending these things for a long time, and I've never seen one of Tilleo's savages handle us like *that*," Bones points out, like we all didn't just witness the same thing.

"What do you think she meant by *she'll be dead before the actual bidding starts?*" he asks, his eyes fixed on the entrance of the tent while one of his hands is still shoved into his pants.

"It means Tilleo is up to something and we need to keep an eye on it," Scorpius points out, and I grunt my agreement.

"That fool is always up to something. I'm not worried," I declare dismissively as I reach over and pick up the abandoned bottle of soap that Slave just used to blow all of our minds.

It's not that she used her feminine wiles against us. The three of us aren't fumbling virgins by any means, and the days of tripping over a pretty piece of pussy simply because we're desperate and don't know any better are long behind us. No. It's more that when you reach the stature that we have, when you've carved out the virulent reputation that both precedes and trails after us in everything that we do, one gets used to others treating you in a certain way.

I've grown accustomed to the scent of fear that wafts through a room when a member of the Order of Scorpions enters it. I revel in the widening of stares and the loss of a fae's bowels when they set their eyes on our bones and know it will be the last thing they ever see. I enjoy watching people skirt around our namesake or apologize to the lone skittering scorpion crossing their path in hopes that it will never invite our wrath down upon them. But none of that was present in that blade slave's tone or her stunning, savage silver eyes.

She was angry at being played with. She surprised the fuck out of all of us when she showed that she'd be more than happy to bite back when we showed her a little fang. It was...enthralling. Thrilling in a way I haven't felt for some time now, and I can tell by my brothers' faces that they feel exactly the same way.

"Her coloring is very unique," Scorpius grumbles, finally folding himself into the tub so he can wash his hair.

The newest glamour makes us all look like we have short, perfectly styled tresses, when in reality mine is down my back, Scorpius's is shoulder length, and Bones likes to keep his shorn and out of the way. I suddenly crave the safety of home where we can all drop the guises and use our real names instead of being on constant alert and working in codes like we have to do when we're hunting.

A flash of that starlight-colored hair splayed all over my bed while I lick Slave's slit from ass to clit flashes in my mind. My dick hardens, and I squeeze the base and absently start to stroke myself.

"Her hair and eyes are something I'd expect to find in the High Courts of the shadow realms, not here in the middle of this sand hole," I point out, agreeing with Scorpius's observation.

"There's something familiar about her," Bones states, his nails scratching at the stubble dusting his cheeks and chin. "I'd bet a caravan full of aurems that one of her parents is a highborn fae while the other is lowborn enough to peddle their progeny for the largest purse offered." Bones gives a derisive snort. "The three of us know better than most how easy it is to sell off a bastard."

"I want to fuck her. That's all I know," I announce as I rest my head back against the rim of the small golden tub and begin to stroke my cock harder and faster.

"Careful, I think that cunt might have teeth," Scorpius warns with an amused but exasperated chuckle.

I smile even wider as my balls start to tighten and my impending release begins to tingle up my thighs. "We're Scorpions, brother; it's not good unless it hurts a little," I tell him on the cusp of a moan, and he and Bones both chuckle.

I come all over my stomach, the pearly streams sticking to the muscles of my torso and floating in the warm water I'm soaking in. I imagine the little blade slave licking the cum from the grooves of my abdomen, and my dick twitches in anticipation of more than a quick tug in the tub. I should have said yes when she asked to wash my dick, but I needed the distraction of her gone. So did the others. She blew in here like a sandstorm, and we need a minute to dust off and recalibrate.

"We need to watch the brazen vixen, learn what we can about her before anyone goes and sticks their cock in something that wants to rip it off. We're not here for long, and we won't be bringing any pets home," Scorpius announces, pointedly looking over at Bones. "Let's not have a repeat of what happened in Nadil," he reminds us, and both Bones and I cringe.

"She's fresh meat, I can tell. There's zero chance that she's a hexed hag wearing a pretty girl suit," Bones defends, and I cover up my laugh with a cough and climb out of the tub to dry off.

"If she tries to eat my soul like that last one, I'm blaming you," I warn Bones, and his smile grows salacious.

"I'll keep that mouth all to myself then if you can't handle it," Bones taunts, and Scorpius groans.

"Stay focused on what we're here to do. Don't forget who owns that slave and what that means. If she thinks she'll be dead long before one of the other Orders can purchase her, then Tilleo or one of his cronies is looking to stir up a mess. The kind of mess *we* don't want to get caught up in with our pants down. We're Scorpions, we don't play their games, so keep the head on your shoulders engaged and the one in your pants tucked away for its own safety," Scorpius warns, glaring at both me and Bones.

"Says the guy who just had her hands all over his sac and shaft," I point out, smiling at the withering stare he fixes on me as I dry off.

Scorpius runs a hand down his face and sighs. "Mistakes were made. I thought I'd call her bluff and she'd back down," he admits, and I shake my head and chuckle at his expense. "We've been at this half as long as that one's probably been alive. Still, I didn't see that coming."

"That's what makes it fun," Bones declares, his wagging eyebrows punctuating his point.

"It is nice to hunt something we're not being paid to slaughter in the end," I confess as I pull a clean pair of trousers from the trunk and a floor-length lightweight vest to go with it.

"Who's to say she won't need to be slaughtered in the end?" Scorpius counters.

"I don't think she'd even mind that," Bones adds, an eager glint in his pitch black gaze. "That one needs it rough while teetering on the edge of death and disaster. I can feel it in my dark and depraved depths," he states matter-of-factly as though the quarter of an hour she spent in our presence allowed him to split her open and stare into her soul.

"You just hope she likes the salty right alongside the sweet," I jeer.

"One truly does enhance the flavor of the other," he agrees, and I hum my own endorsement of his statement as I tuck my hardening cock into my pants.

"Maybe Scorpius is right about watching ourselves around this one," I admit a little hesitantly. I want to play, but not at the expense of letting our guard down and paying for it. The fact that any of us, let alone all three of us, have so quickly been reeled in by the cunning cunny means she's a problem. A dangerous one, knowing Tilleo as we do. "Could be much safer to find a house whore to sink into while we're here," I add, and Bones groans in dismay.

If I happen to picture starlight for eyes and moonbeams for hair while I'm at it, none will be the wiser, I reassure myself. My load and my person will certainly be much safer dripping out of one of Tilleo's sand sluts than some slave who's been broken and rebuilt with the taste of death on her tongue and swords for hands.

"Did you two catch that she filched one of my knives?" Scorpius asks absently, and I'm surprised to hear a hint of amusement ringing in that statement.

I watched the sleight of hand, impressed. I even wanted a better angle of where she stashed it in that almost nonexistent sorry excuse for a dress.

"And you didn't immediately throttle her? I think you might be going soft, brother," Bones quips.

"I'm too interested in seeing what she's going to do with it," he confesses.

"Frame you, is the likeliest of options," I point out.

"Maybe," Scorpius admits, his eyes far away like he's divining all the possibilities of what might happen. "Tilleo knows better than to come for us though. I'd sooner hunt everyone in this place and then burn it all to the ground than fall in line with whatever is going on. He knows we come for the information that can be collected here and to keep an eye on our enemies. He's not Dorsin; he'd never make a move against the wrong people."

"Never swear by never," I chide, and he fixes me with an unamused look.

"I'm going to go find something to play with," Bones announces, pushing up off his bed.

"Stay away from that blade slave," Scorpius warns more seriously. "We need to tread lightly there until we know more. And no marks, Bones," he calls out as Bones reaches the entrance to the tent. "If you need to go there, clean up after yourself and wipe the flesh slave's mind when you're done."

"This is not my first Bidding, Father," Bones provokes, knowing it pisses Scorpius off to be compared to any of the men who sired us.

Sure enough, Scorpius's ebony gaze darkens even more. "Don't fuck around here, Bones. Go talk to the Vulpi, see if you can get anything about that hunt in the Dawn Court that eliminated one of the lords and his entire line of successors. We know it was them, and you know how Kiffin likes to brag when she's riding the high of several good orgasms."

"Do we have an interest there?" I ask curiously.

Scorpius nods. "We have an interest who's very keen to understand how that was sanctioned."

I smile, knowing that Scorpius just waved an exciting scent in front of the nose of a hound that lives to track and deliver. Bones will now be occupied with sniffing out what happened and will hopefully avoid the trouble he's so good at finding himself in the middle of.

With a predatory gleam in his glamoured black eyes, Bones slips out of the tent.

"Where'd she hide the pen knife that she stole?" Scorpius asks casually as he steps from his tub and pulls out new clothes from the chest beside his bed.

A slow smile stretches across my lips, and I chuckle softly, entirely amused at the answer. "She palmed the knife *and* the sheath and nestled the protected blade between her ass cheeks," I inform him, and his eyes light up with heat even as he shakes his head like he disapproves of the move. "That cunny had her cheeks clenched harder than a sailor's cock when he first comes ashore. And you know if she had her ass clenched, *everything* else was nice and tight too..."

I laugh as Scorpius groans at the thought of that stunning creature and the tight pussy she would have been clamping down the entire time she rubbed all over him before stroking a twinkle of madness into his eyes.

"I might need your help, brother, to remind me that playing with dangerous things is a good way to get your throat slit," he admits, and I'm taken aback by the confession.

Of the three of us, Scorpius is the least likely to lose sight of the big picture and all that we've worked to build. He doesn't chase juicy gashes or lose himself in their wet folds like Bones does regularly or I've been known to do from time to time. We all have needs, but that's usually what brothels are for. We've entertained the thought of procuring something more permanent from the various skin markets around, but ultimately none of us liked the idea of having someone who wasn't truly devoted and loyal in our space all the time with access to who we really are and what we truly look like.

Events like the Bidding allow us to pretend for a moment that what we do is civilized and respectable, but there's no mistaking the bloody, brutal truth of what we do and who we are. We kill for coin. No hunt is too big or too small. For the right amount of aurems, we can deliver the end however the purchaser desires. We're all soulless, morally corrupt dealers of death. It's best not to get too lost in the glitz and glamour of this occasion and remember the reality of what's all around us. Tilleo built his empire on the back of fae slaves, and we've built ours in the shroud of murder.

"Are you really that worried about her appeal?" I ask as I study Scorpius's face.

It's harder to discern his thoughts and concerns through the protective layer of the magic he's wearing, but I know him well enough after all these years to see that something about that slave unsettles him, and he's not a man that unsettles easily...if at all.

"I think she's trouble," he tells me evenly, striding over to a mirrored trolly filled with liquor bottles and glasses.

He pours himself a drink, offering me one as well, but I shake my head and wait for him to get out whatever's eating him up inside about this mysterious blade slave.

"My issue with trouble is that it can bring a man to his knees in the best kind of way or it can have him on his knees so it's easier to remove his head from his shoulders. Every instinct I have tells me it's one or the other with that fae. It's a problem that I don't know which one."

"Maybe it's better not to know," I offer, and he answers with an incredulous snort.

"Weren't you just saying that you wanted to fuck her?" he points out.

"I do, but no cunt is worth the risk of tearing apart what we've built. I don't care how wrapped up in moonbeams and stardust it is. Listen," I start, striding over to him and patting him on the back while I pluck a tumbler from the tray and fill it with wine.

I drink deeply, feeling the alcohol sink into my weary body where it works to reinvigorate my sore and tired muscles.

"We've been here for less than an hour," I remind him. "The trip out is always a pain in the ass, and we both know Tilleo will pack so much shit in the next few days that we'll be willing to spend any amount of aurems just to escape. We'll finance the ludere in secret, just like we always do, and then we'll go home alone, just like we always do. We were thrown by a smart mouth set in a pretty face, wearing only strips of fabric. We'll meet the other blade slaves, find a house whore to share, and realize this minx isn't nearly as appealing as we thought," I reassure him.

He chuckles hollowly as he runs his palm over his face. "You're right. We're all travel weary and horny. This is nothing more than that."

I throw back another glass of bloodwine and then pat him hard on the back in camaraderie. "That's the spirit! Now, let's get a little drunk and then head off to this bloody awful dinner we're being forced to attend. I say it's high time Bones spent his night keeping *us* out of trouble," I declare, lifting another glassful in toast.

Scorpius sighs and then clinks his tumbler with mine. "To trouble," he agrees with a deep laugh, and then we both drink and refill until the tent undulates all around us and we both forget the tight body and the full lips of a blade slave, who no longer matters and never will.

8

AUSET

THE SAND RADIATES HEAT UP AT ME LIKE A warning as I cross the wide distance between the ludere and Tilleo's manor. Harsh keeps looking over at me like he expects me to leap at him and slit his throat at any moment. I'm seconds away from growling at him to cut it out.

The night is growing deeper, but the sun's caress over the sand all day is still radiating up at me as I trek across it with the other blade slaves. Bright stars twinkle merrily down at me as though they too are ready for the party. Their touch invigorates me, filling my reserves with a cooling, calm power that serves to reinforce the decisions I came to earlier.

The closer Harsh and I get to the manor, the more music and chatter reaches us from the open windows of the wings closest to the front of the house. I suspect that's where the house whores stay, but I don't know that for sure. My stomach dips at the thought of all the Order members congregating inside, ready to feast, drink, and fuck with the slaves. Worry roosts in my belly at the thought of once again coming face-to-face with the Order of Scorpions. I still can't find it in me to regret how I behaved, but I know I need to be very careful playing with fire so I don't end up nothing but ash before I can go to work on fucking up this place.

Harsh turns and leads the rest of us to the back of the gargantuan property where we go down a small flight of stairs that leads us to the slave's entrance. There are guards and some kitchen servants standing outside of the large door, puffing on pipes and other sticks of inhalants. We pass them with no issue, and Harsh opens the door and leads us into pure chaos.

Cooks and servers are scrambling about, shouting out things and hurriedly placing large dishes of food on trays and in bowls. What seems like a thick invisible wave of scents assaults me as I wind through the loud melee. My taste buds suddenly wake up, and saliva pools in my mouth while my stomach rumbles a request to taste everything. I've never smelled anything like it in my life, or if I have, I can't recall. Savory scents tease me, dancing for my senses and inviting me to track them to their source. A servant runs past me with a stunning cake on a stand, and I find myself abandoning Harsh's lead to follow the pastry instead.

"Out of the way, you useless gash," a lanky fae yells at me as he rushes for a row of sinks with a large steaming pot clutched in his hands.

I jump back, not missing the glare Harsh lobs at me as he gestures for me to follow him. We leave the loud clamoring of the kitchen behind us, dodging more servants who are running food up a steep set of stairs while others run empty trays back down. My stomach growls jealously, but I know there will be nothing more than gruel in the morning for the likes of us. This feast is just one more thing to add to the tally of why all of these fae need to die. The hallways are dark as we wind through them. Clearly, Tilleo doesn't see the purpose in paying for slaves to see down here, although the cool temperature is certainly appealing in the stifling desert heat.

We make our way up another set of stairs where we find the other blade slaves waiting for whatever Tilleo wants us here for. Uncertainty mills about. It settles against me like a heavy mongrel whining for attention. I want to fidget under the press of disquiet, but I fight the urge as I watch my fellow savages study our surroundings with concern or masks of boredom. I'm curious about their experiences with their assigned Orders, but I keep my mouth shut, refusing to ask anyone about what they've been doing, and simply observe everything instead.

Reddish-brown eyes watch my every move. I can sense Leto's gaze pour over my body, his concentrated stare needy and imploring me to get sucked into its rich, demanding depths. I leave him thirsting, unwilling to take his bait too quickly and look over. It's a game I've always played with him, one that allows me to feel as though I'm in control and as detached as I need to be in order to survive this place. He always waits me out, content to allow me to come to him on my own terms and in my own time. He's good with me that way.

We're not close—the ludere is too quick to kill anything of that nature—but I find myself wondering about him in ways I've never allowed myself before. I've never asked how he ended up here, we don't lie around sharing stories and bits of our past, and for the first time ever, it bothers me. I've found moments of power and pleasure at his hands, which is more than anyone can ask for in a place like this. He watched over me at a time when I was a fractured shadow of who and what I am now, and because of that, I gave him a piece of me that I never thought anyone would earn. But we don't really know each other.

Finally, after studying every inch of the bland room we're in, I cave and sweep my stare across the space of unsettled savages until my silver eyes land on Leto's hungry russet perusal. His soft lips tilt up in what I know he thinks is a seductive smile, but really it makes him look like he's been standing too close to a guard who was puffing away on their best pix weed. It's a goofy come-hither grin that somehow makes me want to genuinely smile, even though that's not something that I do.

Leto's eyes flash from mine up to the ceiling, and then he subtly jerks his head in what I think is the direction of the ludere. He's once again asking me to meet him later in our spot on the roof, and I glance at the others all around us, my eyes asking *how?*

He wags his eyebrows at me, and I shake my head at his overexuberant confidence. I shrug once, letting him know that I'll try, but I won't put myself at risk for it. His grin grows wider on his face, and then a loud bang pulls my attention away as Crit shoves the door to the room open and it slams loudly against the wall from the force of his aggressive entrance.

We were standing at attention as we quietly waited, but there's a sudden stiffness to all of us as we pause to hear what required that overdramatic entry by one of Tilleo's guards.

"Tonight is the first feast night of the Bidding and the only one you'll be summoned to attend. You are not to eat, speak, or move from your place against the walls of the hall unless handed something by a server or called forth by Tilleo or an Order member. You will keep your backs straight and your eyes forward, or I'll punish you personally before your test tomorrow and let you bleed while you fight for a place amongst the elite," he barks, and I feel several of us fight the urge to scoff.

Crit doesn't have the kind of authority required to back up that threat, not unless Tilleo is there to remove his muzzle and let him loose, but it doesn't mean that he can't find some other way to sabotage us or make our lives generally miserable.

"Follow me," he orders, and we fall in line immediately, first females, then males, as he leads us down a long hallway, through a large door, and into a tremendous dining hall.

The ceilings are as tall as the manor itself, with huge quartz chandeliers that cage in dancing fairy light at their tips. Tapestries the size of our living quarters hang on the four sandstone walls surrounding us, each a meticulously painted scene that represents the four fae courts.

Images of the Summer Court, or the Day Court, stand tall behind the head table where Tilleo will sit with different invited guests each night. The Autumn Court, or the Dusk Court, is to the left, behind a long table with benches. There are fancy china and crystal goblets set out all over the surface of the tables, with room in the middle for the mouthwatering dishes I smelled downstairs to sit on display in front of the feasting guests. The tapestry representing the Winter Court, or the Night Court, hangs on the far wall. And the Spring Court, or the Dawn Court, guards another long table set up identically to the one in front of the tapestry of Dusk.

Crit calls out our names and points to where we're supposed to stand. I move to my appointed place in the middle of the Dusk Court's stunning artistic scene, where I'll spend the night watching Order members eat and drink their fill. My body once again grumbles its dissatisfaction that all we're running on is this morning's porridge. On our taxing training days, we're fed a meal of mush in the morning and one at night that has enough mystery meat in it to keep our bodies from going soft with starvation. However, Tilleo must have decided today's events didn't categorize as strenuous, which means all we'll be given is this morning's bowl of tasteless oats.

Occasionally when a sand stag dies, we're treated to its meat before it can rot. But that hasn't happened in months, meaning the bugs in the mush are the only thing that changes from time to time when it comes to our diets.

When I first arrived here, I'd have dreams of platters of fish baked in flaky pastry, pies, tarts so sweet and creamy they'd melt in your mouth. I couldn't remember who or where I came from, but somehow I remembered food.

A longing for something I can't quite recall fills my chest. I ache for the first time in a long time as delicious scents call to memories I can't access no matter how hard I try. It's as though a troop of nixies have taken on the task of cleaning my mind until it's empty and sparkling. From time to time, my other senses try to muck it up, but the nixies always win in the end. Nothing surfaces. Nothing ever makes sense. I'm always left feeling bereft, with no true understanding of why.

Crit steps in front of me, and I force my muscles to stay loose instead of tensing at the threat that wafts darkly from his thick frame. He looks me over like Figg does, working to spy a hair or thread out of place. I breathe evenly as he reaches down and straightens Tilleo's crest where it rests between my hips. Thin fabric is the only thing that separates the back of his intrusive fingers from my mound, and I stare blankly at his leather breastplate as he pretends to fuss over my dress in an effort to unsettle me.

Crit's hand hovers where it will never be welcome to play, and I start to wonder if he's who I'm supposed to kill? I recall Tilleo's words from the hashery, and disappointment oozes like liquid tar from my chest into my stomach. Without question, he said it would be an Order member that I'd be expected to kill. Not some lowly guard who thinks he can make me feel small by touching things he wasn't given permission to.

Then again, I've already decided to create as much mayhem as possible before I'm murdered. Why not start with teaching some of these lecherous monsters a lesson in why you don't mess with a blade slave? A trickle of satisfaction drips into my heart with that thought.

Could I get away with it?

Do I care if I don't?

I lean into Crit's hand ever so slightly, not sure how he'll react to the sudden contact. Crit likes to cause pain. He gets hot at the *no* in our eyes, loves the *don't touch me* that we're unable to place on our lips for fear that we'll be punished for it. If there ever was a time to fight back, it's now though, when the ludere and surrounding compound are chaotic, and there's more trained killers here to take the fall than just us blade slaves.

I dare to look up at Crit's face. My heart hammers with apprehension and excitement. He could have me beaten for this. He could track me down later and try to make me pay for what I'm about to do, or he could whine to Tilleo and immediately have me whipped or, worse, racked. I'm counting on his need to get even though, on his hunger to put me in my place. Crit's pupils are blown. His conniving gaze drops to my lips, mistaking my pressing closer for interest. It takes him a breath to feel the blade now resting over the leather atop his hardening cock.

It's a rousing thing to witness the heat evaporate from his eyes like a desert mirage. In its place, outrage sparks, and his body tightens against the threat it now registers I am.

"Touch me again, halfwit, see where it leads," I warn, my voice barely above a whisper.

"Tilleo will flay you for this," he snarls quietly back.

My worry flaps away like a flock of birds as he drops his voice to match mine. If he were going to involve Tilleo, he'd be screaming his head off right now that I have a knife I'm not supposed to have. No, he's going to handle this all on his own, which is exactly what I want him to do.

"Maybe," I agree, even though the threat is obviously empty. "But he'll have your head for taking liberties you were never told to take, won't he, Crit? We both know how well he tolerates disrespect," I counter, and a tic starts in his jaw. "Run along now," I tell him sweetly, pressing the edge of the blade against the suede of his pants a touch harder.

Crit glares at me, but after a tense beat, he steps back. As soon as he puts a centimeter of distance between us, the knife is back in its sheath, the movement so fast Crit could watch it for the rest of his life and still not see where I've hidden it.

"You're a dead whore," he snaps at me, but I drop my eyes back to his chest plate, blank my features, and once again pretend he's not there.

I sense his hesitation for a moment, and then with a furious stride, he moves away from me and leaves the dining hall. If any of the other blade slaves saw our exchange, they're not giving themselves away. All of us stand stationary, ready, with our unseeing eyes fixed on some faraway point in the room.

My head, however, is a mess of thoughts. It's as though I'm waking up from a hundred-year-long sleep. Ever since Tilleo banished me here, I've mastered my ability to shut my thoughts and emotions down. I've followed orders, crushed the anger that collected in my soul. I've extinguished my need to react, to fight back, and come as close to an empty vessel of death as possible. But now everything they thought was tamed is bubbling to the surface. I want to kill, to wreak havoc, to unleash the suffering that's rained down on me for the last six years. They taught me to be a ruthless killing force, and all I want to do is use it against them.

It's hard to be patient about it.

I study the spark of vengeance now glowing in my chest, and remind myself that caution and stealth are key. I could lose myself to the call for blood, barely put a dent in Tilleo's operations before they cut me down, or if I'm smart, I can cut his legs out from under him as much as possible in secret. Then, when I stand over my Master of Masters and slit his good-for-nothing throat, he'll know that his empire, his legacy, is going with him.

I ponder that for a while before laughter and boisterous talking demand my attention. I'm not sure how long we've been standing here, but the lack of feeling in my feet tells me it's been a while. I adjust my weight, inviting the sensation of pins and needles to fill my blood and wake my limbs. Just as I settle again, the doors to the dining hall are thrust open, and in strolls Tilleo with one of the members of the Order of Vulpi on his arm. She laughs demurely at something he tells her as he leads her into the room. They're followed closely by the rest of her Order as well as the members of all the others. I spot the skeletons in my periphery, but thankfully their eyes don't land on me. It's as though we're as much a part of the decor as the furniture and tapestries, but that's fine by me. It's safer to be as insignificant as a dusty vase on a sideboard.

The large group of killers and slavers find their places at the long ornately decorated tables. Orders stick together, some seemingly friendlier with one group over the others. Tilleo saunters to the head table, his guests tonight the Order of Vulpi. Figures. The Vixens, as they're nicknamed, are the only Order composed solely of women. They're a goal of many female blade slaves here, but as I watch them delicately take their seats at Tilleo's table, I can already tell there are only a select few of us who would make the cut.

The four women are gorgeous, each of them very different from the other but stunning all the same. Their dresses probably cost more than any of the slaves in this room, and they're dripping in jewels and layered in products that make their cheeks look flushed, their lips plump and red, and their eyes rimmed with a darkness that looks as though they're inviting sin. They look expensive and decorative, but their gazes are shrewd and their manners exquisitely practiced.

A thick black-haired beauty sits to Tilleo's left. Her eyes are a light crystal blue, and her lips are full and the color of a decadent merlot. Her breasts are pushed up and bound tight, and I wonder if she can even breathe in the contraption I can tell is cinching her stout waist under the satin of her light blue dress. On Tilleo's right is a stunning statuesque woman with the richest, darkest skin I've ever seen. Her entire countenance is regal and smooth, and the updo of locks arranged on her head is just as captivating as the sparkling diamonds woven into the thick strands themselves. She plucks a glass of bubbly liquor from in front of her and laughs at something Tilleo says before bringing the crystal flute to her crimson-painted lips.

The other two women who sit at the ends of the head table are strawberry-blonde and beautiful. I realize quickly that they're mirror images of each other and must be twins. Their hazel eyes survey the gathered Order members at the tables like their namesake suggests, foxes searching for prey.

Slaves carrying steaming trays of food come pouring through the back set of doors. There are more dishes and side dishes than I can count, and soon the long tables are overflowing with options. I catch the slight movement of other blade slaves bordering the room, and I know their empty stomachs are just as enraged as mine is. The room is loud with booming powerful voices and laughter. Surprisingly, this gathering looks more like a collection of long lost friends than a gathering of professional murderers and possible enemies. I know the Orders compete with each other for hunts, but this display makes me wonder if the competition isn't as cutthroat as all of us have been led to believe. I suppose some of this revelry could be chalked up to peacocking and positioning, but certainly not all of it.

Plates are filled and cleaned. Glasses, emptied and replenished. The conversation never seems to lull, and I grow more and more tired by the hour. My eyes land on the Scorpions, my gaze flitting over their presence like a fly checking for fresh meat. Their backs are to me, which I count as a good thing. I don't know what I would have done if I had fallen within their line of sight across the room. One of the skeletons turns his head, offering his profile as though he can feel my eyes on him. I hold my breath and watch for any further evidence that he can.

I can't tell them apart from this distance or while staring at the backs of them. I didn't spend enough time or focus enough of my attention on the things that separate them from one another. None of their gazes ever search me out, and strangely I'm not sure if I'm comforted by that or annoyed.

Raucous laughter explodes from one of the tables, but I'm not able to see exactly where or why, because a frail house slave steps into my line of sight and hands me a glass carafe.

"You need to go down to the cellar and fill this up," she commands, her voice wobbly like she's not used to being the one to give orders.

Confusion fills me for a beat, and I hand the carafe back. "You go fill it. We're supposed to stand here until we're dismissed," I inform her, and her brown eyes shift quickly to the back set of doors before flicking back to me. An awareness tickles up my spine, and I look past the house slave at first to Tilleo and then the Scorpions to see if this is their doing. Neither of them have taken any notice of me or the girl in front of me.

"No. I was told we could use you if we were too busy," the waif of a girl hesitantly argues. "I'm too busy refilling glasses out here to go get more wine. We'll run out soon, so *you* will do it," she orders me, once again trying hard to sound strong and authoritative while pushing the carafe back toward me.

I take it and look over to the doors at the back. There's no one there, but I have my suspicions about who gave this house slave her information. "Fine, where am I going?"

She visibly relaxes, making me even more on edge. "Out

the doors to the right, then it's the first alcove on the left. The cellar is at the bottom of the stairs, and the wine is already set out on the table. You'll see it when you get down there," she instructs, and before I can ask any other questions, she glides away from me. I watch her as she moves to the sidebar and plucks a full carafe of white petal wine and starts moving around the tables.

I take a second to scan the room again, but no one's eyes are on me as I move away from my assigned place and stride to the doors at the back. Blood rushes my ears, carrying with it the heavy beat of my pulse as I push through the doors and follow the house slave's directions. I hurry to calm my breathing and settle my body's reaction to the newfound adrenaline pumping through me.

I'm being hunted.

The problem is I'm not confident I know exactly who's doing the hunting. Is this Tilleo setting me up to kill an Order member? Or the Scorpions getting back at me for my earlier disrespect? My instincts throw Crit into the mix, but it could be some unknown I haven't factored in yet as well. I open up my senses as I find the alcove on the left that encases a flight of dark, shadow-soaked stairs that lead down. I tighten my hold on the empty carafe, careful not to break it in my white-knuckled grip.

With a quick sigh, I start down the steps. I don't know what it says about me that there are so many options for who could lay this trap. I suppose I'm about to find out. It's fine though, they're about to discover that I'm done playing around.

9

I MOVE SILENTLY DOWN THE WINDING STONE STAIR-case. If there is anyone waiting for me down below, there's no way they're breathing. I hear nothing, not even the crackle of fairy light in the sconces barely lighting my way. I move fluidly, aware that the threat could be sneaking up behind me just as easily as lying in wait. The end of my descent comes into view, revealing an arched entryway into the wine cellar itself.

I scan quickly for feet or a flicker of shadow or anything that might give my hunter away, but either they're good enough not to be standing right by the entrance ready to pounce or there's no one down here. I suppose it's possible that the house slave's orders were innocent and she really did just need someone to get more wine, but for some reason, I doubt it.

Suddenly, I leap off the bottom stair, and with a burst of speed, I sprint through the cellar entrance. I'm hoping my unexpected efforts will take any lurkers by surprise. I skid to a stop just before a long wine-stained table and spin, prepared for an attack that could be coming from any direction.

Nothing happens.

Silently. Motionlessly. I wait. I listen. Every muscle in my body is ready, but as one second bleeds into another, nothing happens.

I set the empty glass bottle down on the long table, which is exactly where the house slave said it would be. There are several open bottles of wine, but I don't start checking which one I should be refilling. Instead, I scan the rows of bottles and barrels of alcohol being stored in the dark, cool room, but nothing moves, and my senses and instincts aren't picking up any unexpected presence down here either.

I move past the table to an especially dark corner. I glance around quickly one more time, and then I do something that no one knows I'm capable of. I step into the blackness created by a burnt-out sconce and a tall rack of liquor, and become one with the shadows.

The murk enfolds me, everything growing cooler as I settle into the gloomy protection of the darkness. I discovered that I could do this only a couple of years ago when I almost got caught one night trying to break into the hashery. I was being punished—I can't remember for what—but I hadn't eaten or been given water in almost two days. The food I could go longer without, but I knew if I didn't drink something soon, I wasn't going to make it. I had been forced to train again at midday when the sun was at its most punishing peak, and each step I took felt one step closer to the end unless I found some spare drops in a canteen or a glass of anything.

I don't know why I thought trying to break into the hashery was the safest option; I was probably half delusional with hunger and dehydration. It didn't take long for me to regret that decision when I heard the familiar cadence of night patrol heading my way. I panicked. I couldn't run without getting caught, so I backed as far as I could into the shadows, begging any deity that would listen for them to swallow me up. There was no way in my state that I could survive a whipping or any other kind of punishment, and each step the guard took closer to me felt like a death knell.

I don't know what happened or how, but all at once a strange, cold sensation took over. The next thing I knew, I was no longer standing outside of the locked hashery doors. I was inside, bathed in the dark of a corner in the back of the kitchens. I couldn't move. Whatever I had just done felt like it drained every ounce of energy from my body, but as I slid to the ground and sat there in shock, I knew this: whatever it was would change everything for me.

I brush the memories away and wait, cloaked in the dark. My breaths even out. My heart slows until it's steady. Patiently, I scan the cellar, focusing on the sole way in and out of this dank room. The scent of rotten fruit and stale barley tickles my nose as I debate how long to stay hidden down here. All at once, something in the air shifts. I don't hear anything, but I sense a change as though somehow, unexplainably, there's another presence down here with me. I scan the cellar again, studying the packed tall shelves and stacks of barrels. I can't spot a change in anything down here, and yet my eyes settle on a dark patch of wall near the entrance.

I'd noticed that shrouded area and the surrounding unlit sconces when I first came down here. I only dismissed it as a good hiding place because anyone with a brain would expect an attack right when they first walked through the entrance. Where I am hiding now is a better option for a surprise attack, but I can't fight the inkling that there's someone watching from those shadows like I'm watching from mine. Keeping to my dark corner, I peer into the inky depths as though I can push aside the curtain of black and force it to reveal whatever it's hiding. That's when a scuff of a boot on stone catches my ear.

My eyes snap from the pool of shadows against the wall to the arched entrance. Someone is coming down the stairs. I go completely still. Holding my breath, I listen hard for any other noises that will give the new intruder away, but I don't have to listen for long. In less than another heartbeat, a dark figure slinks from the bottom of the steps through the entryway. His hands are on the buckle of his belt as he unfastens it and goes to pull it from his hips. Crit's skeevy eyes land on the long wood table where he expects me to be standing with my back to him as I fill the carafe of wine as ordered.

Dolt.

Crit's knuckles go white against the brown leather of his belt as he looks around the room. His feet are planted in front of the only exit and entrance into the cellar, and his brow is furrowed with confusion. Fiendish eyes hungrily survey the rows of shelves, and a menacing smile spreads across his thin lips as he concludes that I must be hiding among them.

"Little gash," he calls out in a taunting song as he steps deeper into the cellar. "There's no use hiding from me." He peers around and under the table, wrapping the ends of the belt around both of his hands like some oversized garrote.

Silently, I reach behind me and pluck the knife I stole from its sheath. My gaze once again flashes to the shadowed wall by the entrance, but I still don't see anything there. I focus back on Crit as he prowls closer, checking every nook and cranny as he stalks in search of his prey. I study him, taking note of his size, the way he moves, the weapons he carries. I know he's skilled; he wouldn't be one of Tilleo's guards if he weren't. However, I can't decide if his confidence is alarming or laughable. He knows what a blade slave is, knows what we're molded to become from the moment we're dropped in the sand pits, and yet, he's down here without an ounce of fear or doubt in his voice as he mocks and threatens me. He thinks I won't fight back? He's about to find out just how wrong that is.

Crit strides into the racks of spirits, peering into their depths as he hunts. An excited snicker bounces off the walls of the cellar as he moves deeper into the musty room where he thinks he has me trapped. I begin to question how often he does this. From the ease in his gait and the excitement tightening his muscles, it's more often than I realized. How many of my fellow blade slaves have tried and failed to escape his wrath?

Crit makes a small whistling noise and pats his leather-clad thigh as though he's calling a pet to heel. Anger spills like acid down my throat, burning a path into my lungs. I want to make him hurt. I want his screams to be the song that I recall as I fall asleep tonight. I want the warmth that comes from staring deep into his pitiful eyes as he realizes he's *not* the hunter, *he's* the hunted. But I know I won't get any of that. I'll get a kill, but not a satisfying one. As much as I wish I could, I can't go back up to Tilleo's dinner covered in blood and satisfaction. No one can know what I'm about to do down here. I have to be quick and careful and always a step ahead.

I visualize all the places I can insert my blade to give me a clean kill. It's more than he deserves, but dead is dead in the end. I'll have to find gratification in that alone. Calculating the force I'll need to end this walking shit stain, I *feel* more than hear him moving closer. He rounds the end of the rack to my left, casually strolling toward me, his eyes scanning every possible hiding spot. His smirk is gone, replaced by a furrowed brow and a concerned glint in his searching gaze.

My condemning stare is fixed on his face, and my heart beats steadfast, as though the muscle is dutifully counting down each second that passes as he steps closer. Each thump of my heart in my chest rings like a death bell, and I fight the urge to tighten my grip on the stolen blade clutched in my palm. Anticipation pools in my mouth, and I hold my breath as Crit's brown eyes rove over the shadows draped protectively all around me. They spark with dismissal and disappointment, and he turns to retrace his steps back down the aisle.

My blade pierces the center of his ear faster than heat lightning strikes the sands of the desert. With practiced and deadly force, I muscle the thin knife into his ear canal, breaking his skull and skewering the contents of his mind before he can exhale the shocked breath he just sucked into his chest. I follow Crit down to the ground, twisting the blade to do as much internal damage as possible as his legs give out on him. It's a testament to how well the Scorpions care for their weapons that this kill goes as smoothly and easily as it does.

Crit is dead before his head hits the ground. Blood pools around the guard of the thin, sleek dagger, warming my palm before death begins to cool it. The mess is minimal, just like I needed. I wait a handful of heartbeats before I free the slender blade from the contents of Crit's skull. I jump back just in case any part of him tries to mar any part of me, but nothing does. I wipe the dagger and my palm free of his stain on his treasured guard uniform, staring down at the lifeless guard, scrutinizing his corpse.

I wait for panic or anxiety to surge in me, but it doesn't. I just killed one of Tilleo's personal guards in an unsanctioned hunt, something that's forbidden and punishable by torture and death, and yet I feel nothing. There's no relief—or gratification—pumping in my veins. I should feel vindicated and resolute, but all the dead body does is prove just how over my life and dreams truly are.

With a quick grunt, I rush to push Crit's body into the shadows that sheltered me from him. I can't wrap them around him like I do to me, but this will hopefully keep him hidden until his stench starts to give him away. Tilleo might suspect one of his blade slaves killed him when he's found, but he won't know for sure. Normally, he'd punish us all until someone confessed, but the Bidding and the presence of the Orders should shroud us from any retaliation, lest Tilleo risk not being able to sell us off. I don't think he'll chance that. I'm counting on his hubris to press him to save face. He wouldn't want anyone to know that he's lost control in any way. I'm betting that he'll sell us all to the highest bidder and declare whoever murdered Crit their new Order's problem.

I kick Crit's lifeless body once for good measure and then check over myself as I straighten my scraps of a dress and my belt. I check for any indication on my skin or the blue silk and metal I'm wearing of what just happened down here. I can't find anything. Sliding the thin dagger back into its sheath, I release a deep breath and move to the table to fill the empty carafe I was sent down here to deal with. I don't think I've been gone long, but I don't want to risk anyone noticing that I should have been back already.

I reach for the wine when it happens. That feeling that I'm not alone crawls up my back again. Without questioning the instinct this time, I whirl, sending my dagger flying at that suspicious spot of shadow that made me feel uneasy before. I don't see anything there other than darkness, but just as the dagger is about to hit the shadow-draped stone of the wall, a hand appears and plucks it from the air.

No. Not a hand…bones.

Dread hammers in my chest as I witness a skeleton peel itself from the shadows. Shock rocks me as I watch one of the Scorpions do something I've never seen anyone else aside from me do. The skeleton twirls the dagger around his glamoured bony fingers with expert skill, looking from the blade to me before offering a knowing smile.

"Naughty, naughty, Slave," he tsks at me, leaning back against the stone wall. His black eyes dart from my face to where Crit's dead body is hidden.

I sneak a glance just to be sure that Crit is completely cloaked in shadow as a flood of excuses settle on my tongue. Maybe the Scorpion didn't see. Maybe he's just trying to rattle me. I start to breathe faster, the air moving in and out of my chest keeping time with my ever increasing heart rate. Black eyes settle back on me, and all thoughts of getting away with the murder I just committed evaporate.

He knows.

I felt him down here before Crit swaggered through the cellar's entryway. I should have suspected that there'd be others who could do what I can. In the moment, the possibility didn't even cross my mind, a mistake I know that's going to cost me. I pull in a deep inhale, trying to settle the rapid-fire worry coursing through me.

I was going to die anyway. This just moves up the timetable.

"I see you've been playing with things that don't belong to you," the skeleton observes. His astute stare studies the blade in his hand, and I get the impression that his words aren't just meant for the weapon I stole, but also for the guard I just used it against.

"You might want to wash that," I tell him, nodding at the dagger he's still twirling around his fingers. Jealousy flickers in me as I eye the exquisite weapon that was starting to feel like it was made just for me. These skeletons, these members of the Order of Scorpions, have more blades than they probably know what to do with. I can only imagine that each and every one of them was made and handled with the utmost care. What would life be like with that kind of arsenal? "I've been keeping it—"

"Oh I know where you've been keeping it," he interjects, a cheeky smile stretching across his glamoured face.

I wish I knew which one of the three he was. Have I touched this one's cock? Was he the other skeleton in the tub, or was he the one on the pallet? I think he's Bones, the one who enjoyed the show I put on with his other Order member from the comfort of his silk sheets, but I'm not completely certain.

"While we're on the subject, why don't you hand the sheath over too," he orders, his tone alarmingly light and playful.

Refusing to release the sigh that's forming in my chest, I reach behind me and pluck the sheath from the crack of my ass. I toss it at him, and lithely he catches it. With deft movements that are almost too quick to track, he rehomes the blade and tucks it in a pocket at the side of the floor-length vest he's wearing.

The neck of his top is high and buttoned just below his Adam's apple. It looks to be made of some expensive material that has just a hint of sheen to it, or maybe that's the dim fairy light playing with my eyes. It has buttons trailing down from his throat to the top of his trousers where the long vest splits down the front as well as the sides like it's a paneled dress. The design of his frock would look feminine on anyone else, but on this assassin's thick, hard body, it's the epitome of masculinity.

"Now," he starts, "as much as I'd like to strip you down and have you show me how you kept that dagger clenched in the seam of that tight ass of yours, we have more pressing matters," he declares playfully, but there's distinct heat banked in his onyx gaze.

My nipples tighten at his words, my body responding to the ripple of desire that suddenly fills the space between us. I'm not a stranger to interest, but I've never reacted this quickly to a lust-laced declaration, and it throws me off. I narrow my eyes at the skeleton and try to get a hold of myself. Amusement only grows on the fae's face as I school my features and square my shoulders, waiting for him to declare what pressing matters he wants to discuss. My aurems—not that I have any—are on the guard I just killed.

"Where do you come from, Slave?" he asks with an odd rising intensity.

I'm confused by the direction of his question. I have to keep my eyes from flashing to Crit, as though my subconscious wants to remind him there are bigger issues at play here. I just killed a fae. Why would where I come from matter?

"Who's your sire?" he continues, his black eyes now keenly studying my face as though the answers lie in the shape of my nose or my cheeks and chin.

"Why do you want to know?" I retort coarsely instead of providing him with the bleak truth, which is I have no idea.

"Does Tilleo know you can do that?" he counters, jutting his perfectly chiseled jaw in the direction of Crit's lifeless body.

I scoff at the Order member, the false bravado helping to calm my panic. "It is what he's been training us to do," I sneer.

The skeleton fixes me with a stern stare. "Not the kill-ing," he dismisses with a wave. "The shadow walking."

My stomach both drops with trepidation and tightens with excitement. He knows what it is, which means he could tell me more about it. Is there more that we can do than the few tricks I've picked up by sheer chance? It's on the tip of my tongue to ask him everything, but I stop myself. He could use this against me somehow. I'm not sure exactly the angle, but why else would he want to know? It's not like he and his fellow Order members are here to help. They're here to procure. I would be stupid to trust this stranger with any part of me, including my desperate curiosity.

"I don't know what you're talking about," I answer stoi-cally, and his gaze quickly morphs into a glare.

"I'm not playing games, Slave," he warns me, straight-ening from his casual lean against the wall. The movement alone feels like a threat, but I refuse to be cowed by it.

"I'm a blade slave," I remind him. "We don't play. We obey or we die. We kill or we're killed. I wouldn't know a game if it bit me on the ass."

He steps toward me but freezes when a pair of boots can be heard coming down the stairs. My heart jumps with anticipation, and his menacing gaze roves over me as though he's debating whether to come for me despite the company clomping down the stairs. It sends a thrill flar-ing through me. One, strangely, not tinged with a hint of fear. There's a certain exhilaration that loosens my tongue when it comes to snapping at these Scorpions and not giv-ing them what they want. I've been powerless for so long, and as much as I don't want to die, I have to admit that I like snatching my power from the clutches of the entitled bastards who can't see me coming past their own corrupt and overinflated egos.

I glance toward the entrance and debate whether I should hide. Unfortunately, the closest cluster of shadows is where the skeleton is standing...or was. When my gaze lands back on the spot the Scorpion was just occupying, there's nothing there but a blank dark wall. I try to stretch my senses to see if he's cloaked himself in darkness or if he really is gone, but before I can discern one way or the other, a pair of strong legs cuffed in deep blue silk come into view.

Tension bleeds from my shoulders as Leto descends the remaining stairs and strides into the cellar. He has an empty carafe in his hands, and his russet eyes warm when they land on me.

"So this is where you snuck off to," he declares, heat suddenly glimmering in his gaze. He looks behind him at the stairs and then sets his empty carafe on the long table.

Before I know what he's doing, Leto closes the distance between us. His callused hands cup my face as he drops his lips to mine. The kiss is frenzied, hungry, and I study his closed eyes and pinched brow for a beat before I push him back, breaking the claim his lips have on mine.

"What are you doing?" I demand a hint breathlessly as my eyes snap to the shadows darkening the wall to the left of the entrance.

Is the Scorpion still watching?

"At the rate Tilleo and his guests are going, we'll never make it to the roof tonight," Leto tells me, stepping into me to bring our bodies flush again. "But they're drunk and distracted right now. I'm seizing an opportunity," he adds, his lips once again finding mine.

This time, he doesn't give me a moment to hesitate, to think. His tongue demands entrance and his kiss turns unexpectedly devouring. Leto and I have always had something between us. I wouldn't call it passion or devotion, more like we're a soft spot to land in a world made of iron and spikes. But the way he's kissing me right now has my mind jumping to curious places.

I give in, closing my eyes and relishing the feel of Leto's mouth against mine. We shouldn't be doing this, risking ourselves this way, but I can't find it in me to care. I probably should. My future is nonexistent, but Leto still has a chance. I shouldn't selfishly steal his prospects and possibilities away, but this is just like mouthing off to the Order of Scorpions and killing Crit. It's freeing, and all I've ever wanted to be is free.

Leto grabs my ass, squeezing it once and groaning into my mouth before he lifts me and sets me on the table. I palm the back of his neck, the stubble of his shaved head rough against my hands as I pull him impossibly closer. My thighs spread, offering his hard body a silken spot to settle against. His deft fingers unhook Tilleo's crest and chains from my hips, and I stop myself from running my nails up Leto's back. I can't mark him, I remind myself. It's one thing for me to get lost in this, but I can't leave any hint of myself on his body. I won't make him a target to seal his fate like Tilleo's done with mine.

Leto's lips break from mine, and he drops them down my neck as one hand reaches under the silk strip covering my left breast to pinch my taut nipple. His other hand reaches for the fabric draped over my slit. As though he's pulling back a curtain, he draws the dark blue panel over my right thigh, exposing my center completely. My slit is bare, any hair on my body from the chin down long since magicked away like all the other blade slaves. We say nothing to each other as Leto runs the pad of his fingers over my seam. I'm ready for him, and when he feels it, he smiles that sneaky smile I'm partial to.

"You owe me from last time," I remind him, and his smile grows even more.

We almost got caught on our last adventure on the back roof of the ludere. It made us hurry, which meant he enjoyed it far more than I did. I require more warming up, we've discovered over the years.

"Ah yes, the tally is in my favor, how could I forget?" he agrees, reaching into his flowy silk pants and stroking himself.

Russet eyes sparkle at me from a face that's given me far more pleasure to look at than I'd ever admit. Hungrily, I watch that face drop between my thighs, his stare fixed on mine as his tongue snakes out and licks up my seam. I spread my legs even farther for him, a needy moan slinking up my throat as his mouth parts me and his tongue and lips wrap around my clit. He sucks me into his mouth, his face diving between my thighs like I'm a feast that was just laid out before him.

I grab his head, shamelessly pressing him against me as I throw my head back and grind against his mouth. I quietly pant as he works my body, trying my hardest to keep silent, to keep us safe. His fingers press into me, coaxing out a low moan, and when I bring my head up so I can look down at Leto licking my cunt, my eyes catch on a pair of gleaming black orbs.

I tense and pull in a sharp inhale, my stunned stare landing on the glamoured face of a skeleton. His eyes are suffused with heat as they trail from my face down my body and settle on what Leto is doing between my thighs. My left tit is exposed, and I fight the urge to cover myself, to close my legs and block the Scorpion's view, but for some reason I hesitate. His shoulders are stiff as he studies Leto tonguing my seam. Leto slowly adds another finger to my glistening entrance, the pair of digits rhythmically pumping in and out of me as his lips suck on my core.

All at once, I find myself wondering what it would be like if the fingers now fucking me faster and faster looked like bones instead of the tan skin wrapped around Leto's strokes. I roll my hips against Leto's mouth and fingers, urging him on, but my eyes never leave the inky stare of the assassin hiding in the shadows.

Why is he here? I ask myself as tingles start coalescing in my limbs. Better yet, why am I allowing him to stay? I could call attention to him. I should stop Leto, straighten up, and scurry back up to the party with a full carafe of wine, like a good obedient blade slave is supposed to do. I could even try to kill the Scorpion for taking liberties with his eyes. Yet all I do is stare at him as Leto's administrations begin to culminate and peak.

A white-hot star gathers in my center. A few more rough pumps of Leto's fingers have the star bursting inside of me. I bite my lip and toss my head back, my eyes still transfixed on the skeleton's as I come undone. Mercilessly, I grind against Leto's face, wringing every ounce of pleasure I can from his mouth and fingers. He groans against my cunt, and I can tell by the small twitches in his muscles that he's finding his release too.

Quickly, I wonder if the house slaves will know what we did down here. Will they spot Leto's puddle under the table or smell the forbidden pleasure in the air? Will they keep our secret or rat us out? Then again, they might be preoccupied with the body tucked in the shadows. Crit won't stay hidden forever.

A small smile pulls at the lips hiding under the skeleton's glamoured white teeth, and I realize I have bigger problems than the house slaves. I rage-jerked-off one of the Order of Scorpions, mouthed off to the rest of them, and now I just let this mystery guest watch as I fucked another blade slave's face. I'm pretty sure Tilleo has ordered me to kill one of them, at which point I'll be tortured and executed, and I have a feeling the two remaining Scorpions will be the first in line for that.

I've spent so long being tightly wound and in control, and now I've lost it. I'm dancing with flames as though I'm fireproof, but in truth, my entire existence is dry kindling. Leto rises to his feet, reaching for a rag on the table meant to clean up spills, and uses it to free his fingers and face of any evidence of me. I hop off the table, covering myself with the panels of my dress, and quickly refasten the metal belt holding it all together around my hips. By the time I look up, the skeleton is once again gone.

Leto is tucking himself back into his pants as I fill both our carafes with wine. I don't wait for him to say anything before I take the stairs out of the cellar two at a time and find my way back to the loud and boisterous party. With a huff, a servant takes the wine from me, but nothing more is said or expressed as they whisk off to fill up empty glasses. Heart pounding in my chest, I once again find my place in front of the Dusk Court's tapestry.

Unable to help myself, my eyes immediately land on the three members of the Order of Scorpions. Their backs are all still to me, and a thick-bodied male is engaged in an animated conversation with all three. If I didn't know any better, I'd think I imagined the presence of one of them down in the cellar. Just as that thought flits through my mind, one of the sable-clad skeletons reaches into an inner pocket of his long vest and pulls out a thin, delicate dagger. He uses it to stab a fruit tart on a tray to his right, bringing the pastry to his skeletal mouth where he savors every bite until it's gone.

Goose bumps pebble my skin as I watch. How much longer before he's using that dagger to cut out my heart? I wish I could say never, but everything inside of me is screaming that it's coming sooner rather than later. I just wish whatever is now broken inside of me didn't feel so eager for it.

10

BONES

SILENTLY, MY BROTHERS AND I WALK BACK TO our tent, the cool desert night doing its best to trick us into thinking this place is something more than the hellhole it is during the day. Stars blink down at us as though they're the true rulers of this realm and we're nothing more than insects playing at being more. I can't say that I disagree.

My gaze wanders to the darkened ludere on our left. The large oval building seems like nothing more than a collection of shadows and pain, and I can't stop myself from wondering where she is inside of it. Is she thinking about me or my brothers? Is that other slave balls deep in her seeping pussy, ruthlessly pounding into her while she silently meets him stroke for stroke? I huff out an irritated breath as I once again grow hard. I just talked my cock down twenty minutes ago. I thought I was going to lose my mind, sitting at that table, rock hard, as I felt her eyes climbing all over me. It was all I could do not to pin her against the wall and fuck her so hard she screamed my name.

There'd be no quiet gasps or muted moans when I was inside of her. I'd show her just what her body was capable of taking while I sank my teeth into every inch of her, marking that tan flesh and drinking down the power I know is swimming in her veins. I was almost grateful when Tilleo excused the blade slaves to rest in preparation for tomorrow's tests. Gartox, the brute of a Bruin, was pissed. He'd been staring at a crimson-haired blade slave since dinner was served. She was lucky to escape whatever nefarious intentions were gleaming in his ruddy gaze. He was staring at my Slave first, but I shut that down with a look.

I fucking hate that Bruin. His entire Order goes against the Scorpions' core principles, and it pisses me off that we can't simply wipe them out. I release another sharp disgruntled exhale. They better keep their eyes off of Slave from here on out. I don't care what accords are in place, I'll violate every one if they so much as ponder a thought about her.

Tarek—Scorpius, I immediately correct myself—looks over at my huff of annoyance. He won't say a word until we're in the tent and free to speak, but I can see the questions already brewing in his eyes. I inhale a deep calming breath and try to get a grip. This slave already has me so distracted that I'm breaking protocol and thinking names instead of the codes we've created to protect ourselves while out hunting. I know better than to think there might not be magic here strong enough to breach our tent walls or even our minds. It's rare, but after watching that little speck of moondust *shadow walk* in the cellar, I won't rule any possibility out. Tilleo's been hiding things from us, and we need to get to the bottom of it immediately.

Skull throws the flaps of the tent out of his way, and we all stride into our usual accommodations for every Bidding. Straight away, he moves to the trunk located at the end of his pallet and pulls out a glass orb with a murky gray mist held inside. Walking to the center of the tent, he smashes the small globe on the ground. The glass shatters, immediately releasing a gray cloud that surges to the edges of our tent and then rises until it's converging over our heads.

"We're good for the night," he declares, and all eyes land on me. "What has you so riled up? What did you find out?"

"The Vulpi didn't have anything useful to say," I start, getting the boring shit out of the way first. "They're on high alert, something about another unknown Order stealing their signatures and setting them up."

"Dawn Court?" Skull asks, his eyes jumping from me to Scorpius and back again.

"That's my take on it. Someone wants us to think they're responsible for the annihilation event in the Dawn Court. They could be trying to purge us from their trail, but none of them were up for playing, not even Kiffin, and you know how her addiction rides her. I've never witnessed a *no* out of that female's mouth, but she was not having it today. They're pissed and here trying to track whoever is behind the setup."

Scorpius and Skull nod, their eyes thoughtful as they file this new unexpected information away. We all thought for sure the hunt was them, but if they're telling the truth about their signature being mimicked, this thing is even deeper and more fucked up than it was before.

"What else?" Scorpius asks as he starts to undo the buttons of his vest and strip down.

I pull in a deep breath. "She can shadow walk," I announce, my stare not missing the moment my words freeze both of my brothers in their place.

"Who?" Scorpius asks, but I can see he suspects exactly who I'm talking about.

"Our little Slave, that's who," I declare, feeling the same astonishment from them that *I* felt when I first saw her do it. "Oh, and I also watched her brain a guard with this as though his skull was nothing more than an eggshell," I add, pulling Scorpius's sheathed dagger from my inner vest pocket. I toss it to him, and he looks down at the blade as though it will sing to him all about its latest blood-soaked adventure.

"So she's strong too," Scorpius states, his eyes gaining that faraway look he always gets when he's trying to piece out a puzzle.

"I knew she was some highborn mutt," Skull announces, and I nod.

She has to be from a prominent noble line; they're the only ones capable of passing down that power, but how? We keep an eye on the bastards the rulers of the four courts create. It's not as many as one might think, but it does happen from time to time. The three of us are proof.

"Do you think Tilleo is targeting us?" Scorpius asks, his obsidian eyes now hard.

"I don't think Tilleo even knows," I answer, and I track the surprise my declaration sets off in both his and Skull's gazes. "She hunted a guard in the wine cellar. He moved around like she was hiding in the crates and shelves, not the shadows. He never saw her coming," I explain. "If Tilleo knew she had that ability, his personal guards would know too, if for nothing more than to protect him from it, but more so because they probably would have overheard him bragging about it. We all know how he is. He can't keep his mouth shut when he thinks he has something that will make him rich."

"Unless she's a new weapon and he's making a move," Skull counters.

"A move where though? He never had aspirations beyond taking Dorsin's place and creating his own empire," I argue.

"Can she do anything else?" Scorpius cuts in.

"Aside from face fuck a fellow slave so hard my dick might never recover, no," I state simply, adjusting my rock hard cock in punctuation of my point.

"Fuck, that's all I've been thinking about doing since we kicked her out of the tent," Skull admits, and I can't help the laugh that spills out of my lips.

"I'll be joining you now in that endeavor, brother, I can promise you that," I tell him as I run my hand over my short hair in exasperation.

I could call for a flesh slave to help alleviate my sudden onset of tension. I know Tilleo has them ready and waiting for all of his guests, but I suspect it won't have the effect

I'm hoping for. I don't want just any wet cunt, I want hers. I stepped into the cellar simply intending to keep an eye on her like Scorpius warned, but watching her slip from the shadows to deliver a kill so clean you could eat off it is something that speaks to me on a visceral level.

Her eyes weren't flat or empty as she struck, not like other blade slaves I've observed over the past years. There was no hesitation. The spark of exhilaration in her deadly stare wasn't there through madness or bloodlust. She was delivering justice. It was there, written in her very features. I don't know what that guard did, although I wouldn't have to think hard to come up with far too many disturbing scenarios, but whatever it was, ending him felt righteous to her. In that millisecond before she struck, I saw a fae who lived by the same code that my brothers and I do, and it calls to me. *She* calls to me.

"What is with this slave?" Scorpius asks absently as though he's hoping the answer will form in the air all around us, subsequently freeing us from her strange allure.

It's on the tip of my tongue to answer, but I hold back. I don't think that he's ready to hear the truth yet. Scorpius has always been too analytical. His best laid plans have best laid plans. He analyzes things from every possible angle, and *then* he attacks. He's not there yet. Skull wants to fuck her, but I can tell he thinks once he scratches that itch, he'll be all set to move right along. He doesn't see it yet either, even though he's usually more intuitive than that.

This girl, this Slave, is one of us. She's not like the stock we usually see Tilleo churn out of his ludere. He hasn't broken her. He hasn't turned her into a mindless killer for hire. She kills. She probably even enjoys it when the circumstances are right, like with the guard in the cellar, but there's more there. There's a drive to right wrongs, to punish the deserving. She has a need to restore balance.

Scorpius said we're not bringing home any pets, but I don't think it will take long for him to discover what I already have. She's ours. She's just waiting to be claimed, and I can't wait to put our mark all over her.

"Where are you going?" Scorpius asks as I move back toward the tent's entrance.

"I'm going to deal with the body she left behind. I don't want anyone tracing her to it or the fact that she used your blade to end him," I call over my shoulder before I push the flap of the tent aside and step back out into the surprisingly crisp desert air.

Scorpions always have each other's back. Skull and Scorpius may not know it yet, but our watch begins now.

11

AUSET

"SIT STILL, YOU LITTLE SHIT."

Wilik slaps the side of my face as she jerks my head around by the thick strands of hair gripped in her hands. I grit my teeth but say nothing as I continue to sit as still as a stone, just like always. Wilik always takes her frustrations out on us, but this morning it's extra hard not to turn around and slap her back. It's not my fault that Tilleo ordered a complicated set of braids for all of the female blade slaves today. It's the beginning of our tests, and he has expectations for how we're to look and be presented.

My head is yanked to the side again, and I start to debate how mad Figg will get if I get blood on my cream tunic so soon. The garnet-colored leather pants I'm wearing would hide the stains, but the gauzy, sleeveless top isn't going to fare so well. Deciding it's best not to piss off the two slaves I'm still dependent on for a few more days, I only grunt irritably when Wilik threatens to rip out my hair as she puts the final painful finishing touches on the single braid left to do on my head.

I quickly stand before she can kick the stool out from under me, and hurry out of the room before my newly broken sense of self-preservation comes out to play and gets me in even more trouble than I already am. I wish I could say I barely slept last night for fear that I'd wake to a blade being held at my throat while a skeleton loomed menacingly over me. Or because an alarm had sounded at the discovery of Crit's body in the wine cellar. Oddly, I slept hard, like I hadn't a care in the world. Surprisingly, neither dagger to the throat or a call to arms occurred last night.

This morning though, all I can seem to feel is concern over my total *lack* of concern when it comes to everything that's happening. It dawned on me last night that there's a possibility that Tilleo is fucking with me. I've sifted through his vague instructions over and over again, and as sure as I was that he'd just set me up for failure, there's now a part of me, a small part but a part nonetheless, that wonders if this is all some trick, some kind of conniving game? I don't think it is, but I've been wrong about his motivations before.

"Blade slaves to the pit in ten minutes," a guard calls out, his booming instructions echoing off the walls all around me.

I run my hands over the thin material of my top, smoothing it down for reasons that elude me. It will probably be wrinkled, torn, and stained crimson by the day's end. A sad fact, because it's the second softest thing I've ever worn. I fall in behind Kin and Paryn, who are stoically making their way down to the pits of sand located directly in the center of the ludere. Other blade slaves join our shuffle, all of us ambling toward the place where we've spent most of our time at the ludere training.

As I step into the open space of the largest pit, I notice red fabric draped and rippling over the railings of the walkways on the floor stacked above us. Someone has gone through the effort to make this inner circle of sand and brutality feel more elegant and brighter. It makes me want to rip the decorations down and burn them for the lie that they are.

It's early morning, but the sand is already radiating heat, and I can tell it's going to be a scorching, miserable day. Bright beams of sun slice through the opening above us, and there's not a cloud in the brilliant sky. I want to groan at the endless blue, ask it why it has to be such a shit and chase the fluffy white protectors away all the time, but what's the use? The sky above us hates us as much as the sand below, and both can get in line behind the masters and the other blade slaves.

All the male blade slaves stand shoulder to shoulder on the right and females to the left. I quickly find my place. My line of sight of the pit clears as we all fall into formation, which is when I get my first peek at the tall thick posts that have been driven into the sand in front of us. My stomach drops and I immediately know what is about to happen. I've seen it before and experienced it once, but usually it's reserved for punishment and the posts are dug in outside the ludere.

Risers have been set up on one side of the pit. Velvet cushions are placed atop the wooden benches, and I'm instantly vexed over the show we're going to be expected to put on for the Order members. I knew we were going to be tested, but I thought they'd put us through forms, demand to see our skill with various weapons, and then watch us fight hand-to-hand. *This* is a different level of jumping through hoops.

A whip cracks and all thoughts of masters that deserve to suffer and evil cloudless skies fall from my mind like boulders down a steep ravine. I stare straight ahead, body stiff and mind ready and waiting to be commanded. Master Chen stands in front of us on the other side of the field of poles, his body and eyes mirroring ours.

Excited chatter slowly reaches the pit, and we're forced to wait for Tilleo and the accompanying Order members to appear. In no rush, they languidly find seats on the risers where large umbrellas are hastily opened above them by servants, offering cool shade and solace from the sun. Slaves step from the recesses surrounding the pit with large *rone* leaves gripped in their palms. They begin to pump the dark green foliage up and down, fanning the collective as they find the velvet cushion of their choice and set their pampered asses upon them.

I spot the skeletons as they settle in the very back row, right in the middle, and my heart starts to pick up when I find that each of their soot black stares is trained on me. I force my vision to blur and block out the details of their intense skeletal faces. Today is going to be hard enough, no use adding to the mix things like annoying thoughts and worries about what the skeletons might do to me for my insolence. I need to stay calm and escape to a place in my mind where pain can't reach; it's my only hope of withstanding what's about to come.

The pit goes silent with anticipation as the Order members' eyes rake over our static positions. With a nod from Tilleo, Master Chen cracks his whip once and then coils it like a belt around his waist.

"You have exactly five minutes to locate a pole, pluck the sword from the sand next to it, climb atop the pole, and stand on it until I say you're done. Go!" he bellows suddenly, and like chirp ants, we all scramble for a perch.

Harsh and a handful of other blade slaves who are always vying for number one all rush to the front line of posts. I choose the option right in the middle, surrounded by the pack where I should be partially hidden from prying eyes. As others begin to climb, a couple of us are already planning ahead, knowing what's in store for the rest of the day. I begin to strip out of my pants, pulling the thin leather from my limbs and setting it on the handle of the sword still sticking out of the ground.

I hate the feeling of being exposed in just my undergarments, but I'll hate the strength these pants will strip from me as I sweat in them and dehydrate quicker much more. When I was first dropped in these sands, standing in the unforgiving sun like this would have resulted in a burn that would have required healers to recover from. After all these years, the sun has beaten my skin into submission, and a strong warm-bronze tone has replaced the pale delicate shell I used to be. I pull off my gauzy shirt and quickly tie it around my head. It will stop the sweat from dripping into my eyes for a while at least.

I pluck my pants and sword from the ground just as Master Chen screams, "You have two minutes left!" I hurry to climb the pole that's three lengths taller than me, inwardly groaning as I reach the top and confirm it's only two finger spaces wider than one of my feet. I get my foot in place, and with strength and balance whetted over years in this place, I rise and swiftly wrap the entire sword in my leather pants. It will make it slightly heavier, but it will keep the metal from burning my hands as the punishing desert sun beats down on it until it gives in and tries to melt to avoid the onslaught.

I look around to see far too many blade slaves dressed in exactly what they've been given to wear today. Only a handful of others have stripped down, and only one other blade slave had the same idea I did with our pants. I want to catch Kin's eye, get some sort of confirmation that we did this right, but I'm not sure. Tilleo could have us whipped for ruining the perfect image he seemed to want to create with our clothes and hair, or he could reward us for our ingenuity. I never truly know which way things will go when it comes to him.

Another crack of the whip echoes off the walls surrounding the pit, and I try to relax into my one-footed stance on the top of the thin post.

"Bring your swords forward, keep your arms straight, and do not drop them until you've been given permission," Master Chen barks, and each of us does as we're commanded.

The pit once again goes quiet, and the test starts. We'll stand on these poles until we can't stand anymore. One of us will fall first and be punished for it. Others will follow, and a few of us will push ourselves past all limits for the bragging rights of saying we were last. The Order members will watch until they're bored, and the winner will probably be announced to them when they've abandoned us to return to their magically cooled rooms, platters of food, and realm gossip.

I wish I felt more mad than jealous right now. Anger can be fuel, jealousy is draining. Centering my breathing, I do my best to disconnect from my body and float back into my thoughts like they're a cool pond of water. I imagine I'm weightless as I tear into a juicy leg of succulent meat, pop some sweet berries into my mouth, and chase it all down with a wine that makes me feel alive and unconquerable. I've never in my memory feasted on any of these things, and yet it's as though I can taste them on my very lips like they're real. I welcome the phantom memories that I can't quite explain, inviting them to swarm my thoughts and steal me away from my reality for as long as possible.

It's well past midday when my body demands I surface. Brutally, I'm yanked back into the here and now, my muscles screaming and my foot demanding relief. Looking around, I find all of us still on our perches, but from the look of a few of the others, it won't stay that way for much longer. I adjust my stance for the first time since we started, turning the hands holding the sword from palm up to palm down. It provides a little relief in some of my arm muscles, which is better than nothing, I tell myself as I very carefully inch one foot over to make room for my other. As I shift my weight at the top of the pole, I notice that the wooden risers are empty.

I want to scoff at the Order members retreating so early, but a familiar stern voice draws my attention, and I track it to a few poles down from mine. Master Chen stands beneath a struggling blade slave, firmly announcing something to all the Order members, who are gathered around. Tilleo is in the back, greedily watching the interaction as a house slave furiously works to fan away the sweat slowly collecting on the master's brow.

"She's a passable lock pick and can untangle basic wards. She's trained with all required weapons, but she excels at the use of a gnome pick for close contact and an assegai for distance. Just like with all blade slaves, she has built a tolerance to most dosable toxins, but she's shown to remain susceptible to fir flower and *sarkar* bites. She ranked number one in her enticement training, proving to be quite adept at both male and female satisfaction. Her build is softer than some of the others in this batch, but what she lacks in muscle mass, she makes up for in flexibility. According to Master Dorrow, there isn't a position that she can't be bent into, which is a useful skill in its own right."

Order members nod as they eye Orit like she's some beast of burden who needs its flanks slapped and its joints bent and tested to ensure they're sound. Sweat drips down her reddened face, and her arms shake as they battle to remain straight and to hold the sword out in front of her.

Master Chen moves from the base of Orit's pole to Haryk's, who seems to be faring slightly better atop his post. His shirt is drenched in sweat and clinging to his body, and even though the tremor in his arms is less visible than Orit's, I notice a slight sway to his positioning that has me rethinking my assessment. It's possible Haryk might pass out before Orit does.

Master Chen begins to list Haryk's stats and efficiencies, and I listen, surprised by the detail and observations being made. I probably shouldn't be shocked by the collection of data the masters have compiled, as the whole point *is* for them to sell us off, but the detail in their observations is unnerving. Just like Orit did, Haryk keeps his head up and his eyes fixed on nothing as Master Chen talks about him like he's nothing more than a commodity. I wonder what's going through the blade slave's head as the Order members are told that he's advanced at wards but has little patience for the use of poisons, preferring death by beheading even when a more delicate approach would have been preferred.

Sweat drips freely down my body, distracting me from Master Chen's summary as my attention is once again called to the discomfort peppering every limb. My arms are stiff and solid, the leg I just switched to has hours left in it, and the shirt I wrapped around my head is doing a decent job of keeping the stinging sweat from my eyes. I focus on what's working and shut down the need to move and stretch my stiff muscles. Once again, I return my focus to the crowd of Order members gathered next to me, which of course is when a giant glamoured wolf head stirs and moves to the side, and my gaze lands directly on the face of a skeleton.

Why can't I seem to escape their soul-sucking eyes?

Unwelcome heat gathers at my center, but I can't bring myself to look away. Thanks to their solid glamour, I once again find that I don't know which of the three he is, but dropping my gaze feels as though I'm offering submission that he doesn't deserve. His eyes trace a bead of sweat that runs from my neck down between my breasts, setting a steady course over the muscles of my stomach to meet its end in the fabric of my underwear.

My nipples pebble at his attention, a reaction the thin binding at my chest won't do much to hide, which is just perfect because the whole crowd of Order members is slowly shifting to surround me. I catch a hint of a smile breaking across the skeleton's face before a gargantuan bearded man steps in front of him, blocking the Scorpion from my sight. It's probably unwise, but just like I was staring down the skeleton, I decide to stare down what I suspect is a member of the Order of Crows, based on the feathers he has woven into his hair. He dismisses the challenge in my gaze as Master Chen begins to speak, but I chalk a tally in my favor at what I deem is his surrender to me.

"Auset came to us later than the other blade slaves in this batch," Master Chen starts, and I find myself meeting the eyes of all the Order members surrounding me one by one. "Her late start however has not impeded her skill. In fact, many of the masters have been impressed at the rate this slave took to the conditioning and training. This female excels at any weapon given to her. She once downed an opponent with an empty quiver when the arrows weren't enough to drop him. She ripped it apart and used the suede to strangle him," he continues, and the wolf head I'm currently locked eyes with tilts in interest at the master's words.

"I'd like to see that," the wolf grumbles, and Master Chen nods as though he's a djinn that would love nothing more than to grant that wish.

"This blade slave has a mind that matches her advanced weapons skills. She is calculating and instinctive, often downplaying abilities in order to diminish any difficulties that may occur socially from a high rank in the batch," Master Chen continues.

I want to glare at the master for announcing that to the entire pit of blade slaves, while simultaneously scowling at myself for not realizing that I wasn't hiding what I was doing half as well as I thought I was.

"It's important to note that this slave did not undergo enticement training. Instead, an excellent baseline for withstanding torture and punishment was developed over the course of her time here. She has a high tolerance for pain and a body that takes to healing faster and much better than most. Her status as bait ranks higher than any blade slave we've seen come out of this ludere."

My mind stalls at that declaration, and my gaze flashes to Master Chen. Did he really just tell the gathering of the best assassins this realm has ever seen that I should be used as bait to potentially be caught and tortured over and over again, all because my body could heal from it? My eyes narrow at the bastard, and he immediately wraps a hand around the whip coiled at his waist. For the first time, I wonder if Tilleo's order might be more of a mercy than a condemnation. If my life is destined to be used as bait, there's no question that death is the better deal.

I glare at the master, suspecting he's been biding his time, waiting to pay me back for my defiance over the years. The pardon I was ultimately given over the enticement training refusal was never going to slide with the masters, regardless of what Tilleo declared. I just never realized how they were going to make me pay until now. They talked me up, made my abilities desirable, and then laid the path to a lifetime of pain with only a few well-spoken words.

Fuckers.

"Moving on," Master Chen declares as though my fate is sealed.

My gaze moves to Tilleo, but he's not looking up at me as he wanders below my post and on to the next. I'm reeling and it takes all the control I can muster to rein in my anger and astonishment. I should have known, and yet I didn't. My status with the masters changed the day Tilleo refused to wash me from the batch. I thought his word was final, that it protected me in some way, but I'm discovering just how wrong that assumption was. I want to scream at my own stupidity, but thanks to Tilleo, I've already accepted that my life was going to end before I ever made it to the final Bidding Day.

They can't hurt me. Not anymore. Or so I tell myself as I work to fall back into oblivion while my body fights to stay on top of a narrow post, in the scorching sun, with nothing but retribution flowing through my veins.

12

A NXIETY HAMMERS AT ME AS I LEAN BACK INTO the shadows as deeply as the wall at my back will allow. The footsteps that triggered my alarm slowly fall away, but I don't dare breathe a sigh of relief just yet. I scan the shelves in the alchemy room I've snuck into and carefully sort through the ones filled with healing tinctures and herbs until I find the stack of poisons the healers dose the blade slaves with. We're told that it's to help us build a tolerance to the common poisons used in the death trade, that it could one day save our lives, but far too many healers and guards seem to enjoy the suffering these innocent looking vials cause. It makes their altruistic claims evaporate right out the window like early morning mist.

The bottles and pouches are all neatly labeled and organized. I'm not supposed to be able to read any of it; the neat scroll identifying each poison isn't expected to be a threat to the healers and guards who keep us under their thumb, but today it is. I move closer to the shelf, dismissing label after label until I find what I want.

The healers call it *pokoyn*. I don't know where it comes from or how it's collected, but I do know that it causes a horrid wasting sickness if too much is given too fast. It moves slowly, rotting a fae from the inside out, and it kills more than it saves. When my batch was given this in my second year here, it culled more than half of us. I think it's high time the guards and healers themselves test it out.

I tuck the light yellow vial in the waist of my pants and move gingerly back to the shadows. The poison feels secure enough—I just need it not to break as I step into the shadow that let me in here and back out into the shady hallway on the other side. Casually I stroll out of the healer's wing, which takes up one whole side of the lower floor of the ludere, and move in the direction of the hashery on the other side.

My heart beats frantically in my chest when I stop and nonchalantly lean against a dark wall like I'm taking in the morning appreciatively. Other blade slaves wander past me, but no one bothers to look my way. It's early and the main crowd of us is still in their chambers, attempting to steal a few more seconds of sleep before today's tests begin. I wait until the walkway is empty, and then I crawl through the shadowed wall and into the food storage room at the back of the kitchens.

Relief rides a deep exhale when there's no one in the space but me and bags of grain. If I didn't know already that the bitch hated me, I'd say fate is on my side in this endeavor. I know better than to trust her though. I found this room by accident the night I wandered down here starving and fell through the wall. I also discovered that same night, that the healers and guards aren't forced to suffer the same rancid gruel that's forced on the blade slaves.

Stealthily I move to the cooler and pull the door open. Just like I did before, I find bottles of some kind of milk stacked there. I grab one, quickly uncap it, and pour half of the pokoyn in. I put the stopper back in and shake the milk before setting it back on the cooler shelf. I reach for another bottle and pour the rest of the poison in and then hurry to shake it and put it back.

I sneak down here from time to time when I can get away with it, but I have to be careful with what I take. The cooks keep a tight watch on everything, but the normal anxiety that accompanies one of these trips is dulled by the fact that I'm not stealing anything today. As long as I can get out of here unseen, no one will be the wiser until they all start to get sick. By then, it'll be too late. Carefully I close the cooler door and retrace my steps back to the dark wall. I pull in a deep breath and ready myself for the next part. I'll be walking out into the open corridor of the main floor. If someone sees me, I'm fucked. Then again, I'm dead anyway, so really it will just move up the timetable.

It dawns on me that I should stash the empty vial. I had intended to return it to the alchemy room in case the healers noticed it was missing, but it would probably be wiser not to get caught with it now just in case someone spots me. I dash to the side and tuck the tube of glass in a dark corner behind a large sack of something that's sitting on a low shelf. It's dusty and I hope that means it isn't used often and my hiding spot will go undetected for a while.

Before I can second-guess myself, I step back through the wall, peeking my head out for a quick glance to make sure the sand pits and walkway are empty. I don't see anyone, but I hold my breath all the same as I walk out into the shade-soaked corridor. Hastily, but not too obviously, I move away from the dark wall toward the hashery. I debate for a moment going back to my sleeping chambers, but I've already seen Figg and Wilik this morning, so there's really no reason I'd be up there. Instead, I decide breakfast makes the most sense. My stomach growls at that thought, and I wish I had more to look forward to than putrid porridge, but the thought of the guards and healers diving into their morning meal offers a whole different kind of sustenance to my soul.

They've spent years reveling in our screams. I can't wait to dance to theirs.

I smirk as I queue up for the morning drivel. I think through today's test in an effort to calm myself. I don't want to walk in looking too excited about what I've just done and make anyone curious about what's going on in my head. Fortunately, the test this morning isn't the mystery the previous ones have been. Based on the fighting leathers I was handed this morning by Figg, and the battle braids Wilik plaited in my hair, it seems as though we'll finally get to show the Orders just what we can do against one another.

There are more blade slaves than I thought there would be in the hashery when I walk in, and there's a distinct edginess to the atmosphere as I observe the others all decked out in matching garb.

I accept the bowl of mush that's handed to me and take a seat in the spot that's been mine since I arrived here. Taria is on my left and already halfway through the flavorless morning meal as I scoop up my first mouthful and eye the others slowly filling tables around us. Leto huffs as he takes up the spot to my right. I didn't realize he was so close behind me, and I eye him for a beat as though his face will give away whether or not he saw me climb out of a shadow-flushed wall. He looks like he usually does. Harsh settles in across from Leto, and Yotta slumps down at the end of the bench on my side.

Everyone looks wired and expectant, but no one looks as though they saw anything out of the ordinary. I command my heart to calm down and refuse to look for any more signs that I've been caught. I haven't. The tension all around me is because everyone knows there's a lot riding on this next test. I, on the other hand, have the freedom of knowing that nothing I do in the pit today will have any effect on my impending death.

"You look awfully cheerful this morning," Leto observes, nudging my shoulder playfully as he shoves a large helping of gruel into his mouth.

"Less cheerful, more resigned," I counter, and Harsh grunts at my claim.

I'm not sure what the sound is supposed to mean, but I don't care what Harsh thinks one way or the other, so I don't press to find out.

"You're with the Scorpions, right?" Taria asks, and I nod. "What are they like?" she inquires eagerly, and I recall that she'd mentioned hoping to catch their eye before the mess of this Bidding ever started.

"Yeah, Auset, what are they like?" Harsh adds, making it clear he thinks I should have a lot to say on the matter.

I glare at him, and it seems to remind him of the threat I have every intention of keeping if he doesn't shut the fuck up. His gaze once again finds his bowl of mush, and he's careful not to look up from it again. Leto gives me a curious dip of his brow, but I ignore the question in his face and look around. Sorag is in the kitchen today, and he usually doesn't care if we talk quietly at our tables. I look over at Taria to find her gazing up at me excitedly. I try not to cringe at the eager flecks alight in her bright brown eyes.

I want to tell her that the Scorpions are just like the other masters here, cruel and entitled, but I hate the idea of crushing the optimism in her stare. There are enough things in this horrid place that will do that, I don't have to be one of them if I can help it. I swallow down my opinions about excitement being a dangerous thing to feel in a place like this, and instead shrug my shoulders. I'm not really sure what to even say about the three skeletons that seem to haunt my every step these days.

"I haven't had much interaction with them," I start, making it clear that I'm no expert when it comes to the Order, like Taria is clearly hoping I'll be. "They're very talented," I offer vaguely, thinking back to the shadow walking and dagger catching in the cellar. "When the masters said they were the best, they weren't wrong. They seemed just as pampered and arrogant as some of the other Orders, but they're more independent and capable than I thought they'd be," I add, remembering that first night when they removed their own armor and clearly dressed themselves before the big feast. "That's about all I know."

I leave out my thoughts on the voyeurism at least *one* of them is into, as well as the intimate details I now know about Scorpius's cock. I figure Taria is less interested in the primal draw the Order of Scorpions possess, so I keep it professional and don't mention the list I've been compiling of the desirable physical attributes that are hidden under each of their glamours.

"Do you think they're looking for someone this year?" she asks me, trying and failing to hide her fervor.

I shove a bite of gruel into my mouth so I don't immediately have to answer. I chew and casually observe her while she patiently waits for me to respond. She looks so young, so small. She's the most petite of the female blade slaves, but she's no less skilled and relentless. Her deep ebony skin is flawless, and her rich brown eyes are big and beautiful. She's the kind of pretty that encourages someone to want to protect her, to trust her, and she's a more lethal killer for that fact. If the Order of Scorpions didn't have their heads up their pampered asses, she might be an excellent option. But I suspect Taria has a good shot with the Order of Vulpi. None of that is what she wants to hear right now though.

"I'll put in a good word for you," I offer, as though my word holds any weight with the best Order here.

Taria has to know that, but her smile grows even brighter, and she dips her head shyly with gratitude.

"Thanks, Auset. I'd really appreciate that," she tells me, and I nudge her shoulder playfully with mine like I've seen Leto do before.

I'm not sure if it makes her feel anything. I know I feel a little awkward initiating contact where I normally wouldn't, but oh well. I could be dead any day now. If she thinks it's weird, I'll never know. I have no doubt that this year will be just like every other year when it comes to the Order of Scorpions and the fact that they don't bid on blade slaves. But I'll tell them about Taria anyway. I'm sure it will make for good conversation the next time one of them orders me to wash their dick.

The table grows quiet as the others eat and seem to contemplate their own place in this Bidding. Being that I don't have one, I'm suddenly bothered by the silence.

"What about the Order of Serpents?" I uncharacteristically turn and ask Leto. "You and Haryk were assigned to them, right?"

He looks momentarily confused by the question. Or maybe it's that I'm asking him something other than *do you want to meet tonight.*

"What are they like?" I encourage, and the table turns to look at him, all of us quietly awaiting any insights that might make all of this easier to navigate.

"Quiet, quieter than I thought they'd be. They barely speak to each other let alone any other Orders," he shares, and soon someone else is talking about the Order of Wolves and their penchant for marking their territory.

"I thought the wolf thing was just a glamour?" Paryn asks with a laugh and a disgusted look on her face.

I smile at the thought of man-wolves who aren't potty-trained, but it drops at the sound of heavy footsteps that pound from down the hall. Everyone in the hashery immediately goes silent. The screech of benches scraping against stone fills the air as we all push to our feet when Master Vilde strides into the room. It's utterly soundless all around me, but I can practically hear the inner groans of every blade slave present at the cruel master's presence. He's on my want-to-kill list, just behind Tilleo.

"Today you will fight in the pit until only one of you is left standing," he growls out, his moldy gray eyes hungry for the blood and pain that will paint the pit sands today. "You will be assigned an opponent, but once that opponent is down, you are free to attack anyone you wish. You are only allowed to touch the weapon assigned to you. Do I make myself clear?"

"I am your blade to command," all of us answer back in unison.

A merciless smile crawls across Vilde's face as we show him our complete compliance. I can see his chest puff up and his eyes darken as the power goes straight to his head, just like it always does, and I already know today is going to be a bad one for far too many of us. He starts to call out pairs and assigned weapons. I remind myself that none of this matters. My fate has already been decided. But I can't ignore the rock that starts to settle in my stomach as more and more pairs are put together.

I know who I'm going to get before Master Vilde calls it out. Taur. I can see the conniving move from yards away. Taur is huge. The biggest male in our class. He's faster than he has a right to be at his size, but he's beatable as long as I can stay out of reach enough to tire him out.

"Taur, you're assigned a broad sword. Auset, it's been requested that you show what you can do with a bow."

Master Vilde's face melts into a vicious sneer, and it takes me a moment to realize why. He said bow, not bow *and* arrows. They want me to fight off the biggest brute in the batch with a useless bow and nothing more.

Great. Pissing great.

"Oh, and Tilleo has given the green light for two kills in this match. Nothing gets the Orders going like the scent of blood and death in the air."

His putrid gray gaze fixes on me, the meaning very clear. Two people will die today, and it doesn't take a mastermind or a tactical genius to guess who the bloody master wants one of them to be.

This just gets even better.

Part of me wants to point out that Tilleo has *big plans* for me, so killing me today is not a wise idea. But no one knows about that aside from me and him...and maybe the Scorpions, depending on what they've pieced together from my cryptic declaration that first night in their tent. It does remind me though that I don't have to hold back anymore. I can't risk exposing *all* of my secrets, but I sure as shit can let loose and ride the bloodlust like I've always wanted.

Anticipation slowly pushes out the dread I was feeling, and I study Taur, sizing him up. I don't need to tame my instincts in this fight. A small smile slips across my face. It grows even wider when Master Vilde takes one look at it and the overconfident light in his eyes dims with doubt.

I have to stay alive until two bodies are in the sand. I can do this. Screw Vilde and anyone else who thinks otherwise. Soon they'll be puking and shitting all over themselves, and I can't wait to watch as they slowly and very painfully die.

I BREATHE HARD AS I DASH UNDER ANOTHER BRUTAL slash from Taur and his lethal long sword. Hot sand jumps at my feet with each heavy step, but I ignore the burning pain of the pit under my soles and concentrate on the bastard in front of me. Taur's reach is already more than twice mine, so of course the masters *had* to go and make it even longer by handing him the biggest weapon we train with other than a spear. What I wouldn't give for a spear right now. The bell rang hours ago, indicating two deaths were done and we were back to maiming and not murdering, but it seems Taur didn't get the message.

He swipes for me again, and I jump out of the way, the tip of the sword barely missing me that time. I can see the big behemoth tiring, but I can't lie—it took way longer than I thought it would. My muscles scream at me to slow down and give them a break, but Taur just keeps coming. I scan his face, trying to discern what his next move will be as we start to circle one another again. My gaze flits between the egg-like bumps he now sports on his head like he's about to sprout horns at any moment. I had really hoped that one of the bashes of my bow against his skull would knock him out, but he's proven to be a resilient shit. It seems I wasn't the only one holding back in training.

"You can keep running, but I'm going to cut you in half all the same," Taur grumbles, both of us taking our time to analyze and assess the best move forward.

"Victors don't talk shit about how they're going to kill you, Taur. They just kill you. Threats are for the weak," I lob back, satisfaction warming my chest when a tic in his jaw pulses with annoyance.

I don't know what I ever did to this big oaf to deserve his relentless effort to separate my head from the rest of me, but I'm done with it. It's hot as lava out here, and the punishing heat is sapping my strength from above as well as below. The blazing sand works hand in hand with the sun and the fucking masters to bring me to my knees. Sheer stubbornness and will are the only things I'm still running on, but it's more than enough. This ludere made sure of it.

Taur surges at me like a bull, and I whack my bow against his left thigh as I duck under his swing and sprint to get out of the way of the spinning slash I can feel coming. I've been working on Taur's thigh for forty minutes now. I know I'm only a couple blows away from rendering the leg useless, my hits making it too numb to hold his weight anymore. My biggest worry right now is that one of the hits is going to crack the shaft of my shitty bow, and then I'll really be left with nothing to defend myself aside from my wits and my fists.

Taur stumbles as he twists to try to clip me, and I seize the opening his sloppy footwork offers and bat at the hand gripping the sword. I don't expect much from my attack, so when the sword goes flying out of his palm, I'm shocked. It takes me a beat to process what just happened, but I'm sliding in the sand for the weapon before it can even hit the ground.

Jubilation rockets through me as I wrap a palm around the grip of the long blade. It's heavy, but my body knows exactly what to do. Muscle memory kicks in and aids me in redirecting the blade as I smoothly swing for Taur. I'm fast, far faster than he thought I'd be with the hefty sword. Shock and fear detonate in his gaze as the arc of the blade promises to settle in the meat of his upper arm.

I know the masters won't let me get away with killing him, regardless of how on board they were for my death when the blade was in his hands, so I don't even bother. I *am* going to make this prick hurt though for trying to be their lackey and come for me. Let's see how he likes healing from an almost-severed limb.

Out of nowhere, a whip cracks against my hand. The braided tip clips my wrist so hard that my fingers immediately go numb and I lose my grip on the broad sword mid-swing. The weapon goes flying out of my palm, misses Taur completely, and spins end over end until it hits a wall and clunks loudly to the ground. Taur and I both snap our heads in the direction of the jeering masters, and I glare at Master Vilde as he coils a whip in his hands and sneers at me with undiluted contempt.

"No touching weapons that weren't assigned to you," he taunts, and as much as I want to snarl with frustration, I know it'll do no good. I have to beat these bastards at their own game.

I ignore the snickers of the masters and instead leap at Taur while he's still looking at them as though they'll tell him what to do next. At some point with the whip, my bow broke in half, but I don't let it deter me as I take the piece I still have and hit Taur as hard as I can in the temple with it.

Blood sprays as his skin tears from the force of my contact. He yelps and lifts his arms to protect his face, and I drop the now useless piece of wood in my hand and start in on the body shots with my fists. The masters yell out commands to help the big, bloody blade slave stave off my attack, and rage starts to boil me from the inside out.

Fucking cowards.

My vision goes red as I land hit after hit against Taur's ribs. The noise all around me dims, making it easy for me to hear the delicious crack of bone followed by a pained whimper from my opponent's mouth. It spurs me on, and I reach for an arm that Taur is trying to protect himself with and spin hard enough to break it or pull it out of the socket altogether. Taur screams, and out of the corner of my eye, I see Master Lira hand Master Vilde a coiled rope. I immediately know what I'm in for, what they're going to try to do, and I hurriedly reach for something else on Taur's huge frame that I can break before they get that rope around me and make this fight a hundred times harder for me to win.

It's all I can do to not pivot my attack and rush the horrible masters for what they're trying to do, but I shut that burning desire down. They'll pay soon enough. I've already made sure of it.

13

SCORPIUS

HE SLAPS A SWORD OUT OF A TALL MALE'S hands with the useless bow they've given her to defend herself with. They didn't even provide the slave with arrows, only an impotent bow to use against the melee in the pit. All of this nonsense because Taos mentioned one time that he wanted to see what she could do with a non-weapon. It makes me want to skin the wolf and set his glamoured pelt in the entryway of our home so we can stomp on his ass every day.

Chaos rings from the largest circle of sand in front of the risers where we sit. We're on day three of these shows, and I'm about two and a half days done with the superfluousness of it all. I've never enjoyed these events. I've always understood the advantages they can provide if worked just right, but this Bidding is different. From the first test, where my brothers and I finally learned Slave's true name, to then hearing all about the torture she's endured at the hands of the masters, followed by the days of useless tests and the long nights of pretending like most of the Orders don't want to kill each other, I'm starting to lose the battle with my ever-waning patience and my progressively building temper.

What's worse is it's not as though I didn't know what happened in this ludere. I know the kind of fae Tilleo is, so why does the fact that Auset is here bother me so much? Why are we drawn to her? I'm a sucker for a smart mouth. I figured that was the lure when I first interacted with the blade slave, but Skull and Bones are enthralled too. She's not what we initially thought she was, which now has me wondering just what in the Kings' names we've walked into here.

My suspicious stare once again finds her unique white-gray hair in the tangle of action in the pit. Her skin is sun-kissed and slick with sweat as she weaves and dodges around her attacker's extensive reach. I watch the little moonbeam struggle against everything that's stacked up against her, and it makes me even more wary. The masters weren't exaggerating when they ranked her skill and competency. She's the best option here. Even when she holds back in order to stay in the middle of the batch's standings. However, if Tilleo thinks my brothers and I are dumb enough not to see right through this obvious setup, then he hasn't been paying close attention all these years to what the Scorpions are capable of.

She's too perfect, too good at this game. She's the ideal fit for the Order of Scorpions, and I don't trust it for a second. It's obvious she's a highborn bastard. If her looks didn't give it away, her strength and abilities scream it. She has the perfect wounded fawn backstory, one the masters were all too eager to shove down our throats. They've even gone the extra mile with setting her up for failure with every task the blade slaves have been given. Of course she doesn't fail. Time after time, she finds a way to rise to the occasion.

It's maddening to watch and impressive.

I scowl as I watch her sprint and then gracefully skid through the sand, scooping up the discarded sword as she cuts through the gritty desert floor as though it's nothing more than water at her feet. She attacks, bow in one hand and hard won sword in the other. Her opponent is two heads taller and spans thicker than she could ever be even if they were feeding her properly—which I have no doubt they aren't. I shake my head as I watch her take on the behemoth of her batch with a gleam of reprisal in her silvery gaze. She's the perfect underdog. Her story and circumstances are an intricately woven net in which to ensnare us. As though my brothers and I are that easy. As though we're that dense.

I glance over at the colorfully dressed slave master. He watches the test with a bored mien. He has a glass of bloodwine in one hand while the other pinches at the breast of the house slave that was fanning him before he found another use for her. I glower at him for a moment before looking back at the action of the fighting blade slaves. The slave master has tipped his hand, and he hasn't even realized it. I'm sure he thinks he's playing us just right, but what my brothers and I have can't be bought or infiltrated.

Not even by something as enticing as Auset. She's a plant, an informer of some sort. I've pieced together that much. What I don't know is why.

Our relationship with Tilleo has been cordial since he took over Dorsin's interests. He doesn't know that my brothers and I are the reason Dorsin's interests were even up for grabs, but he's never needed to know that detail. So why now is Tilleo dangling this bait in front of us? What's his endgame here? I doubt he'd want revenge if he found out about Dorsin and the part we played in his death. We also fund his enterprise here at the ludere in exchange for the information collected at these Biddings and long after. Why fuck with that? The only conclusion I can come to is that someone has paid him to infiltrate our Order.

I bite back the growl of frustration that wants to crawl up my throat, and stop myself from running disgruntled fingers through my smooth glamoured hair. I study the other spectators, wondering if one of the other Orders could be behind this, but immediately I dismiss the idea. It would have to be someone with more financial backing than the Order of Scorpions, and the only houses that can claim that are the royal ones.

Mentally, I tally the threats and enemies we've made in the royal houses over the years. No one stands out as being a viable option. Even if one of them was patient enough to come up with this plan, they'd never get the financial backing without one of the Crowns finding out about it. Luckily for us, our fathers have their uses for what we can do and what we've built as an Order. We may be the bastards of kings, but we've proven our worth to our sires time and time again over the years.

Skull hisses next to me, and I focus back on the mock battle occurring in the pit in front of us. Patches of red spot the surface of the circle as fights turn more fervent and brutal. The parched sand greedily drinks down the scarlet splatters while determined grunts and growls bounce off the walls of the ludere. Masters rebuke and cheer with equal frenzy, making it easy to see who they've put money on or bet against. I don't know why Tilleo thinks this manic fighting is beneficial. We're assassins, masters of subterfuge, secrecy, sneaking, and death. Why we'd need to see what these slaves can do in battle, is asinine. What's happening in front of me right now is nothing more than sport.

I watch Auset move lithely as she goes in for the kill. Her opponent leaves his stomach open and she's on it, pummeling him before I can even blink. Could she be from the Winter Court? I wonder as I take in her coloring. I try to recall any of the noble lines there that might have similar features, but we don't deal with the Night Court often, and my memory is hazy. The Night Court is the only royal house currently lacking a seat at our table. I suppose it's possible they're the ones behind this, and yet they have no reason to want to infiltrate our ranks. King Korven is sterile. He hasn't filled the empty throne at his side since Queen Akiruh died. Which means her useless nephew, Leyev, is the sole heir.

Leyev has bred a handful of bastards, but none of them are old enough to make a run for our ranks. The future heir spends his days wine drunk and buried between the legs of anyone willing. His biggest worry in life consists of planning what to wear at the next big party. Nothing more is required of him, and he likes it that way. There's no chance he'd pick a fight with us. The king stoically locks himself away, his kingdom managed more by his advisors than by him directly. We have no issue with him or his court, so the question remains, who the hell is Auset, and more importantly, who is she working for and why?

Bones tenses next to me, and I'm pulled from my thoughts to find the fight still hasn't ended. I thought Auset had the other blade slave, but they're both back on their feet, and the large male is wobbling unsteadily toward her. His face is nothing more than bruises and dripping blood, and he's favoring his left side. Undeterred by his injuries, he swings wildly at her. He's outmatched in every way by the stunning blade slave, but it seems someone forgot to make him aware of that fact.

There's no denying that whoever trained Auset created a lethal masterpiece. Maybe when all the curtains have been pulled back and the players revealed, we'll kill Tilleo and hand over this ludere to the fae who polished this slave and made her sparkle the way she does. The realms know the Orders need more candidates like her. She's a moon-kissed nightmare, and there's no escape for her prey.

A rope snakes out from nowhere, lassoing one of Auset's ankles and pulling her off balance. Immediately I see what's made Bones taut with fury as several masters work to give Auset's opponent the upper hand. They laugh as she struggles against their interference, she bobs and weaves avoiding the other blade slave's sloppy swings while trying to pull her leg free of the rope. A tide of cheers rises up around us as another fight ends. A fight that several of the Orders were keenly watching, but I can't pull my gaze from Auset.

I observe as anger floods her features just as she gets her leg free, only for the masters to quickly wind the rope back and prepare to try to snag her again. She snarls something at them, but there's too much noise all around us to hear what it is.

Before they can interfere once more, Auset leaps for her opponent. She's utterly fearless as she attacks, knocking him to the ground and destroying him until he's no longer moving. There are no cheers for her as she rises off her opponent's wide chest, bloodied and breathing hard. All at once, her hand snaps back, and before I can track the movement, a broken piece of the bow she was fighting with goes flying through the air. It hits the master with the rope in his hands, square in the chest, the force of the blow knocking him on his ass.

Satisfaction flares in her eyes before the reality of what she just did slowly overtakes her indignant stare. The ludere instantly quiets. Apprehension and tension thicken the already cloying air all around us, the atmosphere growing even more blistering with each expectant heartbeat. The master Auset just assaulted is helped to his feet. Embarrassment and rage simmer in his eyes as he steadies himself and rubs at his chest.

He snarls a command that sounds more like a bark from a rabid dog than words to me, but whatever he growls, it makes Auset straighten. Without argument, she turns and strides over to a large log that's been pounded into the sandy ground just outside the ring they're currently fighting in. Her face flashes with fury before she steels herself, a careful mask shuttering down and blanking all expression as she lifts her arms expectantly.

Skull and Bones have both gone rigid, and I can tell that just like me, they are holding their breath. There's a slight tremble from exhaustion, barely visible in Auset's extended arms, but it disappears as another master wraps a leather band around her wrists, securing her to the fixed whipping post in the yard. He says something to her, which causes her to steady her eyes on the pole itself and pull in a deep breath as she readies her body for what's to come.

How often do they do this to her?

The master that tied her hands pulls a dagger from his waist and runs the blade down the back of her pitiful armored chest plate before then shearing the tunic she's wearing underneath it until her back is exposed. It's smooth and muscular, without so much as a mark on it, but there wouldn't be with the healers I know Tilleo employs here. My stomach roils as the fae moves away from her, leaving her alone and vulnerable as the master Auset knocked on his ass takes his place behind her. He tightens his grip on the brutal whip now clutched in his hands, and even at this distance, I can see the manic look on his face.

Fury and disgust constrict around my heart at the enjoyment I know this fucker is about to get from this. I want to rip him in half. I want to cleave his head from his shoulders with my bare hands and spit down his spurting throat while I stomp on his still beating heart. I want to rage, to demand all of this stops now. But I know I can't. I have to sit here, still and silent as they try to destroy something too wild and beautiful for the savage world they live in. To do anything else would open us up to weakness, and that's something my brothers and I can never afford.

A sharp crack rents the air. I fight the flinch that wants to jerk through me as the whip connects with Auset's back, quick as a striking snake. She's a monolith of strength against the large wooden beam. There's no recoil, no gasp of shock or hiss of pain as the tips of the braided leather slice open her skin and muscle. I instantly hate that she's good at this. That she knows what to expect because she's been here too many times before. That keen understanding sinks in my gut like a stone in water, unsettling me in ways I can't look at too closely right now.

My nails dig into my palms as I clench my fists tighter and tighter with each punishing blow and resounding crack in the air. They come fast, a steady rhythm of pain and punishment, and the only hint Auset gives of the agony she has to be in is the white-knuckled hold on the leather straps tying her in place. I stop counting the lashes when it starts to take all my effort not to rise from my seat and bellow *enough*. Blood pools at her feet, and a tremor moves its way down her legs as she begins to struggle to keep her legs locked despite the torture these craven masters are putting her through.

Order members around us go back to their drinking and whispered conversations as though all of this is just part of a typical day. Looking at some of them, it probably is, but none of this sits right with me. It's one thing to keep ranks in line, it's another to torture and take your anger out on the powerless. As assassins, most wouldn't think that we would care one way or the other, but the Order of Scorpions does. Tilleo once did too.

I observe the slave master as he downs another full glass of wine and laughs heartily with a member from the Order of Crows. He's completely indifferent to the cadenced cracks of the whip against Auset's back. It seems Tilleo has lost sight of things in more ways than one. Skull's weight rocks forward as though he's preparing to pounce, and Bones shoots out a hand to stop him. Skull sends an agonized look over his shoulder to me, and it makes my jaw clench and my fists tighten even more.

I look back to Auset, and surprise jolts through me when I find her silvery stare fixed on me. Another lash rings out all around us, the circular shape of the pit and the surrounding building making the sound echo loudly back at us in a taunting, horrific way. Auset looks at me. Her face is frozen and her body is stiff against the pain, but her eyes scream a different story. Like silver daggers, they rip into my soul in search of strength and comfort, and as much as I'm hesitant to trust who she is and what that means for me and my brothers, I can't find it in me to deny her. My black gaze steadies on her moonlight-gray irises, and I offer what little I can through the strange tether that tightens between us. All the worry and mistrust sifts away as I look past the threat she could be and simply see someone who deserves more than *this* in life.

We stare at each other as everything else slowly recedes and quiets. In her eyes, I suddenly see myself. A street thief, who was one savvy shopkeeper away from having a limb removed for stealing or having a permanent place in the Crown's prison. I was young. My mother had just died trying to bring another bastard into the world, and the brothel, the only home I'd ever known, decided I either needed to earn my keep or get out. I was desperate for help, in urgent need of someone to look past my dirt-streaked cheeks and jaded eyes and see a boy who could be more than his circumstances. I found it, and as I regard her fervent silver-plated eyes, I start to wonder if now it's time to be *that* for someone else.

She's likely a spy, but even so, what kind of life leads a person here? Tied to a whipping post, bleeding into the sand, commanding your body not to show any pain, all in hopes of spying on an Order that will kill you at the first hint of disloyalty. People with options don't find themselves in this kind of nightmare. People with hope and a future don't sign up for what happens in a place like this ludere. There's more to what's going on here, more to *her*, and I need to know what that is.

Her eyes are flat by the time the master stops. The emptiness in them claws at my soul, but I continue to watch helplessly as the master winds his whip around his arm. Other slaves move forward to unbind Auset from the post. I can tell she's barely hanging onto consciousness, and still her eyes never leave mine. I watch her until she's carried into the ludere and out of sight. My chest feels heavy, like some unwelcome beast is sitting on it and refusing to move, but I keep my face emotionless. Skull and Bones look over at me, their clenched jaws the only sign of how furious they are. From the outside, we look deathly calm just like we always do, but I can tell my brothers are seething inside just like I am.

Slaves begin to rake the blood from the sand as Tilleo blithely announces the time of tonight's feast. Orders start to depart for their quarters, and my brothers and I stand and casually stride away from today's useless test and poor show of brutality. Eyes watch us as we go, but I don't bother to turn and take note of who is tracking us. We stride through the sand, the sun high and punitive in its reach. It's as though even the celestial body above us is angered by what it just saw. Tilleo's stronghold wavers in the heat, the massive manor to our right tricking the eye into thinking it can be blinked out of existence. If only it were that easy to escape this place.

Ahead of me, Skull angrily shoves back the flaps of our tent. By the time I stalk in after him, he's already working to put up wards so no one can hear us. Bones leans against the large chest at the foot of his pallet, arms crossed and blazing eyes watching Skull finish up. I pour myself a drink, throwing it back as I work to get a hold of my runaway fury and chaotic thoughts. Skull no sooner whispers the last power-laced word of his chant than Bones pushes off from the chest and snarls.

"What in the fae fuck was that?" he demands, his arms outstretched and his glamoured face etched in wrath.

"We've seen slaves whipped before," I point out, hating that I'm playing at casual when I feel the exact opposite. I know that I need to be the voice of reason here. I have to be the calm one. If we all lose our heads simultaneously, it could be catastrophic, and we've worked too hard to allow that to happen. I toss back another drink and try to ignore the tremor of ire in my hands.

"Not like that, we haven't," Bones argues. "We've never watched masters interfere like that with the tests or the prospects."

"We've also never watched a blade slave step out of line like she did," I counter, refusing to acknowledge the heat that climbs up my thighs at the thought of her small act of rebellion.

"Don't play games, Scorpius, you're just as bothered by what happened as we are," Skull snaps at me.

I fill my tumbler to the brim again and drink deeply before leveling Skull with a scowl. "I am, which is part of the problem," I admit, staring down into the amber liquid clutched in my hand. "We're all drawn to her. Tilleo and the masters seem intent on making a target out of her, which clearly is working to pull us in even more. She's a plant of some sort, and although I feel for her"—more than I should—"we need to be careful here," I admonish, barely believing my own words as they slip silkily out of my mouth.

My brothers go quiet, each of them deep in thought and disgruntled. "So we turn her to our side. Show her that loyalty to us will serve her better than whoever it is she's accountable to now," Skull throws out there, and I nod, having thought of the same thing.

"We need to find out what's at stake here, not just for us but for her too. Someone has gone to a lot of work to set this up; we need to make sure we understand the big picture," I point out.

Bones shakes his head and stares absently at the far tent wall. "I know you see threats and enemies around every corner—fuck knows it's saved our asses more than once—but I don't see what you see, Scorpius," he declares on a sigh as he rubs at his temples and looks over at me. "She's familiar, I can't explain why, but I know her somehow. I don't see a spy when I look at her, I see a slave who's tired of being a slave. I see hopelessness and a fae that has nothing left to lose."

"You see us, before Eacon found us," Skull adds, his eyes suddenly contemplative, like he's just now seeing it too.

I'm surprised to hear that what just happened to Auset has stirred up memories for Bones and Skull too, although I probably shouldn't be. We've all shared a unique connection and deep understanding of each other, even back when we were first brought together.

"Maybe that's it," Bones agrees, although his eyes remain troubled. "I just can't shake the feeling that we know her somehow. That we're here for her. That she's one of us."

His words have me examining my own observations and feelings about the blade slave. Is that the draw I feel, some sort of recognition? Could we have known her from before somehow? I shake off the questions and drain my tumbler dry.

"Whatever it is about her, we need to get to the bottom of it and fast. The final Bidding is a day away, and we need to know where we stand with things before we leave here. I taste change in the air, and we need to be on the right side of it," I announce, and they both nod their agreement.

"Change?" Skull teases. "Your palate must be better than mine; all I can taste in the air are weak fae and toxic egos."

Bones snorts with hollow amusement. "I'm only getting sand," he announces, looking around our tent with distaste. "I fucking hate the desert."

I huff a small laugh and wipe my palm down my face, suddenly exhausted. I couldn't agree more. This place used to serve a purpose, but now it's coming off as more of a liability. If my suspicions are right, then this may be our last Bidding, and if Tilleo doesn't come clean about his part in all of it, he's about to learn what Dorsin did. You don't fuck with the Order of Scorpions unless you like the taste of death.

14

AUSET

MY BACK IS ON FIRE. HEAT AND HURT MOVE in waves over me as I slowly come to. A sharp astringent scent mixed with herbal earthy tones gives my location away, and I know I'm in the healing chambers. The taut canvas of the cot beneath me is stiff and unforgiving against my chest, but when I try to move to get more comfortable, I regret it immediately. Agony flares through me, and I hiss in pain, unable to do anything more than lie here and endure until it slowly fades to a more manageable undulation of torture. It appears that lying here all night unhealed is a continuation of my punishment.

Carefully, I blow out a deep breath and cringe at the

memory of what happened. I want to be mad at the masters, and I am, but I'm more furious with myself. I don't know what I was thinking, losing control like that. I could blame it on the adrenaline, on the high of the fight, and the festering fury over everything that was happening. But it had more to do with the loose tongue and careless attitude I've acquired in the past couple days. I let myself get too comfortable, and it caught up with me. I'm lucky they didn't slit my throat...or in this case, unlucky, I suppose, depending on how I look at it. It would have been a faster way to go. Definitely more humane than this slow boil that Tilleo has kindled.

Despair circles my chest, making itself comfortable as it curls around my heart and settles there. My cheek presses against the stiff cot beneath me, and I can see a streak of moonlight that spills in through a window, but there's no way I can get to it. Tears prick my eyes, and in the silent hours of this deep night, I give myself permission to let some of them go. It's the only way I know to purge the poison of what they do to me here from my veins. It hurts too much to reach up and banish the wet tracks, so I leave them to carve tiny streams in my dirt-caked cheeks.

I can't believe that *this* is all my life will ever come to. All the fight I've kept stoked and blazing in my body, the white-knuckled survival I've held onto at all cost, it wasn't worth it. I keep telling myself that even though my life has amounted to nothing, my death doesn't have to, but who am I kidding? I couldn't even stop the masters today. Six years of forging every part of me into a deadly weapon, and I'm no better off than I was that first night when I woke up in a cage.

I let my sorrow slip out onto my cheeks for a second more, and then I shut it down.

A heavy, quivering breath leaves me slowly as I beg oblivion to once again find me. Better yet, maybe I should be pleading with death. The sands know I'll be meeting that reaper soon enough. I wince as I suck in too deep of a breath and my raw back protests.

"Thirty lashes, and she doesn't so much as cry out in pain. And yet here we find her, alone...leaking," a warm, rumbling voice declares.

I jerk in surprise and immediately force my body to go still as torment lights up my back. Scorpius steps into my line of sight and slowly crouches down until we're almost eye to eye.

"Did they break you, Slave?" he asks, his black eyes trailing from my face to my back.

I huff out an unamused breath and notice Skull and Bones standing further back. Bones leans against a wall, one leg bent casually as he runs his gaze over me, but there's nothing casual about the anger I see steeping in his soot-stained eyes. The reaction surprises me. It's almost as though he disagrees with what's been done to me, but that can't be right.

"Give me until just after sunrise, and I'll teach you a lesson in breaking," I grumble to Scorpius, pretending a small tinge of defeat doesn't ring in my words.

Morose or not, I've clearly learned nothing on the merits of keeping my mouth shut. Then again, it wasn't my mouth that landed me here with a whip-torn back, so I guess as long as there's nothing within reach to throw at anyone, I'm probably safe.

A wide grin stretches across Scorpius's lips at my threat. He's still glamoured to look skeletal, but even magic can't hide what that smile does for his face. It's exquisite.

That's probably just the pain talking though.

"Awww, look at the little dagger thinking she can take on a sword," Scorpius teases as he rises and moves to stand next to Bones.

Stupidly, I turn my head to try to follow his sudden movement away from me, which forces me to groan an apology to my back and shoulders. The grin immediately leaves Scorpius's face, and it's as though an unwelcome cloud has stretched in front of the sun just when I was basking in its deliciously warm rays.

"If memory serves me correctly, I've already conquered your sword," I remind him, and I'm treated to another soul-thawing smile.

"Handled, not conquered," he counters, and if my body wasn't already on fire from my wounds, the flames would probably be crawling up my neck right now at the unmistakable challenge I see banked in the skeleton's eyes.

"Is a healer not going to attend to you?" Skull asks, the question a welcome interruption to the stare off I was just having.

I have no idea how to unfurl the heat that is coiling low in my belly now. Skull's gaze moves around the healing chamber, confused by the obvious fact that there's no one here aside from me and them, but I already knew that. I debate asking them to move me closer to the window where the moon and the powers of the night can help alleviate some of my suffering, but I know I can't let that happen no matter how tempting it may be. I close my eyes as an aching wave moves through me. I try to breathe shallowly until it passes, but the state I know the masters left me in isn't going to offer much reprieve from the pain.

It's going to be a long night.

"They'll wait until morning," I finally answer when the anguish isn't squeezing so tightly and I can get more than a pitiful moan out. "Tonight I've been tasked with fighting off shock and infection. They're creative with their punishments at this ludere," I joke, noticing the small tremor that's already started to ripple in some of the muscles of my arms and thighs. The battle with shock I'm about to wage tonight is no doubt going to feel more like a war.

"Bones can help you with that," Scorpius declares, and like a good little Scorpion, Bones pushes off the wall and strides toward me.

"Don't heal me," I frantically stammer, trying and failing to move away from him.

Pain blazes through me, and I press my forehead to the canvas of the cot underneath me as black spots dance in my vision, and suffering goes toe to toe with every nerve ending in my body. A miserable mewl spills out of me as I try to float above the agony long enough to keep Bones away from me. "If you heal me, they'll whip me again twice as hard for not enduring the full extent of my *correction*," I grit out before I finally give in and get pulled under by the pool of searing torment that's lapping at me.

Despite my efforts to keep them locked up, fresh tears march down my cheeks. A strange tension begins to build in the room, and I close my eyes, all at once overwhelmed and completely drained.

"He won't heal you, he'll just take the edge off," Skull offers hesitantly. I can't see him, but I can feel the way his hands flutter in front of him, like he's desperate for something to do. "We won't do anything that could hurt you even more," he reassures.

It hurts too much to open my eyes, but it sounds as though he's speaking through gritted teeth, like I'm not the only one in pain in this chamber tonight. My mind winds curiosity around all kinds of possibilities of why Skull could also be injured, but something warm drips over my mangled back, and all I can suddenly focus on is the ripple of relief that it instantly creates.

I whimper, worried that whatever it is Bones's doing is only going to cause me more pain when the masters discover it, but he shushes me gently and pushes hair away from my face as he continues to drip something incredible across my tattered back.

"I've got you, Auset," he soothes, and a spark of warmth ignites deep in my belly at the sound of my name on his lips.

More numbing drizzles work to chase away my pain, and as the agony starts to recede, the fog in my mind begins to clear. All the warm and fuzzy feelings from the unexpected smiles and kindness are chased away by a broom bristled with reality.

Why are they here?

Why would the Order of Scorpions want to help an insignificant blade slave like me?

I don't know if Bones feels when I suddenly tense, but the atmosphere in the chamber immediately changes.

"What's going on?" I demand, my voice slightly stronger, my body instantaneously feeling the effects of whatever Bones is doing to my back.

"That's exactly what we're here to find out," Scorpius counters, and I'm immediately on edge. "Who are you, Little Dagger?"

The question is soft, even, demanding, and all that's left in its wake is confusion.

"I don't understand?" I state, opening my eyes to find all three Scorpions now staring down at me.

Bones rubs at his wrist, and I'm immediately reminded that this isn't the first time these three have loomed over me and played with my fate. Scorpius steps closer, pulling my focus to him, and I quickly run through what in this room can be used as a weapon. Just as quickly, I dismiss every option that pops into my head. I may not feel the need to writhe in agony anymore, thanks to whatever salve Bones just dripped all over my shredded back, but there's still no way I can get up off this cot and fight anything stronger than a gentle breeze.

The Scorpions are quiet, like they expect me to hurry to fill the silence, but all I can do is picture the last time these three were there for one of the worst days of my life. I run my gaze over Scorpius's glamoured face, studying it and locking it in place with the skeleton that was first out the window that night in Dorsin's office.

"What?" I ask, my eyes fixed on his. "No offer to kill me this time?"

Scorpius's brow furrows at the question. He stares at me as though what I just said will make sense if he simply looks at me long enough. None of them make the connection. Not a one recalls that we've all been here before. What did I expect though? I wasn't significant enough to *help* back then, why would I think I'd be significant enough to be remembered at all?

"Why would we kill you?" Bones asks as though the mere suggestion is ludicrous.

"No reason, I've just been told a time or two that I'd be better off if someone did," I answer, carefully watching each of their faces for the tiniest hint of recognition.

I find nothing.

I deflate a little under the weight of their empty stares, and suddenly my lids feel heavy and my body and soul as wasted as they've ever felt before.

"I'm tired," I whisper with a weary exhale. "Whatever it is you're here to do, just do it so I can get back to wallowing in my misery alone," I tell them, waving my hand in dismissal and appreciating that things don't hurt nearly as bad as they did.

"What makes you think we're here to do anything?" Scorpius starts, and I groan in frustration.

"Fuck the stars! What are you, a bridge troll with all these riddles and inane questions?" I growl crankily. "What do you want, Order of Scorpions? To irritate me to death?"

Scorpius rewards my outburst with a small smile, but I won't be beguiled again. I roll my eyes as the grin grows; it seems my annoyance does things for this pest. Figures. Bones laughs lightly at my frustration, and Skull tilts his head back and shakes it as though all of this is pure entertainment to him.

The smirk drops from Scorpius's face just as quickly as it appeared, and his eyes once again grow intense. "Who are you, Auset? Who are your people? Why are you here, and why are you trying to infiltrate our Order?"

The questions fire out of his mouth like bolts from an automatic crossbow. Each of them hit their mark, but for what purpose, I couldn't say. I narrow my eyes at the skeletal face, taking my turn to try and understand what he means by all of this.

"I'm a blade slave," I answer evenly, as though that's all I really need to say. In truth, it should be. "I'm owned by Tilleo. Brought to this ludere from people and a place I have no memory of, and despite your gargantuan ego and misplaced superiority, I have no interest in your Order," I tell him matter-of-factly. "I was assigned by my master, and I don't know if you know how things work around here, but arguing with orders isn't an option."

I see doubt and judgment bleed into Scorpius's glower, while anger settles in mine.

"Why would Tilleo assign you to us? What makes him so sure that we'd take an interest?" Scorpius demands.

I huff, annoyed, and try not to roll my eyes. "How would I know?"

"Oh, you know *something*, Little Dagger, and we're not leaving here until we get to the bottom of it," he tells me darkly, and I work hard to ignore the enticing bite that sings in the sweet threat of his words.

"We can help you," Bones offers, moving closer, his eyes softer and more imploring than his brother's commanding stare.

I bark out a laugh at the offer. If only they knew how funny those words really are. I once begged for just that, pleaded for them to help me, only to watch them slip out of the window without so much as a backward glance. *They left me to this very fate.* I wasn't important enough to remember, but they would guffaw at their own audacity if they could recall what I already know about their willingness to help.

"And why would you do that?" I snap at him, venom now dripping from every word.

Confusion and a tinge of hurt seeps into Bones's surprisingly gentle stare.

I refuse to let myself feel bad about that.

"It serves all of us to get to the bottom of what's going on here. You've been tasked with infiltrating us, and we need to know why. Things will go far better for you if you're honest and help us put the pieces together," Scorpius retorts, his tone now hard and menacing.

"You don't want to test us, Moonling. We make far better friends than we do enemies," Skull adds, the threat in his words blanketed by a seductive purr.

I stare at them, annoyed and depleted and far too close to the end of my rope, which is probably why I start laughing like some sun-sick pilgrim just a day past pure madness. I gasp when my fit of giggles forces my back to remind me that I should be taking it easy and not acting like I wasn't just whipped within an inch of my life. *Damn all the stars.* I want whatever salve or tincture Bones used on me. I don't care if I only have days or maybe even hours to live, whatever it was is pure magic.

"With friends like you three, who even needs enemies?" I point out, tittering as I work to get a hold of myself. "You're so certain that everyone is obsessed with you, but have you even considered for a moment that it's not about you at all?" I ask, trying and failing to rein in my amusement. "You keep saying I'm here to infiltrate your stupid Order, but how can I do that if I'm dead?" I demand, as though it's all so simple.

Laugh tears slip down my cheeks, and I dash them away as I take in the three skeletons and the pompous expressions on each of their glamoured faces.

"I've been commanded to kill an Order member, and as much as I *hate* to piss on the fine impressions each of you have of yourselves, it has nothing to do with you," I tell them, spelling it out when it's clear they're too dense and sure of themselves to fully grasp what I'm saying.

I know it's stupid to be repeating any of this, but I just can't stand how arrogant they are. I thought in the beginning that the kill order might be for one of them, but after replaying Tilleo's words over and over again in my mind, none of the Scorpions fit the bill. He said whoever it was *likes to play with females who haven't been broken yet.* Yes, I've shown attitude and gotten away with it when it comes to these three, but I'm not picking up any of the *torture the innocent for fun* vibes that I got when Tilleo was vaguely describing who my mark will be.

I could be wrong, but my instincts are telling me I'm not. Either way, I've got nothing to lose, and I can't pass up the opportunity to put these self-righteous pricks in their place, not when that gift has landed right in my lap like this.

"Tilleo's going to violate the sanctum?" Skull points out, as though it alone is proof that what I'm saying is impossible.

"Like I said, I can't infiltrate shit when I'm dead," I lob back, sighing against the bone-deep fatigue that's working hard to sap me of every ounce of energy I have right now.

I close my eyes for a beat and then decide it's not worth the effort to try to open them again.

"Now, if you don't mind, I'd like to pass out. But have fun stroking each other's cocks while cooing away about just how big and important you all are. This whole time I thought the realms revolved around the four kingdoms, but now I know how wrong I was. It's been all about your little circle jerk this whole time. I can die happy now that I know," I say with a tired laugh and far too much mirth. "Remind me to bow down when I'm all healed up, wouldn't want to waste the opportunity to worship you like you so clearly worship yourselves," I add, the words slipping closely into an unintelligible slur as my limbs grow heavier and sleep nips at my heels.

"Who has Tilleo ordered you to kill?" Scorpius demands, his face suddenly so close that I can feel the heat of his words against my mouth.

He smells good, like rich leather and sleek elven steel. There's a hint of something sweet there too, something oddly floral, but I don't know what it is. I resist the urge to shove my face closer to his to sniff out what it might be... but just barely.

"I don't have a name, just a description. Go ask him yourself if you want to know so badly," I grump, trying to wave him away, but my arm feels too leaden to actually move at the moment, so it's more of a solitary wobble.

"What does he look like?" Bones asks, and I can taste the sliver of desperation in it.

"He looks like the end of everything I ever wanted for my life," I tell them sullenly, and then, just like that, my mind and body decide they've had enough, and everything around me fades away.

15

SKULL

WHAT IN THE ORC TITS WAS THAT?" I ask, rounding on my brothers as the flaps to our tent close and the wards envelop us.

"I don't even know," Scorpius admits, running his hands through his hair, his stare far away and equally confused.

"I didn't see things going down like that," Bones adds, his own gaze also contemplative like he's shoving around everything we just learned until it all lines up in a way that makes sense, except none if it does.

"Who the fuck would Tilleo want to kill bad enough to violate the sanctum of the Bidding?" I throw out, knowing that neither of them have any more information than I do, but I need to say it out loud just to try to wrap my mind around it.

"We were so certain the trap was for us, but—"

"She could be lying," Scorpius interrupts, but I can tell not even *he* believes that.

"Why does she talk like we've all been here before?" I ask, again needing to put a voice to my inner confusion so I can try to see what it is we're all missing here.

"I told you that there's something about her that's familiar to me," Bones emphatically reiterates.

I didn't put much stock in his claim before. Bones can be like that, seeing signs and hints of destiny where there's nothing. But right now, I also feel like I've somehow forgotten something. It's on the tip of my tongue, so close and yet somehow impossible to reach. I pace at the foot of my pallet, grumbling with frustration as I smooth my hair back. I think through everything Auset just said to us, examining each word and syllable like the clues I know they are. Her rich voice teases my memories, her questions demanding my attention, and then I see it. I see *her*. Plain as day, younger, terrified, huddled in a corner, clutching blades covered in orc blood.

"Fuck," I whisper on a weary exhale as the memory comes crashing to the surface with a force that rocks everything inside of me.

Both of my brothers look over expectantly, and I know my face looks haunted as that night plays out again in my mind. I've never given it much thought since then. There were bigger things at stake, so why would I have wondered about what happened to the frail creature we found in the corner that night? But now, seeing her again, seeing what became of that scared, doomed girl, I realize just how fucked up that is.

"She was there," I tell them, my tone tortured as I drop my head into my hands and feel a wave of shame move over me. "She was there the night we executed Dorsin," I continue, and realization dawns in Bones's face while Scorpius runs through everything that happened that night in his mind, trying to place her.

"Fuck," Bones echoes, and I plop down on the soft cushion of my pallet, my legs suddenly shaky with guilt. "The girl in the corner," he recalls, paling just like I did, finally understanding what Auset was talking about.

"I offered to kill her," I croak as Scorpius exhales his own *fuck* and then stomps over to grab a glass from the liquor cart and promptly fills it with bloodwine.

He pauses, staring at the deep red of the liquid clutched in his hand. Then, instead of drinking it, he throws it across the room. Glass shatters against the side of an empty golden tub, and I'm drawn back to the night we arrived here, a vision flashing in my mind of Auset on her knees scrubbing down Scorpius. I don't know what he's madder about, that he didn't make the connection sooner or that there's a connection to be made at all. We don't usually leave witnesses.

I'm sure we all thought that the girl that night in Dorsin's office wasn't going to survive long in the world she found herself naked and chained to. We were all content with allowing fate to run its course, not wanting undeserving blood on our hands. Instead, we doomed her to this life. She's back to teach us just how wrong we were for thinking fate was going to tie up our loose ends.

"Do you think Tilleo knows?" I ask, my mind whirring with all the possibilities of just how fucked we might be right now.

I doubt the slaver would care that we took out his boss, but if he's trying to discover what we took from Dorsin's vault that night, we might have more serious problems on our hands than we realized.

"He kept her alive," Bones points out as though it somehow answers my question. "He must have thought that massacre in his office was her doing," he goes on, and I see what he's getting at.

"That's possible," Scorpius concedes. "But what's the likelihood he didn't torture her for every detail of what happened that night, and now we're being set up?"

"She said Tilleo's target wasn't us," Bones argues, and Scorpius shoots him a look that tells him to pull his head from his ass.

"We all knew from the beginning that something was off about her and this whole situation. Now we have a lead, and we're not going to give the little killer the benefit of the doubt because she grew into your ultimate wet dream, Bones," Scorpius chides.

Bones snorts out a derisive laugh. "Riiiight, *I'm* the only one hard for her," he snarks with a scowl. "If we had kept her from the beginning like I wanted, we wouldn't be in this mess."

"Oh fuck off, Bones. She's not a hound that you can collar, feed, and scratch behind the ears when it's convenient for you," Scorpius snaps.

"No. She was a scared female, who was chained to the floor in the room of a monster, and we just left her there,"

Bones snarls back, and I step between my brothers, drawing both of their attention to me.

"Firstly," I interject, looking over at Bones, "you never said anything about keeping her that night when we executed Dorsin. You only asked if we should do anything about her," I point out, shutting down my brother's heroic delusions. "Secondly, we don't need to give her the benefit of the doubt, and we also don't need to be stumbling around in the shadows here. There's an easy way to get to the bottom of all of this," I declare, looking from Bones to Scorpius. "I think it's time we pay Tilleo a visit."

Neither Scorpius nor Bones say anything, and I can see them both weighing the cost and benefit of cutting out the middleman and going straight to the source of our suspicions.

There's a possibility that it could bite us in the ass. That it might put Tilleo on the back foot and encourage him to be more desperate. That is if he's behind some sort of plan to take us out in the first place. However, if he's not scheming behind our backs and we're reading this situation wrong...

"If he's plotting against us, we'll have to kill him," Scorpius states coolly.

Bones scoffs dismissively. "He's more or less an employee anyway. We fund his enterprise here. We can promote someone else to run it, or get out of the business altogether," he points out. "Tilleo and his Biddings have been a good opportunity to collect information, but we knew the well would dry up at some point. None of the other Orders are even in our league. It might be time to see things as they are and move on."

"And what about Auset?" I inquire, a heavy cloak of finality settling on my shoulders.

"Let's deal with Tilleo first, then we'll know how to proceed on other fronts," Scorpius declares, and both Bones and I nod our agreement.

I walk over to one of the stands encasing a large ball of fairy light to help illuminate the inside of our quarters. With a wave of my hand, the light sputters out, sending a corner of the tent into shadow. Flickers of light from the other stands dance across the hide of the tent wall, and I can't help but recall the way Auset's gaze fixed on mine in the healing chamber. The pain that filled her gaze and yet there was still that hint of challenge even before Bones did what he could for her.

I wanted to heal her completely, scoop her up and get her as far as possible from this place. Every fiber of my being was calling for me to be for her what Eacon was once for me. She'd found me in a horrid state, tied up, abused, covered in filth and hopelessness. I thought I'd been sold to her. That she was just another of the ones who wanted to take from me, who wanted to break me. Then she led me out of the caravan I'd been chained in and sold from for longer than I could remember, and I saw the bodies and the blood. She hadn't bought me, she'd saved me, fed me, let me get cleaned up, and then brought me to Scorpius and Bones. Together, they helped me fight the nightmares and trauma, and taught me to never let another fae fuck with me again.

Bones steps up to my side, and I shake away my thoughts. I tamp down on the longing that surges through me to help her, and instead step with my brothers into the dark. The shadows welcome us happily, just like they always do. We're pulled from the planes of our realm and invited into a corridor of enigma and in-betweens. We shadow walk seamlessly from our tent to Tilleo's home, stalking through the shadows of his halls until we find the master in his study.

He stares sightlessly at a roaring fire, a half-filled glass of spirits clutched tightly in his aging hand. I try not to roll my eyes at the absurdity of a fireplace, let alone a *cozy* fire in any home in the heart of the desert. The waste of magic to cool the room to a comfortable temperature scratches at my skin, but I let the annoyance roll off my shoulders. We have bigger concerns than all the ways Tilleo is clearly squandering his resources.

We watch and wait from the dark corner by the window, eyeing the master who's lost to some thought or memory as he stares off into nothing. Deep lines etch his brow, his mouth is dipped into a pensive frown, and there's a tightness around his eyes that speaks of agitation and aggrievement. We settle into our silent spying, observing from the darkness long enough to see that Tilleo doesn't appear to be waiting on anyone. He doesn't drink from the tumbler gripped in his palm. He doesn't blink. He doesn't impatiently check the time or relax his taut posture in any way.

Scorpius taps on my shoulder and then, using hand signals we've created over our years together, signs that we should split up. He indicates that each of us should take a murky corner in the room so that the master can't escape or call for help before we get the answers we're here for. Bones and I nod and step back into the recesses between realms, shadow walking to our subsequent corners.

The darkness wraps around me like a cool hug, the shadows of my corner deeper than where I was watching from before. I can feel when Bones and Scorpius are in place, and all at once, we step from the dark into Tilleo's study like the reapers we are. The slave master shoots up from his seat with a shocked exclamation. He pulls back one arm, ready to launch the thick crystal tumbler in one hand while his other reaches for a knife sheathed at his waist.

"You can go for that knife and then meet mine instead, or you can dip into your wits and breathe for a little longer," Scorpius warns, stepping further into the light to make it clear why his words ring with promise.

The tumbler falls to the ground, the thick layers of carpet cushioning its impact as the honey-colored liquid spills into the dark indigo of the rug. Tilleo's hand drops the dagger and clutches at his heart instead. He bends forward, placing his hands on his knees as though this position will dampen his fright and help to expand his chest with soothing deep breaths. He doesn't look scared or like he's been up to anything he shouldn't be. He certainly doesn't look like a fae who ordered one of his slaves to murder an Order member and violate a sanctum.

"Shit, Scorpius, I didn't realize it was you," he grumbles, his eyes manically bouncing around to find Bones and me slightly further back. "What's going on? Why is the Order of Scorpions paying me a late night visit?" he queries, doing a good job of hiding the sudden quiver in his voice.

There it is. There's the guilty tell I've been waiting for.

"Can I get you anything to drink?" he genially offers, gesturing to the cart of bottles and glasses, his eyes now wary and soaked in trepidation.

He probably thinks we're here to kill him. Who knows, depending on how forthcoming he is about what's going on around here, maybe we are. Scorpius waves the offer of drinks away and settles his large frame in the only other chair in front of the fire. He turns it until it faces Tilleo, while Bones and I continue to stand, ready and waiting for anything.

"Something is off and we're here to find out why that is," Scorpius starts, keeping things casual and friendly as he folds his hands in his lap and studies the master.

"Off?" Tilleo questions, his uneasy gaze once again skipping around the room, landing quickly on me and then Bones again before darting away.

He looks entirely too much like the short-haired, long-bodied *celairats* that I used to hunt for food when I was a boy. Those beady-eyed little bastards were afraid of their own shadows.

"Mmmm," Scorpius hums, refusing to offer any more information than that.

Typical Scorpius. He's always ten moves ahead of everybody before they even realize they're playing against him. I know this mystery around Auset has been gnawing him alive, and he's as keen as we are to finally make sense of it all. We're here to confirm what she told us, but who knows what the slaver will cough up to get back into our good graces.

"I don't—" Tilleo starts, but I cut him off.

"Before you finish what is sure to be a denial reeking of fetid *coro* shit," I start, leaning nonchalantly against a cabinet that probably houses priceless stolen items, "I want you to think long and hard about our tolerance for nonsense. We wouldn't be here digging at the roots of *nothing*," I point out, already tasting the lies in the air that Tilleo has yet to speak.

He pulls in a sharp breath like he's readying himself to argue, and then he slowly deflates and runs a tired hand down his face. "What do you know?" he asks, his tone worn and his body language all at once submissive.

Well, that didn't take long at all.

"The sands whisper that the sanctum is about to expire," Scorpius cryptically informs him, and each of us studies Tilleo carefully for his response.

He tenses, as though the words are a physical blow, and then his fists clench and his skin flushes with anger. "Fucking Crit," he snarls, slamming a fist down on the padded arm of his chair. "If I ever see that good-for-nothing guard again, he's dead," Tilleo announces, and I realize that he thinks the guard who Auset killed in the wine cellar has sold him out and somehow managed to disappear.

"Shed some light on the situation, and we'll handle him for you," Scorpius offers, not missing a beat.

Tilleo glares at him and then seems to recall exactly who he's glaring at, and promptly blanks his face. "I know this probably doesn't look good from where you're sitting, but I promise it has nothing to do with the Order of Scorpions," Tilleo attempts to reassure.

All that earns him is a scowl from all three of us.

"Violating the sanctum of this event most definitely has something to do with us, or have you forgotten who pays you?" Bones questions, and Tilleo jerks his head in surprise in my brother's direction as though he'd forgotten the assassin was there.

Jumpy little celairat.

"It's not as though you three don't benefit from what goes on here," Tilleo argues and then immediately looks as though he regrets it.

The hard look in Scorpius's black eyes confirms that the master is walking a very tight and perilous line. Tilleo huffs and collects himself. We all know there's only one way he's walking out of this room alive, and that's if he tells us everything. Even then, if he's put our Order at risk, what comes next for him will be very painful and very drawn out. Our arrangement with Tilleo has been fruitful, but we won't hesitate to cut ties or throats if it's warranted.

"My niece was a chambermaid in Lord Craxon's house," Tilleo starts, and it's as though he ages ten years right before my eyes. Like some kind of magic spell, the words spilling out of his mouth seem to drain him, syllable by syllable, of every ounce of vitality he possesses. "Craxon had a wagering habit that made him a good source for information when he was down on his luck. But it seems he got himself caught up with a collector that had run out of patience for the lord's *speculative* ways."

Tilleo leans back in his chair and sighs, his listless stare once again fixed on the fire as though he's locked in some haunting memory.

"If the assassins that were tasked to deal with Lord Craxon had stopped there, the sanctum would be as solid as it ever was, but they didn't."

Realization moves over me like frost over leaves before dawn. All at once, Tilleo's rage suddenly makes sense.

"It wasn't enough to punish the lord for his covetous ways, they fell on the house like they were to blame too. It would have been better if they had cut my niece's head from her body like they did Craxon's, but no, instead they left her with a baby growing in her belly and a mind too broken to even know it," Tilleo laments, and I drop my head, the weight of his pain heavy on my shoulders.

"Bruins?" Scorpius asks without even having to. We all know which Order lacks the honor to do something like this to innocent fae.

"Who else," Tilleo confirms hollowly, fury banking in his brown eyes. "He has to die," he whispers vehemently, and the seething wrath in his tone makes goose bumps crawl up my arms.

"And exactly how are you going to make that happen?" Scorpius demands, further covering Auset's confession to make it look as though the dead guard is our informant and not her. "Gartox is a brute, but he's skilled and cunning. His Order isn't going to take the murder of their leader lying down."

"No," Tilleo concedes. "The remaining Bruins will get their justice. Gartox's *needs* will set him up all on their own, and he'll just so happen to pick the wrong slave to play with. No one else will be implicated. And the loose ends will tie themselves up," he explains with a proud smile, like he's a school-aged boy awaiting high marks in strategy for the brilliantly thought-out plan.

"What does that mean, that the loose ends will tie *themselves* up?" I demand, biting back the snarl that starts to wind up my throat.

This hypocrite wants to kill Gartox the Bruin for attacking his niece, and yet he's more than happy to throw a blade slave to the mercy of first Gartox and then the remaining members of the Order of Bruins, damning her to an even worse fate than just death. I stare at the master completely disgusted. Here he is, pained and furious over what's been done to his family, with *no* thought to what happens under this very roof or the fact that he himself trades in flesh, only caring about the highest bidder and nothing more.

"I have a girl who's up for the task," the master reassures us, tension sloughing off of him as though that thought is all the reassurance he needs.

"A blade slave?" Scorpius asks, his tone relaying none of the agitation I see tightening his body.

Tilleo snorts. "Don't let your righteous indignation get away from you," he gibes. "This one *needs* to be put down. *I should have killed her when I found her in Dorsin's office*," he confesses with a shake of his head. "I let my curiosity get the best of me. She was a waif of a thing. I found her with knives in her hands and Dorsin's cold body lying at her feet. She slit his throat and killed two orcs while she was at it. I wanted to know how she got the jump on him, so I dropped her in the ludere and watched her. It didn't take long to see she was made for this," he tells us, gesturing to the moonlit ludere outside of his wide windows. "She's not fit for an

Order, too headstrong and combative. I was going to wash her from the program. I have buyers who need a more robust kind of pet, but then Gartox happened, and I realized this was the purpose she could serve."

Fucking Crowns and stars.

I'm once again struck by the illogicality of Tilleo's double standard, but I stomp the embers of my outrage until they're nothing. We're here to get to the bottom of Auset's claims, not to fix the world, no matter how much it needs it.

"Is this the blade slave that the masters seem to be targeting?" Scorpius inquires, his body language once again relaxed even though I know he's itching to shove a dagger in Tilleo's eye right now, just like I am.

"Like I said, don't waste your time even observing her," the slaver counters.

"This isn't about her, it's about protecting our investment here," Scorpius snaps, and Tilleo's arrogance immediately deflates. "We'll help you with Gartox but not until *after* the Bidding. We'll make sure there's no connection or threads that lead back here," Scorpius announces and pushes up from his chair, done with the conversation and ready to leave.

Tilleo rises with him as though he's going to see us out as opposed to watching us trace back through the shadows. "That's generous of you but not necessary," he states confidently, and I freeze from where I was backing into the dark corner behind me.

"That wasn't an offer up for debate," Scorpius informs him, his voice dropping to a dangerous level that leads to very bad things. He looks at Tilleo in a way that would flay his skin from his body if only he had the thura for it.

Panic seeps into Tilleo's face, and he winds his hands in front of him suddenly very obviously distressed. "I would never argue with you, Scorpius, you know that. It's just that it's a done deal already."

"Make sense quickly, slave master, I'm out of patience," Scorpius warns, stepping forebodingly closer.

"I...I sent Auset off to deal with Gartox not too long ago. By now, either she's dead or he is."

Tilleo's words ring in my mind like the loud bells of a clock tower sounding an alarm. My eyes snap to Scorpius's enraged onyx gaze, and I immediately disappear into the darkness at my back. We were just with her, she was injured and passed out in the healing chambers.

There's no way she's gone already.

I step into a black, cloaked corner in the healing room. Healers scramble about, cleaning up after something that was obviously eventful. A blade slave lies on a cot, her stare empty and soulless. A healer is wiping up pools of blood on the floor and on the cot from several wounds torn into the female's dark skin. She's dead—and the only fae in here aside from the healers.

Fear and anger wage a war in my chest as I frantically look around to confirm what I already know.

Auset is nowhere to be found.

While we were off trying to figure out who she was and what that meant for us, she was sent off to her death.

16

AUSET

SET HER DOWN HERE! SHE'S LOST A LOT OF BLOOD. Pack the wounds as best you can. Farren, grab every bottle of *hemoc* we have, and tell Zinny to start making more immediately!" a commanding voice orders, and I'm pulled awake by the frenzy of healers and servants that frantically pour into the healing chamber.

What was a quiet solitary room is now a hive of hectic activity. I'm confused at first as to what's going on, and then to my left where all the commotion is coming from, two healers step away from each other, and I get a clear view of dark silken skin and agonized bright brown eyes.

"Taria?" I whisper as I take in the blood dripping from her chest. All too quickly it stains the cot beneath her and joins the growing red pool on the floor.

Alarm and worry explode in my chest, but all I can do is watch as the healers scurry around the small blade slave, trying to help her.

"Are these bite marks?" someone asks, but I don't know which of the healers voices the question. "Kings' justice, what did they do to her?"

No one answers what they suspect the trauma to the little fae's body might be from.

"Stay with us," one of the healers by Taria's head coaxes urgently, and I watch, utterly helpless, as the pained gleam in her eyes suddenly dulls and then, like someone extinguishing a flicker of fairy light, it goes out entirely.

Shouts and curses fill the room, and someone steps into my line of sight, blocking me from the girl I've fought beside and against during my time here at the ludere. I watch dazed. I've listened to the whispered dreams she confided late at night when it soothed us more to dream awake than asleep. I can still see the spark of pride that would ignite in her beautiful gaze when she did well in front of the masters. She was sold to Tilleo by her mother. Taria said there were too many mouths to feed in her house and not enough of anything to feed them with. Like many of us, she'd always boast of her plans to pay off her debt and then take care of them. Now, she never would.

The noise in the healing chamber grows somber and heavy. I can almost, for a moment, convince myself that the healers actually care about losing one of us, that they feel the absence of the light that twinkled in tiny Taria no matter what she was up against. But then I catch a few worried whispers about Tilleo and what he's going to do when he finds out about his lost investment. There's no mourning going on here; they're scared, and she's nothing more than a thing they've been tasked with protecting and failed.

Empty brown eyes stare at me, and I can't help but stare back and wonder if this is what I'll look like soon. Will my face relax and my body sag as the blood slowly stops falling from my wounds to dapple the floor? Will death kiss me quickly and steal all my pain away, or will it be drawn out until I'm begging for the sweet release of nothing?

"What the fuck is going on here?" Tilleo demands, the bark of his voice making me jump and then immediately bite back the hiss of pain that works to overwhelm me.

"We're sorry, Tilleo, she was too far gone by the time she was brought to us," a healer informs him, and I can see him battle the cringe of fear that wants to flash across his face as he awaits the master's response.

"Too far gone?" he snarls, stomping closer to take in Taria for himself. "Who did this?" he bellows as his cruel carob glower travels from one brutal injury to another and another and another on the small blade slave's battered body.

Several of the healers look over to the small huddle of house slaves, who are now shaking in the dark, murky corner. One of them steps forward, his eyes fixed on the ground and his hands clutching his bloody tunic as though it'll give him the strength he needs to speak.

"She was in the south wing, master. She was crawling down the hall," he announces, his voice frail and wavering and his movements jumpy and unsettled. "There was screaming still coming from the other side of one of the suite doors," he timidly adds, trailing off as though he hopes nothing more needs to be said.

Tilleo's back is to me as he stares down at the broken creature on the cot. I can't see his face, but the way his shoulders tense at the house slave's words makes it clear that nothing more does need to be said. He knows exactly what's going on. Calculating eyes snap to mine, and I all at once feel like prey that's been seen by a hunter and now there's nowhere for me to escape. I expect him to lash out at me, offended that I've looked him in the eye, but he doesn't. I don't know if looking away will trigger the violent response he normally has to any kind of eye contact from a slave, so I look on, knowing I'm probably fucked either way.

"Heal her," Tilleo orders, pointing a stiff finger in my direction.

Four healers stammer their agreement as they rush to my side without question or argument. I don't dare to break my stare with my master or show him any of the pain that heats my blood to a boiling point as too much magic is forced into me. The quilt of open wounds on my back starts to close up. Sweat collects on my upper lip and brow in the seconds it takes them to reverse the damage done to me earlier. A breath-stealing crack of my ribs is the last thing to hit me as they realign and seal themselves back together. I don't even know when they were broken.

Job done, healers immediately move away from me, skittering as far as they can from Tilleo's volatile direct line of sight. Slowly, I sit up, shakily clutching my dirty bloodstained tunic to my chest. Tilleo looks furious, and

I wonder for a moment if he's going to have me whipped again for embarrassing him the way I did at the trial earlier or if he needs a target for his anger right now and I'm here. I know he expects me to paint my features with contrition and cower at his anger, but I don't have it in me anymore. I've been careful and tried to be appropriately meek the majority of my time in this hellhole, and it's gotten me nowhere. Tilleo hasn't broken me so far, and no matter what he thinks, what's gleaming in his eyes right now isn't going to do it either.

Tilleo glances over at Taria's body as a healer draws a sheet over her face. His eyes harden even more, and he works to control a confusing flood of emotions that hit entirely too fast for me to interpret, before turning back to me. I wait to hear him demand to know who did this to her, to rage that someone dared break what was his, but instead he levels me with an enraged stare, and it's all I can do not to shrink away from it.

"It's time," he announces as though I should immediately know the plan contained in those two simple words.

I don't, but my heart picks up regardless, as though it can sense the doom spilling out of the vague instruction. Sinisterly, Tilleo bends down, his mouth inches from my ear so only I can hear what comes next.

"I thought things would come together differently, but this is as good a time as any," he frostily whispers, and the air around me grows even thicker with malice. "Slave, you will make your way to the south wing of my manor, and you will not leave it until either you or Gartox of the Order of Bruins is dead."

My heart stutters as understanding skitters over me like starving sand voles. This is it. This is when it all ends for me.

I'm about to die.

I stare at the blank wall of the healing chamber, not sure what to say or do. It feels so different when you see it coming. Life here has always been kill or be killed. But if we were good enough, if we worked hard, it meant we could outrun death for some time. I've trained the way the masters wanted, the way Tilleo demanded, and it should have meant that there would be another day and another hunt on the horizon until I was too old and frail to lift a blade anymore. At best, I would earn enough to buy myself and then I could walk away from it all. But it was a lie. I was dead the moment Tilleo set me in the sands of this ludere. I just didn't know it.

Tilleo steps back, his severe scowl doing its best to shut down the dissension now dripping from my mind into my mouth like sap from a cut tree to the forest floor. I want to tell him no, to slit him from torso to throat for toying with me the way that he has, but I have no weapons. The healers and guards would be on me before I could so much as squeeze one breath out of the bastard with my bare hands. So instead, I do what's been beaten into me since the day I got here: I drop my eyes and submit.

"I am your blade to command," I reply, as is expected, and then I push to my feet as though I'm not rising simply to meet my own end.

Tilleo and I stand across from each other, slave and master, master and slave, our places in this world carved into stone as though that's how it will always be. But I don't accept that. Not anymore. Tilleo wants death to coat the walls of his manor tonight, fine, but it won't just be mine or Gartox's—I'm coming for every single fae that runs this place. I won't get them all, I know that already, but I'll end enough of them not to die in vain. Enough to make my tortured and brief life worth *something*.

"Hord, take her to the armory and get her what she needs. Then you will escort her to the southern wing and report back to your post," Tilleo barks at the familiar guard, who steps forward with a stiff nod.

At that, I'm dismissed, like the insignificant mongrel that Tilleo thinks I am. The master of my fate gives me his back while he speaks with the senior healers in the room. I vow, in this moment, that he'll regret treating me as though I'm nothing.

Clutching my tattered tunic to my chest, I move to follow Hord out of the healing chamber. Cool desert air caresses me in a way that feels comforting, like the elements themselves are offering their support when there's none to be found anywhere else in this Kings forsaken place. I'm led out of the ludere and into the quiet of the early hours of the morning. This day is about to wake up to a massacre. The thought makes me feel lighter.

I'm surprised at first when Hord heads in the direction of the stables. I consider for a fleeting moment that he might try to help me escape. Hord has watched over the ludere in some way or another my entire time here; could he feel pity over everything that's happened and want to help? Then I realize that he's not taking me to the stables, but to the guard's barracks just on the other side. He's guiding me to the guard's armory for weapons. When Tilleo ordered him to arm me with whatever I needed, I pictured the room in the ludere where we pick up weapons to train with. But given what I've been tasked to do, I should have known that Tilleo wouldn't want rusted swords and dull spears for this hunt. He wants death done right this time.

I shiver as we make our way across the warm sand. My body is exhausted, and my muscles feel battered and tight with tension. I want to stop and stand with my face tilted back to the waning moon so it can really work its magic on me, but each moonlit-soaked step helps me feel stronger, more fortified. I have no idea what my connection to the celestial body is. When I was younger, I used to think that I must be from the Night Court and therefore the moon is looking out for me when there's no one else who can. Then I grew up and realized I must have some kind of affinity for it, but who knows if that's true or what it could mean.

The mystery barely plagues me anymore. I realized a long time ago that there's no point wondering or trying to figure it out when it wouldn't change anything. I was a blade slave, I was trapped, and no sudden flash of memory or understanding was going to change that fact.

Hord pushes a door open that leads into the building, and ushers me inside. The barracks are steeped in quiet, the late hour wrapping everything around me in a thick blanket of calm and peace. I try to absorb it as I step into a large room with rows and rows of weapons fixed to the walls, and racks and crates full of more set off to one side. Hord disappears through a doorway to the right. After a minute or so of the distinct sound of rustling fabric, he reappears with a gray guard's tunic. I take it, showing him my back as

I drop my soiled, useless top to the ground and pull the new one over my head. It's a little big, so I grab a dagger and cut a slit in the front of the fabric up to my stomach and then wrap the tails of the top around my back, tying them off at my front just above my pants.

"There's armor in there too. I wasn't sure what would fit you," he offers, not his usual jovial ass-slapping self. He's probably gleaned what I'm here to do, or maybe my pokoyn plan has started to work.

Hord does something to the fairy light sconces, and they brighten, allowing me to see the metal and hardened leather options hanging on long racks in the other room. I squeeze my hands into fists once and then relax them, only allowing myself that small show of emotion before I shut it down and focus. It's tempting to kit myself out in every-thing, to adorn myself in so much protection that nothing could get through, not even death, but I know that will just delay the inevitable and mess with my range of motion.

I reach for a leather chest guard, waving away Hord when he steps forward to help me get it on. I'm not some spoiled guard who requires help, I'm a blade slave. No one does this shit for us. It makes me think of the Scorpions as I carefully tighten the laces at the side until the leather molds to me as much as it can. It was made for a male, but every other piece of armor I've ever worn was too; I'm used to working around it. The Kings know, if I ever got a kit that actually fit, I'd have to retrain completely and figure out how to fight and kill without the bulky mass of male armor in my way.

Guess I'll never know.

I leave the room, urgency all at once tugging at me. Anticipation settles into my limbs, and I consider my choice of weapons carefully. My hands are eager to grab everything I can and find a home for it on my body, but my mind warns me that doing that might give others something to grab and use against me if they get too close. With what I'm planning to do tonight, someone is bound to get too close.

I need to think things through carefully.

I close my eyes and try to picture the Order of Bruins. I'm not sure which one is Gartox exactly, but I plan as though he's the biggest one of the group. He probably is. Fate thinks it's funny to pit me against mountains that can walk, talk, and fight. If he's like all the other giants I've fought over the years, he'll probably throw his weight and size around. His reach will be an issue just like it was with Taur. Maybe I should thank the masters for the fight I had earlier. In a way, it was good practice for what's about to go down.

A pair of curved daggers as long as my forearm catch my eye. I grab them along with some leg sheaths holding thin knives that I buckle into place around my thighs. A handful of push daggers go into guards on the belt I knot around my waist, and lastly I slip a penknife down my back, my armor keeping it snugly in place between my shoulder blades. I take a deep breath, locking any stray thoughts or emotions down once and for all, and turn to Hord.

"I'm done."

Without a word or even a nod, he leaves and I follow. We walk silently toward the manor, and I work through all the possible scenarios of how this will end for me. Will it be fast? Slow? Painful? Tilleo might have guards waiting to capture and silence me just as soon as the job is done. Or maybe the other members of the Order of Bruins will discover what's happened and slit my throat before Gartox's blood is even cold.

The lazy desert wind flings sand against my clammy skin as I mentally stomp on all worry and thoughts of *what if*. I move silently behind Hord, who seems oddly nervous as he keeps looking back over his shoulder to check that I'm still there.

Something about his fear calms my nerves. It reminds me of everything I've been through to survive this place. I get to come face-to-face with the monster they've created and then forced me to keep locked up and leashed. I get to set her free once and for all. No more cages for us. No more piss-stained tunics, unearned whippings, or cowering in fear. Everything they've beaten, starved, and tortured into me is about to come out and play. Whatever happens from here on is because *I* decreed it, because *I* made it so. This may be it for me, but I'll spend my final moments making all of the bastards here sorry for it.

I'm led through a maze of foyers and corridors, one looking the same as another. I map everything out as we go, matching it up with what I learned about this place when I was first pulled from a cage and later when I was marched out and carried down to the ludere. After what feels like forever, Hord stops at a wide, barely lit hallway. With a brief nod of confirmation, he hastily disappears back the way we came. I can't help but scoff at his unapologetic and speedy retreat.

Where does Tilleo find such big tough guards?

Reality drums in my chest like a call to arms as I stand amidst the closed doors of the strange corridor. I have no idea where I'm supposed to go. Am I expected to knock on each room, inquiring gently for Gartox until I find him and then try to slit his throat before he can get the jump on me?

I stand frozen like an icy boulder in a storm, uncertainty making me hesitant as I look from the dark wood of one door to another and then another, all the way down the hallway until darkness keeps me from seeing any more rooms.

Why am I even here?

I start to wonder as I stand there. Maybe it's time to cut the puppet strings and hunt down Tilleo and his cronies instead. I don't owe him anything, especially not some Order member's death. An uneasy stillness settles in the air. Warning calls to the hair that starts to rise on my arms and the back of my neck. Tension practically whispers that something dangerous is out to play tonight...and it's not me. Alarm tightens my muscles, and I start to think that plan B might be the better way to die, just as a scream rips through the deadened night and sinks its terrified talons into my gut.

I don't know who the horror-filled plea belongs to, but three doors down on my right, the dark wood vibrates against the shriek as though it can barely contain the sheer agony in it. My stomach drops, and I rush silently toward the door just as another scream rips my hesitant caution away. I surge into a thin patch of shadows on the wall, the blackness soaking me up and delivering me seamlessly to the other side. In front of me, I find a large entryway with a small round table in the middle and a dark hallway further back. The distinct sounds of a fight lure me down the bleak hall, and then I don't know what happens, because one moment I'm shrouded in the shadows by the door of the suite, and in the next breath, I'm standing in an unfamiliar dark corner and trying to get my bearings. I've used shadows to hide or move from one connected place to another, but I've never jumped entire spaces like I just did.

I'm disoriented by the strange new ability I accidentally unlocked, but the sound of glass shattering and fabric ripping clears the haze, and I focus. The room is huge and dripping with luxurious furnishings. There's a large round bed cocooned in hanging drapes that flutter even though there isn't the slightest breeze in the air. One panel is hanging askew and in tatters, and through it, I see a behemoth of a man pressing down on the neck of a much smaller female. She's clawing at his massive hands, teeth bared and eyes wide with fear and pain and rage. Red hair fans out all around her, and I immediately recognize Sennet.

In a heartbeat, I catalog her torn tunic, her missing pants, the bruises, cuts, and...bite marks that pepper her skin and face. Another beat is all it takes for daggers to be clutched in my hands as I move in behind the Bruin. He's the giant I remembered. I still don't know with one-hundred-percent certainty that he's Gartox, but it doesn't matter anymore. Whoever this is needs to die.

Like a wraith, I hunt him, moving toward his naked back as I quickly work out the best option to take the colossal Order member down. I want to go for his throat—it would be my best chance to mortally wound him quickly—but the way he's scrunching his shoulders as he does his best to strangle Sennet means I won't get the clean deep cut I need. Fairy light flickers in the room, and it's as though the shadows themselves are reaching out to help me. A strip of darkness moves down the Bruin's arms, and at last I see it, I see where to attack.

There's no hesitation, no deep preparatory inhale or adjusting of my angle. I leap for him like the savage I am, flicking my daggers from an underhand grip to an over-handed one. Like a pouncing feline, I land on the Bruin's back and reach around to slice the underside of both arms.

My blades cut through his flesh like it's nothing more than a hot juicy roast that was just pulled from the fire. A bellow of pain fills the room, and blood arcs up the wall at the head of the bed before splashing Sennet and soaking the bedding beneath her.

I flip off the monster as though I'm capable of walking on air the way I walk through shadows. I crouch and ready myself for what I know is going to be a brutal, unforgiving fight as the Bruin turns to me. Images of Taria's empty eyes flash in my mind, and I blink back the sight of the marks on her body. This fucker didn't just kill her, he tried to destroy her. He shattered her body right along with her hope, and now he needs to pay for that.

Sennet and Taria are decent fae. They didn't target the weak. They didn't stand on the backs of others in order to climb high in the ranks. They deserved to have a rich life in a prominent Order, to find some semblance of content-ment and peace. They sure as fuck didn't deserve *this*.

Blood drips from my blades as the Bruin pushes off of Sennet and slowly studies me like I'm nothing more than a swamp gnat buzzing obnoxiously in his ear. Green eyes the color of stinging nettle lazily move over my body and my weapons, landing and staying on my crotch for far too long. The threat is clear in his gaze when his eyes eventually find mine. I have to strangle the molten urge to charge him when I see the laces of his trousers are undone. His features are sinisterly unapologetic as he reaches down to stroke the grotesque bulge in his leathers. The monster's eyes darken with painful promise, and he licks his lips as though he's some kind of reptile who's scenting me.

Sennet isn't moving on the bed. I can't tell if she's even breathing, and there's no way I can take my eyes off the fucker in front of me to try to help her. Fear simmers in my stomach, and a foreboding chill crawls up my spine.

I took too much time getting here.

The room is eerily quiet now as the Bruin touches himself and watches me. I can hear drops of blood as they fall to the carpet at our feet, and my gaze flicks to the rivulets of crimson flowing steadily down the Bruin's inner arms. There are scratches on his face and chest, but I can't focus on that. My soul doesn't need any more scars.

My cuts under his upper arms must not have been deep enough, because he's not bleeding to death nearly as fast as I was hoping he would. It doesn't help that he's gargantuan. He was huge from afar, but close up, his size is even more daunting. His arms are bigger than my thighs, his thighs thicker than my waist. My heart hammers as I take him in, and I realize, with alarming certainty, that I'm going to have to rethink my plan of attack. I could spend all night hacking away at him and still not take him out.

He doesn't say a word, doesn't ask what I'm doing in his room or why I attacked. He doesn't look toward Sennet, doesn't feel the need to reassure himself that his prey is where he left her. No, the Bruin looks at me like he discovered something that's guaranteed to be more fun than what he was previously doing. I want to gag on the revulsion that bubbles up my throat, but I manage to tamp down the bile.

I can do this.

I know I'm good. I hate that I ended up in the ludere, but there's no question that I take to death and violence like a bird to air. But staring this monster in the eyes has doubt festering in my chest. I may not be enough tonight. And if this bastard wins, I'll wish for oblivion long before I'm blessed with it. Here's to hoping I can get a blade through my own throat first if it comes to that.

17

"Gartox?" I confirm to break up the silence and give my mind a few more seconds to scramble for a plan B.

His green eyes light up with interest, but he doesn't answer. I start to wonder why no one else has kicked in his door to investigate the screaming, but they're all Order members; maybe bloodcurdling fear is just what they need to sleep easy throughout the night. I guess that means I'm really on my own here. No one is coming, no matter how much I might beg for it if things go badly. Three glamoured skeletal men rise to the surface of my thoughts before I shut everything down and prepare myself for whatever is about to happen.

"Good enough for me," I grumble, done stalling, and then as fast as fangs, I step to the side.

I see Gartox stiffen, preparing for the attack we both know is coming, and then I see his head snapping left and right in shock as I step deeper into a shadow and disappear altogether. I pop up in a dark recess to the Bruin's right, and I'm on him before he can track me. Fairy light flashes on the metal of my blades as I bring my two daggers down his naked chest from shoulder to ribs. Swiftly, I retreat back into the darkness again, moving myself to a pool of shadows at his back. This time he reaches for me, but I'm gone before he can so much as whirl around.

The gouges I leave in his back and front are deep but not deep enough to bring the colossus to his knees. They'll weaken him, and that's half my battle. He howls as I strike out at him again. It rings of rage more than pain as I vanish once more just as he turns to face me.

"Stand still, you miserable cunt!" he snarls, his body and muscles taut as he spins around in place, frantically searching for me.

My only response is to step back into the light across the room and pitch two push daggers at him. One sinks into the base of his neck on the left side, while another blade buries itself hilt deep just below his collar bone on the same side. I'm gone before his furious eyes can track me, and then he does what I was hoping he wouldn't do until I'd gotten a few more hits in. He steps as far from the shadows as he can and growls an incantation that makes the fairy light in the room flare. The light doesn't banish every shadow in the room, but it illuminates enough that things just became pointedly harder for me.

"It seems Tilleo has been holding out that he owns a highborn bitch," Gartox snarls, plucking the two push daggers from his skin and muscle like they don't even faze him. "Shoulda known as much when the Scorpions didn't want me to even look at ya."

Blood gushes from the wound at his throat, but not enough to give me hope that he'll drop dead from it or that it'll force him to shut the fuck up.

"Does that highborn slit taste sweeter with all that rich blood pumping between your thighs?" he asks, reaching down to cup himself again as his eyes dart around the few shadows that still remain in the room. "Is that what the Scorpions like so much about ya? Why ya mum sold ya off? Your highborn cunt too much of a distraction for your pa?"

He starts to laugh, but I ignore the taunts and debate where to attack from now.

"Did you think you could save your little friends?" he mocks. "It's the brave ones who always end up screaming the loudest," he jibes just as I step out of the left corner behind him, wrath seething from every pore.

Before I can so much as raise the knives in my hands and leap for him, a *whoosh* fills the air and then pain slams into me. I stumble back into the stone nook at my back and then look down to find both push daggers buried deep, side by side, in my shoulder. The blade I had ready in my palm clangs to the ground as my right arm goes completely numb.

Shit!

I push past the alarm that sounds in my mind and shut down the pain. The shadows pull me back into the safety of their cool embrace a mere millisecond before two huge arms try to wrap themselves around me. Gartox yells his frustration and then starts to stalk from one shadow to another, waiting for me to appear. My options are severely limited. There's a sliver of darkness by the large wardrobe that he hasn't noticed yet, or I can hide beneath the bed; I'm screwed either way.

"If you run, little gash, I'll find you," he snaps when the room once again grows quiet and I stay hidden for too long. "Tilleo can't help ya now, ya stupid whore. The moment you interfered in my business, you became *mine*. If I have to bid on your cunt to own it, I will. I will rip ya open and fuck you till you can't scream anymore. Then I'll get ya a healer and do it all over again and again and again. You'll wish you'd left your wee friends to die before I'm done with ya," Gartox shouts into the room, his threats bouncing from stone wall to stone wall, making them impossible to escape.

A chill slips down my back as I watch him from the safety of the gray darkness that's both a part of this world and yet isn't. The Bruin grows even more enraged as I refuse to step into the light and give him an easy target. Warmth drips down my chest, and the tunic under my chest plate starts to grow tacky as it soaks up my blood. Gartox picks up a chair and throws it across the room with an unhinged howl, and just as the chair comes to rest askew against a wall, I see an opening.

I jump from one shadow to another, crouching in a new pitch black pool made by the leaning broken chair, while Gartox rips a panel of fabric from the ceiling around the bed. I leap for him while his back is turned and, with my one good arm and hand, sink the long blade of a dagger into his upper back. I hit bone, and the blade sticks. Panicked, I push against his body with my knees, trying to free one of the few weapons I have left.

Before I can stop it, I'm ripped from Gartox's back and pinned against a wall. Air abandons my lungs as quickly as a plan abandons me. I struggle against his hold, a salacious smile all I see as Gartox presses his thumb into the blades still sticking out of my shoulder. I left them in, not wanting to deal with the damage and blood loss of taking them out, but now I'm regretting that choice as the small, serrated edges start to dig deeper. I bite back a whimper, and Gartox's dark chuckle fills my ears as he slams me back against the wall to try to stop my attempts to break free of his strong grasp.

The rich smell of blood drowns out everything else as I fight the dread and pain that starts to take hold of me. My instincts scream for me to get as far away from this beast as I can, but he's so damn strong I can't break away. He presses into me, the blood from his own wounds stamping my armor as he does. A familiar tingling starts in my gums, and I lift my good arm and dig my thumb into Gartox's eye, pressing as hard as I can and hoping the shock of it will loosen his grip.

He laughs even as I feel his eyeball start to give way. I push harder, trying to destroy his eye, but the fucker just grinds his disgusting length into me as though nothing matters more than that terrifying promise of things to come. Fangs drop in my mouth, my fear entirely too potent to keep my body from revealing my secrets. Before I can question the instinct, I lean forward and sink my two razor sharp canines into the fucker's neck. I tear into the wound left by my push daggers, the very same daggers that are now digging further into my shoulder. I rip at him with my teeth, trying to do as much damage as I can while reaching for the long knife I left in his back.

Gartox roars in pain and shock, and it spurs me on as he reaches for the braided tails of my long hair. He wraps them around one fist and yanks hard in an effort to force me to pull my teeth from his throat.

"What the fuck are you?" he bleats, just as I involuntarily swallow a mouthful of his blood.

I'm shocked and disgusted at just how good he tastes. I suck down another swallow, unable to help it, while I simultaneously question what the fuck I'm doing right now and fight the growing need to gulp down more. I've known about my fangs since the first time the masters starved me, but I've never felt the urge to drink blood from another fae before. I always thought the fangs were a response to either being too hungry or too emotional, but there's no denying I'm getting something from this, that Gartox's blood is working *for* me.

I've done everything I can to keep this part of me hidden. I learned all too quickly what happens if you stand out or show how different you are from the other blade slaves. But if my secrets can save my life, I'll use every weapon I have in my body's mysterious arsenal.

I clamp my teeth down harder and greedily suck more blood down. It heats through me like a soothing balm, healing and strengthening as it works through my system. I'm stunned by the sensation, lost to it, and then pain blinds me when Gartox gives up on ripping my hair out of my head to get me off of him and starts punching me instead. My ribs break with the first hit, and I gasp against the throbbing sting of it. He punches me again just as I finally get my hand around the knife in his back. I pull for all that I'm worth as he pounds against my head and abdomen. But his blood in my body works to counteract the damage he's doing. I hiss from the anguish of him battering my outsides, while his blood painfully fixes things from the inside.

The dagger in his back just starts to come loose when, out of nowhere, something stabs into my chest. I ignore it at first, all of my focus on getting the weapon free from his back and into my hand so I can shove it through his throat. Then, all at once, Gartox gasps and slackens against me. His fist glances off my cheek, but not nearly as hard as before, and then his hand drops away altogether. I rear back, preparing myself for the new attack he must be mounting, but all I find is a shocked look on the Bruin's face, and then he stumbles back away from me.

As he does, the tip of a sharp sword pulls free from my chest just above my right breast, and I discover the glinting metal is also protruding from Gartox. It pierces through the exact spot where his heart is. Astonishment paints the Bruin's face as he reaches for the pointy tip sticking out of his chest, like he can't understand how it got there. My heart pounds like it's banging on a door to salvation, begging to be let in, but it won't budge. Confusion battles my relief as I look up to see who just stabbed the bastard, but there's no one standing around eager to take credit for it.

Blood starts to leak out of the beast's mouth, and he wavers on his feet. I slide down the wall, my body and face throbbing with pain as the blood I stole continues to try to erase it from the inside out. Gartox falls to his knees, and it's then that I see the lean girl with the bright red hair now tangled around her shoulders standing behind him. She looks at me once, her hands limp at her side and covered in blood. She blinks and then pitches forward, her body finally giving out and taking her soul with it. I try to grab her, to keep her from falling next to the fucker who did this to her, but I'm too hurt and too slow.

I scramble over Gartox's dead body, fumbling to get to her. When I do, I carefully brush the red strands of hair from Sennet's face, hoping against hope that there's still a chance for her, but there isn't. Just like Taria, her eyes are empty, fixed, and what made Sennet who she was is absent. Her shirt is in tatters, her body bruised and broken. The wounds cut and bit into her aren't bleeding anymore, and her face is in that far-off land that only death holds the key to.

She's gone.

We survived against the odds. We made it to the Bidding. And now, she's died saving my life even though I was too late to save hers. She's escaped to a place where my gratitude can't follow, and it all hollows me out in a way that's far too familiar and crushing. My eyes sting as I close her lids, forever hiding away her now empty hazel eyes. I crawl back and lean against the wall. I simmer in defeat as I stare at the two dead bodies, debating the merits of curling up alongside my fellow blade slave and hoping to join her in whatever awaits us after death.

Too bad for me, my body is awake and buzzing thanks to Gartox's blood. With my good hand, I reach up and pull the daggers from my shoulder. I drop them, the noisy clangor they make when they fall against the stone floor too loud in the eerily quiet room. I wince but swallow down a hiss, no longer worried about bleeding out or doing more damage to my shoulder. The evil fucking Bruin's life force is working inside of me, mending and healing my body despite the fact that I just helped destroy his.

I need it to heal me and yet I want to purge it from my veins at the same time. I wipe my mouth with the bottom of the guard's tunic I'm wearing and try not to think about the blood that comes away from my face as I do. I take in Gartox's dead body and run my gaze over the puncture marks in his throat that I know I need to hide. The likelihood that I'm going to live beyond tonight is low, but it feels right to take my secrets with me when they finally slit my throat. These bastards have gotten enough of me over the years; they won't be getting any more.

With far less effort than it should take, I grab the push daggers from the floor, and one by one, I slam them into Gartox's neck. The little blades erase any signs of fang marks, and I once again sit back against the wall, breathing hard and unsure of what to do next. Do I leave Sennet here? Do I clean up and hunt down Tilleo and his people like I vowed to do? Or do I just sit against this wall, in shock, angry, tired, overwhelmed, and saddened by the horror that is this heinous, fucked-up life?

Before I can decide one way or another, three tall, muscular, skeletal apparitions step calmly from a dark corner and then freeze as they take in the room. Intense black stares land on the streaks and splatters of blood, the broken furniture, the chips in the stone walls, and then finally the dead bodies before landing on me.

"Fuck," one of them whispers with awe, and then a skeleton is crouching in front of me, his two warm hands cradling my face as he looks me over with both shock and worry.

His touch is soothing in a way that threatens to break me open and leave all of my soft spots vulnerable, but I can't bear to pull my face from his grip or my eyes from his probing stare. I want to harden myself against the questions I see floating in the onyx abyss of his gaze, but I can't help but wonder what it would be like not to have to. A thumb caresses my cheek, and I wait for the questions to come, the ones I'll offer up lies to because that's what you do when someone asks if you're okay when *okay* is impossible. But Scorpius says nothing. I don't know how I know it's him when they're all magicked to look the same, but I do.

"Gartox is as dead as dead gets," Skull declares. He's crouched over the bodies, wiping blood on his black trousers from where he checked the Bruin for a pulse. "So is the slave," he continues, gesturing to the other body next to him.

"Sennet," I speak up, surprised by how even and calm my tone is.

I don't know why I expected to sound as raw as I feel, but the fact that I don't makes me uneasy, which is stupid. I've killed before. I've watched people being killed before. So why does *this* sit differently with me? Is it because it's the start of my end, or could it be that I'm finally embracing all of who I am, just in time to die?

"Her name was Sennet," I offer again, and Skull nods, his dark eyes gentling as they find mine.

"Do we need to cover anything up?" Bones asks as he kicks at the broken leg of a chair that rests by his feet. "It looks cleaner than I thought it would," he admits, looking around clinically. "It looks like Gartox attacked a couple of blade slaves and they got the better of him," he observes, and Skull nods and stands up.

He surveys everything slowly, and I get the impression he's making sure that he's not missing any details or hints of anything that could disprove the scene that Bones just described.

"Are you hurt anywhere else?" Scorpius inquires softly, dropping one hand from my cheek to pull my tunic away from the wound in my shoulder. The fabric makes a sticky sucking sound as he peels it back from the punctures, but the bleeding has slowed already, and I know some time soaking in moonlight can do the rest.

"No," I answer, but Scorpius's gaze drops down my body like he needs to check for himself before he'll believe me.

I would be offended by that, but truth be told, I would have told him *no* even if I were on the brink of death. Scorpius reaches down and runs a finger quickly inside my leather-clad thigh. My breath hitches, and when Scorpius pulls his hand up closer to his face to reveal the blood on his fingertips, the malevolence that fills his face makes the hair on my arms stand up in warning.

"It's not mine," I rush to tell him, unsure of why I feel the need to reassure him or console away the baleful look in his eyes.

I don't even know why he'd care if it was. But with the way he stares at me, hard and intense, as though he's reaching into my soul in search of the truth, there's no denying that it matters to him, however nonsensical that may be to me.

"It's not mine," I whisper again, gently, soothingly, as a tic starts in his jaw and the room grows thick with tension.

"If he touched you, I'll bring him back and then kill him far more slowly for it," Scorpius declares, his tone a lethal purr that should do none of the things it's doing for me right now.

I scoff at the ridiculous statement. Dead is dead. Not even the Scorpions in all their glory hold dominion over that.

My eyes flit back and forth between his lethal heated stare, trying to interpret what I'm seeing. I know I'm misreading possession for something else, I just can't figure out what that something else could be. There's absolutely no way the Order of Scorpions gives a shit about what might or might not happen to me.

"Why are you here?" I ask instead, my senses once again firing off and trying to comprehend everything that's happening.

"Because we failed you once, and we weren't going to fail you again," Scorpius answers quietly.

My brow furrows as I puzzle out what in the crowns that means. I look over at Bones and Skull, who are both staring at me too, and I realize something feels different about it. Before, they looked at me like I was something amusing, an intriguing problem that would be entertaining to solve. Now, there's more in their eyes, in their countenance. A hint of promise maybe, dedication...guilt?

Realization hits me harder than Gartox ever did, and I suddenly know what I see in their faces.

They remember. They know I was there that night in Dorsin's quarters.

I shut down so fast it makes Scorpius reel back in surprise. I douse every flicker of heat that was building in my chest. Deaden my eyes. Fortify everything inside of me and set any stray emotion on fire until it's nothing more than ash and emptiness in my head. I don't know what's going on here, what they'll do now that they know, but alarms blare loudly inside of me.

"Are you here to kill me?" I ask, a shell of what I was mere seconds ago.

As though my body is giving permission that my mind hasn't agreed to, I flip the dagger that I somehow pulled from Gartox's back until the hilt is facing Scorpius and the blade is pointed toward me. Silently I offer him the weapon. He looks down at it confused, and then his head snaps up, the remorse in his eyes suddenly replaced with rage. He grabs the dagger from my hand, and I flinch when instead of using it on me, he throws it across the room.

"No one will be killing you," he seethes at me, and for some reason, it lights a fire of indignation in me instead of cowing me like I think it's supposed to.

"But Tilleo..." I start to argue, anger banking in my stare as a telltale tingling starts in my gums again.

Shit.

"Fuck Tilleo and anyone else who even thinks it," Bones counters, but I have no idea what that means.

Annoyed, I try to push up to my feet, but it's hard to do with Scorpius looming over me like he is. I shove him away from me with a glare, and surprisingly, instead of stabbing me for it, he gives me room to get to my feet.

"Fuck Tilleo?" I scornfully repeat. "Big words for some-one not *owned* by him," I snap.

I don't bother mentioning anything about how I planned on hunting him down and killing him tonight. I didn't miss Bones's accounting of how Gartox's murder could be seen from the outside. If that's possible, then it means *I* was never here. The sanctum was never violated. None of this has to be the death sentence I thought it would be. One look at Scorpius stops that train of thought. The Order of Scorpions knows. How long before they tell the others?

"Tilleo doesn't *own* you," Skull starts to insert, but fury takes off with my tongue before he can get another word in.

"That's odd," I snark venomously. "I tried to tell him that very thing when he first brought me here. I spent at least three months being beaten almost to death, healed, and then beaten all over again. When *that* didn't work, they starved me. Finally, to really *prove* just how wrong I was about who I *belonged* to, Tilleo loaned me out to some lord. When that bastard was done with me, he let his guards take their turn before I was dropped back off to the ludere like a sack of garbage. So fuck you," I snarl, my every edge feeling grated and raw.

"He what?" Skull barks furiously, stepping toward me like he wants to wrap me up, but that can't be right.

What is wrong with me right now? Why am I seeing every-thing so backward?

"Oh, save it," I interrupt, as though I'm not walking a tightrope over death. I know I'm not doing myself any fa-vors by talking to the scariest Order of assassins known in all the realms this way, but I can't find a fuck to give. "This isn't your first Bidding; you know what happens here. *No is not in a slave's vernacular. Isn't that right?*" I ask, pointedly staring down at Scorpius's crotch. Or do these idiots really think fae are just falling all over themselves to clean their dicks?

My enraged glare bounces between the three skeletons, and even though the details are hard to make out under the thick magic hiding their features, I can tell they're probably above average in the beauty department. Maybe they do have fae falling all over themselves to willingly wash every inch of them...among other things. What do I know?

"We didn't know you'd end up here," Bones defends.

It's everything I can do not to leap at him, let my fangs drop into his throat, and then drink him dry.

Damn. Why is that thought enticing?

"Have you lost it? *You* thought I'd end up somewhere worse!" I caustically remind him. "You figured I'd end up at the flesh markets. That's why you so kindly offered to kill me, right?" I demand, my heated stare jumping from Bones to Skull and back again, because now that I can pick them apart in a group, I know who did what that night. I can fit their faces with that memory.

Scorpius slit Dorsin's throat and got something from his vault. He was also the first one to climb out of the window while demanding that the others leave me to my fate. Bones was the first to notice me and take an interest, and Skull was the one ready to slit my throat if I just said the word.

"Enough," Scorpius snaps, ever the leader. Eager to regain his chokehold of control over everything around him. "We can't save everyone, no matter how hard we try, Auset."

"But how hard did you try, really, Scorpius?" I counter, and I see the moment I've pushed too far. The moment when his face drops into a cold emotionless mask.

Is that what I look like when I shut down?

"We can debate this later. Right now, we need to leave before someone stumbles in here and the story we want the other Orders to come up with gets tainted by our presence. Right now, it looks as though Gartox got what was coming to him by messing with the wrong blade slave. We need to keep it that way."

"Sennet and Taria screamed. They didn't go quietly. If no one came to check on that, I doubt they're just going to wander in here now," I argue, unable to shut down the need to fight, to dig at them until I can see what's happening underneath the cool skeletal veneer.

"The other Order rooms are warded," Skull informs me. "I'd guarantee all of them have magic in place so no sound comes in or goes out."

"But—" I start.

"Gartox removed his wards. He liked to let the screams out," Skull continues, cutting off the start of a new argument. "Part of his perversion was challenging anyone to come and stop him. As you can see, no one did."

"Until now," Bones points out, once again staring at me with something that looks alarmingly close to admiration.

"I got lucky," I dismiss, hoping to shut down whatever it is that's happening with these three.

Scorpius snorts but doesn't elaborate on what the hell that means, his eyes once again fixed on Gartox's body. "I'll go deal with Tilleo. You two get her back to the tent," he orders. He looks up at me for a moment, his stare unreadable, and then he steps back into a pool of shadow and disappears.

It dawns on me, again, that these Scorpions can do something I've never seen anyone aside from me do. I open my mouth to ask about it, but Skull steps toward me, and I tell myself that this isn't the best place to get into it. I'll get answers. Right now, though, I need to go. Scorpius wants me tucked away, nice and neat in their quarters, probably to keep me close in case things change and they decide I need to die.

Yeah, that's not going to happen.

I need a safe place to figure out what Tilleo is going to do now. Gartox is dead like he wanted. The sanctum is, surprisingly, intact from the outside looking in, but thinking things are now going to work out for me is asinine. Slave masters and assassins don't like loose ends. Like Scorpius said, they can't save everyone.

Skull reaches out like he's going to take hold of my arm, but before he can, I step back into the same shadow Scorpius just used and melt into it. I hear Bones shout out a curse before the shadows of Gartox's room give way to the shadows of the girl's bathing chamber. I wait, tense and ready for Skull and Bones to follow me. I know they can shadow walk too, but I don't know how hard it is to track someone through them. I don't even know how I'm using the shadows now to jump distances. Before, I could only slip from room to connected room. This jumping would have been seriously helpful before. Maybe I could have figured out a way to shadow walk all the way out of the ludere entirely. Not that I would have known where to go if I ever did get away from this place.

I sigh as the placid hush of early morning wraps around me like a thick cloak. The last of my fight drains away, and I'm left standing in the dark bathing chamber, feeling empty. My defenses seem to have more holes than the aged tin of the tubs all around me. I lumber from the dark spot I just escaped to and run a hand over my face, exhaustion seeping into my deepest recesses and making me feel worn and used up.

I choose a bathtub soaked in moonlight by the far back window and start to fill it up. Robotically, I pick Wilik's braids out of my hair, massaging my sore scalp from where Gartox tried to rip chunks out. I can tell that the last dregs of night will heal the bruises by the time I'm done with my bath. I strip out of my bloodstained clothes. A knife drops to the ground as I pull off my chest plate, and I realize I forgot that I hid it there between my shoulder blades.

I shake my head, disappointed in everything that went wrong tonight. I let myself get overwhelmed and then pinned, but what's worse is I forgot what weapons were on me that I could have used to end that fucking monster. Maybe if I'd remembered, I could have saved Sennet.

That thought floats around in my mind like the moon's reflection on the water of my slow-filling tub. I absently study the dried blood on my pants that's from my whipping earlier, and then I look down at the blood on my chest, unable to tell how much is mine and how much is Gartox's. I feel numb. Like I need to play back every second of this day over and over again just to try to process all that's happened. My life has completely changed, and yet here I stand in the bathing chamber of the ludere, and there's nothing different about any of it. I'm still here. I'm still a slave. My future is still uncertain. And none of that means what it did before the Bidding started.

Threadbare washcloths in one hand, and soap and hair cleaner in the other, I step into the lukewarm bath. Water sloshes over the tin rim as I sink into the cooling liquid, hoping it will wash the *horrible* of the day away. I scrub furiously at my body, wasting no time in getting the sticky residue of death and violence off my skin. My nose and eyes start to sting as the grime and blood are washed away, and for the second time today, I feel the need to break.

I don't know if it's the guilt over not being able to help Sennet and Taria, the brutal, tragic way they were killed, or the relief I feel that my life didn't end like I thought it would. I shouldn't be here in this tub, trying to figure out what comes next, but I am.

I am, when they're not.

Tears trail down my cheeks and plop soundlessly into the dirty bathwater, as though my pain hopes to cleanse the pool of all the blood and anguish. I bite down on a clean rag to help muffle a sob that refuses to be swallowed down and denied.

I open the doors in my mind to the horrors of what happened to them. To me. To the others that have come and gone in my time here. Distress shakes through my limbs as images of Gartox's sinister face and evil words flicker in my head. It adds new cuts to my soul. I'm already so scarred, so filled with wounds I have no idea how to heal from. I gave the Scorpions a peek, and I couldn't even say why. The moment I mentioned what Tilleo had done, I unlocked and opened a vault that I should have left well enough alone. Now, I'm scrambling to shove all the loose memories and emotions back inside when they don't want to go. I suppose I can't blame them; who wants to spend their entire existence in a cage?

For the first time in a long time, I try to force my way past the wall in my mind that keeps me from going further than the night I woke up in the room of cages. Maybe it's knowing that the Scorpions remember that has me trying so hard to be able to do the same. But nothing I do or try uncovers anything new. Just like always, everything beyond that night is gone. *This* is all that I am, no matter how much I might wish otherwise.

I wipe at my eyes, drain the tub, and fill it back up again. I try to find solace in the routine of washing my hair and my body until everything on the outside is once again a perfect mask for what's going on inside. Fading moonlight kisses my skin, healing the last of my physical wounds and helping to fortify my defenses once more. Brick by brick, I sit in the cool water of the tub and shore myself up. I breathe through the sorrow until, once again, it's a quiet hum at the back of my mind. And then I step out of the tub and ready myself for whatever is going to come next.

18

I STARE AT WILIK'S STOOL IN THE DARK OF THE adornment room, wondering if I can smash it without anyone hearing. Arched windows leak pre-dawn light across the table that Figg is usually perched behind, and I can barely make out the togs on the shelves at the back of the room. I move silently and pick out a pair of leather trousers and a tunic from the piles she usually pulls my clothes from. I add chest bindings and underwear to the collection, and then I step back to the other side of the table and start to pull everything on.

It's strange to be in this space while no one else is here. It feels dead without Figg and Wilik and their fussing and walloping. I hate that their abuse and griping feels normal, that I feel off because they're not in here with me to administer it. The tunic fits snugly, but I'm too tired to try to find a bigger size. I run a comb through my hair until the teeth can't find any more tangles, and then I break it. I can't get away with shattering the stool we're forced to sit on while she pulls and yanks and slaps at us, but I can ruin her tools well enough. I leave the pieces all over her station in the corner, wishing I could see her face when she waltzes into the room in the morning.

A self-satisfied smile is stretched wide across my mouth as I slip out of the adornment room and turn and run hard into a large body. I reach for the dagger at my back that's tucked in the waist of my leathers, ready to cut down whoever this is, when a familiar voice whispers down to me.

"What are you doing here?" Leto asks quietly as his arms reach out to steady me.

Relief warms me as I look up into a gaze I would know anywhere.

"What are you doing?" I demand instead, pointedly looking around at the female end of the hall.

Behind me is our bathing chamber. The males bathe on the other side of that, and their quarters are all the way down at the end of the hall.

"I was looking for you actually, but you weren't in bed," he admits, and I'm both surprised and confused by that. He rubs at the back of his neck, and a sheepish gleam enters his stare as he shrugs his shoulders, aiming for flippant but falling short. "The final day of the Bidding is later today, so I just thought…"

I study his face, too tired to feel enticed by what he's saying. Then again, maybe my sleeping quarters aren't the wisest place to wait out whatever Tilleo or the Scorpions might send my way. Actually, now that I think about it, I'd be dumb to think that isn't the first place someone would look for me.

It's the time of day that isn't quite night or morning, and a purple tint paints the walls of the hall around us. It won't be long before the sun starts to inch closer and closer to the horizon, and who knows what the day will have in store for me after that.

"Okay," I offer softly, and amusement flares in my chest when Leto looks pleasantly surprised.

"Really?" he presses and then shakes his head as though he's a dolt for even questioning it. He grabs my hand and pulls me down the hall and out into the inner walkway of the ludere.

I stiffen when he guides us around a corner without even pausing to check for a guard, and Leto smiles at me over his shoulder.

"Don't worry, the guards were pulled a little while ago. I was up to piss when something happened up at the manor. They were pulled in to help with it," he assures me, and my stomach drops. "That's why I thought I'd come get you; no better time to sneak off than when there's no one around to notice." Leto smiles, and he's so genuinely happy about this turn of events that it makes me want to feel it too.

He turns back, and for a brief moment, I wonder what the Scorpions look like when they smile. Not the cheeky, controlled, arrogant grins that I've been given since I met them, but an overjoyed and gleeful widening of their lips, until their entire face was alight with pure happiness. Maybe I'll ask for that before they kill me. That is *if* they try to kill me. But really what other option is there? I don't see Tilleo putting me up for sale to the other Orders. The Scorpions don't buy blade slaves. And I'll slit my own throat before I get sold at a flesh market.

Leto gestures for me to go first up the ladder that leads to the roof, and I try to push down my wayward thoughts and pay attention to what I'm doing.

"Do you know what happened up at the manor?" I fish as I ascend higher up the rungs.

"Not sure, but I think it was something to do with the Order of Bruins. They were arguing with Tilleo out front when I was watching to see if the guards were really all leaving. Some slaves ran out to the stables to hitch sand stags to a carriage. I figured I'd ask Yotta and Taur about it in the morning since they're assigned to them. Maybe they took a hunt or something," Leto hypothesizes from behind me.

"Maybe," I agree, my mind whirring at what I know is really going on.

Did they buy that Sennet got the best of Gartox? Technically it's the truth. Not that I can tell anyone I was there and saw it with my own eyes. There's also the small fact that I tried to rip his throat out with my bare teeth. What if I didn't cover it up as well as I thought? I want to ask Leto if he saw the Order of Scorpions out front with Tilleo and the Bruins. Scorpius said he was going to talk to the master, but I keep my stupid questions to myself.

The sky lightens even more in the short time it takes for us to reach our spot, and I can already tell today is going to be blazing hot. The air is getting thick and choking off the chill of the desert night. I keep low, knowing the half wall that encloses the roof only blocks so much until we get closer to the guard room built in the middle. I step into the dusty space that's only big enough to fit a few cots and a stool. There are cutouts in the sandstone walls, which allow the guard posted here a full view of the ludere and surrounding property, but a patrol hasn't been assigned to this place for over a year.

Apparently, Tilleo feels more than safe with sentries only walking the top of the wall surrounding the stronghold, as well as an occasional check inside the ludere itself. It didn't take long for some of the more cunning blade slaves to claim this spot for ourselves. I straighten when I toe the corner of the threadbare blanket that someone stole and laid up here. The cots and stool are long gone, and I tap one of the rocks that keeps the thin blanket from blowing away with my foot for good luck. I know I'm going to need it.

Leto grabs my waist and presses me to the side so he can tap his foot against the small stone too. I don't know if this is *our* thing or if it's a ritual passed down from other blade slaves, but we always do it when we sneak up here.

"We survived this place," Leto declares, his proud stare now fixed on the world around us. His words settle against my skin like the warning mist of a rare Corozean rain, and I want to shush him so he doesn't curse it. Then again, everything about today feels like a never-ending curse.

"I didn't think Tilleo was going to heal you until morning, but I'm glad to see he showed a little mercy," Leto tells me, and I scoff at the thought of Tilleo's mercy. Leto should know better.

I study his face and shake my head, tempted to tell him about everything that's happened, but I quickly decide against it. We don't share those parts of each other; why change now on the eve of never seeing each other again?

"Where do you think you'll go?" I ask to fill the silence that starts to stretch between us. Usually he's pulling his clothes off by now or doing his best to get me out of mine. I'm surprised at the lack of urgency tonight. Then again, I didn't exactly come up here for a quick fuck, I came because I wanted a decent place to hide. Maybe he can tell I'm not in the mood.

Leto offers me a warm smile and reaches up to wrap a strand of my hair around his finger. "You don't usually have it down like this," he observes as he plays with the straight lock that looks bluer than it is from the bruised light of early morning. "I think I have a good shot at the Order of Corvus or maybe even the Order of Wolves," he answers, his eyes roaming over my face as though he's working to memorize it.

"No Order of Serpents?" I ask, because I can't think what else to say when he looks at me like that and something thick and uncertain starts to build between us.

I look away from him as I try to figure out what's going on here and why it feels so different. Tilleo's manor stands tall and forbidding in the distance. The sandstone peaks that tower over the wings of his residence paint pointed shadows on the sand as the sun starts to consider waking up. The tall wall that surrounds us hides the sandy hills beyond that stretch as far as the eye can see, or so we're told by anyone who's allowed outside of the large front gates.

"I think they're looking for a female this Bidding," he answers absently, stepping closer until our chests tease each other every time we breathe in.

I study him, trying to interpret the intensity I see in his gaze. The light skims across him in a way that encourages his tan skin to glow. He looks ethereal in this moment, and if I didn't know better, I could be convinced that salvation might be found in his eyes.

"You're beautiful, Auset," he starts, brushing the back of his hand over my cheek.

"Did one of the guards let you puff from their pix weed again?" I question, ensuring my tone comes across playful, but everything about this is putting me on edge.

Leto and I don't do this. There's no softness or poetry in how we are with each other. He's behaving as though I'm some dimwitted female in need of admiration and approval. But I've never needed or wanted flowery words and bullshit promises.

Sweat starts to collect at the small of my back, and it has nothing to do with the sun's imminent rise or the way it will heat the desert's sands to unpleasant and punishing degrees. I study the male who helped me find myself when I thought I was lost and beyond saving. I take in his straight nose and sharp jaw and the lips that aided me in taking back control and finding power in what happens between a male and a female when they both want it to. I chased gratification against his hard body and found an escape that helped me survive this place.

Now, as Leto looks down at me, the hint of nerves alight in his brow as he puts on an act that he should know I've never needed, I start to suspect that I'm about to find betrayal in his arms too.

"What did Tilleo offer you?" I ask, all hesitancy and pretense gone between us.

I step back and casually drop my hand to my side so I can reach for the dagger at my back. His amber gaze tracks my movement, and I pause not wanting to give myself away just yet.

He sighs and rubs the back of his neck. "Why would he offer *me* anything when he can simply order this?" he counters, the heat that was simmering in his words gone as though it was never there.

He has a point, but something in his face tells me this is a choice and not a command.

"You're about to be bid on later today," I remind him. "Tilleo knows sending anyone after me is a risk. He would have sweetened the deal; we both know it."

If Tilleo *ordered* this, if he was going to force someone's hand, he'd choose the blade slave most likely to succeed. According to the ranks that would be Harsh, not Leto. Harsh recently learned that I'm more formidable than he thought. Leto, on the other hand, doesn't know that...yet. I know him and he only takes risks when there's something in it for him.

Carefully, I inch my hand closer to my dagger, trying hard not to draw any attention to the slight movement.

"I think I deserve to know what he offered you to kill me," I press, needing just another beat before my weapon is in reach.

Leto pulls his hand from his neck, and my heart drops. I realize too late that he wasn't rubbing the back of his neck out of nerves. He had a chakram hidden behind his back.

The perfectly circular blade slashes down at me, and I don't have enough time to grab for my dagger. My arm goes up to try to keep Leto from burying the chakram in my throat. The sharp blade sinks into my forearm, cutting me open to the bone. However, it's the sudden punch of another razor sharp chakram deep in my gut that makes me gasp in shock.

He had two.

Two deadly weapons somehow hidden behind his back, and now they're both mortally embedded in me.

"Any Order I want," he grunts in answer as he tries to pull the bladed circle from my stomach.

I snatch his hand and use all my strength to hold the chakram there, knowing if he pulls it out, it will eviscerate me. The times we fought in the ring or trained against each other, I always let Leto think he was stronger than me. Surprise flashes in his determined gaze when he realizes that he's not. Immediately he stops struggling to pull the chakram from my stomach and targets the blade still in my arm to finish this once and for all.

Before he can, I yank him closer, trying not to think about the damage the chakram is doing to my gut as my movements force it even deeper. I let my fangs drop as Leto stumbles into me. I revel in the terror that washes over his face as we show one another the true monsters that have been lurking within all this time.

I rip into Leto's throat, and the scream that tries to rush out of him morphs into a wet gurgle. Leto has none of the thick corded muscle that Gartox had to protect his neck, and all too quickly, I feel his throat start to collapse under my bite. Hot blood pours out of him, spilling down my throat and drenching my chest. Blood sprays the roof and the walls of the abandoned guard house as my fangs puncture something vital in Leto's neck. He immediately weakens, his jerky defensive strikes and efforts to get me off him slowing until they're nothing more than muscle twitches.

I drink Leto down until his body sags and grows too heavy to hold. The betrayal tainting the flavor of him begins to taste of death, and with one more deep gulp, I peel his fingers from the round blade in my stomach and then shove Leto's body away from me. He hits a wall and crumples to the ground, death spasms already draining the last of his life as the remainder of his blood starts to puddle beneath him. Pain ripples through me, and I whimper, which makes my stomach muscles tighten, and the horrifying wounds there flare with agony. I wipe my mouth but remember too late that my other arm is injured badly and bleeding too.

With a brutal yank that feels like it saps the last of my energy, I pull the chakram from my arm. It drops with a clang to the floor of the roof. I cry out as I try to step out of the guard house. Agony rebounds through me, and I quickly realize that I'm not going to be able to get to the ladder, let alone climb down it and stumble to the healing chamber. I consider calling out for help, but all the guards are gone, and everyone else in the ludere knows better than to go searching for the source of someone's screams or pleas. I don't even know if the healers would help me or if Tilleo has already ordered them to let me die too.

A shuddering sob works its way up my chest, and I decide to do the one thing I probably shouldn't do. The only thing I can think that *might* save me. I step back into the shadows of the guard house and beg the darkness to take me to *them*.

19

BONES

I RUN THE TIP OF MY FINGER AROUND THE RIM OF the half empty glass in front of me, my thoughts restless and heavy and nowhere near calm enough to allow me to sleep. Skull's soft snores fill the otherwise quiet tent, and the chair beneath me creaks as I lean back and stretch. The draft Scorpius took before bed knocked him out. I've noticed, since we arrived, that he's relied on the sleep aid more here than he normally does. He won't admit it, but I know Auset is the reason.

The crystal tumbler is cool against my lips as I take a sip of the thick golden liquid. I stare at nothing as I try—and fail miserably—to see anything other than *her*, sitting on the ground in that fucker's room with her knees pulled up to her chest like she was trying to make herself as small as possible. She looked completely devastated and scared and surrounded by death.

We did that to her.

I know, at the time, we didn't have any options. We were on a hunt and had one more target yet to deal with. Dorsin's stronghold was warded—something my brothers and I remedied shortly after—but we couldn't shadow walk anywhere. It wouldn't have been safe to take her, not for Auset or for us. Or maybe I'm telling myself that to assuage the guilt currently coursing through me like a tidal wave.

The truth is that we might have gotten too good at ignoring the plight of the fae we come across as we move about the realms to hunt. It was a defense mechanism at first. Something each of us had to become adept at because it was impossible to save everyone we came across who needed it. We looked at Auset, but we didn't want to see her. We didn't want to find a way to help her. We'd grown too apathetic, too selfish. A certainty made worse by the fact that each of my brothers and I were rescued by someone who would never turn her back on anyone.

I never viewed any of it through the lens of dishonor, but I can't see it any other way now. We dishonored Eacon. We dishonored ourselves. We left Auset in Dorsin's chambers, and *this* is what they did to her. She couldn't have been older than thirty-five, on the cusp of maturity, scared, and innocent. It's only been a handful of years since the night that we abandoned her, but the change is undeniable. I remember her fear, the plea in her eyes as she looked up at us from her chains. All of that is gone now. She's hardened now, brutal, enraged. We threw her to the wolves, and the battle being waged inside of her because of it is condemning. One moment she looks capable of burning the world to the ground to get where she wants to go, but in the next blink, she's hollow, lost, like she's ready for it all to be over. I can't stop seeing that war in her eyes, and I hate that I don't know which side of her will win.

Liquid burns down my throat, the stinging pain almost a kiss of penance as Auset's words swirl around in my mind. She talked about being beaten and starved and sold off to monsters as though it was an everyday occurrence. The reality that it was for her is driving me mad. I can't stop thinking about it. I can't stop hating myself for what they did to her. I can't stop loathing that it's our fault.

It can be easy to feel privileged and important as a Scorpion, given what we do and what we've worked to build. My brothers and I have more than earned the awe and the genuflection, but I feel lower than sarkar shit right now. I know the world we live in is a cruel one. The three of us alone are proof of all the ways the realms can wrong us, but we've tried to create some semblance of balance through our actions. We don't *just* hunt for coin. The Order of Scorpions takes pride in destroying the depraved and deserving. The realms should be rid of the monsters that plague them. My brothers and I are all too happy to cut them down, but it's not enough. I understand that now in a way I haven't before.

I've never cared about what went down in this ludere until now. Our connection to this place was about results, about placing integral pieces that we controlled on the board the realms are playing on, but we fucked up. It took a pair of silver eyes, a smart mouth, and an unhealthy lack of fear for us to see it. The Order of Scorpions hasn't been paying enough attention, and that's a serious fucking problem. Now, all the ways we mucked shit up are screaming in our face, and I don't even know where to begin to fix any of it.

I tilt the rest of the contents in my cup down my throat and try not to choke on the liquid fire that spills from my mouth down into my stomach. I should feel relieved that Scorpius told Tilleo that we're claiming Auset later in today's Bidding. It should ease some of my worry, that my brother made it clear to the master that he's not to bring any more batches of slaves into the ludere until we tell him otherwise, until we can fix everything that's fucked up. But it's done nothing to alleviate the tension and shame still churning in my gut. It's not enough. I don't know if anything we ever do will be to her, or the others here that deserved better.

A weary sigh escapes me, and I run a tired hand over my head, the rough feel of my short hair against my palm grounding. Out of nowhere, the atmosphere in the tent suddenly changes. I freeze. Every muscle in my body is suddenly on high alert as I discreetly scan my surroundings in search of what's triggering my internal alarms.

"Bones," her frail voice pleads, the sound barely more than a pained whisper. Auset staggers out of a shadow, and my heart plummets as I take her in.

Like she used up all of her strength just getting here, she starts to pitch forward, and I rush to catch her. She's covered in blood. The muscle and skin of one of her arms flaps precariously away from the bone it should be attached to. But it's the chakram she's pressing into her stomach, and what I know it means, that sends terror hammering away at me. Scorpius and Skull both rush out of their beds as I catch our little moonbeam before she can hit the ground and do even more damage to herself.

I hate the groan of pain that leaks out of her bloodied lips, but there's no safe place to touch or good way to carry her that isn't going to hurt. There's too much damage.

Why is there so much damage?

"Who the fuck did this?" Skull snarls as he rushes to her side while I carry her to the black maple table and set her gently down on top of it.

She looks half dead already, and my heart races with panic as it tries to settle heavily back into my chest. Sticky blood coats her mouth and lips as though she's been coughing it up. Streaks and splatters of crimson are drying in the light strands of her long, wild hair. The rich tan of her skin is sickly and sallow, making the smattering of freckles across her nose and cheeks darken and stand out. Her tunic and pants are soaked with scarlet, and I start to question if she has any blood left in her small body.

"Skull, go get a healer," Scorpius barks from Auset's other side as he positions the linens from his bed around the chakram and then pushes down on the split in her abdomen.

He hurries to pack the wound and apply more pressure, as Skull soundlessly steps into a shadow and disappears. I rip my tunic off and hurry to wrap her shredded arm, ignoring the flashes of bone the deep gash reveals as I do. She writhes and whimpers against what Scorpius and I are doing to her, but there's no avoiding it. I apply as much pressure as I can and hold her arm up to try to help with the bleeding.

"I thought you said Tilleo knew he wasn't allowed to fuck with her anymore?" I snap at Scorpius as another pained keen from Auset sets every nerve in my body on edge.

I need to stab something. Tear into someone. Scream until my voice is gone and the rage has dulled to a low roar in my chest, but I can't. All I can do is watch helplessly and hope with everything that she doesn't die before Skull gets back.

"He's fucking dead," Scorpius snarls in answer, and he repositions his hands to keep the chakram from digging any deeper while also making sure that Auset's intestines don't spill out.

"Mine," Auset gasps out. "Tilleo is mine," she croaks more harshly, but first we need to save her, then I can go about giving her whatever it is that she wants in this world.

I drop my fangs and press my mouth to my inner wrist. Quickly, I pierce my flesh with the sharper canines, the pinch of pain a small payment for the healing I'm calling on. Blood fills my mouth, and I pull my fangs out and position my arm above her stomach. Carefully I direct the steady flow of blood to spill from me onto the circular chakram blade, and then watch as it drips down into her wounds. My blood won't be enough to heal her completely, especially not when the damn weapon is still in her, but it can start to repair what it can, which could make some difference before the healer comes.

Skull strides out of the shadows with a lanky elderly healer in his grip. The balding fae is being carried into the room by his nape, as though the fucker was unwilling to come, or maybe Skull didn't waste time on the invite and just grabbed him. His robes dangle around his feet, the dirty fabric swaying jerkily from Skull's rough treatment as he shoves the healer at the table where Auset is lying.

"Fix her," he barks, his tone filled with promises of death and agony if the healer doesn't do exactly as commanded.

"Tilleo ordered us not to," the healer squeaks out, and if the situation weren't more dire, I might be impressed with the set of balls this shit must have to talk back to a member of the Order of Scorpions.

"You either start pumping her full of healing magic right this fucking second or I won't just kill *you* very slowly and very painfully, I'll track down every member of your blood, every person you've ever talked to or even looked at, and I'll do the exact same thing to them," Scorpius seethes, and all the color drains from the healer's wrinkled face.

He looks down at Auset, his eyes softening and his hands hesitating above her as though he doesn't know where to begin. The entire front of her tunic is soaked in scarlet, and I realize at the same time the healer does that she might have other wounds that we can't see.

"Skull, take her arm," I call out, and my brother is there before the command is all the way out of my mouth. "I'll check her for wounds up here, you fix her stomach," I tell the healer, and he nods and starts chanting as he begins to pull out the bed linens Scorpius packed into the grizzly gash in her abdomen.

Scorpius holds the chakram still, and we all work in tandem as though we're a finely tuned team. Auset's eyes are closed, and I think she's passed out, the blood loss and injuries all too much for her body to handle. But when I pull a dagger from my thigh and start cutting away at her tunic, silver eyes snap open, her gaze luminescent, pained, searching.

"Hey, little moonbeam," I soothe as I cut the blood-soaked fabric from her body, careful not to jostle anything that Scorpius and the healer are working on in her stomach.

My eyes stay fixed on hers, and I wish, not for the first time, that I wasn't wearing this fucking glamour so she could be staring into *my* eyes and not the black orbs that Scorpius's power, his thura, morphs them into.

"You're going to be okay," I reassure her, and she nods once weakly, like she believes me.

She makes a fist with her good hand, squeezing it tight once before relaxing, and I reach out and grip her delicate palm in my larger callused grip.

"I'm going to check you for other wounds, is that okay?" I ask as I pinch a corner of her bloody tunic with my free hand.

She licks her dry, blood-caked lips and nods again. Wasting no time, I quickly peel the sticky top away from her skin and look down to search for stab wounds or more cuts. Her chest is wrapped, and I scan the crimson-stained fabric for puncture wounds or pooling blood, but I don't see anything. Urgently, I look over her throat, trying to figure out where all of this blood is coming from, but I don't see any seeping cuts or scratches or anything else that would account for all of it.

Auset cries out, and I jerk my head up to see that the healer and Scorpius are pulling the chakram from her stomach. I look away when a lake of blood pools in her abdomen and starts to form a river to the ground.

No. No. No. No. No!

Her agonized wail rips into my depths and demands that I do everything in my power never to hear that sound torn out of her again.

"Shhh," Skull whispers soothingly as he smooths hair away from her face and tries to pull her attention away from what's happening to her.

"It hurts," she pants.

It breaks my fucking heart.

I'm going to track down whoever did this to her, and I'm going to rip them into tiny pieces, bit by bit. I'm going to scatter their parts across the realms so all fae know that you don't fuck with the Order of Scorpions. No one will so much as glare her way by the time I'm done making it clear that to do so is a death sentence.

"I know, but it'll stop soon," Skull answers comfortingly.

The healer wipes at his sweaty head with his sleeve, the few strands of hair he has left soaking with stress and perspiration. His hand is covered in Auset's blood, and I know it's a sight that's going to haunt me.

Shit. Maybe we need another healer. This one looks ready to keel over soon.

As though he can read my mind, Skull grumbles, "More are coming. I took this one and shouted for the others to grab supplies and then run here." He looks over at the flaps of the tent expectantly, and I blow out a tense breath.

Auset's hand tightens in mine, and I look down at her. She's so pale. Her eyes are squeezed shut tightly as she grits her teeth and tries not to make a noise.

"Hey," I call to her, moving closer to her face and trying to think of what might distract her from the tugs at her abdomen and the frantic chanting of the healer while Scorpius clips orders to the now shaking and quickly draining fae.

She opens her eyes and levels me with a stare that silently begs me to make the pain stop. I would do anything right now to be able to do just that. I scramble for something to say, for some way to make this better, but nothing comes to me.

"Tell me about where you grew up? What's it like? What's your favorite memory?" I stammer in hopes it will do the trick and pull her mind momentarily from the trauma of everything that's happening right now.

Auset's moonlit gaze narrows, and I can't help the smile that warms my face at the tiny irate fire that sparks in her eyes.

"Why are you Scorpions so dim?" she rasps, the words requiring far too much effort as they slip out of her lush, blood-stained lips. "I already told you, I don't remember anything before I came here," she whispers, her words brittle and fissuring.

The flaps of the tent are shoved open, and in pour several more healers with leather cases clutched tightly in their hands. Worry loosens its talons around my throat, and Scorpius immediately starts snapping orders and instructions as healers join us around the table and add their own voices to the sacred chant that focuses their magic, guiding it to stitch and seal and smooth all of the injuries away.

A healer takes her arm from Skull, and my brother moves to the top of her head, running his fingers through her hair and whispering things in Auset's ear that are too quiet for me to hear. I've never seen him be so tender with anyone. If there were any doubt about how far Auset had already sunk under our skin, the display between Skull and the little Moonling would chase it all away.

"Fine, you're right," I concede, recalling that she did tell us that she doesn't know where she came from or how she got here. I thought she was just being evasive, but now I see maybe we read that wrong.

"Tell me about yours," she asks faintly instead. "What was it like where you grew up?" She leans into Skull's touch, her eyes once again closing as though she doesn't have the energy to keep them open anymore. Her hand starts to go slack in mine, and dread takes flight like a million crows flapping around in my chest.

"Stay here with me, Auset," I snap, getting in her face, like my will alone can keep her from slipping away.

Her lids flicker back, and once more, stunning silver eyes find mine. I teeter on the edge of what to do, looking over at the group of healers working on our moonbeam. Resignation rides my deep exhale, and then I lean closer to Auset and chant a ward that will keep what I say between her and me and Skull.

"I grew up in a palace," I proclaim calmly, allowing none of the trepidation that's tightening my throat to leak into my words. My eyes sparkle invitingly, and I force smooth, practiced charisma into my tone, daring Auset to follow where I want my story to take her. "Before you rush to perfect your curtsey," I warn her playfully, "I wasn't a prince. Although, many have said over the years that I have the countenance for it," I tease, and Skull scoffs.

Not even his amused judgment can keep the grin from spreading across my face as one corner of Auset's mouth tilts up in fleeting enjoyment.

"My mother was a kitchen maid, and if you ask me, being her son was even better than being the heir to the throne," I hurry to continue, ignoring the twinge of pain that stabs at my soul as thoughts of my mother rush forward from where I normally keep them buried. "I got to run all around the castle, learning every private passage and secret held within the dragon stone walls. And then me and all the other children of the palace slaves sat through boring lessons with haughty tutors, learning the same silly things the princes and princesses had to learn, all because the king thought it made him look more magnanimous than he really was." I scoff and then fake a dramatic gag, and that small twitch of amusement at the corner of Auset's lips appears again.

All too quickly it turns into a pained gasp, and Skull smooths his fingers over the agonized clench of her features. "Almost done," he assures her, leaning down to kiss her forehead as though sealing that promise into her skin.

"My mother made the best food," I start again, recalling fondly the times that we braided pastry crust together or basted a big fat pheasant in the oven. "She always let us sneak the scraps the royal family didn't eat. And on rest days, we'd pack baskets of victuals that were going to turn soon, and we'd carry them down into the city and pass it all out. We played tag in the streets as we slowly walked home to the palace afterward. The sun made the dragon stone of the palace glow blue, and the wind would sing a song to us as it snaked through the tall stalks of crops that filled the fields in rows all around the city."

"Sounds beautiful," Auset murmurs so quietly I almost don't catch it.

"It was, until it wasn't," I agree, running my thumb softly over her cheek while I hold her hand in my other fist. "I'll show you sometime," I promise her, but I can see unconsciousness wrap her up in its hold and finally pull her under.

A healer brings a basin of warm water to the table and starts wiping blood from Auset's skin, looking for anything else that needs attention. It feels wrong to let them handle her this way when she's not awake, and I have to fight the urge to rip the cloth from the healer's hands and do it myself. Skull picks up the discarded chakram and shoves it into a pack in his trunk. I don't question what he'll do with it; Skull always has his reasons.

I fidget and remove the ward I cast to keep my words to Auset private as the healers continue to work on her. I know the damage was worse than I thought simply by how many of them already look like they're going to pass out, and that understanding makes it impossible to sit still as they continue to work. They've only been here a short while, but the thura required to bring our moonbeam back from the brink of death is taking an obvious toll on many of the gifted fae. I will let her drain each and every one of them dry if that's what it takes, and I won't even blink twice about it.

Skull moves next to me, handing me a pitcher of water before crossing his arms over his chest as though he's standing guard over something priceless and precious. That's exactly what she is.

"What do we do now?" I ask, my stare fixed on the slow rise and fall of Auset's chest as she sleeps while the healers continue to clean her up and chase away the last of the damage.

Scorpius steps back from the table, that action alone supporting that she's stable enough for him to accept that the healers can take it from here. The apprehension I've been wearing like a second skin from the moment Auset stumbled out from the shadows starts to crack and fall away. She's going to be okay. We'll make sure of it. Scorpius looks as exhausted as I know we all feel. The adrenaline is crashing in all of us as the worst of this drops back to trail behind us. He looks over at me and Skull, and I can see that he's plotting and planning and working out how to maneuver everything so that we're once again a step ahead of anything that could come our way. He reaches for a rag and starts to methodically clean Auset's blood from his hands and arms.

"Now..." he answers, his black eyes growing even darker as he looks from us to the tiny blade slave that's passed out on the black maple table. "We get the fuck out of here, and we take her with us."

20

AUSET

I GROAN, EVERY MUSCLE IN MY BODY STIFF AND tight as though I haven't moved in days. I'm lying on something soft, and I nuzzle deeper into the velvety warmth, teetering on the edge of sleep and consciousness. Somewhere in the back of my mind, I'm faintly aware that there should be pain. The last thing I remember was hot agony and sharp suffering before cold numbness crawled through me and snuffed everything out.

My mouth is dry, and my eyelids feel gritty as I finally come to enough to realize that I've never slept on anything warm and soft my entire time here at the ludere. That's enough to send bolts of alarm zinging through my mind, and I open my eyes and sit up with a gasp.

Am I dead?

My head spins and I jerk away from a figure that rises from a cushy wingback chair in the corner of an unfamiliar room.

"It's okay, Auset. You're safe," the female reassures me, her arms out in front of her as though she's hoping to calm the wild animal in me.

"Safe?" I croak, the word tasting strange on my stale tongue.

I look around, keeping the woman in my line of sight as I try to absorb where I am.

The orange-brown of the sandstone walls and floors I've known since I can remember, are missing. In their place are deep gray rock walls and rich umber-hued wood for floors. The fairy light that floats in the sconces all around the room has a purple hue to it instead of the yellow tone I've looked at my entire time in Tilleo's stronghold. A chill runs up my arms as a thick fur pools at my waist, and I realize the air here is heavy and cold and completely different from the arid desert atmosphere I'm used to.

"Where am I?" I demand, my voice parched and panicked as I scoot further back in the massive bed until my back hits the cold wood of an elaborately carved headboard.

A large tunic envelops me, the material thick and fluffy and distracting, but I ignore all the confusion and questions swarming inside of me and watch the tall female as she reaches for a silver pitcher and the matching cup that's sitting on the bedside table. She offers me a warm smile and the cup of water she just poured, but I stay pressed against the vines that are carved into the wood at my back.

"They're going to be upset that they listened to me," she answers cryptically, tilting the cup of water closer in encouragement. "I just convinced them to go clean up and rest. I should have known you'd choose that time to wake up," she teases, as though we know each other well enough to laugh about something like this.

Her face scrunches up in a way that tells me she smiles a lot and finds joy in her day-to-day life. Her azure blue eyes are soft and comforting, her gray dress drab and made of a thick material I've never seen before. Her hair is the same color as her dress, which I realize is the same color as the stone walls, but she has thick white streaks that add a bright dimension that makes her look lovely instead of worn. The rosy hue in her cheeks speaks of good health as does the lean muscle I can just make out under the thick layers of her simple floor-length dress.

I don't know what to make of her, but she looks entirely too disarming to be trusted. I tense, hoping my legs will support the sprint I'm about to make for the door, but she shakes her head, her kind blue eyes filling with a knowing glint that gives me pause.

"I know you're scared, Auset, but I promise you're safe here. Nothing bad is going to happen."

I'm already shoring up my defenses with wary mistrust before she can finish that sentence. With a resigned look on her face, she unsheathes a long knife from the belt that's cinching her waist. With comfortable and practiced movements, she flips the weapon until the hilt is facing me, and it's as though she's just pushed back a cloak to reveal the seasoned warrior hiding beneath her amiable surface. She stretches out her arm, offering me the small dagger, and I snap it out of her hand like a striking snake. She gives me an even wider smile.

"My name is Eacon. I help run the orphanage in the village," she explains, and my brow furrows with bewilderment.

Why am I in an orphanage?

What village?

As though Eacon can see the questions written all over my face, she laughs softly. "You're in the castle of Scorpions, my dear. The Order brought you back with them, which I must say was a very pleasant surprise," she tells me, her benevolent mien warming even more. "You've been asleep for three days, and according to the Scorpions, for the two-day journey before that. You've been through a lot."

She studies me in a way that makes me think that the last part wasn't just about my unconscious travels here.

"Are you not a Scorpion too?" I query, getting the impression that she isn't, but I never did find out how many members of the Order there are.

She laughs quietly, the question apparently more amusing than I intended it to be. "No, there are only three members of the Order of Scorpions...for now," she answers somewhat cryptically.

Her revelation surprises me. That can't be right, but my thoughts are a chaotic whir, and all I can seem to absorb are my strange surroundings. Closed floor-to-ceiling drapes the color of early morning mist cover what I think are evenly spaced windows in the wall opposite the bed. There's a round table and two matching chairs to the left of me, and a huge fireplace tall enough for a fae to walk right into on the right rock wall. I suspect a closed door over Eacon's right shoulder leads out into the rest of the Scorpions' castle, while a darkened entryway to her left probably leads to a bathing chamber if this castle is as opulent as it seems to be at a glance.

I stare, hesitant and unsure, as I catalog everything, and then it hits me...I'm not at the ludere anymore. My gaze bounces around the room once more as though I need everything I see to ground me in reality. I'm not surrounded by sand, and heat, and masters. Somehow I got away.

I pull in a deep shocked gasp and press my palm to my lips. Each beat that passes feels like it pushes against the boulder of captivity and subjugation that's been crushing me for as long as I can remember. The brutal weight of it all teeters and tips until the gray rock walls and the cold air of my new surroundings pull me from the onerous force that's been bearing down on me for too long. My heart gallops as reality catches up with my drowsy mind. I reach down to clutch the fur throw to my chest, desperate for some semblance of comfort and reassurance as everything sinks in. My eyes prick with tears, and my mind snaps momentarily from worry to relief to trepidation like a pixie that can't make up its mind where to land.

I made it out.

I don't know what I've made it out to, but I did, and that's enough right now. I blink back tears that threaten to spill over onto my cheeks, and pull ragged breaths into my chest. Eacon moves a step closer, her arm still outstretched and offering me the cup of water. Shakily, I reach up and take it, swallowing down the cold liquid like it's the best thing I've ever tasted. When it empties too quickly, she takes it back from me, fills it up again, and gently returns it to my palm. I sip slower and try to get a hold of my frenzied emotions. I'm not in the ludere. I'm not in the Corozean desert. But I'm not free either. I've been bought by the Order of Scorpions, and I have no idea what that means for me.

Eacon watches me thoughtfully, and just when I think she's going to start asking a bunch of questions I doubt I have the answers to, she steps away from the bed and starts to pull the tall drapes open across from me. I balk as she goes, staring out at an endless expanse of slate blue water. The sky is saturated with moody dark clouds, and I smell rain on the salty breeze that slips through the glass pane Eacon just opened. I can't tell what time of day it is, the lack of sun and the unfamiliar setting make it impossible to gauge if it's early morning, afternoon, or if the day is about to succumb to night's claim.

There's a large balcony that a set of glass doors leads out to. The tall windows on each side are framed by deep ledges wide enough to sit on. It's so different and strange from anything I've ever seen; I don't even know how to process it. Knife still gripped protectively in one hand, I'm out of the bed before I even realize what I'm doing. I touch my fingertips to the clear glass of one of the massive windows and marvel at how it looks as though we could drop into the cresting waves below at any moment. It's beautiful and alien and terrifying all at the same time.

"The castle is set on the Verdyn peninsula," Eacon explains, as though I should know where that is. "The village is on the other side of the Tinisk forest. It's not a large establishment, but we get or make everything we need," she continues conversationally. "The Scorpions have a small circle of trust, and many of the villagers don't know that they're anything more than privileged fae who've been given this land to watch over and govern. I ask that you keep that in mind as you find your place here. That you protect them like they will protect you, Auset," she states, leveling me with a steady, unwavering look. "Don't do anything that might put the Order in danger. If you do, you'll have more than them to answer to," she continues casually.

I say nothing as I watch her once again start to fuss about the room, pulling more drapes open on each side of the gargantuan bed before then straightening the wrinkled and tangled bedding I left behind. She doesn't seem to expect a response to her clear warning, which is good because I'm not sure what to do or say in answer to it. I'm utterly out of my depth right now, and my mind is a jumble of confusion and wariness.

I'm standing in someone else's clothes, in a strange home, with a woman who's obviously important to the Scorpions, and they her, based on her subtle flash of claws just now. I don't know which way to step or what's expected of me. I've fought so hard to get away, to arrive at the day when the ludere and Tilleo were far behind me, but now that I'm here I feel fucking lost.

"I should be getting back now that you're awake," Eacon announces, surprising me.

I don't know why, but I figured she'd guard me until the Scorpions showed up to tell me what in the stars is going on.

"There are some clothes in the chest," she tells me, pointing to the tall cabinet on the other side of the black table and chairs. "There isn't much to choose from, but the

Scorpions will get you sorted in time, I'm sure. It was nice to meet you. We'll talk again when you're settled and more up to it."

A kind smile stretches across her face again, and then she's moving toward the door, the skirt of her dress swishing as she goes. Part of me wants to ask her not to leave. I don't like the idea of being stuck here in a place I don't know with fae I don't think I can trust. But I say nothing as she opens the door and closes it softly behind her.

I stand there unsure about what to do. She said she just sent the Scorpions off to rest; does that mean they'll be back soon? Do I want them to be back soon? I look down at the small dagger still clutched in my hand and realize Eacon forgot to take it back. Or maybe she knew I'd feel better if I had it. Even that odd but caring thought throws me into a spiral of confusion I don't think I'll be surfacing from any time in the near future.

Why am I here?

The Order that never bids at the Biddings bought me, that much is obvious. I just wish I understood why.

Could they be as strangely drawn to me as I seem to be to them?

I ponder that for a moment. It's the first time I've admitted it to myself, but I'm here now and I can't pretend that it's not something I need to be cautious of. I shake my head at myself and huff out a vexed breath. I'm being foolish. They clearly want *something* and there's no way that's going to turn out to be a good thing for me.

My stomach grumbles, and I can't tell if it's from worry or hunger. Cautiously, I wander into the darkened doorway. Relief trickles through me when I discover it *is* a washroom, a well fitted and fine looking one at that. I use the toilet, grateful that the Scorpions have the magic for this instead of chamber pots. The tap creaks shrilly when I turn it so it can fill the large bath in the center of the room. I look around nervously, worried that someone will storm in here at any moment and flog me for touching things I shouldn't. Nothing happens.

Steam starts to rise from the stream of water that's pouring from the spout and I stare at it with pure astonishment. Any heat in the water at the ludere was pure happenstance and thanks to the brutal sun and sand warming the pipes all day. It's colder here, which means this warm water is a comfort the Scorpions are providing, and I'm shocked by it. They've put me in a comfortable room with soft things and warm water, and I don't know if I want to curl up in all of it and relish the offering or keep as far away as I can so I don't miss it if and when it's all taken away.

I adjust the knob until the temperature feels tolerable and then strip out of the large tunic.

I have nothing on underneath, which should feel unsettling, and yet all I can do is run my hands over my smooth stomach and marvel that there isn't even a scar from the chakram. I look over my arm, already knowing I won't find anything there but checking all the same. I've been healed on the brink of death before—more times than I can count now—and yet it still surprises me every time I'm brought back when it seemed so impossible.

My thoughts are fuzzy after what happened on the roof. I remember struggling to get to the tent. I was terrified the shadows would dump me somewhere else, but by some miracle they didn't. It was as though my thoughts guided the murky depths to take me exactly where I needed. I can still hear the skeletons as they yelled and barked out orders. I can feel their phantom hands on me as agony staked a claim. Whispers in my ear, quiet promises I couldn't grasp beyond the pain, but I reached for them all the same, and now...I'm here.

I sigh, running my fingers through my hair to push it back. It's tangled but clean, which shouldn't be the case unless someone bathed me while I was unconscious. I raise an arm and sniff at my armpit. I reel back as the aggressive stench of sweat, dirt, and blood assault me. Maybe they just washed my hair then. I cringe. Plucking what I need from an assortment of options from a cabinet in the corner, I then slip into the bath to scour myself until I'm squeaky clean. I try to picture the gruff, arrogant Scorpions caring for me, scrubbing blood from my hair, gently changing me into clean clothes. It doesn't fit with who and what I thought they were. Maybe their slaves did it.

I work rapidly, worried the Scorpions or someone else might come looking for me at any moment. I have no sense of whether that would be good or bad, and the uncertainty rushes me through things I wish I could take my time with. I drain the tub and hurry to fill it back up, still shocked that the faucet continues to proffer more blissful heat. I'm tempted to soak, to lie back in the water and float until all my worries trickle away, but I scoff at the ridiculous urge and hastily scrub my hair clean. The large basin of liquid warmth and comfort drains as I stand and sprinkle oil on my tresses to help keep it smooth and tangle free.

A surprised squeak sneaks out of my mouth when I reach for a towel from a stack by the tub and discover that it's the softest thing I've ever felt. I stare down at the fluffy fabric in awe as I run my hands over the plush downy material. I almost hate to taint it by using it to dry me. I check to see if there's anything else I can use, but there's only the large tunic I woke up in. I debate air drying, but it's cold. Hesitantly I rub the towel down my chest. Instantly, I want to lay it on the ground and roll around on it, it's so fluffy and nice and comforting. I stare at the stack of dreamy softness and barely fight the urge to create some kind of weird cocoon. Instead, I wrap the towel around me and tip toe back out into the main room.

It remains empty, but I pause in the doorway, listening for any signs that I'm no longer alone, just in case. Everything is still and quiet, so I sneak to the tall cabinet, open the doors, and cringe. Two dour looking brown dresses are hanging there.

Yeah, that's not happening.

I ignore the repellant clothing and pull open the first of four drawers that make up the bottom of the wardrobe. I huff out a deep sigh of relief when I discover several stacks of black tunics folded next to stacks of black trousers. The other drawers are filled with more of the same, and even though I'm not thrilled that there are no undergarments or chest bindings, this is better than nothing—and far better than the two heinous dresses.

I don't know what material the pants are made of. They're thick and pliant, almost like flexible armor. I have to stretch and force them over my legs, and the strange black material clings to me as though it's a second skin. Oddly, even though the bottoms are tight, the tunic I pull on is huge. It looks more like a dress than a shirt. It's as though they gave me tunics that fit them, but bottoms from someone tiny. I suppose it's better than tripping over a pair of baggy trousers if I need to make a run for it though. With that in mind, I rip the huge tunic up the front to my navel and then wrap the halves tightly around my waist before tying them. I tuck my new knife in one of the shirt loops and tug at the neck to keep it from falling off my shoulders.

My stomach growls angrily, and I stare longingly at the door that Eacon left through. I'm ravenous, but I don't know what to do about it. The Order of Scorpions are my new masters, and I don't know how long it will take before they check on me or what will happen when they do. Will I be allowed to eat? Will it be just like at the ludere? Another demanding gurgle sounds off, and I press my hand to my stomach as though I can silence it. If Eacon is telling the truth, I've been down for at least five days, and it's not as though I was well fed and could spare a meal or two before that. I start to pace, agitation and frustration building with each pass in front of the balcony doors.

Fury begins to fill every footstep, my anger growing with each second that ticks by. The more I think, the more I start to question everything. Why did I go to them? I thought they could save me, but I didn't think through *what* they'd be saving me for. I'm not in the ludere, but I'm once again trapped, a slave waiting on her masters, waiting to be commanded because I'm not allowed to have a mind of my own.

A frustrated growl slips out, and I turn to stare at the tumultuous sea, the frothing, undulating waves oddly similar to how I feel inside right now. I should have let myself die. I could have stopped fighting, and then I really would be free instead of sold and starting over as though it's my first day back at the ludere. I can't go through that again. I won't.

I thought I wanted a place in an Order, to work off my price until I was finally free, but what happened during the Bidding changed me. What Tilleo forced me to do awoke something in me. I got a taste for how good it felt, how freeing it was, to take back my compliance and submission. For the first time since I can remember, I stopped chasing survival at all costs and just...lived. I want more of that, and not later, dozens upon dozens of years from now when I *might* be able to pay off what the Scorpions purchased me for. I want it now.

I can't go back to being a slave. I won't cower and bow to another master, let alone three. I want to be my own and nothing more, and if I can't have that, I'd rather slit my throat right now.

I stare at the door knob as though it's some powerful force that can either condemn or liberate me. I wrap a palm around the handle of the knife Eacon left behind, pulling what strength I can from it as I reach for the knob with my other hand. My mind screams warnings about how fucking stupid this it. Leaving this room without permission and nosing about a castle that belongs to the strongest, scariest Order in all the realms is pure madness. I already know that Tilleo doesn't hold a candle to what Scorpius, Skull, and Bones are capable of. They could probably show me a world of hurt, the likes of which I've never seen, and yet I'm undeterred.

Maybe it's because somewhere deep down, I don't think they would do that. Or perhaps I'm too resentful and fed up to care anymore, but I'm starving and I refuse to wait another second before I do something about it. I hold my breath as I turn the knob and pull on the door. The hinges are silent as it swings open, and I let loose a tense exhale. I assess the empty corridor just beyond this room as though it's one gigantic booby trap. Maybe that's why Eacon was fine to leave me without supervision, because she knew as soon as I walked out alone I'd lose a leg or something.

On high alert and prepared for anything, I peek my head out and find more gray rock walls and dark wood floors. I try not to cringe as I take my first step outside of the room, but as my weight settles on the wood plank completely, nothing tries to tear off a limb, so I take another step and then another. As though I'm on the most important hunt of my life, I tread carefully, testing the floor beneath my feet for creaks and pops, and learning how to move silently in this new environment.

Very few of the sconces dotting the hall are lit, leaving plenty of shadows for me to hide in if needed. I'm tempted to try to use them to get the fuck out of here, but I don't know exactly how to do that and I don't have time to waste trying to figure it out. I need to get food in my belly and figure out what to do beyond that. I sneak down the hall. Every once in a while, I pass a window that brightens the corridor, but to my surprise, I don't find any guards wandering the halls. No salivating dogs come snarling out of the dark recesses, and no traps are tripped or alarms set off. I don't know if I find that comforting or not.

I round a corner and freeze when I discover a wide staircase that leads down to an even wider foyer. At the front are two massive rectangular doors with carved panels of flowers, vines, and scorpions. I hold my breath and scan the area for hidden sentries, but there's no one standing around to keep me from opening those doors and running.

I once again debate the merit of just running, but there are too many things working against me to get very far. I have no money, no supplies, no idea where I am, and most importantly I have nowhere to go. I need to think things through. I don't want to be owned or ordered around anymore, but I need to get the lay of the land and come up with a viable plan before I can run. I need to make sure whatever I do next actually gets me out and free, not hunted and destroyed.

I fill my chest with a deep fortifying breath as I step gingerly onto the first stair. A crossbow bolt doesn't sink into any part of my body, and none of the Scorpions stride from the shadows and ask me what the fuck I'm doing, so I speedily make my way down. When another set of stairs descend from the foyer down, I follow them. Tilleo's kitchen was in the lower level of his manor; perhaps all big castles and houses are set up the same way.

Finally, I step out into a well-lit hall that makes me proceed with even more caution. I'm bound to run into house slaves down here, and I don't know what they'll do about me lurking. I doubt they'll point me in the direction of food and ignore me beyond that, but I'll deal with whatever happens when it does. I stand and listen at a few closed doors, but either the rooms on the other side are empty or the wood of the door is so thick that I can't hear anything or anyone through it. I gently feel for any wards, but I don't sense anything there.

I continue on until the end of the large hall leads to exactly what I was hoping to find, the kitchen. What I don't expect, however, is to find it empty. I haven't spent much time in one of these, but I thought there'd be cooks and slaves scurrying about to prepare meals and snacks and whatever else it is they do all day. It's probably a long shot that I'll find something edible sitting out and asking to be taken, but I look around expectantly anyway. Unfortunately, the wood counters are clean, the large ovens look cold, and the sinks are empty. The pans hanging in the corner are most certainly not going to cook something up on their own, and I sag in defeat.

I wouldn't know how to make something if all the ingredients were lined up on the long prep table directly in front of me and someone told me step by step what to do. My stomach growls as I sigh. The heavy door to my right suddenly slams open out of nowhere. My shocked yelp is only drowned out by the bang of the door against the stone wall behind it. A tall, well-built male jumps when he sees me, almost dropping the heavy vegetable-laden basket clutched in his large hands.

"Shit," I gasp as I watch the house slave nervously.

I clench my hands at my side, unsure what the big male is going to do, and I try to get control of my runaway heart that's surging from the spike of adrenaline and the need to do *something* that just shot through me.

"You're up," the slave points out, shocked but not concerned that I'm standing in his kitchen. "Eacon said it would be a while..." He trails off as he moves to set his heavy load on the massive rectangular table in the center of the big kitchen. The top of it is stained and has score marks probably from chopping things in preparation for all the fancy dinners they must have in this place. My mouth starts to water, and I wipe at the corner of it, hoping I haven't started actually drooling when the only food here is in my head. The male fae looks behind me as though he expects someone else to be there, and his features fill with confusion when he realizes it's just me.

His hair is ash brown, but the light catches a few blond flecks scattered about his head. It's short, like it's just started to grow after being shaved. I recognize the cut—Tilleo made his male slaves wear their locks shorn too. A short, neat beard does nothing to hide the square shape of his jaw or his full lips. His nose is straight, and bright hazel eyes observe me as he uses his sleeve to clear his brow of sweat.

"How are you feeling?" he asks, his eyes dropping to my stomach as though he knows I was almost cleaved in half only a few days ago.

Maybe he was the slave who attended to me?

"Hungry," I answer as I study the streaks of dirt on the otherwise clean cream-colored tunic that hangs down to the thighs of his dark brown britches.

His skin is sun-caressed but not desert-baked like mine now is. The corded muscles of his arms and back, and the tapered waist his well-fitted shirt outlines, tells me he spends a lot of time doing manual labor here. His thighs are huge, and I just barely stop myself from asking what kind of slave he is. He doesn't look like a cook. I suppose he could be a crop tender, not that I would know one way or another. However, his basket full of soil-crusted vegetables makes me think I could be on the right track.

He rubs his hands together and strides confidently over to the sink to start washing his hands. "Of course you are.

You've had a long journey," he agrees, offering me a warm smile over his shoulder.

I'm surprised that he knows that, but then again, it would make sense for the Scorpions to inform their slaves that I'm here. I'm not sure if he attended to me or maybe saw his masters carry me in. I definitely didn't get here by the power of my own two feet.

"What would you like to eat?" the slave asks jovially, and I go still.

I figured he'd just give me whatever he wanted or what might be about to go bad, but now he's earnestly looking at me as though whatever I tell him I want, he'll provide.

"Uh...um," I stammer, not sure what to say. Would it be weird to ask for sand stag? We were allowed to have that sometimes in the ludere, and I know my body could use the nutrients. I hesitate, my eyes flitting from his sincere expression to random spots around the kitchen, as though the answer will be carved in the wood of the counter or the black metal of the cooktop. "Do you have porridge?" I finally ask, trying not to cringe as the question spills out.

The way his face falls with dismay tells me I didn't do a good job at hiding my revulsion. "We can do better than porridge," he encourages, and my stomach flips unexpectedly when he looks at me, a wry glint in his hazel eyes.

"What...what do you normally eat?" I counter, hoping that will force him to list some options.

I don't know why I feel so awkward about the fact that I don't know what else to ask for, but I do. I guess I could just ask for meat in general, but I'd feel like a dolt. For reasons that are lost to me, I don't want this slave to look at me like that. I already feel like some strange interloper. I'm adrift in a sea where everything is unknown, but I don't want to see that reflected in his eyes just yet. I don't want him to confirm just how lost and out of place I am right now.

"We normally have *quddock* eggs, maybe some tubers, steak, fruit," he explains. "It gets mixed up depending on what's in season, but that's a typical morning meal."

I try to hide my shock, but he smiles, and I realize my mouth is open and my eyes are wide. I slip an indifferent mask into place and clear my throat awkwardly. The Scorpions make their male slaves wear their hair like Tilleo demanded, but they obviously take care of their people far better than my former master ever did. It should make me feel better about the fact that I've been bought and brought here, but I know better than to think things will work out like that for me.

"Have a seat," the slave gestures to one of many stools tucked under the large prep table. "I'll get some things going. The others will probably be down soon anyway," he confides, and I hesitate to pull out a stool and sit down. It feels too comfortable, too casual, and my presence here is anything but that. "It's okay," he reassures softly. "You're safe here."

We stare at each other for a moment, and I let loose a deep breath and relent.

"Yeah, so I've been told," I grumble, still not buying it.

I don't care how kind his eyes are. Or that my cheeks start to heat as he traces my movements with an intense gaze until I sit down where he told me to. This *safe* thing is all nonsense. I don't know the meaning of that word even if I did believe him and Eacon. Ignoring the house slave as he starts to move about the kitchen, I look out the broad window above the sinks and decide that it must be early morning. Something about the light gives the impression, but I could be completely wrong. It's quite gloomy and gray outside, and I wonder if that's normal or if the day will brighten as it progresses.

I could probably ask the slave. He seems amiable enough, but I can't bring myself to let the questions slip off my tongue. It might be wise not to get overly friendly too fast, or he may not tell me and then things would be awkward.

"I'm Auset," I offer instead as the silence in the kitchen starts to feel itchy against my skin.

He laughs and looks over at me, a curious glint in his hazel eyes as he cracks orange eggs into a bowl. "I know who you are, little blade slave," he declares with an amused smile.

I'm taken aback by his use of the title from the lud-ere and the overly friendly nature in which he speaks it. It throws me just like the long journey comment. I study him closely, questioning if there's more going on here that I don't understand or if I'm reading too much into it. I have a leery, overly cautious habit of thinking there's a hidden meaning beneath every word that's ever been spoken to me. Sometimes I'm right, but other times I'm merely assigning depth that isn't there.

The slaves would have been told about me. That's all this is, nothing to freak out over.

He stares at me expectantly, but after a moment when he doesn't find whatever he's looking for, he shakes his head and turns back to the bowl of eggs. I think I see his smile grow even wider, but I can't be sure.

"I'm Riall," he finally calls out as he starts stirring the contents of the large bowl and sprinkling different things from jars into the mixture.

When he's done with that, he opens an oven door and pulls something out. He slices it up with a thin, delicate knife that I have to stop myself from trying to steal, and then sets the sliced up thing in front of me.

"It's bread," he states, and then he turns back to what he was doing before.

Starving, I snag a thick oval slice of whatever *bread* is. It's warm and spongy in my palm, and I immediately shove the entire piece in my mouth. Riall laughs, and I look up to find he's watching me. I probably look like some desert rat stealing scraps under the table, with both my cheeks puffed greedily as I test the limits of how much they can hold, but I don't even care. Bread is a*mazing*. I definitely like bread. I eagerly add it to my list of things I now know to ask for, and ignore the warmth that washes through me because my list isn't just gruel and sand stag meat now.

The slave's eyes twinkle merrily as he watches me try to chew my huge mouthful, and there's something oddly familiar about the look on his face.

"Iss goo," I mumble, already reaching for another slice. I don't know if I want to shove it in my mouth too or hide it for later in the shirt halves I wrapped around my waist.

Riall's laugh deepens and grows even louder, but a noise from behind me pulls my attention away. I spin, puff-cheeked and swelling with chagrin, to find two other males standing in the doorway watching, surprise—and could that be relief?—etched in both of their faces. They're big like Riall is, their muscles and bulk filling out their tunics and trousers in an equally appealing and astonishing way. Once again, I'm curious as to what these slaves do around here to look like bigger versions of the warriors I'm used to training next to, but my mouth is too full of delicious bread to demand answers.

Maybe they're guards?

The male with wavy, shoulder-length, dark brown hair is the first to snap out of his stupor and stride into the room. His eyes are a startling light blue that makes me think of snowflakes, even though I've never seen one. The beginnings of a beard dust across soft, warm-ivory skin. The dark scruff highlights his strong jaw and high cheekbones, and I struggle not to stare at him.

Where Riall is more feral looking and gruff, this male is pretty, but in a deadly, masculine kind of way. He leans back against a wood counter, crossing his large arms over his wide chest and watching me like I'm something to hunt. Instead of challenging that look like I want to, I turn to take in the other fae still standing in the doorway. When my eyes land on him, it also seems to pull him from some sort of trance, and he joins us in the kitchen.

He moves like a feline, more prowl than walk, and I recognize the gait, but I can't immediately place it. His hair is long, layered, and gorgeously full. It's the color of shadows with a few pieces around his face that are the same color as the pale-gold that often streaks the sky at dawn. His hooded eyes are a rich hickory, and his complexion is a shade darker than mine but with an olive undertone. He's wearing a black tunic like I am, but his trousers are an inky suede and not the weird skintight material I found in the drawers of the room I woke up in. His dark brown eyes fix on my shoulder, and I realize the neck of my tunic is currently sliding down my arm. I rush to pull it up, and a small smile threatens to spread across his plump lips before he catches it and blanks his face.

I manage to swallow my mouthful of the bread while the three fae silently study me. I try not to squirm. Riall chuckles again and then gestures to the long-haired fae, who I swear is debating whether or not he wants to eat me up right now like I'm the best option for breakfast, or maybe it's dinner time, I'm still unsure.

"This is Curio, and this is Tarek," Riall states, his arm waving from the long-haired fae to the one with ice for eyes and dark brown hair teasing the tops of his muscular shoulders. "Boys, this is Auset," Riall tells them, and Tarek looks from me to Riall, like he's trying to read what's really written in the slave's amused tone and gleaming eyes.

I survey them and the loaded reaction. Maybe I'll be working with them while I'm kept here? They're probably just as surprised by my presence as I am. They don't seem cruel—surprisingly polite, if I had to categorize it. I'm uncertain if that's a testament to the kind of fae they are or if it's because the Scorpions are good masters. I shove the thought away. Good or not, I'm done with it.

Riall rubs a hand over his shorn hair as he and the other two exchange another veiled look. I have no idea what it means. Warnings trill in my head, and instead of shoving the new slice of bread in my mouth, or hiding it away in my clothes, I set it in front of me and pick off a small chunk while watching each of the slaves more suspiciously. I'm missing something here, but I haven't the foggiest clue what it could be.

"Don't tell me our little *Slave* has forgotten us already?" Curio asks, a teasing lilt to his deep tone, and Riall lets loose an exasperated groan.

"Really, Curio?" Tarek asks.

I stare at Curio, his question taking its time to seep in and tickle a memory. Understanding crashes into me like a runaway beast I'm not fast enough to avoid, and the blood drains from my face. My startled gaze jumps from Curio to Riall to Tarek and back again, my heart dashing away entirely too fast for me to keep up, as I finally connect what is so oddly familiar about these three strangers.

They're not slaves.

They're fucking Scorpions.

I'm staring at Skull, Bones, and Scorpius, only now there's no shadow and bone glamour for them to hide behind.

21

THE STOOL BENEATH ME HITS THE GROUND with a loud thwack as I scramble off it and struggle to get my legs and feet under me. Unsteadily, I back up, pulling Eacon's knife from my shirt loop and clench it tightly in my hand. Light flickers on the blade as my stricken gaze jumps between the glamour-free Scorpions. They cautiously watch me, exchanging loaded looks like they're trying to anticipate what I'm going to do. I catch signals in the silent communication they pass back and forth, but frustratingly I can't decipher what they mean.

"What's going on?" I demand, feeling duped and stupid and entirely unsure of what game they're playing here.

"It's okay, Auset, there's no need for that," Riall purrs at me, his hazel eyes flicking from me to the knife and back again.

I realize as he talks that I know the sound of his voice. I don't know how I didn't hear it before. It's unquestionably Bones. I've just gotten used to associating the sound of him with the glamour he's always worn. I study his face, trying to lay the image of a magicked skeleton over his fae features. I attempt to line them up, fit them together, so I can reconcile the glamoured assassin I was getting to know with the unfamiliar male currently standing across from me.

Bones is Riall, with his short ash brown hair and beard, hazel eyes, and thick muscular frame. Curio is Skull, the short, perfectly styled hair he had while wearing his glamour is gone. It's still black and beautiful, but now it falls to his mid-back. Warm hickory-brown irises have replaced the black orbs I'm used to looking at, and he appears much larger in his own skin than he seemed before. They all do. Scorpius's, or Tarek's, creamy skin is smooth over bulging muscle, his ice-blue gaze watches me shrewdly, and the waves of his shoulder-length dark brown hair soften his square jaw and the angles of his high cheekbones. Somehow I managed to forget that they were fae underneath the camouflaging layer of magic, and now here they are, defenses down, and it makes me want to scream.

Eacon's words chime in my head, *the Scorpions have a small circle of trust,* she'd warned. *Not many know they're more than privileged fae given this land to govern and watch over.* So what in the name of the stars does it mean for me that they're letting me see them for who and what they are now?

It means I'm fucked beyond belief, that's what it means.

I won't be allowed to roam free in the realms with secrets like *where they live* and *what they look like* floating around in my mind as though they aren't weapons that could be used against them at any moment. My last shred of hope searches for any sign that they're still wearing any kind of glamour, but I don't feel the slightest tingle. This is who they really are. Anguish and grief clash within me as once again I feel the freedom I crave slip through my grasping fingers like desert sand.

I didn't ask for this.

I don't want to see past the façade or dive into a deeper understanding of who they are. It's a fucking trap if I've ever seen one, and it has rage curdling in my stomach. I glare at them and start backing away, needing immediate space between me and the fuckers who are stripping me of everything I want like I'm unworthy of it, like freedom is too good for me. I was sold and now I'm being robbed. They're trying to steal my future as though it's something owed to them.

Why is there always some entitled bastard trying to snatch away everything I want?

I thought I could eventually run, that in time, if I planned it right, I could finally seize the life that's owed to me and find my way in this messed up world. The Scorpions would probably be pissed, but I'm just some lowly blade slave. They wouldn't trouble themselves with hunting me. But they've shown me their faces and ruthlessly sealed my fate. I hold secrets in my hands now, and I wish more than anything I could shake them off, fling it as far away from me as possible like the filth it is.

Scorpius, or Tarek—or whatever his name is—is suddenly there next to me. His ice-blue eyes are commanding and sure as they settle on mine like a key trying to access a lock. He's saying something either to me or the others, I don't know, because all I can focus on is the need to wipe the imperious look from his face, a face I wish I didn't know.

A wrathful snarl rumbles out of me as my fangs drop, and before I can second-guess how wise it is, I leap at him. I'm rewarded when shock flashes in his cool gaze, but a thick, hard arm wraps around my waist, keeping me from connecting with the bastard leader of the Scorpions. I'm slammed back against the cold stone of a wall, and I redirect my irate growl to Riall, who's abandoned the meal he was cooking and is now pressing into me in an effort to pin me in place.

I didn't even see him move.

The beast inside of me takes interest, and I'm suddenly unsure if I want to rip him apart or bury my fangs in him and drink him dry. My lip curls as I viciously snap my fangs at him, but instead of being rattled by the sight of my razor sharp incisors and the threat that's practically dripping from their tips, wonder fills Riall's face. A stunned smile slowly slinks across his lush lips, and he presses against me even harder.

It's the exact opposite of what I expect to happen, and it throws me off completely. One-handed, he lifts me up on the wall by the waist until we're face-to-face. And then, in an astonishing flash that I do not see coming, his canines lengthen and he snaps them back at me, the motion more of a lurid promise than any kind of a threat.

"There's my little beasty," he proclaims, his tone deep and sensual, and his pupils so blown all that's left of his irises is a tiny ring of dark green.

I jolt back, thoroughly startled by not only his strange reaction to my secret, but the fact that he has one of his own. I glance from the banked heat in his gaze to the sharp fangs peeking out below his ample top lip. My fury drains like the sight of his sharp teeth have poked invisible holes in me and all the anger has nowhere to go but out. In its place, astonishment and wonder seep in. I run my tongue over my own piercing canines, cataloging the similarities and differences. His are so much bigger, and I suddenly want to test the edge of them with my tongue.

What would he taste like?

As though he can read that thought, a quiet growl vibrates from Riall's chest into mine. I snap my astonished gaze back to his. Ragged breaths saw in and out of my chest as we stare at one another.

*Who **are** these fae? First the shadow walking and now the fangs? This whole time, I've been so careful to keep these unusual abilities a secret, but are my secrets theirs too? Is that the draw to these fae? Like recognizing like?*

I'm all at once aware that my breasts are pressing against Riall's hard unyielding muscles with each gulping inhalation I take. His hips anchor mine, holding me in place, and we breathe each other in, our faces so close that I can count his eyelashes if I want to. Someone peels my fingers from Eacon's dagger and plucks it from my palm, but I can't even be bothered to care. I'm stuck in a stupor of amazement, and no other emotion seems to be able to penetrate that. My every thought is pulled in the direction of Riall as though he's the sun and I'm merely the day with no choice but to bow to him.

"You're like me?" I whisper, and his eyes drop to my lips as though he's tasting my words and not just hearing them. "How?" I demand, my eyes fixed on the sharp points of his fangs. "What are we?"

"No," Tarek interjects from over Riall's shoulder. "First, *you* explain what just happened. Surprised to see us without the glamour, I can understand, but why the fury? Why are you angry? We saved you."

I pull my stare from Riall and take in Tarek and Curio over his shoulder. Do they have fangs too? They both watch me with guarded, severe expressions, and I don't know what to make of any of this. My feet dangle above the ground, and the rocks in the wall dig into my back. Somehow, it makes me feel centered instead of trapped, and I'm sure that's some kind of testament to how messed I might be.

Something in me hammers away at the shock enough for other thoughts and feelings to rush in through the cracks. I try to sort through the deluge of questions and astonishment, but I feel as though I'm drowning. Riall doesn't move, doesn't give me any room, and I can't decide if I want him to put me down or if he's the life preserver I need so I'm not pulled under by the mayhem that is my mind right now. I want to wrestle control of my future from the claws of these Scorpions, but what if they can keep me from being swept away by the maelstrom that has fucked up everything in my life?

"Why am I here?" I ask, leveling Tarek with a hard expression as I work to affix the apathetic mask I mastered at the ludere.

"Answer what I asked you first," he counters, and just like that, my flimsy controlled veneer dissolves as I sigh and fight not to growl with frustration.

I want to rage, but it's being overpowered by other things that are teasing the back of my mind. Startling things I shouldn't be thinking about right now, if ever. I shouldn't be focusing on how Riall feels against me. Or that Curio's blistering gaze is leaving a hot trail over my exposed skin, while Tarek's cool perusal works to soothe the delicious burn.

I don't know who they are or what they're doing to me, but I need to get a hold of myself. I need to take back my control. With great effort, I retract my fangs as I force my emotions to level out. I swear Riall groans an objection, but it's drowned out by the screech of a stool being pulled out so Curio can plop his huge frame down as though he's settling in for the exchange that Tarek isn't going to back down from. Curio pushes his long dark locks back from his face and eyes me like he's not sure what to expect next and he loves it. Skull wore that same wickedly amused look when his eyes were glamoured black, and it further cements that they're one and the same.

"You want me to kiss your feet for saving me, but all you've done is unlock Tilleo's shackles and then put on a pair of your own. I am not your slave. I don't want to be caged," I snap at Tarek, and his eyes narrow with menace.

"You don't look as though you *don't* want to be caged," Curio remarks, peering pointedly at the way Riall is pressing against me.

Both of his large arms are boxing me in against the wall. I can't even say when he did it.

Warm breath skates over exposed skin, and I realize that the neck of my tunic has sagged down my arm again. Riall leans closer as though my bare shoulder has sent out a personal invitation to his mouth. A tingling tremor works its way up my back, and goose bumps crawl over my flesh in a way that makes me feel flushed and chilled simultaneously. I try not to think about what it might feel like for him to run the tips of his fangs up my throat, or better yet, sink their sharp depths into the juncture of my neck and shoulder. I ignore the shiver of pleasure that snakes up my spine and instead, focus on the smelting judgmental glint in Curio's gaze as I try to push Riall away.

It takes him a moment to realize what I'm doing. It's like shoving a mountain—a warm, muscular, delicious-smelling mountain—for all the good it does me. But then Riall registers my efforts and backs off, giving me space. He peels his body from mine, his arms dropping from around me after a slight pause as though he doesn't want to let me go. I don't acknowledge how it feels to drag my body against his as I slide down until my feet are back on the floor. I ignore the emptiness that fills the space between us as Riall steps back to give me the room I stupidly demanded.

Reluctantly, I force myself to step to the side away from the wall. I need room to attempt to think clearly, and yet as Riall moves further away from me, I want to command that he stop and climb back into his arms.

What in the blood moon is wrong with me?

Riall shoots a vicious glare at Curio as I try to clear my head of all the confusing and conflicting thoughts. I want to hurt them, take from them like they're taking from me, and yet there's a part of me that doesn't want that at all. They flipped my switch from rage to reeling in less than a beat, and now I'm nothing but churning chaos and confusion.

"And what gives you the impression that we want you to be our *slave* as opposed to our...guest?" Tarek demands.

I get the impression that he was about to say something else other than *guest*, but his icy eyes are frosted over with indignation, and I can't see even a hint of what could be hiding in their fathomless depths.

I glower at him, defiance sparking in my gaze. "Guest?" I challenge.

His scowl deepens. "For now, yes," he vaguely supplies.

I huff an unamused snort at the ambiguity in that statement.

"You bought me. You've brought me here. You removed your glamour and exposed me to secrets I didn't ask to know." My frustration rises with each unfettered fact. "I know what this means," I continue, waving at them, at the absence of the glamour that kept *me* protected. "You've made me a liability. You've filled my mind with shit I don't want in there." I look at Riall and Curio. "Which of you wants to remind *Scorpius* about what happens to fae who know too much in this killing business?" I snark.

Tarek's gaze narrows, not amused by my cheek in the slightest.

"Why the fuck did you heal me?" I demand, trying to tamp down the savage storm brewing inside of me. "I would have rather died that night than trade one master for another!"

"You speak like all masters are the same," Tarek retorts, obviously offended at being compared to Tilleo.

"Are you not?" I counter. "Was I asked what I wanted? Do you even care?"

Tarek chuffs with exasperation. "So we should have left you there in the desert?" he growls. "Let our ma—let *you* die, or worse?"

"You've done it before, why should this time be any different?" I snarl.

Tarek steps closer, danger written all over his face. I square my shoulders, refusing to let the heat that tries to surge through me at his threatening advance drown my outrage.

"This time was different. We weren't in a position to do anything for you before; now we are," he counters as though it's as simple as that.

"Now that *I* have something you want, you mean," I correct him.

Icy blue eyes glint with promise as they drop down my body and slowly rise until they're once again fixed on my now flustered stare. I try not to squirm under his perusal, angry that part of me likes it. I've never had anyone look at me the way these Scorpions do. It feels like a scalding promise that's also laced with a frigid threat. I both relish it and hate that my body is so quick to succumb to that call, whatever the fuck it may mean.

"I understand that, up until now, life has shown you a very limited view of things. You may think all of this is very black and white, but I promise you, Little Dagger, our existence is far grayer than you realize. Yes, we want *things* from you," he admits, his deep voice dropping even further as he practically hums the word, "but we're offering you everything you could ever want in return."

His promise washes over me, but I refuse to let it settle where it wants to.

"I don't want to be owned." I growl at them. "I don't want to be bought and sold on the whims of greedy, *weak* fae. I'm not an animal. I deserve more."

"We are not greedy or weak, and we didn't buy you," Riall defends, cutting off whatever Tarek was about to say.

"What does that even mean? Did you steal me?" I question, not understanding the latter part of that statement.

Fear flutters through me at the thought that they took me without permission. Will Tilleo send someone after them? Am I being hunted as we speak? The twitchy need to run begins to overtake me, but I work to calm myself and think things through. It's the Order of Scorpions we're talking about here, the most prolific house of assassins anyone has ever known. Even if Tilleo wanted me back, who would he send to get past these seasoned killers? Who would survive an attempt to drag me back to the ludere?

No one.

It would be a suicide mission, and I doubt some lowly blade slave would be worth the wrath of these three powerful fae. My racing heart slowly calms as I inhale deep reassuring breaths. Bewilderment replaces my apprehension, and I cross my arms over my chest as I glance back and forth between the three Scorpions, still waiting for an answer to my question.

Curio sighs and leans back against the table. "We didn't buy you, because we technically already owned you. We finance the ludere."

I reel back in shock, the admission hitting me harder than any master or blade slave ever has. "You...you own that place?" I stammer, as though not even my mouth can wrap itself around the truth of those words.

They own me?

Tilleo and the ludere belong to them?

Flashes of all the torture and brutality I've experienced in that hellish hovel flash in my mind. Pain suddenly explodes in my shoulder as though I'm reliving some long forgotten injury. I rub it absently as I stare them down. I don't know what in the crowns is going on.

Is this why they killed Dorsin that night? They wanted what he'd built?

No wonder they left me there, they probably thought I'd been bought and paid for. Why would they take me from exactly where they wanted me to be? Every ounce of interest and need simmering inside of me goes sour. I try to breathe through the mess of emotions bombarding me. I can't believe I thought for even a second that these Scorpions might be different. They're just as rancid and evil as every other master I've ever met.

I was dying, and it was their skeletal faces that invaded my thoughts. I dared to believe that the strange draw to them might be fate working on my side for once. And here they've owned me this entire time. All the abuse, the mind games, the constant struggle for survival was because of them. Maybe not by their hand directly, but surely by their purse. They paid for it all.

Pain and anger pit my soul. A brutal haze coats my vision. Everything in me is crying and begging for me to move, to strike, to kill. I want to make them pay for every lash, every broken bone and attempt to break my spirit. Every disfiguring scar slashed into who I am, now has their names etched inside too. I want to rip their fucking heads from their bodies, but I know I can't. It's a fight I won't win, and they don't deserve my end. They don't deserve another second of my life. They've taken enough from me.

I refuse to submit to the anger that's broiling me from the inside out, so instead, I shut everything down. I deaden every feeling, every flicker of fury, every unwelcome brush of betrayal. My expression goes blank, and my body relaxes as I let go. I can't take all three of them. I'm not delusional. I'll do what it takes to survive today, just like I have for too many years, but a reckoning is coming. Maybe not today or tomorrow, but they'll pay. I'll make sure of it. I already promised myself that I'd destroy the ludere if it was the last thing I ever did. These three just added their names to that list.

As though the sudden change in me has charged the air in this room with warning, Tarek steps back, his tall hard body almost shielding Riall and Curio. It's a silent declaration that to get to them, I'll have to go through him first. I like that he sees me as a threat.

He should.

I don't know what the kind of devotion and partnership that he's showing the other two feels like; all anyone has ever done for me is turn their back when I needed them most. If I think about it long enough, it might sting, but I shut all of that out.

Fuck them.

"Stop," Tarek commands, and my enraged focus tunnels until all I see is him.

I taste magic in the air, and his order moves over me like an encroaching fog. It doesn't nip forcefully at my skin like

I expect. It's as though he wants me to know that he could compel me to listen, but he's not. I had no idea fae could do this, that they could feel this powerful. I should probably be terrified, but all it does is piss me off even more.

"We know that your life hasn't been easy," he starts, the tinge of power winking around me like sun sparkles over water. "But before you act on the righteous indignation simmering in your eyes, you need to understand that there's more to this than you think, Auset. We help condemned fae have a chance at more. The ludere and the Orders are the best option any of them have. You may not like the methods, but we give fae an opportunity to overcome their shitty circumstances at birth. We show them a way to fight what fate had in store for them."

His message sounds noble. Maybe if I hadn't spent the last six years having their *methods* and *opportunities* whipped, beaten, and scored into me, I might fall for the earnest gleam in his blue gaze, but it's all bullshit. No one in the ludere has a choice. Maybe things get better for the blade slaves once they leave, but everything that happens up until that point nullifies any *good* the Scorpions think they're doing.

I scoff and shake my head. "Whatever you tell yourself to help you sleep at night." I glare at each of them. "You can paint pretty pictures about where you get fae from, but you still make slaves of them. You're as rotten as every other powerful person who preys on the unfortunate."

"They would have been slaves whether we stepped in or not," Skull counters. "Whether the skin trade got them or they were pulled in by a thief's guild. Maybe, by some miracle, they find a job, but in the end, it's all some form of slavery. One fae slogging away for another, dependent on them for everything they have. It could all be stripped away in a second, and often is. Don't pretend that the realms don't work the way that they do. We're *all slaves* to something or someone."

"So that makes it okay?" I demand, disgusted by the rationale.

"It makes it what it is," Riall offers grimly. "We at least give fae a chance. We don't doom anyone to a lifetime of nothing but suffering. The ludere teaches the skills needed to crawl out of the shit-ridden holes the Crowns would rather see them drown in. It's something, which is infinitely better than nothing."

"Like we said, it's gray, Auset, even you have to be able to see that," Tarek adds.

I stare at him, his words swirling all around me like pecking birds looking for a place to swoop in and perch. I refuse to give them one. I smother the flames of fury that try to flicker through my chest and offer the Scorpions a cold smile.

"I don't think you want to know exactly what it is I see," I challenge, my tone so saccharine that it makes Curio's mouth pucker against it.

"We're offering you a place with us, Auset. We don't offer it lightly, and you shouldn't dismiss it simply because we see the world differently. Being one of us won't right the wrongs done to you—no one can do that—but it can give you what you truly want in life," Tarek offers, and it's almost as though the other two are holding their breath as he stares at me pointedly.

"And what would you know about what I want, Scorpius?" I bite back.

"More than you'll admit," he smugly retorts, one of his eyebrows ticking up as though he's daring me to deny it.

I want to argue, but it would solely be for argument's sake. I know nothing about these three fae in front of me, and he's right, knowing that what was done to me is wrong doesn't erase that it was done. The notches in my soul are a permanent part of who I am now. I don't know much about the realms outside of the ludere, but it's not hard to see that too much about them is severely broken. It makes me want to burn it all to the ground, but that's nothing more than an unrealistic fantasy, and I think the Scorpions are delusional enough for the both of us.

Even if the abominable systems could be toppled, I have no doubt that something equally as heinous would find a way to rise from the rubble. I know all too well that life is nothing more than a brutal dance between predator and prey. I've had the keen misfortune of being prey since I can remember, but now, if I accept the Scorpion's offer, that could change. I wouldn't have to live the rest of my life being hunted. I could finally be the hunter.

Like he can sense the chips in my resolve, Tarek's shoulders lose some of their tension. "You wouldn't be alone anymore," he tells me as he steps to the side and leans back against the table next to Curio.

He must think the worst that could happen between us has passed.

"You'd be a Scorpion, and you'd be entitled to everything that comes with that designation," he continues as though this conversation has shifted from chaos to casual in less time than it takes to blink.

I wish I could say the staggering flip back and forth hasn't been our entire interaction so far, but I keep flashing from wrath to wonder so fast that I don't even know what I'm feeling anymore or why. Tarek stands there as though he's not working hard to dangle an irresistible lure in front of my face.

"You're one of us, Little Dagger. I know you feel it," he tells me, and it's exactly what I need to hear to see this for what it is.

"You don't know me," I contend, scowling at his presumption.

"Then let us get to know you," Riall counters, as though it's as simple as that.

He's a mere arm stretch away, and his body tightens as though he wants to move closer but is stopping himself. I brush off the longing and justifications that try to seep through the cracks in my armor. They know exactly what to say to coax out my deepest desires and buried insecurities, but I know I can't trust it. The offer is enticing, but it lacks the one thing that's kept me going all of this time. I don't ever want to bow to anyone again. Whether it's three powerful assassins or the kings that rule over these shitty realms.

Let them all leave their castles and their cooks and their servants. Let them be bought, sold, and used as they come up in a ludere, and then maybe they'd be worth listening to. Until then, they can fuck themselves with an iron dagger for all I care.

I don't remember who I was before I woke up in a cage, but I hadn't been starved. I didn't have any bruises, broken bones, or a mark on me until the iron bars burned my back. Dorsin and the orcs expected to ransom me, which makes me think that I came from a place where I was wanted, valued. There were people somewhere out in the realms who would have paid a great deal to get me back. I was once cared for, maybe even loved...and now I'm nothing.

I've been fractured beyond all repair, and I'm now standing in the home of the fae who helped—in more ways than one—to break me. I've had enough.

"I belong to no one but me. I never did and I never will," I proclaim, my head high and my stance proud. "I want nothing more than that. Dressing up the cage doesn't change what it is. I don't give a fuck how comfortable you make your chains or what benefits might come with them, they're still chains."

"We're not trying to chain you," Riall argues.

"Speak for yourself," Curio interjects, his tone a seductive purr.

"Not helping," Riall snaps at him, his hazel eyes enraged as he fists his hands at his side.

Tarek rolls his eyes and then blows out a deep exhale. He studies me with a contemplative eye, like he can see what he wants but he's still unsure how to get it. Silence grows heavy in the room. It presses against me, demanding I lift the pressure that's slowly growing, but I refuse to give in. I won't speak first. I won't be the weak one.

"Fine," Tarek finally clips. "If that's what it takes, you're free. You can walk out the door right now, and no one will stop you. No one will hunt you down. Your life is your own."

I suck in a sharp breath at the indifferently spoken pronouncement. I don't miss how both Riall's and Curio's heads snap in Tarek's direction. It's obvious neither of them are in on what their leader just declared, which makes it all the more confusing. Unable to help myself, I glance over at the door Riall walked through when he first found me in this kitchen.

Through the window inset in the wood, I can see the fluffy gray clouds are even darker, and the smell of rain is potent in the briny air.

"We can help you, if you stay," Tarek proffers. "If you give us a chance we can show you who we really are and how you could fit in that."

I jerk my stare back to Tarek, his words a sprinkle of enticing crumbs on the barren ground, a trail he's hoping I'll follow. "You said you don't know where you come from or how you ended up at the ludere. We have contacts that could help point us in the right direction. There's no one in the realms more driven or adept at finding things than we are. We can help you."

"Why?" I ask, completely bewildered.

Curio and Riall study me earnestly. They're silent as Scorpius does what he can to reel me back in. It's written all over each of their faces that they're keen to keep me here. I doubt it's because they want answers too, but this can't just be about fucking, can it? I'm not daft, I know what each of them is not so subtly hinting at. Under different circumstances, with less crushing truths between us, I might not be opposed to the physical implications of staying.

Fucking and emotion are not connected things for me. It's a release, a need, an opportunity to control what happens to my body when I want it and how I want it. But I can't trust these fae. I just met them, and there's already too much damaging history between us to turn a blind eye to. I don't understand what it is about me that they're fighting so hard for, but in the end, it really doesn't matter.

"What you can do, Auset...what all of us can do for that matter, is rare. *Shadow walking* and *blooding* are not talents that we stumble across often, if ever. We can help you develop those abilities while we search for answers. We can prepare you better than anyone for what's out there in the realms. Let us show you what it's like to be one of us."

Tarek's words do their best to ensnare me. They try to wrap around my cold shoulders like a warm cloak. I can see the promised answers, offers of inclusion, and hints of so much more sewn into the seams of the hopeful protection he wants to drape over me. But I know where hope leads. I know how quickly sweet promises can be ripped from your heart, leaving gouges not even the best healers can smooth away.

They can't see them, but I'm covered in those scars. Besides, it's not lost on me that he didn't actually answer my question. He's being cagey about something, they all are, and I'm not interested in figuring out what it is or how it will bite me in the ass in the end. It always does. I've learned that lesson too many times now to care to repeat it again.

I watch the three Scorpions as they watch me, their offer dangling between us. I don't know what they expect me to say. I want answers, I want to find my place, but trusting anyone, especially them, is too dangerous a trade. These three left me chained to a floor in a manor as it passed hands from Dorsin to Tilleo, with them watching from the shadows. They abandoned me to my fate, and now after all this time, they want me to braid that fate with theirs as though a few answers would earn them that sacrifice.

It doesn't.

Like the night they crawled out of the window in Dorsin's chambers without so much as a goodbye or a backward look, I turn for the door. A stool scrapes against the stone floor behind me, and the sounds of a soft scuffle trail in my wake as I reach for the knob. My hands tremble as I hear Tarek whisper commandingly to the others.

"No, let her go. She deserves to choose this."

Finally we agree on something. I *do* deserve to choose whatever happens to me from here moving forward, and I'll take my chances with what's outside this castle. Tarek said I was free. I'm not going to give him a chance to take it back. The stars know my odds of surviving outside of these walls are probably better than what could happen to me if I give in to the Scorpions' overtures. I have no doubt that each and every one of them is laced with poison.

I don't turn around to see what I expect is the big leader with the snowflake-blue eyes ordering the other two Scorpions back. I offer them no consideration as I walk out the door and into a world I know nothing about. As the latch clicks closed behind me and I take my first steps away from the castle, I yearn for them to feel as wronged and defeated as I felt that horrific night when they abandoned me to fate's cruel clutches. I curse them to spend as much time as I have suffering for all of it.

22

CURIO

What the fuck, Tarek?" I snarl, shoving his hand from my chest as he tries to moor me in place.

All too quickly, Auset disappears beyond the window in the door, and the need to stomp after her and drag her back here is overwhelming. I knew I was drawn to her that first night of the Bidding. I didn't understand the pull, so I dismissed it, but something solidified in my chest for her the night she almost died. Now she wants to walk out of here, possessing pieces of me she doesn't even know she has, and I can't allow it.

I'm not a soft male. I can be impertinent as fuck when I feel like it, but more often than not, I'm happy to fall back and astutely observe. I was born for a hard life. I've never shied away from backbreaking work or hesitated to do whatever needed to be done to survive. Auset thinks we're immune to these hard lessons, but she has no idea what the three of us have traversed to get where we are today. I thought she would listen, that she would want to understand why we brought her here, but she's more stubborn than I anticipated. I'm hard as fuck because of it, but she can't leave, we just found her.

I move around Tarek, intent on the door, but he steps in my way again.

"You're my brother and I don't want to hurt you, but she's my mate. If you don't move, I will fuck you up," I warn.

"I'll help," Riall announces from behind me.

Tarek lets loose an exasperated exhale. "You need to trust me," he states evenly, like Auset walking out isn't fucking with him too.

I know it is, he's just better at hiding it. There's a tightness around his eyes, a subtle clenching and unclenching of his jaw, and the racing pulse in his neck all give him away.

"I do trust you, but even you aren't infallible," I remind him as I frustratedly shove my fingers through my hair and pull at the roots until the small bite of pain serves to calm me. "Letting her go is a mistake. She's ours! She belongs with us!"

"I know that. We all know that, but we need to be patient while *she* realizes it," he counters.

Riall scoffs and Tarek scowls at him. Patient is the last thing Riall will ever be.

"Why didn't you just tell her she was our mate?" he snaps at Tarek.

"Do you really think she wants to hear that right now?" he snips back. "You heard her, the *owned* part of all of this is what she objects to. She doesn't want to be trapped or tethered to anything right now, and can you blame her?" he demands, gesturing out the door as everything we want starts to slip further and further with each step she takes away from us. "She probably has no concept of what a mate is or how that connection works. She'll see it as nothing more than fetters right now. Yes, she belongs *with* us, but she doesn't want to belong *to* us yet. That's an important difference to her. If we don't honor that now, we'll never have her the way we want, not truly," Tarek argues.

"So, what, we just sit here and wait? Twiddle our thumbs and watch the door, hoping someday she walks back through it?" I demand, misery already clouding the thought of giving up that easily.

A smile breaks across Tarek's face, and an all too familiar cunning gleam illuminates his light blue eyes. I should know better than to doubt that he has a plan, but I want to punch it out of him right this minute. Smug prick. He relaxes back against the table and crosses his arms.

"Did you not see the state of her when she left?" he asks.

My brow furrows and I think past the trepidation hammering in my chest and try to follow his meaning. Riall considers his question for a moment too, and then out of nowhere he starts to laugh, patting Tarek hard on the back twice. Clearly, he's arrived at the answer far faster than me. It's not surprising. I'm struggling to think past all the lurid graphic thoughts I've been grappling with since I walked into the kitchen and saw Auset in my togs. I groan at the images that once again push to the forefront of my thoughts, unsure if I possess them or if they possess me.

The neck of my tunic kept falling off her strong shoulders and flashing her golden skin in the most delicious way. It was as though the fabric knew who its true owner was and was giving me peeks of exactly what I needed. Eacon said she brought Auset some clothes, so I don't know why she's wearing mine, but I like it. From the waist down, she was wrapped in the tight rinds we put on under our armor when we hunt. I've never been more grateful for the clinging fabric that leaves nothing to the imagination.

Every curve of the muscles in her calves and thighs was on full display, as was her round, firm ass. The seam between her thighs was a cruel taunt, and that was before Riall pinned her against the wall and I watched her struggle with how much she liked it. Everything in me was begging for him to bite her. I wanted him to send her into a haze of need more than I wanted my next breath.

I could see exactly how it would all play out. He would sink his fangs in her shoulder and then bury his cock deep in her dripping pussy. Tarek and I would watch, the carnal images and sounds fueling our own mindless hunger. I'd steal her before Riall could finish. He breached her first, which means he can be the last to mark her with his seed. I'd lay her out on the table. Lick and suckle every inch of her until she was begging me to pound into her deep and hard. I'd bury my face in her cunt for so long there'd be a puddle of desire beneath us by the time I came up for air. Our Moonling would writhe and plead and scream my name as I thrust into her and showed her just what it would mean to be one of us, what it would mean to be our mate.

We'd prepare that tight weapon of a body to take the three of us all at the same time, and we'd claim her over and over again until not only she but the kitchen was dripping with all of us. Then we'd mark every inch of this castle exactly the same way.

I run my fingers through my long hair, frustrated and still searching for what Tarek wants me to find. When Auset pushed Riall away, I knew she was close to accepting us but not quite ready. We'd have to take things slow, make our intentions clear, but wait for her to come to us. Just as Tarek has always taken charge, I sense a similar need to control in her. That drive doesn't fuel her every move like it does his, but when it comes to opening up, it *has* to be on her terms. I'm more than happy to wait for her to need me the way I need her, but how will that happen if she's not even here?

Anxious anger shoves out all rational thought. She walked out of here completely unprepared for the wilderness all around us. She has no supplies, no idea where she is, and I suspect not the slightest clue where to go. She survived the ludere, but can she survive the wilds of the realms? Something could happen to her. Someone could take her and show her that Tilleo is the least of the monsters lurking in the realms. We're just standing here...

Understanding kicks me in the gut, and my eyes flash to Tarek's knowing stare.

"She has no supplies. She's not even wearing boots," I announce, finally crossing his bridge of thought.

"How far can she truly get?" he agrees, solidifying the picture even more. "We want her, and she wants freedom. So she'll have it. Our mate is smart, she's cunning and calculating, and she'll realize soon enough that she's not thought this through. That there's a better way for her to get what she wants."

His statement sparks an ember of hope. Auset is all of those things, but she's also headstrong. Her sharp tongue and unwillingness to bend call to me. She knows her mind, and it's a mind I want to know too. She's unlike anything I've ever come across, and I want to unwrap her secrets and thoughts layer by layer until I'm as deep in her as I can be.

"She'll come back, even if it's just for supplies, and that's all the opening we need," Riall states appreciatively, and I can see plans already forming in his mind for how to convince her to stay.

Once again, I pull at the roots of my hair, the slight sting helping to dissipate some of the tension tightening my shoulders. "But what if trouble finds her before she finds her good sense?"

The subdued deep rumble of distant thunder moves through the kitchen as though it's reaching to answer my question. Riall laughs again and moves over to the table where he happily starts chopping vegetables. The eager, slightly unhinged gleam I know all too well is back in his eyes. A game is afoot, and for him, there's nothing that he likes more. All the panic and concern that was just thickening the air is chased out of the window and replaced by the scent of an impending vicious storm.

It smells like victory.

Tarek grasps my shoulder and gives it a reassuring squeeze. "She's ours," he affirms. "She just doesn't know it yet."

His words wash through me, and I try to let them purge me of my apprehension.

"She will," I proclaim, and he nods his agreement as he moves to perch against the counter.

It's not lost on me that his eyes are trained on the window etched into the kitchen door. I fold my arms over my chest and take up a similar stance. I try not to count time as I wait, but it's impossible not to feel as though it's purposefully slowing just to fuck with us. A few raindrops patter against the glass, the sound a whisper of warning that the storm is ready to unleash its wrath.

I usually love when the sky gets angry like this. The ocean always answers its fervor, and for a spell of time, the world mimics what too often rages inside of me. But today... today I feel as though a sliver of my soul is out wandering in this danger, and it's entirely too fragile to risk.

"I thought she would listen," I offer when the sounds of Riall making breakfast become too much to bear in the otherwise quiet kitchen. We're all in our heads as we stand here impotently waiting, and that can be a dangerous place to spend too much time. "I figured it would be a shock, learning of our involvement, but I didn't think she'd do this," I continue, pointing at the door I need her to walk back through any moment now.

"I'll admit, I expected a touch more gratitude," Tarek agrees, and Riall gives a derisive snort.

"You both are clearly forgetting how we were when we first got here," he points out, pouring things from one bowl into another before hardily stirring everything together.

I smile as I think back to the early days. The fights, the challenges, the time it took until I saw these two as a part of who I am. Tarek looks as though he's taking the same trip down memory lane.

"Maybe," I concede, but I can't help but feel uneasy about everything that just happened or the fact that we're having to wait for her to come back to us, and only then because she doesn't have a better option.

We shouldn't have to try to convince her to stay in the first place. She should feel the same pull that we do. Tilleo has been running the ludere like it's his own. We had no idea about some of the horrendous things he and his masters were doing behind our back. We probably still wouldn't if Auset hadn't caught our eye and then snatched each one of our souls as though they always belonged to her. We all agreed to let her deal with the master and his people when she was ready, but if Tilleo fucked her up so badly that she can't recognize her mates, I'll spend the rest of my days making him pay for it.

"She'll come around," Tarek assures. "She doesn't know what we do about the realms. All she's ever experienced is that ludere. She's probably spent most of her time there dreaming about what it would be like to leave. Reality will replace that fantasy soon enough," he asserts, and I nod.

"And when we find out where she's from and how she ended up there?" Riall questions, wiping his hand down his beard, and I narrow my eyes at the nervous gesture.

We all go silent.

"She's ours," I reaffirm, the declaration pushing her even deeper beneath my skin.

If my brothers weren't feeling the exact same way, I'd question the overwhelming need to tether Auset to us in every way possible. I've never felt something like this before, and it's concerningly all-consuming. But I can't get the image out of my head, of her bleeding on the table, pallid and on the cusp of death. I can't push away the overwhelming drive I felt to save her or the way I knew without a shadow of doubt that she was a part of us the way we are a part of each other. I never hoped to find anything like this, and now that it's punched us all in the face, there's no letting go.

It'll take time to know her, to show her who we are and what she could be to us, but she needs to give us a chance first. While Riall is the worst of us when it comes to patience, Tarek and I aren't much better. We've worked too hard and been through too much to be denied. We're the Order of Scorpions, and Auset needs to learn quickly that we're hers as much as she's ours.

I glance over at Tarek and silently communicate that I'm already growing tired of waiting. He sighs but says nothing. I attempt to redirect my focus from my impatient frustration to the plan. I can't deny that it makes sense despite how much I hate just sitting here. I do understand the importance of Auset working this out and *choosing* us, but my patience can only be stretched so far. If she forces me to bring her back, I'll do it happily. Tarek will just have to sort out some other way to convince her to stay, if it comes to that. And if it happens to involve locking her in my room and teasing her until she begs for more and promises to never leave us, so be it.

23

AUSET

An endless horizon of trees is all I can see as I pick my way through bushes and the lush greenery creeping across the forest floor. The moist air is thick all around me, but it's not hard to breathe, and my skin seems to appreciate it more and more with every second I spend tracking through the rich atmosphere. I've pushed myself for a while now. At first because I was worried that, despite what Tarek said, someone would track me and force me back, but surprisingly, that hasn't happened, and the rush to get as far away as quickly as I can is starting to recede.

When I first stepped out of the kitchen and into the strange world of green, blue, and gray, I gave myself a moment. I took in the foreign sites, hoping I might recognize something, but nothing came. I've long since given up trying to understand how I can sometimes recall random things like the way a particular food smells even though I can't think of its name. Or the title of a person, place, or object when I possess no other memory about it. It's as helpful as it is frustrating. When I study the black rocks and the ground that's almost the same color, nothing about this land registers any kind of familiarity.

I don't know what the lines of trees all around me are. I don't recognize the clusters of needle-like leaves, and nothing is triggered when I smell their sweet woody scent. The cliff the gray castle is built on is as foreign and strange as everything else around here. The roiling ocean doesn't call to me in any way, nor does the smell of salt, lush vegetation, smoke, and an undercurrent of something floral on the wind. None if it strikes me as anything I might have experienced before.

So instead, I walk. I stomp into a world I don't know and don't recognize, trying to put as much distance as I can between me and the Order of Scorpions. I don't know how far I've managed to get; I can still hear the ocean crashing against rock and the whistle of wind as it ruffles the trees and the bushes all around me. The sky is growing darker with each step I take, and I'm starting to accept that I have no idea what I'm doing.

I wince as I step on a sharp rock. Hissing in pain, I pick up my foot so I can rub the sting from the pad of it. I curse myself for letting my mulishness lead the way as I walked out of that kitchen. If I had been thinking, I would have packed some supplies, demanded a sack full of aurems, stocked up on weapons, and then put boots on before I stormed out. The burning sands of the Corozean desert have hardened the soles of my feet a fair amount, but the sticks and rocks of this unfamiliar terrain are already taking their toll.

I brush a few pebbles from my feet and stare at the soot-dark stain the soil has stamped there. I brush the pad of a finger over the inky darkness, and I can't help but think of the skeleton glamour I was growing so used to seeing every day. So much has changed in such a small stretch of time, and I feel like my head and heart are playing catch up.

Tarek's words swirl in my mind. The offer to become one of them tugs at me as I look down and imagine what my hand would look like if it were draped in a skeletal glamour instead of the dark soil that's there. I jostle the strange feeling from my mind and set my foot down. Straightening, I once again look around before sighing and shaking my head. I don't have the first fucking clue where to go.

I know the castle is at my back, and the sound of waves having a conniption as they crash against the rocky shore is off to my right. The clouds block the sun, making it impossible to use it as a guide, and I worry when night falls that there will be different stars winking down at me. If that happens, I won't be able to use the sparkling strangers in the sky to show me the way, and then what will I do?

I throw my head back and groan. Leave it to me to finally get away only to have nowhere to go. Reality nips at my neck, and I start worrying about how I'm going to survive in a world I know nothing about. The only skills I possess involve fighting, killing, and biting my tongue. That last one seems to be broken these days though, and speaking my mind isn't exactly working out so well for me. Even if I can make it to some town or village, how in the bloody moon am I going to make a life for myself?

"No," I order, slashing out my hand with finality.

The word bounces back at me from the bark of the leaning trees I'm surrounded by. They tilt as though they're eagerly waiting to hear a secret, but they'll be waiting forever, because I'm all out. I've revealed everything I know to three strangers who title themselves after arachnids and body parts. Now I'm here wandering through a sea of trees, with no clue what the fuck I'm doing.

I sigh and start moving again. It doesn't matter if I don't have the answers, I tell myself. I've never had the answers, and I've always found a way. This will be no different. I'll make it, because that's what I do, and now I'll do it all as a free fae. I smile at that, muted shock and triumph dancing with one another in my head.

I'm free.

"I'm free!" I scream at the trees, as though I'm daring them to prove me wrong.

I close my eyes and relish the way they scream it back at me like we're all celebrating together. I stop and throw my hands out, twirling as the declaration slowly fades on the wind. And all at once, just like that, the weight of those words settles over me. I drop to my knees, the dark soil cushioning my fall, and I stare at my surroundings in a new light.

I am my own.

For the first time since I can remember, there's no master breathing down my neck. There are no demands forcing my hand or expectations to meet. No one stands by with a coiled whip, waiting to punish some stupid thing I do or say. I don't have to give or concede because I've been ordered to. I don't have to bend for anyone ever again.

I stare down at my hands with disbelief.

I did it.

I got away.

A drop of water kisses my palm, and I look up to see if the slowly encroaching storm is finally ready to come down and play. But it's not raining. It's me. I swipe at my cheek and stare down at my wet fingertips. A broken laugh warbles out of me, and more tears drip down my cheeks. I dig my fingers into the forest floor and bow until my forehead touches the soft soil. I offer the ground my tears and soak in the verity of this moment. Gratitude and anger battle in my chest, as determination and relief settle in my soul. Every step I make from here moving forward will be because *I* make it. Every result or repercussion is now mine to own, and that's both incredible and incredibly overwhelming.

After some time, I sit up and wipe my face with the sleeve of my tunic. I stand and brush dirt and twigs from my hands and inhale a deep grounding breath. I want to stretch this moment for as long as possible. I want to bathe in it, inscribe it in my skin, but life and my circumstances insistently tap at the edges of my newfound peace. Like it or not, I need to think about the best way to move forward from here, and I need to do it without letting fury or fear drive me.

If the Scorpions are right—and I have no reason not to believe that they are—the world I'm wandering into is just as dangerous as the ludere. I have to ensure that I'm the predator in these realms, because there is no alternative for me, not anymore. But how?

I rub my hands down the thin material of my trousers and do my best to come up with something, but try as I might to chase them far from my thoughts, three faces keep barging into my mind. I've known them for barely any time at all, and yet I feel as though they've been haunting me in some way forever.

Tarek's protective countenance. The way Curio watches me, drinking down my reactions as though he can't get enough of their flavor. The playful gleam in Riall's gaze that's both a warning and an invitation. I picture them glamoured, the way I knew them back at the ludere, and then it fades to reveal who they are now. I wish my chest didn't tighten and the air in my lungs didn't feel utterly insufficient for what was lying beneath the magic. I don't want to appreciate lush lips or square jaws. Stunning physiques and intriguing minds aren't enough to erase the damage they've done. I refuse to be bewitched by heated stares and warm promises.

I attempt to shut their words and faces out of my plans, but every time I weigh the risks of something viable I come up with, the Scorpions are there, whispering in the back of my head that there's a better way. What's worse is that I can't even say with conviction that they're wrong.

I have nothing and nowhere to go.

I know I can make a shot of this newfound freedom. I can figure out how to land on my feet, I always do, but I don't have to make it so hard on myself. I can find boots, pocket a little bit of money, and put together a better plan than wandering around a mysterious forest and blindly thinking *who needs boots or a skillset beyond killing?* I groan irritably as the path away from the Scorpions grows dimmer, while the path back to them sharpens, suddenly lined with paving stones of reason and wisdom.

I kick at a small rock and then immediately regret it.

"Fuck boots!" I shout into the murky sky, but this time, when my own voice echoes back at me from the surrounding trees, it feels more like a taunt than encouragement.

"Ugh," I growl.

I don't have to stay forever, I tell myself, and even though I know it's the right choice, it still feels so wrong. I have to go back.

I have to go back, and I hate it.

Just long enough to make walking away the next time easier, because there *will* be a next time. However, there's no denying that my very survival in these cruel realms is hinged on *not* allowing my pride to blind me from the best path forward. That doesn't mean I have to do things on their terms though. The Scorpions might have a role to play in a *good* plan, but it doesn't mean I have to give in to what they want from me. They offered me a place in their Order, probably as the official cock washer, among other things, but I don't have to accept anything that doesn't serve me and my goals.

They want to lure and entice, and even though I skipped that training in the ludere, it can't be too hard to play that game too. I can give just enough to get what I need without compromising myself. Supplies, aurems, a little time to find my way, these are the things I need. I also want answers, and if the Scorpions are as good as they say they are, it shouldn't take long to find something. Anything that can point me in the right direction, and then I can take it from there. I can be cautious. I can make things work for me instead of against me.

Just as I'm ready to pivot and start back the way I came, doubt begins to fester. I wrestle with my thoughts, weighing and advocating for and against, but I suddenly feel as lost as I did when I first wandered into these rows of towering trees. I shake my head, uncertainty making it impossible to step forward or go back. I know I need to be smart, but how wise can it really be to trust the Order for anything? They'll only give to me as long as they're getting, and what if they demand too much?

Maybe Eacon would help me?

I immediately eliminate that thought. Even if I was lucky enough to find her village, there's absolutely no doubt that her loyalties lie with the Scorpions. In fact, I'd be better off avoiding any nearby villages for a while. Who knows which fae might gladly hand me back over to them simply because it might gain them favor?

I survey my surroundings, determined to find another way. I'll walk until something else presents itself, but there has to be something I'm not seeing. Just as I come to that conclusion, a flash of lightning streaks across the sky, immediately followed by a terrifying crack of thunder that's so loud my bones vibrate from the sound. If I didn't know better, I'd think this storm was arguing with my plan. The clouds choose that exact moment to rip themselves open and dump down on me, as though fate itself is bathing me in tears of dissension. I glare up at the clouds, unamused by their obvious efforts to dissuade me.

"Did you not hear them in there?" I demand of the weeping sky and rumbling thunder, gesturing behind me to where the castle sits somewhere far at my back. "They're slavers," I argue as lightning whips across the dreary gray to strike down somewhere far off in the looming forest. "What the fuck am I supposed to do with that?" I challenge.

Pushing sopping strands of hair out of my face, I wrap my arms around myself as the temperature drops and the cold rain pelts me. I stop moving and then waver as the sky grumbles above me. I swear it sounds like sonorous approval. With a huff, I stare at the soaring walls of trees around me. This forest will lead me either on a path of mystery and uncertainty or back to the castle, where I'll have shelter and the time to come up with a better plan. I scrub at my face and shove my long hair off my shoulders. My stomach then pointedly reminds me that it's empty and not at all happy about it. I scoff at myself; I don't even know how to forage for food or what kind of beasts I can hunt and eat. I doubt I'll find desert rats or scarabs scampering about. And there's that delicacy called *bread* back at the castle...

All I can do is stand there as the storm picks up like a wailing child that just found its lungs. I once again vacillate over what the right choice is. I don't believe in signs, but I do believe that stupidity is a choice. I can stubbornly keep walking with no shoes, no cloak, no money, and no idea of how to function in these lands. Or I can see the obstinacy for what it is and make a decision that doesn't leave me dying at the base of a tree either from starvation or the elements.

I groan into the wind and rain, hating the feeling of being trapped, even though in this case, it's of my own choosing and for the best. I know what I need to do. In accepting that, I also have to admit to myself that I can't step back into that castle without being honest about the pull I feel to the three fae. I'm pissed at them, but I'm also intrigued. All of it is too dangerous a game to pretend it won't be a factor. As much as I wish I were, I'm not immune to the effect they have on me. Now that I know who they are and what they've done to me as well as so many other blade slaves, I need to find a way to extinguish this, whatever *this* even is between us.

The Order of Scorpions can't be trusted. I need to reconcile what I thought they might be with who I know they are now. I just wish that was more easily done than I suspect it might be. From the moment I walked into their tent in Tilleo's stronghold, I shed the masks, embraced the anger, and showed them a piece of who I really am at my core. I didn't do it on purpose, but that didn't change how empowered I felt. What I didn't realize could also happen was that it would leave me vulnerable.

If I admit the truth to myself, I crave what Scorpius, Bones, and Skull have with each other. I don't *want* to be alone. I need more than a solitary life of death and barbarity, even though it's foolish to think I'll ever find it. Most days, it's easy to ignore my desire for these things, because they have always been figments of my imagination. And yet, now, they're not so out of reach.

I don't want to get a taste of this life and love it, only to find out that it's poison.

Uselessly I wring water from my hair, even though the rain hasn't let up in the slightest. I stare up at the storming sky as though it will reveal what I'll be getting into if I stay.

"What? No flicks of lightning or grumbling thunder to tell me if I'm doomed or not?" I accuse, and then I snort out a laugh because I'm standing in the middle of a downpour and arguing with a tempest. I guess it could be worse, I could still be at the ludere doing this with a sandstorm.

Surrender—and an eager flutter that I have every intention of ignoring—throbs through me as I finally decide. I know I need to be cautious, that expecting too much is dangerous, but for the first time since I can remember, I wonder if maybe the key to my survival here is to demand more. My wishes and needs have never been a consideration before, but I can ensure that doesn't happen here. For reasons that I refuse to look at too closely, the Scorpions want me to stay. I can leverage that to keep me safe and to get what I need.

If it goes wrong, I'll leave. I'd be no worse off than I was at the ludere—or than I am now, trekking through this unknown forest with nothing but a chip on my shoulder and the ability to strangle a man to death in less than a minute.

I smile at that.

I can do this. I can find my way riding on the backs of a few Scorpions for a while.

I shake my head at the optimism that tries to lodge itself in my chest. Hope is a dangerous mistress, but I don't have to rely on that bitch, I only need myself. Well, myself and a good dagger wouldn't hurt. I exhale a deep, resigned breath and turn around. I start walking back the way I came, doing my best not to think too much about the warmth that dips low in my stomach as I do.

Step one of the new plan is find a dagger. Step two, do whatever I need to do to get away and survive on my own two feet. Step three, vengeance. I'm free, and no matter what, I'm going to make sure I stay that way, and then I'll make anyone who's ever hurt me, pay.

24

THE CASTLE SLOWLY APPEARS THROUGH THE trees, and I refuse to feel relieved by that. It grows bigger as I draw closer, and yet it's more unpretentious than I thought something called a *castle* would be. It's made of gray rock that's been amassed together and held in place with matching mortar. A large cliff wraps itself around the base of the building, which has layers of wall towers, stacked wings, and battlements with ornate crenulations. There's a large round turret in the middle at the top, and even though the Scorpions' home is smaller than Tilleo's stronghold overall, it somehow possesses a more imposing visage.

Waves crash around the cliff face. The unbridled storm urges the ocean to rage against the black rock that looks like stacked books on a shelf, as though it's personally offended by the obstruction. The wind howls and the rain pounds at me, like it too is a cruel master, demanding that I do whatever it tells me to. My eyes burn from the salty drops and the ocean spray the gale slams unforgivingly against me.

Surprisingly, I hear arguing as I stride closer to the kitchen door. The voices are booming, angry, and loud enough to be heard over the burgeoning turbulent storm. I can't make out what they're yelling at one another, but I sneak closer and try to pick out the individual threads of the jumbled mess they're lobbing back and forth.

Lightning snaps down somewhere behind me, but it's close enough for me to feel the pulse of power and heat before thunder explodes in the air. It sounds and feels as though the sky is falling all around me. I shove back through the thick wood barrier to the safety of the kitchen faster than the storm can scream, *"And stay there!"*

Silence greets me as I press my back to the closed door as though it will shut out the threats the sky's been making since I dared to step under its insolent cover. I pull in heavy breaths, water dripping down my face and body to pool quietly on the floor as the Scorpions just stare at me. Neither of us hurry to say anything, but I notice each of them is positioned around the large prep table in the middle of the kitchen as though they needed it between them to keep the peace.

Riall's eyes trace drops of water as they plummet from me to the floor, and when he spots my bare and now muddy feet, a smile oddly threatens the corners of his mouth before he stifles it. Curio has his arms crossed over his chest as though he wants to ask me what I have to say for myself, like I'm some cria who was just caught doing something I wasn't supposed to be doing. Tarek has a blank mask in place, and I don't like that he doesn't want me to see what he's feeling—or that I even care to know.

"I'll give you a month," I offer, my voice loud in the stifling quiet of the kitchen.

"Five," Tarek counters without missing a beat.

I scowl. "Two."

"Three, at a minimum. We need time to make quiet inquiries about you and then chase the credible leads that may come forward. You'll also need some time to train and get kitted," Tarek argues, and I scrutinize him as I consider his words.

The leader of the Scorpions stands across from me, his eyes shrewd, his body language assured and intimidating. But I've held his cock in my hands, so the big-scary-killer demeanor just doesn't have the impact it once did.

"Fine," I concede, and it's as though the word creates a leak in the kitchen's atmosphere, allowing all the tension to hurriedly stream out. "What is blooding?" I immediately demand, wasting no time diving right into the pool of answers I know these three possess.

I wait to see how they will play this. Will Tarek shut down the question again? I've just made it clear that I have no intention of staying. I wouldn't be shocked if Tarek and the other two refuse me any answers that will make them even more vulnerable than they already are. Riall's eyes rake over me, and he slowly smiles. He brings the tip of his tongue to the smooth curve of his now perfectly ordinary canine before snapping out of whatever trance he was just under.

He turns and grabs a pan from the rack attached to the wall before lighting the cooktop. I linger and silently study the muscles of his back as they flex and roll with his movements. Grabbing the large bowl he was cracking eggs into, he pours the mixture into the warming pan with one hand while adding colorful cubes of other things into the same pan with the mixture. I suddenly don't know which I want more, answers or breakfast.

"Blooding is pretty much what it sounds like," Riall finally starts as he shuffles the eggs around in the pan with a wooden spoon.

Relief washes through me as he starts talking, but I worry if I do anything, like move too quickly, he'll stop. He grabs another pan and begins to warm it over a new set of ignited flames before turning to a tall cupboard—which turns out to be some kind of cooler—and pulls out large medallions of red meat. My stomach gives an impatient rumble that's so loud Curio looks over at it with a raised brow. I ignore him and my impertinent, demanding empty belly.

"We can drink from other fae, other beings in general really, and it does things for us," he continues vaguely.

"All of us can?" I press, looking from Riall, while he fusses with pans on the cooktop, to Curio and Tarek.

Riall turns until his eyes find mine.

"No. Just me...and now you," he answers reverently. "In all of the realms, I've only known of about a dozen other Sanguinna who can do what we can. All of them are male.

It's thought that any females with this ability died out long ago," he supplies, and I'm both surprised and bewildered by his statement. "Shadow walking is rare. Usually only the elite of the elite are predisposed with the ability to manipulate shadows on some level. Even that doesn't guarantee they'll actually learn how to master the ability. Blooding, however, is even rarer," he goes on, turning back to what he's cooking.

The kitchen starts to fill with delicious smells I can't identify. Riall's large back blocks much of what he's doing, and I can't trace which scent goes with which pan. My stomach starts moaning again, and I beg it to stop trying to climb out of my throat in an attempt to crawl closer to the cooking food.

"Why?" I question, moving closer to the table to pull out a stool. Maybe if I put more obstacles between me and whatever Riall is cooking, then I'll be less likely to pounce like a feral beast because it's taking too long to get it from the pan into my mouth.

I sit and reach up to wring out my hair as a small shiver quakes through me.

"Here," Curio declares as he reaches over his shoulder, grabs the back of his tunic, and pulls it off. He tries to hand me the heap of black fabric, but I just stare at it and then him, confused.

Why is he giving me this?

Curio leans closer, as though the distance between us is the reason why I haven't plucked the top from his outstretched hand. I look down, still unsure of what he's doing, and my eyes lock onto everything that's now on display.

His warm brown skin is the smooth, mark-free surface that Tilleo always required of his blade slaves. It makes me wonder if Curio was once a slave like me or just lucky that life hasn't marked him up. All of the exquisite detail I can now trace with my eyes was lost under the thick layer of glamour, but luckily for me, it's all on display now. My gaze drops greedily over his honed and hardened body. His firm pec jumps as he pushes his tunic closer.

Slowly I reach for it, but I can't seem to tear my eyes from the display of rippling muscle and sinew. I've seen chiseled bodies before; some of the guards and all of the other blade slaves exhibited their own versions of the eye feast before me. However, what I'm used to seeing significantly lacked the bulk that these Scorpions are working with. Males in the ludere are more scant and far less brawny. That is not the case here at all.

Heat pools low in my belly, and my mind feels as though it's stuttered to a stop. I blame the all-consuming trance on why, in a daze, I untie the ripped halves of my tunic, pull the dripping fabric free from where it's wound around my waist, and then tug the soaked top off over my head. Nudity and shyness isn't a luxury blade slaves are allowed at the ludere. All of us quickly get used to the exposure and learn how to not feel vulnerable because of it. But all it takes is the cool air against my skin and the shocked look that overtakes Curio's face for me to remember that I'm not in the ludere anymore. I also sure as fuck don't have a binding wrapped around my chest like I usually do when I have to undress.

The sopping fabric of the black tunic I was wearing hits the ground with a wet slap as I quickly drop it. I fumble to pull Curio's tunic on, internally cursing myself for getting distracted and then partially naked, all because the muscles were too pretty not to stare at. Someone clears their throat, and I recognize a hint of a chuckle before a cough covers it up. Thankfully, I still haven't pulled the neck of the tunic down and I can't see anyone, which means they also can't see the mortification currently flushing up my neck.

If I could crawl into a shadow right now and disappear, I would, but I don't want to give these three the satisfaction of seeing me flustered. Their egos are entirely too robust as it is, so instead, I feign nonchalance as I push my head through the neck, and then I reach down and shove off my wet skintight trousers as well. The hem of Curio's tunic drops until it skims the middle of my thighs, and I nudge the rain-soaked clothes into a pile next to the foot of the stool, as Curio's warm scent wraps itself around me.

I refuse to draw in the deep pulls of Curio's smoky masculine bouquet like my mind is begging me too. No. I won't try to decipher if there are notes of charred cypress mixed with something light and crisp, some kind of sap maybe? I'm also not going to even bother to attempt to figure out how I know what any of those things smell like, because I'm not even smelling them. Nope. I'm sitting down on a stool, scarcely aware that I'm wearing Curio's shirt and that he's still bare from the waist up. Definitely not noticing that.

"I'll...uh...get you a blanket," Tarek declares, and there's far too much amusement in his tone as he breezes past me.

The kitchen is once again quiet, and I think I see Ri-all's broad back shake as though he's stifling a laugh as he scoops things from pans onto plates. Curio adjusts how he's sitting on the stool he's occupying, and I do my best to pretend that I'm unaffected by what just happened.

So I flashed them; I have no doubt that they've all seen tits before. Probably more than they can keep track of. There's absolutely nothing special about mine, so there's nothing to fret over. I try to focus on whatever we were talking about before Curio went and scrambled my brain, but it takes me a moment. I have to practically slap my wandering eyes to keep them from searching for Curio's naked chest in the corners of my vision. I saw two-thirds of these Scorpions naked in their tent back at the ludere. I knew they were large in every way and cut as though they'd been carved from stone, but it did nothing to prepare me for how all of it would affect me when the glamour was finally shed.

"Right...so...um...why is blooding rare?" I stammer as I do my best to put blinders on my thoughts in an effort to point them at what's important here. I need answers, and I doubt any of them are found in the lines of Curio's exquisite arms, or chest, or back, or...

Slavers, Auset! They're dirty, rotten-on-the-inside slavers. Focus!

"Right," Riall echoes as though he's resetting things in his thoughts too. "Blooding... Blooding is rare because the lines of ancient fae that had the ability have died out for the most part."

"Sanguinna?" I ask, picking up on the title he mentioned previously in passing.

"Exactly. They, *we*," he corrects, "are a blessed line of fae who can siphon power and other abilities through blood. Fangs appear here and there with some fae, but that doesn't mean the Sanguinna line is strong enough in them to allow them to drink and use blood for their benefit," he explains as he pulls other items from the cooler and adds them to the plates he's preparing. "But I have a feeling that you can not only drink, you can siphon, can't you, Beasty?" Riall asks.

The question is casual, but he turns to look at me, and the hopeful glint in his gaze gives me pause.

"I can drink and siphon, so it would make sense that my *Blood* would be able to as well," he explains, his green-brown gaze growing molten as he holds my stare.

The way he wraps his lips and tongue around the word *blood* is distracting. What he said doesn't make sense to me, but his tone is a distracting sensual tease that makes tiny interest-fairies wake up in my stomach and start fluttering about.

"I wondered if there might be more to what happened on the rooftop," Curio interjects. "I should have recognized the bite marks in his throat, but Riall's kills have been clean for so long I forgot it could get so...messy. It looked like you clawed through the throat of that blade slave."

"Leto," I interrupt. "That *blade slave's* name was Leto," I tell Curio with a scowl.

The bastard may have tried to kill me, but he belonged to them after all, just like the rest of the slaves at the ludere. The least they can do is remember a name. Curio fixes me with a look but wisely doesn't say anything about my snappish tone.

I wait for the flash of pain I expect to feel, hearing and talking about Leto, but the sting of what happened between us doesn't resonate. I feel nothing. Not anger or even disappointment. I thought betrayal might ring more strongly in my veins, but if the roles were reversed, and Tilleo had offered me a choice of any Order, I could easily see me on the roof of that ludere burying a chakram in Leto's stomach. It's always been about survival, even at the cost of each other. We always knew that. What does bother me though, is Curio saying my kill wasn't clean. He's not wrong. But I can't help but hear a reprimand in that statement regardless of whether he means it to be there or not.

I shoot a glare his way, but Riall is watching me as though he'll happily stand there smoldering for all of eternity until I answer him.

"Yes," I finally respond. "I can...drink. It seemed to do *something* to me, so I'm guessing that's siphoning, I couldn't say for sure," I admit. "I didn't know I could do any of it until recently. I thought my fangs were an emotional response; I didn't realize that they served more of a purpose than that," I offer hesitantly, hating that the admission affirms just how little I know about my own body and abilities. "I've never felt the urge before to...uh...bite. The drinking was an accident," I admit.

"Who?" Riall asks, a hint of snarl in the question. The covetous gleam in his eyes confuses me for a beat as I process what he's asking me.

"Gartox," I answer. "He had me pinned. I thought I was going to die, and it just happened. I bit him, and...well, you saw the rest. Leto was the same thing. He was close and I didn't have any other weapons. The fangs felt almost like a fail-safe."

"Are you craving it?" Riall inquires.

My brow furrows. "Biting? Blood? Or someone trying to kill me?" I snark, unsure of where this is going.

Is it bad if I crave it?

Riall gives me another bright, mind-numbing smile, and Curio laughs. I like his laugh; it's deep, and I can hear all kinds of dark hidden things in it.

"Blood or biting," Riall answers, his smile cheeky and his eyes now glinting with mischief.

"No," I answer simply.

"Good," he replies just as casually, and then he grabs two plates and sets them down in front of me and Curio.

What would he have done if I had said yes?

"Take this," Tarek announces as he walks back into the kitchen and hands me a blanket.

I pause for a moment, wondering why he handed it to me and not Curio; I'm not the one who's half naked here. But when his cool blue eyes fall to my legs, I realize that I sort of am. I stand up and wrap the thick wool tartan around my waist and then sit back down. I bring a corner of the blanket up to help dry my hair, not bothering to gauge any of their reactions, even though I can feel their eyes on me. I ignore the burn of their stares and focus on the heaping plate of food in front of me.

Steam rises off the soft orange of the eggs. There are small chopped-up colorful vegetables—I think—speckled amongst the fluffy peaks, and next to the healthy pile of eggs is a seared, round cut of meat. It glistens and has a sprig of something green placed on it, but I snatch a spoon from the table and start shoveling eggs into my mouth before I can bother to ask what any of it is called.

The eggs burn my tongue as I stuff my maw full of the soft, mouthwatering heaps, but I don't care. I barely even slow to recognize the small pinch of searing pain as I shove even more past my lips. The delicious tower of orange is gone too soon, and when my spoon does nothing against the thick cut of meat, I abandon the utensil—and all pretense of civility—and snatch the juicy meat from the plate with my hands and tear into it.

My fingertips singe, but an explosion of flavors detonate in my mouth, and I close my eyes in an effort to catalog what I taste on my tongue. It's warm and juicy and seasoned with things that make my mouth feel alive and happy. The meat practically melts in my mouth, the texture nothing like the sand stag I've had only a handful of times. I can almost feel the vitamins and nutrients going to work in my starved body, and before I know it, I'm licking the juices from my hands and wishing I had more.

I eye the three Scorpions, weighing which would be the easiest to fight for their food.

"Take it," Tarek surprisingly concedes, his plate sliding across the table to bump the empty one in front of me.

I watch him warily as I fist his eggs into my mouth like some wild brute, but he doesn't look angry or exasperated, he looks amused, and maybe a little sad.

"Take mine too, Beasty, fuck knows I'm getting more out of watching you eat it than I would if I was. Do you always make those noises when you eat?" Riall asks me, a salacious grin spreading across his full lips.

A tiny growl rattles in my chest, but then I rip into Tarek's meat, and all annoyance is sucked right out of my body and replaced by the undiluted excitement of eating. There's no comparison between what I'm heaving eagerly into my mouth versus the bug-laced slop we barely survived on at the ludere. It makes me angry to have forced down that rancid porridge when there are things like eggs, and bread, and melt-in-your-mouth meat out in the world, but I shove my indignation away. I'm here for a short while because I have to be. My outrage isn't going to do anything for me now except encourage me to walk back out into the forest and never look back. Better to bury it...for now.

Riall reaches for a slice of bread, and another rumble of warning sneaks out of me. He laughs and holds his hands up in surrender as Tarek slides the board of doughy goodness closer to me. A huff sounds next to me as I stack Riall's plate on my empty one and start in on his feast. Curio scoots his food in my direction, and I light up with elation. I should probably care that I'm fully living up to the stupid name Riall keeps calling me. Hunched over my food like some feral creature and demanding that they sacrifice their meals to me, but the desperate way I need every bite overwhelms every sense or desire for decorum.

"You're a cutthroat little thing, aren't you?" Curio asks amused, and both Tarek and Riall laugh softly.

"Was there any doubt about that before now, brother?" Riall teases, and Curio chuckles and shakes his head.

"Suppose not," he agrees, mirth chiming in his tone.

"You're brothers?" I ask around a large bite of eggs and bread.

"Not by blood," Tarek informs me.

"By choice," Curio supplies.

"Careful, you'll choke," Tarek commands as he rises and opens the cooler to pull out a pitcher.

He plucks four glasses from a different cabinet, filling the first one and handing it to me. I swallow what's in my mouth and bring the cup to my lips. The drink is sweet and waterlike. There's no bite of hidden spirits in the cold liquid, so I quickly gulp it down before returning back to the last plate. My movements slow, my stomach now starting to stretch and fill, but Curio's food is mine—I don't care what my stomach says. I know I can't finish off the bread too, but maybe when they're not looking, I can hide it in my blanket and stash it in my room. I nod approvingly of that plan as I finish off what's left on my last plate.

Tarek clears his throat, and my eyes snap to his. "Well, we've established you can shadow walk and siphon. Any other abilities that we need to know about?"

I consider him for a moment. "Like what?"

"Can you manipulate any elements? Persuade others with just a look or command? Any gifts with glamour?" Tarek asks, and I dismiss the idea I was just entertaining about licking the plates clean, and focus on him and the last of Curio's cutlet.

I deliberate whether or not it's wise to tell these killers what else I can do, but after a beat, the desire to find more answers outweighs the need to keep the few secrets I have left to myself.

"I'm strong and fast, or at least stronger and faster than I ever let the masters see. I don't know the limits of either. I've never been able to test them, but it's more than the average fae, I think."

Tarek nods as though this isn't a surprise to him.

"I don't know about the other things you mentioned. My instinct is to say no, but I've never tried. What I can do now, I discovered by chance, and I'm nowhere near close to mastering any of it," I admit. "Oh, and I can heal with the help of moonlight...and blood. Again, that last part I just learned."

Riall stands up from his spot at the prep table and starts cracking more small orange eggs into a bowl, but I don't miss the look he levels at Tarek.

"What?" I demand, looking over at Curio to see a similar contemplative look on his face.

"Just your appearance alone has us speculating that you are probably from the Night Court. The Dusk Court is a possibility too, but the fact that the moon is healing to you supports the Night Court theory," Curio answers.

"Is it normal for fae from the Night Court to heal with the moon's help?" I question.

"Not normal, but I recall reading about a group of fae that were once thought to be moon blessed. I'll have to look for the passage again to see if there are any other clues. We could be wrong, but it's a place to start," Tarek explains.

I look at each of them in turn while his words steep in my gut.

The Night Court? Could that be home? Am I moon blessed?

As expected, the words rolling around on my tongue and in my mind trigger nothing but curiosity and contemplation. There's no sense of awareness or recollection. There never has been, but for the first time, I look around and know all of that is about to change. I've been here for less than a day, and already I'm clothed, fed, and learning things I never thought I would. Who knows what will happen in three months before I leave for good? I could very well have found family by then, found a place in this world that isn't at the end of a whip or a knife or under the thumb of some slaver.

Something warm settles in my chest. If I didn't know better, I'd think it was hope, but I've long since learned my lesson from playing with that poison.

Riall slides plates piled high with fluffy eggs and crisp vegetables in front of Curio and Tarek. He sits down in front of his own plate, and they all look at me as though they're waiting to see if I'll try to commandeer their food. Awkwardly, I lean away from the table. I'm not really sorry, and I'll probably do it again next meal, but it's odd to have the three killers defer to me like they are. When it's obvious I'm not going to demand more from their plates, they dig in.

"Eat up, boys. When you're done, we'll go see what this Beasty can do," Riall declares with a smirk.

He smiles more than anyone I've ever met, but I can't say that I hate it. I want to, but it's proving more difficult than I thought it would be.

The green in his gaze brightens as he fixes it on me. "Your ass is mine."

I study the look in his eyes and easily surmise there's more to that statement than just training. For some reason, it feels as though *that* might be more trouble than anything I've faced up until now. I have to shut this down, but I don't know how. I need things from them, but I need to figure out how to get what I want without it costing me more than I'm willing to give.

25

MY FANGS DROP FOR THE THOUSANDTH TIME today, and I try not to growl in frustration. The momentary lapse in concentration throws me off my attack, and I lose the advantage I just worked for the last hour to gain. Riall deflects my overhand hit and drives my bow staff to the side with the top part of his while the bottom end swipes up toward me. I flip back, barely missing his strike aimed at my chest.

Tarek and Curio are off to the side, talking back and forth, most likely about me and the mistakes I keep making, but I tune them out and concentrate on the arrogant Scorpion in front of me.

"What's wrong, Beasty?" Riall taunts, his eyes dropping to my pointed canines when my lip curls up in a snarl. "I thought you said you weren't craving blood," he jeers, spinning so fast I shouldn't be able to track it.

Thank the stars I can, or I'd be covered in more bruises than I already am. I'll need to sleep on the roof directly under the moon at this point to be ready to go again by tomorrow.

"I'm not," I snap back before diving underneath his swipe and aiming my staff at his knees.

I'm not completely lying. I'm not craving blood exactly, I'm craving a fuck ton of other things I have no business thinking about, and it's driving me mad. He jumps over my charge, rolling forward and popping back up like some maddening roach that refuses to take the hint and die.

"Craving something else then?" he teases as he starts to circle me.

I glare at him, sidestepping his effort to put me on my back foot and force me to lose ground. "No, Bones. No cravings to speak of. I can't say I care for bugs," I snark, hoping he can't see right through me, but the bite I try to infuse in my tone doesn't deter him in the slightest.

He just laughs.

If only I could find it all so amusing, but I'm pissed. I can't figure out how he's setting me off, but I know he is. No matter what I do, I can't sort out how to stop my fangs from reacting to whatever it is he's doing to me. He's forcing me to literally fight through the driving need that's currently hammering at me like a battering ram. At this point, I'm not sure what will satisfy it: blood, sex, or death. I'm so incredibly frustrated that I suspect it'll take all three.

Every time my fangs drop, it's like an off switch to my mind. Gone are the maneuvers and tactical plans for how to wipe the floor with Bones. In floods all kinds of thoughts about what Riall might taste like. What would his blood feel like in my veins? Better yet, what would it be like to drink at his throat while other things work in and out of me faster and harder and...

Ughhh!

I shake away my thoughts and once again glare at the knowing smirk I'm determined to wipe from his lush mouth. I want to quit, but that's not in my nature. Regardless of the fact that I *need* distance from him. Space is the only thing at this point that can clear away the thoughts and images I know he's somehow shoving in my mind.

He's a bad fae. It's a fact. One not even he would deny. So why is it so hard to stick to the plan I was committed to before I walked back in the kitchen door and stuffed my face? Riall doesn't matter to me, he shouldn't; I just wish my fangs—and now my cunt—would get on board with that.

I feint a leg sweep to the right and then, quick as a striking whip, redirect my weight and my staff for a lateral hit to Riall's ribs. He blocks me with annoyingly little effort, and I'm once again reminded that fighting a seasoned Order member is nothing like training with a fellow blade slave, or even a master for that matter. If I couldn't do what I can, Riall would have walloped me at least a dozen times already.

"Now, now, Beasty, you're so quick to protest, but it's clear you're in desperate need of something," he taunts.

"Yeah, to rip your head from your body and spit down your throat," I growl back.

Riall's smile grows even wider. "I'd much prefer you to swallow, Beasty," he quips, and I wish I could strangle him with his own conceit.

I parry as he advances, but just as we get started, he backs off. He's toying with me, poking me for weaknesses both physically and mentally. He wants an opening past my defenses.

I refuse to give him one.

"Does the shit pouring out of your mouth usually work for the females you want to bed?" I ask, fixing him with a derisive scowl.

"I've had no complaints," he states confidently.

"Maybe, but slaves paid to pretend they like it are never much for complaining in the first place, now are they?" I counter, but my vitriol falls on deaf ears.

Riall laughs harder as though he's proud of my dig instead of offended by it like he should be. It's aggravating. I've never been more sore and tired in my life, and this bastard looks like he could go days without needing so much as a break. Sweat drips down my back and chest from the hours I've spent being tested on different weapons and showing the various forms of combat I know. Riall appears to be fresh from the bathing chamber with crisp, dry togs and a bright smile I want to smack off his face but can't because he's too bloody brilliant.

He's put me through it so far, and what's odd is that I know more than I should. I haven't said anything about it, but I'm using forms and tactics that I was never taught in the ludere. I doubt Riall knows. He probably thinks Tilleo is just that good at being a master, but I've been meeting Riall blow for blow all morning, and I have no idea how.

He's good. Incredible even. I've never seen anything like it, and yet I'm keeping up despite there being no logical explanation for it. He's a seasoned member of an Order; I should have been stomped to dust ages ago. I'm certainly not winning, but I'm not exactly losing either.

Looking back, I realize that a similar thing happened when I first started training at the ludere. Somehow it was like I knew the drills they were hammering into us. I moved and absorbed it all as though it was dormant muscle memory. There's a strange familiarity to the way Riall is pushing me to move, and it's more than an instinctual reaction to his attacks. It's as though we've learned the same techniques side by side, which makes no sense.

I don't know why or how any of this is happening, but really that's not a new sensation for me. I can't count the times that a word or random thought has popped up in my mind, answering a question I never knew I'd asked. At this point, I've grown used to ignoring the unexplainable. The phantom pains, a grasp of techniques I shouldn't know, the name of something, or a scent I can identify with no understanding of how. It's all part of the list of things in my life that I can't make sense of.

"Focus, Auset," Riall barks at me, tapping me on the ass with his staff as he whirs around to avoid the answering blow I slash at him.

I pull in a deep, frustrated inhale and try not to give in to the anger that's simmering inside of me. I'd prefer that he just hit me full out than pull his attacks and land irritating little jabs instead. It's insulting, like he thinks I can't handle it. Why do they want me to join their Order if they think I'm too fragile to withstand the blows?

I remind myself that getting angry isn't going to help. Fighting mad is about as effective as fighting blind, a truth I know all too well. I'm letting Riall get into my head, and I need to stop. I plant my staff against the floor and vault at the Scorpion. He flips to the side, evading my leap, and swats at the anchored end of my bow. I land in the spot he just vacated and snap my weapon up so he can't make contact with me. I try to use the momentum of his swing against him and sneak inside the reach of his staff, but it's like he can read my mind, and he evades me once again.

"You know the fae I hunt aren't going to pull their hits. You're not doing me any favors by going easy on me," I pant as we both analyze one another, searching for an opening and working out a plan of attack that hasn't been tried yet.

"That's what we're there for," he counters, as though that makes any sense. "They'd have to go through us to get to you, and no one gets through us," he declares, and I stop moving, completely taken aback by that ridiculous statement.

"You seem to be forgetting the fact that I won't always be with you," I argue.

"You're with us now; that's all that matters," he arrogantly replies, and once again I feel as though there are so many unspoken things taking up the space between what he is saying and what he means. It's oddly cryptic and annoying.

"So you're just wasting my time?" I demand, lifting my bow with an indignant shrug. "If they'll never get past you to attack me, why bother training me at all?"

My question is met with another of his obnoxious grins. Then, faster than lightning, he swipes his staff up, hitting mine so hard that it pops out of my lax grip and flies up in the air between us. He ducks under the downward trajectory of my weapon, spins around me until I feel his chest against my back, and then presses the unforgiving grain of his wood bow staff against my throat.

"Because," he whispers in my ear. "It's good for the lungs...and for the body."

His breath tickles the shell of my ear, and he runs the tip of his nose up the side of my neck. I barely hold back the shiver his closeness coaxes out of me. I wish I could say that it was pure revulsion pumping through my veins, but I'd be lying.

I grab his staff and use it as leverage. I kick my feet up and then immediately swing them down, dropping my weight at the same time, and flip Riall over my head. The staff leaves my throat, and I dive for my weapon, which is on the ground. Impossibly, Riall lands on his feet and whirls around to try to stop me. It's as though the wood staff is a complete extension of his body, more limb than weapon. I'd marvel at his skill more if he weren't using it to beat my ass in every possible way.

I somersault away from him and then kip up onto my feet. Annoyingly, my bow is rolling away from me, and now Riall is standing firmly between me and it.

"Are you ready to submit yet?" he asks.

"To you?" I question, and his eyes light up, the thought clearly doing things for him. I scoff. "Let me make this as clear as crystal for you, Riall," I tell him, dropping into a defensive stance. "I will *never* give in to you in any way. Not in a training room. Not in a fight. And sure as fuck not in a bed."

Riall's eyes practically glow with eager anticipation as I once again face off against him. My declaration doesn't seem to be serving as the deterrent it was supposed to be. Instead, Riall looks as though I've thrown down a gauntlet and he has no choice but to pick it up. My words have drummed a call to advance, when the rhythm I was searching for was retreat.

His fangs slip out in a blink, and his smile goes from playful to challenging. My body responds, but not in the way I fear it might. All at once, I feel the threat tightening my muscles, and a white haze shutters over my mind. I stop reacting and defending, and instead, like a stone in water, I sink down into instinct and untamable drive.

All light and easygoing pretense is immediately sucked out of the room, and in its place, tension and urgency settles. I kick out at Riall, my heel shattering the staff in his hands and connecting with his chest. I kick him hard enough to knock him back, and he struggles to stay on his feet. The shock written on his face quickly morphs into rapacious excitement, and he tosses the two pieces of his bow to the ground and charges.

We become nothing more than a blurred cyclone of fists, elbows, knees, and kicks. We crash and flow against and around each other like tempestuous river rapids, blocking and connecting in a fluid but savage poetry of motion. The thwacks of skin and bone meeting skin and bone fill the air all around us. The cocky smile is permanently wiped from Riall's lips and replaced by determined focus and wonder.

I inhale and exhale destruction. Riall meets me hit for hit, no longer holding back but embracing the force between us. The deleterious dance we take up is a ruthless thing of beauty. If I weren't so intent on making Riall bleed, I might marvel at the way we ebb and surge, hit and spin like we've been doing it together all of our lives. Just as I reach the pinnacle of what I think I can give, Riall demands more. Impossibly, I meet the call, tapping into reserves I never knew I had and coming for him even harder.

My knuckles crash against Riall's nose at the same time his knee sinks into my stomach. The force and momentum of our blows have us both skidding back, and before either of us can launch a new attack, a booming staccato of applause wrecks our violent enthrallment. My dangerous daze fractures, and Tarek claps as he moves closer. Curio is casually leaning back against the wall, arms crossed over his chest, one leg bent while the other supports his weight. He looks relaxed, but the intensity in his stare betrays him.

Riall and I are both breathing heavily, but strangely, I feel like I could go on forever. Riall finally broke a sweat, and whatever just happened broke the smooth, calm veneer he's been fighting with since we walked into the training room.

"I fucking knew she could tap into more," Riall pants.

I stare at him, bewildered. How would he know anything? I didn't even know I was capable of that. I've hit a focused and determined stride before in training, but what just happened was a whole other tier of unusual.

The way we moved.

The skill and speed.

I study my hands, astonished that they still look the same when everything inside feels different. An energized hum sings in my blood, but I don't mention anything. I don't even know what I would say if I wanted to.

Do you suddenly feel invincible, because I sure do. Let's see who can punch through the wall first.

Yeah, I don't see that going anywhere good. It's on the tip of my tongue to ask if this is because I'm Sanguinna? I hesitate though, worried I might be wrong. What if this is something else?

"Impressive. With time, she might even be able to best Eacon," Tarek agrees, stepping close and leaning toward me as though he's trying to listen closely to something my body is whispering to him.

I go still, wanting to hear whatever it is too. He studies my eyes for a second longer than normal, and I immediately want to find a mirror to see whatever it is that's making the curious glint in his gaze gleam with a hint of concern. Is it the blood and bruises bothering him, or something else?

Warmth drips from a split in my lip, and I wipe at it with the back of my hand. Tarek tosses me a towel, and I use it to clear my brow and the back of my neck of sweat. Riall reaches up and resets his nose. The cracking of bone and cartilage as it's realigned fills the silence that starts to uncomfortably sift through the room. Tarek hands him a towel too, and he presses it to his nose to staunch the bleeding. A large lump is forming beneath one of his eyebrows, and his left cheek is red and slowly growing puffier. I turn away from the crimson patch slowly soaking into the towel. It's getting harder to disregard the pang of hunger that's growing deep in my belly, but I'm not giving into this *blooding* nonsense.

Not with him.

I've never needed it before, and I won't start needing it now. I test my jaw, wincing at the pain that streaks up into my cheek and ear. My right eye isn't opening as wide as the left, and I suspect the lid will probably bulge and blacken. My ribs and one of my hips throb with pain, and there's absolutely no doubt that I'll be sleeping under the light of the healing moon tonight to deal with all the damage.

Despite my injuries, I feel good. Really good. Whatever just happened, whatever I just unlocked, I want more of it.

"Something about the way she was matching me, I've never seen it before. It's hard to explain," Riall tells Tarek, his voice pinched from where he's holding the towel to his nose. "You'll both need to see for yourself, but if you push, she'll show up for it. It was by the book at first, nothing but the ludere's forms and counterattacks, but the more I pissed her off, the more she showed me hints of that raw power we all just saw."

They all look over at me, observing me like I'm livestock that's being considered for purchase. It's demeaning and all too familiar, and I'm entirely done with anyone looking at me as though they're trying to determine my worth.

"I'm right here," I snap, offended.

"Yes, you are, Beasty," Riall coos at me, and it's all I can do not to try to strangle him with his bloodstained towel.

I'm vexed and begrudgingly impressed, and what's even more annoying is that I feel relief. I loathed the idea that they were trying to sit me in a corner and dismiss what I can do for the sole sake of their pride. I also hate that it bothered me in the first place at all.

"Now that we have a true idea of what you're capable of, we can start building on that," Tarek states, and Riall nods his agreement as he runs his palm over his short brown hair.

Riall's hazel eyes glaze over with thought, like he's already formulating a plan for what comes next. I suppress the urge to discuss it with him, shoving down my interest like it was something that bit me and now needs to be punished. I wish all of this didn't feel so exciting. The idea of building on the savagery we just unleashed makes me eager. There's an undeniable thrum of excited anticipation buzzing under my skin right now, and I've never felt that before when it comes to training.

"Either of you in need of immediate healing?" Tarek asks, his icy blue gaze once again looking me over as though he can see what hurts beneath the layers of linen and skin.

Maybe he can, what do I know?

Quickly dropping my eyes from his assessing gaze, I stretch a little, checking if there's anything to be concerned about. I shake my head in answer. Riall does the same, and I catch a twitch of pain in his face as he rolls one of his shoulders. Suddenly *I'm* the one wearing the snooty smirk. It's good to see that I'm not the only one affected by the hours we've spent going head-to-head. I was trying to weaken the force of his hits at the end by targeting that shoulder and upper arm. I hit him so many times in the exact same places I'm surprised he can feel anything at all from the elbow down.

Riall catches me watching him, and instead of a gleam of retribution igniting in his eyes, heat simmers there. His ardent stare moves down my face and settles on the slowly weeping cut on my lip. His tongue sneaks out, and he licks the lower brim of his mouth as though the cut mars his lip and not mine. I look away, entirely too close to burning up in the flames of his stare than I care to be. A deep chuckle taunts me to look back over at him, but I've been provoked enough today.

"Eacon is stopping by later to bring some things for you, Auset. If you change your mind, she can heal whatever you might need then," Tarek informs me, stoking my confusion.

Why would she bring me anything?

I stare at Tarek as though the answers will slip from his lips, but he doesn't continue or offer any details about what she might be bringing.

Hopefully not more dresses.

The impression I got after first meeting Eacon was that she knew and cared for the Scorpions in some sort of maternal manner. However, Tarek's earlier comment about her fighting prowess makes me wonder about her even more. Who is she to them? My first meeting with her was a bit strange. Then again, everything about waking up in this place has been.

Already it's as though I've been here for weeks, when in truth I haven't even been awake for a full day. At this point, someone could tell me that Riall and I have been going at it for a month in this training room, and I wouldn't question it. So much has happened, and yet I find myself stuck and waiting for more to pile on.

It's all entirely too much while simultaneously feeling like it's not enough.

I take in the wooden practice weapons tacked to the walls. My gaze trails to the double doors at the back of the big training space, which lead into their impressive weapons room. Curio gave me a tour of it when I was guided here after breakfast. I've never seen so many stunning and deadly weapons in one place. I could probably spend forever in there and still find something new to play with every day.

The training area is on the same level as the kitchen, but on the opposite side of the castle. Compared to Tilleo's manor, there aren't an abundance of rooms in this one, but the quarters that do exist are colossal. On this level alone, there's the kitchen, laundry, training facilities, the armory, and an alchemy chamber. The main floor boasts of a library, a dining hall, and a wing designated for guest rooms, which happen to be empty. The sleeping and bathing chambers of the Scorpions take up the entirety of the top floor, along with a study and what looked like a rookery tower from outside, although I didn't hear any evidence of birds when I was sneaking down the hallways in search of food. The Scorpions haven't offered to show me around the top floor, but Curio mentioned the layout during his cursory tour earlier.

I start to make a plan to come down here later, once the house is asleep, and relieve the Scorpions of some of their cache of blades. I need weapons when I leave here, and if I haven't figured out how to stock up on the necessary aurems needed, I can always sell some well-crafted pieces. There was an endless array of options that would no doubt fetch a good price. I doubt these fae would even miss them.

"Alright," Tarek claps loudly, jolting me from my thoughts. "Let's get cleaned up, break for luncheon, and then, Auset, you'll be with Curio this afternoon and finish the evening with me."

Luncheon?

"What is luncheon?" I ask before I can stop myself.

Everyone looks at me for a moment too long.

"It's our mid-day meal," Riall supplies, all playfulness and teasing suddenly gone.

He mumbles something else, but I can't make out the words, only the incredulous and slightly angry tone. The shift in demeanor between the three of them is unsettling. All at once, I feel self-conscious. I do my best to swallow down my shock over the fact that they're going to feed me again so soon. I was disappointed earlier when I couldn't manage to steal the bread like I was hoping to. I figured I'd just add it to the list of things I plan on pilfering tonight when I sneak about the castle, getting the lay of things. I eye Riall for a beat and then look at the other two males. Another question sticks in the middle of my throat as though I can't decide if I should swallow it down or spit it out.

"How...how many meals a day do you normally have?" I question hesitantly.

A soft smile quickly replaces Riall's scowl, and I instantly feel better and then worse because he shouldn't be able to do that to me so easily.

"We have three or four meals, depending on the day's agenda. Breakfast, luncheon, a light supper if dinner is going to be late, and then dinner. We also nosh between meals if we need it," Riall explains.

I attempt not to look flabbergasted by everything he just said, but based on the way Riall's and Tarek's eyes soften, I doubt I achieve the blank mask I'm trying for. I don't know what nosh means, but I decide it doesn't matter.

Three or four meals a day?

I don't even know what to think about that. If they're as good as breakfast was this morning... I shake my head, completely baffled.

"You are welcome to eat anything in the cooler or pantry, Moonling. Your days of gruel are over," Curio calls out from where he's still leaning against the wall, and my throat suddenly grows tight and my eyes start to sting.

I look to the others, waiting for them to contradict Curio's offer, but they say nothing as they watch me. My mouth flops open and then shut as words fail me. Feelings I try not to feel, bubble up. I'm both astonished and grateful. Suspicion crawls just under the surface of it all, and I pet it like it's a sweet furry companion that's worked hard to keep me alive despite fate's efforts to do the opposite.

"No tricks," Curio adds as though he can read the concern that just flashed through my mind.

I scrutinize him for a few breaths before nodding.

"Okay, no tricks," I repeat, needing to say it out loud, as though that will help the truth chase away my misgivings.

No tricks, I repeat again in my head, still unsure how it could be true.

"Wash up and meet back in the kitchens in thirty minutes?" Tarek asks.

"Make it forty, I need time to wh—" Riall looks over at me and stops talking.

The room goes silent, and there's an awkward ambiance that fills the space.

"Right. Forty minutes," Tarek agrees, dropping his eyes to the ground and palming the back of his neck.

Judging by the unusual combination of both censure and amusement written over both Tarek's and Curio's faces, it appears they both knew exactly what Riall was going to say before he stopped himself. I, on the other hand, have no idea. Tarek's dark shoulder-length waves fall forward, helping to curtain his features, and I look over to Curio in an effort to puzzle out what just happened. He stares at me, his hickory gaze giving nothing away, but the smallest hint of a smile begins to play at his lips the longer we both look at each other.

I huff out an exasperated breath. They can keep their secrets. What do I care anyway? I turn to leave, ignoring the furtive pests, and try to remember how to get back to my room. They say nothing as I go. I'm on the first step leading to the top floor before I realize Riall is right behind me. I pause, not liking him at my back, and his arm lightly skims mine as he passes me, taking two stairs at a time.

"Think about me as you wash up," he commands, his voice quiet and dripping with all kinds of wicked and alluring things. It's the kind of tone used to whisper late at night when you don't want anyone else to overhear what you're saying. Goose bumps threaten to climb up my arms, and I order the fluttering sensation trying to flare in my gut to fuck off.

Against my will, my fangs drop in my mouth. The sensation stokes my anger as I glare up at Riall's back while he ascends to the top floor. He turns, his gaze liquid fire. He smiles wide, showing off his own set of fangs, his grin pure provocation.

"I know I'll be thinking about you as I do," he adds, and before my mind can dig itself out of the gutter it just fell face-first into, he's gone.

I climb the stairs, perplexed, and hot, and pissed at my-self for feeling any of it. Riall's words play out again and again in my mind as I find my room. I close the door behind me and lean back against it. I pull in deep calming breaths and run my tongue over my sharp canines. I smile as I get a hold of myself and move toward the bathing chamber.

I think I'll take Riall up on his offer. No one has to know. I can scratch the itch, and none will be the wiser. It's the perfect way to get them out of my system once and for all.

26

EADY?" Curio asks as he brushes his hands together to free them of any crumbs.

He pulls the cloth napkin he set in his lap for the mid-day meal and wipes the corners of his mouth before placing it on his empty plate. I notice my napkin. It's still folded on the table. I should try to use it properly at dinner. That is, now that I know I'm supposed to be using it at all and not simply licking my face and hands clean.

Or not.

I think we're all well past manners and civility at this point when it comes to meals. I should probably feel oafish at the feral animal that gets unleashed as soon as someone places food in front of me, but I don't care what these fae think of me. At least I managed not to steal anyone's plate this time. Riall made me four times the amount he made the others, which helped. Quick learner, that one.

I nod my head in answer to Curio's question, and we both stand up. I groan as I rise from my stool and slightly twist back and forth as though that's going to relieve some of the pressure in my full gut. Maybe I shouldn't have eaten that fourth helping?

Nah. Worth it.

I thought bread was good on its own, but I just learned you can stack things on it and eat it all together. Crowns, it's incredible. There was this meat that made my mouth feel like it was on fire, but I loved it. Tarek showed me that when you combine it with some cooling vegetables and this thing called cheese, it's even better. The little food towers are my new favorite thing. Well, that and everything I ate at breakfast...and probably everything I'll eat at dinner, or supper, whichever one comes first.

Food is the best.

The Scorpions don't seem too fussed at my beastly ways, even if their impressions of me did matter. Which they don't.

Riall stares at my mouth like he's wishing I'd tear into him the same way I attack a meal. Tarek puts more on my plate as soon as there's room for it, and Curio adjusts himself in his seat...a lot. Especially when I get particularly vocal with my appreciation. They're too easy to mess with. It almost takes the fun out of it. Almost. They think they're subtle with their charms and lures, but I've set a few snares myself, and they're too wrapped up in what's happening between their legs to pay attention to what they're walking into.

Typical.

I expect Curio to lead me back into the castle for whatever it is we'll be doing together, but when he moves toward the kitchen door and then outside, I follow curiously. A cool breeze tickles my cheeks as we leave the confines of the castle. The sky is still gray, but the clouds are wispy and frail now instead of the threatening stacks of thunderheads that filled the sky before.

The world around us is wet. The storm stopped only a few hours ago. I can still taste it in the air. The scent of rain-kissed moss teases my nose, as do the deeper notes of wet stone and fertile soil. I recognize better the subtle hint of the tall needle-leaf trees on the breeze after spending so much time with them earlier today. The sun is still hiding, but the overall light of the day is dimmer, as though the bright orb is already in a downward arc, eager to meet the horizon so they can lie together for a while.

Curio says nothing as he leads me into the dense surrounding forest. I don't question where we're going, but I see the thin, worn path at our feet, indicating that wherever the destination is, it's visited often. I study him as we go, prodding my instincts for a read on him. He's quieter than I thought he'd be, based on how he interacted with me at the Bidding. It makes me wonder if I did something to make him act like this or if this is how he is when he's home and comfortable. Just as soon as that curious thought enters my mind, I drop-kick it out.

I. Do. Not. Care.

Maybe if I repeat it enough, my wayward thoughts will finally catch on.

Up ahead, a building comes into view. It's a fair size and made of the same gray rock as the castle. It's one story, but the middle of the roof towers tall enough to be another story before pitching down to connect with the building on both sides. There are two large chimneys, one on each end of the peaked roof, and a faint stream of smoke slithers out of them before disappearing in the somber sky. Large barn-like doors make up the side of the building facing us, and I surmise that they probably keep animals inside. There's definitely a stale unwashed fur smell to the place. However, it's mixed with a distinct metallic scent that I can't place. It's not overpowering or horrible, just unusual.

Curio slides one of the huge doors open and gestures for me to enter the structure before him. When no animal pens appear or any noises come from inside, I suddenly find myself hesitant to step any closer. The interior is dark and dreary, and I can't make out what this place is even in the light of one massive open door.

"If we wanted to hurt you, don't you think we would have done it already?" Curio asks, and I twitch when the sonorous sound of his voice shatters the silence. His tone gives me the impression that he's faintly entertained by my initial reluctance.

"You could have been luring me into a false sense of safety," I counter, glaring into the murk to try and make out what's on the other side of it. "Wouldn't be the first time," I add, absently rubbing where there should be a scar on my abdomen from the last time that very thing happened.

"Fair point," Curio concedes, and he gives up on his supposed gallantry and steps into the building first.

I don't immediately follow. The shriek of metal sliding angrily against stiff metal makes me jump again, and I swear at myself to get it together. In front of me, Curio muscles the other gigantic wood door open.

"I've been meaning to oil that," he tells me, stepping back to reveal what's behind him.

Light finally spills in, unveiling the building's secrets, but I still have no idea what I'm looking at.

"What is this?" I ask as I take it all in, my curiosity coaxing me to step closer.

"My workshop," he supplies, turning to take in the interior himself as though he's also trying to see it for the first time. "I'm an armorer," he explains, nodding to the metal table with nicks and hammer marks all over it.

Blackened tools hang on one wall, and two massive hearths with glowing fires simmering inside of them are situated on opposite ends of the building. Hulking animal hides hang from the ceiling, some of them in their natural state while others have been treated and now dawn the rich black color of shadows. I suppose that explains the animal smell. I stare in awe as I make sense of what I'm seeing, and then I slide my wide eyes to Curio's hickory gaze.

"You make the armor for the Scorpions?" I ask, not even trying to hide my admiration.

I recall the three of them removing their onyx protective plates and defenses that first night in the tent. I had marveled at the luxurious craftsmanship then. That, and the fact that they didn't require help to take it off. It fit each of them as though it had been poured over their bodies instead of painstakingly fit to every inch of them. I stare at Curio and try to picture him crafting something so stunning in this very workshop.

"And the weapons," he adds, and I quickly go from impressed to downright reverent.

I picture that gorgeous little knife I nicked from Scorpius—I mean Tarek—when he asked for me to bathe him. Instantly, I want to ask for one, but I shut it down. What right do I have to make that kind of request? They're already feeding me and giving me a room in their home. I need to tread lightly with how much I take. Each of them is pretending that there are no strings attached to any of these things I've been given, but it's also been made clear to me that this world exists with plenty of gray to watch out for.

What will be the gray they ask of me in the end?

Curio strides further into his repository, oblivious to the turmoil of my thoughts. He shovels black crystalline rocks into one fire and then another, and I watch as they grow brighter and hotter instantly. The heat forcefully shoves the touch of the cool afternoon away, and I inch closer to the warmth. Corozean desert nights could get very cold, so it's not like I don't have experience with cooler temperatures. But something about the wet air here makes it feel as though the chill is sinking into my depths and declaring that I'll never escape its clutches again.

"So what am I doing here?" I ask as I look around.

I have a feeling I'm looking at a whole lot of manual labor in my future. Hammering things, probably washing dirty pelts, cleaning tools maybe. I don't look forward to it, but it's better than the other ways I can be asked to pay for their *kindness.*

Curio lifts a large bag of something that oddly resembles sand and drops it on the large metal table. I refuse to admire the way his muscles flex and strain as he picks up another sack and sets it next to the first. Nope. Doesn't affect me. Not one little bit.

"I need to make a mold of your form," he tells me, his eyes darting to mine for a moment before flashing away in search of something.

"Why?" I query as he strides over to a huge bucket, picking it up and placing it under a long tap that's sticking out of the wall.

The knob squeaks as he turns it. Water suddenly sputters out of the mouth and begins to fill the bucket that's big enough to bathe in.

"You need a kit," Curio answers, one of his eyebrows ticking up in challenge.

It's like he already knows I'm going to have something to say about this. He's right.

"I do," I agree, and I relish the flicker of surprise in his face at my agreement. "However, kits cost money, and I'm currently lacking the extra funds to pay for one," I continue, stating the obvious.

I lack *any* funds altogether, but I'm pretty sure we're both very aware of that. I doubt Curio will have any interest in buying back the weapons I plan to steal, especially since it seems he *made* all of them. That understanding drops in my gut like a massive rock, and I try to breathe through the intense astonishment that ripples in the shock-boulder's wake.

Shit, how can I steal them now, knowing he made the exquisite weapons with his own two hands?

Despite the fact that I've vowed not to care, I immediately start to wonder what else is worth knowing about him.

Curio snorts and shakes his head. "I told Tarek you wouldn't make this easy."

"What can I say, I'm not an easy fae," I reply, extra emphasis on every word in hopes that he can clue Riall in and all the leering and unwelcome invitations can stop.

"And you don't need to be, but you can give us the benefit of the doubt on occasion," he counters. "You're here. No one has hurt you. Your belly is full. Your body is clothed. You can come and go as you please. Does that not earn some faith in us?" he asks, gesturing between us and then behind me as though he's including his absent brothers in this conversation.

"If you truly understood my position, you'd know that faith in others is a luxury I can't afford," I impatiently reply, already fed up with the direction of this pointless discussion.

"You say that, but your actions show otherwise," he accuses, far too much self-importance settling in the features of his face.

It should make him ugly. It's annoying that it doesn't.

I fold my arms over my chest and glare at him. "And how do you figure that?"

"When you were hurt at the ludere, you came to us." He allows that sentence to hang between us for a moment before continuing. "You also left this morning and then came back. Even if you tell yourself it's for a short time, you still trusted us, in one way or another, to help you. Does that not speak to some level of faith between us?" he asks, his brown eyes banked with imperious challenge, while one of his black eyebrows hikes up as though it's punctuating his point.

I offer him a scathing look. "You give yourself too much credit," I counter. "It's less trust and more that you're the *only* option."

"But we *are* an option for you, and that should speak volumes to the truth of how you see us, regardless of what you tell yourself because your feelings are hurt."

I stiffen at the callous insinuation.

My feelings are hurt? My feelings...

Hot anger sears at that belittling minimization, and it's all I can do to not reach for one of the tools hung on the wall behind him and then beat the *cocky prick* right out of him with it. He eyes me as though he can read my mind, and the twinkle in his eyes right now makes me think that he just might like that.

He's obviously cracked.

"I can assure you, Skull, that more than just my *feelings* have been hurt while being owned by you and broken by Tilleo," I snap at him, and he holds his hands up in surrender as though he thinks the bogus gesture will calm me.

"We're not bad fae, Auset, we're simply survivors."

I scoff at that. "You're both, at best," I contend, not buying this innocent act for a second.

He laughs, which both surprises and infuriates me even more. I never quite know what to expect with these three.

"Fine, paint us with whatever brush suits you, but if you think your colors don't look a lot like ours, you're wrong, Moonling," he asserts.

I shake my head and glower at him, completely bewildered as to how he can think that.

"This life is all any of us know," he states, gesturing to the tools and weapons all around us before waving his arm toward the open doors and the peaks of the castle that can be seen over the tops of the trees behind us. "My brothers and I have had our own fair share of *masters*, Auset. Do you think we ended up here because we had other options? We could have stomped around complaining about how unfair it all was, thrown away the opportunity that was presented to us based on some useless moral high ground that serves no one, but we didn't—"

"No," I interrupt. "You became part of the problem instead."

Curio laughs again, but it's harsher this time, less amused. "No," he counters as though he's speaking to someone who's too dense to follow at the pace he wants to set. "We took a broken system and made it work for us, made it work for countless others too," he defends. "But you're not ready to admit that, are you, Moonling?"

"Stop calling me that," I bite out, dropping my hands to my side as though I'm searching for a dagger that's not there. Outrage crawls up my throat, ready for me to release it like flames all over this fae and his warped view of right and wrong, but Curio cuts me off.

"Have you even thought once about any of the blade slaves that you left behind? Do you care at all about what happened to them, or only that *you* got out?" he questions, his face alight with accusation as he steps closer. "One of them nearly killed you, and you don't even seem to be upset by that."

Fury moves my feet toward him, but I stop myself before I close the distance completely. "That's because—"

"Because you knew that's how it would always be?" he interjects. "You've already accepted that life is every fae for themselves. You don't begrudge that fucker who shoved a chakram through your gut for choosing himself over you, but you begrudge us for doing the best we could with what *we* were handed?" he demands.

The fiery words sitting on my tongue crumble to ash in my mouth, and I stand there, gaping at Curio, with no idea how to respond to that.

"What happened to you was unfortunate, but you survived it. That's more than many can say. No fae in their right mind would condemn you for doing what you had to do; all we ask is for that same courtesy," Curio insists.

His words peck at me relentlessly, and what's worse is they're getting through. He pushes his hair back, the light strands in his otherwise inky locks catching the light of the fire in a captivating way. His hickory stare hunts around in mine, like he's looking for the part of me that sees the truth in what he's saying. I wish he wasn't going to find it, but he will.

I want to shut him down. Bark at him about how wrong he is and how he can take his words and shove them up his round and entirely too firm-looking ass, but I can't. I search through his statements, looking for cracks and fractures that will help me pull them apart, but too much veracity fortifies what he's saying.

It's infuriating.

I haven't been here long, and the day so far has been packed full of revelations and adjustments and coming to terms with my new reality. I can pretend that all of this is the reason I haven't given any thought to what happened to the other blade slaves, but I'd be lying. The truth is I don't care...and neither did they. We couldn't. Like Curio pointed out, we were just trying to survive. If that meant someone else fell so that you could climb, so be it. I've stood unapologetically on others' backs without a second thought, because it meant another day, one less beating, one more chance...for me. It felt necessary at the time, but was it?

Like a curtain has just been pulled back to reveal what's on the other side, I can't yank my eyes or thoughts away from the inescapable truth that Curio just shoved my face through. Shame coats my insides, tainting everything with its touch. I don't know if I'm ashamed that I'm understanding this brute's perspective or that I'm looking at the truth of who I am and realizing I'm not as different as I thought. I kill without compunction. I was willing to buy my freedom and future with the aurems I would make ending *any* life for the right price. I chose myself over all else, and even though I see the flaw in that, see how that mentality leads to the faulty broken world we live in, I know I won't stop.

If I don't look out for myself, no one else will.

I expect Curio to see the wound his argument has cut into me and go for the kill. I wait for him to hammer in more evidence of my hypocrisy, to chisel away at what I think about him and his brothers until I don't recognize my convictions anymore. But he does none of that. Instead, he leaves me to stew in my uncertainty while he rips open one of the bags he slammed onto the table earlier and adds it to the water in the tub-sized bucket. He turns off the faucet, and with a large metal-wired bar, he begins to stir the mixture.

"What are you doing?" I ask, moving closer to the fire as though the hot flames will burn up the doubt and confusion now blanketing me and making everything feel heavier and more burdensome.

"Like I said, I need to make a mold of your form so I can start on your kit."

"And what am I going to have to do to pay for that?" I ask warily.

His brown eyes snap from the mixture he's stirring to mine. "Not a fucking thing you don't want to do," he growls, and his words and tone sink deep in my stomach like fluttering, falling feathers. "We're not monsters...I mean, we are, but at the end of three months, if you choose to leave, you can take everything you've been given, because it's yours. You can do nothing more than eat, sleep, heal, train, and hate us while you're here, and it will all still be yours no matter what. We're not trading, Auset, we're giving."

A million thoughts and accusations and concerns flare in my mind, but I shut it all down and focus on one thing instead.

"*If*?" I press, picking at the tiny, seemingly insignificant word that screams out at me over everything else he just said.

He stares at me, his face slowly slipping from frustrated to radiantly confident. His hooded eyes narrow slightly, but not from anger, they're heavy with promise and heat. He searches my face for a moment, and when his dazzling gaze once again locks onto mine, it's as though I'm pulled from my axis and sucked right into his.

"Yes, *if*," he confirms, his large body squaring up to mine. "Because even though we won't demand anything from you, we're still going to do everything in our power to make you *want* to stay."

An inferno quickly blazes to life and tries to consume every inch of me. I feel it wanting to jump from me to Curio and back again, eager to incinerate all reservations and misgivings between us. I breathe through the rushing need, knowing it will pass, and reason and logic will come flooding in at any moment. My eyes bounce back and forth between his scorching stare, and I refuse to look at his mouth, or anywhere else, regardless of how much I suddenly want to drink every part of him in.

"Why?" I ask, my throat suddenly dry and my voice reedy and brittle.

He studies me for what feels like forever before his grin grows slightly. Just when I think he might show me instead of telling me, he shakes his head, breaking whatever spell is thick between us, and steps back. I'm both relieved and bothered by the distance he puts between us. His eyes drop from mine, and he returns his focus to the mixture he was stirring.

"You're not ready for that answer yet, Moonling," he finally replies. "But don't worry, I think you will be soon."

I watch his arms flex as he resumes his efforts to stir the thickening concoction in the huge bucket. Strands of long black and sandy-blond hair fall toward his face, and I don't miss the knowing smirk still painted on his lips as he works. I try to fortify my defenses around the holes this exchange has left behind, but it's difficult. Parts of me I've never looked at too closely are peeking through, and I'm hesitant to brick everything back up and pretend this never happened.

I'm still fighting for survival here amidst these Scorpions, but the rules have somehow changed and the stakes are even higher than they were before. It's not just life that's hanging in the balance here, it's as though they're coming for my soul. No one ever taught me how to defend against that, and I worry I'm already losing the most important battle I may ever fight.

27

CURIO

I'M SUPPOSED TO LIE IN THIS?" AUSET WARILY ASKS, her silver gaze watching me with both interest and hesitancy as I lift the heavy bucket of thick paste and start pouring half of it into the large wood frame I've laid out on my work table.

Auset walks further into the workshop from the washroom in the back, where she just took off my tunic and replaced it with the skintight rind top I gave her. She's now decked top to bottom in the protective material, and I know if I look at her, the black, clinging coverings will show off every curve and line of her body.

So I don't look, even though I want to.

Stolen glances and private gawking aren't going to win me anything. Not when Auset deserves better, and especially not when I'd rather memorize every part of her *after* she's begged me to. I sigh at that thought, both eager for it and painfully aware that we're not there yet. The little Moonling came back though, just like Tarek said she would. So truly it's only a matter of time before fairy light dances across her skin as I press her back into my bed. I'll map her body with my hands while my eyes and mouth trace a careful path over every inch of her. I want her gasps and her pleas, my name on her lips, first whispered and then screamed, while I work her over until she's dripping with desire.

I can be patient. I hate it, but I can be.

With a grunt, I stabilize the heavy bucket, pulling it away from the frame when there's enough adhesive there for the back layer of the mold.

"Yes," I answer, Auset's tentative question still hanging in the air between us as I work.

I grab a thick board to help level out the mixture, and she moves closer to observe what I'm doing. I like that she's interested.

"You'll lie here," I explain, nodding my chin at the mixture already starting to set in the wood-planked frame. It's too big for her, I'm used to doing this with Riall and Tarek, but I'll make it work. "This plaster will mold to your shape and dry. Once you lie down, I'll place a blanket made out of the same material as the rind that you're wearing, and then I'll pour more of the mixture over the front of you to get a full cast."

Auset nods her head, but the way her teeth worry her plump bottom lip tells me that she's not completely on board with any of this. I know it's not just casting this mold that's making her uneasy, it's accepting anything from us at all. I wish she could trust that I won't let anything bad happen to her. I'm all too aware that will take time though.

I know our conversation just now made a dent in some of her doubts and judgments, but I also know I didn't demolish them completely. I'm certain that our effort to help Auset see past her misgivings is going to be a tricky dance of a few steps forward and then giant leaps back. That's how it was for all of us when Eacon brought us here. If Tarek, Riall, and I can find family and purpose with each other, Auset can too. I have a feeling it's going to be a challenge though. Good thing we're all up for it. The sooner she sees her place with us, sees us for who we really are, the easier all of this will be.

I set the leveling board aside and step closer to Auset until she looks up at me. Her eyes sparkle with uncertainty and warning, and I have to fix my face so the smirk wanting to form there doesn't get me into more trouble than I already am. I don't think she'll be as amused as I am by the way she vacillates between wanting to slit my throat and asking a bunch of questions about what I'm doing and why. It's fascinating the way she clocks the exits and weapons in the room while also closely watching everything I'm doing just in case the knowledge might come in handy someday. Auset is constantly planning and preparing while also observing and reading a situation. It's incredible to witness, and it has to be exhausting for her.

"It won't hurt," I reassure her as I study her face. I want to reach up and drag a strand of her hair through my fingers, but I tamp down the urge. "Once the plaster dries, I'll lift off the top layer using the rind barrier, then you can get out. It should only take about thirty minutes to dry from start to finish."

"And then what happens?" she inquires as she eyes the plaster-filled frame in front of her.

"After that, your part is finished. I'll attach the two pieces together, fill it with a resin I make from the sap of the *liex* trees outside, and that will give me the mold I need to start fitting armor and other protective gear for you. Are you partial to any kinds of weapons?" I ask, pulling out my mental list of things I think she'll like for comparison.

Back in the ludere, and again earlier when Riall was getting a feel for what our little Moonling can do, I noticed that she likes small daggers and close contact hits. I figure Riall, being the overprotective bear that he is, will try to push her to hunt safer by staying out of an opponent's reach. I, however, am not interested in pushing Auset to do anything other than what feels natural to her. She likes to be close to the kill, and Tarek is the same way, which means the best way I can help her stay safe is to make sure her blades are so sharp that one flick could separate a fae's head from their shoulders. Then it won't matter if she's within reach. The other fae will be dead, and all Auset will need to worry about is the cleanup.

I can easily imagine how cleanup with Auset could become a new favorite pastime. The three of us will be all too happy to help her wash all the blood away and more.

"What? I just list off what I want, and you give it to me?" Auset challenges, and again I have to bite back a grin.

She's so fucking gorgeous...even when she's pissed.

"That's exactly how it works," I answer.

She scoffs and stares at me for a long pause as though she's waiting for the truth to rip out of my chest at any moment. When that doesn't happen, she huffs out a resigned breath and starts to think about my question.

"Daggers, plenty of daggers and knives, is what I'd like most. Oh, and a slew of places to hide them on me, of course," she mocks as though this is all simply some game.

"Of course," I parrot back, and her scowl deepens.

"Keep going while you get in," I command. "This stuff is a pain to pull from the frame, and I'd rather the hassle be worth it," I tell her, tilting my head in the direction of the plaster.

Auset watches the frame for a minute longer, like she's waiting for something to jump out and bite her. Nothing does, and she sighs.

"Fine," she agrees, and it's clear how much the capitulation pains her.

Auset presses her palms to the table as though she's about to push herself up onto it, but before she can, I move in behind her and pick her up. She yelps in alarm as I wrap one arm around her back and the other beneath her knees. I freeze, surprised by my own actions. I don't know what in the Crowns just came over me, but I pause, waiting for—and fully expecting—her to strike out at me or demand that I put her down. She does neither, which is even more confusing. I look down at her face, and I'm surprised to find her looking up at me, her pupils dilating as she does and her chest rising and falling rapidly, like we've been running for weeks and she's working to catch her breath.

"I thought you might need help," I offer awkwardly, and I want to slap myself across the cheek so I stop acting as though I've spent too long sniffing plaster fumes.

Auset's unique scent suddenly overwhelms all of my senses, and I find myself pulling her even closer so I can breathe in the hints of night-blooming snowdrops, sun-warmed leather, and the fresh scent of *tist* leaves. It's an unusual combination, and yet it makes perfect sense for the enigma in front of me.

I hold Auset tighter than I have any right to, like I'm trying to show her that in my arms is where she was always meant to be. I can see that she doesn't know what to think about this, but she's not trying to stab me, so I take it as a win. She's yet to discover this about me, but I always get what I want. And I want my mate. I don't care how long it takes or what I have to do. I'm tenacious in my focus and drive when I want something. I never give up.

The draw to her already morphed from enticing interest to unquenchable need when she almost died back at the ludere. I couldn't bear the thought of losing her before I'd ever had her, which forced me to admit that I wanted her in a deeper sense. It was then that I stopped pretending that she was nothing more than some forbidden conquest and instead started to see all the ways that we were destined to fit together. Tarek, Riall, and I have been ready for more. We all sensed that there was a missing piece waiting out in the world for us, and then all at once, there she was.

"Did you do this for Riall and Tarek when you needed molds from them?" Auset asks, a cheeky gleam in her moonlight-soaked eyes. Her plush mouth is tilted up in a sexy *I see through you* kind of smile, and I find the corners of my own lips ticking higher to match hers.

"Of course," I answer nonchalantly, trying and failing not to stare at her lips or think about the fact that I'm dying to taste her.

The tiniest sound sneaks out of her. It's almost like a quiet whimper of need, but she all too quickly clears her throat, the gruff sound working to overpower the squeak of vulnerability I swear she just made. I pretend I didn't hear it even as I catalog it in my mind.

"Tarek isn't usually a fan of being carried about, but Riall is all for it," I tell her, continuing with our humorous exchange and offering her a sly grin.

"Why can I see that being true about Riall?" Auset asks with a breathy huff, and a chuckle rumbles out of me.

"Ready?" I ask, hesitantly pulling her away from my chest and positioning her over the middle of the plaster-filled frame. I want to continue holding her tight, but I also want to give her the best kit imaginable, and I need a mold of her body if I'm to have any hope of doing that.

Auset pulls in a deep breath and nods. "Ready."

I set her down slowly, and I'm unable to hold in my laugh when she makes contact with the plaster and squeals.

"It's cold!" she squeaks out as she tries to climb my arms to get closer to my chest and further away from the thick mixture. I keep her in place, and she glares at the grin on my face. After a moment, she accepts her fate, and I set her down the rest of the way. The plaster rises up the sides of her black-clad torso, and I get excited knowing half the mold is already well on its way.

"It will warm now that you're touching it," I explain, moving down the frame so I can position her legs the way I need them. "Spread like this," I instruct as I cup one of her thighs and pull it until her legs split apart.

I watch a shiver sneak over her as plaster seeps up her legs, hugging the shape of them. I set her limb down until it's straight and check that the other one is aligned the same way. Auset rests her neck in the padded cut out at the top of the frame that allows her to be free of the mess from the neck up. After a few adjustments with her arms and pressing her hands flat while I splay her fingers, I give her a nod.

"Stay just like that while I grab the barrier for the next part," I instruct, and she nods somewhat begrudgingly. I don't know if it's the order I just gave or the vulnerability she's feeling right now that's bugging her, or maybe it's both. "You okay?" I check, watching her carefully as I move to the side to unfold a large sheet of the protective rind material we wear under our armor.

Auset has already been wearing my rind bottoms, and as much as I like to see her in them, I need to make her several sets of her own. When the material fits correctly, it compresses and protects all of our vital organs and biological weak spots. She may think my one of a kind togs fit her, but they won't hold parts of her together as needed, because they're technically too big. She needs the right size.

"Fine, I think," she assures me, and then she makes a concentrated effort to relax into the plaster. "I've just never experienced anything like this before. Is this how all armorers fit their customers?" she asks, and I snap out the raven-black fabric so that it billows above her and then slowly floats down until it's covering the frame.

"I can't speak for all armorers; I've only met one, but this is how she did it, and I learned from the best," I tell her as I press the fabric down until it's skimming the plaster and adhering to Auset's shape.

I work quickly, knowing the mixture in the bucket is already setting. I need to get it poured over her before it crosses the threshold from being pliable to uselessly stiff.

"Okay?" I check with Auset again, pausing what I'm doing to read her face. Her eyes flick up to mine, and she nods once more.

Grabbing some small tacks and a hammer, I fix the edges of the rind to the wood frame. I tack fabric around Auset's neck so that the plaster can't leak out, and then I grab the big bucket and pour the remaining mixture into the frame.

"Will I be able to breathe as this gets hard?" she asks, looking down as the gray mixture settles over her. The barrier at her neck prevents her from seeing what's happening past it, but I know the sensation is strange as the plaster works to surround her and set.

"There's give to the plaster itself as it fixes into shape. It will dry giving you the room you need to pull in air and let it go. Which is good because the armor I design for you needs to be able to do the same thing," I answer, an amused smile sneaking over my face. "It's hard to explain how exactly it all works, but I promise you'll be fine."

She nods again, but I don't miss the tight set to her shoulders and jaw. I don't like that she's once again apprehensive, but this will all be over soon, and she'll see that she was always safe, just like I said she'd be.

"So, weapons," I encourage, reminding her that I'm still interested in what she might like.

"Right," she answers, inhaling a deep breath and trying to focus on the question at hand. "Daggers, but I already said that," she states more to herself than to me. "I like the feel of a sword in my hand," she tells me, and immediately images of her fighting in the sand pit at the ludere and training with Riall earlier flash in my mind.

She's good with a sword. Lithe. Strong. No hesitation. I nod approvingly, and she takes it as encouragement to keep going.

"I'm used to making the bigger long swords work that we trained with at the ludere, but one made for me would be...well, I'd like that."

The small confession wraps itself around my heart and squeezes. I remember the first time my brothers and I had the means to craft something of our very own. I spent almost three months perfecting everything about our first weapons, all the way down to how they gleam, or rather don't, in the light. That moment was unlike anything I'd experienced. It was the first time I really felt as though we could forge a life despite what we were up against. I want that for Auset. I want her to have everything that we did, that we still do.

An eager thrill streaks down my arms as I picture what I could make for her. Blades that mirror her curves and the way she flows from movement to movement as though she's water, fire, and steel simultaneously. Blades that are worthy of her resilience and determination. She needs weapons that will drink down the blood she spills and make her even more formidable than she already is. I can give her that, that and so much more, and all at once, I itch to get to work because I can't wait to see the look on her face when she realizes that too.

"I'd also like an ax," she tells me, but it sounds more like a question than a request. "I'm good with the double-sided variety. Maybe the armor could allow the handle of the ax to sit above one shoulder while the grip of the sword sits above the other, for easy access," she states, her eyes suddenly far away and thoughtful. "That's probably it. If I can't dispatch someone with a sword, an ax, and a bunch of daggers, then I'm dead anyway."

My brow furrows with dismay. I don't like that thought. None of us would ever let that happen, but she's still refusing to see that.

She will.

"Oh, and is there any way to get gloves that have metal bits embedded over the knuckles? I saw a guard who had protection like that, and I always wanted some. A little extra oomph in my punches when in close contact would be fine by me," she adds.

I smile. Having seen the surprised look on Riall's face the first time she decked him full out, I know her hits pack plenty of punch, but if Auset wants metal knuckles, she'll get metal knuckles.

"I'll add gloves to the list," I respond evenly, hoping the amused shimmer in my eyes is taken for what it is and not because I think her requests are lacking in any way.

I like her answers, respect them even. Regardless of how much she objects to my doing this for her, she knows her strengths well and chooses wisely. She didn't go overboard, which is easy enough to do. Tarek asked for so many weapons at first he could barely walk out of here once he was fully fitted. It didn't take him long to work out what was the most useful and what wasn't. I bite back a small chuckle at the image of Tarek waddling around while everything he was wearing clanged loudly with every step. It was as though the armor and weapons themselves were mocking his poor overeager decisions.

Wind kicks up at my back and blows into the forge. Strands of Auset's hair tickle across her face, and I reach down to brush them from her cheeks. The strands feel like the softest threads of silk against my fingers, and her golden skin is warm to my touch as though she's trapped the heat of the Corozean desert just below the surface. Her lips part as though they're allowing a surprised gasp to escape, but I can't hear it over the pounding of my own pulse in my ears.

I study Auset's eyes, my gaze darting back and forth between the silver of her irises. I don't know exactly what I'm looking for, but panic isn't it. A shard of hurt works its way under my ribs, but I ignore it. Instead, I observe as her nostrils flare and the even breaths she was just taking all too quickly morph into gulps of panic. The black of her pupils expands, drowning out all but the thinnest ring of silver in her eyes, and I step back, hating that my touch has triggered this primal release of fear.

"I won't touch you again," I reassure her as I watch her battle the terror that's trying to pull her under. I don't know what to do or how to make it better, but I'll never go near her again if it means she never has to suffer like this again.

"Not...you..." she pants, completely panic stricken, and even though she's offering me reassurance, I feel horrified at what's happening. "I thought I'd be fine. I just have to lie here. I didn't realize it would feel..." She trails off, and instinctively I step closer.

I want to punch myself in the throat for crowding her even though I just vowed to myself that I wouldn't, but she neither flinches or shows any sign that *my* presence is what's bothering her, so I don't immediately step away.

"What? What happened?" I press, my every heartbeat hanging on her breaths as they begin to grow shallower with each hurried pull in and push out.

She's hyperventilating.

I take in the frame and plaster that's encasing her, and panic unfurls in my own chest. I need to get her out. I start ripping out the tacks in the rind fabric with my bare hands as a soft frightened mewl fills the air between us.

"I'll get it off," I assure her as I rush to make my way around the frame. "You're safe. Just breathe," I encourage her, my hands starting to shake with the need to move faster.

"Tilleo gave me something," she blurts as I start frantically working on the tacks at the foot of the frame.

"What do you mean?" I demand. I look from the blood starting to well at my fingertips from the tacks I'm desperately working to pull free, and then my eyes snap up to Auset's.

"When he sold me...my body...before. He gave me something so I couldn't move. I couldn't fight," she labors to say, and each word drops like an anvil on top of me.

Realization stampedes over everything else in my mind. The plaster is hardening around her, trapping her, and making it impossible to move more than a twitch.

"Fuck, I'll get you free," I bark out, renewing my efforts against the tacks.

Just a few more, and I can rip the top layer off.

"No," she argues, but I ignore the word, only hearing the fear that's seeping out of it. "Skull, I mean, Curio, stop," she stammers desperately. "If you take me out now, you won't get the mold, right?" she demands between panicky huffs.

"That doesn't matter. I'll get what I need some other way," I snap, and the *tink* of a tack dropping to the floor is music to my ears before I move on to another one.

"I can stand it," she rasps, but I can tell she's trying to convince herself more than me. "I can stand it," she shouts louder as another plink from a falling tack fills the air between us. "I want this," she argues. "I need a kit, Curio."

The plea in her voice is my undoing. It's so small and fragile, and this stunning creature before me is anything but. I can't stand to hear her beg. Not like this. A force like Auset should never have to. The hammer stalls in my hand. I don't even know when I grabbed it. Blood stamps the handle, and my frantic gaze snaps from it to Auset. The need to get her free, to make sure she's okay, wars with the need to never hear her plead for anything again.

"What do I do?" I entreat, utterly torn.

"Distract me," Auset heaves, and the hammer drops to the ground as I abandon the rind, the tacks, the effort to pull her out, and go to her instead.

"I didn't know," she starts as I lean over her. "I didn't know being stuck like this would be a problem."

There's a hint of apology in her tone, and I want to brush it clear of not only her voice but her mind as well. There's not a thing to be sorry for. Everything in me wants to demand to know who took advantage of her when she was so vulnerable, but the truth of it all is that this is my fault. Auset's terror rests on the shoulders of me, Riall, and Tarek. We knew when we left her in Dorsin's office that fate most likely wouldn't be kind to her. We didn't care. That was life. Each of us had endured our own horrors. It was the way of things, and there was no escaping it. But now, staring in her fear-soaked eyes, seeing only a hint of what I know she's had to endure, I hate myself for it.

"Distract you how?" I ask, dismissing her contrition outright.

Auset's eyes search the ceiling frantically, and I can practically feel the dread as it tries to drown her. I move to the head of the table and lean over her until her eyes lock on mine.

"May I touch you?" I ask quietly, soothingly. "Only your hair," I add, and her anxious gaze studies my face for a second before she nods.

Relief floods me, and I quickly thread my hands through her hair and start skimming her scalp with the tips of my fingers. Over and over again, I draw soft calming lines across her head and down the length of her long hair. My blood lightly stains some of the strands, but there's nothing I can do about that now. All I can focus on is banishing Auset's terror and showing her she's safe here with me.

"T-tell...tell me something, pull my head out of the past," she pleads, and I continue to run my fingers over her head as I try to think of something.

I look around the forge as though it will serve as inspiration, but all I can see is my work and evidence of a past I wish I could forget.

"My mother," I start, looking down, but Auset is gone, and in her place is my mother's battered and broken body. "My mother taught me all of this," I continue, gesturing to the workroom with my chin while willing away the macabre image of the past so I can focus on the here and now. "She was the Royal Armorer for the Day Court. It was a family trade, but when my grandad made no sons, he employed his daughters. Said it was the best thing to ever happen to him, or so my mum said. The man died long before I came around," I tell her with a little shrug. A snarl in her hair catches between my fingers, and I gently work through it and continue my soft strokes. "She was a master at what she did. She headed the clan of armorers who fitted the king's guard and army, and she worked directly with the royal family herself."

"That must have been quite the honor," Auset replies, but there's no veneration to be found in the statement.

I both scoff at her comment and laugh at the fact that the royal family of the Day Court doesn't impress my Moonling in the slightest. I notice, however, that her gasped breaths are quieting, and the frantic inhalations are slowing down enough to make me think my story is working.

"I promise there's no honor or privilege in being the bastard of a king," I assure her. "Riall and Tarek will attest to the same."

"Wait," she interjects, her eyes looking me over in earnest. "Your sire is the Day King?" she asks, both equal parts shocked and disquieted.

I offer her a wide smile. It's the one that usually shows the asker of this question the resemblance between me and my sire. I have my mother's coloring, but everything else about me is him.

I realize, as Auset stares back at me blankly, that she doesn't know what the Day King looks like. Something about that resonates with me. Whenever I've revealed this piece of information in the past, all anyone sees after is the fucker who wears the crown. I like the idea that all Auset will see is me.

"Not just me," I answer on a laugh. "Tarek's sire is the King of Dawn, and Riall's is the King of Dusk. We're the Order of Scorpions, but we could have just as easily gone with the Order of Royal Bastards," I tease, but Auset doesn't laugh.

"H-how? Why?" she stammers, and I find her flummoxed reaction diverting.

Auset relaxes a little, and I hide a relieved sigh under an amused snort.

"The others deserve to tell you their stories in their own time, but if you think bastards are ever wanted in this world, the three of us are proof of how wrong you'd be," I start. "The king was fond of my mother; she wasn't brought on as a royal consort, but he did allow me to live after she had me, so some affection was there. After she died though, I was told there was too much of her in me and it pained the king. I was thrown out of the city gates and told to be on my way."

Something shutters in Auset's gaze, but I don't know what it is she's hiding from me as she asks, "How old were you?"

"Thirty or so. My voice was just beginning to drop and my body to fill in. I was still young enough to be of interest to the flesh slaver who found me on the road between realms all on my own."

This time, it's my gaze that disconnects from hers. Her silvery stare asks silent questions we both know I won't answer. I'm past the torment of those years but won't revisit them. Not even for the Moonling who's staring up at me with a knowing look I wish neither of us possessed.

"Your mother?" she inquires gently, and I relax at the diversion I know she's offering me.

I stroke my thumbs over her temples and stare down at her for a moment while I wait for the echoes of overwhelming emotions to settle down to where they were before Auset and I began to trade our tragedies.

"She was killed in an uprising. It seems the people of the Day Court didn't take kindly to the king throwing a lavish ball in celebration of a legitimate child's birth when they were starving, suffering, and watching their own babies wither and die because of it." I shake my head in disgust. "I was in my mother's forge, tasked with making arrow tips perfect enough to meet her approval. She was meeting with the clan to take stock of what was needed for the following months. They were some of the first to be overrun by the mob."

Auset nods but thankfully doesn't offer anything beyond that. We both know it's pointless. Things are as they are, and no amount of pity or empathy is going to change it.

"I took the chakram we found in your stomach," I blurt randomly.

Bewilderment fills her face just as quickly as it fills my chest. I have no idea why I'm confessing this to her, but there's no taking it back now.

"I wanted to break it down and use it for one of your new weapons. I don't know exactly what I'll make yet—we'll see what the metal asks to become—but I thought you should know," I explain.

"Oh," she retorts, like she's unsure how to respond to that.

She stares up at me, her breaths once again even and her eyes searching for something. I hope it's trust she finds in my eyes, but I know that will probably be harder to earn than I would like.

"What doesn't kill us fortifies us," I offer gently, my strokes through her hair slowing as we stare at one another. I feel as though a part of her is reaching out to me, and something in me takes a hold of it and vows to never let it go. "We can take those things..." I continue, my voice growing deeper as purpose and regard settle like a tether between us. "Melt them down, mold them, and reshape them until they work for us instead of against us. Then, when we have weapons instead of wounds, we make the fuckers pay for what they did to us."

I watch as my words stoke something primal in Auset. Uncertainty drains from her eyes, and all that's left is fierce determination. The strength she shows, the fortitude, it speaks to every part of me, tying us together in ways I never thought I'd find. Yet, here she lies, hanging on my every word as though it's the lifeline she desperately needs despite her claims to need no one and nothing.

"They will," she whispers, and even though it's quiet, the power in that statement is undeniable. "They will pay," she vows, and even though she's looking at me as though I might be on that list, I can't find it in me to fault her.

I'll burn to nothing if that's what she needs, and then I'll show her just how I rise from the ashes and take what's mine. I nod, hoping she sees that I'm more than prepared for anything she may throw my way. We both go silent, lost to our thoughts for a time, and before I know it, thirty minutes have come and gone.

"You did it," I declare, pride and respect blooming in my tone.

I reach for the hammer once again and watch as a small smile sneaks across Auset's face.

"I did," she agrees, and it feels pivotal, deeper than simply surviving plaster.

I don't say anything more as I pull the tacks out of the rest of the rind and lift off the top layer of the mold. I keep my thoughts to myself because all I can think is *that's my girl*, and despite what happened here in the workshop today, she doesn't want to hear anything like that yet.

Soon, I tell myself as I lean the top layer of the mold against a workroom wall. I lift Auset out of the frame, and her hands wrap around my neck as I do. I set her on her feet, and too quickly her hands drop away from me and she steps back.

Soon is all that floats in my mind as she disappears to the washroom to change.

Very soon.

28

AUSET

I WAKE ON A GASP, SITTING UP WITH A STARTLED jerk. Immediately, I scan my surroundings for the threat my subconscious is warning me of. Adrenaline works to flush away the grogginess of sleep, but all I see around me is night-draped walls and shadow-brushed furniture. I search, but there's nothing alarming lurking anywhere. Consciousness is slow to chase away my confusion as the booming rhythm of my pulse sounds in my ears. I try to quiet the noise and orient myself.

I look around, expecting to find sweaty bodies lying all around me in some stage of rest, but no one's there. The peppering of the night air with soft snores and sleep-filled groans is the cadence I've slumbered to since I can remember, but I'm not in the ludere anymore. There are no other blade slaves here. No one turning in their sleep in search of a more comfortable position on the hard sandstone floor. Not one telltale pinched brow in sight indicating that someone is in the throes of a nightmare. There are no quiet tip toes as someone sneaks off to the washroom for either a late night piss or a clandestine tryst.

I'm alone.

It's something I've longed for, and yet now that it's in my grip, there's an undeniable unease that's tightening my chest. Glancing around, I take in the dark looming furniture surrounding me. The subdued sound of waves crashing against the shore drifts in, and streaks of moonlight reach through the open window to my left. The moon is high in the sky, bathing me in its healing rays where I lie on the floor. I'm surrounded by a nest of soft towels and a supple bed sheet is crumpled around my ankles, as though I angrily shoved it down there at some point in the night. My pulse starts to calm as I quickly deduce that there's nothing in here that poses any kind of threat.

It's just me.

Me and the empty bed that's too soft to sleep on; a tall wardrobe filled with neat, folded piles of the same tops and bottoms; and a darkened, empty bathing chamber. Exhaling a deep breath, I lie back, crooking an arm behind my head to cushion it against the dark wood floor. I study the silvery light that filters through the smooth glass of the raised windows and encourages a quiet calm to wash over me. I don't know what woke me, but I'm safe and, from the feel of things, already healed from today's exertions.

The stone of the ceiling captures my attention as I try to drift back to sleep, but out of nowhere, my stomach lets loose a deep indignant growl. I sit up and stare down at my abdomen, not at all appreciating the tone it's taking with me.

"The sun handed the day over to the moon less than a handful of hours ago, and already you're greedy for more food?" I ask, clutching a hand to my stomach when it gurgles another impatient demand.

With a scoff, I shake my head, but I push up from the ground, like I've been commanded, and tiptoe toward the door. Slowly, cautiously, I open the thick wood barrier and peek out into the dark corridor that looms on the other side. The Scorpions have made it clear that I'm not their prisoner, that I'm free to come and go as I please, but I sneak to the stairs anyway, looking around as though I expect one of them to come bounding out after me at any moment.

No one does.

When I snuck around the first time after I'd just woken up here, I thought the house slaves must still have been asleep or maybe they were required to keep a low profile and stay hidden. Turns out that the Scorpions don't have any house slaves. According to Tarek, there is a clan of imps that live somewhere on the property. It seems their magic is tied to the castle itself, so keeping it in good shape is beneficial to them as well as the Scorpions. However, Tarek also stated that none of them ever see the imps at work. He doubted I would either. I wouldn't know what to expect even if I did.

The only imp I've ever known is Figg, and that leaves a lot to be desired for her kind. It's hard for me to picture several rotund and grumbling versions of her doing anything as strenuous as cleaning a whole castle. She could barely manage to sort out our togs at the ludere when required. When I mentioned that to Curio, he informed me that there are many different clans of imps, and each of them derives power from their surroundings in different ways. I have no idea what kind of imp Figg was, but if I had to guess, she charged up through whining and bossing others around unnecessarily.

My descent to the kitchens is uneventful, but unease tightens its hold around my chest even more as I'm met with nothing other than a strange and foreboding stillness. Of all the things I thought I'd feel once I was away from the ludere, loneliness was never one of them. I thought after all the years of being packed in far too tightly with too many fae in a sleeping chamber, a washroom, the hashery, the pits, that I would revel in the quiet that blankets this place, but there's nothing soothing about it. I thought I'd settle easily into peace if ever given the chance, and yet all I feel is threatened by the tranquil hush all around me.

It seems I'm not as cut out for the calm as I'd hoped I'd be.

The large placid hall that leads to the kitchen greets me as I force myself to conjure images of some remote cabin in an unidentifiable land, where I sit in a large chair on a porch, serenely watching the weeks pass by. It's a vision that I've harvested of what I want my life to look like once I've bought my freedom and forged my own path. No more death. No more violence. No more endless noise or a life so crammed with problems that there's barely room for *me*. I'd live out the rest of my years in peace and relaxation, as I was due. However, as the stagnant, serene silence grows thicker all around me, it's as though reality is setting my long-collected plans alight, the flames of which now mock my naive delusion that a simple, quiet life could ever be for me.

I hate to admit it, but as I make my way through the dark, sedate castle, I find myself longing for noise, for a touch of chaos, for something dangerous that feels familiar and right. I step into the kitchen, doing my best to dismiss these late night apprehensions. I'm probably just tired. I've only been here a day, which is really no time at all to adjust to the many differences between this place and everything I've ever known. But I find myself wondering. Do I like the taste of destruction because I was forced to stomach it for so long? Or do I *need* it? It's probably too soon to say one way or the other, but it's worth pondering.

Despite my efforts not to, I think back on my first months at the ludere. How I took to training. The way I flowed into it all like a stream to a river. I always saw it as survival, but what if it's more than that? What if I was made for death and simply couldn't see the truth of that past the chains and the whips and the masters?

I shrug that thought off. Maybe it's the fact that I'm finally away from Tilleo and the ludere that makes me feel as though I have to decide everything right this very moment, but I don't. I'm away from the chaos for the first time. It's bound to take some adjusting. I need to be patient with myself—I've sure as fuck earned it.

I shut down all the disquiet and indecision spiraling through me, and close in on the cooler in the kitchen that's disguised as a cupboard. Cold air kisses my worry-flushed face as I pull the doors open and take stock. I want to crow in victory at the shelves filled with food, but instead I hurry to grab a wrapped plate that has reddish strips of what looks to be dried meat on it. My stomach rumbles in approval as I pluck out more dishes and jars of things, my midnight feast coming together quite nicely. The cooler doors click shut, and I turn my attention to one of the ovens. I bite back the squeal of delight that tries to tip past my lips as several loaves of bread adorn the rack inside. I quickly free one and move to the drawer that I saw Riall pull knives from.

I select a long, tapered, sharp blade, ignoring that my heart skips with excitement at the sight of it, just like it did at the sight of food. I refuse to condemn myself for that though. I'm sure plenty of fae appreciate a well-crafted weapon in any environment. It's not a sign. It's natural.

I close the drawer, eagerly moving back to my fixings, when the air behind me subtly changes. This would probably mean nothing to the average fae. A breeze to be ignored, but I'm a blade slave, and the hair on the back of my neck rises with warning. Without hesitation, I spin to face the threat head-on. The knife that was just in my hand, the one that was making my heart patter with excited appreciation, is now flying dangerously in the direction of whoever just popped up behind me.

I have no idea who or what has crept in here, but as I whirl and loose my weapon, a shirtless Riall wasn't high on my list of guesses. He plucks the incoming blade from the air a mere hairbreadth from his throat. He snatches the knife I sent spinning at him so easily and effortlessly that I'm momentarily awed by the skill of it instead of being immediately irritated that he snuck up on me in the first place.

He doesn't look put out in the slightest that I almost just murdered him. Instead, he flips the knife in his hand until the handle is firmly cushioned in his palm, and then he looks down at it with a fond smirk stretching his plump lips.

"What the fuck?" I demand, my pique finally rising to the occasion.

Hazel eyes find mine, the shadows of the dark room almost caressing his high cheeks and strong straight nose. Moonlight glimmers in his gaze and brushes across his bearded chin, dripping down his body and highlighting the firm muscle etched across his arms, shoulders, chest, abdomen—fuck, he's chiseled everywhere. There isn't an inch of him that isn't honed and taut and ready.

I swallow thickly, my mouth growing dry as the moisture all at once evaporates from my tongue and pools… other places. Like he can read my mind or my face or whatever it is that's giving me away right now, his smirk widens even more and he steps closer.

"Couldn't sleep?" he asks smoothly, his eyes flicking from me to the stash of food spread across the counter behind me and then back again.

Riall's lethal mien, the hint of danger and uncertainty that follows each of the Scorpions, is like a warm balm to my unease. The tightening in my chest unexpectedly loosens all at once, and I pull in a deep breath as though I haven't been able to until now. Slowly I'm steeped in his presence, and everything inside of me that was tense with agitation and restlessness goes lax.

He's the touch of chaos I've been craving, and that realization slaps me across the face hard.

I want to step back, to create distance between us, between my disconcerting thoughts and the uninvited reaction of my body to his sudden proximity. But the kitchen counter is already digging into my spine, and I don't want to give Riall the satisfaction of knowing that he's unnerved me beyond the surprise of finding him down here at this late hour.

"Fodder for good dreams," I answer lamely, jutting my chin over my shoulder as though he hasn't already cataloged every item I've pulled from their stores. "What are you doing down here?" I ask, refusing to cringe at the high-pitched accusation ringing in my tone.

Amusement glimmers in his eyes, and he reaches out to hand my knife back to me. I hesitate to take it right away, which only serves to make a quiet laugh rumble out of his wide, hard chest. My brow furrows with annoyance. He's laughing at me. It's obvious, and I'm giving him every reason to by acting like some wide-eyed, flustered simpleton. I clear my throat and reach out to snatch the knife from his palm. My fingers graze the warm calluses of his hand, and I fight off the shiver that wants to crawl up my back and down my arms.

"Fodder for good dreams," he parrots back, only his eyes don't stray to the contents of the counter behind me.

No.

They drop down my body, heatedly tracing the wrinkled tracks of my tunic and languidly regarding my bare legs and feet, before stroking back up and settling pointedly on my face. Desire spills from his stare, thick and hot, and I feel it everywhere despite my concentrated efforts not to.

It's not the first time Riall has looked at me this way. I know the kind of games he likes to play, but why then is his needy gaze starting to tickle over me uncomfortably like an itch that desperately needs to be scratched? Why am I breathing harder and fighting the need to clench my thighs together for relief?

I've never had much of an issue with scratching pesky itches, but this is not the ludere, and Riall is not Leto. I don't know if he's safe. I don't know where he stands. Riall studies me, his molten stare open and inviting. It's as though his warm hazel eyes are brimming with all kinds of promises to chase every speck of my loneliness away. I try to dismiss it, to tell myself that these Scorpions are dangerous, that what feels like an itch could easily turn into a full-blown pox. I have no idea how they might perceive me simply satiating a carnal need. They seem concerningly possessive for reasons that escape me, and that can't be a good thing. Fate doesn't work for me like that.

"What are you doing here?" I ask again as I try to wrangle my conflicting thoughts.

"I warded the kitchen to alert me if you came down," he tells me evenly as though it should be no great concern of mine.

"What? W-why?" I sputter, tightening my grip on the knife that's once again in my possession. *How in the stars did I not notice the ward?* "Worried I'd rob you and take off in the night?" I accuse, happy to let outrage trickle in to help wash away the confusing desire that was rising with unwelcome fervor. "I gave Tarek my word. That may not mean anything to you Scorpions, but it means something to me."

"Relax," Riall coos at me, the amused smirk on his face annoying me even more than it usually does. "It's none of that. Tarek keeps some ingredients in the cooler that might look edible, but they sure as shit aren't."

He leans closer to me, and my heart kicks up as his arm brushes mine. I hold my breath, suddenly unsure of what's happening or what I'm even hoping will happen, when Riall pulls back a jar from my stash with a light green substance, now clutched in his hand.

"This might look like pickled cabbage, but I promise it's not something you want to add to your late-night snack," Riall reassures me, setting the jar of what I now suspect to be worms or maybe brains on a different counter far away from the rest of my hoard. He's so tall, his arms so long, that he doesn't even need to move away from me to do it.

"Oh," I respond stupidly, just barely resisting the urge to step further away from whatever Tarek was saving in that jar.

Laughter dances in Riall's hazel eyes, but he doesn't let it loose. "I figured you might need some guidance for the next couple of days when it comes to what you might or might not want to be putting into your mouth."

Heat once again pools low in my belly, and I'm no longer sure if we're still talking about food. I try to glare at him, but the effect is ruined by the shuddering breath I pull in and the slight fidgeting I do before I put a stop to both. Riall steps even closer, as though he's reading things written across my skin that I, myself, can't see.

"Of course, if there's anything else I can assist you with tonight," he declares, his tone suddenly a deep whisper that speaks to parts of me that shouldn't be awake in his presence, "all you have to do is ask."

I want to close my eyes, float in the sensual tone of his tempting offer, which makes absolutely no sense, because this isn't me. I don't take risks like this or grow weak and simpering because of a pretty face that dares to hint at dark and delicious things in the deep of the night. And yet, here I am doing that very thing. I'm a handful of days free from the ludere, and already the person I thought I was is flying right out the window.

"Stop," I demand, straightening my spine and fortifying my defenses against Riall's allure.

I ignore the tingling of my fangs and the pang that starts in my belly that has nothing to do with food.

Riall's ash brown eyebrow lifts, and somehow it makes him look both curious and defiant simultaneously. "Stop what, Beasty?"

"This," I exclaim, gesturing between us and then around us as though the movement alone explains what I'm referring to.

Riall takes that as an invitation to move even closer. All at once, he's barely a blade's width away from me, and I try not to gulp down air as my heart takes off as though it's being chased. He's not touching me, but he's close enough that I can feel the warmth radiating from him. If I let myself, I could drown in the shadows that currently paint slashes over both of us in this dark kitchen, a kitchen that abruptly feels entirely too small. He stares at my throat for a beat, my racing pulse probably telling him all kinds of things I'd prefer to keep to myself, but I clamp my lips shut and fix my face with warning.

"And why would I ever do that, Beasty?" he asks softly, but it feels more like a purr.

"Because it's enough," I snap, every part of me drawn entirely too tight to hold the weight of the rising tension between us. "I've had enough with the three of you looking at me like something you need to conquer. I am not yours to own, Riall. I never will be," I declare, grateful that I hear hard determination reinforcing my words and not the breathy invitation I was worried might show up in that statement.

"And what makes you think any of us want to own you?" Riall counters, the confident smile he's wearing not dimming in the slightest as his gaze traces over my face like he's looking for something hidden beneath my frustrated scowl.

"Isn't that how all of this works? The world we live in," I supply, mocking Tarek's words from earlier.

"I'd *love* to show you how all of this works, Beasty, but you'd have to let go of the bullshit preconceived notions you have about us...and yourself, for me to do that," he asserts, and I'm slightly thrown by it.

"Me?" I challenge.

"Yes, *you*, Auset. You live in a world where horrible things happen to everyone, and yet somehow you have this fucked-up notion of what *good* should look like. But when has *good* done anything for you, or for us, or anyone else you've ever known for that matter? You know better, Beasty. You know what you crave. What gets your heart racing with excitement, and need dripping down your thighs. It's not *good* that's doing any of that for you, is it? You just don't want to see the truth yet."

"You don't know shit about me," I retort, but even I can hear how weak that argument sounds.

"You'd like to think that, but it would just be another thing you're too afraid to admit," he growls back, caging me in as he presses his palms against the counter on either side of me. "I've never met a being in this land or the next that doesn't take, that doesn't snatch up what they need and want, because that's our very nature as fae. You understood what it took to come out on top in the ludere; you need to understand it again now that you're out."

His heated gaze drinks me down, and despite myself, responding warmth moves over me. I want to pretend it's only anger, but with the muscles of his arms barely brushing mine, and the way his mouth edges closer with each breath, I know I'd be lying. I try to shake free of his words—of the grip his proximity and presence has over me—and lean into him, needing to show him that he's wrong. I'm not scared to admit anything; there's simply nothing to admit. But the moment I press against the hard planes of his body and the warmth of his skin, I know I've made a mistake.

I pull in a shocked breath as the sudden contact sends a flare of undeniable awareness shrieking through me. And then the next thing I know, our lips crash together in a violent, passionate frenzy.

29

I CAN'T SAY WHICH OF US MOVES TO THE OTHER FIRST or if we're both pulled together at the exact same moment. All I know is that Riall's large hands cup the sides of my face, and his long fingers thread through my hair as our mouths and tongues clash and fight and demand everything the other has to give. I want to battle for dominance. To take, exactly like he just said I should, but he nips and strokes and sucks at my mouth like he was made for this and this alone, and it stokes an unyielding need in me to see what it would be like to follow instead of lead.

Riall's hands drop from my face, and I moan as I feel them dip lower and grip my ass tightly. He lifts me up on the counter, stepping into me as plates of food and jars are pushed out of the way. Something falls to the ground, shattering loudly, but Riall parts my thighs with his thick body, grinding his hips into me, and I'm lost to anything else but him.

My tunic is pushed higher by our position, and I gasp at the delicious sensation of his leathers against my bare cunt. My nipples harden and my breasts grow heavy as desire blazes through me. He's hard as a rock against the seam of me, and I suddenly can't decide if I want to shove my hands down his pants or continue to grind against him while I feel the taut muscles of his torso.

I palm the back of his head, his short shorn hair scratchy against my skin in a way I want to feel everywhere. Riall growls into my mouth, pulling me tighter against him. Our tongues dance and stroke, and I feel the hint of a sharp canine that sets everything inside of me alight while also terrifying me. I want to feel his fangs against my neck, and yet that animalistic yearning unsettles me more than anything else.

It would be brutal and rough between us, but that's not what makes me pause. It's what something between us might do to me and my plans, because what if he's right? What if I am ignoring the glaring truths in front of me? What if I am afraid?

As though my doubt starts to flavor our kiss, Riall responds by kissing me even harder. He drives his hips into my spread thighs and sucks on my bottom lip, like he's showing me what it would feel like to have his lips wrapped around my clit. I'm lost to him once again, need drowning out every logical objection trying to form in my mind.

Fuck, he feels incredible.

Riall is large and hard in every possible sense. I feel dominated and yet protected in a way that's both confusing and invigorating. With Leto, I always led. I took what I needed, how I needed it, and he was happy to let me. Riall is different. He's pure unfiltered fervor. He's manic need to dominate and claim and wrench every drop of desire out of every touch and stroke and thrust. It's all consuming, powerful, and I want to drown in it even though I know how dangerous that could be.

"I'm going to fuck you here on the counter, and then again on the table. I'm going to fuck you on every stair that leads upstairs until you're in my bed where I'll have you screaming my name long past the point when your voice gives out," he declares against my lips, threading his hands back through my hair to angle my mouth the way he wants before drinking me down in a kiss so deep and intense that my toes curl and the first signs of release start to collect at my center.

Bless the realms, can he make me come from this alone?

Something about that realization makes all of this feel entirely too intense. I've never experienced anything like this before. I've had needs and desires, but *this* is on another level. What I'm feeling right now is beyond not wanting to feel lonely. It's consuming in a way that could burn everything I know, everything I am, to ash when it's all so tenuous.

What would be left in the wake of the detonation that's building between us?

I've barely gotten a grip on what I want for me, and now I'd have to factor in Riall? How am I supposed to know how he fits into a life I've barely had a chance to peek at? I wanted to find connection, to feel tethered to something again, but *this* is entirely too potent to think I'll walk away unscathed, and I have to be able to walk away.

"No," I manage to get out, but I don't know if it's a declaration meant for me or for Riall.

I push against his bare chest.

"No, what?" he demands, swallowing my panted word down as he nips at my lower lip with his fangs.

Shit.

Riall runs his tongue against my own sharpened canines, moaning at the sensation. I don't even know when my fangs came out to play, I've been so wrapped up in... everything.

"No to all of this," I try again, grinding against Riall's leathers in a way that very much doesn't align with my words. I run my hands down his back, reveling in the hard planes one last time before I shake off the need to lick every inch of him. "No, Riall," I get out with a little more bite, and Riall pulls back to look at me.

I want to whimper with objection at the distance now between our mouths while simultaneously thanking him for stopping, and it needed to stop. Things have already gone altogether too far.

"Tell me *yes*," Riall commands, his tone a passionate plea and a delicious order all rolled into one, but he doesn't claim my mouth again. He waits and watches as a myriad of mucked up emotions flash across my face.

"I can't."

"You can," he argues warmly, his hands still cupping my cheeks as his stare sears into me.

"I won't," I counter, and he studies me for a beat before dropping his palms from my face and stepping back.

Riall runs his hands over his shorn head and down his face as he starts to pace.

"What are you so afraid of?" he finally asks, but it feels less like a whip of accusation and more like a riddle he's trying to work out.

Good luck. I don't even have all the pieces to that puzzle myself.

I throw my hands up in exasperation as I try to catch my breath. "I don't know. Nothing. Everything maybe. But that's the fucking problem. I've been free for no time at all, and it's all wrong. How I feel. What I want..."

"It's not wrong to embrace what the ludere showed you about yourself," Riall interjects.

"Showed me, tortured into me. I guess it's all the same to you, isn't it, *Bones*, or should I call you master?" I jeer.

"Don't do that," Riall snaps. "Don't tally me in your *bad* column when you know it's not that simple."

"You want to know what *I* know, you pompous prick?" I lob back, jumping off of the counter so I can get in his face.

I won't sit here a second longer with my tunic riding up my thighs and the taste of him on my lips as he preaches at me like he has any right to. I kissed him, I didn't hand over my soul. He has no idea what I'm dealing with right now. He can pretend otherwise, but *I* don't even fucking know, so who in the shithole of all the realms does he think he is?

Pain slices through my foot as I hop down. I remember too late about the dish that shattered on the ground when Riall lifted me up on the counter. I hiss as I reach for my foot and try to back away from the shattered platter sprinkling the wood floor. I step on another shard with my other foot, but before I can even cry out, Riall is gripping my waist and lifting me away from the broken porcelain. Quickly he sets me on the long prep table in the center of the kitchen. Warm blood drips down the pads of my feet as Riall pulls some towels from a drawer and rushes back over.

I notice that even though he forgot his shirt when he came down here to meet me, he didn't forget his boots. The heel of his unlaced footwear comes down on a piece of plate and crushes the sliver of porcelain underneath the sole. Riall lifts my foot, eyeing the bottom of it for a few beats before plucking a large shard and dropping it to the ground. He examines the rest of my heel, arch, and toes for a moment more before wrapping everything in a towel and reaching for my other foot to repeat his fussing.

"I'm fine," I grumble as I reach for the foot he just wrapped.

He slaps my hand away as I pull at the corner of the towel so I can inspect things myself.

"Excuse you," I snarl, but he pulls the wrapped appendage away and tucks it under his arm while he pulls pieces of plate from my other foot.

"Do you like killing?" he demands out of nowhere, the question stopping me from kicking him in the face and instead making me pause.

"What?" I ask, taken aback.

"Do you like killing?"

"I'm good at it," I answer without missing a beat, holding back a wince as he pulls out another small sliver from my heel.

"That's not what I asked," Riall counters, giving me a pointed look as he finishes with my other foot and starts to wrap it in a towel too.

I anchor my arms behind me and lean back on the long prep table, studying Riall while trying to suss out the point of this question. Streaks of moonlight gently dance across his long lashes, and his eyes look dark and fathomless as he inspects the wrapped towels to make sure I'm not bleeding through them already.

"Does anyone *like* killing?" I query as I struggle to source my own answer to his odd question.

"I do," he answers bluntly.

Riall looks up from my legs, his intense eyes once again settling on mine like he wants to gauge my reaction. I stare back measuredly, refusing to give anything away. A heart-stopping smile slowly stretches across his face, like he's seeing something in my eyes anyway.

"I love the smell of fresh blood. Relish the look in someone's eyes when they realize you're the last thing they'll ever see." He closes his eyes as though he's savoring that thought. "The hush of a last breath. A final plea from lips that have never granted mercy. I love it all," he impenitently confesses, a fervent fire flickering through his features as he speaks. "From planning a hunt with my brothers to feeling my blade sink through skin and muscle to find that sweet spot that will end it all"—he pauses and levels me with a molten look—"it's my second favorite thing to do ever."

I'm caught in the net of his words and hooked by the suggestive look in eyes. Slowly Riall's hand caresses up my calf, and it's not hard to guess what's on the top of his list of favorite things. His callused palm skims up the inside of my thigh, and it takes everything in me not to spread my legs in encouragement. I know I need to keep a level head, but his hands on my body might be my new favorite thing.

Instead of allowing my baser needs to drive me over a dangerous cliff, I force myself to scoot away from him. Riall's hand falls away as I do, and he says nothing as I inspect my feet. I unwrap the towels, double-checking the Scorpion's work, and then I stretch my legs out into the pool of moonlight grazing the far end of the table to help my feet heal.

I lean back again on my hands, getting comfortable, already feeling the telltale healing tingle at the bottoms of my feet. Riall runs his gaze over me quickly before turning and striding over to a closet. He pulls a broom and towels from its depths, and I keep my mouth shut as I watch him soak up my blood with a rag and then start sweeping up the mess on the floor. His back and arm muscles contract and release as he works, and I try not to get mesmerized by the sheer magnificence of him. I suddenly want to see him train and fight naked for the sole purpose of allowing me to study every lethal exquisite inch of him while he does.

Riall's words wind around me in comforting coils as I observe him. His love affair with death sinks deep beneath my skin to join my own warm sentiments on the subject. I don't know that I've thought much about what I do and don't like in general, but I have spent more time than I'd ever admit thinking about death. I used to beg for it at one point. Locked in the ludere's hot house, tortured day and night, the masters always pushing for me to fracture, to give in and agree to enticement training, to hand over every piece of me to Tilleo and submit to his wishes.

Death refused to wrap me up in its arms no matter how many times I tried to crawl into them. And I did, over and over again, until my pleas eventually dried up like a puddle in the desert. I was angry and bitter for a while, but with time, I saw it all as the gift that it was. If I hadn't been brought so close to the end, only to have it all ripped out of my grasp repeatedly, I might not have understood the beauty and power that could be found in those final moments. I came away from all of that not only stronger, but it made me see things very differently. I've never talked about it before, but that fucked-up experience cut me open and left me exposed. Death slithered in, only instead of letting it claim me, I claimed it.

"I like the instant it dawns on someone that they can't beat me. The look in their eyes when it happens is...glorious," I confess quietly, my admission joining the tinkling sound of broken porcelain as it's swept up.

Riall hums a soft sound of approval, but he doesn't take his eyes off the ground or his task.

"I feel powerful knowing I alone weave someone's end. On a hunt, I can make a fae's last moments as barbaric or gentle as *I* choose. That fortifies me in a way it probably shouldn't," I admit, my gaze moving from Riall to the starlit window above the sinks behind him. "I never got nightmares like the others after our first kills. I felt..."

"Exhilarated?" Riall supplies.

"Sustained," I counter, shrugging. "I felt fortified, indomitable, like it no longer mattered who owned me, who I had to answer to, because in the end, *I* held life in my hands.

I decided what to do with it, and no one could ever take that away from me. It felt right."

I drop my gaze to my hands, flipping them over and tracing the lines of my palms with my eyes. They're simple hands, callused but feminine and fragile-looking on a passing glance. The things I've done with them, though. The things I can do, I should be horrified, and yet all I find in my depths is pride and validation.

"As it should," Riall declares, not unsteadied at all by my ruthless revelations. "You're a powerful, magnificent force, Auset, and there isn't a fucking thing wrong with that."

A small smile hints at my lips with his words, but I smooth it away. I look up at him, not sure how to respond, but thankfully, he pulls his impassioned stare from mine and continues to clean up the kitchen floor.

I want to sneak off while he's distracted. Grab all the food from the counter and dash away as fast as I can from the cumbersome weight of what's been shared between us tonight. I feel raw in a risky and hazardous way, but I know there's no running from this, not really. So instead, I sit there feeling entirely too exposed and vulnerable, while he sweeps the sharp threats sprinkling the floor into a safe pile by the door.

I wait for Riall to say something, make some kind of effort to either entice or soothe. I'm prepared for him to bolster me, to attempt to pull me closer to his side of things so I can look out at the world from his point of view, but he's silent as he works. Somehow, that's almost worse. All kinds of thoughts and realizations that I never knew were locked up inside of me have been freed. Things I don't know what to do with or how to reconcile.

My lips still tingle from our kiss, and I feel both trapped and liberated by that and the dark declarations now dangling between us. I've always looked at my skills as a blade slave as a means to an end. Yes, things came naturally to me, but that was because I was a survivor, not because I liked it.

Right?

I sigh, wishing I could fold all of these frustrating revelations back into neat little boxes that I'd promptly chuck far into the ocean where I'd never have to acknowledge them again. Who has time for all these confusing *feelings?* I want to fuck Riall and then stab the shit out of him for doing this to me. It was all so much simpler when it was just about survival, about freedom. I had no idea how hard it would be to simply *live.* To *choose* a life and figure out what makes you happy. I don't think I've ever said that word, let alone thought it might be within my grasp. It's all so much more complex than I ever thought it would be.

"Beasty—" Riall starts as he tucks the broom back in the cupboard and moves toward my stash of food on the counter.

"Just...stop," I interrupt, not wanting to hear whatever it is he wants to tell me about myself or the way the world works.

"Stop what?" Riall contests, turning to study me.

"Stop telling me who I am or what I need to be. Can't I decide that on my own? Am I not allowed to have more than a day to figure things out?" I demand.

"That's what we're trying to help you do."

"No," I argue. "You're trying to steer me in a direction that has me landing on your cocks. That's certainly in your best interest, but who's to say it's in mine?"

Riall smirks at me while he crosses his arms over his bare chest and leans back against the counter. "Trust me, Beasty, it's definitely in your best interest."

I release a frustrated growl and shake my head as I thread my fingers through my hair with exasperation. "I'm serious, Riall," I snap, and his eyes narrow at me.

"As am I, *Auset*," he mocks. "Why would accepting a place here be such a bad thing?" he demands. "Yes, we'd fuck you senseless each and every day, but what's wrong with that? We'd also care for you. Look out for you. Accept you and give you an outlet for your darker needs. You'd never want for anything again. You'd be one of us, Beasty, now and forever. Why is that such a horrid option?"

"Nobody actually means *forever*," I contend.

"I mean fucking forever," he growls back, pushing away from the counter and closing the distance in two long strides. "My brothers mean it," he insists, and he leans over me, forcing me to look up at him and the searing intensity in his gaze. "Fuck every fae out there. We're not them. If you choose us, you'll have us. That's it," he tells me vehemently, slashing a hand through the air in finality.

I study his face, his fervor, the fight gleaming in his gaze as he readies himself for my argument. It all washes over me, anchoring me while somehow also unsettling me at the same time. I don't understand his conviction, and there's no doubt, as I stare into his eyes and see the truth blaring back at me, that he means everything he's saying.

"Why?" I ask, the question constantly plaguing me since the moment I woke up here. "Why me?"

"Why not?" Riall counters. "You're strong, powerful, smart, rare, resilient, and you happen to be the most fucking beautiful creature I've ever seen. I could build lists for you, Beasty. I will if you want, but none of them are as convincing as what I feel in here," he implores, touching his palm to his chest. "I feel it here. I have since I saw you sitting in that bastard Bruin's quarters covered in blood, looking as though you'd burn the world to the ground. I knew then that I'd happily light it all up right alongside you if that's what you asked of me."

Riall's fangs drop as he speaks, and I feel my own tingle in response. He cups my face, his eyes begging me to see what he does, and for a second, for the briefest of moments, I wish I could. But the night Dorsin took me, the night Riall and his brothers left me to my fate in his stronghold, it hollowed me out beyond recognition. I don't think anything or anyone will ever truly be able to fill me in again.

"You left me, Riall," I tell him, and he winces as though the statement just slapped him across the face. I can see that my words claw at him, not because they're laced with anger or accusation, but because my tone is as hollow as I feel right now. "I'm all of these things to you now, but then...then when I needed everything you're offering me, I was nothing. Not even worthy of a final glance back."

"I didn't see you then," he admits, his thumb stroking softly over my cheek. "But I see you now."

My eyes flicker back and forth between his, and I can see the sincerity that sits heavy in his stare. I shake my head, pulling back until his hand drops from my face.

"That's the thing though, *Bones*, you're too late."

The locks affixing my barriers click into place, and I push off the table, getting to my feet on the other side. My soles feel tight from the healing time spent soaking up the moonlight, but there's no pain as I give Riall my back and make my way out of the kitchen and down the dark hallway to the stairs. My stomach groans in protest, but all it does is fortify my decision even more. I decided that night in Dorsin's office, as Tilleo and his men looked down at me as though I was nothing more than overpriced meat, that I'd never beg for help again. I'd never hope that someone would come rescue me. I'd figure out how to rescue myself.

I've leaned on these Scorpions too much. I've let their tempting promises and charm weaken my resolve, but it's time to get back to the truth I *do* know about this world. I am the only one I can really count on, and I need to figure out who the fuck I am and what the fuck I want, and I need to do it soon.

30

TAREK

THE DOOR SLAMS OPEN SO HARD THAT IT RAT-
tles every shelf in the room and forces the
dust resting on some old tomes in this study
to plume in the air. The loud boom of the
thick wood hitting the stone wall reverberates
through me, and I drop my missives on my desk and look
up to find Riall storming in like a squall of pure fury and
rage.

Curio shoots up from the settee in front of the fireplace,
bewilderment chasing away his sleep, and we both watch
as Riall stomps over to a case of tinctures and starts rifling
through them.

"What's wrong?" I demand, pushing up from my chair and the communications I was just sorting through. My gaze flashes to the now open door as though I'll see something or perhaps someone there to explain what's going on, but the doorway is empty.

"I...just...need..." Riall growls out as he abandons the tinctures of one case for the bottles of another, "to find something..." He hurriedly knocks over several dismissed vials, and I force myself to bite my tongue as I watch him continue to frantically search.

"Is it Auset, is she okay?" Curio demands, his voice gravelly with sleep as he gets up and moves toward the door as though he needs to get a head start on whatever Riall might say.

"There has to be something in here that will let the three of us shitheads go back in fucking time," Riall snarls, picking up a large decanter of sylph sap and throwing it against the wall.

The crystal shatters violently, and I step out from behind my desk, unnerved by my brother's unusual tempestuous behavior.

"Of everything in here, there has to be something that can help us go back and fix what we fucked up. We have to go back for her," he bellows, picking up another stoppered bottle and launching it at the wall too.

"Sit the fuck down and stop destroying my things," I bark, but all it does is force Riall to turn his enraged attention to me.

A furious stare connects with mine, and I'm jolted by the pain I see there. This, more than anything else, sends alarm coursing through me, and then it blares even louder as Riall deflates with sudden defeat. He runs his hands over his face, mussing up his beard and scratching over his shaved head.

"She's never going to forgive us for leaving her there," Riall declares, and then he strides over to the settee that Curio just abandoned and slumps down.

Curio and I both follow him over to the sitting area, not sure what to make of any of this.

Something obviously happened with Auset. There's no one else he would be this upset over, and it's all I can do to wait patiently for him to explain. I know he needs me right now, but it's difficult not to rush out of here to make sure Auset is okay too.

"What happened?" Curio presses as he leans against the thick stone mantel above the fireplace.

The room is silent while we both watch Riall on the couch, elbows anchored on his legs while he cradles his head.

"We were in the kitchen," he starts, just as my patience nears its limits. "We were kissing—"

"What? How?" Curio interrupts, and Riall scowls up at him.

"My lips were on hers, her tongue was in my mouth, she was grinding her bare pussy on my leathers—"

"I know *how*, you ass," Curio snaps, and I catch a flash of a smug, teasing smile wink across Riall's face before he seems to remember whatever happened after the kissing part of his story and grows sullen again. "I meant how did she go from hating us this morning to tongue fucking you at night?"

"Who cares," Riall dismisses, throwing himself back on the settee dramatically and resting his head on the cushion. "She was right there with me, needing, demanding, she was ready, and then all of a sudden she wasn't. We went back and forth about the same shit she's been saying since she woke up. But then she looked at me in this way that fucking took a hammer to my insides, and reminded me that we left her that night at that useless fucking ludere," he tells us, his tone pained as he covers his face with his hands as though it will block the sting of it all. "She's never going to get past that."

The tight band of worry that's been constricting around my chest loosens, and I sag down into an armchair and run a hand down my face with a sigh.

"Why the fuck are you smiling?" Riall snaps at Curio, and I look over to find a grin widening across his face.

Curio shakes his head and collapses down on the other side of the settee that he's been calling a bed since Auset took over his. The furniture we ordered for the empty extra rooms on the ground floor has been delayed, and I'm undecided if that's a blessing or a curse.

"Only *you* would think it's all hopeless, completely ignoring that she went from trying to leave this morning to almost riding your dick by night," he points out, his smile broadening even more as he does. "I'd say that's progress, not failure."

"You didn't see the way she looked at me before she walked the fuck away. There was no progress in that shit. It fucking cut...deep," Riall counters.

"She's been through a lot, Riall, we all knew we'd need to be patient," I remind him, but he shakes his head.

"We fucked up," he sighs, dropping his hands to his lap as he continues to stare at the ceiling.

"She was young; there was nothing we could do then," I remind him. "We've been over this and over this—fate brought us back to her. She may not see all the reasons why right now, but she just got here. Give her time."

"And if she doesn't?" he challenges.

"Then we serve what purpose we can in her life and hope she finds her way back here again," I tell him evenly as though that statement doesn't feel like razor blades in my mouth.

"Screw that, Tarek, I'm not letting her go," Curio argues.

Shocked, I snap my attention to him. I expect a statement like that from Riall, as he's always been the more impulsive of the three of us, but not Curio.

"You will if that's what *she* wants," I correct him.

Shoving out of my chair, I start to pace in front of the fireplace. The drive to move, to process the sudden volatile emotions flinging about the room, makes my legs ache. I swallow down the trickle of panic that laces my saliva, and look for ways to solve all the problems suddenly creeping into my periphery.

"I shouldn't need to remind you two that we all knew this wouldn't be easy. Her desire to be one of us wasn't a guarantee when we brought her here. We all understood that, and now what? You want to tie her up and force her to accept you?" I accuse.

Riall opens his mouth to argue, but I give him a glare and hold up a hand to silence him. Wisely, he shuts his mouth.

"She was taken, abandoned, abused, and now you expect her to just *trust* us as she falls on her back and spreads her thighs for you? What about Auset makes you think that's a viable expectation? She'd sooner slit your throat and remove your balls," I warn them, shoving away the amusement I feel at the thought of her savage nature.

Curio snorts, the sound equally appreciative of the visual I just created, and shakes his head. "Yeah, that's not our girl," he agrees, relaxing a little into the cushions of his chair.

"I know it's hard. None of us are very patient when it comes to taking what we want. But you both need to think less with your cocks and more about what she needs to see from us so she can begin to work through what's happened to her. The nightmare we inadvertently helped create," I point out.

Both of them lower their heads as though the shame of that fact is suddenly too heavy to bear. I ignore my own guilty stirrings and bolster myself as best as I can against the useless emotion. What's done is done. We didn't know what Tilleo was doing, how bad he'd strayed from what the ludere was supposed to be there for. We also didn't know who the girl chained in Dorsin's office would become, what she would mean to us some day. How could we? She wasn't who she is now, and it's because of who she is *now* that she's ours. I equally hate and respect what she's been through, but I can't help feeling that in some way it all needed to happen just as it has.

"We owe her some answers about how Dorsin got her, which I'm already working on," I point out, gesturing to the stack of sealed missives sitting in a tray on my desk. "We need to show her who we are and who she is to us, who she could be *with* us. She's smart enough to figure the rest out."

"She's stubborn," Riall argues.

"Good, it'll make earning her all the more worth it," I contend.

"You act like it's a done deal," Curio points out with a cheeky smirk and an eyeroll.

"It is," I assure him. "She's special, we all know it. She's one of us. She'll get it, and then we'll get her," I state confidently, and there's nothing about my certainty that's fabricated.

I know in my depths that all of us belong to each other. I knew it when Eacon brought the three of us together, and I've known it on some level since the moment Auset walked into our tent, all sharp tongue and raw power.

Riall shakes his head while slowly exhaling a deep weary sigh. "She's Sanguinna," he professes, the statement pained. "A female. I didn't think they existed anymore, and now here she is wandering around my home in Curio's tunic and nothing more, loathing me and everything I stand for. She's my Blood, I don't think you two understand how hard it is not to sink my fangs into every inch of her, to claim her and demand she claims me right back," he admits, and I know how much the confession costs him, how hard it is for Riall to embrace this kind of vulnerability.

My concern softens as I take him in. He's come so far since the day Eacon brought him here. I'd never seen someone so jumpy and feral. He was filthy and terrified and absolutely savage in every possible way. I can still recall the cold night that Curio and I sat by the fire while Eacon recounted how their paths had crossed. Riall had been on the run and hiding for years. He'd been forced to survive solely on others' blood, and he'd attacked Eacon and tried to bite her. Somehow she'd gotten him to come here with her, but she wasn't sure if his Sanguinna side would ever give way to the calmer more civilized parts of him again.

I shake away the memory of the dirt-caked wildling Riall used to be, and focus on the lethal fae before me now. He'd once been hunted by the most feared fae in the Dusk Court. Khartik the Cut-Throat was no one to Riall when he showed up out of nowhere, back from war. Riall had never been told that his mother was married to the brute who led the king's army. Khartik had been gone for a long time, conquering lands at the king's behest. Riall's mother probably thought the monster was dead.

Riall used to have nightmares about the night Khartik killed his mother and tried to kill him. The cruel bastard refused to hear a word in explanation of why his mate mothered a welp that wasn't his. But Riall survived. He ran and hid and evaded for years until Eacon found him.

It took ages for him to get his instincts and urges in check. To think with his head instead of his fangs. Now, here he is fighting who he is at his core, all for a female his kind would raze the realms to find if they knew she existed. I empathize with where he's come from. That the restraint he's showing is unfathomable. I just wish Auset knew it too.

"She's yours," I reassure my brother, pride swelling in my chest not only for him, but for Curio and me too. "She's ours," I affirm, as Riall's gaze intently fixes on mine, his faith in me so absolute that to hear me say so makes it an irrefutable fact.

We aren't those younglings anymore that Eacon first brought here. We've long grown past the traumatized, thrown-away nothings that we were. From bastards to trusted advisors, we're blades to the kings, and the fae that wrong us now bleed out at our feet. Body by body, we've built an impenetrable fortress around our family, one so thick and solid not even our sires can contend with it. Not that they'd ever step far enough from their thrones to realize that.

"We are the Order of Scorpions," I assert, looking from Riall to Curio. "Auset will realize that *we* are where her fate has always been leading. Be patient."

We stare at one another, the power of the moment thick and validating. Riall and Curio both harden with resolve, spines straightening and jaws clenching with determined strength. I smile, and with a satisfied nod of approval, I'm met with their matching grins.

"Good. Now that we've settled that..." I state, striding over to my desk and the two letters that are now my sole focus. "I heard from Kiffin," I start, turning back to Riall and Curio, missives held carefully in my grip. "The Vulpi have been digging deeper into that issue in the Dawn Court, and they're asking for our assistance," I explain as I make my way back over to the sitting area.

I debate claiming my chair again, but my body is still too restless to relax; there's too much to do.

"From what they can gather, Lord Daeral recently returned from some kind of trip. Being that whoever killed Daeral also eliminated his entire bloodline and all of his servants, the Vulpi are having a hard time pinpointing exactly where he went. However, the ladies are currently working through the lord's friends and acquaintances, and they've requested that we reach out to our contacts in the other realms to see if anyone had contact with the lord before his untimely death. Where he traveled could be unrelated, but we won't know one way or the other until we've tugged on every thread we can," I explain, and both Riall and Curio nod their agreement.

Curio extends his hand expectantly, and I hand him the two letters.

"If the two of you agree, I'll reach out to the other realms and see what we can learn."

"Fine by me," Riall offers, and Curio grunts his approval as he reads through what the Order of Vulpi sent.

"They think the hunt was unsanctioned," Curio points out, looking up from the parchment in his hand with a raised brow, his eyes filled with both surprise and concern.

"They do," I agree, flicking a hand at the empty hearth. A spark flits from the tip of my fingers to the stack of logs, the small ember growing as it begins to consume the kindling layered there.

"You're getting better at that," Riall points out with an impressed nod, and I shrug as the fire crackles higher.

"The cast feels like muscle memory now, so there's that, but the spark is still fragile," I admit, doing what I can to level the frustration I feel over that fact. "Anyway, Kiffin didn't come outright and say it in her message, but reading between the lines leads me to think that there's either a new group of killers readying themselves for a place at the

Order table, or something else is going on with this Daeral issue, and we've yet to find the right piece that will help us make sense of it. Either way, we need to be careful with how we proceed."

"It is strange," Curio states as he continues to study the missives. "If it were a new group wanting a shot at an Order, then why copy the Vulpi's signature?"

"Maybe that's *their* signature," Riall offers. "They copy the rest of us and never establish an original calling card."

"Fuck," I sigh, pushing a few wavy strands of my hair back from my face. "I didn't think of that," I confess.

"It would be a good way to create some chaos," Curio agrees.

"It's also a good way to piss off the other Orders. Anyone coming up would know they need a majority vote to be sanctioned. Otherwise, they're just asking to be picked off and plundered by the rest of us just as soon as we can get a grasp on who they are," I point out.

Curio shrugs and goes back to reading, and I go back to steadily pacing, the fire now large enough to provide some welcome heat.

"What's the other letter?" Riall asks, gesturing to the wax seal that's hanging from the second missive in Curio's hands.

I hesitate for a breath, knowing what I'm about to say is going to send Riall into a shit mood, which is the last thing I want to do since we just pulled him out of one. Unfortunately, it can't be avoided. "The Dusk King was enquiring if we'd be taking on any hunts in the near future," I answer, and just as I knew it would, Riall's inner defenses shutter at the first mention of his sire.

"What does that pile of shit want?" Riall growls, and I suddenly feel too fucking tired to take another step. The load on our shoulders has been entirely too heavy for too long, and I think each of us is feeling the wear of that.

I collapse into a chair, considering for the thousandth time just letting Riall finally kill the raping puddle of piss that is the Dusk King, but we all know it will set too many things in motion that could lead to an all-out war between the realms. As tempting as that is on certain shit-infested days, we all know the people will be the ones who suffer the most. None of us are selfish enough to bring that down on any fae's head, which, some days, can be an overwhelmingly maddening reality.

"He's not identified a target yet, only inquired about whether we'd be free to discuss it further. I'll blow him off if you want," I offer, but Riall's gaze is already far away.

Curio studies him before looking back over to me, and I can practically hear the silent question glittering in his concerned stare. Will Riall need to drown what's happening in his mind right now in pix weed, pussy, or pain? On the really bad trips down memory lane, it can take all three.

Surprisingly, it's Riall who breaks up the silent standoff. "Find out who he wants killed and why. We can decide then if we want to play obedient little assassins or do something to fuck with his plan," Riall sagely advises, and I give him an impressed nod.

"I'll do that," I agree, doing my best not to sound shocked that he isn't spiraling like I anticipated he would.

He still looks thoughtful, pensive, but whatever it is that he's pondering, it hasn't sent him plummeting into the depths of despair, so I'll take that as a good sign.

"If we hunt, will we take Auset with us?" Curio asks, handing back the letters.

I take them from him and fold them up neatly, setting them on the arm of the chair.

"That will be up to her. If she wants to come, she'll come; if not, Eacon can come keep an eye on her while we're gone."

"She'll come," Riall declares, a smile hinting at the edges of his mouth. "She's learning she needs the violence as much as we do."

Curio grins at that, as though the statement is music to his ears. I know it's *my* new favorite song. Death is an outlet for each of us. It's a means to an end, but it also fortifies us individually and as a family. I never thought we'd find someone who would fit with us in the same way. A mate capable of appreciating the dark and the brutal things in life the way we do was more than I ever thought to hope for. Couplings like ours aren't unheard of, but they're few. Finding Auset is fate righting all its wrongs against us.

I exhale deeply, feeling some of the tension that's been trapped in my shoulders since we brought Auset here start to slacken. I know there's a lot of work to be done, that she'll more than likely take a few steps forward and then go sprinting in the other direction when things start to feel too intense. But fuck if I don't like the chase. I'll like the catch even more, but tracking my prey has always been a favorite pastime. Pursuing Auset heightens the sweetness of it all even more.

Suddenly, Curio stands and starts collecting his things from around the study. Piling his clothes, daggers, and a few books in his arms, he surveys the space for anything else that belongs solely to him.

"What are you doing?" I ask, confused, as he grabs a tunic that's been strung across the back of an armchair.

"I'm moving back into my room," he announces, and my brow furrows with confusion for a second before understanding sinks in.

"Our Beasty might not take too kindly to you invading her space, regardless of whether or not it was your room first," Riall points out, but the barely stifled laugh in his tone betrays just what he really thinks about all of this.

"Guess we're about to find out," Curio declares dismissively, and then he takes his pile and strides confidently away.

I laugh as he goes, Riall's amusement quick to join mine.

"She's going to slit his throat," Riall states with a deep chuckle.

I shake my head, a wide smile affixed to my face. "She'll try," I agree. "But we both know that's just foreplay to him."

Riall pushes up to his feet, practically giddy as he stares at the study doorway that Curio just exited through.

He walks over to me and pats me on the shoulder, the mischievous gleam in his eyes a far cry from the desperate anger he was feeling when he first stormed in here.

"Don't pull that *watch from the sidelines and plot* thing you love to do," he orders warmly. "It's all hands on deck now. She needs to know exactly where each of us stands if we're going to convince her that we're the right choice."

"Don't worry about that," I reassure him. "I've got plans for our Little Dagger, and none of them involve playing it safe. When I'm done with her, *yes* will be her new favorite word, and each of us will know exactly what it feels like for her to come on our cocks while she screams it."

Riall groans and adjusts himself in his leathers. I laugh and stand up, grabbing the letters off the arm of the chair as I do.

"Patience, brother," I warn playfully as I make my way over to my desk. I pull out clean parchment and ready a pen and ink for the replies that we just discussed. "This is about the long game," I remind Riall, dipping my pen in the well and starting the first of the many missives I need to write tonight. "Auset's about to learn that the Scorpions play for keeps."

31

AUSET

M Y GAZE DARTS OVER TO WHERE CURIO IS lounging in the bed, reading from an old hide-bound book. The silver paint of the title is so faded I can't read what it says, and I refuse to ask the Scorpion, despite my curiosity growing by the day. Slowly, my eyes wander from the deep green of the ancient-looking book to the warm brown of Curio's skin. I study the lines and curves of his shoulders and smooth chest.

Curio reaches up to turn a page, and I dart my stare from him to the rays of early morning light that are streaking through the small crack in the drawn curtains next to me. If he notices that I'm awake, he doesn't say anything as he continues to read silently, something I've learned over the past month that Curio enjoys doing every morning. I try not to shift where I'm lying on the ground or draw any other attention to myself. Often, if I'm careful, I can watch him lazing about for a while before he gets up for the day.

When Curio first stormed in here to reclaim his bed and his space despite me still occupying it, I thought I'd go mad. I was on edge at first, waking up to him every morning and falling asleep with him in here every night. I threatened to move to another room regardless of the fact that they were empty, but for some reason, I never followed through with that threat. Instead, I anticipated his possible ulterior motives and watched my back carefully, but nothing ever happened.

Nothing bad ever happens with any of them.

Curio has long stopped trying to offer me half of his bed or eyeing my pallet of towels and sheets on the ground just under the windows with distaste. He's keeping his grumbling to himself now, but I know he doesn't accept that I'm more comfortable on the floor, no matter how true it is. He never forces conversation, but rather seems perfectly happy to sit in silence and just...be. I've never been made to feel unwelcome or uncomfortable in our shared space, and I've slowly come to terms with the fact that he's always just there, sleeping at night, bathing in the mornings, reading, walking silently with me to breakfast. It's strange, and yet studying him, watching him the way I do, has become an odd little routine of mine. I don't really know what to make of that, so I don't bother thinking too hard on the *whys* of any of it.

I've been doing that a lot lately, just going with things instead of trying hard to puzzle it all out. Between training and eating, I've had far too much time to think, to process. I can't say what I support or oppose anymore. I itch for answers about myself, which is inconvenient because at this point I might never get them.

Tarek has reached out to different contacts throughout the realms, but we've yet to hear anything back. It's only been just over a month, but already I try to prepare myself for life to remain as much a mystery now as it ever was before. I thought if anyone could figure out who I am and where I come from, it would be the Order of Scorpions, but I might never know who I really am.

I started a list in my head of all the things I know but don't know *how* I know. I can read, but I have no memory of ever learning. I know scents and the names of things that I never encountered at the ludere. Every bite of food I like, I grill Riall about where it comes from or how it's procured. I thought it might help me narrow down a region or area to look at more closely, but all I really have is an infuriating list that doesn't make any sense and still no answers.

I observe Curio as he casually turns another page in his book. Maybe mystery isn't the worst thing to ever happen to me though. I don't know what there could be to go back to even if the Scorpions do find something. I'm not the young fae I would have been when I was taken. Whoever she was died in the sands of a fighting pit. I rose in her stead. Maybe it's better to never know what might have been and focus solely on what is happening now.

My stomach growls enthusiastically, and a small smile sneaks across Curio's face before he schools his features and looks over at me. Our gazes connect, and I realize immediately that I've made it obvious that I was just staring at him. His hickory-brown eyes glint with mirth, and I'm all at once certain that my morning ritual of appreciation hasn't gone as unnoticed as I thought it had.

"I could set time by your stomach," Curio teases, his voice gruff and gravelly like it always is first thing in the morning.

My stomach grumbles again as though it's daring Curio to do just that. Ignoring both it and the Scorpion whose eyes are tracing the lines of my legs as I get up, I tug my tunic down and make my way to the washroom. I wish I was as unaffected as I pretend to be by the way Curio's gaze follows me as I go, but the way my heart picks up and the touch of extra hip I put into my stride leaves me with absolutely no denial to hide behind. I close the washroom door and then stare into the mirror, both judging and appreciating the fae that stares back at me. I'm ignoring every inclination I have that's encouraging me to do anything about the way the Scorpions hunt me with their eyes whenever I'm in the same room. The way my mere presence seem to reel them in so effortlessly is a heady thing to experience, and it never gets old.

I wash up and then curse myself for not bringing a change of clothes in here with me. I was too flustered and in a hurry to make my escape after my stomach got me caught practically drooling over Curio. I'm sure he'll enjoy when I have to go back out there and face him with nothing on but his damn tunic. I'm sure the fact that I still wear the long black tops at night instead of the sleep dresses Eacon has brought me isn't lost on him either.

I could easily explain that I don't like things tangling around my legs at night because I'm used to sleeping in thin worn garments that were barely more than a few threads that refused to give in, but it's a weak argument even to my ears. Curio doesn't seem to mind that I'm going through his wardrobe faster than he is. We both keep our mouths shut on the matter and go about our business.

Inhaling deeply, I prepare myself to face the Scorpion once again, and I pull open the washroom door, striding confidently out. I freeze at the sight of Curio partially bent over as he pulls leathers up his corded calves and thick thighs. His round bare ass practically stares me in the face, and for some reason, my mouth starts to water. The muscles in the globes of his cheeks flex, and I'm so distracted by that and the sack just barely visible between his thighs as he straightens that I don't notice he's now watching me over his shoulder.

Before I can get a hold of myself and find somewhere else in the room to focus on, Curio turns around and blatantly offers me an unobstructed view of the front of him. The smile on his face is salacious and proud, and I'm reminded of the arrogant Skull I met that first night in their tent at the ludere. The way he stripped down and sank into the steaming golden tub as though worthy of worship and admiration slaps me out of my stupor. He looks exactly the same way now, only I can't find it in me to disagree. I snap my eyes from his long thick cock up to his entertained brown eyes and do everything I can to banish any heat or appreciation from my stare.

Brazenly, Curio simply watches me as he tucks his hardening dick into his leathers and slowly laces them closed.

I'm immediately struck by all the times I pulled trousers from the drawers of the armoire behind him. Did he wear any of those without undergarments too? I don't know if I'm disturbed by that or turned on. Curio doesn't immediately reach for his shirt, and I suddenly question whether or not I want to yell at him to put it on or beg for him not to. We both stand there, staring at each other from across the room as something starts to build.

Curio's stare slowly morphs from playful and teasing to banked heat and stoked fervor. Warmth pools low in my belly, and it's all I can do not to fidget or clench my thighs with anticipation. I open my mouth to say something—I have no idea what—when a knock sounds at the door. Both of our heads snap in the direction of the intrusive sound, the building spell between us collapsing like a buckling knee that's been kicked from behind.

"Enter," Curio calls out, and I swear I hear a tinge of frustration and threat in the barked invitation.

The door opens and Eacon steps through donning a wide warm smile. She has a pile of clothes stacked in her hands, and her grin grows even wider when her azure blue eyes land on me.

"Oh good, you're up," she declares cheerfully, stepping more fully into the room.

Her smile falters slightly when she turns to find Curio. Eacon's gaze bounces between us, and it's clear that she knows she's just walked in on something. However, what that something was is a mystery to all of us. Or maybe not, judging by the sly gleam that enters Eacon's eyes. She clears her throat, and it almost sounds like she's covering up a small giggle.

"I brought you some more togs, Auset," she offers, extending her hands and the pile of fabric folded neatly there. "Some more trousers and chest wraps since the last ones were getting tight."

With a bashful smile, I take the stack of linens and leathers from her. "Thank you, my ass especially appreciates it," I joke stiffly, but Eacon takes mercy and laughs lightly.

I feel bad that I already need new items since it's only been a little while since she brought me the first few stacks, but eating whenever I want while training hard every day is rapidly impacting my body. I'm filling out and hardening in places that I never have before, and I love it. I feel strong and healthy, and Eacon's been amazing at making sure I have what I need to be as comfortable as possible. She dotes in a way that makes a person feel precious and treasured, and I can see how she wielded that magic to bring the Scorpions together all those years ago.

"I was hoping you'd have a moment to chat, Auset, but if you're busy, I can come back later," Eacon states, looking from me to Curio and back again.

Ignoring the twinkle in her eye as she studies me, I shake my head and smile at her. "You're fine, I was just about to get dressed and head down for breakfast."

Pointedly, I look over at Curio, daring him to argue. After a beat, he gets the hint and grabs a black tunic from behind him.

"I'll just see myself out...of *my* room," Curio grumbles, scooping up a pair of boots as he leaves. "Stay out of trouble," he warns, eyeing Eacon purposefully.

Eacon laughs lightly as Curio saunters down the corridor and out of sight. I make quick work of the new togs.

Everything fits perfectly, and I marvel at the colors. My tunic is a deep red that almost leans purple, and my leather pants are a dark blue gray, a color that reminds me of the sea outside when it's stormy and churning. There are rich yellow tops and soft blues. I'm drawn to one that's a gray so light it could rival my eyes, and trousers in different decadent dark colors. Everything is so soft and lush it all feels more like skin than clothing. I've never had so much in my life, and I wish I had better words for Eacon than the inadequate *thank you* I always offer her.

"I'm so glad Tarek guessed the right measurements. If he weren't so good at killing, he'd have a career as a tailor for sure," Eacon jokes, and I smile.

"It is strange that he always gets it right," I agree, ignoring the warm sensation that moves down my breastbone at the thought of him knowing my body in such an intimate way and yet not.

"He always has been attentive to detail," she observes, and I notice for the first time that Eacon isn't wearing the long gray dress I normally see her in.

Today, Eacon's abandoned the drab frock in favor of her own tunic and trousers, both the color of lush garnet. The bright white streaks in her hair stand out even more against the darker smoky-gray of the rest of her strands, which have been pulled back and plaited tightly at her nape. She looks ready for something. What, I couldn't say.

Quickly I plait my own hair until it falls over one shoulder. Thank the realms, Wilik isn't an issue anymore; she'd cane my hands for the hasty job and then threaten to shear all my locks if she saw the state of me right now.

"Let's talk as we head downstairs," Eacon suggests, and I nod, curious about what she wants to discuss as I follow her out.

I study Eacon's back as we stroll slowly down the corridor. There's so much I still don't know about this place, and Eacon is high on that list. Questions begin to pile up in my head, and I start stacking what it is I want to know most toward the front of my thoughts.

"Tarek mentioned to me that life after the ludere is proving to be complicated," Eacon starts.

I'm surprised to hear that Tarek was talking about me with her, although I probably shouldn't be. The Scorpions obviously trust and admire this fae, but it's hard for me to picture Tarek going to anyone for advice. He seems so sure of himself and his decisions all of the time. I don't know how much I like being the topic of anyone's conversation or that Tarek probably asked Eacon to look in on me, but I swallow all of that down and offer her a small shrug.

"I'm adjusting," I answer dismissively as we make our way down the stairs. "I never knew what to expect. I barely dared to expect anything," I admit with a scoff, "certainly not this." I gesture to the castle all around us, and Eacon's gaze warms as she gives me a nod of understanding.

The lines around her eyes and mouth crinkle as she smiles, and I wonder what it would be like to be so happy that it's physically etched in the planes of your face. I don't know if I'd be capable of feeling that kind of cheer even if life knelt before me and offered it. Perhaps it takes a certain kind of person to find joy and contentment despite the circumstances.

"My madar sold me and all of my siblings off when I was young," Eacon tells me unexpectedly, stepping off the bottom level of stairs.

The word *madar* gives me pause for a moment. It's familiar, but I can't place from where, which is odd because I've never been anywhere aside from here and the ludere. I must have heard it there. Many blade slaves had different terms for their parents depending on where they were from, so it's not unusual to hear a different term to describe relationships, but I can't recall who would have used it. I add it to my list of things I know but have no idea how I know. I doubt they will ever make sense, but it's become a habit now to track them all the same.

Eacon doesn't turn toward the kitchen like I expect her to, instead she pivots and strides the other way. I do my best to ignore the delicious smells wafting down the corridor from the opposite direction, as well as the distant sound of the Scorpions talking, and follow Eacon.

"My madar fancied a new male, who had no interest in children that were not his own," Eacon offers casually. "That's all it took for her to clear us out like we were spoiled goods. I ended up somewhere not so different from your ludere. That was after I killed my first patron at the brothel that initially purchased me, of course," she nonchalantly continues, and I keep quiet, unsure how to respond to what she's sharing or why.

As though Eacon senses my incertitude, she offers me a small smile that doesn't make it all the way up to her azure-blue eyes.

"I tell you this, not because I think it entitles me to give you any counsel on how *you* should feel in your current circumstances, only that perhaps you might glean something helpful from my experiences. Maybe find some hope."

"Hope is dangerous," I retort without missing a beat.

"Ah, yes," she solemnly agrees. "I used to think so too."

We turn down the hallway that leads to the training area, and my interest is piqued even further. Is Eacon going to train with me today? The Scorpions say she's formidable, that they can barely beat her on her worst day. Suddenly, missing breakfast doesn't seem so bad, not if it means I finally get to see Eacon in action.

"Instead of my drawing the eye of one of the Orders that existed in my time, war broke out and I was conscripted into Queen Galayas's army."

"Queen Galayas?" I ask, not recognizing the name.

"Yes, Queen of the Dark realm, before it and the Light realm were split into the courts we have today."

I'm taken aback by that. I knew Eacon was older, but this dates her beyond what I thought. I've never heard of a time before the four courts existed. That could very well be because I've been secluded in the desert, or maybe the fae that lived in that time are all but gone, taking that part of history with them.

We bypass the training area, and Eacon guides me into the armory. She waves an arm invitingly at the walls and racks of weapons.

"Pick anything and everything that pleases you," she orders, and I hesitate for exactly one beat of my heart and then do exactly that.

I don't know what I'm arming myself for, but experience has taught me not to waste time on questions when I could be adding another blade to my body, one that might be the difference between life and death. Eacon peruses a line of swords, touching each of the blades until she finds one that must speak to her. Plucking it from the display case, she tests the weight and balance of the weapon. Satisfied, she finds the scabbard that fits the sword and begins putting it on.

"Battle was chaos," she starts again. "I went where commanded, killed who I was ordered to, and played follow the leader until one day it was all over and we were sent on our way, free to do whatever we pleased with our lives. The only problem with that was I didn't know how to do anything other than fight and kill. So I simply kept on fighting and killing until that's all that I was, all that existed inside of me. And then one day, I met Yaren."

"What are you doing?" Tarek demands, his tone accusatory and angry as it bounces off the metal, wood, and stone in the armory.

Tarek's vexation circles me like angry crows. I stop sliding a dagger into a sheath I've tied to my arm and snap my gaze over my shoulder to his. Only he's not looking at me, his enraged stare is leveled at Eacon. Tarek takes a menacing step toward her but stops when Eacon pulls her sword from the scabbard on her back and levels the steel in front of her.

"Ah ah ah," she tuts at him, and a flash of shock, rage, and apprehension flickers fast over his face.

Unease froths in my gut as I look from Eacon to Tarek.

"I told you *no*," Tarek growls at Eacon, the anger simmering in his gaze making the hairs on my arm stand up. "If you need help, *we* will help you. This isn't the way."

Eacon shakes her head at his declaration, disappointment and steely resignation pooling in her features.

"You're wrong, Tarek. You'll see that when it's all over."

"Don't," Tarek warns when Eacon moves closer to me.

"Don't do what?" I demand, confused and alarmed and not sure what's going on here.

I thought the Scorpions practically worshipped the ground Eacon walked on, but Tarek looks as though he wants to cleave her in two right now.

"This, Little Scorpion," Eacon declares, and somehow she's behind me even though I never saw or felt her move.

Before I can even think to spin away from her, she's gripped my shoulder with one hand. Pain flares in my chest and then explodes through me. I gasp, expecting the tip of a sword to exit between my breasts at any moment. But as I look down in shock, I'm yanked back by an invisible force, and the last thing I see is blistering rage on Tarek's face as he reaches for me. Then everything around me swirls black.

32

I LOSE CONSCIOUSNESS. OR I THINK I DO AS MY surroundings disappear in a blink. In the next blink, however, I'm somehow still awake. The pain immediately disappears at the same time I realize that I'm no longer standing in the armory of the Scorpions' castle. Gone are the gray stone walls mounted with every kind of weapon imaginable. In their place is a bleary alley, reeking of hot refuse and piss. A briny breeze whooshes around me, pulling strands of my hair from my plait while, thankfully, offering some temporary relief from the stench. My blurry vision begins to sharpen, and I discover a choppy blue body of water on the other side of a distant, bustling dock.

I whirl, pulling the sword sheathed at my hip as I do. Eacon backs away from me, her hands up in surrender and an apologetic look on her weathered face. I grasp at my chest, still unable to believe that she didn't just run me through with the sword that she pulled on Tarek. It felt like she did, and yet I can see the weapon is once again tucked safely in its scabbard on her back. I'm all at once enraged and confused and...scared.

I look around the alley we're standing in as though it can offer some kind of testimony that I'm okay, that I'm safe. My thoughts whir as I take in the small buildings on either side of us. The gray wood planking on the exterior looks brittle and sea-weathered. White chalky salt has started to build up in the cracks and crevices, slowly eroding the integrity of the siding altogether. The walls look like they could give at any moment.

"What the fuck just happened?" I snarl at Eacon, eyeing her warily while gripping my sword tightly. I don't know what she has in store for me next or what she intends to do now that she's shed the beloved savior mask she wore so well.

"I'm sorry to have sprung that on you, Auset. I was going to explain everything before it happened, but Tarek reacted far worse than I anticipated, and there wasn't any time."

Gulls squawk above us as they drift lazily in the cloudless blue sky. The smell of fish starts to encroach on the stench of the alley we're standing in, and I look down, grateful that my boots are protecting me from the mystery puddle at my feet.

"I swear on all the realms, if you don't tell me where we are and what's going on right now, one of us won't be leaving this alley alive, Eacon," I warn. "And before you convince yourself that you'd win this fight, I've been holding back for a while when I train with the others. You have no idea what I'm capable of."

I'm lying but she doesn't know that. Her brow furrows, and I get the impression that she's more bothered by my admission of holding back than the threat I mean to pose.

"I'm not here to hurt you, Auset. I would never do that," she gently assures me. "We're in Salak, which is on the southern border of the Night Court. I thought you might need to get away for a bit, to breathe without one of the brothers watching you like some circling falcon that's tracking prey. I needed to do some work, and I figured you might not mind getting your hands dirty for a good cause."

"What?" I demand, even more bewildered by her explanation. "But how did we get here?" I ask, gesturing with my sword to the buildings bordering the strip of dirt we're standing in.

"Thura," Eacon answers, as though whatever sound she just made should solve the mystery for me.

Eacon stares at me for a moment, clearly waiting for the moment where understanding dawns over my features, but that doesn't happen. Her brow crumples under the weight of confusion as she studies my face and clear lack of reaction.

"Thura," she tries again, but I shake my head, still not following whatever crumbs she thinks she's laying out for me right now. "You can shadow walk, and you're Sanguinna," Eacon starts again, and I begin to wonder if she's senile or if speaking in riddles is a talent I never knew she possessed before. "Those abilities, your powers...including any others you've been keeping secret," she states pointedly with a cocked brow that clearly communicates her disapproval of secrets. "These things are your thura," she expectantly explains as though she's once again waiting for the word to trigger some kind of lesson or memory on the subject.

Too bad I still don't have the foggiest fuck what she's talking about.

"Tarek can shadow walk, manipulate heat, lightly compel, and cloak—those are his thura. Riall can also shadow walk and is Sanguinna, like you," she continues, studying me carefully.

I shrug. I knew some of that, just not that those things had a general title.

"Thura," she chirps again. "You know, the abilities that you and only some other fae have? My thura allows me to jump from one place to another simply because I will it. It's called tracing. You and the Scorpions can do something similar; however, your thura requires shadows to move from place to place. I thought Tarek would have explained all of this by now?" Eacon declares, her own features steeped in bewilderment too.

"Thura?" I repeat curiously, the word sounding odd and yet tasting right on my tongue.

Eacon shakes her head and lets loose a deep, tired sigh.

"It seems you're not the only one who's been holding back," she observes, looking past me like she needs a moment for her astonishment and dismay to settle.

Unnerved by that statement, my thoughts turn to Tarek. It would seem that there's more to his absences than simply being busy with Scorpion matters. I thought he was working on his brothers' behalf as well as mine, but there's obviously more to it than that. Suspicion collects in my chest, and I'm surprised to find hurt there too. It's not as though the Scorpions owe me anything, but I didn't think they were hiding things from me, especially important things like this. It's not even just Tarek that kept it from me, Curio and Riall obviously know all about thura too. Why wouldn't they tell me?

Eacon clears her throat and pushes her shoulders back, visibly collecting herself before me.

"Thura is the term the fae use in reference to the abilities that some have. It grows rarer in our kind with every year, and it's said that no two abilities work exactly the same. I thought Tarek was already working with you on this," Eacon confesses, and I immediately shut down the disquiet that further surges through me.

"Why did it hurt?" I ask, as I absently rub my chest again.

"It doesn't always. I thought since you can shadow walk that my thura would feel similar. I'm so sorry I didn't think to warn you that it could be uncomfortable the first few times."

"Uncomfortable?" I exclaim with a huff. "I thought you stabbed me."

Eacon cringes. "Forgive me, Auset. I wasn't thinking, only reacting to Tarek's anger. I should have explained everything ahead of time. I would never hurt you intentionally."

I debate for a breath if I can trust what Eacon is saying. She looks sincere, but what just happened was intense. As alarming as all of it was though, my instincts aren't screaming that I'm in danger. Eacon could have run me through when she had the chance, and yet I'm still standing, unharmed, and learning that there's a word for what I can do.

Thura.

When I get back, it seems Tarek and I are long overdue for a conversation about abilities. Being that it solves nothing at the moment, I tidy up my anger and set it aside to be revisited later. Instead, I focus on Eacon, who's still standing at the dead-end side of the alleyway with her hands raised. She's calm and her gaze is assessing. I push through the loads of questions currently bombarding me about thura and how it all works, and concentrate on the bigger issue at hand...where I am and why.

"If you're not here to hurt me," I concede, and a wave of relief moves through Eacon's gaze and countenance, "what are we doing here then?" I ask, just as a boisterous group of sailors strides past the mouth of the alley.

I turn slightly so I can keep them in sight as well as Eacon. My sword is clutched in my hand, but my body blocks it from view of the sailors. They don't even glance our way as they pass, teasing one another and hollering about their plans for the evening now that the cargo has been unloaded and the ship they work on is docked for the night.

The alleyway begins to quiet again, just in time for me to hear Eacon say, "We're here to right some wrongs."

I turn fully back to her and lift one eyebrow with annoyance.

"Is it a fae trait to answer every direct question with cryptic bullshit?"

Eacon laughs lightly, her gaze lighting up with fondness. "You and the Scorpions are a lot alike, no patience for sarkar shit or clandestine adventure."

I scoff.

"Please, those three seem to be full of nothing but sarkar shit and clandestine everything."

Eacon laughs harder.

"Maybe so, but it's not hard to see what it was about you that transfixed the Scorpions so completely. You four fit perfectly," she warmly proclaims, but I'm done with the *you were meant to be* shit that I really don't need shoved down my throat right now.

I've heard it all before from lips more appealing than Eacon's, so she can cut the nonsense. I sigh, and Eacon smiles wider. She runs her gaze over my face and nods as though she can perfectly read how I'm feeling about all of this.

"A long time ago, I met a fae named Yaren. She found me when I was lost and helped me discover not only my way, but myself. She was one of the most beautiful souls I've ever met. I thought we'd have years upon years together, learning and loving and making this world a better place than we'd found it. Fate had other plans though. Some vile bastard happened upon Yaren and decided all of that loveliness needed to be shattered."

Eacon grows quiet, the look in her eyes suddenly tortured and heavy. Her hands and arms curve in front of her as though she's holding something that isn't there, and then her eyes squeeze closed as though the memory she just quickly recounted to me is as fresh today as it was the moment she found her Yaren...and I have no doubt that Eacon was the one to find her. It's evident in her every breath that she discovered her love, dead or dying. It's in the way her hands clutch at a phantom body, at the horror and pain that radiates out of her like it's seared into her very being forever.

It all happens in less time than it takes to inhale. The way the strong and warm Eacon seems to fold in on herself with a sadness so thick and pervasive that it makes my chest grow tight.

I've felt and witnessed my share of pain, but what I'm witnessing right now feels so much more visceral. I can't even imagine what it would be like to live with all of that inside of you every day. It's a kind of loss I've never known and hope I never do.

"I looked for him, the man who stole her from me," she tells me softly, her eyes still closed and her hands still clutching at a love that's no longer there before her arms fall slowly to her sides. "There were times I thought it would be impossible to track him down. I had almost nothing to go on. A scrap of cloth Yaren ripped from him. A few strands of hair. The impression his boots and hands left in bruises on her body. But I never gave up."

Eacon opens her eyes, the azure blue of her gaze alight with determination and fury as it settles on mine with unfaltering purpose.

"I wandered the four courts and beyond, always searching. It's how I found the Scorpions before they were Scorpions. Once, I would have left the lot of them to suffer and not given it a second thought, but I saw things differently after Yaren. She chose good where possible. She fought for justice and decency when *I* didn't even know what they meant. I learned though.

"In those moments when I could have either walked away or intervened, it began to feel as though there wasn't really a choice. I didn't seek any of the orphans or other downtrodden out, but when they fell into my path, it was as though I could see perfectly what Yaren would have done, and in those quiet moments, she was with me. I still feel her every time I take the path I know she would have," Eacon confides as she presses her palm to her chest.

I'm touched by the pure reverence radiating from Eacon as she speaks, and my throat constricts with emotion. Goose bumps rise on my arms, and a shiver scurries up my spine as though the world is telling me that *this* is important. That Eacon isn't just speaking for herself, but for the divine, for the fates themselves even.

"I choose good when I can find it," Eacon declares, moving closer to me. "At first, it was simply so I could feel Yaren again, but now it's a part of who I am."

At some point while listening to Eacon's story, I lowered my sword. I debate for a moment whether to ready myself once more or to put the weapon away and follow wherever it is Eacon wants to lead me. Or maybe it's something else that's guiding my path right now.

I've never believed in the spirits or the things that might lie beyond. It always seemed pointless to dwell on something that couldn't be proven one way or the other. It's not as though some mystery force has ever done much for me, but the conviction in Eacon's eyes as she talks about feeling Yaren's presence past the veil of death, about living for someone she loved even though they're gone, it resonates with me.

"How do you do that?" I ask as I slip my sword back into the sheath belted around my hips. "How do you see the good beyond everything else?"

Instead of answering, Eacon walks past me, and I turn to follow her. She steps from the alley out onto a stone path that runs past the entrances of several shops and taverns. In the distance, fae stroll casually down the wide walkway, some veering off into one establishment or another. Not many are wandering as far down as Eacon and I find ourselves. I look around and guess that's probably because the taverns on this end are more worn and dilapidated. I don't have much experience with things like this, but I'd wager a fae could find a good amount of trouble behind the worn doors of the establishments all around me versus what they'd find within the others down the way.

I'm both wary and fascinated by everything I see. It's overwhelming. Every fae feels like a threat even though most of them are simply minding their own business and not anywhere close to me and Eacon. I find myself tensing and ready for an attack at any moment, regardless of the easy strides and warm smiles painted across the faces of the strangers on the street. Eacon's gait is smooth and her steps sure. She moves toward the busier end of the pathway, crossing over until we're closer to the commotion and activity of the docks.

Huge ships are moored to long piers, and fae move about like chirp ants busy loading and unloading things, while more vessels float off in the distance awaiting their turn. Orders are bellowed out from every direction as we get closer to the water. I'm astounded by the organized chaos of everything that's happening all around me. It's as mesmerizing as it is baffling. Questions start to pile up in my mind as my senses quickly become overloaded by the smells, sounds, and sights. I don't know if I want to shut it all out or throw myself in the mix until I've mastered it all.

Inhaling deeply, I attempt to ground myself against the onslaught. The scent of excrement isn't so cloying, but now it's been replaced by pungent sweat, salt water, and too many bodies who reek of both as well as a mixture of other things my nose and mind can't identify.

"Over here," Eacon directs me, and somehow I hear her command despite all the shouting and calling back and forth that's ringing in the air.

I follow the mysterious fae away from the clamor and craziness, the deep red of her leathers making it easy to keep my eyes glued to her. Fae hustle to and from everywhere, and I'm grateful that no one ventures too close. It's like they can sense the overwhelming desire I'm struggling with to stab anyone who gets within reach. I didn't realize it would be this difficult to be around so many beings at once, but everything in me is screaming that it's not safe, and I'm battling to get control of the panic that's starting to crawl up my throat.

Just when I feel like I'm on the brink of screaming, Eacon veers off to the right and pushes through a set of swinging double doors. Like a pup chasing after its master, I lumber in after her, and I'm immediately hit with a refreshing blast of cold and the smell of something floral and pleasant. Blissful quiet sneaks around with the dim lighting of the place, and I feel instantly soothed and all at once capable of wrangling my wayward faculties.

Swallowing down a ragged breath, I try to quiet my inhales and exhales, hoping my heart will quickly follow suit. I don't know what to think or how to feel about what just happened. I'm one of the most lethal things to come out of Tilleo's ludere, and yet I was practically bested by a small crowd and a bunch of loud noises. The Scorpions have convinced themselves that I'm ruthless and ferocious enough to be one of them, but I doubt they'd feel the same way if they were here to witness the freakout I'm on the verge of experiencing.

"Eacon!" a rich, full-bodied, feminine voice calls out with relief. "We were worryin you would'na get here in time," a scarred, curvy fae declares with a thick accent as she pushes through a set of curtains and rushes into the dark, quiet space.

Blonde curls are piled on the top of her head and held in place by a colorful scarf that's wrapped all about as though it can't decide if it's taming the mess or submitting to it. One green eye fixes on Eacon with both exhilaration and apprehension, while the other eye seems to wander, all color bleached from the orb, leaving it a stark milky white. I suspect the scar that runs from her temple through said eye and up into her hairline is to blame, and I try not to stare at it, even though that's all I want to do. The female's arms are a quilt of slashes and burns as she lifts them and pulls Eacon into a fierce embrace.

"Tyvanna suckered in tha First Mate, but tha Master is gettin' impatient. Most floaters stay for a day or two as a kindness to tha sailors, but this rank fuck don't give a toss. Knowin' what we know about him though, I ain't all that surprised."

"I owe Ty then, Rink," Eacon offers as she rubs the voluptuous fae's back, pulling away to look at her.

"We both do," Rink agrees warmly as she takes Eacon in like she's the first burst of sunlight on a cold winter morning.

"I got here as fast as I could," Eacon reassures the other female, and Rink's smile grows so wide it looks as though it will split her face in half.

"We're gonna get him, ain't we, Eacs?" she asks, but it feels more like an eager declaration than a question.

"He was dead the moment he came back here," Eacon assures her smoothly, and the look in both of their eyes is one I know well.

Death and pain are about to rain down on this place, and the vicious fae in front of me are going to enjoy every bloody moment of it. Just like that, I'm anchored. All the trepidation and tension strumming through me is forgotten. I don't have the first clue about adapting seamlessly in a crowd, but I do know death and pain. If they're leading the way, I'll be right at home.

"And who's this little poppet?" Rink asks, having just noticed me standing in the entryway.

"Rink, this is Auset. Auset, Rink. She's like us," Eacon informs the other fae, and I grow even more curious about Rink and her story.

"Ahh, always noice to meet kin," Rink declares, and then she's wrapping me up in a hug so tight that even if I wanted to stop her, I couldn't.

My arms are locked down by my side, Rink's vise-like grip so solid that if she decided to squeeze me to death, I have no doubt that I'd be done for. I don't even have time to panic over her touching me before Rink lets me go and steps back to take me in.

"You'll get used to those with time, Poppet," Rink assures me. "I'd take it slow out of respect as I can sees you're fresh out the pit, but with our kind, it's best to shock the system before the ol' instincts kick in and ruin it for us. Ya didn't stab me, and I know how hard it was not to. You're strong, and you're gonna be just foine."

I nod, a little surprised by how much sense her explanation just made, and Rink's buxom lips split into another grin that seems to have no end in sight.

"Where'd you catch this beauty?" Rink asks Eacon, jutting her chin in my direction.

"Didn't. The brothers did," Eacon answers, and I don't miss the mischievous twinkle in her eyes as she does or the way Rink's face lights up even more.

She slaps her leg with amusement, the sound echoing in the small space thanks to her leathers amplifying it. "'Bout time those three saw past their own peckers and ego, and settled in," Rink declares, and a laugh bursts out into the air.

I bring a hand to my mouth, surprised the sound is coming from me, and both Eacon and Rink grin as though the most miraculous thing just happened. I laugh, usually in a mocking or scornful kind of way, but what just tore out of me was something rare and unusual altogether.

"Oh yeah, you're going to be just foine, Poppet."

"Did Tyvanna deal with the First Mate yet, or do we need to head to her place before we go?" Eacon asks, her countenance instantly shifting from tender and blithe to dangerous honed killer.

I really like her.

"Ty had the First Mate's head off his shoulders before he could get his other head outta his shorts for her. We're good to go aboard straight away," Rink confirms. "The dock master and nearby vessels already ken who's prowling about. They don't want no taste of our cookin' this eve. We'll have no trouble about, not even if you wanna take your sweet time with the filth, and I truly hope ya do. Yaren was a light. Let that fucker feel what light can do when ya get too close. Let him melt with it."

The scars on Rink's body make her look even more formidable as she speaks of pain like it's dessert. I don't know how Eacon and Rink found Yaren's killer, and I don't care because I suddenly need this like they do. I didn't know Yaren, and I've never felt the light that Eacon and Rink speak of, but justice sounds like decadent perfection right now. I tasted it that night in Tilleo's wine cellar when I ended Crit and again when I ripped Gartox's throat out with my teeth. The promise of more retribution has me salivating, and I have to admit that I could get used to this. Hunting because I want to, because I can see the good that will sprout by removing some of the bad, is a heady thing.

"You ready?" Eacon asks, and I realize both she and Rink are watching me.

Rink is donning weapons that she wasn't wearing earlier. I have no idea when she strapped a small arsenal on, but I'm impressed nonetheless.

"If this doesn't feel right, you can wait here until we're done," Eacon kindly offers, but I don't need to consider it.

"Ready," I confirm, not needing to debate or ponder any more than I already have.

Eacon was right, I need this, and I needed to experience it without the interference of the Scorpions and their *you're one of us* agenda. I offer Rink and Eacon a small smile, and their own feral smirks join mine for a moment and then quickly fade away. Like a cloud that's wandered in front of the moon, darkness overtakes each of us. The lighthearted banter and warmth is shoved into our depths as each of us taps into the savage creatures that we are at our core. I suddenly feel tethered to these fae as though dark sees dark and revels in it, but I set those thoughts aside.

Now, it's time to hunt.

33

"THE TRICK IS NOT TO LOOK AT THEM," EACON whispers to me as we keep a swift pace behind Rink. "Treat them like they don't exist. It helps to move through a crowd unnoticed when you look past the people. Don't make eye contact unless you have to. It will feel less overwhelming that way," she continues.

I nod and do my best to breathe through the unease I once again feel as we navigate through a bustling crowd. I do my best to heed Eacon's advice and look past the other fae all around me as though they're not there. It's a difficult trick to see nothing while simultaneously seeing everything, a skill every assassin has to master, or they don't survive long. I was excellent at it in the ludere, but out here in the realms, it feels entirely different. There's just so much noise, so many bodies and smells. My training is second nature, but all of these new experiences and exposures require more adjustment than I realized they would. I knew on some level that I'd have to learn and adapt; I just wish I had more time to do that before Eacon and Rink were counting on me.

Apprehension hums in my veins, and I don't know if it's steeped more in worry from my unfamiliar surroundings or excitement for what's coming. No one on the streets or docks pays the three of us any mind as we stride with purpose down several winding paths. I thought our weapons might draw some attention, but I spot plenty of swords and axes sheathed over shoulders, and daggers tucked into belts.

Females and males hock wares and food from carts they pull down the rickety planks of the docks. They weave in and out of the other fae who are unloading cargo or loading supplies. Eacon, Rink, and I blend into the mayhem far better than I suspected we would, and it helps calm me slightly. Expertly, Rink winds us further down to a part of the long, extensive port where the wharfs aren't as crowded and hectic. The difference in activity and noise is so drastic from what we just trekked through that it's almost as though this part of the harbor houses sleeping giants that the fae don't want disturbed.

I've never seen a giant, only heard tales of their size and brutality, but the ships that are moored at this end could rival a whole family of the behemoths. They look more like the skeletal remains of small mountains than boats, with their reaching masts and bulging bows. Nets and ropes are tethered to the tops of towering poles, giving the appearance of empty spiderwebs that are eagerly awaiting prey. There are fewer ships down here either anchored out in the harbor or secured to the wide wooden wharfs that stretch out like fingers on a hand. I presume it's because of their size, but many of the ships on this end look to be more opulent and ornate, so maybe prestige has more to do with it.

The dock narrows, and Eacon files behind Rink to make way for the few others who are traveling in the opposite direction. I take up the end. I keep my eye on the two females in front of me, prepared and alert, but it's impossible not to be awed by everything else all around.

Massive sails are rolled up and tied off, ready and waiting to be hoisted and driven by the wind. The decks of some of the ships we pass are quiet and surprisingly empty. It's like they've been abandoned, and it makes me want to sneak onto a few of them and explore. Some vessels look newer and fitted with luxurious things I don't see on other more worn and sea-tested ships. I spot what I think is a royal crest on a flag flapping high above one colossal boat, but we're moving too fast for me to stop and truly study it.

The distinct sensation of being watched crawls up my neck, and I casually glance over the main deck of a ship as we advance past it. I spot several eyes and faces just barely peeking out from rigging or around a post or railings. It's as though the crew members are hiding, which seems odd. The eyes earnestly track our movement, and it dawns on me that they very well *may* be hiding from us. Rink did say something about none of the other vessels wanting a taste of our cooking. The phrase makes me smile, but it quickly drops as we approach the end of the dock and the lone ship that's floating there.

Rink stops and both Eacon and I do the same.

"Glamour?" Rink asks so quietly that I almost don't hear it above the water lapping at the wood of the pier.

Eacon stares up at the ship as though she's listening patiently to it spilling all of its secrets.

"No," she finally answers. "I want him to see exactly who's coming for him."

Eacon pulls in a deep breath and then reaches over her shoulder to the hilt of the sword at her back. She frees the long weapon as Rink plucks a double-bladed ax from her back. I immediately fill one of my palms with a sword and the other with a dagger. Eacon uses a series of hand gestures to tell both me and Rink where she will go on the ship and where we're expected to go. I'm a little surprised that the hand gestures are familiar—I'd assumed each ludere would use their own signals—but it seems the language of the hunt is universal.

I nod, silently agreeing to clear the main deck as ordered, and then she turns to scan the boat one more time before looking back at both Rink and me. Eacon drags her hand across her throat and then circles her face once in a fluid gesture that spikes my adrenaline.

No survivors. No one gets off this ship alive.

With that, Eacon leads the way to the steep platform that bridges the gap from the wharf to the boat itself. A distant whistle sounds off somewhere behind us, almost like a signal to begin. The incline onto the boat is sharp, but it feels good to ready my muscles for what's about to happen. Eacon and Rink move like shadows as they slink onto the deck and quickly shift to their parts of the vessel.

The ship creaks as it softly rolls in time with the tides. It's a strange sensation, the feeling of standing on water instead of land. Planting my feet and bending my knees just slightly, I start to get a rhythm for the way the hull moves as it floats. Eacon glides like a wraith toward what looks to be a large set of quarters at the upper back of the ship, while Rink practically floats to the entryway that leads below. There are several stacked rows of window-like holes in the boat, and I know Rink has her work cut out for her, clearing the lower levels. All too quickly, both of them disappear, and then it's just me and the bright sun alone on the deck.

I stand there, the warmth of the sun kissing across my skin as I scan my surroundings. I feel him before I hear him. It's the slightest shift behind me to the side. Maybe it's the change in air pressure or the tiniest vibration in the wood at my feet that sets my instincts off. Spinning, I barely catch sight of a large male off to the right, but he's closing the distance between us swiftly with long hurried strides.

"You can't be on this—" he starts to order, but the dagger in his throat stops his words and his advance toward me mid-step.

Shock fills his dark brown eyes, but he doesn't go down. Before he can attempt to pull the dagger from his throat and use it against me, I run my sword through his gut. The blade is crafted perfection; it makes me want to sit and watch Curio work for hours on end to see how he does it. With barely any effort, I angle my thrust and lift, halving the fae's torso as I go until the vitality empties from his eyes and his heart gives way. Grabbing the hilt of my dagger in his throat, I kick the sailor off my blades. I don't bother wiping blood from the steel or hiding the sailor's body as I step back to my position in front of the bridge to the deck and wait.

Cool wind plays with the wisps of my hair that have come free from my braid. I breathe in the salty tang of the morning, enjoying the unique flavor on my palate just as muffled shouts and yelling begin to seep up from the wood deck under me. I soak in the fright and surprise I hear, suddenly wishing I was below with Rink and feeding more blood to my blades as we silence screams. Panicked stomping up the stairs on the other side of the entryway Rink disappeared into is the only warning I get before bodies begin to spill out on the deck. Several fae trip over each other in their terrified attempt to escape the horrors below. They fall, inadvertently blocking others from getting free of the stairs while everyone is trying to force their way up.

I'm on the unsuspecting boat crew before they even realize that it's just as dangerous at the top of the stairs as it is at the bottom. Blood splatters and sprays as I do what I do best, slicing and stabbing and claiming life after life after life. I take souls like they belong to me, like I'm entitled to them for no reason other than I've decided that it's so. All thoughts of right and wrong are wiped clear from my mind. All I can see is the next threat, the next countermove, the next body as it crumples lifeless to the floor of the deck.

My fangs drop as the sweet scent of blood rides the teasing breeze. The cool current carries screams and pleas and the sound of me silencing all of it until I'm standing amidst scattered heaps of bodies, breathing hard. I look around to find that, once again, I'm the only thing alive at the top of the stairs. I search the corpses littering the deck, double-checking that each one has been properly dispatched, like I've been trained to do.

Blood and death pool all around me, and I feel more free and alive than I have since I can remember. This, all of this chaos and loss, is because I chose it. I wasn't forced, threatened, or coerced. I was asked and entrusted, and I showed up in a way that feels right...even if ultimately it's wrong.

I don't know whether or not each of these deaths was earned. I can't say what, if anything, these fae did to deserve a brutal end like this, but as I step from one corpse to the next, retrieving daggers and wiping them clean on the rags of the dead, I find that I don't truly care.

"Nicely done, Baby Scorpion," Rink calls from the entryway as she takes in the mess.

I turn and discover she's covered in gore. Blood drips from loose strands of hair framing her face. The color is no longer golden blonde, but spattered and streaked with deep scarlet. Rink's face is speckled with ruby drops of death, and what's soaked into her cream tunic is already drying to a dark reddish-brown. Blood and bits of other things drip from the ax she still has clutched in one hand. She looks like annihilation in its purest form, and it's beautiful.

Rink leans down and flicks a dead man's vest open. She studies the body for a moment and then nods appreciatively.

"Any of these bastards have more than two wounds in 'em before they died, Baby Scorpion?"

"Don't call me that," I retort immediately as I look around before offering Rink a shrug.

I don't know how many times I stabbed, cleaved, or slashed someone before they died. I wasn't exactly keeping count as I went.

"Doubt they did. I'd expect nothin' less from anyone worthy of the brothers' notice," Rink states as she stands. "And thank you very much, Poppet, but I'll call you what you are, and this..." she declares, pointing at the dead fae spread around the deck, "this shows me that you're a Scorpion."

I sigh and shake my head. Rink grins at me, and while I'm tempted to argue with her, I decide against it. I feel good. Calm. Centered. There's no point chasing all of that away to try to convince a stranger that the situation isn't as easy to read as she's convinced herself it is.

Rink lifts her ax and points it at me, her smile stretching even wider. "That stubbornness confirms it even more," she teases, and I can't help but smile at the goofy grin on her face.

Agonized screaming starts up somewhere toward the back of the boat, and I tense, preparing for some kind of attack. Rink tips her head back and closes her eyes, like she's relishing the sound instead of being alarmed by it. I realize then that no one is going to come running at us, sword raised, ready to take us on. No. That's the sound of Eacon going to work.

Satisfaction warms me as begging begins to pepper the shrieking. I can't make out whether the fucker is pleading for Eacon to stop and let him live or to kill him quickly and end whatever torture is being administered. Rink wanders over to the far rail of the ship and makes herself comfortable. She sits down and leans back against the wood rim of the massive boat, soaking in the screams like they're the most soothing thing she's ever heard. It makes me think back to the times at the ludere when I've done the very same.

I take in the other ships that are moored further down on the pier. I expect crowds to be gathering on their decks as they search for the source of the tortured screams, but there's not a soul in sight. Whatever Rink did to scare the fae nearby, it worked. I stroll over to where she's sitting and slide down next to her. Stretching out my legs in front of me, I balance my sword on my thighs and relax. I have a feeling we'll be here for a while.

"After all these years, I still can't decide if the best thing in all the realms is incredible sex or the sound of some vile piece of shit breaking. It's a tossup for me," Rink confesses as the screaming suddenly cuts off and the faint sound of weeping takes its place. "How 'bout you, Poppet?"

I ponder the question, my thoughts suddenly drifting to that night in the kitchen with Riall. The way he kissed me, what it did to my body all on its own merit. I don't know if I'll ever get it out of my head. My heart speeds up at the thought of what it might be like to have more. More than just his tongue in my mouth and the hint of fangs nipping at my lips. What would it be like to have him moving inside of me, kissing and sucking? A sudden image of Curio flashing me his cock makes me fidget, and my thoughts quickly pull him into the mix. How would Curio kiss me? What would he taste like? Would he watch or join if I let him?

Hastily, I shove those musings away and clear my throat. I know it's the bloodlust speaking, the thrill of the kill demanding even more release to feed the high. I've no doubt that's to blame for being all at once parched and craving things I shouldn't be. I do my best to ignore the building need and focus on Rink's question.

"I don't know that I've had either," I admit bluntly before immediately wishing I could take it back. It's a little too honest and deep to be discussing with someone I don't even know. Even if I like her and we did just massacre the fae on this ship together.

Rink tsks and then shakes her head, but the smile on her face and in her eye gleams even brighter. "I'll check back in a couple months and see if that's changed," she playfully taunts, and I can't help but groan and press my head back against the wood of the rail behind me in exasperation.

"Oh come now, Poppet, ya cannae pretend with me. You're good, great even, but the Scorpions will make you damn near invincible. They learned from the best and then became even better. We both know it's not the worst deal you could stumble inta," Rink defends. "I know those boys, have since Eacs collected each and every one of 'em and set them right. They don't let anyone in, not anyone, and yet here you are."

"So, what? I should show my gratitude by letting them own me?" I demand, the angry edge I try to infuse in my tone falling flat and sounding more petulant than indignant. "Should I throw away what I want and need all because the mighty and benevolent Scorpions stepped down from their pedestals long enough to choose me?"

"Partnership isnnae ownership, Poppet. That's not how mates work. Trust takes time to build. You need to nurture it, give it a chance to take root, and then tend to it thereafter," she advises kindly yet firmly. "Hell, I've loved Eacon since the moment I watched her charge into battle like a raging *phanzu* mother protecting her cubs. She was fearless as she impaled everything within reach of her sword, while bellowing threats that quickly turned into promises. She was the most beautiful thing I'd ever seen, still is, but I knew right then and there that I was lookin' at the other part of my soul," Rink confesses, and surprised, I turn to look at her.

"You and Eacon? I thought Eacon and…"

"Yaren?" Rink finishes for me.

"Right," I admit.

Rink smiles and pushes back some of the loose bloody strands of hair that are sticking to her face. "All I'll ever need is Eacon, my ax, and death. But Eacs was still finding her way when I met her. We had a couple hundred days before Eacon met Yaren, and it was easy to see that she was the piece that Eacon was missing all along. Yaren helped Eacon in ways that I never could, and I loved Yaren for that. Eacon was our center, and everything was just as it should be, until…"

A tortured scream shatters the sounds of squawking gulls and sloshing waves. I pull my gaze from Rink's, the pain in her stare suddenly overwhelming.

"After Yaren died, I lost Eacon for a bit. She needed to find her purpose again, and I knew in time she would find her way back to me."

"You waited for her?" I ask reverently, simultaneously stunned and in awe of that kind of devotion.

"I love her, Poppet. That means I will rip the realms apart if that's what she needs, destroy anyone who'd dare ta stand against her. But it also means I'll wait. Wait fer my strong incredible mate ta mourn and grieve and come back ta me. I'll hold every piece of her shattered heart safe in my arms until she's ready to put it back together. And do you know what's so beautiful, so astonishing about it all?" Rink asks as my eyes begin to sting with emotion. "She would do the exact same for me."

"Without question," Eacon agrees as she strides out from the direction of the cabins.

Rink shoots up and in four strides meets Eacon halfway across the deck. They stare at one another for a beat, and then Eacon deflates into Rink's arms. Rink wraps her in a hug so tight and secure it makes my chest ache. I feel like an interloper on a very vulnerable and raw moment, but there's nowhere for me to slink off to without drawing attention to myself.

I stare at the ground, doing everything I can to give them the privacy I'm sure they need in order to break down and be there for one another. Surprisingly though, neither Eacon or Rink dissolve into tears or start to purge what has to be years of pain and loss. They simply lean on each other, silently, like there are no more words to be said or tears to be cried.

"I only got halfway through what that evil fuck did to Yaren before he died," Eacon whispers, and Rink brushes a soothing hand over her head and down her back.

"Males always think they're so tough. Ridiculous, if you ask me. They get a mere taste of what they've spent their lives doling out, and they crumble faster than a sand house at high tide."

Rink scoffs and Eacon sighs. They step back from one another, the blood spattered on each of them making their tunics stick together. Something about that must be hilarious to them, because they both start laughing...a lot. Trilling guffaws and cackles rent the air as Eacon and Rink collapse into each other. They lean on one another precariously, looking as though they could topple over at any moment. Blood drips from Eacon's sword onto the deck, and I watch the drops steadily, rhythmically fall to their end while the two fae lose themselves to a fit of hysterical laughter.

My chest aches with longing as I watch Eacon and Rink cling to each other. They both have experienced such profound loss, and yet here they stand in the peals of exquisite love despite what someone tried to take from them.

What would it be like to have that?

Someone who you could kill beside one moment and lose yourself to laughter in the next? Someone who not only understood what my soul needed but reveled in those needs themselves? What could it be to have someone willing to not only rip the realms apart, but also quietly wait, wait for me if that's what was needed? The distinct faces of three someones rise to the murky surface of my mind.

Could I have all of this with them?

Is that what I'd be choosing if I said yes to what the Scorpions are offering?

"How do you feel?" Rink asks Eacon as she plops back down next to me, pulling Eacon to her side and wrapping an arm around her shoulders.

Eacon sighs, her eyes far away for a moment as her gaze tracks the flight of a large golden sea bird who's enjoying a smooth float through a strong current in the air. "I don't know. I wanted him to suffer more, but it's done, and that's more than we thought it'd be at one point."

Rink nods and kisses the top of Eacon's head as she pulls her closer. Part of me feels odd lingering here among the slain, while another part dares anyone to cross the bridge from dock to deck and do anything about it. The three of us grow quiet, each of us lost to our thoughts while still being sustained by the tranquil support of the other. I think about what both Eacon and Rink have said, what they've taught and shown me in their way, and I know I'll walk away from this seeing things differently. I just don't know exactly how that will impact all of the choices I have yet to make.

"Why didn't Tarek want me to do this?" I ask Eacon after some time, the question growing hotter and hotter on my tongue until I have no choice but to spit it out.

I recall the small argument he and Eacon had before she used her thura to steal me away. The look of fury on his face when she refused to listen is an image burnt into the back of my lids. I worry I'll see it every time I blink for who knows how long.

"The Scorpions are the best at what they do, and this..." Eacon states while gesturing to the bodies and blood dotting the deck, "is not what they do."

"I don't understand," I confess.

"They stalk and silently annihilate. Fae don't see them coming until it's too late. Winding through a busy dock, stomping up to a ship, and then destroying everyone on deck during broad daylight is an exposure risk they felt was unnecessary. They had a different plan," Eacon explains. "I thought *my* approach was better."

Rink laughs at Eacon's statement, and Eacon smiles. "Aye, there's no arguing with Eacs once she's made up her mind. I can attest to that," Rink teases.

"But why'd you want me to come?" I press.

"If I'm being frank, I felt there wasn't an exposure risk for you, Auset. No one knows who you are, including you." Eacon winces as though she expects me to be offended by that, but she's right. "Aside from that though, I truly did hope that this might help you find what you needed. I know the Scorpions want the best for you, but how they go about convincing others to see things their way can be a bit..."

"Stifling?" Rink offers.

"Arrogant and insufferable?" I pitch in too.

We all laugh and Eacon nods her head. "Yes, that," she agrees. "They'll be mad for a while, but they'll get over it."

"I'll pound on each one of their arses if they don't," Rink threatens, and Eacon tilts her head up and places a soft kiss on Rink's smiling lips.

I look away and study the blade still balancing on my knees.

"The thing I want you to know, Auset," Eacon starts, and I glance over expecting to find Eacon's eyes on me. Instead, her gaze is fixed to Rink's adoring face. She brushes a strand of hair back from her mate's cheek, her blue eyes filled with matching tenderness and veneration. "No matter what you choose after today—death, life, Scorpion or not—you deserve to be loved. You deserve to find others who make you happy. Build a life around that, Auset. I vow to you that you can never go wrong if that's what's at the center of your purpose."

Eacon's weighted stare moves from Rink's eye to mine, and I feel the impact of her words through every fiber of my being. It's simple advice and yet far more complicated than I ever thought anything could be.

"Let's get you home," Eacon offers, and with that, Rink pulls Eacon's mouth to hers in a devouring, passionate kiss.

I push up from where I'm sitting on the deck and wander away from them, offering what little privacy I can as the word *home* floats around in my mind. The more I think about it, the more the concept settles unexpectedly deep in my chest. I realize as it does, that I might not be as opposed to the thought as I once was. Maybe *home* isn't as far off and foreign as it used to be. Maybe.

34

THE DOOR TO THE WASHROOM FLIES OPEN, slamming against the gray stone of the wall with a sonorous boom. I'm on my feet, the sword and dagger I perched on the lip of the tub now gripped firmly in each of my hands, before I register that it's Curio in the doorway and not some other unanticipated threat.

"What are you doing in here?" he snarls, his nostrils flaring and his eyes narrowing with fury.

"What does it look like I'm doing?" I bark back, pissed that I was so relaxed that I didn't hear Curio in our room until he was busting down the door.

My heart feels like it's trying to race right out of my chest, and I'm breathing hard in preparation for a fight that I now know isn't coming. Instead, I get to deal with a pissed off Scorpion, which I knew was an inevitability when Eacon dropped me off in my room, but I was really enjoying my soak and thought I'd have a little longer.

"Why are you in the bath?" Curio demands, his hickory-toned eyes dropping down my body for the first time.

Desire instantly begins to swirl with the vexation in his gaze, but he blinks and shutters the heat almost immediately. My body responds to the flash of need I just witnessed. My nipples go hard, and a warm tingle settles low in my belly, but if he can fight his need, so can I.

"It is what one does when they're dirty and don't want to be," I snark, and Curio's glare deepens.

He steps closer before noticeably stopping himself just past the threshold.

"Not *why* are you bathing," he grumbles menacingly. "Why are you here in my room at all? When did you get back?"

"My room," I correct.

"Our room," he counters. "You know what? Leave it."

Just as abruptly as he arrived, he spins on his heel and marches out of the bathroom. I can hear his angry stomps all the way out of *our* room and even further down the corridor until they finally fade away. Sighing, I step out of the tub. I set my weapons down on the window seat and grab a large towel. I expected to feel some frustration from the Scorpions over what happened, but Curio's display is unwarranted. I was with Eacon. They knew what she wanted and what we would be doing, so why are they being so dramatic about it? Yes, there was a moment when I thought Eacon was trying to kill me, but they knew she wasn't, so what else is there to freak out about?

I run a comb through my hair, having to pull my ends forward over my shoulder to get to them. It's getting too long, and I can't decide if I like it or if it's time to take some shears to it. I've never had control of how I look before. My head was shaved when I was first thrown into the ludere, and Tilleo only approved Wilik growing it out after I'd begun to prove myself in the pit. I've always been coiffed and styled to his liking. In the past, I've associated the length of my locks with success, but now that I can choose how I want to look, I'm not sure what suits *me* best.

The towel is soft and cozy against my skin as I wrap it around my body. I turn toward the door, ready to dress and deal with a little Scorpion drama, when the distinct sound of heavy tread reaches me. I thought maybe Curio ran off to sulk, but I was wrong, he went to get reinforcements. Squaring my shoulders, I prepare for the onslaught that's headed my way. Just as I pull a fortifying breath in, three tall, muscular frames spill into the large washroom perfectly in sync. They move so fluidly and confidently that it's impossible not to be slightly intimidated and impressed. Eyes filled with fire, arms crossed over broad chests, and clenched jaws meet me as I look them over.

I exhale. It isn't laced with the irritation I intended, sounding more relieved instead.

"You're back?" Tarek asks, but it feels more like a declaration than a question.

"I am."

"When?" he demands.

"Forty minutes or so," I supply, keeping my eyes on his even though I can feel the heat of other gazes grazing my damp skin.

"Are you hurt?" Tarek stiffly inquires, and I narrow my eyes at him.

He's in front of me in three long strides, forcing me to look up into his angry ice-blue eyes, and I don't know if I like the challenge I see there or if I want to stamp it out.

"Don't give me that look, Auset, it's a fair question. The planning of this hunt was nonexistent. The outcome could easily have been disastrous," Tarek practically growls.

I meet his angry glower head-on and match Riall's and Curio's stances at the doorway by crossing my arms over my chest. In doing so, I brush the soft material of his shirt and feel a hint of the hard muscle hidden beneath.

"You have little faith in the fae who saved you," I retort, feeling protective of Eacon and everything she showed me today.

"I love Eacon, but hunts go wrong when they're rooted in emotion instead of strategy and skill," Tarek states matter-of-factly.

We stare at one another for a moment, and just when I think the Scorpion is about to double down on being hard and unyielding, he blows out a breath and softly asks, "Are you okay?"

My eyes flick back and forth between his in an effort to glean where this change of heart, this hint of vulnerability, is coming from. I thought the Scorpions' overreaction was based on control, on their desire for me to give in, but maybe I'm wrong.

Was he worried for me, is that what this is all about?

Habit and routine would have me crushing this show of emotion under my boot, treating it like the dangerous pest I used to think feelings were, but I ignore that instinct and choose instead to remove my internal armor. Piece by piece, I take down the wall. I swallow the daggers waiting to be released on my tongue and quiet the defensive ire humming in my limbs. I douse the indignation in my stare and unclench the stubborn set of my jaw.

I'm not sure where this ceasefire might lead or if I'll regret it. All I know is that I don't want more of the same things that have poisoned my existence up to this point. I crave death and destruction in some facets of my life, but I don't want to battle and bleed and run in *all* aspects of who I am.

I want more than that. I just never knew it until now.

"I'm not hurt," I reassure Tarek and the others. "There wasn't a blade or hand that came close enough to even threaten injury let alone inflict it. It was nice to help Eacon," I answer, and Riall snorts from somewhere behind Tarek.

I lean to the side so I can take the Scorpion in, and he shrugs.

"What? I find it amusing that slaughter lands in the *nice* category. I couldn't agree more," he explains with a playful grin.

I roll my eyes but can't deny the small smile that plays across my mouth. I look back to Tarek and find his ice-blue stare is now fixed on my lips.

"I'm glad Eacon trusted me with something so important. I learned a lot today," I go on, and Tarek's gaze once again meets mine.

"Eacon got him then?" he asks.

"He died faster than she wanted, but it's done."

"Anyone give you trouble?" Tarek presses.

I huff. "Just you," I retort, a little stunned by how saucy and almost playful I sound.

Tarek smiles and I hear two deep chuckles sound off behind him. He lifts his hand, and I freeze, unsure of what he's going to do. He brushes a thumb across my lower lip, and I feel as though I can't breathe while simultaneously fighting the need to pant incessantly at his touch. I search Tarek's eyes as his stare traces the trajectory of his soft stroke.

"Good," he declares, the word more rumble than speech, and then out of nowhere, he grabs me and throws me over his shoulder.

Before I can register what in the realms just happened, I'm being marched out of my room and down the corridor. I start to put up a fight but quickly realize that entirely too much of my skin feels the air right now. I stifle a frustrated groan. If this were the ludere, my nakedness wouldn't even faze me, but the way I'm starting to react to these three means I can't afford to be so cavalier. The towel I've wrapped around me is starting to feel precariously loose as it climbs up my legs until my ass is on the verge of hanging out. I growl my frustration at not grabbing clothes *before* I decided to clean up earlier.

"What the fuck?" I demand, punching Tarek hard in the back, but he doesn't even flinch at the contact.

Knowing the brute, I bet he probably likes it. I press against his muscles, pushing up until I can see the two Scorpions trailing after us. I shoot both of them a threatening glare, but my *I will end you* stare must be broken, because all

I get in return is an amused snicker from Riall and a cocky grin from Curio.

"Put me down!" I snarl as Tarek strides through a doorway and into what looks to be a study.

There are dark shelves lining most of the walls packed full of books and different artifacts. A large desk sits off to the side made of some dark wood I can't identify. Fire crackles almost in greeting in a large hearth that's surrounded by a long settee and two armchairs. And the back wall houses a collection of bottles and vials with a large mystery door nestled in the center of it all. The space is warm and masculine, boasting of rich dark wood and deep green textiles. It's clean and organized and smells of worn leather, elven steel, and magic. Tarek's scent and presence is stamped all over this place.

"If you don't put me down right now, I'll—"

"You'll what?" Tarek challenges as he pulls me from his shoulder and sets me on my feet by the fire.

I flounder as he glares at me, the look in his eyes contesting my interrupted threat. I wasn't actually expecting him to give in to my demand yet, and I suddenly question what exactly my threat would have been. Would I promise to fight him? Draw blood? Admit that a small part of me liked the manhandling? I shake away those thoughts and ignore Tarek's defiant stare, embracing my own outrage instead.

Whether it's him or myself I'm more outraged with right now, I can't say.

"You have no right!" I sputter, my rage blinking out momentarily when Tarek steps even closer, his hard chest skimming mine in a way that feels entirely too promising to me at the moment. "Who do you think you are?" I exclaim as I wrap my indignation in a stranglehold, refusing to acknowledge the fluttering Tarek's proximity is causing deep in my body.

"Who do you think *you* are?" he parrots back, only he doesn't sound nearly as unsettled as I do. He's once again calm, cool, and collected, and I don't know if I need that right now or if I want to do something that shatters it. "You could have been hurt or worse today, and I speak for all of us when I say that is unacceptable."

Is he serious?

Riall and Curio arrogantly saunter over and plop down into an armchair and on one end of the settee. They silently lend their support to Tarek's ridiculous statement, Curio offering me a raised brow and Riall nodding once in agreement as he makes himself comfortable. My glower grows darker, and Riall holds up his hands in a gesture that says *there's nothing I can do here*, while Curio dawns that annoyingly attractive half smirk that he does when he's trying to be antagonistic.

I scoff and turn back to Tarek. "Do you not remember where we met?" I ask acerbically. "What was safe about any of that? You didn't care then, why care now?" I counter, unsure if I'm talking about the first time I saw them in Dorsin's office or later in the ludere.

"Because I do—we do," Tarek corrects, his gaze searching my face for something.

I cross my arms over my chest and shake my head at the Scorpion. "I'm a trained killer, Tarek, with or without weapons. I'm immune to every major poison on the market, and if all else fails, I have *thura* to back me up."

"Not all poisons, Auset, and you've *barely* tapped into your abilities," Tarek argues.

My ire peaks and I clench and unclench my fists as I try not to lose control. "Whose fault is that?" I accuse, pressing even closer and fighting the urge to shove him. "You want to complain about what could've happened on that hunt with Eacon, but you're not even doing everything you can to prepare me for what's out there!" I snap, gesturing all around me.

Riall fidgets in his chair, and Tarek scowls at me, but I can see in his hard eyes that he knows exactly what I'm talking about.

"I know nothing about thura or that fae abilities are even called that. I had no idea how hard it would be to navigate a crowd or how overloaded I could feel from simply being out there in the world. The three of you said you would help me if I stayed, but I need more than food and sparring, and you know it! Don't you dare lecture me about safety when you aren't doing everything you said you'd do to keep me that way."

The room grows quiet, and I prepare myself for the volley of excuses and temper I'm sure are about to be flung my way. Tarek's eyes stay on mine, each second that passes making the face-off feel more and more uncomfortable. Aggravation swirls through me, but I'm also all too aware of how close we are. I can feel his even breaths against my chest, see the dark blue ring around his irises, that same color striating thinly through the crystalline blue making his eyes look even brighter and ethereal. If I lifted up on my tiptoes, our lips would meet. I should be glaring daggers and focusing on all the ways Tarek's wronged me, but all I can seem to do right now is wonder what it would be like to kiss him.

"You're right," Tarek agrees after what feels like weeks.

I open my mouth, ready to launch into another biting argument, when his words sink in. I stare at him, my lips now parted in shock, unsure of what to do or say. I didn't expect him to be so reasonable. I study Tarek's face and am forced to admit that I don't know this fae at all like I thought I did. I've pegged him as controlling, stiff, and combative, but I've seen none of that on display since I got here. I hate to say it, but maybe I've misjudged him. Maybe I've misjudged all of them.

Tarek steps back and runs his fingers through his hair. The dark brown strands immediately fall back in place around his face as though not even they are willing to go against him. I feel both relief and disappointment at the distance he creates between us, and I internally slap my face and shout at myself to get my head out of the dark and broody, sexy fae clouds.

"You're right," Tarek repeats. "I was hoping we'd know more about you before diving into your thura. Riall has been trying to track the lines of the last known female San-guinna, and I've been cross-referencing that with the fae lines on record that can shadow walk," he explains.

Confusion sweeps across my face, and seeing it, Tarek quickly continues.

"We were hoping that connecting your thura to existing records would give us a lead on who you are and where you come from. But knowing these things can also help you, and us, to navigate your abilities. No two thura are exactly alike. Each of us can shadow walk." Tarek gestures to Curio and

Riall. "But Curio is the strongest with the affinity. Riall's thura works better when it comes to long distance as opposed to short walks, and my ability works better when I walk with all three of us. For me, it's almost like my thura can feed on others' power and grow stronger. The differences can be subtle, but they're important."

"We've also learned over time that the fae lines that carry certain thura often have similar strengths or weaknesses when it comes to that ability," Curio provides, and Tarek nods.

"Exploring thura can be dangerous. I was hoping we'd have a clearer idea of what you might be able to do before we started down that path," Tarek states.

"Fine," I concede. "But why not tell me that from the start?"

Tarek sighs and leans back against the thick stone mantel above the fireplace. "You don't trust us. Which is understandable given the circumstances," he hurries to clarify. "But I was worried that bringing it up would make you want to test your limits on your own or that you wouldn't believe our reasons for waiting. I didn't want you to think we were trying to hold you back on purpose, so I chose to say nothing, figuring we'd have some answers soon and then it could be addressed."

"*We*," Riall corrects. "We discussed it and thought it would be better to focus on helping you adjust and get healthy before dealing with your thura. It wasn't just Tarek's decision."

I study at the three of them, a flicker of respect pushing through my frustration at the way they defend and decide things together. I want to be annoyed, to feel offended at being cut out of the conversation, especially when that conversation was about me, but I can't deny that their concerns might have been justified. There's a strong possibility that I wouldn't have believed them. They're right in that I have been so busy trying to adjust to this newfound freedom that I haven't given my abilities much thought. Not until Eacon reminded me that I should know more.

"Okay," I say, the word a combination of me trying to process everything they just told me and accepting their explanation.

"Okay," Tarek parrots, only his expression has a touch more question in it. He watches me like he wasn't expecting that reaction, and a small smile flickers at my lips. Looks like neither of us gave the other credit for a calm and rational side.

"You made a decision. I can't say whether it was right or wrong, but it's done. In the future, I would like to be a part of these discussions. I feel as settled as I can, and I think it's time to start preparing me for life outside of the castle walls."

"Fair enough," Tarek concedes, and both Curio and Riall nod.

A large smile sneaks across Riall's face as he looks around at all of us. "Look at all of us being a team," he teases, and Curio and Tarek both chuckle quietly.

I shake my head, but a grin splits my lips anyway. I'm uncertain that any of this means anything other than we can be levelheaded when we want to be, but I suppose time will tell when it comes to everything else. I know I want more in life than I dared to want before, but I still don't know exactly what that looks like or even how to get it. I'm willing to consider that I may have been too dismissive of these Scorpions from the beginning, but it doesn't mean that they're the answer either.

I wasn't lying when I told them that I feel as settled as I can. I also know that I wouldn't feel that way without all of their help and support. I'm uncertain where any of this leads, but I don't think that's necessarily a bad thing. I'm open to possibilities. I didn't understand the importance of that before, but I get it now. I guess we'll see where that takes me.

35

I THINK IT'S TIME WE INTRODUCE AUSET TO THE Empress," Tarek states, his gaze bouncing from Ri-all to Curio as he squares his shoulders and crosses his arms over his chest. He radiates strength and power, and there's no mystery as to why he's the un-spoken leader of their Order. "Even if she chooses to go, I think it's wise."

Some sort of silent exchange born from *eons* of knowing each other occurs between the three of them. Try as I might, I can't follow what their eyebrow flicks, mouth twitches, or intense eye contact mean. I also have no idea who the Em-press might be. The realms are ruled by kings and, for the few that have taken them, queens. There are other lands that exist far outside the borders of the realms, but I've never heard mention of other rulers before. We weren't fed regular realm news at the ludere, but the powers that be have always been well known and discussed amongst the masters and guards.

"You think you can handle it, Moonling?" Curio asks me, a roguish glint in his hickory-brown eyes.

"Handle what exactly?" I question, looking at the three of them in turn.

"Our namesake," Riall answers, but that only serves to confuse me even more.

"You said we weren't doing everything we could to protect and prepare you; this would help protect you," Tarek supplies cryptically, and it's all I can do not to huff in frustration and walk out.

"Someone make sense, I'm begging," I gripe, and Riall chuckles.

"I do like when a beautiful female begs," Curio taunts.

I glare at him, ignoring the flash of heat that strikes through my center. It's entirely too easy to picture kneeling in front of him or, better yet, watching him kneel in front of me as he slowly parts my thighs. I quickly retreat from the provocative direction of those thoughts. I don't know what in the stars has gotten into me. It started with that kiss in the kitchens, and now it's blazing a path through me, making it hard to think about anything else. Eacon's advice and the easy intimacy I witnessed between her and Rink hasn't helped dissuade these deepening desires either. In fact, it's only served to muddy the waters of my mind even more.

With Leto, I was a master at separating emotion from sex. I needed that then. What we did on the rooftop of the ludere under the watchful eye of the moon, soothed scars that had been clawed into my soul. I took back power that had been stolen from me, found a way to enjoy my body and what could be done with it, and to it, when *I* allowed it. There wasn't a thing that Leto and I didn't explore together, but it's not just physicality and pleasure that I'm craving these days. It's starting to become a distraction, and distractions are dangerous.

I want to give in—I would if I thought it would get this growing need out of my system—but I worry instead of dousing the fire, it would just serve to kindle something that could ultimately consume me. The idea of working out my stress and frustrations on and against a rock-hard, sweaty body while they moan and plead for more is beyond appealing, but I find myself needing more than just that. I'm craving a connection I've never wanted before, something to tether myself to, and that terrifies me more than anything ever has. I've never needed or wanted anyone else. It's always been too perilous to even consider, but I'm not in the ludere anymore, and everything I thought I knew about myself and the world is changing faster than I can track.

"Have a seat," Tarek orders softly, his hand suddenly skimming the small of my back.

Goose bumps immediately erupt down my arms, but no one says anything about it as I move to the armchair opposite Riall and sit down. I tug at my towel as it climbs up my thighs, trying to force it to behave and cover more of me. I look up to find Riall studying the newly exposed flesh of my legs, and heat washes over me. I start to question whether staying here with the three of them is a wise choice. I'm one sharp pull of fabric away from being naked, and I can't seem to keep my thoughts from wandering down titillating but treacherous paths. I should leave, and yet I can't bring myself to push out of my seat and walk away.

"Our first hunt together didn't go exactly as planned," Tarek starts before he moves from in front of the fireplace, striding confidently toward the door nestled at the back of the room.

Riall snorts, the sound one part amusement and one part annoyance. The sound draws my attention to him. "We trained harder than we ever had in preparation for it," he recalls, his gaze far away as though he's been transported back to that time in his mind.

I turn back around in time to see Tarek disappear through the tall back door. The room on the other side is draped in darkness so thick that I can't make out a single detail of what exists within its confines.

"So imagine our shock and frustration when we snuck into our mark's quarters only to find the fucker dead already," Riall states, and I turn back, all my attention instantly focused on him and the story that just took a turn I didn't see coming.

"We hadn't made a name for ourselves at all yet, but the only conclusion we could come to was that the Orders were sending us a message," Curio recounts with a humorless chortle. "We were plotting revenge within minutes of finding the body. They didn't know who they just fucked with..."

"But then we met the Empress," Tarek interjects from somewhere behind me.

I pivot around, wondering if I'll find some frail female clutched to Tarek's side, or maybe he'll have a scroll held ready in his hands to explain what they're talking about. What I don't expect to find is Tarek holding a scorpion the size of my foot. I'm not usually squeamish around things that creep and crawl. I've lived in the Corozean desert since I can remember, and every living creature that survives in those sands creeps and crawls—me included—but nerves skitter through my stomach all the same as I take in the huge creature clutched in Tarek's palms. He draws closer from the back room, and firelight begins to dance across the hard onyx shell of what must be the Empress herself. Tarek holds her with care and esteem, and I take her in, both impressed and unnerved. I can't decide if I want to marvel or back hastily away.

"Out of nowhere, this surprising little menace crawled out from under our mark, and that's how the *Scorpions* truly began," Tarek confides as he crouches down in front of me.

"What...what is she?" I ask as I fight the urge to press back in my chair.

I've seen many scorpions in my life, but never anything like this. The Empress is more than worthy of such a regal name based on size alone. I don't even want to think about how potent the venom in her tail might be. Cautiously, I watch the creature for signs that it's perturbed and looking for a fight, but oddly she seems at peace in Tarek's hands. I keep what distance I can though.

Tarek chuckles at my obvious unease, but thankfully he doesn't push her closer.

"She's a *fettik* scorpion," he answers simply. "They're incredibly rare, if not almost extinct. We probably house the largest bed of fettiks in all the lands, and that's saying something, as they're near impossible to breed," Tarek explains warmly.

I can't discern if that softness is for my benefit or for the Empress's.

"Why is that?" I query, hoping that if Tarek keeps talking, then he won't remember he wanted to properly *introduce* me to the Empress. I have a sinking feeling that introducing me to their namesake involves more than simply showing her off while offering a lesson on what she is and why they have her.

"Because fettik venom is the most potent toxin there is. It's even deadly to their own kind. That's why they're dying out and so hard to breed. Females can only procreate with males who are immune to their sting. Most males die in the process of trying to find a mate. Only one in several thousand is capable of creating and releasing an antitoxin through their system that can withstand the sting of a female, and there's no way to tell that a male fettik has the ability to become walking antivenom until after it's been stung."

"They're an incredibly brutal species," Riall provides, scooting to the edge of his chair and leaning closer with interest. "The female stings the male when he approaches her to mate, and then he stings himself until he either counteracts her venom or dies. Seems fitting," he adds, his hazel eyes once again fixed intensely on me.

I work not to fidget under the thick fervor that saturates Riall's stare or to see any link in his description of fettik scorpions versus what me and my Scorpions are doing. What we do and what we are *is* brutal, but I'm not some creature that could end them because they want to claim me...am I?

Tarek is saying something about breeding lines and males, but I struggle to focus on the details of his explanation with my mind now whirring the way that it is. I take in the three of them, recalling their offer to me when I first woke up in this castle and learned who they were and why I was here. I think back to the interactions we had at the ludere, and even skim over the memories of the first time I saw them while chained in Dorsin's office. The journey to where we are now has been a winding, precarious thing, and yet here we are. Here I am, sitting amidst the realm's fiercest and finest hunters. Hunters who have shown me nothing but the same care and veneration as they're currently showing this rare and toxic creature cupped in Tarek's hands.

They've taken something that most others would consider a threat, a hazard that should be immediately destroyed, and not only saved it, but respected and revered it. I've convinced myself that I could be nothing more than a passing fancy to them. I've done what I could to keep a firm distance, to not take what they say and do at face value. I'm always looking for ulterior motives and trying to stay several steps ahead of how they could turn things against me. But as I look at the Empress in all her alarming glory, held so gently in hands capable of ruthless violence and callous annihilation, I question the way I've been seeing things.

How many times will I watch the Scorpions sting themselves in an effort to prove the sincerity of their actions and words?

I've been quick to deny that I have anything to gain by

trusting them, but the truth is that they have more to lose by trusting me. Their home. Their stories. Who they really are and where they come from. The veil has been pushed aside for all of it, yet I haven't been able to see it for what it is. Even now, doubt creeps in, whispering that I should slink back into my safe and jaded ways.

"Auset, did you hear me?" Tarek presses, and I'm jerked from my turbulent contemplation.

"What?" I ask, flustered, my gaze dropping to his lips. It's more of a struggle than I want to admit to focus on his words and not the lush mouth that's speaking them.

"I'm going to let the Empress sting you," he states, emphasizing each word to ensure I don't miss anything this time.

"No," I immediately argue, but I already know it's pointless.

There'd be no reason to show off their little treasure—or freakishly hulking treasure, I should say—on the pretense that it will be something that prepares and protects me, unless the goal is to create an immunity to the venom.

"Yes," Tarek contends evenly, a determined glint gleaming in his gaze.

I groan and eye one scorpion and then the other Scorpion, no longer sure which is the greater threat to me. I want to fight this, but the blade slave in me insists that removing something from the list of things that can kill me is never a bad thing. I also understand on a deeper level what this offer really is. It's their way of showing me that they're willing to protect me even from them.

I haven't agreed to stay. I've never expressed a hint of desire to become one of them. I've made it perfectly clear that I'm here for answers and as soon as I have them, I'm gone. Yet despite all of that, they're offering me assurance and a kind of sanctuary. I may have never heard of fettik venom before, but I have no doubt that they use it in their hunts, that it's a calling card for their Order. If I leave, knowing everything that I know about them, they won't be able to use that calling card against me. It evens the potential battlefield between us, which is not something to be taken lightly.

The Scorpions are willing to sting themselves to keep me safe.

It makes me want to punch them, but it also opens my eyes.

Fuck, this is going to hurt.

"I hate this," I admit uncharacteristically. "I'd rather take on a *sint* cat without any protection."

Curio barks out a laugh, but sints with all their spikes and razor sharp claws are a picnic compared to what some venoms can do, and according to them, Tarek is cradling the worst of the worst. I lay my head against the back of the chair as flashes of the healers and masters dosing me with different venoms and poisons runs through my head, making my stomach churn with anxious unease.

"It's not too bad, Beasty," Riall reassures me softly. "A little pain, and then you never have to fear a scorpion again."

The double meaning in that statement is not lost on me.

Curio scoffs and rubs the back of his neck. "I did almost die."

"Great," I quip, blowing out an apprehensive breath while offering him my most withering glare. "That's very helpful, thank you."

Out of nowhere, the Empress's tail goes up in warning, and I flinch at the sudden movement.

Tarek shakes his head at Curio. "That's only because you fancied yourself an owl and tried to jump out of a window," he scolds.

Curio just shrugs, his unapologetic grin growing even wider. "I was a beautiful owl though," he defends, and I laugh.

Apparently, my momentary mirth agitates the Empress even more, and she snaps her claws in front of her as though she's reaching for some invisible prey. I slam my mouth shut, not looking to rile her up, especially since I'm about to be on the receiving end of that temper. Like most royalty, she lacks a sense of humor, or so I've heard.

"He was in the fairy wine all morning that day, Beasty; don't let him scare you," Riall contends.

"Had to if I was expected to get anywhere close to *that*," Curio argues, a shiver quaking through him.

Curio's aversion makes me feel better about my own reaction to the overgrown arachnid. Maybe if the Empress wasn't the size of an actual empire, it would be fine, but she looks like she thrives on nightmares and dines on small children.

"It hurts, but you've been through worse," Tarek assures me. "Fettik venom is worse the longer it sits in your system, but I'll bring her mate out right away, and he'll give you the antitoxin. We won't let you suffer unnecessarily. You can trust us."

I study the dark blue rims of Tarek's eyes, running my gaze down the straight line of his nose, across his high cheekbones and voluptuous lips. My perusal pauses as I stare at the beast in his hands. Before I can talk myself out of it or work myself up even more, I lift my arm and offer it to both scorpions.

"Good girl," Tarek purrs, and where once those words might have rankled, now they wind through me, tightening and stimulating and settling warmly in needy crevices I don't want to think about right now.

Wasting no time, Tarek moves the Empress closer. I try not to tense, but it's difficult knowing, while also not knowing, what's to come. I'm very aware that this isn't going to feel pleasant, but just how unpleasant it'll be is yet to be determined. I expect the scorpion to strike right away, but she doesn't. It isn't until Tarek leans closer and blows softly on her that she reacts. The stinger strikes faster than I expect, she gets me twice before Tarek pulls her away, and I'm instantly pissed that they undersold just how shitty this is going to be.

Fire climbs up my arm, and I grit my teeth and settle back in the chair, my strength immediately sapped. My vision blurs, but whether that's an effect of the venom or the tears welling in my eyes, I don't know. I feel like I'm melting from the outside in. I gasp, prepared to smell the scent of charred skin in the air, but strangely it's not there. The inferno and agony coursing through me should result in my combusting into ash as I sit here, and yet I'm still whole and supported by the velvety chair beneath me. Everything hurts, which makes it all the worse when I seem to grow even more acutely sensitive to all the stimuli around me. Murmured voices try to talk to me, but I'm lost to pain and sudden overwhelming sensation. A new prick against my arm douses me in frigid water, and a shiver wracks through my system.

Fire and ice war for a claim over my soul. I have no choice but to writhe while I wait to see who wins, to see who will be my new master as I thrash and silently plead for all of it to stop. I've never felt anything like this. I hope to never feel anything like it again. Vows pour from my mind in an effort to bargain with the pain, but in the next minute, it's so all-encompassing I can barely think at all. I'm taken to the edge of what I can take, of who I am, of what I can survive, and just when I think I'll be dropped over the cliff to finally succumb to the darkness I've left unchecked for so long, I feel something tug me back.

Awareness creeps through the molten blaze and glacial chill. Arms wrap tightly around me as a gravelly voice croons sweet promises in my ear. I can't piece together what's being said, and yet I know on some visceral level that it's soothing and comforting and everything I need to pull me safely from the edge of anguish. I submit to the touch, the tone, the claim of the power that's anchoring me here. It's fighting my battle when I'm too weak, and I cling to that sliver of salvation with fierce desperation.

I've been tortured and beaten, violated and poisoned, abandoned and stripped of who I am for as long as I can remember, and I've had to survive it all alone. But now, as I struggle to find the surface of this suffering, I feel *them*. Hands caress my limbs. Fingers rake through my hair. Lips skim the shell of my ear as calm assurances pepper my skin. Their strength laps against me like rippling water as they try to pull me from the pain.

I surface with a gasp, panting, as Curio wipes sweat from my brow.

"There you are, Moonling," he drawls, the resonant sound of his voice dripping over me like warm honey.

Fingers caress my cheek as Curio runs a cool rag down my neck. I bite back a moan at how good it feels, my skin seemingly still hypersensitive even though the pain is starting to fade to a small echo of what it was. Palms skim up the tops of my thighs, and I find Riall crouched in front of me, his brow furrowed and his eyes soft and attentive. Tarek's feather-light touch trails across my cheek and down my jaw.

"It's over," Riall assures me, absently running his rough callused hands up my thighs again.

But he's wrong, because in this moment I know, without a shadow of doubt, that nothing is over, it's all just begun.

36

A PAIR OF THICK, MUSCULAR, LEATHER-CLAD thighs rest against the outside of each of mine. A hard chest presses against my back, and I realize that I'm not sitting in a chair anymore, I'm sitting on Tarek. He has one arm banded around my waist while the other is bent over my chest so that his fingers can trace gently across my face. Riall is crouched between my thighs, his hands slowly rubbing up and down in languid lazy strokes that I feel…everywhere. Curio is running a blissfully cool rag over every inch of my exposed skin, which is a lot because my towel is bunched up on my hips and just barely covering my cunt, while the top has loosened so much that it's threatening to slide down.

I'm pretty sure Tarek's arm is the only thing that's keeping it from dropping to my waist.

My breaths start to come faster, but I don't know if that's because I'm coming down from the pain or because of their proximity.

"You're okay, we've got you," Tarek rumbles, the scruff on his jaw teasing the shell of my ear as he does.

A shiver works through me, but thankfully it's passed off as a reaction to the antivenom currently soaking through my system. I don't know what to say or if I even want to say anything. I wait for panic to trickle through me, to signal that it's time to run, but it never comes. I force myself to think through all the reasons it'd be foolish to cross the lines each of us are balancing on like a tightrope. I don't know them. I don't even fully know myself at this point. They're frustratingly imperious and cryptic, bossy even. Each one of them is depraved—then again, so am I—I don't know if I can hold that against them completely. They left me that first night, just walked away and resigned me to fight the monsters on my own.

But they're here now.

I wait for all of the damning evidence I've been collecting to bolster my resolve, to dock me to the reality of why getting closer to them is a horrible idea that could never work. But the time I've spent with them, what I've witnessed and learned, all of it has poked too many holes in my reasons for them to bear the weight of any true protest. Where once my justifications were solid stone, thick and immovable, now they feel like sand in my palms. It's like I'm watching the pummeled grains of my excuses slip through my fingers to reveal possibilities I couldn't, or wouldn't, see before.

Instead of feeling uneasy or threatened as each Scorpion holds or caresses or comforts me, I feel safe, tranquil. I feel so relaxed and comfortable that I could easily close my eyes and drift off to sleep right here and now. It's been a long morning. I cut down a group of sailors, survived fettik venom, and now I'm cocooned against large, hard bodies, watching the thick impenetrable walls I've worked tirelessly to fortify around myself slowly crumble to nothing. If anyone deserves a nap, it's me. But as Riall's palms stroke back up the tops of my thighs, the thought of sleep is rapidly replaced with notions of other things.

Warmth travels from the tips of his fingers to settle at my core. I grow wet as the strokes, caresses, and embraces become all that I can focus on. A small whimper tickles up my throat, but I swallow it down as I try and fail to pull myself together. The fettik venom has run its course; however, a different trio of Scorpions are now to blame for the burn currently building in me. I don't know what I want to do about it, about them.

I could spread my thighs further, offering Riall better access to the intimate parts of me. It would take the barest hint of pressure to guide Tarek's arm from my waist and settle his fingers over my clit instead. His other hand could easily be redirected from my face to my breast, and if I demanded it, I know Curio would be all too eager to let me taste his lips. It would be no hard feat to turn the comfort they're currently offering into so much more, but can I do it? Can I push for more from them when I don't know what I'm willing to give in return? Handing over my body is the easy part; it's what they might want afterward that troubles me.

As though Tarek can hear my tumultuous thoughts, his hand drops from my face. I hold my breath, all at once eager and tentative about where I want it to settle.

Is he going to make the decision for me?

Will I let him?

Long, thick fingers wrap around my throat, administering the barest hint of pressure as the short stubble of Tarek's chin scrapes deliciously across the crook of my neck.

"I can practically hear the debate going on in your head right now, Little Dagger," he tells me, the faintest trace of some blossom I can't identify mixing with the rich scent of leather and steel that is all Tarek.

I gasp as he nips the lobe of my ear, his teeth sinking in just hard enough to enhance the pleasure. Riall's languorous strokes up my legs shift, and I feel the slightest kiss of his thumbs as they dip deeper down my inner thighs. His palms slowly rise higher, the sensation whispering a silent promise against my skin as they do. Tarek nuzzles my neck and cheek, and goose bumps rise on my arms. Curio looks on, his pupils now drowning out the hickory tone of his irises until all I can see is the faintest ring of warm brown.

"I can feel your need," Tarek purrs. "But I can also feel your hesitation."

I try not to squirm in his hold, but his grasp of my unspoken thoughts and feelings is unsettling.

"We don't want what isn't fully and freely offered, and make no mistake, we want *all* of you, Auset. If I peel this towel from your body right now, we can give you what you're craving. We can have you so thoroughly wrung out with pleasure that you'll lose count of how many times you come, how many times you scream our names, and how many times we'll have you begging for more. But…" He pauses to trace his lips around the shell of my ear, the light touch teasing me so thoroughly that a pulsing ache starts between my thighs. "I know I'd rather do all of it when I'm certain that you won't wake up after and try to rationalize or convince yourself it didn't mean what it did."

"It's all or nothing," Riall agrees, his thumbs inching tantalizingly closer to the lips of my pussy.

Can he feel how hot and wet I am?

"I'll show you what it means to be one of us—*when you're one of us*," Curio concurs, licking his lips and dropping his eyes down my body like he's already marking the path he'll take when they finally get what they want.

My chest rises and falls rapidly with need. It's hard to think past the haze of desire that's coursing through me, but I know they're right. I shouldn't be talking myself into leaping off the cliff, hoping that the rocks below don't break me beyond saving. If this is right, then I should dive off headfirst because I know I won't fall, I'll fly. Still, a small part of me hates that they're telling me no. It's just so typically arrogant of them, even though, in this instance, their argument is sound.

Fucking Scorpions.

"Now," Tarek continues as he runs the tip of his nose up the side of my neck.

Now he's just being a shit.

"Curio left a set of rinds for you on your bed. Go put them on," he orders, and it's exactly what I need to snap out of my lust-filled daze, because now I'm back to wanting to punch him in the face.

"Any particular reason for your *command*?" I snip, and I can feel his quiet laugh not only in my ear, but against my back.

"One of our contacts has some information. We'll be meeting them to see what it is," he answers smoothly, but I hold my breath at his words.

Twisting in his hold, I turn until I can see his face. *Information?*

"About me?" I ask hopefully.

Tarek's eyes suddenly look cautious, and my heart starts working faster.

"We don't know for sure, but it's possible," he tells me, and I let loose a shocked exhale as nerves begin to skitter about in my stomach like chirp ants.

"Don't get your hopes up yet, Moonling," Curio warns. "We have feelers out about you and another issue. I don't want you to be disappointed if this turns out to be a dead end."

I nod, doing my best to rein in my frazzled thoughts. I school my features and pull in a deep fortifying breath.

"That's it, Beasty," Riall praises, his hazel gaze locked on mine, and once again those words do all kinds of things to me that they shouldn't.

Riall smiles as though he knows that too and stands up. I immediately feel the loss of him as he moves away from me, but it's time to get my head on straight. Whatever is happening here between me and them can wait. It's time to hunt down some answers.

"Meet me in the kitchen when you're done getting dressed. I'll feed you, and then Curio can fit your armor.

You've seen how Eacon hunts; it's time you experience what we can do too," Riall tells me, his eyes wandering up my bare legs and settling pointedly at the apex of my thighs before rising to meet my fiery gaze.

I fight the smile that wants to sneak across my face at the struggle he's obviously dealing with. I decide a little payback is in order for the *no*—regardless of how justified it might be. I'm playing with fire, but right now I like the burn. I've never been one to back down from a challenge no matter how dangerous it might be, and that's exactly what this feels like. They want me to come to them, to split myself open and give them everything I have. Well, maybe they need an idea of who they'll be fucking with if they don't honor that gift the way they should.

"Fine," I agree, pushing up from Tarek's hold.

His grasp hesitates for the smallest fraction of a second, but then he relaxes his hold and drops his hands. I let the towel fall too.

"Anything else I need to do to prep?" I ask, casually turning to the three of them as though I'm not completely bare and haven't a care in the world.

My nipples pebble, and the firelight flirts with the curves of my body as I drop my hands to my side.

Tarek smirks, but he drinks his fill as he takes me in. Curio's eyes narrow, but I don't miss the shift of his leathers as he grows hard. Riall groans, and I get the distinct impression it's all he can do to hold himself back. No one answers my question, but I'm not fussed. I got exactly what I needed. I turn and saunter out of the study, debating whether or not it would be overkill to pretend to drop something and then bend over to pick it up.

"Fuck me," somebody laments as I make my way out to the corridor.

A smile is the only thing I'm wearing as I walk away, and I have to hold back the laugh that wants to punctuate the frustration I feel at my back from the Scorpions. I don't know exactly where I stand with them after everything that happened today, but oddly, I don't have any desire to examine it or dissect things. This is fun, and the stars fucking know I could use more of that in my life.

37

OU WON'T NEED THAT," CURIO TELLS ME AS I reach for the sword I selected earlier with Eacon. The hunt with her already feels as though it was weeks ago even though it wasn't. So much has happened since this morning that I'm scrambling to catch up with it all. I stare down at the first sword I used to deliver death outside of the ludere, and hesitate. It served me well, and it's crafted so perfectly. My eyes flit to Curio and the eyebrow now cocked in challenge. I sigh, shoving the sentimental urge aside that wants me to ignore his order and grab the sword from where it's leaning against a leg of the long prep-come-dining table that sits at the heart of the kitchen.

I eye the last remaining pieces of lunch, grabbing one for the walk down to Curio's workshop, and Riall chuckles. I was too wired to want to sit down and eat, but Tarek threatened that we wouldn't go anywhere until I had. I'll never confess it, but I'm glad I was forced to eat my new favorite thing. Dough with some kind of white sauce, cheese, and different meats and vegetables sprinkled across the top greeted me, hot from the oven, when I arrived. The burns I sustained to the roof of my mouth and tongue as I practically inhaled it are well worth it. I suspect feeding me like this is part of the ploy to further convince me to stay. It's working, not that I have any intention of telling the Scorpions that. Then again, the lewd noises I make every time I put something new and delicious in my mouth have probably given me away at this point.

I had hoped that experiencing new foods and surroundings would help trigger recognition or memories from before the ludere, but I'm still as blank as I've always been. Perhaps, though, I won't be for much longer. If the Scorpions' contact has useful information, the answers I've craved for so long might be closer than ever.

I follow Curio outside, picking out the familiar path that leads to his forge. I've ambled down it quite a few times now to have him check the fit on certain things. He's always been adamant that he wasn't close to done, so I feel absurdly giddy at the thought of finally seeing what *finished* looks like. I recall the incredible armor the Scorpions have donned the few times in the past they've walked into my life battle-ready and hunting. I try to picture what I would look like in all that finery, but it's difficult to envision. In my head, I still see the dirty blade slave with the threadbare clothes and the rusty sword clutched in one hand. I know I'm not her anymore, but I don't know how long it will be before *that* truly settles in.

Steady meals have thickened me. I'm harder in many places than I used to be now that my muscles are getting what they need. Curio has had to redo more than a few things on my kit because of the changes, but he's never complained once about having to. A smirk tilts across his mouth as he watches me stuff my face. The eager bounce in my step might have something to do with that smile too. I wonder if this is as exciting for him as it is for me. He gets to take in the fruits of his labor, and I achieve another stride away from the blade slave I no longer am.

It's not lost on me what the Scorpions have done for me. Stay or not, it's a debt I don't know how I will ever repay. It's clear that they don't look at it that way, but I don't know how not to. With Tilleo, everything was marks in a ledger. From the gruel to the cost of fairy light to the rags we were given to wear, not a thing escaped being tallied and tracked. But here, they give so freely. I didn't trust it at first, but I've seen enough to know now that as much as they want me to stay, they won't ask an aurem from me if I choose to go.

"I want you to do something for me," Curio announces as we round the last bend before his workshop comes into view.

"What?" I ask, wiping my mouth with the back of my hand and then dusting a few crumbs from my chest.

"I want you to close your eyes while I fit you. When I'm finished, I'll tell you when you can open them."

I regard him for a beat, a smile hinting at my lips. Where I typically see a cocky glint in his gaze, I notice a bashful gleam instead. I doubt he's ever asked Tarek or Riall to do this, which somehow makes it all the more endearing. My small smile hatches into a full-blown grin.

"Sure," I answer casually with a shrug.

The way Curio beams at me before he catches himself does interesting things to every part of me.

"It's just that I'm sure you'll have lots of questions about things, and it will be easier to address them once you're fully suited," he explains nonchalantly, rubbing the back of his neck.

"Makes sense," I agree, my grin growing even brighter.

"What?" he taunts, but I just laugh lightly and shake my head. "You're addled, Moonling," he teases, but he's not fooling me.

He's excited to deck me out, to see my face the first time I take it all in. It's an unexpected side to the male who lives for either riling others up or brooding. It's surprisingly... charming. Of course, if I said any of this to him, he'd deny it and probably act more like a dick to prove me wrong, so I keep my lips sealed, even though I can't keep them from arcing with amusement.

We reach his forge, and I wait as he pushes the doors open. I close my eyes immediately, not wanting to see a thing and spoil the fun for both of us. An elated thrill works through me as he tucks my hand in the crook of his elbow and carefully guides me into his workshop. The heat of the fires that blaze on opposite walls of this place envelops me instantly. I fervently welcome their flickering caress as the days grow colder here. Riall said it might snow soon, but I'm not sure if that's a welcome thing to me or not. I'm eager to see it; the way he described the blanket of white that covers everything and how it quiets the forest all around sounds magical. However, I'm not completely convinced that I'm cut out for the cold. I also don't love the desert heat either, so who knows where that leaves me.

It's hard not to peek as I stand bathing in the warm light while Curio moves about, making all kinds of noise. I start to think he's doing it on purpose to throw me off the trail of what I think he's doing, and then he's once again in front of me, running his hands over the tops of my shoulders and down my arms. Goose bumps trail in the wake of his touch, but the black long-sleeve rind I've been given to wear hides my reaction to the contact.

I thought Curio's rind bottoms were tight on my legs when I first pulled them on, but I discovered today, as I forced myself into a pair made for me, that I had no idea just how snug these things could get. I look less like I'm wearing clothes and more like someone painted my skin with a layer of obsidian. The rinds have a binding feeling when they fit like they should, but it doesn't hinder movement, which is both impressive and incredible.

"I put several sets of rinds for you in the drawer, next to mine," Curio tells me as he steps away.

His tone is offhanded, his focus elsewhere, but the statement is soaked in a comfortable intimacy I didn't know we had until now. We share a room, so maybe I shouldn't be so surprised, but we're only in there together when we sleep, and I prefer the floor to the bed.

Would that change if I...

Curio taps my thigh, and I focus back on him. His hands tell me that he wants me to lift my leg, so I do. He rests my foot on what must be his knee and presses something cool and hard against my outer thigh. Deft fingers make quick work of the straps that run up my inner thigh to hold the cuisse in place. I try not to *feel* things as his fingers work up my leg, but all I can seem to do since this morning *is* feel. A tall boot is slipped up my calf and hooked closed along the inner seam of my rind. The tops of the boots sit just above my knee, skimming the bottom of the cuisse that was just attached.

My booted foot is set down, and Curio taps me for the other, repeating the same steps of cuisse and then boot. After that, he fixes something around my waist. It ends below my hip bones and rises to just under my bust. Once that's affixed at the side, a chest piece follows.

"Cup your breasts and adjust them until they don't feel compressed," Curio instructs, his breath tickling the skin of my neck.

The sensation ushers a shiver up my spine. His chest skims my back as I do what I'm told, reaching into the breast plate and adjusting myself until it feels right. As soon as I drop my hands, Curio tightens the armor around my chest and then moves on to fit my arms. Supple rerebraces and vambraces fit to my upper and lower arms, and then the next thing I know, Curio is pulling fingerless gloves over my hands.

It's hard to think past how he's touching me as he buckles, laces, and fixes me into the kit. The smell of him and his workroom is surprisingly comforting, and I wander through the memories of the first time he brought me here. The way he stroked my hair and worked to soothe me as I fought off an unexpected rush of panic. Curio let me in that day, he let me peer into his past in order to help me banish mine, and now he's giving me a priceless piece of my future. Warmth blooms in my chest, and I try not to fidget as it slowly spreads through me.

I don't know what I look like, but I can already tell that everything he's attaching to my body fits like a glove. It's hard like metal yet contoured to my form perfectly like boiled leather. Nothing seems bulky or without purpose. Curio has masterfully crafted something that's thoroughly protective but still allows me to move as though I'm only wearing the rind. He's spent hours upon hours out here working on this kit for me. Hammering, shaping, and painstakingly caring for every piece that he's now strapping to my body.

It fills me with a tender regard I've never experienced before. His generosity, skill, and effort will protect me in more ways than I ever thought anyone or anything could. And it's not just him either. The meals, the training, the time and space I've been given to lunge forward or retreat back as I figure out my way in this world. There's been subtle guidance mixed in with answers and brazen commands. And then there's the soft and sometimes not so soft invitation that underlies everything, the offer to have all of this at my fingertips forever, if I'll just give in.

The thought of bogging myself down, of tethering my future to anyone or anything when I'd only just gotten a grasp on my present, was too much. What they were offering, what they hoped for in return was more than I could give. But I'm realizing that I don't feel that way anymore. This place, them, I stopped picturing a future without either. I don't know exactly when it happened or how, but the hunt with Eacon opened my eyes and made me aware that things have changed. *I've changed...and so, I'm discovering, is what I want.*

Something slips into place on the outer side of my boot, and I realize with an excited rush that Curio is sliding blades into the sheaths he's hidden throughout my armor. It makes me think of that first night in the ludere when I was disarming Tarek before his bath. I thought I'd never stop pulling knives from the hidden compartments that Curio is now arming on me. If someone had told me that night that I'd end up here, I'd have probably tried to slit their throat for attempting to curse me. Now look at me being fitted like the princess of death, all because three Scorpions decided I was worthy.

I hope I am.

"Almost done," Curio assures me, and I hear him moving around the workshop again.

Rolling my neck, I shift my weight and start getting a feel for the kit now encasing me. I know Curio made a mold of me to help him fit everything just right, and that he's had to make several adjustments as I've filled out more, but I didn't anticipate that armor could feel like a second skin. If Curio is this good at kits and weapons, I can't wait to watch him kill. I'm all at once certain that he must be primal poetry in motion. I bet they all are. The thought sparks an ember of bloodlust that starts to glow and warm my chest. I know we're not headed out to hunt per se—we're merely collecting information—but I'm suddenly excited to see the Scorpions in their element.

Scaling the walls of the manor to take out Dorsin the way they did is a feat I now know to be just shy of impossible. How they even approached the ludere from the empty desert surrounding it, let alone breached the walls and then the manor without being noticed, is something I still can't wrap my mind around. Dorsin apparently had the manor and compound warded so the Scorpions couldn't rely on their thura. In the end, it didn't matter; they're deadly with or without their abilities. They're the best of the best, and I'm being allowed a front row seat to all of it. That used to make me wary, but now I feel more honored and grateful for everything they freely teach me and demonstrate.

Something slides into place diagonally behind my shoulders, and I realize Curio must have strapped a scabbard there. I'm practically jittery with anticipation. Curio better let me look soon; I don't think I can hold off much longer. Another weapon is strapped in place behind the other shoulder. I teeter slightly as two other blades are slipped into position at the small of my back, and then Curio grows still as silence slinks into the space between us.

"You can look now, Moonling," Curio declares, his voice heavy with pride and wicked promise.

I pull in a deep breath, letting it out slowly, as I take a moment to center myself before I open my eyes. A tall, simple mirror has been leaned against the work table, ready to reflect my image back to me. It takes me a moment to process what I'm seeing.

She's fierce, the stunning fae who's staring back at me. Bright hair is plaited back from a face that glows with health and contentment. Even the sun spots that dot the bridge of her nose and cheeks look pleased. Raw, wild power simmers in her eyes as she stands there encased in protective perfection. She's strong, intimidating, formidable...she's...me.

From head to toe, the armor looks exactly as it feels, utterly perfect. I'm covered in a smooth black that hugs my every curve as though the shadows themselves have hardened to adorn me. I pivot slightly, the inky-black of the armor almost absorbing light instead of reflecting it. A pattern of onyx moon cycles line the outsides of my legs. I reach down to touch the different lunar phases, awed by the subtle detail of them, and gasp when I realize they're the handles of push daggers.

"Full moons, half-moons, crescent moons, all the moons, now just as deadly as my *Moonling*," Curio tells me, and my eyes flick from the gorgeous little daggers hidden down my legs to his warm ardent eyes.

The weight of what he's done. The care. The *why* behind it all suddenly makes my throat feel tight. Then I notice that Curio's fully kitted in his own armor and weapons. I stare at our reflections, at the way we seem to complement one another, to match. In his own profound way, Curio's just shown me how I fit within the dynamic of the Order, and it does more to banish my fears and worries than anything else has. There's no doubt in my mind how he sees me, as I take in the two of us standing shoulder to shoulder.

I'm his equal in every way.

Not some slave stolen in the dark of the night. Not a conquest to capture and then cast aside. I'm worthy of veneration and fervent regard needed to create something this exquisite. I'm worthy of the blood, sweat, and time that went into the stunning, thoughtful details that I'm discovering on my body one by one. A scattering of stars down the black handle peeking above one shoulder. Clouds and raindrops etched into the grip of the weapon guarding the other side. The hidden blades of two daggers are tucked horizontally low on my back. Scorpions are carved on the handles, the stingers of their tails barely visible past the sides of my waist. Another set of daggers are sheathed at my hips, their scabbards have small vines and even tinier flowers etched into the borders.

How Curio feels about me is written all over his work, and I'm both awed and overwhelmed.

"These are how the stars looked in the sky the first time I wanted you to be ours," he tells me, pointing to the handle of what has to be a sword sheathed at my back. "Your ax has the day you left and then came back to us," he continues, drawing my eyes to the other handle with the rain and clouds. "Moonflower vines." He gestures to the daggers belted at my waist. "They grew all over my mother's garden, and you carry their scent... Maybe fate was trying to tell me something even then," he muses, his fingers tracing slowly up to my arms. "These are the same style as the one you stole from Tarek that first night in the ludere."

Curio pulls the knives from a hidden spot on the inside of my vambraces, and I laugh at the memory. I really did love that knife.

"But this might be my favorite," he confesses as he unhooks my ax.

Curio brings the pitch black weapon in front of me, and I immediately notice that the edges of the blades aren't black like the rest of it. Confusion furrows my brow, and then recognition flares through me.

"The chakram," I exclaim as I take it in, pressing fingers to my mouth as though it will keep my emotions trapped there.

He made the edges of my ax from the weapon Leto tried to kill me with. He split the solid circle, melding the silver halves with the sable metal he forged the rest of the ax with. It's a breathtaking, poignant fusion of my past and my future, and my eyes start to sting.

"What doesn't kill us fortifies us," I whisper, reciting what he said to me when he first told me that he'd kept the chakram and wanted to use it in my kit somehow.

I run my thumb along the vicious edge and marvel. I've spent as long as I can remember surviving and adapting, and now it's as though I'm holding the physical manifestation of that struggle in my palms. Something that should have killed me but didn't, something that I survived will now cut down anything that stands in my way.

Tears well in my eyes as I look up at Curio. Somehow, completely unexpectedly, he's wholly and unequivocally rocked me to my core.

I take the ax from his hands and in two strides set it on his work table. Then two more strides after that, I reach up and pull Curio's mouth to mine.

38

CURIO

USET KISSES ME LIKE SHE'S DROWNING AND I'M her next breath of air.

I'm stunned at first by her reaction. I wasn't sure how she'd take the professions I etched into every piece of her kit. Worry's been eating at me all day, knowing I'd finally show her pieces of me the only way I know how to expose them. I didn't even get to reveal the grooves I painstakingly carved into the metal of her blades to help direct the blood that will eventually bless them, away from her grip. Or the blades of the daggers that I shaped to look like scorpion tails. I carved fettiks into the handles too, wanting her to have a constant reminder of where she belongs, even if she chooses to leave us.

But the flick of Auset's tongue at the seam of my lips is all it takes for me to forget everything but her mouth on mine. The feel of her in my arms, the way her lips beg me for more, it pulls me from my shock and launches me into something I've been dreaming about since I first laid eyes on my Moonling.

Hunger unfurls and smelts my veins. My cock hardens and I grasp her face and begin to claim her right back. Her hair is braided tightly in a line down the middle of her head, the plait hanging long down her back. I wrap the tail around one hand and pull, forcing her to tilt her face back and relinquish some control to me. Greedily, I swallow the moan that escapes her, instantly needing to feast on more. I back her up to the edge of my work table and drop a hand to lift her on to it.

She welcomes me between her thighs, and I take my place pressing her to me as we devour each other. Tongues clash and twine, as our mouths envelop, suck, and nip. She tastes like home and fucking vengeance, two things that call to my soul and anchor me to this world. I growl as Auset soaks all of my senses in everything that is uniquely her. I'm drowning in her, and yet it's still not enough. I need to sink into her hot, wet pussy and fuck her until my brothers and I are all she can see and all she'll ever want again.

Our armor collides unforgivingly as we try to crush our bodies closer. I want to peel her out of each piece I just meticulously fitted to her, but I know there's no time. I want to scream with how much I want her, but duty fucking calls. Tar and Riall gave me a little space to get Auset ready, knowing what I've been working on and that she'll need help the first few times getting in and out of her kit until she can do it herself. But I know me fucking her on my shop table while they wait back at the house isn't going to go over well. Especially when there's vital information waiting to be collected.

I give myself another moment to get lost in the taste and feel of my Moonling. I nip her top lip and then suck the bottom into my mouth, my thumbs caressing her cheeks as I angle her the way I need to let my tongue show her exactly what I want to be doing with my cock right now. I grind up into her thighs, the rind covering her there just tight enough for me to feel the beckoning heat of her cunt. She moans again and I pull away from her before I lose all sense of right and wrong and take her here and now.

Our foreheads press together, both of us panting and lost to each other.

"Fuck," I lament, skimming my lips against hers for another quick sip before denying myself any more. "Listen to me right now, Moonling, and listen good," I growl against her mouth. "I'm going to fuck you so long and so hard that you'll need a month to recover from it, but it will have to wait until after we meet our contact," I promise her, and the frustration that flashes through her features makes me bite back a disgruntled snarl.

Auset's silver eyes are glassy with desire. Her lips are kiss-swollen and the same pinkish-red as *siru* berries. My fingers pulled a few strands from her braid, and they now hang free, framing her gorgeous face. All I want to do is rumple her even further, to finally crack through her failing defenses and dig into the center of who she is and why she's ours, but we need to go.

A resigned huff falls from her lips, and she leans back on the scarred and worn table that I do all my best work on.

"You Scorpions keep promising things to that effect, and yet here I sit...unfucked," she practically pouts in the *I will slit your throat* kind of way that is an adorable expression of Auset's displeasure.

It makes me even harder.

I want to soak in her ferocious displeasure, listen to her growl warnings at me while I tease her body, edging her until she's on the brink of murder and insanity, but I'm pushing it as it is already. I give her a smile that speaks of all the foul and dirty things I plan to do to her when we get back.

She just glares at me.

"I thought you'd be in as much of a hurry for answers as we are," I question, balling my fists so I don't try to pull her closer.

"I am! Fuck...I am," she sighs almost as though she's reminding herself of this fact. "I can't help it if you fuckers always overwhelm me at the most inconvenient times. I'm starting to think you're doing it on purpose."

"Who? Us? Never," I assure her, punctuating my lies with a wide smirk.

She slaps the back of her hand against my chest, a small laugh escaping her as she does. I want to pluck the melody from the air and seal it in a jar so I can hear it again anytime I want.

"Soon, Moonling, so fucking soon," I vow, which is maddening.

All of us have been dying to get her exactly where she is right this very moment, ready and wanting, and now I can't do fuck all about it. This informant better have what we need, or I swear I'll string them up by their entrails.

"First, our contact, hopefully some answers, and then maybe you'll get to test out your new kit?" I encourage Auset, and maybe myself a little too.

The frustration stewing in her stare gives way to an avid gleam. I chuckle and reluctantly step back. Every instinct I have demands that I step back between her sweet thighs, but I shove the aching need aside. Fluidly, Auset hops off the table and grabs the battle ax next to her. The way she twists it expertly in her hand like she and the weapon have known each other forever isn't helping me to not want to bend her over and fuck her ruthlessly while she holds it. I reach underneath my guard and adjust my cock in my rinds, trying to find a position that feels less torturous, but my armor doesn't exactly make that easy.

Auset steps to the side, executing a couple practice swings, and I almost lose the battle with my will.

"It's perfectly balanced and lighter than something this incredible has any right to be," she marvels almost to herself.

I try not to puff up with pride as I do my best to talk my dick down. I enjoy mastering my craft and kitting me and my brothers with the best, but there's something significantly special in gifting Auset her armor and blades. It's like I know a part of me will always be there to protect her, and it soothes and reassures me in ways I didn't know I needed until I saw her outfitted in my best work like she was one of us already.

I feel things in me click into place like a key that fits in an old forgotten lock, ready to open me and make room for her. There was a time where I would have run from this, where the thought of ripping myself open for someone else would have felt more akin to torture than destiny. But as I look into Auset's silver eyes, watch her run her fingers over every detail of my gifts, I know the only place I'll ever run again is to her. She may not fully want to admit it yet, but I know it's only a matter of time before she feels it too.

Auset fixes the ax in place behind her back and turns her penetrating silver gaze on me. It's as though she's baptizing me in molten mercury as she surveys me, her shoulders pressing back as she once again bricks up her defenses. I want to take that ax to her walls immediately, but I reassure myself that we'll get her to crush them once and for all when we get back from this hunt. There's nowhere she can run, nowhere she can hide at this point, not from us and not from what she's realizing we are to her.

She doesn't know or comprehend what it is to find your mate, or mates in this case, but we do, and I know that bond is solidifying between all of us with each minute that passes.

"Thank you," Auset offers proudly, her palm running down the armor protecting her abdomen as though she's suddenly nervous and not quite sure what to do with her hands. "It's not really an adequate sentiment for how I feel right now. I wish I had something that expressed this better," she tells me, touching her palm to her chest, "but thank you will have to do for now," she continues, moisture glinting in her moonlit eyes once more.

For now, I think in my head, but on the outside, I nod once, not wanting to draw out Auset's discomfiture more than it already has been. She relaxes. It's a small act of trust, but it's there all the same, reinforcing every sign I'm seeing that my Moonling is going nowhere. It makes me feel like I've done everything right, seeing her let go, a little, of the tension and uncertainty that always seems to plague her.

Stealing one more quick glance in the mirror, I watch as Auset shutters all vulnerability away and lets her inner darkness weave a new impenetrable barrier around her. She morphs into the merciless huntress my brothers and I met on the first night of the Bidding, and all at once, I'm eager to see her hunt with us. She may not have agreed to join our Order yet, but if it walks like a Scorpion and slaughters like a Scorpion...

"Let's head back. Tarek still needs to glamour us before we can go. I can hear the lecture on tardiness he's probably pacing and preparing to deliver as we speak," I tease.

With a playful huff, I hold out my hand to Auset, ready to lead the way back to the house arm in arm. She eyes it for a minute before halfheartedly slapping it away and striding past me. I laugh, I should have expected nothing less. I can drink down my Moonling's mewls and moans with my tongue in her mouth and my hands roving all over her body, but treat her like some frail, frilly-frosted female, and she'll shove a dagger somewhere unpleasant.

She's perfect.

She'll hear no complaints from me as she strides on ahead. Now I get to watch her exquisite ass as she does her best to show me who's boss.

I sigh like some lovesick pup. Auset isn't denying that she's one of us anymore, but I'm tense with the need to make it official as soon as possible. *Fuck*. I've never been so eager for a hunt to be over.

Tonight, I assure myself, and then I trail after my Moonling, intent on following her wherever she may lead for the rest of our days.

39

AUSET

WITH A WHISPERED WORD, TAREK DIMS the fairy light sconces that are set high on the walls. Instantly the shadows slink from the edges and corners and start to swallow up more of the front room we're standing in. Two large double doors that I've only ever seen closed loom in front of me, while the stairs that lead up to the rooms and study guard my back. Nerves scuttle through my veins as I watch Tarek grab a bundle of smoking herbs from a small table. More muted words slip from his lips, and it's all I can do not to lean closer and try to make out what he's saying.

Questions scamper relentlessly in my head as Tarek works through the ritual that he does before every hunt, the glamouring of us being the last part of it. I'm entranced by every move he makes, cataloging the twitches of his brow, the flicks of his hands, and the pattern of his pacing so I can ask questions about all of it later. Riall and Curio stand patiently as Tarek quietly mumbles and winds his bundle of herbs in invisible patterns that only he can see.

Each of the Scorpions is fully kitted, their obsidian armor and weapons marking them as the daunting dealers of death that they are. I've never seen anything more breathtaking. I keep thinking that I'm teetering on the precipice of something when it comes to these three males, but if I'm being honest with myself—and at this point, I *have* to be—I think I've tipped over the edge. I can't say if I'm falling or flying, but whichever it is, there's no fighting the trajectory at this point. I'll land where I land and deal with the fallout of wherever that may be when it happens.

Tarek moves from Riall to me, and I hold my breath as he waves his smoldering bundle around me. A thick herbal scent collects in little clouds that surround my face. I'm not sure what it is, some kind of musky juniper maybe, but it feels thick and sticky when I eventually breathe it in. I can sense the white smoke adhering to my insides as I inhale, the cloying vapor waiting and ready for whatever Tarek is going to do next.

"I'm going to glamour the others first so you can watch and see what to expect," Tarek tells me, and I'm so surprised to hear him actually speak at an audible decibel, using words that I can identify, that I stare at him for a beat before what he's saying sinks in. "It won't hurt, but it can be an unusual sensation. What's important is that once I start, I can't stop; it's draining and dangerous."

I nod and pull in a deep breath. Nothing like an ominous warning of potential doom to get the adrenaline flowing. Tarek studies me for a moment, a glint in his light blue eyes that I can't identify. Whatever it is, it's been glistening in his gaze since Curio and I walked in here. At first, I thought my slightly mussed braid and my puffy lips were to blame for the look I'd like to explore, but now I'm not so sure.

Tarek runs his ice-blue perusal down my face, stopping when his eyes land on my chest. He tilts his head ever so slightly as though he's listening for something, and I study the high point of his ear as he does, curious as to what it could be. A satisfied smile stretches slowly across his face, and then he moves to the small table, dousing the herbs in a bowl of water. Once again I'm left confused and curious and wanting more, but what else is new? They should really consider a name change from Order of Scorpions to Order of Confounding Cunt Teasers.

Keenly, I watch as Tarek moves in front of Curio. I scrutinize them both, trying to memorize what they're doing so that I can mimic it when it's my turn, but when Tarek leans in and *kisses* Curio, my mind careens to a complete stop. My mouth drops open, and my eyes grow wide. But the longer I watch, the more I realize it's not a kiss in the romantic sense. There's no threading of fingers through each other's hair, no angling of jaws or swirling of tongues. Not an ounce of passion permeates the interaction. In fact, I can't be sure unless I get closer, but I think there's a hairsbreadth of distance between their mouths. I want to crank up the fairy light to examine what's happening in greater detail, but I was just warned not to do anything to mess with the process.

My focus is drawn from their mouths when pitch-black patches start to spread over Curio's exposed skin. They first appear over his jaw, erasing the three-day-old stubble that just grazed my chin and cheeks less than a handful of seconds ago when our lips clashed and our tongues danced. Onyx flows up Curio's ears until the pointed tips are lost to the inky shadows of his hair. The lighter streaks around his face darken, and the loose strands suddenly look as though they've been pulled tight in a knot behind his head. The white of a skull claims parts of his face, and vertebrae work down the center of his neck. His hickory-brown eyes are eaten up by liquid obsidian, and all too quickly, the Curio I've been getting to know is gone and in his place is Skull of the Order of Scorpions.

I don't know if it's on purpose, but when Tarek pulls his mouth from Curio's and steps back, I realize that Skull looks exactly like he did that night in Dorsin's room. At the ludere, their glamour gave them short smoothly styled tresses. It was one of the things that threw me off about them at first and made me wonder if they were the same fae from that fateful night. But now Skull is here in all his glamoured glory, and I suddenly smell orc blood and fear in the air.

I shake away the lingering olfactory recollection, not wanting to be sucked back into the memories of that night. The reality is the girl who was kidnapped, beaten, and chained up in that room died that night. Someday maybe

I'll find out who she was and discover what her life would have looked like had she not been robbed of it. But who I am today was born in the pits from blood and brutality. I don't know if it was a fair exchange, but it's done. I could choose to be angry about it, try to lay the blame at the Scorpions' feet, but they didn't steal me and chain me up. They owed me nothing that night. It's not pleasant to admit or accept, but that's the cruel world we live in. Crying about it changes nothing.

It would be easy to wrap myself up in a safe and familiar cloak of rage and resentment, but it's pointless. I don't just see Skull when I look at the Scorpion now, Curio is there too. He's the one who kissed me like I was all he'll ever need in life to be happy. The male who carved his adoration in my blades and subsequently my heart.

There was a time I thought all I would ever see is the three of them crawling out of Dorsin's window, my battered and broken body huddled in the corner, too shocked and scared to beg them to take me too. But my eyes are open now, and I can't seem to stoke the hate that I once could.

Maybe I needed everything that came after, to be who I am today, to be able to stand here ready to claim my place as one of them. Or maybe that's the shit we tell ourselves to feel better about the times that try to break us. Either way, I'm ready. I'm not afraid of what's to come.

Tarek strides to Riall, and when they kiss, I'm far less shocked by it. Once again I watch them, mouths pressed together in almost a cold clinical manner. Riall and Tarek are closer to me than Curio was, and I can almost see a hint of something moving from Tarek's mouth to Riall's. I stare, feeling a little deviant as I do. The darkened room still robs me of the details I'm so hungry for. Just like with Curio, inky splashes begin to anoint Riall's skin, the golden tan slowly receding to the claim of thick black shadow.

All too quickly, Riall fades away and Bones emerges.

I have the strangest ache that strikes me as I take both Skull and Bones in. It's as though I've missed the *Order* sides of the males. I've been sharing my meals and training with one part of them, but now the other part is here again, and I can breathe a little easier.

With Skull, Bones, and Scorpius, things are simpler, smoother. I can brush aside my worry about the future with Tarek, Curio, and Riall. I can ignore the debate about what I want, stop caring about what *they* could mean to me, and instead fall back into the arms of death and destruction, a place that has enabled each and every one of us to become who we are today.

Bones's namesake flashes white amidst the black of his glamour. His skeleton is a twin in height and bulk to Skull's. They share no blood between them, but they truly look like brothers when they're draped in doom like this.

Abruptly, Tarek steps away from Bones and starts to advance on me. My heart kicks up, and I clench and unclench my hands as he comes to a stop. His impressive figure towers over me, and I feel lost in his shadow in more ways than one. Tarek's breastplate knocks against mine as we stand and stare at one another.

What would the tips of my nipples feel like against the heat of his skin?

"Do you hear it, Auset?" he asks me, his crystal-blue eyes boring into mine and snapping me away from my lurid thoughts.

"Hear what?" My voice is nothing more than a whisper, as though the space between us has been baptized holy and now deserves reverence.

"Your heart is beating in tune with mine," he whispers back, watching me, like he's waiting for the exact moment I hear the truth of what he's saying.

Astounded, I strain to hear the rhythm thumping in my chest. Mine is a steady staccato of apprehension and anticipation. I try to hear past that, to hear if what Tarek is claiming is true, but all I can make out is the steady thrum of my own heart. I lift a hand to press to his chest, but his armor blocks that path. Then I see it—my gaze snags on the steady bounce of a thick artery in his neck. My fangs drop as I observe the steady pulse. He's right, the beat matches the cadence of my own heart.

My eyes widen as synchronized rhythms grow louder in my ears. I can suddenly hear the confirmation of what my eyes just witnessed. I open my mouth to say something, to ask how this is possible or why it feels so significant, but Tarek's mouth presses against mine, and I go still. I shut my eyes and quiet the questions blazing through me, afraid that I'll do something to fuck up his thura while he's using it to glamour me.

I press my mouth harder against his, not able to help it, but it isn't until Tarek's large hands cup my face to hold me still that I realize he's *not* kissing me, not exactly anyway. His mouth is cushioned against mine, but instead of nibbling on my lips or deepening the contact between us, he's breathing into me.

It caresses my tongue and drips down my throat, tasting of smoky need and biting steel. It cools my insides at first, but then a prick of warmth starts at my center. It sluggishly ebbs out and begins to coat everything it touches. The sensation and flavor of his power slinks over me, masking my tan skin and freckles, tucking away my silver eyes and moonbeam-stroked hair. Each breath of Tarek's thura shutters protection down around me. It shields me from the monsters by showing them that I am one too.

Bit by bit, Tarek's influence begins to wane. All too quickly, the consuming deluge becomes nothing more than a trickle. I'm tempted to grab his head to keep him here. The drive to force him to stay pressed against me, feeding me from the depths of his strength, is abruptly all consuming. A new hunger arises, one that I suspect is solely linked to the Sanguinna in me. The staggering demand for blood hits me so hard and so fast that it triggers a flare of panic. Cold alarm hammers through me, and I think it's the only thing that allows me to shackle the pounding urge and keep my hands down and my sudden thirst in check.

The stream of power from Tarek stops completely, and the thrumming need for blood quiets from a pummeling demand to a manageable tap against my senses. Tarek's hands continue to hold me in place, and a spark of confusion flickers through me. Why is he not stepping back? And then his stationary lips, where they're still pressed against mine, start to move.

His mouth is tentative at first, searching. Doubt drips through me, not having watched him do this with Skull and Bones, but then he lightly suckles my bottom lip, and my uncertainty unravels. This isn't about glamour; this is a surrender to the driving desire that's been building since the first night that I washed his body and tempted his soul.

Gone is the thura that Tarek was pouring into me, and in its place is his tantalizing and tortuous tongue as he begins to insatiably plunder my mouth. I mewl softly, ready to drown in the feel of him, the feel of us as we finally collide and ignite. He works expertly around my fangs, careful not to nick himself, although the prickling in my gut that wants his blood to be streaming down my throat right now wishes he would.

I once again freeze, disturbed by the direction of my desire, but Tarek growls his objection to my sudden inaction, and the carnal sound crushes my hesitation under the weight of his voracious hunger. Abandoning all inhibition, I dive into the want and possession I feel in his kiss, meeting it with my own. We nibble and imbibe, trading fervor back and forth, and then Tarek slows, taking our mouths and connection from a frenzy to a measured, methodical devouring. Each stroke of his tongue against mine, every pull and suckle of his lips, has potent need coursing through me like venom. I burn and transform from the contact, no longer sure of who I'll be on the other side of this, but there isn't an ounce of me that cares.

If the three of them are the bargain for my soul, they can have it.

I thread my fingers in Tarek's hair only to find his loose waves have been pulled tightly behind his head. My eyes snap open, and I discover that Tarek's snowflake-blue eyes and ivory complexion are now hidden underneath the same black and white glamour that the rest of us are draped in.

Scorpius is here to play.

Just as that thought registers, Scorpius starts to pull back. Irritation begins to ripple in my gut, and I know at once that there will be no *playing* right now. I sigh, already suspecting what's about to come spilling out of his mouth before he can bother to open it.

"Let me guess, you'll fuck me until I can't walk, or remember my name, or know how to talk at all, but not now, because *now* would be too *convenient* and we have other shit to do," I grump. With a huff, I step away from him, tired of being the one they walk away from. I'm starting to acquire a distaste for being left with desire dripping down my thighs and racing thoughts that try and fail to work out why *later* feels so much like rejection.

I know there's information waiting for us, that it could be something that points us in the direction of where I come from, or it could outright tell us who I am altogether, but these Scorpions keep getting me worked up at the most inopportune times. For males who've been posturing about me being theirs and what they plan to do to my body when I'm ready, they sure are lacking on the fucking follow-through.

I'm *not* impressed.

I shouldn't be focused on that at all, but they make it so hard to concentrate on anything else at the moment. It also probably doesn't help that I just might be stalling. All I've wanted for so long is answers, but there's a part of me that's not ready. What if I learn something that changes everything? I don't know if I want that anymore. It was one thing to daydream about it in the ludere or when I first woke up here, but now, now that I'm just starting to find my footing, just starting to see a life with them, to want it, I'm not ready for all of that to come crashing down. Not when we've barely even started.

I seethe internally at how ridiculous I know I'm being. I hate that this weakness still exists in me, that I'm nervous about what might be waiting on the other side of what I thought was an impenetrable veil. It's my fault that I'm feeling so fragile right now, but I can't help feeling like the Scorpions are to blame for it too. This is exactly what I didn't want, to compromise on what's best for me because of some pretty-faced fae. What's more confusing though is that the Scorpions were starting to feel like *they* were what's best for me, and if that's true, where does that leave everything else?

"Hey, where'd you go?" Scorpius asks me, leaning down so that we're eye to eye while he reaches up and strokes my face.

I step back, breaking the contact.

"Does it matter?" I snip, and then I put even more distance between us. "Right. So where are we going?" I ask, as I try to regroup and focus.

Scorpius stares at me for a beat, but I refuse to look at him in hopes that he'll get the message to drop whatever is smoldering in his eyes at the moment.

"Why don't you kiss Skull and me like that after we're done being glamoured?" Bones demands with faux outrage, his hands planted on his hips.

It's the distraction I'm desperately in need of, because Scorpius huffs out a hollow laugh and turns his attention to his brother.

"Watch out, Skull, I think he's playing favorites already," Bones jeers with a wink.

"*I* didn't mind the show," Skull counters, and even

though his hickory-toned eyes are now black, I can practically feel the heat coming off them.

The tiniest smile twitches at my lips. Bones points at the two of us, like we were just caught doing something naughty.

"I *knew* you were up to no good earlier, I fucking told you, Scorpius! Was it the daggers or the ax that convinced her?" Bones asks, and I can't decide if I'm annoyed by his question or amused by it.

The easy banter between the Scorpions lightens the ache in my chest in a way that nothing else could. I'm reminded that each of them has faced their own battles and nightmares to get here. Their scars run as deep as mine, in some cases maybe deeper. They are the unwanted bastards of kings from different realms, but it doesn't make them anything less than the brothers they are. The three of them have gone head-to-head with their pasts and come out better and stronger on the other side. If they can do it, so can I.

"Let's go, I'm ready," I declare, and each of their black eyes flick to me.

"You're almost ready," Scorpius corrects, and my glamoured brow furrows. "First, you need a name."

Bewilderment has me ready to remind him that I *have* a name, and then I realize what he means.

"Okay, so give me a name, *Scorpius*."

"One is not simply *given* a name, one is *chosen* by a name," Bones corrects, his tone laying on the omnificence a little thickly.

I snort at his antics.

"And how does *one* do that?" I snark.

"With a very ancient and revered ceremony," he answers immediately, the twinkle in his eyes giving me pause.

I have no idea what it could be, but I've come this far. I knew before I walked into this room to be glamoured that there was no going back from here. I may not have said the words, but my actions are speaking loud and clear. I'm all in, and I can see in the black depths of each of the Scorpions' piercing gazes not just that they know it, but that they are too.

Three predatory grins stretch across the maws of three skeletal faces, and all I can think as I look at them is *bring it on.*

HOOD?" I ask, incredulous. "YOUR ANCIENT and revered ceremony is pulling a name from the hood of a cloak?"

"Not just any cloak, *your* cloak," Curio points out, as though that distinction makes all the difference.

In my head, I chastise myself for using the wrong name. He's Skull, that's how I have to see him and refer to him when we hunt. The last thing I want to do is leave the walls of this place and fuck up the anonymity they work so hard for.

"Was it made with thura or something?" I question as I assess what looks to be a simple sable wool cloak.

"I'm sure the seamstress that fashioned it did so with the highest affection for the coin she'd be making when done. Does that count?" Bones inquires with a cheeky smile.

I shake my head and stare down at the hood in Scorpius's grip.

And here I thought they'd want a blood sacrifice or something.

My fangs threaten to drop again despite just managing to retract them a few seconds ago. I need to talk to Ri—shit!—Bones about why I'm craving a carotid all of a sudden, but it'll have to wait until we get back.

"Alright," I concede, reaching into the hood of the cloak and feeling for one of the slips of parchment that Scorpius dropped inside. "Is this really how you three chose your names?" I ask as I pinch a folded slip between my fingers and pull it out.

"Trust me, this beats the hours of deliberation and arguing that happened *before* we all agreed to leave it in fate's... hood," Skull assures me.

"Arguing?" I press as Scorpius plucks the parchment from me.

"*Who* was going to be Scorpius was an issue that almost came to blows," Skull whispers conspiratorially, and I laugh as I look over at Bones and then the clear winner of the name.

Fate chose well. Maybe it's because I met them with these names initially, but they seem so fitting. I can't imagine calling them by different designations or picture Bones being the *Scorpius* of the group.

A tiny tingle of excitement makes me hold my breath as Scorpius unfolds the name that *chose* me from the hood.

"Claw," Scorpius announces, his eyebrow quirking up with contemplation.

"Claaaww," Bones repeats as though he's testing it out.

"Claw?" Skull questions, his onyx perusal moving down and then back up my body as though he's looking for a way to make the name fit.

Bones snatches the parchment from Scorpius's hands, confirming the name with his own eyes. "Claw," he concurs, a little flat, his shoulder lifting in a half shrug. "Nope. That's not it. The hood's obviously rusty. Try again," Bones suddenly declares, and Skull nods his agreement while Scorpius hastily offers me the hood again.

Thank fuck.

There is nothing intimidating or threatening about *Claw*. In fact, Bones made a meal of some that he plucked off a crustacean. They were delicious. However, I don't want a name that's more likely to spark hunger than fear.

I try to hide the relief I feel behind a small laugh, but it sounds stiff and awkward even to me. I reach inside the hood again. This time, I mix up the collection of slips before picking out another one. My heart picks up as I hand it to Scorpius, and he quickly unfolds it.

A smile flashes across his face, and I exhale some of the nerves fluttering around in my chest.

"Telson," he reads off, his mouth wrapping around the name in a way that has me thinking about his tongue twining with mine. It makes me want to hear it fall from his lips while my mouth is wrapped around his cock.

"Telson?" I ask, not opposed but unsure of how it fits with their obvious theme.

"It's what a scorpion's stinger is called," he explains, and goose bumps crawl up my arms.

"Telson," I whisper reverently, and it feels...right.

"Tels," Bones announces, already playfully shortening it.

"That's the one," Skull affirms, and just like that, another piece of the *we* we're now becoming clicks into place.

Auset is tucked away for the time being, and in her stead is Telson of the Order of Scorpions. Warmth floods my chest, and a heavy weight of purpose and belonging serves to anchor me. I never knew how much I wanted this, how much I needed it, but now that I have it, I'll never let it go.

"Telson..." Scorpius addresses, the commanding tone pulling me from the internal acknowledgement that has my eyes starting to sting.

I blink away the sensation and focus on the task at hand.

"Skull is our strongest shadow walker. You'll be *walking* with him to our destination," Scorpius tells me, and I nod my assent. "I'm sure you'll have plenty of questions as we go, but I ask that you stay quiet and vigilant unless there's a threat. When we hunker down for the night and it's safe, we will answer anything that you may want to know."

"If we somehow get separated, you are to shadow walk to our first destination and then wait for us there," Skull adds. "I'll point out the best way for you to find it when we first arrive," he assures me.

"Got it," I confirm, and he nods once.

"Let's go," Scorpius commands, and with that, each of them moves to the darkest corner of the room.

I follow closely behind Skull, my pulse now humming in my veins. Excitement flows through me, and even though I don't know where we're going or who we're meeting, I know I'm ready. I've trained for this, and the Scorpions have expanded on that, refining and sharpening me even further. We're not out to spill blood on this hunt, but even without it, tonight will be poignant. It'll be a night I will always remember because it will be the first time we go out as a team. The first time I step into the light of the moon as a Scorpion, fully relying on the others to bring me back in one piece. Everything that comes after this, my future...*our* future, will be built on the foundation of what happens under the stars tonight.

I never thought in a million years that I would be here.

I used to spit the taste of hope from my mouth. It was a venom that exacted a steep price, a price that I refused to pay. However, a different venom now runs in my veins, one I'm learning is so potent that it burns away everything until all that's left is hope. A hope that's survivable because it's wrapped in safety and acceptance, devotion and respect, adoration and so much more.

And it's all mine for the taking.

Scorpius disappears into the shadows, and Bones traipses in after, offering me a wink before he's swallowed up by the inky depths.

"Ready?" Skull asks, and I pull in and then release a deep breath as I nod.

I've only traversed the shadows fewer than a dozen times. I was always too aware that I could be caught at any moment in the ludere, so I used the surprise ability sparingly. It was a means to breach a wall or two, that was all I ever risked. Scorpius and Bones aren't popping into the next room over though, and the only time I've ever traveled more distance than that was after I'd ripped Gartox's throat out. So when Skull presses into my back, one arm circling my waist while the other snakes across my chest, I blow out the worry that was settling in my lungs.

He's got me.

"Try to sense the signature of the space," Skull murmurs against my ear, and I automatically lean back into him. "It's instinctual with this thura; the more you use it, the more you'll be able to discern one collection of shadows from another. Step into it," he guides me, pressing me into the shroud that just claimed his brothers.

Skull's tone is assured and comforting, and his physical presence grounds me, making what's being asked seem far less impossible than it ever has before.

"Do you feel the little tug?" he asks me, patting his hand low on my stomach.

"Yes," I answer.

"That's the thura inviting you in. We're going to follow that tug until the stones in front of us melt into an infinite number of shadow patches."

I nod and try to keep my breath even and my jitters settled.

"Once we step into that in-between, I'm going to take over. I'll walk us to where we need to be, okay?" Skull asks me, his cheek softly nuzzling mine.

"Got it," I tell him a little breathily, and then he plants a soft kiss just below my ear.

It's a battle, but I refuse to get distracted by it. Instead, I follow the pull exactly as he just instructed. Like a rake through sand, I'm gently dragged from the front room of the castle into a gray space filled with endless speckles of dark possibilities. I know Scorpius said that Skull was the best at this, but a part of me didn't think I'd be able to do what he was asking so easily.

"That's it," Skull rumbles, the vibration of his approval tickling my neck and moving down to settle at the top of my shoulder.

Cool pressure entwines around us, and then in a puff, Skull is pressing me out of the gray in-between and into a dark storeroom. The scent of herbs and onions weakly permeates the thicker smell of hops. Large wooden barrels are stacked against the back wall of the chilly, white-washed stone room. Shelves occupy the other side, piled high with various root vegetables and spices.

I look over to see Scorpius and Bones waiting at the bottom of a flight of stairs. Skull presses on my stomach, and my attention snaps back to him.

"Every shadow has unique qualities, the thickness, the temperature, its proximity to light. Sometimes even scent is a component. If you want to shadow walk back to this room, you'll need to recall how this particular shadow feels to you and then use that to locate it amidst all the others. It sounds complicated, but when you step into the void between light and dark, all you need to do is call the shadow of the destination you want, and then you'll be connected to it."

I think back to when I shadow walked from Gartox's room to the female washroom in the ludere. I didn't understand how I did it then, I was simply chasing my instincts, but I remember wanting someplace safe and quiet. The tiled room with its rows of tubs popped up in my mind, and the next thing I knew, I was stepping out of a shadow into the very space I'd just pictured.

"The more you shadow walk from place to place, the more familiar you'll become with the shadows themselves. That will make it easier to come and go," Skull assures me before he pulls his arms from around my body and moves away from me to join the others.

I take a quick moment to close my eyes and get a better sense of the shadow we just exited. When I feel like I've cataloged it well enough to call on it again, I move from the dark depths and fall in step behind Bones as he begins to ascend the stairs.

Wherever we are, it's quiet. I feel both wary and soothed by the hush that wraps around us as we climb up the narrow stairwell. The top step gives a small squeak of protest as Scorpius treads on it, but the sound doesn't give him pause or make the others tense. They're not sneaking around, even though they move with pure predatory grace. I want to ask where we are, but no one else is talking, and I *was* told to keep my queries to myself until later. I swallow down my curiosity and tabulate the first of what I'm certain will be many questions by the time this hunt is over.

When we left Scorpion castle, it was dusk, but as I file out of the storeroom stairway into a large kitchen, the view through the large windows shows that it's much later here. Waning moonlight spills into the large room that's built to feed an army, and I realize the placid lull of this place is the sedate quiet that accompanies the early hours of the morning. It's too late to deny sleep and too early for the first risers of the day to be shuffling out of bed.

Scorpius pivots left through a tall swinging door, and I follow him and Skull out into a sprawling tavern. I exit into a throughway that leads out to clusters of tables and chairs. To my left is an immaculately stocked bar with bottles of spirits stacked to the lofty ceiling on rustic metal shelves. Butted up against that is a wall of spouted barrels that are heaped sideways, ready and waiting to be drained. A dark oak counter stretches in front of it all, only leaving room for the passageway we're all standing in, which I assume is how servers get food and drinks to patrons from the back.

Arched stone ceilings curve above us with chandeliers hanging from the towering heights, looking like giant spoked wheels made of more dark oak and slate gray metal with globes of fairy light hanging down in a scattered array. The floor is the same light teak-colored stone as the ceiling, and there are colossal, rich oak pillars and walls holding the entire structure up.

A man fitting of the vastness of the tavern is sitting at the bar with a ledger opened in front of him and a pen that looks like a tiny twig gripped in his massive hand. He rises as we spill into the tavern, and rises before rising some more. I thought the Scorpions were tall and built, but this male has to have giant blood somewhere in his lines. His thigh is the size of a tree trunk, and his shoulders look as though they could easily carry the weight of the world on them.

"Scorpius," he greets warmly, his voice as deep as the sound the realms make when they quake.

He pushes away from the bar and strides over to grip forearms in delighted greeting.

"Summix," Scorpius returns, pulling the behemoth into a hug that keeps one of their arms trapped between them while the other hand pats heavily against the other's back.

I study Summix as he releases Scorpius and pulls Skull into a half hug. His eyes are vivid pewter and his complexion a deep sorrel. Alabaster patches leach the hue from his skin in several places, most notably around the outer edge of one eye, a streak across his jaw to his ear lobe, and a mixture of pale speckles down both of his arms. Bones steps around me as Summix loosens his strong grip on Skull, and I step back, not wanting to intrude on the reunion. Fairy light shines in the curls of Summix's crow-black hair. It's styled into a dense mohawk, the sides shorn close and revealing more light patches on one side of his head.

"Did you close down for us?" Bones asks as he claims a hug. "Usually there's a straggler or two in here to threaten when we arrive."

Summix gives a derisive snort as Bones chuckles. "King Ergen raised taxes a few days ago. It'll be quiet until folks adjust," he grumbles.

I look to Scorpius to see if this news about his father is surprising, but his skeletal face gives nothing away. We're in the Dawn Court, I deduce based off of what Skull told me before about where each of them are from and who their sires are. Scorpius was born in and rescued from this realm, but it's clear nothing about that is currently fazing him. He looks as confident and comfortable as ever.

"Your visit is well timed in that regard," Summix declares. "I've only got one room occupied for the night and nothing more coming in. You'll be freer in your comings and goings, and once the whispers start, I'll probably get an influx of fae who are willing to part with some aurems to try to catch a glimpse of the renowned and terrifying Scorpions," he states with a chortle as though he finds the well-earned designations amusing. "Your room is rea—" Summix's pewter gaze lands on me, and he stops mid-word, his black eyebrows shooting up with surprise.

Bones chuckles and steps to the side, exposing me further to Summix's stunned stare.

"And what do we have here?" he asks, bewildered interest tinting his tone as he looks from me to the others in search of an answer.

"Summix, meet Telson. Telson, Summix," Scorpius introduces, nodding his chin from the half giant to me and back again. "Telson is one of us," he offers somewhat vaguely, and I wonder if that's by design either for Summix or for me.

"I can see that," Summix stammers, his gaze bouncing around the group with astonishment. "Mated?" he asks, his eyes growing even wider as he takes all of us in.

"Working on it," Skull answers, and I suddenly choke on nothing.

I slap my chest as I try to calm the cough sputtering out of me and narrow my eyes at Skull. I've never framed the Scorpions or the place they've been vying for in my life with the title of *mate*. Our situation has always felt more complex than that simple title makes room for. I don't know much about mates, but I do know that it's a moniker that carries a binding weight to it, a weight it seems Skull and the others have already decided they want fettered to what's dawning between us.

I don't know who Summix is, but he must be a close friend for them to be making such addled declarations.

"Shhh, don't tell Telson though," Bones whispers loudly as he conspiratorially leans toward Summix. "She's still pretending that she's considering her *options*." Bones gives me a cheeky wink.

These fucking Scorpions.

Summix's mouth splits into a wide grin, and he chuckles softly. "It's an honor to meet you, Telson."

I'm taken aback by the genuine regard and sincerity that's brimming in his gaze. I nod once, not sure what else to say. I'm curious about him, curious about his relationship to Scorpius and the others, but I'm not allowed to ask questions right now.

"I'll adjust the pallets in your quarters," he states, and I open my mouth to argue that I actually prefer to sleep on the ground, but a look from Skull reminds me that I agreed to keep my mouth shut. "That reminds me, this arrived for you not too long ago."

Summix strides back over to the bar and plucks a folded missive that was tucked in the pages of his ledger. He hands it to Scorpius and then looks back at the rest of us. "I've kept a pot of scouse and some loaves of bread warm for you if you're hungry. I've also got your tankards ready if you'd rather drown in some cider or ale instead. I've been tinkering with that mead recipe, Bones, and I think you'll like the results. I put *cet* root in it, and *by the stars* did that enhance the sweeter flavors while also cutting back on the bitter bite that last batch had."

"You're too good to us, Sum, I'd kill for a—"

"It'll have to wait," Scorpius interrupts Bones. "There's been an issue with the informant," he announces, holding up the opened parchment. "The quad is requesting we meet with them right away."

41

W HO IS THE QUAD?" I INQUIRE AS WE STEP out of a block of shadows that takes up almost an entire alley.

Skull steps away from me now that we're at the desired destination, and I take a moment to register the unique things about the shadow we're standing in so I can add it to my ever-growing network of shadow walking options. No one immediately answers, either because they're scanning our surroundings or enforcing the *keep your thoughts to yourself* decree.

I roll my eyes. I understand the need to mind my manners when the Scorpions are interacting with other fae or realm contacts, but there's no one here except us, and I can't hold in the curiosity anymore. I'm not the greatest at following orders on my best day, which is something the Scorpions *should* know given what happened when we met at the ludere. Really, they should be proud as fuck that I've managed to stay quiet for this long. I'd call it progress.

Scorpius sighs and I take that as permission to pepper him with every question that I've been obediently storing.

"You've actually met them. Well, more like you've seen them," Scorpius corrects as we move out of the alley and down a placid street.

Dim light from sporadic street lamps spills over the cobbled road, and closed shops border the walkways on either side of us. I can just make out the dark tipped roofs of the turrets that crown the Dawn Court castle over the tall buildings lining this street, and the rows of even taller houses hide the horizon beyond that. I get the sense that this city must be colossal, and I'm grateful that we're wandering its depths while it's still quiet and sleepy.

"At the ludere?" I ask as I rack my brain for any talk of *the quad*, not that it could have possibly been anywhere else. I've only met Eacon, her mate, and the Scorpions since I've left Tilleo's sand pits.

"They're the heads of the Order of Vulpi," Skull supplies, and I stop.

"Oh," I utter, the images of the four female fae who sat with Tilleo on the first feast night of the Bidding, the night I killed Crit in the wine cellar, solidifying in my mind.

I don't know why I thought I'd never see any of the attending Order members ever again, but I did. I realize now how stupid that was. They're Order members. There are alliances and assemblies and protocols between them.

Running with the Order of Scorpions means I'm now woven into the fabric of all of it, like it or not.

Skull and Bones observe me, a glint of concern stewing in their black glamoured gazes. I couldn't say if the concern stems from my reaction or *who* it is we were going to meet. Either way, I don't like it. I start to walk again, and each of the Scorpions falls into step around me.

"Enay is the *Scorpius* of the Vulpi," Skull tells me as we round a corner and make our way down another dusky street. "Mayden and Myrka are usually the muscle, and Kiffin is the astute tactician."

"Of all the Orders, we cooperate with the Vulpi the most, but it doesn't mean they're not a threat, so stay alert and cautious," Scorpius advises, stopping at a tall metal gate.

He reaches for the handle and pulls it open. Moonlight catches on the metal designs of the entryway, and I discover images of foxes running and wrestling and napping on the borders and bars of the gate door. The details of the playful metallic art are captivating. I can practically smell the steel wildflowers that have been welded to the bottom half of the gate, little fox heads and ears peeking up through the blooms.

A steep set of stairs leads us down below street level, and almost immediately I sense a change in the atmosphere. It morphs from the tranquil early hours of the morning to something heavy, something seedier. It's as though the air has a taint to it, and I'm all at once alert and wary. Skull knocks on a towering metal door that waits at the bottom of the stairs. A peephole opens up high on the door with a clunk, and a hint of red light spills out. One large eye peeks out and takes us in. The iris inspecting us is a soft purple surrounding a pupil that looks more like a cut gem with all of its rainbow-like facets and angles.

"If you dare dine on fox, beware the fangs," Skull intones, and after a slow blink of the eye at the door, the peephole shuts and the large door opens.

Thick treacly incense practically slaps me across the face as I step into the grand entry. Soft reddish-orange firelight blankets the room, but there are no hearths or flames in sight. Sultry music winds its way around the space with no identifiable source. The floors are black and buffed to shine, making them look more akin to the surface of a glassy lake than whatever stone they might be. The walls surrounding us are a creamy, soft tangerine with thick black molding at the ceiling and floor and around the various doorways that lead elsewhere. But none of that is the reason why my stomach drops and my muscles tense.

No.

It's the fae that are draped on the fox-orange settees dotted around the entrance hall. The ones wearing scraps of fabric or nothing at all. Males and females alike, sitting, waiting, and some playing with one another, tells me exactly where I am...a flesh house.

Dozens of eyes take us in, assessing, calculating, anticipating what we might want, what we might need. Unease climbs up my back as a male rises and sensually strides toward us. Silky garnet-hued hair falls down his back, undulating behind him as he moves closer, like a well-fed cat appraising its next meal. Steel bars run through both of the male's nipples, and I notice the same treatment in a line down the shaft of his flaccid dick.

"Is it business or pleasure that brings the Order of Scorpions into the Den on this fine fortuitous morning?" the male asks, his velvety rich tone slipping out of his mouth like some unspoken promise of debauchery and licentiousness.

"We seek the quad, Nero," Scorpius answers, and the male nods, a salacious smile spreading swiftly over his face.

"Very well. Follow me, Scorpions," he invites, his rich brown eyes falling on me for a half a beat longer than anyone else, before he turns and saunters toward a dark doorway.

A fox tail catches my eye as it swishes behind the fae as he strolls ahead of us. I study the movement, unable to help myself, wondering what it would be like to have a tail. Then I realize what it is and feel daft as fuck. It's not a limb. It's not a part of him at all. It's a furry accessory that's attached to the plug that's seated in his ass. I look away quickly, only to land on a room draped in dark orange light. There's plush seating edging the small space, offering observers the perfect view of the female dangling from the ceiling by the chains at her wrists. She's bare and breathing hard as she squirms to get away from a male who has his hand working between her thighs.

A dagger is in my palm and I'm stepping toward the room when a strong hand grips my shoulder.

"It's pleasure, not pain," Bones tells me as he points back toward the room while holding me in place. "The Vulpi aren't slavers; the fae that live here do it of their own free will," he explains as I turn back to the chained female.

Her face is still scrunched up like she's suffering, but just as I start to doubt Bones's assessment, she throws her head back and starts a steady chant of *yes*. I can't hear her, only read her lips, the room must be warded, but her obvious exclamations morph into what looks like a euphoric scream, and then release surges out of her in a deluge that sprays around the room. The spectators cheer, rubbing her shower all over themselves or licking it off one another, and I turn away, shocked.

My dagger slips back into its sheath, and I train my eyes on the knot of hair at the back of Skull's head as we're led deeper into the *Den*. Lurid sounds dare me to peek, but I hold strong. The guards back at the ludere talked incessantly about their favorite flesh houses and what went on in them. It's how Leto came up with half of the things he wanted to try, but none of the crass conversations I've overheard prepared me for something like this. Especially not Bones's comment about how no one here is being forced to do anything. That should make me feel better, but I mostly feel like I did with Eacon walking through a crowd for the first time. I'm out of place and being bombarded by smells, sounds, and sights that I don't know what to do with.

My body is reacting to the stimulation, which has me feeling even more on edge because I don't want anything to cloud my judgment while we're in here. I don't want to think about the reasons that Scorpius knows the name of the male in front of us. Or why Nero *asked* if they were here for business or pleasure as though it could be either. I'm not bothered by their sexual history or that a place like this might be appealing. The stars know that Bones watched

Leto devour my cunt that night in the wine cellar and has never uttered a complaint about it, but I can't stop wondering what they do here when the answer is pleasure and not business.

Would they do it to me?

Are they intimately familiar with the piercings in Nero's dick? Do *they* enjoy squirted showers of desire? Do they watch, like to be watched, fuck as a group, or go off on their own? I want to know, but that's not what we're here for. I'm distracted, and I don't *do* distracted. If this were the ludere, my back would be in raw strips right now. The masters had no tolerance for wandering thoughts. I don't either, and yet here I am struggling. I've crossed a line with these Scorpions, and now I'm wondering how they like to have their cocks sucked instead of watching the shadows for potential threats.

What is wrong with me?

A small growl of disapproval snakes out of me. It's loud enough to have both Skull and Scorpius glancing back at me. I ignore them as I do my best to shake off the lusty cloud of this place and sink into a hunting frame of mind.

Nero pushes open a set of double doors and guides us into a large room. Chairs and sofas take up the middle, a large desk occupies a corner, and a bed and open washroom comprise the rest of the space.

"Kiffin and Enay will be with you shortly. Is there *anything* I can do for you until then?" Nero asks suggestively, his gaze flicking between the Scorpions before once again landing on me.

Bemusement flashes in his eyes while he catalogs me in a skilled way that makes it look as though he's interested when really he's counting daggers and evaluating just how dangerous I might be.

"Very," I tell him, not answering his spoken question but the one floating in his silent perusal.

The suggestive smile that slinks across Nero's face makes me realize that this fact serves more as an enticement than a deterrent. He reaches down and strokes himself once, his decadent and depraved brown eyes never leaving mine.

"Would you make it hurt so good, Slayer?" he purrs at me.

His length hardens in his hand as he arches an eyebrow in both challenge and invitation. It's all I can do not to gawk at how large he's getting.

"Because I know I can," Nero promises wickedly, running his palm down a shaft that's easily three times longer and thicker than it was before.

The male has dick thura, no question.

"Out!" Scorpius barks, and now it's Nero's grin that grows even wider. "Now!" he commands once more, and Nero offers him a conciliatory half bow.

"Come play, Slayer," Nero urges as he starts to back up toward the double doors. "Let me unwind that tight coil of need at your center. Your Order can watch if you'd like," he taunts, finally looking away from me and back to the others. "I don't mind showing them how it's done."

A cacophony of snarls fills the room just as Nero backs out all of the way and shuts the doors behind him. I can make out a low chuckle from the other side of the wood barriers before the fae with an obvious death wish moves on.

"Fucking prick," Bones grumbles, staring at the doors as though he's debating whether it's worth it to go chase Nero down.

"You okay?" Scorpius asks me, his black eyes filled with agitation.

I laugh. "If all it takes is some pierced enchanted dick to unsettle me, then we might have bigger problems than you think."

"Nothing about that was enchanting," Skull grunts.

I offer him my best smirk. "Agree to disagree," I counter, and he glares at me.

Bones chuckles and plops down in the middle of a sofa, content to make himself right at home. I try not to think too hard about why he might be comfortable here as he throws his hands behind his head and stretches.

"What do you think the problem is?" Skull asks as he wanders over to the desk and takes in the things on display there.

"We'll find out soon enough," Scorpius states, moving closer to me as though he's not sure if he wants me to sit or stay right where I am.

It dawns on me that I'm not the only one trying to figure out how I fit in the dynamic they've honed for so long now. I know they want me here, but it's clear it's going to take time to adjust for all of us. Scorpius looks me over as though he's confirming for himself that I'm good. The pad of his thumb brushes down my bottom lip, and I'm taken aback. Maybe this place is affecting him too. As much as I like the small show of affection, I don't know if it's wise. He's the one who said we need to be vigilant, and yet here he is seemingly more worried about me than what we're here for.

I step back from him, and his brow furrows as his hand drops to his side. Before he can question me, the doors to the room fly open and my head snaps in that direction. A buxom and completely naked woman strides in dramatically, her face alight with welcome and her voice practically singing, "Scorpions!"

Her full tits bounce and her nipples tighten as she moves closer. Her crystal blue eyes and long black hair are the same as what I remember from the ludere. She either didn't wear a glamour to the Bidding or she's wearing the same one now.

"Kiffin," Scorpius greets, stepping closer to her, and I get the sudden urge to step between them.

Whether it's because I don't want *him* near her or *her* near him, I can't say.

When all they do is grip each other's forearms in the formal way of the fae, I let loose a relieved breath. Only to instantaneously suck it back in, when Kiffin shoves her ample bosom in Bones's face as she leans over to hug him on the sofa. It doesn't help that the gesture gives me a clear view of the jewel-encrusted butt plug shining like a beacon between her very round ass cheeks.

Looking around at the opulence of this room and the Den in general, I think it's safe to say that whatever the orange jewel is that's decorating the depths of her derriere, it's more than likely real. Which means the tool she uses to stretch her ass for pleasure probably costs more than I did at the ludere.

Great, just great. If I didn't want to stab her before, I sure as fuck do now.

Kiffin pulls Skull in for a quick hug, and then ignoring me altogether, she bounces toward the washroom.

"Sorry to keep you waiting, I had to finish up with Count Gerrin and Count Zhao, and neither one of them are happy until they've come at least three times in every hole and then licked it all up," Kiffin announces casually as she steps into a tiled area in the corner and pulls a lever.

Water sprinkles down from above her, and she steps into it, squealing and then moaning after a moment when steam starts to waft off the water. The tactician of the Vulpi, as Skull previously described her, turns so that her front is on full display as she tilts her head back and wets her hair. Then the show truly begins when she grabs a bottle of soap and starts to work it all over her body.

"Enay will be right in and we can get started. Hope you don't mind me cleaning up while we wait," Kiffin declares, and I'm tempted to offer an objection, but I keep my mouth shut.

I glance at the Scorpions, but each of them is focused on something that isn't her, and my hackles lower slightly. Skull is very focused on the dagger in his hands, Scorpius is scanning titles on the spines of books that fill up a shelf over by the desk, and Bones is watching me. I can't read the look in his eyes but decide it doesn't matter when not even Kiffin's soft moans entice a glance in her direction.

I never knew that one's cunt requires several minutes of fingering in order to ensure that it's properly clean, but Kiffin's apparently does. Then again, I haven't personally played with the counts, so what do I know? I study the Vulpi, trying to garner the purpose of this erotic display, but not knowing her or the history between her and the Scorpions makes it hard to say. This could simply be something she does because she's comfortable. Or she could be trying to make them uncomfortable, and then there's always the message that she could be trying to send to me.

When she pulls the plug from her ass and then bends over in *search* of something, I have to keep myself from snickering. I also have to keep myself from informing her that her counts missed a spot when cum drips out of her now unstoppered hole. I shake my head at the ridiculousness of it all and move to sit on the arm of a chair. If Kiffin is trying to make me jealous or encouraging me to make some sort of scene, she's going about it in the wrong way. If anyone in this room was truly interested in her, she wouldn't be trying so hard. If she's simply trying to make me uncomfortable, then she should spend more time in the sleeping quarters of blade slaves. There isn't a thing about what can be done with or to someone's body that makes me uncomfortable, just so long as it's consensual.

I relax, and a small chuckle pulls my attention to Bones. He's still looking at me, but now the mysterious glint in his eyes has made way for amusement. The water turns off, and I'm ready to leave before this meeting has even started. I'm not even sure if these females have legitimate information for us or if the summons here was all about...whatever Kiffin is trying to do.

"Bones, I had Dar fetch some peaches for us. I know how much fun we had playing with them last time," Kiffin giggles, and then she's suddenly standing in front of him, now wet and naked, with her hand outstretched.

Because Bones is still staring at me, I catch the lightning-quick flash of a grimace as he reaches up and takes the fruit from Kiffin's palm. Instead of biting into it, like he's being set up to do, he offers it to me instead.

"Have you ever had a peach?" he asks, a cheeky smile on his face.

"No, silly, that's for you," Kiffin objects as she grabs his arm.

My blade is pressed to her throat before she can so much as tighten her grip on his wrist. Her crystal blue eyes narrow instead of widening, and I know the game she's been itching to play has just officially started. Scorpius and Skull both draw closer, but I lift a hand telling them to back off. Thankfully, they do.

Kiffin isn't the only astute tactician here. It's loud and clear to me that *this* is what Kiffin is really after. She wants to know what my place is, test my mettle, see for herself what it is about me that made the immovable Scorpions move. The Vulpi and Scorpions are allies—that's not an easy feat when it comes to what we do. On some level, each of them probably knows what drives the other Order, what their tells and pressure points are, how to get what they need when they need it. However, I'm an unknown, and how *I* will affect that important dynamic is really what this vixen is after.

I suppose it's time to show all of them the kind of Scorpion I intend to be.

42

THREATENING THE ORDER OF VULPI IS UNWISE," Kiffin states, her tone just shy of a growl.

"So is what you're doing," I counter, purposefully dropping my eyes from her infuriated stare to where her hand is still holding Bones's wrist.

A challenging smile tips her lush lips up. "Cria, I've touched more on this male's body than we have time to recount. *This* is nothing," she disputes, her pale blue eyes searching mine as she tightens her grip on Bones's arm.

"*That* has nothing to do with me," I tell her evenly. "*This* does," I declare, drawing a line between how things used to be and how they will be from here on out.

It would be one thing if Bones showed any indication that he welcomed Kiffin's advances, but he isn't. He won't even look at her, none of them are. I don't know if the Scorpions' lack of reaction is out of concern for their alliance or because they also want to see where I stand on things, but Kiffin is crossing a line and she knows it. This isn't about marking territory, it's about respect.

I press the small blade more firmly against her throat. It's one of the knives that Skull made for me that resembles the one I stole from Scorpius during his bath. I really like the idea of using it to cut this presumptuous bitch up. Blood pools at the edge of the blade, but instead of pulling away, Kiffin leans into it and laughs breathily.

"Well, now you're just giving Bones exactly what he wants," she taunts as she reaches up with her other hand and spreads blood down her breast and around her nipple.

Kiffin's eyes light up like she's certain she's proved that I'm out of my league. I can't fight my smile. My assured grin throws her a little, but she hastily banishes the doubt from her features and doubles down by smearing more blood down her chest with a small moan.

I keep my smirk wide and beaming as I drop my fangs.

"Am I though?" I mock.

Kiffin's eyes finally grow wider, and she gasps as she takes a step back. "You're...you...you're Sanguinna?" she stammers, looking from me to Bones and back again several times before she turns and snatches something from her bed.

"She is," Bones answers, his black eyes still fixed on mine, only now there's an undeniable heat broiling in his ebony stare.

Kiffin pulls on a robe, securing the tie around her waist, and I bite back the *fucking finally* I want to huff out as she does.

"I had no idea. I thought they'd disappeared," she murmurs as she looks at me as though she's seeing me for the first time. "I get it now. Forgive me."

Kiffin's demeanor morphs from hostile and challenging to contrite so fast it makes my head spin. I expected the fangs to help her realize that I'm more of a threat than she realized, but I didn't expect an immediate and almost reverential response. I figured I'd have to fight harder than that to get her to back off, or maybe that was just wishful thinking on my part. I really was looking forward to breaking more blades in. I thought one of them would look lovely stabbed through the middle of her wrist. I suppose there's always next time, although judging by the way Kiffin is now looking at me, *next time* might be off the table.

"I'm so happy for you, Bones. If anyone deserves a miracle like that, it's you," Kiffin declares, and there isn't an ounce of jealousy or malice in her tone or countenance, only respect and genuine regard.

"Thank you, Kiffin, that means a lot," Bones offers, his tone warm and appeased.

I realize then that he's still trying to hand me a peach. I take it, not sure what else to do. Bones stares at me like he's waiting for me to take a bite, but he's going to be waiting forever, because I'm sure as fuck not eating it. I meant it when I said that whatever happened between Bones and Kiffin before me was none of my business, but that doesn't mean I have to eat the bitch's *fuck me* fruit, and that's exactly what this little fuzzy orange thing is.

Pass.

Kiffin offers me a genial smile, but I'm not there yet. She doesn't seem deterred by my lack of response in the slightest.

"Please sit," she encourages, and I drop back down to the arm of the chair I deemed was safe to sit on earlier. "Enay should be here any minute."

As though conjured by her name alone, a statuesque woman pushes through the doors and surveys the room and its inhabitants. Her skin is as dark as night, her lips full, and her almond-shaped, dark brown eyes assessing. At the ludere, she had a stunning array of locks arranged in an updo, dripping with jewels. Today, she's abandoned the gowns and finery and instead has a bright white tunic on and a pair of amber leather pants. Her black locks are now stunning braids that fall around her shoulders, and I count at least ten blades tucked on her person, which means she's probably carrying thirty.

The Order of Vulpi is ancient. Their craft and the way it has shaped parts of fae history is legendary. Many of the masters at the ludere speak of them with devout worship, and for the first time, I'm starting to see why. The Vulpi have been referred to as Realm Breakers because of the kind of influence they carry everywhere. Having the support of their Order in anything is like a magic wand that opens doors and makes things happen. I looked for evidence of that designation at Tilleo's feast, but all I saw were rich, extravagant, polished fae who enjoyed stroking Tilleo's ego. But as Enay walks confidently into the room, I see it.

She's a fucking Realm Breaker.

"Scorpions, thank you for coming," Enay greets as she moves to stand next to Kiffin. "Myrka and Mayden left a short while ago to help secure the informant," she explains, and then she strides over to me.

I stand, and even though I'm by no means short, Enay is easily two heads taller. "We've yet to be introduced. I'm Enay, the leader of the Order of Vulpi," she tells me, as though there could be any confusion as to who she is.

I take her offered arm, gripping her tight around the forearm as I do.

"I'm Telson, the newest member of the Order of Scorpions," I reply, and I don't miss the almost imperceptible way that Scorpius goes still.

It's the first time I've said it out loud, and I know the declaration has shocked him. I could have simplified things and maybe said *I'm Telson* and that's it. It would probably be wise to give myself more time to be sure about what I'm doing and committing to. But as I look into Enay's piercing gaze, as I take in her no nonsense demeanor and her matter-of-fact countenance, I know that claiming my place right now is crucial, that it's significant. I won't let fear guide me down a different path when the one I want, the one I *need*, is right in front of me.

"It's an honor to meet you, Telson. I hope our relationship will grow with trust and esteem just as it has with the other members of your Order," Enay professes, and I offer her the warm smile that Kiffin was hoping for.

"Me too," I agree, and with a firm squeeze of my arm, Enay moves back to Kiffin's side.

I feel as though I've just passed another test, but I have no idea what it was.

Kiffin sits in the chair opposite mine, and Enay claims the end of the sofa that Skull dropped himself onto earlier. Scorpius stays standing behind Bones, but this must be normal, because no one says anything or objects to his looming over the rest of us.

"So," Scorpius starts, as though he's the one to call this meeting and not the Vulpi. "What's going on exactly?"

"It seems that the Vulpi we sent to procure the informant have noticed a tail," Enay starts, leaning back into the sofa and putting her feet up on the large oval ottoman that sits at the center of all the seats. "Now, whether that tail is related to the Vulpi or the informant, we haven't determined as of yet, but we've holed up in Porrin longer than we initially intended and called in reinforcements."

"Mayden and Myrka?" Skull confirms, and Enay nods.

"Do we know who they're bringing back to us?" Scorpius asks, and he starts to pace behind Bones's sofa.

"His name is Hatus Orill, he's the brother of Lord Daeral's stable master, and he was there the night Lord Daeral and his whole house were slaughtered," Kiffin answers, and the words drop like a boulder in the middle of the room.

Shards of questions explode everywhere as the Scorpions express their shock. A pit opens in my chest, and disappointment and confusion plummet in its depths. The informant witnessed a murder. That's the information he'll be sharing with us. Not that he knows anything about me. My feelings were so jumbled, so fragmented about what this mystery person might know or say. There are no answers for me here, and I feel stupid for thinking there would be.

"What was he doing there?" Scorpius asks at the same time Bones questions, "How did he get away?"

Kiffin holds up a hand to slow the barrage of demands.

"Mr. Orill was passing through on his way to visit his wife's nephew. All we know right now is that it was an unplanned stop and no one knew that he was sleeping on a pallet in a stall that his brother put together for him. He wasn't willing to tell us any more than that until he felt safe, which is why we decided to bring him here," Kiffin explains. "From what I understand, Mr. Orill watched from a stall as a group murdered everyone inside the house. He stole a mount and fled."

"And the fae responsible didn't hunt him down?" Skull questions. "They didn't seem like the type to not notice someone fleeing the scene of a massacre."

"He's been hiding with family and friends. We only found him because our network included the cook at one of the houses he holed up in for a while. She's the one who convinced him that we could help him," Enay answers.

"So why do you think whoever is following his collection party isn't the group responsible for killing the lord and his line?" Scorpius queries, his shrewd gaze studying Enay.

"Because they've had opportunities to tie up loose ends, but they haven't. Like you said, Skull, the original hunt wasn't disorganized, which means whoever it was that executed it should have capitalized on the first chance they got to slit Hatus Orill's throat, but he's still alive," Kiffin tells us.

I consider what the Vulpi are saying and what they're not. Enay mentioned that there was a possibility that the tail had nothing to do with Hatus, but the way Kiffin huffed a little at that makes me think they don't believe that. Which means if the group following the informant doesn't want him dead, there are only so many reasons why that would be the case.

"You think Hatus is involved," I announce after watching the two Vulpi leaders for a moment.

Enay's brown eyes flick to mine, a smile ticking at one corner of her mouth as she nods her head. "That's our theory at the moment."

"And what, whoever's tailing them is *his* backup?" Skull asks, his brow furrowed as though that doesn't quite fit with the pieces of the story he's collecting.

"We can't say for certain one way or the other. It just seemed odd that a lowly cobbler managed to survive something that almost a hundred other fae didn't. Whoever erased the Daeral line and anyone closely associated with them isn't the type to let even one thread slip from their grasp. Which means either Hatus Orill is coming here to discover how much we know and whether or not we pose a threat or whoever is hunting him is drawing it out on purpose," Enay cautions.

"You suspect an ambush," Bones observes with a hollow laugh. "And now we know why you sent for us."

"Precisely," Kiffin agrees. "Any information we glean benefits us both, so why should we bear the brunt of the risk? Your contacts have asked you to look into this, and we want to end whoever is trying to set up the Order of Vulpi. It's a win-win."

Scorpius shakes his head. "You should know better than anyone that when you let a wolf into the paddock, the sheep always lose."

"Good thing we're not sheep," Kiffin counters.

"True, but even a fox isn't a match for a wolf," Scorpius points out.

"Then we'll have to hope a Scorpion is?" Kiffin retorts.

Enay studies Scorpius, and her brow furrows. "You think we're making a mistake by bringing him here?"

Her question holds no ire, only genuine curiosity rings in her tone as she looks from Scorpius to the rest of us. Scorpius stares at nothing for a long moment, and then he shrugs as he focuses back on her. "I suppose we'll find out tomorrow."

43

EACH OF US ARE CONTEMPLATIVE AND SILENT as we slip out of the gate that leads down to the Dawn Court Den of the Order of Vulpi. Things feel different after the time we spent inside, but whether that's for better or worse is debatable. On one hand, I feel more rooted to the Scorpions and secure, which is good. On the other hand though, foxes in general now make me want to stab something, and there's the high probability that we're walking into some kind of ambush tomorrow—or maybe it's later today, I'm not sure of the timeline anymore.

Instead of retracing the path we took to get here, Scorpius turns in the opposite direction. I follow, focused and scanning our surroundings for anything that might be off as we thankfully get the fuck away from this place. With talk of traps and massacres, I'm a little tense and a lot restless, but the streets and walkways remain as empty and sedate as they have been since we arrived.

Like a bruise, the sky above us is just beginning to fade from dark blue-black to deep purple. The stars are fading as they submit to the command of the oncoming day, and I can taste the approaching dawn in the early morning air. I brush the push daggers hidden on my thighs as we walk, grounding myself with the feel of steel and accessible weapons. My kit and the small armory I'm carrying aren't weighing me down even after a long day of wearing them. *Maybe Skull has thura that helps him create such utter perfection?* It's hard to imagine that only raw skill and regard went into the masterpieces that are the Scorpions' armor and weapons.

"Well, that was interesting," Bones comments when we pass down another street and make a left.

I laugh hollowly at the benign description. "Why can't we shadow walk into the Den?" I observe as we continue to move further away from the Order of Vulpi in the opposite direction from how we arrived there. "I'm sure Kiffin wouldn't mind you popping right into her room of *romance*," I snark.

Skull snorts.

"Need me to carry you, Beasty?" Bones teases, wagging his eyebrows at me.

"You don't get to touch me until you've bathed at least a dozen times," I retort, and Bones's mouth drops open with indignation.

"Don't be jealous, Beasty, I swear to you there's no need."

"Please, I'm not," I scoff. "But the Kings know who she's fucked on those couches and how much of them is now"—I gesture to his entire frame—"*on* you," I finish, my face crumpling with disgust. "In fact, all of us need to be boiled before we sit on or touch anything. I'm for pleasure and sexual freedom, but I'm not for having someone else's escapades stamped all over me, especially when that seems like something Kiffin would get off on."

She eagerly waved her exploits with Bones in my face, and while I don't care about that, I wouldn't be surprised if she tried to stake some hidden claim that only she would know about.

The Scorpions laugh and shake their heads at me as though I'm being dramatic, but my concerns are valid. I'm going to have to take lye to my kit first thing, just in case.

"Our arrangement with the Vulpi doesn't allow us to shadow walk within a certain distance of their dens or safe houses. In exchange, we get unfettered access to them. We also have codes that our network can use to do the same," Scorpius explains.

"And what do they get?" I question, noticing that the scales of the deal seem tipped in the Scorpions' favor.

I may not care for Kiffin, but she's too sharp not to get something substantial from the agreement, and if they say Bones, I will deck each of them.

"They get to see us coming, and we assist them on certain more complicated hunts at no cost to them," Skull supplies, and I look over at him, impressed.

"Do you work closely with the other Orders too?"

"We trade information with the Order of Crows on occasion, but that's the extent of it. The other Orders we don't see unless there's either a Conclave or a Bidding at one of the luderes," Scorpius answers.

"*One* of the luderes...exactly how many more are there?" I demand, stopping in the middle of the street. "Do you own them too?" I accuse, suddenly feeling witless for not realizing or thinking to ask about any of this sooner.

"No," Scorpius hastily assures me. "There's only one other ludere. It's funded by the Order of Stags. Luderes and blade slaves as a practice started to die off after there was a coup inside the Order of Wolves a long time back. Since then, the Orders have found other ways to recruit.

"We got involved after Dorsin's death because it was an opportunity to source information and plant potential informants. Plus, after the hunt ordered on the former ludere master, we thought it wise to keep a closer eye on what was happening there."

I'm drawn back to that night in my mind, the way they snuck into his room without even a sound or change in air pressure to give them away—not that I would have noticed any of those things back then, but I'm certain Dorsin would have. The look on the master's face as Scorpius drew his blade across his throat and the vindication I felt at watching the fae who had just beaten me to the point of wanting to die, bleed out in front of me instead... I couldn't appreciate it then like I can now, but the retribution was a thing of beauty.

Something in me almost wants to thank them for what they did that night, but they didn't do it for me. It was a hunt, nothing more. Any praise or gratitude I might feel after so long is misplaced, because it's not truly what they did that I'm grateful for, it's that I survived it.

"Why was Dorsin executed anyway?" I voice instead. "What did you take from him that night?"

"He stole a contract and some other documents from an Elix," Skull tells me.

My brow furrows. "What is that?"

"*Potionists*. They're fae with a thura for tonics and philters. Their lines are very rare, very powerful, and they should never be crossed. I don't know what Dorsin was thinking," Bones answers.

"She wanted her stolen things back. She was very concerned about a particular fertility covenant if I recall correctly. She didn't say more than that though. Most Elix's that are worth anything pride themselves on their secrecy. They have to be, or fae won't go to them for help. She wanted Dorsin dead for crossing her, all of the stolen documents back, and the apprentice who sold her out returned to be dealt with. We found the traitor in Dorsin's stronghold after we dealt with him and retrieved what we needed from his vault," Scorpius explains.

"It was an odd hunt to say the least," Skull notes. "Dorsin traded in flesh not secrets, so why he got himself caught up with an Elix was irregular."

"He finally fucked with the wrong fae," Bones finishes. "The ordering of the hunt was very clandestine and hush hush, but that's Elixes for you. She paid us five times our normal rate to make Dorsin's hunt a priority. We used that surplus to wedge our way in with Tilleo afterward."

"What were the other documents aside from the fertility thing?" I ask, intrigued by why it was so important to get them back. Dorsin's greed was his end, but he had to be good at what he did before that. There's not a trace of who

I am or where I came from floating in the wind anywhere, it seems. He tied up loose ends the way Wilik plaited hair, painfully and inescapably. Whatever it was he was hoping to find in those documents was important enough that he left himself open to retaliation.

"We were paid not to look, so we didn't," Skull answers simply.

I frown at that, but I suppose I can't say that I wouldn't do the same thing now. Some things simply aren't worth the cost; Dorsin certainly learned that lesson the hard way.

"Our ludere—" Scorpius starts.

"*Our?*" I challenge, astonished by the claim and a little incensed.

"Yes, *ours*," Scorpius enunciates. "You're a Scorpion now, Telson. That means anything and everything that we have is now yours too."

As profound and incredible as a declaration like that is, any warmth it might stoke is snuffed by the sick dread that roils through me like thick smoke. Since leaving the ludere, I've come to understand that the realms and way of life for most fae is some fucked-up cycle of the strong and powerful preying on the weak and unfortunate. On some level, I've come to terms with the reality that there isn't much I can do about that.

It's a "grain of sand against a tidal wave" kind of situation. And I've spent the entirety of the life that I can remember being pummeled by those waves. All I want to do now is dry off, heal, and make sure that I'm never pulled under by those punishing forces again.

Scorpius's use of the word *ours* feels like a punch to the gut, regardless of the sentiment behind it. I may not be able to fight the powers that be, but even so, I don't want any-thing to do with any of the fucked-up things that were done to me in that ludere. I don't want to be a part of *ours* if that's what it entails.

"Hey," Bones soothes as he cups my cheeks and draws my untethered focus to him. "I see that stunningly ruthless mind spinning in all kinds of directions, but here, with us, is where you need to be," Bones tells me, hunching over so that he can bring his eyes level to mine.

Scorpius and Skull move closer to my sides, each of them caging me in a way that I realize I need desperately right now. Bones's swirling black gaze pulls me in and an-chors me, but I find that I want to tear through the glamour and stare into Riall's hazel eyes instead.

"I can't," I start. "I fucking won't…"

"You don't have to, Moonling," Skull assures, pressing further into my side as I look over at him. "If you want to burn it to the fucking ground, then we'll burn it to the fuck-ing ground."

"We'll hunt the masters and string Tilleo up in the training room. We can bring in healers, and you can beat the piss out of him every day until there's nothing left," Bones adds.

"You can bathe in the blood and tears of anyone who's ever hurt you, including us, all you have to do is say the word and it's done," Scorpius vows, and his fingers tenderly graze my cheek in a touch that feels so reassuring that I can't help but lean into it. "We haven't done anything with the ludere yet because we were waiting for you," he tells me softly. "Pick your poison, Scorpion, and we'll help you strike at everyone who ever hurt you."

I close my eyes as their fervent promises and devotion wash over me like warm water. Their adoration and allegiance lap at my soul, and I don't have words for what's singing in my heart right now. I have more at my fingertips than I ever dared to reach for, and for once in my life, it all feels...right.

I open my eyes, not sure how to communicate what I'm feeling but determined to do it anyway. I focus past Bones's shoulder, trying to collect my thoughts, when my gaze lands on a tall peak in the distance, one that looks oddly like an eagle's talon. I freeze as recognition bubbles like acid through my mind. It burns away every other thought until all I can process is the talon-tipped mountain.

"I know that summit," I whisper as festering rage rises in my chest.

"What?" Bones asks, leaning closer to hear my muttered profession.

"I know that fucking mountain," I snarl, and then, without warning, I'm pushing away from the confines of the Scorpions' bodies and running as though my life depended on it.

Confused shouts fall away somewhere behind me as I dash in the direction of the familiar landmark. Memories try to crawl to the surface of my mind, the sharp barbs of the horrors they contain slowly shredding through my defenses. Fear does its best to smother me, but I'm not the youngling I was when I stared out of a window at the peak of that mountain and wished that the eagle's talon would come carry me away. Fury and vindication rage in my chest like a sandstorm, the grains of rage and promise smoothing away the pain like a pumice stone.

I push my body harder, needing to find the house more than I need my next breath.

I'm a streak in the night as I sprint through yards and streets, the houses growing larger and larger as the base of the mountain draws closer. Clustered homes give way to sprawling manicured properties. Lofty fences and gates enclose lush lands that surround opulent buildings big enough to fit several luderes.

They're all in my way.

I skirt around what I can and climb over everything else that can't be avoided...until I find it. There, nestled in the shadow of a sleepy, talon-topped mountain, is a palace that once haunted my nightmares. For a time, I thought the ludere was the worst that it could get for me. Then I was drugged and brought here. Tilleo handed me over, eager to count the aurems he earned trading my flesh while I fractured. I was returned to the ludere after as though nothing had happened.

For too long, I thought that I wouldn't come back from what happened to me in this house, that it didn't get worse than that. Now, after all the years I've survived at the ludere, I don't know that I can choose a *worst thing* that happened. All of it scarred me in different ways, but it scarred nonetheless.

I pull the two daggers from my lower back, the stinger shape of the blades glinting in the waning moonlight. I study the dark manor, pushing away all of the painful recollections as I concentrate on remembering things that can help me. Things like the layout of the rooms inside and the faces of the fae who took from me then and will die for it tonight.

A flash of being carried through the front door like a prized pet and then taken upstairs to the bastard's quarters lights up in my mind. I use it to quickly map my hunt. I plan the path I'll take from the outside gate, choosing the most camouflaged part of the outer wall to climb over, and the quickest path across the lawns to a lower window that's been left partially open. I watch expectantly for guards, but surprisingly, no one is walking the perimeter at this hour. It's as though fate has wrapped this moment up in a neat little package, and all I need to do is tear it open and let the blood flow.

Silently I stalk to the part of the stone wall that's sheltered by a massive tree. I push through the ivy that's climbing up both the tree and the wall, and just as I find my first handhold and start to climb, arms wrap around my waist, and I'm yanked into a hard chest.

"Shh, it's just us," a deep, familiar voice whispers in my ear.

Skull pulls me back against his chest. Scorpius squeezes me gently once as though confirming that he's here and then releases my arm, the one he just caught mid-swing to keep me from slicing through Skull on pure instinct. I drop it to my side, my dagger still clutched tight in my palm, and breathe through the rush of adrenaline and shock.

"I could have stabbed you," I whisper-scold Skull, and I feel more than hear the vibrations of his quiet laughter against my back.

"Want to tell us why you ran off like your ass was on fire and are now trying to break into Duke Andross's home?" Bones asks, his tone light but his gaze searching and troubled.

"He's a duke?" I demand, my attention jumping from Bones back to the manor.

I glare at it and tighten my grip on my weapon. I can only see the peaks of the roof over the tall rock wall guarding the property, but it's enough to rankle more ire.

"Why are we here, Telson?" Scorpius asks, his own stare locked in the same direction as mine as though he'll be able to identify whatever it is I'm scowling at.

"I was sold to the bastard who lives in this house. It was only for a night, but it was enough. Now I'm going to kill him," I tell them, tensing in preparation for the objections I know are about to fly my way.

They're silent for several heartbeats as though my declaration needs time to slowly sink in. I shift my weight from one foot to the other, already working through how I'll fight my way through them if they try to get in my way. I won't enjoy it, it will damage us in more ways than just physically, but I will fuck them up with everything I have, because the duke is destined for my blade tonight, and there isn't a damn thing anyone can do to stop it.

"How are we getting in?" Bones asks, all levity gone from his tone and replaced by sharp focus.

"There's a window open on the bottom left, but if you want to avoid any potential run-ins with staff inside, the vines running up to the second floor on the outer right might be a more secure point of entry," Scorpius observes.

My head snaps to first Bones and then Scorpius. I stare at them both for a moment, bewildered by their reaction. They're not going to stop me? They're not even offering a word of censure or a grunt of admonition. I study all three of the Scorpions' faces, looking for traces that this is some kind of trick. I watch for any hint of doubt or concern, but all I see are three fae who are willing to do exactly what they said they'd do...give me anything and follow me any-where.

Their unwavering support and validation from the moment I woke up free from the ludere until now, takes my breath away. They stand guard around me, three of the most deadly and ruthless fae in all of the realms, ready and willing to ensure I get the retribution I need no matter the cost.

I don't know how I ever thought that I was just a game to them, a simple passing fancy.

How did I not see sooner what's etched so plainly on each of their faces, that I'm the *everything* they swore I was right from the beginning, and now...they are *everything* to me.

"I say we go through the front door," Skull states evenly. "Fuckers like this never lock up; they think they're untouch-able. Let's walk right in and show them that they aren't."

Rage bleeds into their voices, and fury tightens their shrewd stares. I swallow the lump of emotion in my throat and turn from them to the huge house that will be ringing with screams soon.

"The front door would make it easier to trace the path they carried me in from before," I agree, and all three Scor-pions nod.

It's decided.

"You want a boost to the top, or would you rather go the easy route and shadow walk to the front door?" Scor-pius asks me, his eyes moving from the ivy-covered stone in front of me to the dark shadows on the other side of the large tree trunk. "Technically, we can shadow walk right into the fucker's room, but we usually like to get a feel for the layout and exits when we move in on a hunt. Your call though."

It's all I can do not to bash my head against the wall for my stupidity. I'm so used to hiding my thura and relying on my body that it didn't even dawn on me to shadow walk to my destination.

Scorpius reaches up and presses a black strand of hair out of my face. "It'll get easier in time," he assures me, and I'm not entirely sure if he's talking about using my thura or wading through what was done to me. "Until then, I'm always up for the hard way."

I smile at his cheeky grin and push up on my toes, needing to taste that cocky smirk. I sink into the kiss for a beat, and then it's over before it even started. I pull the other blade from the small of my back and let the dark part of me stretch and slip into every nook and cranny of who I am.

"Shadow walk it is," I whisper, and in perfect synchronicity, we all move to the dark cloak on the other side of the tree.

"We'll follow your lead, Telson," Skull announces, as though there were any doubt, but there isn't. I know who I am to them and who they are to me, and I'm ready for anything and everything that comes next.

With a nod, I access the in-between. And just like they taught me to, I slip into the shadows, eager to make the world bleed.

44

THE DOOR OPENS SILENTLY, AND I ALMOST want to scoff at how right Skull was. The duke has everything but basic sense. He assumes there isn't anyone in the court who would dare to take what's his, to stand against him. History should have taught him better, but it'll be a pleasure to remind him of who I am before I feed him his own cock and watch him choke on it.

We step into a foyer that is a perfect match to my memory. The red-carpeted stairs look the same, as do the faces that stare out with dead eyes from paintings hung on the walls. Flashes from the last time I was here bombard me. I stop, one foot on the bottom step, and try to shake free of the shackles of pain and fear that are echoing through my thoughts.

"You're not her anymore," Skull mumbles quietly in my ear, his hand pressed to the small of my back. "You are not defenseless. You are not at their mercy. You are the dangerous one now. *You* are their reckoning."

His lips meet my neck in a brief but mooring kiss, and with a deep breath, I banish the memories from that night. I'm not here to relive them. I took back my power and my body a long time ago. Tonight is a new chapter, one that will stamp justice on the pages of everyone the monster within these walls has hurt, and I know there are others. Tonight is my gift to all of us, whether any of them ever know or not.

The stairs welcome our ascent silently, and we bank to the left at the top. We stick to the shadows as we slip down the long wide hallway. Closed doors line our path, but I don't bother to check whether they're occupied or not. Only the duke and his personal guard are calling to my blades. If anyone else on the other side of these doors chooses to add their name to that list, Skull, Scorpius, and Bones are there to deal with them.

I stop outside of the room I was brought to at the end of the hall. I use my hands and the language of assassins to signal that this is the place and what the plan is on the other side of the door. I'll slip in first, and they'll follow. They'll check for any secret entrances into the room and guard all of the exits while I get the names of the duke's guards. When I'm done with him, we'll hunt them. That is if the shit stain's screams don't have them rushing right into our blades. One can hope they make it that easy.

I press my ear to the seam of the door, making sure no one on the other side is up taking a piss or something. The faint sound of snoring is all I hear.

I twist the knob and carefully push the door open. Moving in like a wraith, I immediately note that it looks different from how I remember it. The deep green velvets and dark wood accents have been replaced by soft yellow silk and warm walnut furnishings. There's a feminine touch to the space that wasn't here before, which makes sense when I spot the blonde hair fanned out on a pillow at the head of the bed.

If there were any doubt about the owner of the room, it vanishes when I look to the other side of her and see the duke on his side, deep in the clutches of sleep.

I stalk to the bed, tracing the details of his face with a rage-filled gaze. His light brown hair is longer than it was but holds the same curl that kept falling into his face when he was on top of me. His pale skin is the smooth, line-free display that the rich can always afford to maintain. There's a scar on his upper lip that wasn't there before. I hope one of his victims gifted him the mark by biting him. His face is serene in sleep, but I know all too well the evil smirk he likes to wear when taking things that don't belong to him.

I raise a hand, signaling to the others that it's about to begin, and then I lean over the duke and press my dagger to his throat. He gasps as the sharp edge of steel violently pulls him from his slumber. I ready myself for the putrid green eyes that will open in shock any moment now, eyes that stalked me in my nightmares, eyes that I'll never fucking forget.

With a jerk that helps my dagger find his blood, he stares up at me, fear crumpling his features and floating in his...*blue* eyes. I startle, confusion shoving at me as I take in the monster, but I shove my bewilderment away and press harder at his throat.

"You promised me as you handed me off to your guards that you'd remember me and my sweet cunt. I hope that's true," I snarl at him as I press my face closer.

He blinks those fucking blue eyes up at me, his stare filled with nothing but terror, and I yank a memory from the vault I locked them in to try to figure out how I got his eyes so bloody wrong. I stare down at him, like he stared down at me, but the blue in front of me and the green from my memories don't reconcile.

"Oh stars, no!" the female next to me cries out.

She sits up with shocked terror, looking around the room and pulling her bed sheet to her chest as though it will protect her. She whimpers when she spots the Scorpions, and tears begin to trail down her sharp cheeks and drip off her chin.

"Who...who are you? What do you want?" she gasps out as she scoots back into the cushioned fabric of her ornate headboard.

"You know who we are," Scorpius tells her casually.

"And *you* know why we're here," I growl at the duke. "Did you really think no one would ever stop you?" I seethe at him. "That you could rape and torture to your heart's content and there'd be no reclamation?"

"I...I've never r-raped a soul. I would n-never," the duke stammers as he lifts his hands in what he hopes is an innocent gesture.

"I'm going to make you swallow your cock like you expect us to swallow your lies. Tilleo drugged me. *You* carried me to this very room, cut my clothes off, and tied them around the poster of your fucking bed."

His gaze alights with recognition, and I smile cruelly down at him as I witness it.

"Not...not me," he argues as a tear falls from the corner of his eye. "You want my brother."

I almost laugh at his pathetic defense, but then another tear falls from his blue eyes, and I pause.

"You're not Duke Andross?" I snap at him, my eyes roving over his face again.

It's him, it has to be.

The female next to us starts to cry harder, but I ignore her panicked sobs.

"I am," the duke confirms, and I press my other blade to his limp cock at the confession. "No! Wait! Please!" he yelps.

I could dine on his horror all night. It's so dense and enticing.

"I'm the *new* Duke Andross. My br-brother, the old duke, and his guard were murdered half a month ago. I...I *just* inherited the title."

His words unsteady me like a cut to the back of my legs. The blow hammers my chest, and I fight to hold on to the air in my lungs.

"What the fuck are you talking about?" I snarl, and the female scrambles off the bed.

"It's true. We just moved in a handful of days ago. I can prove it," she wails, taking a step toward a desk in the corner.

Bones has a knife to her throat before she can take two steps, and she starts crying even harder.

"I have no fight with the Order of Scorpions. I swear I've never tortured or raped in my life. My...my brother was a sick bastard. You want him, not me. Please don't hurt my mate," the duke implores.

"I've heard nothing about Duke Andross being murdered," Scorpius declares, and my need to end this fucker wars with the need to make sure he really is the one that should be gutted. Scorpius walks over to the desk the duchess was trying to get to and starts rifling through the missives there.

"I'm s-so sorry Pate hurt you. Please. It wasn't me," the duke pleads, and I glare at him.

"What color were his eyes?" I demand, the blood from his neck seeping into the light yellow silk of his pillow case and starting to slowly spread.

"What?" the duke asks, confused.

"His eyes, what color where his fucking eyes?"

"Green. Like dead grass. They were light green," he rushes to answer.

I want to scream. I want to slit this bastard's throat regardless of who he is. The same sick blood has to run in his veins. Blue eyes, green eyes, what does it really fucking matter? I have to make them pay. My gut knots with rage, and my heart pounds so hard it feels as though it's trying to tear itself from my chest to attack the duke all on its own.

"The king is investigating the murder. It happened outside of an inn while Pate was on a diplomatic assignment. His death hasn't been announced publicly. We swore to keep it quiet while the court looks for whoever is responsible. Even the servants were sworn to secrecy."

"Mommy?" a tiny voice calls from the door, and I look in time to see the brass knob start to turn.

Skull is there in a flash, pressing his body against the door to keep it from opening. The duchess starts to hyperventilate, and the duke presses up from the bed like he's forgotten a dagger is at his throat as he tries to go to the little girl calling from the other side of the door.

"Mommy, I had a bad dream," the little voice calls out again, and my heart feels more like a battering ram against my chest.

"They're telling the truth, Telson," Scorpius announces as he lifts a long sheet of parchment from the desk. "This is the transfer of title and a letter advising Carn Andross to take residence in the manor for his own safety."

A ringing starts in my ears as I glance from the scrolls held in Scorpius's hands back to the duke. His pleading blue eyes stay fixed on mine, his stare begging me to be merciful.

I don't know if I have it in me.

I've killed indiscriminately since I can remember. I just destroyed every sailor on a ship who dared to step my way. I didn't ask if they deserved it. I did what Eacon brought me there to do—help her find her long earned justice. Why should this be any different?

"Mommy, please," the girl begs, her frail voice now wobbly with tears. There's a small thump, like she's pressing her little body against the door to gain access.

"Please don't hurt her," the duchess beseeches, and Bones looks over at me as though all he needs is a nod and he'll gut her where she stands.

Another tiny thump hits the door, and the sound of crying grows louder on the other side.

"I'll be right there, Jovie. Go back to your room. I'll come tuck you in," the duchess shakily calls to her daughter, her spine straightening and a defiant light sparking in her eyes.

"I need you," Jovie pleads at the door.

Anger shreds me as I focus on the dagger held against the duke's throat. The unfairness of what's happening, the justice I'm being denied, burns in my veins. Rectitude demands that I do something, but I'm drowning in indecision. Maybe *this* duke deserves a bloody death. Maybe he doesn't. But what does the little cria at the door deserve? What right do I have to destroy her young life? What right do I have to take from her, like so many have taken from me?

I could kill her parents. Kill her and stop every beating heart in this house, but where does it end?

I am death's hand, but I won't destroy for destruction's sake.

I lift the blade from the duke's throat, and he blinks up at me in shock. Frustration screams in my mind as I step back from the bed. My hands shake with the effort to hold back, to deny the bloodlust coursing through me. A tempestuous thirst for ruination pounds at my resolve, and I falter under the force bearing down on me to shower the room with blood.

"Get me the fuck out of here," I demand quietly, the order a mangled mix of warning and an urgent plea to rescue me from the edge of vicious violence I'm teetering on.

Without another word, Scorpius, Skull, and Bones are at my side.

"Don't ever give us a reason to come back," Scorpius warns as someone pulls me to their chest and backs me into a shadowed corner.

My breaths grow short and volatile as I battle my inner petition for pain and savagery. I've never refused it before. I've always leaned into it, and now I feel as though I'm falling, and the landing rushing up at me promises nothing but agony.

"I'm sorry," the duke laments as he rises from his bed.

His mate rushes into his arms, wrapping him up in a fierce hug, but his words aren't for her. His blue eyes are fixed on mine, anguish and regret pouring down his face in a steady stream of tears.

"I'm so sorry for what he did to you."

The in-between washes over me as his sorrow and his words wrap around my ribs and compress them against my heart. The last thing I see is a streak of long blonde braids and a pink night dress as Jovie flies into her parents' arms.

I chose her innocence over the roar of death, and as the shadows in the corner swallow me whole, I can't help but wish that someone had once done the same for me.

45

TALL GRASS SWAYS AROUND MY THIGHS. COOL, wet air slaps at my cheeks. My boots press into spongy ground. I pull in gasping breaths of leather and steel, smoke and salt, and something sweet and blooming.

The Scorpions.

A thunderous crash reverberates somewhere below, and a sky of angry clouds stands guard over the turbulent sea that reaches out and kisses the horizon. Arms are still wrapped around me, and I'm pretty sure they're the only thing holding me together. I shiver against the crisp spray that rises over the edge of the cliffs we're standing on, but

I'm not cold. My body is fighting against the decision I made, and I'm paying the price in every way.

My head is a jumbled mess of anger and admonishment. I don't know if I'm more furious with myself or fate for dangling justice and punishment the way it did, only to snatch them away when I needed them as badly as I do right now. I was robbed and denied, and it's all so fucked up I'm being torn apart by the injustice of it all.

I craved the death of the duke and his personal guard for so long, long before I knew that's who they were. I had no real way or hope of ever finding them, but that didn't stop me from planning, from envisioning how I would storm into that fucking house and destroy everyone who ever touched me. I worked it out in my mind over and over again, meticulously planning in the quiet hours of the night when I was afraid of what nightmares awaited me if I closed my eyes and succumbed to sleep. I didn't know when or how I would find them, but I've steeped and stewed on exactly how I would make them suffer when I did.

The mountain was just...there. A beacon of requital that'd been waiting patiently for me. Retribution should have been mine for the taking. I walked into that horrible fucking room, knowing it was destiny, that I was meant to be there to take back the final piece that they stole from me, a piece that only their horrific deaths could restore. But someone already cut the fuckers down, and now I'm left shaking and panting from the loss of what should have been mine. Vengeance pressed against my lips, whispering dark vows of justice and punishment, and just when

I leaned into the promised kiss, it all disappeared with a taunting laugh echoing in the air all around me.

"What do you need, Beasty? What can we do?" Bones demands, his face so close I can taste his breath, the heat of his presence coiling around me like it's trying to temper my defenses.

But I feel so far away.

I feel so fucking lost.

"I need to fucking kill a dead man," I snarl out before a new rush of rage and misery tries to bowl me over.

Arms tighten around me from behind, but I'm smothered by overpowering emotion. I want to rage and lament, destroy and keen. I vacillate between unbridled fury and drowning sorrow for who I was, what they took. I couldn't discharge any of this emotion in the ludere. It would have only gotten me killed. I had to find other ways to cope, other ways to snatch power from the masters who tried to hold it out of reach. Leto helped. He gave me the strength to take back my body, to find pleasure and passion in what I could do with it, in what could be done to it when I wanted. We had no limits between us. We explored every inch and crevice so that all of it could be reclaimed by me. Reclaimed by my consent. Reclaimed by my enjoyment.

When my body was my own again, I poured every drop of wrath and every tear I wanted to cry but couldn't into the fighting pits during the day and fucking Leto under the stars at night. Gradually, bit by bit, the pain started to dull. Different wounds were carved into my body and my heart by the masters, and my dark thoughts and haunting memories quieted. What happened in that house became something I survived. Something that happened. But I'm more than that now, more than what they tried to take from me. I'd whittled away at everything inside of me until all that remained was the ruthless savage that Tilleo always wanted.

I'm free, and now that I'm standing on a cliff and staring out into a raging sea that's begging me to rage alongside it, I can finally let go. For once, I don't have to hide. I don't have to shove it all down or grit my teeth and bear it. I can finally scour it all from my soul.

My knees give out and force me to the ground, dragging Skull down with me. I rip into the wet soil with my hands and press my face to the stalks of grass and small yellow flowers sprouting beneath me. A scream builds in my chest and then pours out of my mouth, clawing across the ground until it leaps from the cliff and charges at the crashing waves. Another one tears out of me just as the first one dies, and the violent crush of the sea against the cliff face sounds like an answering roar. The water bellows with me as I try to purge the fury and torment from my veins.

I wail and scream as I expel the pain. I rip open the soldered doors trapping everything I was forced to bury and ignore. I expel everything I've choked down for too long, uncovering layers of loss and torment. The agony evolves as I scream, the source transforming from my body being sold and used without my permission to the beatings and torture at the hands of Tilleo and his masters. I rage and disgorge until I'm back in Dorsin's quarters. Time and my memories rewind in a slow crawl as I relive being carried down the hall by brutal orcs and then waking up in an iron cage.

A black wall slams into me then. My anguish tries to push past it, tries to raze it to the ground, but no matter what I do, all I see is the blank reminder of the nothing that I come from. My wails wane. My screams are ripped away by the cleansing wind and drowned in the dark ocean beyond. I'm left lying in the grass, the flattened flowers as empty and blank as my origins are.

I don't know how long I lie there. I can't say when Scorpius and Bones move to surround me. Put their hands on my back or my leg in silent support. Skull's arms are still wrapped around my waist like he's worried I might fly away on the wings of my fury if he lets go. The Scorpions don't speak. Instead, we bask in the sound of the waves as they try to wash all the harm away.

There's no judgment. No promises that it will get better. No exchange of horror stories to help me feel less alone.

They just sit with me.

Breathe with me.

Hurt with me.

Each of us floating in the abyss of unfair fate and the countless wrongs against us.

A hollowness sits in my chest where everything once sat heavy and onerous. I know the demons of my past won't disappear forever. No matter how much I wish they'd been shoved over the cliff, never to return, they'll crawl back. They'll once again settle silently inside me until another day like today wakes them up and forces me to fight for what they try to claim.

I will.

I'll never let them win no matter how bloody they leave me after our battles.

I look over at the Scorpions, and something resonates within me. Maybe if I fill the caverns in my chest with other things, replace the hollow with the happy, there will be less room for the monstrous things that plague me.

A trail of crimson drips from gouges in Bones's arm.

Shit. Did I do that?

My fangs drop as I watch the trails of blood spill over to spatter against the bright yellow petals of the flowers below.

"You can drink," Bones offers, his black gaze studying my empty eyes and the tips of my sharp teeth that are just visible between my lips.

I stare at him, confused at first by the offer.

Drink?

I taste the invitation on my tongue, trying to discern if that's what I need right now to fill the crater in my chest.

"Take it, my Blood, take whatever you need," Bones implores, but it isn't what's spilling down his arm that's calling to me the loudest.

It's his mouth. His fangs. The way his tongue strokes the words he's bestowing alongside his blood, that's the siren's song I want to answer right now.

I grab his arm, but instead of lapping up his scarlet offering, I pull Bones to me. My lips crash into his. I'm rough, unapologetic, and one of his fangs slices across my bottom lip. A sweet tang blesses the joining of our mouths. My tongue searches for his, and he moans into the kiss when they finally meet. He sucks my lip hard, and I groan into his mouth as he swallows me down, his hands in my hair as he pulls me closer and deepens the kiss.

The void in my chest fills the tiniest degree, and if I could crawl inside of Bones right now to escape the sting of the anguish that still remains, I would. He captures my face between his hands and presses into me as he kisses me fiercely. It's as though the ache is inside him now, too, and the only thing holding it at bay is the way our mouths fuse together and our tongues dance. Bones leans me back until I bump into Skull, who continues to guard me from behind.

I moan at the sensation of being caught between the two of them, and Bones greedily steals the sound for himself. I pull my mouth from his and turn to pull Skull to me. He claims me just as fiercely with a molten kiss that feels as though it melts me and then reshapes me all in the span of tangled tongues and enthralling lips.

Scorpius is there when I reach for him. His thumb runs across the small cut on my lip. I disregard any concern he might be harboring and instead consume him. He meets me nip for nip, stroke for stroke, until the frigid ache inside of me begins to warm from the growing fire their mouths and touches start to stoke. I pull back, panting for a whole new reason.

"I don't know what the fuck that was," I admit breathily as I look at each of them in turn.

I feel as though I need to explain myself, even though none of them are looking at me like they need answers. My *take me or leave me* personality feels inadequate for what just happened though. I just lost it in an epic and all-consuming way, and I want them to know that they can still trust me and rely on me despite my...moment.

"Where I'm from, we call it a kiss," Bones teases.

I laugh at Bones's joke, something that felt forever out of reach only a few moments ago, but I'm suddenly light. I'm unburdened, and now there's room for the Scorpions where there should be, instead of only pain and anger.

I assess the warm gleam in Bones's dark gaze, taking in the heat banked in Skull's and Scorpius's stare, and it's clear my explanations aren't needed. There's a knowing in their eyes, like they've been exactly where I am now. But of course they have. They haven't shared every dark detail of their pasts, but they've told me enough to know that each of them has been powerless, shredded, beyond all hope, and then it all changed.

Just like me, they were forced to work through it, to face the horrors and the injustices. They built an Order on top of that foundation instead of allowing the weight of such heavy things to bury them. The Scorpions rose from the dregs of what was done to them, and they grew into who they are now. And what shines back at me in each of their gazes is the unwavering faith that I will too.

The four of us are kneeling in the tall grass and flowers. Skull is at my back, Bones at my front, and Scorpius by my side. Each of us is breathing heavily from the kissing and adrenaline of everything else that just happened. I move to get up, and the Scorpions do the same, each of them watching me carefully as though I'm far more fragile than I am.

"Can we go home, or is there somewhere nearby that's safe?" I ask.

"Safe for what?" Scorpius questions at the same time Skull answers, "We should stay in the Dawn Court. It's easier for the Vulpi to summon us if they need something."

I don't answer Scorpius.

"Summix's tavern is safe, our quarters are warded, and he's as loyal and trustworthy as they come," Bones offers. "What do you need, Beasty?"

Again I don't answer, leaving the question to drip to the ground like the slowly closing wounds on his arm. I step away from them and stride to the shadows that brought us here.

"Safe for what, Telson?" Scorpius demands more insistently, moving to cut me off.

I stare up at him, annoyed. I know what I want, but I also don't want to be talked out of it or told I need to wait for a list of reasons that I don't give a searing shit about right now. I'm not the fragile little flower they think I am no matter how unhinged I might look. I needed to get some things out. Granted, I didn't realize just how badly I needed it until the screams were shredding my throat, but now I need *them*. I've never been more certain of anything in my life.

Scorpius reaches for me, pulling me into him, and I go, fighting the urge to try to burrow into his soul like he's burrowed into mine. I pull in a deep breath and look into his sooty gaze as I answer.

"To fuck you," I tell him evenly.

Scorpius's eyes widen with surprise, and I feel satisfaction at catching him off guard. Really that kiss should have told him everything there is to know about what I want right now, but I'll take the win of throwing him off-kilter, even if it's only for a moment.

"I'm in," Bones declares, and he starts traipsing toward the shadows as though it's a race he's determined not to lose.

"Auset—" Scorpius starts.

"That's Telson to you, *Scorpius*," I correct, and a possessive glint sparks in his glamoured inky stare. I glare at him.

"If the word *later* so much as slips out of your mouth right now, I will make you regret it," I warn.

"What you just went through, what I think you're still going through right now... I don't want to make it worse. I don't want to set you off," he argues, his tone deep and worried, but I hear the need bleeding through the edge of his agitation.

"I know my own mind, Scorpius. This isn't me running from what just happened or looking for a haze of sex and orgasms to get lost in. I need you. I want you...all of you. I'm not being driven by bloodlust or loss. You're not taking advantage or disregarding my emotional state. There are still walls between us"—I gesture between our bodies—"and I want to tear them down. I'm ready."

His eyes study mine, and I hate the uncertainty I see etched in his face. His hesitation makes me want to scream. They've been pushing for this. They've been edging me closer and closer to joining with them in every possible way, and now that I'm making it clear that I'm here for all of it, Scorpius is...wavering?

Fuck that.

"You said I was a Scorpion..." I snap at him. "That I was your future and you were mine. Well, I'm right fucking here! Take me already!"

My heart plummets a little as he just stares at me, his chest heaving as hard as mine is right now. I can practically see the debate in his mind, and it's maddening. I want to shake him, tell him to just—His mouth is punishing as it meets mine. He grabs my ass with both of his hands and pulls me up. I wrap around him as he devours me, finally letting go of everything that's been holding him back. The handles of the blades hidden in his pants rub against my inner thighs, and it turns me on as much as the feel of his hard cock through his leathers does.

The in-between wraps around us while flames lick down my body and settle between my thighs as he shadow walks us away. Instead of stepping back into the storeroom of Summix's tavern, he strides out into a large room with four pallets that have been pushed together against one wall. There's a roaring fire blazing in the massive hearth, and a large furry animal skin is lying in front of the glimmering flames, taking up almost the entire center of the room. When Scorpius moves to set me on the makeshift bed, I unlatch myself from him and stride instead to the pelt on the floor.

His brow furrows and he looks at the comfy bed, but I don't need the softness of tangled sheets and a feathery mattress. I need the hardness and familiarity of the floor, and I *need* all of them right now. Skull breaks the standoff by striding over and kissing the ever loving fuck out of me. I groan at the power his mouth gives and takes, and then I'm lost to him and his dominating, demanding, exquisitely perfect kiss.

"Strip her down while I check the wards," Scorpius orders, his voice gruff and dripping with need.

Bones's hands are on me then as he slowly, sensually starts to pull my weapons from my rapidly overheating body. Skull works his mouth against mine until I'm a mewling mess. His tongue swirls and strokes, a rough mimic of how I want his cock to be sliding in and out of my drenched cunt. Tingles of release are already collecting through my limbs, and none of the Scorpions have really started to touch me yet. I'm still fully kitted and on the verge of coming in my rinds. It's not exactly how I envisioned breaking in my armor, but now it might need to become a tradition every time I put it on.

The driving urge to claim them grows even more insistent, and I've never been overly patient. It may take me time to decide things, to move in one direction or another until I've worked through all the possibilities and consequences of my actions, but once I've decided on something, I go for it with a single-minded focus that helps make me the best at what I do.

I don't doubt.

I don't question.

I take.

Skull begins to unclip my chest plate as Bones continues to pull the small arsenal of blades from my body. He places everything on pegs that have been secured to the far wall, the knives, daggers, sword, and ax joined by Bones's larger weapons as he starts to pluck them from his kit. Pieces of my armor are handed off as it's peeled from me. I never knew something as simple as removing vambraces could feel so fucking erotic.

It's as though every plate of protection isn't just pulled from my body, it's armor that's being removed from my very soul. They're laying me bare in every possible way, inside and out, and while it's an alarmingly vulnerable experience, I've never felt more powerful in my life.

Scorpius's whispered chant as he secures the wards harmonizes with my shallow breaths and whimpers. The last of my kit is set aside, and Skull pulls his mouth from mine, his fingers finding the hem of my rind top as his black gaze consumes mine with overflowing desire.

"I've wanted my hands on you like this since the first night of the Bidding. You wrapped your grip around Scorpius's cock and mouthed off to each of us like you owned us already. We didn't know it yet, but you did," Skull whispers possessively against my mouth.

Goose bumps chase his touch as he unhurriedly begins to push the onyx fabric up my torso. Bones drops to his knees on the fur behind me and starts to pepper lazy nibbles and kisses up my back as Skull pulls the top over my head. The leather tie binding the coiled braid at the back of my head is pulled free, and Bones unravels the plait as Skull hooks his thumbs in my bottoms and starts to work them down my hips.

"The wards are reinforced and I've blocked any sound from leaking out," Scorpius announces as he moves to the wall of weapons and starts adding his own.

His glamoured gaze takes in what his brothers are doing to me before steadying on mine with such naked need. I'm certain his searing stare alone could make me come if he looks at me like that long enough.

"Are you ready to scream for us, Telson?" Scorpius purrs.

Deft fingers begin to unhook the binding around my chest, and it falls away, the warm air a sensual caress against my heavy breasts and tightening nipples. The groan that falls out of Scorpius's mouth as his hungry eyes fall to my chest has me feeling predatory and wild for them to take me now.

I fix the leader of the Scorpions with a challenging look, more than ready for the dark promises gleaming in his eyes. Purposefully I drop my gaze to the bulge between his thighs and cock an eyebrow in sultry defiance.

"Are you ready to make me?"

Scorpius's answering grin calls to the pulse of longing thrumming at my core. They're mine, and it's time each of us cements that unshakable truth.

46

LIGHT FLICKERS OVER MY SHADOW-AND-BONE-soaked skin as Bones wraps his large palms around my hips and slowly spins me until I'm facing him. Even on his knees, he's chest high, and he nuzzles my nipple with his nose as he looks up at me like I'm the moon to his stars and he's prepared to worship me for the rest of time.

Bright white slashes trick the eye to make it look as though I have a skeletal abdomen, and I realize that the glamour is the last barrier between me and my Scorpions.

"Take it off," I order softly, my fingers tracing Bones's glamoured face, but my command is aimed at Scorpius.

There will be a time and place where I'll fuck them in full glamour. That Telson will take Scorpius, Skull, and Bones and wring every ounce of pleasure from them while riding the high of a successful hunt. But right now, this first time, I *need* Tarek, Curio, and Riall. The compulsion to take in every detail of who they really are without the guise of the Order cloaking their features is demanding. I need them as stripped and bare as I am. I want nothing between us as we finally come together and for nothing to ever get between us again.

Stripped down to nothing but his skintight rinds, Scorpius nods, understanding exactly what I'm craving as he strides over to Skull. He presses their mouths together, only this time Scorpius inhales, reclaiming the thura coating Curio's skin instead of bestowing it. The power exchange between them is far more titillating in the light of a soft fire while Bones kisses lower and lower on my stomach.

I want to feel each of them everywhere.

"Spread that pretty pussy for me, Beasty," Bones sensually orders, his hands sliding up my thighs as his lips skim just over the crest of my mound.

I gasp as he presses his face harder against the lips of my cunt. Bones growls his approval as though he can scent the desire that's collecting there for him.

"I watched from the shadows as that little fuck at the ludere spread these thighs and licked you until you wiggled and gasped your release," Bones confesses, but he seems to be talking directly to my cunt.

His soul-owning black eyes suddenly flicker up to mine.

"You looked like the goddess of death herself when you stabbed that guard in the head that night. Destruction and damnation pumped through your veins instead of blood, and I wanted to lick you head to toe and taste all of you right then and there. That unworthy little shit got to feast on you instead, and I've dreamed that it was my face buried in your pussy every fucking night since."

Bones's tongue snakes out and flicks at the seam of me.

"Give it to me, Beasty," he implores hungrily with a growl that I feel all the way to the darkest recesses of who I am. "Give it to me until it's all I can smell and taste. I want you dripping off my fucking chin, your pleasure stamped all over me, now give it to me!"

Need ricochets through me, and I widen my stance my for him. Bones wastes no time grabbing my knee and throwing it over his shoulder. I grab his head so I don't lose my balance as he spreads my lips and licks me from ass to clit in one long leisurely stroke. I groan as he slurps me up, circling my clit before sucking it into his hot, talented mouth. I throw my head back, reveling in the way he devours me.

Scorpius presses against me. His strong hands turning my face until our eyes meet. He studies me, his gaze scorching and seductive. Slowly, he brings his mouth to mine, the stubble on his chin and cheeks tickling me. Instead of kissing me, he inhales deeply, drawing his power from my very pores as Bones begins to shove his tongue into my cunt. Curio's callused hands knead my breasts, and I pant and growl into Scorpius's mouth as each of them work me over.

I've known for a while now how good it feels to be sucked on and touched like this. But what Leto and I discovered on the roof of the ludere is nothing compared to how the Scorpions make me feel. One body plying mine with pleasure is incredible, but to have all three of them pressing against me, kissing, sucking, and preparing me for what's to come is a gift from the fucking stars themselves. It's not just physical; it's not just chasing our release. There's so much more between us, and it heightens every caress, every kiss, every heated look until all I can see and feel is them, and all I need is this.

Scorpius swallows his magic and my needy noises, and Bones presses his fingers into me and then starts to rhythmically flick his tongue over my clit.

"You like that, Moonling?" Curio silkily asks, his breath a warm caress against the shell of my ear. He pinches my nipples, the pressure and release of his fingers against the taut buds in perfect sync with what Bones's mouth is doing between my thighs. Scorpius reclaims the last of his thura, and then he sucks on the bottom of my lip, nipping it hard once, the slight sting of pain enhancing the sensations of pleasure I'm feeling all over.

Scorpius steps away from me, and Curio moves in at my back.

"Bones," Scorpius calls, and his brother lifts his face from my cunt, his mouth shiny and coated in evidence of just how badly I want them.

Scorpius leans down and presses his mouth close to Bones's lips. They're both right over my clit, and when Scorpius inhales deeply, it's as though his thura is stroking over my sensitive bundle of nerves while he steals away Bones' glamour to reveal Riall.

Riall's fingers begin to thrust in and out of my wet cunt faster and harder, and Curio kisses my neck while his adept hands pinch and pull at my heavy breasts. An orgasm detonates through me hard and fast. All I see is red as the tide of delicious, tingling ecstasy roars through me. I'm so used to having to be quiet while I come that I automatically clamp down on the euphoric shout that tries to erupt from my mouth, and it comes out sounding more like a feral snarl. My hips roll and my body twitches as ecstasy ripples through me. My legs start to give out, and I'm grabbed by Curio's strong hold before I fall to the fur pelt at our feet. Curio twists and maneuvers me into a different position, while the potent pleasure still buzzing in my limbs leaves me dazed and happily pliant.

"Now, now, Auset, that will *not* do," Tarek scolds, his glamour now gone too and his tone dripping with dark wickedness. "I want each of those screams. I want the sound of you coming ringing endlessly in my head. Don't you fucking hold back on us now, Scorpion."

I'm sitting on something wet and warm. Curio's hard naked chest is pressed against my back as I lean on him. I open my eyes as the echoes of my release begin to fade. The glamours are gone. Needy ice-blue eyes look down at me, and I realize that Riall's on the floor and I'm now strad-dling his face. Tarek has his impressive cock gripped in his hand, and he's languidly stroking it while waiting for me to submit to his will. I don't know what I do, or what he sees in my face, but he rewards me with a devastatingly beautiful smile. I lick my lips as a bead of desire drips from his tip, and I have to fight the urge to bend over and lick it from the floor where it fell.

"That's our girl," Tarek coos at me, as though I'm the most magnificent being he's ever beheld.

He bends toward me and kisses me fiercely. I try to lean into his delectable mouth, demanding more, but he pulls away, smiling at the small noise of outrage I make when he does.

"I want you to fuck Riall's face. Then Curio is going to get your ass ready for me," he orders against my kiss-swollen lips. "That ass was mine since the day you hid my dagger between those cheeks. I'm going to take it now."

A delicious shiver of anticipation drips from my breasts, trickling down my abdomen and settling wetly in my core.

"It's about fucking time," I half moan, half sigh, and then I pull Tarek's mouth back to mine, claiming him as thoroughly as I can while I begin to grind unabashedly against Riall's mouth and tongue.

"Can you take all of us at once, or do you need us one at a time?" Curio asks me as he bends me forward and starts to massage the globes of my ass as I ride his brother's face.

I don't even have to think about it. "I need you all. Right. Fucking. Now."

It's intoxicating and overwhelming, the way I feel in such a short amount of time about these three fae. If I hadn't survived this long trusting my intuition and my instincts, I might have never given them a chance. But it's right. In every possible way, this was written in the stars. Tonight has incinerated any worry I ever held about how we'd seal our bond. I'm going to give myself to them wholeheartedly and with wild abandon. And it's going to be life shattering in the best possible way.

"You're fucking exquisite," Curio declares, his hand caressing my ass before he dips his fingers into my wet pussy alongside Riall's tongue.

Curio pulls my release and my need back over my ass, circling me in a promising way that has me rolling my hips in a plea for him to deepen his touch while Riall tries to consume my cunt whole. Curio slowly, expertly slips his large finger into my ass at the same time Riall sucks on my clit. I don't know how they know the perfect way to strum my body into a chord of mind-blowing pleasure, but they do, and I'll never be the same after this. There's no going back to anything I had before, not when I know this kind of perfect pleasure exists. Not when the three of them seem to be made to stroke, suck, and fuck me like this.

An orgasm begins to build again, and I look over at Tarek, whose burning blue gaze is glued to the way his brothers are playing with me.

I need more.

I need all of them.

"Fuck my mouth," I command Tarek as Curio inserts another thick digit into my ass.

Riall presses his face deeper into my now sopping cunt. Curio nips and sucks at my shoulder, his other hand, the one that's not deep in my ass, wrapping around my chest and tugging at my tits. Tarek's ice-blue gaze grows molten at my order. Holding his long thick shaft, he moves tauntingly closer to my mouth.

"Now," I plead as another orgasm begins to tingle and coalesce at my center.

I'm close, so fucking close, but I have to have him in my throat before I can detonate the way I need to. I want to feel all of them as I'm worshipped into another shattering orgasm.

Tarek lines the head of his cock with my mouth, and I stretch out my tongue and lick the tip of him. He hisses and frustratingly tries to control the slow slide between my lips. I'm on the edge of maddening euphoria, and *measured* and *gradual* are the last things I want right now.

Fuck respectful. I want feral.

Roughly, I grab his ass and shove him deep into my mouth. His cock rubs against the barrier in my throat that makes me want to reject his size, but I swallow him down, forcing him as deep as he can possibly get. The dark brown curls at the base of his shaft tickle my nose, and I dig my fingers into the cheeks of his ass, refusing to let him pull back or put any space between his cock and my throat. The primal growl that tears out of him and the way he starts bouncing his hips and making his cock dance in my mouth and down my throat is exactly what I need to explode again.

I close my eyes as sparks of satisfaction bloom and burst all through me. Tarek pulls out, uncorking the rapturous scream that rips out of me as I ride the peak of my orgasm and tip easily over the edge to exultation.

Riall's accompanying mumble-shouts of exhilaration are lost to the folds of my cunt as I drench him in my cream and my cries for more.

Curio scissors and stretches my ass, pressing more of my cum into me, easing the way his fingers work in and out as I ride the ebb and flow of my release.

"She's ready," Curio declares, his proclamation dripping with salacious satisfaction as he picks me up off of Riall's face and spins us until he's on the ground and I'm being held over his rock-hard cock.

My cunt clenches in eager anticipation of what I know is coming. I've already had two life-shattering orgasms, and we're just getting started.

"Yes, fuck yes," I whimper greedily.

I don't know how this is my life, but I'm thanking the stars and the moon with everything in me that it is. Everything up until now has been about survival, about brutality and the hunt. I've claimed a hard-won seat at the table of blood, bone, and blades, and I thought that was all I would ever have. I take in Tarek, Riall, and Curio, and it once again hits me, there's so much more to life and love, so much more to what I have with my Scorpions.

I might not know how I ended up at the ludere. I might have scars on top of scars from everything I've endured to get here, but I'm here. I made it. I'm in their arms. In their blood. In their soul. And they're in mine.

Forcing my legs to support my weight, I pull away from Curio's grip and his waiting dick. Halfway boneless, I crawl over to Riall.

He's lying in a daze in front of the fire like he's floating in his own pool of bliss. It's adorable and I can't help but laugh at the dreamy look on his gorgeous face. He's soaked.

Desire drips down his chin and throat, and he licks his lips like he still can't get enough. It's obscene and tantalizing and makes me impossibly more turned on than I already am. I kiss him thoroughly, the taste of my orgasms seasoning our lips and tongues, creating an ambrosial combination of flavors that I could sip on for the rest of my days.

I love the way he tastes with my cum all over him.

Riall crushes my mouth to his as roughly as he crushed his face into my pussy. I revel in the way he dominates me until Curio grabs my hips and steals me away.

I'm used to being the aggressor when it comes to fucking. I thought I would always need that control in order to ride the high of intimate contact the way that I want. But handing the reins over to the Scorpions is a lesson in rapture I'm eager to learn over and over again for the rest of my fucking life. I had no idea how hot I could get simply following their lead and being manhandled into one orgasm after another. I have no experience with this level of intimacy, and there's something incredibly erotic and alluring in giving others control and knowing that it will be used *for* me and not *against* me.

I press my palms against Curio's hard chest and watch his gorgeous face as he aligns his cock with my pussy. I sink down onto him, his already hooded eyes growing even heavier as I bury the entirety of his massive length in my wet cunt.

"Fuck, that's so good, Moonling," he grunts, and we sit there for a moment as I adjust to the size of him, and he relishes the feel of me.

All I can do is moan my agreement. Words are too complicated to form past the pure pleasure that's wracking my body.

"Fuck me. Show me how you like it before we all take you at once," Curio commands, his heated hickory gaze focused on my cunt as I lift off his shaft to the dark tip and then drop back down until he's deep inside of me again.

I watch Curio like a predator hunting prey, and he watches the way I roll my hips and grind my clit against him as I start to fuck him the way I've needed each of them to fuck me. Curio feels incredible. The way he fills me, the depths he touches as I ride him, it's almost indescribable how good it is. This carnal connection unlocks parts of me that will only ever be for him and his brothers, and I wouldn't have it any other way.

"You feel so bloody perfect," I purr as I ride Curio's cock, loving the sound of our joining and the feel of my tits bouncing heavily in tandem with the rise and fall of my hips.

Tarek grabs handfuls of my swinging breasts, pulling me back until I'm flush with his chest, and his dick is rubbing against the crack of my ass.

"Are you ready for me, love?" he asks, the question resonant and rumbling as he licks the shell of my ear and nips at the lobe.

"I've *been* ready for you," I groan-growl in answer, but it sounds less assertive and more like a breathy needy mewl.

Tarek's kisses trail down the side of my neck, over my shoulder, and then down my spine. He holds my hips, his touch telling me to sink down on his brother and wait. Riall sits up from his dazed dozing on the floor just as Tarek starts to push into my ass. I breathe through the tight, stuffed sensation and do my best to relax into the exquisite invasion of Tarek in my ass and Curio deep in my pussy.

"Fuck, I can feel you sliding into her, Tarek," Curio grunts, his fingers pressing harder into my hips as he struggles to hold himself still.

I moan and tighten around both of them as soon as Tarek pushes all the way in. I'm bent over, my chest is flush with Curio's, my back covered by Tarek's wide frame. I've never felt so surrounded by undeniable strength while also feeling safe and cared for in every possible way.

"That's it, love," Tarek groans. "Take us both, feel us claiming every part of you while you claim us right back."

Curio and Tarek work together as they take turns easing out of me and then pushing back in. The pace is slow, almost leisurely as we all settle into the rhythm and sensation of one another. As my body opens for them I push up from Curio's chest, my palms resting on his pecks as he starts to thrust up into me harder and faster. Tarek holds my hips as his pace begins to match his brothers and I moan in approval. Riall's heated gaze roves over my bouncing tits, my thrown back head, the way his brothers tightly hold on to me as they carefully, expertly edge me closer to ecstasy. His libidinous stare flares to an inferno as he watches Tarek and Curio fuck me like it was all we were ever made to do.

"Faster," I beg, and with satisfied grunts, Curio and Tarek eagerly comply.

The pace starts to pick up, accelerating until we're nothing more than slapping flesh, delirious groans, and undiluted desire. I reach for Riall.

"I want you dripping down *my* chin," I demand, parroting his eager edict from earlier, and Riall moans in time with Curio and Tarek.

We're a symphony of wordless praise and encouraging moans and whimpers. My Scorpions start to fuck me harder as Riall runs the tip of his cock across my lips. I open, fervent, bordering on desperate, to take him in. I'm not going to last long with each of them inside of me like this, as the building orgasm is already making *everything* feel so incredibly sensitive. The three of them together feel better than I could have ever imagined. I thought I might feel overwhelmed, but all I feel is hungry for more.

Giving me what I'm begging for, Riall thrusts into my mouth. Each Scorpion pistons their cocks into me at exactly the same time, as though they've trained all of their lives for this moment and the tempo has to be perfect. Curio kneads my tits and pinches my nipples as he hammers into my pussy. Tarek fucks my ass as though he's stamping his name there with each slam of his hips. Every wild and savage thrust drives me closer and closer to blissful oblivion. Riall mumbles words of adoration that string together into a hum of worship and praise as he threads his fingers in my hair and loses himself to my mouth and throat.

They work together perfectly to show me exactly who I am to them, and I do the same as an orgasm rips through me so brutally that everything blurs and becomes disjointed except the sound of their names spilling out of my mouth on a pleasure-soaked scream. The staggering and wondrous climax feels like it yanks my soul from my body, wraps it up in ecstasy, dips it in delirium, and then places it back covered in pure paradise.

Riall's growl is feral as he comes down my throat. Lost in complete euphoria, I drink him down, savoring every last spurt. Curio and then Tarek both press as deep inside of me as they can and then bellow out their own release. I'm held firmly, like I'm something infinitely precious and fragile as hot ropes of cum fill me, and each of the Scorpions takes what they want while giving me exactly what I need.

I'm completely spent.

I breathe hard, certain that I no longer contain any bones in my body. I'm nothing more than a puddle of satisfaction as Riall pulls out of my mouth and once again drops to his back on the fur rug as though his body is more jelly than muscle too.

"Fuck," Tarek pants. "Better than I ever dared to dream," he declares breathlessly, his tone rough and euphoric as he rides the waning waves of his orgasm.

"You're ours," Curio declares from beneath me, his hand cupping my cheek with gentle adoration.

The sentiment behind his words warms me in ways I have no words for. It sings of home, of safety and belonging. But I won't be *owned* by anyone ever again.

"I belong to no one," I assert evenly, my eyes fixed on the rich hickory of his steady gaze.

He studies me for a moment as though the pain and history etched in those five words hangs in the air between us.

"Very well, Moonling, we're *yours* then," he tenderly assures me.

Warm gazes and soft hands caress me, each brush and affectionate press of their lips against my skin an acquiescence to my terms. With that, the last link required to bind us together slips into place.

They're mine, and we'll possess and protect each other long past our last breaths, because even death will know it has no claim here.

47

RHYTHMIC RAP ON THE DOOR STARTLES ME awake. A sleepy groan sounds off behind me, and strong corded arms wrap tighter around my waist. Curio buries his face in my hair as he pulls me back into his chest. Tarek rolls out of the bed and moves to answer the impatient knock. I stretch and nuzzle Riall's bicep, which is currently serving as my pillow. I've never slept with anyone like this. Especially not the downy beds that had been pushed together so we could all lie side by side. Normally, the plush bedding and soft mattress would have my body aching—and not in a good way. But sleeping against, and partially on top of, three hard bodies might be the key to solving that problem. I've never felt more rested in my life.

Then again, that might have less to do with the sleeping arrangements and more to do with the dozens upon dozens of orgasms wrung from my body before all of us passed out in a heap of limbs and sated lust. I was genuinely worried at one point I might actually die from *orgasm overdose*, a notion that had the Scorpions rolling with laughter before growing determined to show me just what my body could take. I'm pretty sure they broke me somewhere around twenty-two, because all I was capable of doing after that was mewling the word *yes* and endlessly writhing as they did their worst... which happened to be their best.

They're bastards. Each one of them is a fucking scoundrel in every possible way...and I loved every moment of it.

Tarek speaks quietly with whoever is at the door, while I soak in the moonlight that's piercing through the open curtains of the window behind us. It seems we've fucked and slept the day away. The soft beams of silvery light paint my skin, chasing away the aches and twinges—which I fully blame on the Scorpions—and I sigh contentedly as the moon works her magic.

"Mmmmm," Riall groans as he presses closer. "I'll never get tired of hearing all the satisfied noises you make, Beasty."

I smile at his adorable sleep-rumpled rambling. I feel lighter tonight, lighter than I've ever felt in my entire life. I've carried the weight of being alone, fighting alone, surviving alone for so long that I didn't realize how oppressive it all was. I was managing. It was fine. But something clicked into place between the four of us as we fucked and made love and basked in each other. Knowing that the Scorpions are there to help with my heavy shit, that I'm there to help with theirs, it makes me feel like I can breathe, *really breathe*, for the first time since I woke up in a cage. I can rest because there's someone to watch my back while I do. Maybe I can dare to hope again, because I'm not the only one fighting for better days.

The soft smiles and satisfied moans, the tender touches and possessive declarations, they aren't just for me, they fuel all of us. Violence and death brought us together, but it's the stolen kisses, the way our bodies fit under the sparkling stars and the searing sun, the laughter, and the precious moments between the blood and brutality, that ensure we'll never be torn apart.

I moan quietly, encouraging the naughty twinkle in Riall's eyes. A surprised squeak sneaks out of me when Curio suddenly rolls us until I'm fully lying on top of him, my back to his chest. My small squeal morphs into a groan as Curio's big palms spread my thighs. Needing no more invitation than my freely offered and accessible cunt, Riall crawls over until he's lining up his cock and pressing into my wet heat. Curio's palm moves from my thigh, and his rough fingers start to stroke my clit.

I don't know how these two still have the stamina and will to fill me and fuck me. Though I might be just as bad, as I release a wanton moan and reach up to knead my breasts. I doubt I'll ever get enough of what we do to each other.

The sound of a door clicking closed reaches me between the whimpers I'm working hard to keep quiet. Tarek is suddenly there, prowling back into bed, his hot mouth instantly claiming one of my nipples. Riall starts to pound into me mercilessly, and in no time flat, I'm a mewling, needy mess. Each of my Scorpions makes quick work of my greedy body. My orgasm floods me hard and fast, and Riall comes just as quick. Once again, we're nothing more than overlapping limbs and absently stroking hands, as labored breaths pepper the air and Riall's cum starts to drip down to my ass.

"We need to bathe and be suited up within the hour," Tarek announces. He shoves his face deeper into the plump pillow as though he's hoping the soft linen and feathers will save him from the day. "The Vulpi just sent word. The informant will be arriving at their northern safe house soon."

With everything that happened last night, I almost forgot what we're here to do...almost. I rub my cheek on Curio's chest, hesitant to climb from his arms. I'm not eager to leave this bed and shatter the intimate cocoon we wove around ourselves. I'm not ready for the world to infringe on what we've created together just yet.

"Come," Tarek encourages as he gets to his feet and extends his hand to me. "I'll bathe *you* this time."

I smile at the reminder of how far we've come and let him drag me out of bed against the groans and objections of Curio and Riall. Their over-the-top antics make me laugh as I'm led into an attached washroom. I salaciously study the bitable curve of Tarek's ample ass as he bends to fill a large tub with water.

"Save all the deplorable thoughts I can see you thinking for later, little moonbeam. As soon as we get what we need, we'll be heading home, where I'll gladly pick up where we've left off."

"Do you think it will be that easy?" I ask, taking his proffered hand and stepping into the hot water.

Tarek gets in behind me, pulling us both down until I'm sitting between his legs and resting back against his chest. Soothing steamy water eddies around us as the tub continues to fill, and he runs his fingers, feather light, up and down my arms over and over again. The touch is so drastically different from the first interaction we ever had in a tub. I can't help but smile and relax into him as I think about those first days. It feels like years ago, when I wanted nothing more than to gut Tarek and stopper his taunting. If someone then had suggested the possibility that he'd become everything he is to me now, I would have thought they were suffering from sun poisoning and delusional beyond saving.

Fate just might be a fettik scorpion. The stars know I've been poisonous for everyone except these three.

"Every time I've ever thought something was going to be easy, it was the exact opposite," Tarek rumbles, the stubble on his chin and cheeks scratchy as he buries his face against my neck. Strong corded arms wrap around me, and he pulls me even tighter against him. "So no, I don't think today will be easy. The Vulpi are good at what they do, and if they think there's some sort of trap that's waiting to be sprung, there more than likely is."

"Is there anything we can do to mitigate it?" I ask.

"I've been thinking through our options since we left the Den yesterday." Tarek sighs, clearly frustrated by the conclusion he's come to. "Other than abandoning whatever information Hatus Orill might have for us, there's nothing we can do but meet what's coming our way head-on and hope our skill outmatches what we'll be up against."

I snort at the uncharacteristic humility in that statement.

"You're the Order of Scorpions. Who stands a chance against that?" I tease, and his answering laugh vibrates through me in a delicious way I've been told not to think about until later.

"*We* are the Order of Scorpions," he corrects, wrapping his palm around my throat.

He tilts my head to the side and nibbles where my neck meets my shoulder. "And no one stands a chance against us."

"Then what has you worried?" I press, a shiver chasing the goose bumps that scatter across my skin as he sucks and nips up my neck.

"I'm always worried," he admits, his lips skimming the shell of my ear. "We just found you," he continues, and a trill of surprise rings through me.

"You're worried about me?"

"Not about you, *for* you, love. I know you're a force to be reckoned with; it's not an issue of questioning what you can do. It's that I have everything I've ever wanted in the palms of my hands, right now," he tells me, squeezing me possessively before forcing himself to loosen his hold. "I'm waiting for something to come and strip it all away."

I turn to look at him, the ache in his words calling to me as I stare into his pale blue eyes. I brush a wet wave from his face and trace his jaw with my fingers as I try to work through what to say.

"If I die today, it will be the freest and happiest I've ever been in my life. What you and your brothers have given me is so much more than I ever dared to dream. I will take my last breath with no regrets in my heart, needing nothing more than what the three of you have already given me."

His soft snowflake-blue gaze takes me in, and he reaches up to cup my cheek as my confession bobs in the water between us.

"We would follow you. There'd be no choice in it. Where you go, we go," he whispers, as though he's trying to hide his words from fate.

The promise that rides his breath tickles my face and sinks deep into my soul.

"Then follow me," I whisper back. "What do we have to fear from death? We are its faithful servants, it can give us *this*."

I circle the tip of my nose around the tip of his as I press my hand to his heart.

"Worry about having plenty of weapons. Worry that they're sharp enough. Worry about your bowels turning to liquid from nerves and fear."

Tarek's eyebrows lift with shock at the last part.

"Telson of the Order of Scorpions has shit herself because of nerves?" he teases with a hardy laugh.

I scoff and roll my eyes at him. "Never," I indignantly exclaim, slapping at his wide muscular chest for even thinking such a thing. "A boy during my early years in the pits had an issue with it. It seemed like something worth worrying about until I knew I was made harder than he was."

"Mm-hmmmm," Tarek rumbles. "It seems we're both hard," he confesses, rolling his hips and drawing my attention to his stiff cock.

I laugh but spin until I'm straddling him in the large tub. I press up on my knees, making me taller than him as he leans back against the tub. I stare down at him, my thumb pulling down his bottom lip as I cradle his face and marvel at his incredible beauty. Each of the Scorpions is sculpted perfection from the tips of their toes to the tops of their heads. It makes my heart race and my breaths shallow when I get to stare at their utter perfection like I'm doing with Tarek right now.

"Time isn't often fair," I tell him as I sink down on his thick length.

He inhales sharply, his strong hands moving to grip my ass as he tilts his hips up to fill me completely.

"Life promises us nothing," I continue, lifting up and then dropping back down on him.

Fuck, he feels good.

"Don't let *might* and *could* rob you of what *is* right now."

I start to fuck him faster, my last words hanging in the air between us, as the rib-high water starts to slosh over the sides of the tub from my movements. Tarek palms my breasts as I ride him. He leans in to suck one taut peak into his mouth, flicking his tongue over the sensitive bud until he has me whimpering, and then he moves to do the same to the other.

"I will fight with everything I have to stay right here," I tell him, punctuating the last two words by dropping down harder and harder onto him. "I know you and your brothers will do the same, and that's all any of us—"

I hiss as Tarek drops a hand to my clit and pinches it hard.

"That fucking mouth," he growls at me, sucking in my bottom lip as his fingers start to work my clit in circles. "I don't know if I like it more when these lips are professing adoration, screaming my name, or threatening me with bodily harm for pissing you off," he admits, grinding his hips into me as my pace becomes more frenetic.

"Make me come, *mate*, or I'll cut your fucking balls off," I taunt, but it morphs into a needy mewl.

Tarek laughs, and then he lifts me, stepping out of the tub as though I weigh nothing.

"Two out of three," he exclaims happily before kissing the shit out of me.

My back is slammed against a wall, and Tarek starts to fuck me so hard and so fast that all I can do is hold on and greedily cry out as he does.

"Now, to go for the third and make you scream my name."

Six hard thrusts and a bruising, all-consuming kiss later, I do exactly that.

48

BONES

WELL, THIS LOOKS FAR LESS OMINOUS THAN I thought it would," Telson mumbles as we cautiously approach the Order of Vulpi's safe house.

Now, more than ever, I wish that we'd never agreed to the *no shadow walking within three court blocks of their havens* part of our alliance. All I want to do right now is crawl into a shadow and step out exactly where we need to be. We all know the stakes are high tonight. We could scrap the hunt, but we are who we are because we don't shy away from shit like this. We're the best because we charge in no matter what, taking what we want out of sheer will and drive and a whole lot of well-honed skill.

Scorpius walked out of the washroom earlier much calmer than he looked when he entered it. I have no doubt that the muffled moans I heard through the closed door and the addicting smell of Beasty's cum in the air had something to do with it. I fucked that sweet cunt first thing this morning too, but apprehension and wariness are slowly slinking in despite the incredible things that happened between me, my brothers, and our mate. The Sanguinna in me is demanding more, but the Blood Bond will have to wait.

I pull two swords from my back, Scorpius regarding me as I do. There's something in the air tonight, the taste of blood on the breeze, that has my hackles up. Silently the four of us move to the stoop at the front of the plaster-walled house. We're cloaked in glamour and shadows as Scorpius moves up the steps to the front door. The house is dark and quiet, but I sense the presence of others inside. The stars are hiding behind a dense wall of clouds, making the dark night even darker. It's almost as though the moon itself doesn't want to witness what might happen on her watch.

Scorpius doesn't knock, he simply opens the door to the modest home and strides in as though it belongs to him and not the Vulpi. Skull pulls in a deep breath as he follows in after, and I can tell he's feeling tense too. Auset—Telson, I snarl at myself—moves into the house as though she hasn't a care or worry in the world. She looks around at the bare walls and minimal furniture as though they're of some interest to her, but I know she's really tabulating the threats in the room and what might be a concern to her.

She's such a fucking natural at this. I'm excited for her to blood her blades. This is supposed to be an information gathering hunt, but I have a feeling she might be breaking in the beauties Skull gifted her with sooner rather than later. It makes me hard just thinking about us fighting side by side, destroying anything that comes against us and tearing out the throats of our enemies.

Flashes of fucking my Beasty on a pile of broken and dismembered bodies while licking blood from each other has me biting back a moan as I close the safe house door behind me. Two of the Vulpi's enforcers stand like statues in opposite corners of the room. They almost look as though they're the only decoration in the room, with the hue of their burnt-orange armor and their helmets made to look like a fox's face. A long spear is gripped in each enforcer's hand, and they say and do nothing as we move through the main area of the home toward the room in the back that's the most defensible in the house, which is exactly where the Vulpi and the informant will be.

"Will they be here soon?" a male asks, the words of his question wobbling around the tenor of his voice as though they'll plummet to the ground from fright at any moment.

I don't know what the Vulpi plan to do with Hatus when we're done gleaning what we can from him. If it were up to me, I'd probably kill him. I can't abide stupidity or cowards, and that's what this male radiates, and we're not even in the room yet. I don't necessarily fault him for running from the Daeral massacre. The instinct to flee is a hard one to fight—I know from experience—but he had to know that he was going to be hunted. To take that kind of trouble to the doorstep of the people you say you love and care about, to ask them to hide you and keep you safe, it's a kind of recklessness I don't tolerate.

I've been in this male's shoes. Going about normal easy life one minute only to have it all ripped away in the next. When my mother's mate showed up unexpectedly from a long, drawn out war—one that started before I was born, in a land I couldn't find on a map if asked—my life ended just like Hatus's did the night of the Daeral murders. It wasn't Hatus's fault that it happened, just like it wasn't my fault that my sire, the king, had raped my mother and cursed her with me.

My mother never treated me like the affliction I had to be to her. She'd done the best she could by me despite the heinous way that I'd been forced into the world. But none of that mattered to Khartik. He could have been there for his mate after discovering what she endured. He could have let me go off to squire for another court like I was supposed to do in less than a month.

But no.

I existed.

Which meant both my mother and I had to die.

I was young, not quite thirty. Still a handful of years away from reaching the point where my body would start to transform from boy to a mature fae male. But even I knew not to run from Khartik to the people I loved. I couldn't drag my problems to the ones who would *want* to help me, just to watch them die by Khartik's hand because of it. If I could figure this out as a *child*, there's no excuse for this grown fae.

I'd lived in the woods, surviving off of raw hare—because a fire would have brought the trackers right to me—and berries that made my guts feel like they were going to explode. I learned to travel by climbing trees and crossing the land from branch to branch in order to keep from creating any tracks that the fucker Khartik and his men could follow.

I learned, as my hunger and desperation grew, that my repugnant sire had not only blessed me to be a bastard, but thanks to him, Sanguinna blood also flowed in my veins. As I grew, I started to risk sneaking closer to towns and drinking from some of the livestock. That alone is probably why I'm alive today. I learned quickly that blood did more for me than any scrap of scavenger meat I could consume. I got stronger and stopped hunting defenseless animals and started hunting fae.

Scorpius opens the door to the large bedroom that's empty of everything save Mayden and Myrka and a thin, reedy fae sitting in a chair in the middle of the room. Stress and apprehension are etched into the male's face. His skin slightly hangs from his chin and limbs as though he's lost a fair amount of weight in a short period of time. His dark gray eyes remind me of the hares I used to catch—wide, terrified, and all too aware that death has caught up to them.

I love when I find that look in a pair of eyes. It reminds me of how powerful I am, that the days of being hunted mercilessly and running for my life are long gone. I'm the hunter now, and there is no escaping me or my brothers when we come for you.

Hatus releases a pitiful squeak when we slip into the room. He looks over at the Vulpi as though he's silently begging Myrka or Mayden to do something. What he thinks they can do is beyond me. The very reason that Hatus is here is to tell us what he knows. Although looking down at the unwashed, greasy male, reeking of fear and too many days on the road, has me questioning any valuable information this pathetic creature could really have.

Either he's the best actor in all of the realms and this *is* a trap—like the Vulpi suspected—or whoever was following them was doing it because they wanted something from the Vulpi and not this guy.

How has he survived this long against a group of killers that slaughtered an entire bloodline in one night?

My gaze rakes over Hatus as we all silently settle in the room. I don't begrudge him the help he's getting from the Vulpi. Fuck knows, Eacon and my brothers saved my life. But if he wants to survive what's breathing down his neck, he's going to have to get smarter and more determined, and he's going to need to do it right now.

Telson leans against the wall between Mayden and Myrka, who are occupying opposite corners like the Vulpi always do. They're taught to find the most defensible point in any room and place themselves there. They look like Vulpi bookends around Telson, and I would smile at the odd picture if we weren't about to question an informant and therefore needed to maintain appearances. Scorpius and Skull stride to the other side of the room opposite me, and I take up position next to a large window, the only other exit and entry point in the room aside from the door.

"You know who we are?" Skull asks Hatus, his tone bored and put out.

"Yes," Hatus answers, his hands now shaking harder than a banner in the wind.

"And you know why we're here?" Skull continues.

Hatus gulps. "To keep me safe from…from…them."

Skull snorts the small puff of air, derisive and indignant. "*Safe* is between you and the Vulpi. If you give us every detail of who *them* is exactly and what you saw at the Daeral manor on the night of their deaths, the Order of Scorpions won't do anything to jeopardize the safety you were promised."

Skull's words are barbed with aristocratic nuance. It's a trick he's mastered to make those he converses with either feel unsettled and challenged or inferior and beholden. It also keeps others guessing as to who we are and what footholds we may have in the upper echelons of the realms. He's good at these subtle manipulations, so good that I always find *I* want to punch him whenever he slips into this hoity role on a hunt.

I watch Telson to see what she thinks of Skull's new persona, but she's watching Hatus like she expects him to pull a claymore from his ass and charge her at any moment. The challenge in her black eyes makes me hard, even though it's not aimed at me. I brush away the images that flash in my mind of all the ways I fucked her and she fucked me earlier, and tell myself to pay attention to what's going on before I fuck up and miss something important.

"Now, start at the very beginning. Be slow and thorough, and tell us what you saw. We don't want conjecture.

Keep your suspicions to yourself. Give us only what *you* witnessed," Skull instructs, and I can tell that he's also questioning how helpful whatever Hatus saw is going to be for us.

Hatus nods solemnly and pulls in a deep shuddering breath. He looks at my brothers and then me, our skeletal visages reflected in the growing black of his eyes as his pupils expand with fear. Then he looks over at Telson and loses just a little of the rigid tension in his shoulders.

This time, I can't fight the smile that curves at my lips. Hatus sees a softer option, one less intimidating to him than me, Scorpius, and Skull. He doesn't know that Telson would cut his tongue from his mouth just as quickly as the rest of us would. It almost makes me want to see her do it, if for no other reason than to teach a lesson in underestimating any member of the Order of Scorpions.

"I...I was sleeping," Hatus starts, his shaky hands reaching for the hem of his tunic.

He begins to absently wind it around his fingers as though the movement soothes him. Enay mentioned Hatus was a cobbler in his previous life, the one that died when he survived something he shouldn't have. The movement must mimic how he works, probably helps him focus, but I watch his hands and body for any tells as I let the others focus on his tone and words.

"I had stopped to visit my brother Fet. He didn't know I was coming, but he was excited to see me all the same. Fet mentioned that the house was just getting back from some travels and that things in the manor were a bit chaotic. He didn't want to ask any of the staff if they'd make up a room for me, which was fine by me. Fet and I'd spent most of our youth in the barns sleeping with the beasts. It was no issue to cozy up to them again instead," Hatus explains with a shrug.

He clears his throat, and his eyes twitch from Telson to Myrka and then back again, but I take note of the chagrin that seems to suddenly weigh down his back and fill his features.

"Fet nipped a bottle of wine and some victuals from the kitchens," Hatus admits more quietly, as though he thinks we're going to report the theft to Lord Daeral and get his brother sacked.

Being that they're all dead and buried, his concern and embarrassment is wasted.

"We drank and ate and caught up with each other, and when it got late, I hunkered down in a stall and Fet went to his cottage that he shares with the stable boys and carriage staff just down the way. I...uh...I drank more than I usually do. The wine was good, much nicer than the likes me and Fet were used to. I must have slept through..."

Hatus wrings his tunic in his hands, his eyes closing with shame, as he takes a minute to collect himself.

"When I woke, it was to one of the house girls screaming. I don't know if she was a maid or a cook or something else, but she was running from the servants entrance at the back. Running for her life and hollering with blood curdling fright. There were no other sounds. No birds. No insects. Not even the mounts snorted in fear. Just her shrieking, terrified, and sprinting away as though a ghoul were on her heels. And then I saw what was..."

Fear wafts off Hatus like heat from desert sand. His eyes snap open, and he stares at Telson, but his gaze is far away, locked in whatever horror is playing out in his mind. I've seen this look a thousand times, and it makes me stand a little straighter and actually believe Hatus might be useful for the first time since we walked in here.

"What?" Mayden prompts.

She leans forward, clearly invested in whatever Hatus is holding back, and I recall that the Vulpi want these answers as much as we do, because whoever it was had carved a fox in one of the bodies, which made it seem as though the Vulpi sanctioned this hunt. Something they were adamant they didn't do.

"Ghosts," Hatus exclaims, his voice barely above a whisper. "Ghosts were after her."

His eyes never leave Telson's, and I glance at Skull and Scorpius, wondering if they're thinking this fae is as fucked in the head as I do right now.

"There was this small knot in the wood, and I could see the courtyard. I thought maybe the wine was poisoning my dream, turning it into a nightmare. They moved so fast. One minute, there was nothing, and then the next, the wraiths were just there."

I look over at Skull and shake my head. All this fucking trouble, and the Vulpi brought us a loon. Skull's answering look tells me he's equally unimpressed. My vexed gaze flits to Mayden and Myrka, but they're looking at Hatus as though they can will some semblance of sense into the bastard.

"I've...I've never seen anything like it. I can't sleep without seeing the eerie way they moved. They threw a knife at her. Threw it so hard that her head almost came clean off. It just hung to the side like it would fall away completely at any second," he exclaims, his eyes filling with panic as though he's still hiding in the barn, watching it happen right in front of his face.

"Who did?" Skull asks, but his tone isn't very hopeful that we'll get anything useful out of the hysteria that's quickly building in the cobbler.

"Her body kept running," he wails, tears spilling down his cheeks as he clutches his hands in front of him as though he's pleading with us to believe him. "It was awful, her body didn't know that her head wasn't where it was supposed to be; it kept running, and then she crashed to the ground, and they laughed. They laughed like it was the funniest thing. I can't stop seeing it and hearing their evil laugh!"

Hatus presses his hands to his mouth as though his palms will hide the terror-stricken whimpers he's now making.

"Then I heard another scream somewhere deep in the house," he whispers after a moment, and he wipes furiously at the tears spilling down his cheeks. "That's when I knew what they were doing. That there had to be more than the three I saw. There had to be. Because they were killing them....all of them."

"Who was?" Skull demands again.

"The ghosts!" Hatus repeats with more frustration in his tone this time.

"How did you get away from these *ghosts?*" Myrka practically sneers, and Hatus's pale face pales even more.

He looks around the room, assessing the rest of us as though he's searching for anyone who's buying this story. He takes another deep shuddering breath and tries to calm himself.

Mayden looks over at me, just as pissed as I feel about this waste of time. The Vulpi dedicated valuable resources to retrieving this fae. I wouldn't be surprised if she's seconds away from slitting him navel to neck. She'd be doing the addled fool a favor at this point.

"I was going to get Fet, get us both away as quickly as possible, but when I snuck out to try to get to his cottage, I saw the door was already open. They had... I was too late." A sob snakes out of his mouth, and he works hard not to let another slip by as he wipes his nose and ruddy cheeks on his sleeve.

Scorpius cringes, his gaze filling with disgust at the unsanitary gesture.

"I grabbed a mare and I ran. I didn't go toward the front gate. Not after...what I saw, so I angled the mare to the trees behind the stables. Lord Daeral loved to hunt, and he owned a lot of forest as part of his property. There was only a small fence that the mare could jump over, and we got away."

"Where had the lord and his house been?" Telson asks, pulling Hatus's focus back to her.

She must be getting just as impatient as the rest of us are to get this over with and go. Hatus stares up at her, hopeful but confused by her question.

"You said that the lord and his house had just come back from traveling. That the house was chaotic. Where did they go?" she reminds him.

"Right," Hatus chirps, his brow furrowing as he seems to search his memories for an answer to that question. "The Sagor Coast. It's in the Night Court, I think."

Fucking Night Court, I grumble internally. King Korven has been next to useless since the queen died. All kinds of fucked-up things seem to grow roots there before they spill over into the other realms. We haven't crossed the Winter Court's borders since the Elix overpaid us for Dorsin and her apprentice. I for one would be happy to keep it that way for another dozen years. It's no surprise that trouble followed Lord Daeral home from that lawless realm.

Scorpius moves toward the door with an irritated shake of his head. "You owe us, Vulpi. This was fucking useless," he calls over his shoulder, and I push off the wall to follow him.

"Wait, no!" Hatus yelps, falling out of his chair and onto his knees. "I told you everything that happened! That's everything that happened!" he shouts at Scorpius's back. "Please, they can't find me! I don't want to die!" he begs.

"For the last time, cobbler, who the fuck is *they*?" Scorpius bellows as he whirls around, his face a mask of fury and his shout dripping with impatience.

"The ghosts! The fucking ghosts! There were three of them. They moved like the wind itself. They threw a knife so hard it almost took the girl's head off. They had white hair. Gray eyes. Skin and armor the color of fresh snow. I'm telling you the truth, please believe me! They were ghosts! I don't know how to hide from ghosts. I don't want to die!"

Every Scorpion in the room freezes at Hatus's shouted and frantic description. Telson's face snaps in his direction so fast I hear the bones in her neck pop. The Vulpi go still at our obvious reaction, their eyes searching our faces for a clue as to why we're all now staring at Hatus—who's sobbing into his hands on the ground—like he's no longer shit we just found on our boots.

That's when I hear it. A soft, barely there sound on the roof. It's a gentle scraping, something I probably wouldn't have caught if the room hadn't just plunged into astonished silence at the perfect time. Or maybe it's the days I spent as a cria, scared and alone in the woods, listening for anyone or anything that might be sneaking up on me, that made me so sensitive. Either way, I hear the careful quiet steps above us like they're loud stomps through the room.

Someone is up there, and they've been listening to everything we've said.

49

AUSET

MY HEART PLUMMETS AS HATUS'S WORDS dislodge it from my chest and send it careening to my feet. I swear the shocked organ rolls across the floor as I reel and try to think through what the fuck he just said.

They had white hair, gray eyes, and skin the color of snow.

Hatus's voice repeats over and over in my mind. Does he know? Can he somehow see what's hidden beneath my glamour? I stare down at the pathetic, trembling heap, suspicion and shock spiraling through me. All I can see is my own unusually light-colored hair, my silver eyes, and skin that was once pale before the Corozean desert and the searing sun burned it enough times that it tanned to adapt.

Ghosts.

He screamed that title enough that I'll probably hear it every time I look in the mirror now. My heart races, or maybe it doesn't because it's still on the floor while my gut churns with astonishment and unease.

The Vulpi say something to Scorpius, and Skull barks a question at Hatus, but everything is muffled by my confusion and the explosion of questions that detonate in my mind. I'm trying to rein in my emotions and my stupefied reaction, knowing the Vulpi are watching everything we do and say right now. I need to be smart. I need to not fuck up my first hunt as a Scorpion simply because Hatus Orill might have answers that I desperately need.

I force myself to breathe.

In.

Out.

Get control, collect the barrage of questions in my head, and sort through what needs to be asked first. Maybe Scorpius can kick the Vulpi out of the room. Then we can cut to the heart of what we need. I look over at Scorpius, but my attention catches on Skull, who looks as though he's trying to calm Hatus. I don't think the cobbler can hear Skull over the sound of his terrified sobbing. He's rocking on the ground, begging us not to let him die. His hands are wrapped around his head as though he expects a killing blow at any moment.

Shit.

If my heart was in my chest, it would plummet again. Hatus has answers. Answers to things I was starting to give up on, but now we've broken him, and I'm suddenly terrified that everything I need is locked away in his panicked and traumatized mind forever.

I look to Bones. He was good with me when I first woke up in their home, so maybe he can help. Bones's head is tilted up, and he's staring intensely at the ceiling. Goose bumps skitter across my arms at the look of concentration on his face. Instinct tells me to stop, shove everything aside, and listen.

My soul yanks my heart back in place, and I'm forced to concentrate past the anxious staccato and target whatever it is that Bones is intently focusing on. He goes still, tension building in his shoulders, and it's as though that alone shuts down all the emotion and turmoil swirling inside of me. The pounding of my pulse quiets. My senses sharpen, and that's when I hear it, a subtle shift of weight above us.

I fist my hand and then release it. My fingers itch for the feel of blades in my palms, but I keep myself under control. I let it slip once today, and it won't happen again. We're on a hunt, and in all the bewildering confusion, I lost sight of the fact that we were preparing for trouble tonight. From the sound of things, trouble's here.

Bones fluidly moves closer to the window, his focus now peering out of the thick pane of glass.

"Telson, on me," he orders, and then he shoves the window open and jumps out.

I barely hear Scorpius order the Vulpi to get Hatus out of there, before I leap out of the window too. Part of me wants to climb back in and wring Hatus's neck until he tells me everything I want to know about the ghosts, but this isn't about me anymore. I'm Telson of the Order of Scorpions, and they're counting on me not to be a selfish cunt and to watch their backs no matter what.

I pull a scorpion tail dagger from my back as I scan my surroundings in search of Bones or a threat. It's late either because the Vulpi like to do things when the court and its citizens are fast asleep or because the Scorpions do. The houses around me are plain and humble. They're built close together and look similar with only subtle differences here and there. Narrow alleys run between the abodes, which is where I spot a streak of black sprinting through the shadows and then a flash of white jumping from roof to roof ahead of him.

Ghost!

It's as though I've conjured them straight from my hopeful mind. Shock and a longing to understand what the fuck is going on pummel me as I take off, racing to catch up to Bones's long stride. I scan my surroundings, my gaze bouncing between everything around me to ensure I'm not missing anyone who might be lurking in wait for an ambush, and then pick up speed when there's no one else around.

Oblivious fae slumber in their homes as an apparition, one that probably has more answers than broken Hatus ever did, jumps from roof to roof above while two Scorpions hunt from the narrow streets below.

The streak of white bounding above is getting smaller as the phantom expertly navigates the slight slope of the slate roofs. They angle their escape so there are more alleys and streets for us to run through in order to follow the same path. A chill runs up my back like a desert rat when I take in the white armor and white hair of the roof runner. We're not only chasing a ghost that possibly helped massacre a whole bloodline in one night, we're chasing a potential key to my past.

I've waffled over my need to know where I come from, doubted why it would matter, and worried about what knowing could change. I've yearned for the moment I would learn who I am, only to be disappointed when it seemed to disappear like a puff of smoke in the sky. My chance to know anything is losing us as it leaps deftly from roof to roof, and I won't let it slip away no matter what I have to do to catch a ghost.

"Boost me up," I call to Bones as I gain on him in the alleyway.

"Follow from the roofs. I'm going to shadow walk and see if I can cut them off," Bones calls over his shoulder.

Then he bends at the exact time that I leap for a wall at our side. Using my momentum, I spring off the wall and onto his shoulders. Without missing a beat, he straightens and I go flying up to the roof of the house next to us. Bones doesn't so much as slow his pace as he charges a shadow and disappears.

I leap from one roof onto another, my stride even and sure. The stars and the moon guide my path, the night quiet and cool as I stealthily and speedily stalk my prey. They never look back once, so either they don't know I'm here or don't care. The ghost is fast and nimble, but they're running out of small houses to vault across. Up ahead, there's nothing but a massive walled-in courtyard.

The phantom stops abruptly when they finally run out of roofline. They stand there for a moment on the edge of what must be a market that's closed for the night. I can just make out the tops of several stalls as I get closer. There's a flash of fairy light against steel, and then the ghost disappears. I can't tell if they jumped or fell or disappeared altogether.

My heart leaps with panic at the thought of them vanishing without a trace. I press harder to close the distance. Dread tries to override my training, as the ghost seems to evaporate into nothing. I can't see them anywhere. Only a handful of houses are between me and where the specter disappeared, but something in my gut tells me to slow down and sneak to the edge of the market. The drive to charge forward, to seize the key to everything I want to know, is riding me hard, but I shut it out and listen to my instincts.

Like a prowling sint cat, I pour myself over the remaining rooftops, moving to the side and then forward to make sure I don't appear in the same place that the ghost just disappeared from. I'm liquid shadow as I silently slink forward until I'm able to peek discreetly past a slate gutter and take in what's happening in the empty market below.

Bones stands lethal and menacing in the middle of the open space, empty carts and stalls butting up against the walls on all sides. He has two swords in his hands, ready to take on the six cloaked figures surrounding him. They don't move, as though they're waiting for him to strike first, but judging by the crumpled body of the ghost I was just chasing and the pool of blood that's slowly spreading beneath them, Bones already has.

Anger and apprehension mix to create a lethal combination that has me desperate to coat every blade on my body in enemy blood. The ghost is dead, and if the cloaked fuckers aren't with him, then I've just lost something vital that I might not ever find again. I ache as that realization punches deep and painful in my gut. I was so fucking close. I force myself to tamp all the anguish and frustration down and focus on what's happening in front of me and not on everything I might have just lost.

Bones shifts his weight, like he can tell the moment is quickly coming when this standoff morphs into battle. I shove away every unhelpful emotion whirring through me and calm the need to jump haphazardly into the fray.

Six against one isn't an impossible clash, especially not for Bones, but I need to figure out how to make it six against two and do it in a way that gives us the advantage. Large hoods bathe the features of the cloaked figures in shadow. I can't make out any details or faces no matter how hard I try. The thick clouds blanketing the sky part, letting the soft light of the half-moon they've been hiding escape. It catches on the lush, light gray fabric of the protective cloaks, and it's as though twinkling stars have been sewn into the hems as they sparkle and preen for the moon itself. Something about that calls to me, scratches at my mind as though I should know it, but the wall of nothing in my head is as impenetrable as it always is.

"You don't have to die brutally tonight, Scorpion," one of the cloaked figures declares, his voice a silky tenor that rings with authority. "Lay down your weapons, accept the inevitable, and I'll make it quick."

I can't tell which one is speaking, but the fact that they're negotiating instead of attacking outright is telling. There's an arrogance to their words and their attack formation. Taking in the way that they stand and seeing the glint of the sword tips just visible past the front seam of their star-speckled cloaks, I suspect the audacity radiating off of them is probably earned. They're used to being the biggest threat in a room.

They obviously haven't met the Scorpions yet.

As I watch, I also notice a few hoods turning in the direction of the dead ghost on the ground. Whoever they were, they're now lying face down in a pool of blood, but I can't see more than that beyond the cloaked figures in the way. The death, or maybe it's more the loss of another warrior needed to go up against Bones, is clearly unsettling the cloaked collective. They seem to be waiting for some kind of upper hand or maybe reinforcements. Either way, they're not willing to charge in blindly right now and risk losing anyone else to Bones's punishing skill.

"Brutally, quickly..." Bones shrugs. "Makes no difference to me. It's all death in the end. The least you can do is show me your face before you try to shove a blade through me. What are you hiding from?"

Bones's taunt floats on the tense air, and a few unimpressed huffs sound off around him.

"This would be easier for you if we were afraid of you, Scorpion. We're not," the leader jeers, and then the group does the last thing I expect them to do.

They pull back their hoods.

Hatus was wrong.

Perhaps fear tinted his eyes or time leeched the color from his recollections, but it isn't a group of ghosts standing in the middle of the empty market. No wraiths surround my Scorpion, mocking what they think is his certain death. All I see are answers to every question I've ever had about where I come from and who I really am. Keys are dangling in front of me, but all I need is one to free what's been sealed in my mind for too long.

Their hair isn't white. It's a peculiar shade of not quite white, nor light gray, or even light blue. It's somehow all of those colors, a hue I have no name for despite all the times I've run my fingers through my own locks and wondered what word could possibly capture such an unusual mix of pigments. Their eyes aren't simply gray, they're a familiar bright silver. A color I've studied in every reflection of myself I've ever seen. My skin was once pale and creamy just like theirs is now, and I want to rip the glamour from my body and demand they tell me who they are, because I am too.

The leader's hand twitches. He sends a silent signal to the rest of the group, and the air around them grows taut. As much as it pains me, I know if I want to save Bones, there's no time for questions, there's only time for action. A month ago, I would have taken what I wanted with no qualm. But now everything has changed. I *want* the keys to my past. I *want* answers. But I *need* a future with my Scorpions more.

It's an easy choice.

One handed, I unclip my ax from my back as I spring from the roof. My scorpion tail dagger is still gripped in my other palm as I land behind two of the largest males in the circle. I eviscerate all thoughts of who these men might be or why they look like me. It doesn't matter. They're standing in the way of what's mine, and that's only ever going to mean one thing to me—they're dead.

Before the noise of my landing can even bounce off the walls surrounding us, I shove a dagger between the ribs of one male and then swing my ax at the neck of the other. The fae's head goes flying with such force that it slams against the dove gray chest plate of the smirking leader. He wobbles back in shock as the head tumbles to the ground. A pained bellow joins other surprised gasps and shouts. The noise fills up the empty market, making everything sound more frenzied and hectic. I pull my blade free from the chest of the fae I stabbed and step past the falling headless body that clears a direct path to Bones.

"Careful, Beasty," Bones cautions as I press my back to his and join him in staring down the remaining enemy.

"Yes, Bones," I chime back, and his deep laugh fills the circle of threats around us.

"Did you just *yes, dear* me?" Bones asks, amused.

"Did you just tell me to be *careful?*" I counter, a wide smile stretching across my mouth.

"What in the festering realms is going on? Who the fuck are you?" the leader demands, as though the shock of my presence has fried his good sense.

He should be attacking us, not demanding answers. It's five against two now and one of them is injured. They should be running or trying to catch us by surprise, like I just did.

"There are only three," a statuesque female on Bones's side of the diminishing circle insists. "Innis confirmed that they were keeping the other two distracted while we caught this one."

My eyes narrow at her words, and I itch to make her eat them. Hopefully, Bones is as tired of the jaw wagging and posturing as I am.

"Surprise...you're all dead," I croon, and then Bones and I do what they should have done in the first place.

We attack.

"Keep one alive!" I call over my shoulder as I charge.

Bones grunts a confirmation, and then all I see are the two males in front of me, both of them now marked for death. Steel sparks against steel as blows viciously rain down. We spin and strike, lunge and prance, lost to death's dance as we dart in and spring back, narrowly avoiding the sharp edge of a deadly weapon or the clip of an elbow or knee. When they didn't engage like they should have, I'd started to question if these bastards were as good as they thought they were.

They are.

I don't know if it's the newly unleashed feral side of me that likes that this is a challenge or if fighting alongside Bones for the first time is making all of this feel far more romantic than it has any right to be, but I can't stop smiling as I push even harder to cut these fuckers up into unrecognizable pieces.

One of my attackers advances when he should have ducked back, and my ax comes down hard on his shoulder. I cleave into him almost all the way to his heart, and I abandon the ax and ready my sword instead. My blades slice through bones and sinew like they're nothing more than warm lard. When this is over, I vow to myself to fuck Curio on every surface of his masterful workshop for creating such flawless and deadly weapons.

A dagger comes flying at me, and I reach up to pluck it from the air. It slices across my palm as I stop its fatal trajectory, and I hold on to the blade in search of who I'm going to return it to. The palm of my hand sizzles and blisters as the dark gray blade scorches and scalds. I drop it with a yelp and look down at the angry burn now marring my hand.

Iron!

"These fuckers have iron blades," I warn Bones as I dodge a charge from a female who slips from the other fight to join mine.

She tries to slide past my feet and pick up her iron dagger, but I shove a stinger-shaped dagger through her throat instead.

"Ours are poisoned; I'm not worried," Bones yells back, and the male who was just about to advance on me hesitates.

I capitalize on his cowardice and lift my hand to the shaft of moonlight that's thankfully still streaming into the courtyard above me. As soon as it kisses my palm, the burn starts to mend. The fighter in front of me gasps, his eyes going wide and searching as they flick from my healing hand to my face. He squints as though he's trying to see past my skeletal glamour, which is when Bones walks up behind him and smashes the hilt of his sword into the back of the shocked male's skull. He crumples to the ground with a resounding thud.

I look from Bones to the surrounding courtyard and stalls, ready for another attack, only to realize everyone wearing the light gray armor and moonbeams for hair is down. I start checking bodies for heartbeats. Poison blades or not, I have the one hostage I needed, but I want to make sure the rest of these shits are dead; otherwise, they can come with us too.

"You good, Beasty?" Bones probes as he watches me check everyone over.

Blood dapples the painted white bones of his glamour, and I'm sure the black patches hide their own fair share of gore. I want to lick it from his skin. A salacious smile tips Bones's mouth up, growing wider and wider the longer I stare. Then he winces, and the building heat between my thighs takes a back seat to instant concern.

"You're hurt?" I demand, abandoning the last body left to check and striding over to him.

"It's shallow," Bones assures me as he presses a hand to his chest.

Blood seeps from the wound, arguing against his claims of *shallow*, but he threads his fingers in mine to keep me from inspecting it.

"It was one of those fucking iron daggers," he dismisses as I glower at him. "We need to go make sure Scorpius and Skull are okay."

"Well, that would certainly save us from having to check on you," Skull calls as he steps out of the dark shadows behind an empty fruit cart.

Scorpius appears right behind him, and they scan me and Bones before taking in the courtyard and the bloody bodies scattered all around us.

"Looks like they underestimated you too," Scorpius observes, and I notice the blood dripping from their skin and armor.

"Did you get all of them?" Bones asks.

Skull shakes his head. "Only three, they ran when the Vulpi escaped with Hatus."

"So are we just not going to talk about the fact that they bear a striking resemblance to a certain slave we all know?" I point out cryptically in case there are listening ears nearby.

"No resemblance to a *slave* we know, but they could definitely pass as kin to a goddess we often cross paths with," Scorpius states matter-of-factly, his eyes warm and sparkling with mirth.

I snort and shake my head, but a sweet smile pulls at my lips.

"Let's go before anyone comes looking for the source of all the noise," Skull points out.

"We kept one alive."

I point to the unconscious fae at Bones's feet, and Scorpius grins like I just gave him the best present in the world. I love how fucked in the head we all are. Who needs romantic overtures and jewels when you can have *fights to the death* and the *torturing of your enemies?*

It's good to be a Scorpion.

Scorpius flicks a spark of fire at the pile of bodies Skull collected, and they go up in flames. I stare at him, impressed.

"I didn't know you could do that."

Scorpius's shrug is casual, but there's pride in his half-cocked smile. "I could try to teach you."

And now *I'm* smiling like he just gave me the best present in the world. He scoops up our newly acquired prisoner, and with a wink, he and Bones move to the shadows.

"Shall we…"

Skull offers me his arm, and I take it as though we're some hoity elite couple decked in all of our finery and not dripping blood and stinking of death.

"We shall," I concur, doing my best to mimic the tone and accent he used earlier when questioning Hatus. "It's a fortuitous day to solve a massacre and hopefully a mystery in one fell swoop. I've always enjoyed killing two birds with one stone."

Skull chuckles at my over-the-top affectation. "Or just killing," he counters with a cheeky grin.

I laugh. "You know me so well, *mate*."

Skull's onyx eyes gleam with pure joy and deep satisfaction as he wraps his arm around me, hugging me to his side as we step into the shadows.

"That I do, *mate*, that I do."

50

Bones hisses as Scorpius helps him sit on his bed back in the castle. I would feel relieved to be back, but now we have a captive to deal with, and Bones looks worse. I watch him wince as he tries to perch more securely on the edge of the fluffy bedding and too soft mattress. Scorpius shoots me a curious glance, and I sigh and then quirk an eyebrow at Bones.

"Still pretending it's a shallow stab wound that's of no consequence?" I demand, crossing my arms over my chest as though I'm daring him to keep the tough-fae act up.

"It *is* shallow, and it only hurts like a dry fuck because it was iron. It's nothing a warm bath and Eacon can't handle," Bones dismisses.

I roll my eyes. "Lovely visual."

"Thought you'd appreciate it," he snarks right back, and fuck if that doesn't make me want to smile.

I don't because the daft shit won't admit to how badly he's really feeling right now, so he gets no smiles from me.

I watch him start to sway slightly as he sits on his massive bed, which is tucked into an alcove of a very rustic and cozy room. I realize I've never been in here, what with my being convinced that I'd never trust any of them let alone love them, but now that I've gotten over that delusion, I'm craving access to all of the details I didn't think mattered before.

Scorpius leans down and starts to remove Bones's glamour, and I take the opportunity to peep around his space. A deep and very comfortable-looking chair is angled in front of a tall hearth. It's a rich yellow-orange that reminds me of desert sunrises, and there are stacks of books leaning against the intricately carved feet. Riall's room creates a softer impression, with its richer textures and colors than Curio's room, which seems more utilitarian. It suits Riall in a way that I find intriguing. It's masculine but warm, functional but slightly indulgent. I haven't seen Tarek's room yet, only his study, but it's interesting how much I like each of their spaces even though they're so different. Then again, I feel the same way about the fae that occupy those spaces, so maybe this isn't the revelation I'm thinking it is.

"I'll call Eacon," Scorpius announces, pulling me from my stray thoughts and nosing.

I step closer to Bones when his swaying grows more pronounced. His pallor unnerving. There's no hiding his current resemblance to trampled shit now that the glamour is gone. Scorpius doesn't look overly concerned, and I try to let that reassure me.

"Mine too before you go," I call to Scorpius when he turns for the door.

I circle my face with a finger and then crook a finger to coax him back to me. He's in a hurry to head down to the torture rooms they conveniently left off the tour they first gave me of this castle. I should have known then that all castles have torture rooms and dungeons, but it won't be something that slips past me again. Skull is already down in the dungeons I just learned existed, getting our new guest *comfortable*. I have a plan in that regard, however, and it involves getting cleaned up and not missing any spots camouflaged by the skeleton skin I'm currently wearing.

Scorpius grins at me as he stalks back in my direction. He presses his lips to mine and pulls the glamour from my skin before nipping my lip with a promising love bite. He doesn't say a word as he swaggers out of the room like the arrogant Scorpion that he is.

I might sigh dreamily as I watch him go.

I ignore the gooey, silly feeling in my stomach and turn back to Riall. "Let's get you in the bath then. You strip and I'll get us set up."

Riall only nods weakly as he leans heavily on the footboard of his bed.

Annoying tough-ass fae nonsense.

I shake my head but keep my lecture to myself. I leave him to sort his weapons and his kit, and I start to fill the huge inground tub I find in his washroom. I thought Curio's bath was big, but Riall's can probably fit all of us and then some. I set everything we'll need around the rim of the massive sunken oval basin and then head back out to find Riall...exactly where I left him, weapons, kit, and all.

My brow furrows when I take in how he's shivering. It's cooler here than it was in the Dawn Court but not so cold that he should be quivering.

"Hey," I coax him softly, brushing my fingers over his cheek and the short ash brown beard that's dotted with blood along his jaw.

Pained hazel eyes look up at me, and I soothe the anxious line between his eyebrows with a gentle brush of my thumb. I was going to ask him if he was okay, *really okay*, but it's obvious now that he's not. Gnawing on silent concern, I start plucking weapons from his body. I set them on the far side of the bed to be dealt with later and then strip him out of his kit. When it seems like a struggle for Riall to even pull his rind off, I borrow one of his knives and slice down the front of it.

What the fuck?

A hiss sneaks out of me when I see the wound on Riall's chest. The puncture through his right pec looks like it's started to heal—it's not bleeding anymore—but there are alarming dark gray lines feeding away from it in the direction of his heart. The lines haven't made it past the center of his chest, but his weakened state and failing energy makes more sense now. I've never seen it with my own eyes, only heard horror stories about what iron can do to a fae, but I'm getting a front row seat now, which makes my stomach roil with unease.

"The iron is poisoning you," I whisper, hoping he knows what to do about it, because I have no fucking clue.

"It's okay," he assures me, but he looks as though just those words are costing him. "I just need to clean it out so it can be healed."

His breaths are more labored now, and I feel tendrils of panic tightening around my throat. I nod at him and then cut the rest of his shirt and trousers off. He's a beast of a fae—something I thoroughly enjoy under *and* on top of me—but trying to drag and carry him from his bed to the bath is definitely not one of my favorite things about his size. I almost go down twice, and I'm not even through the doorway.

Fuck. How am I going to get us through the doorway?

Sweating and panting like I've been training for two days straight, I finally guide Riall into the hot bath, muscling him into the seat that takes up one side of the large basin. I shove my bloody, dirty, sweaty hair out of my face and wait, hopeful that the water will help Riall rally and he'll start cleaning his injury. He just sits there like he's too spent to do anything else.

I strip, not even bothering to pull my weapons off first as dread starts to steadily drip like lead in my gut. My experiences with iron are limited to the bars of the cage I woke up in and some tools used for special occasions in the hot house at the ludere. As far as I know, most fae can't stand to be exposed to the metal for too long, which makes it all the stranger that the ghosts were so comfortable using it. Whatever is happening, it's moving fast. A fact that makes it feel like there's a sand stag standing on my chest.

I wade into the sunken tub, the invitingly warm water sloshing at my thighs. Immediately I cup water into my hands and pour it over Riall's chest. He gasps, but his eyes stay closed and he doesn't try to stop me from doing it again and again. It does nothing to stop the slow crawl of dark lines across his chest.

"Talk to me, Riall. Tell me what's going on. Tell me what to do," I plead as I run my hands over his closely cropped hair and down his jaw.

He leans into the touch but doesn't answer me.

"Fuck fate. Fuck the moon, and fuck her cunt-ass star sycophants," I snarl as I stare at the even edges of the stab wound.

It was just a dagger. An iron one, which burns like lava, but it shouldn't be doing all of this. Their iron burned the shit out of my hand too, but it didn't start poisoning me before the moon helped me heal.

I press my fingers against the seam of the puncture and palpate. Maybe there's—a hard piece of something sits just inside the flaps of his broken skin. My heart starts to race as I press against it again just to be sure it's there.

"Bloody bastard dagger," I growl when I realize that the tip of the blade must have broken off and is still sitting in Riall's chest. "Bloody stubborn fae," I add when I look up at him. I should have checked his injury right away. Not that I'm a healer, but these Scorpions obviously can't be relied on to watch out for themselves. They did bring my deadly ass home, which worked out in the end for them, but I could have just as easily slit all of their throats.

I dig my fingers into the gash. Gritting my teeth against the pained howl that tears out of Riall, I try to pinch the remaining piece of the dagger between my fingers and pull it out. Blood starts to dribble out of the wound steadily, making everything more slippery and harder to grasp.

The iron burns my fingers until I can't feel the tips anymore, but I don't give up.

I won't let this tiny shard of nothing take anything from me. Not my determination, not my fingers, and sure as fuck not Riall.

His head snaps back, and he groans exhaustedly in pain as I press in deeper. He's too weak to put up much of a fight, which I hate, but it's probably a good thing that he can't punch me in the face right now. His arms jerk impotently at his side, and I mumble apologies over and over again as I go.

Thankfully, Riall was right when he said the wound was shallow. I'd probably chuckle about that if I weren't losing it a little right now. *Finally* I get a good hold on the piece of the dagger and pull it out. As soon as the poisonous shard is free from Riall's skin, I toss it as far as I can. It plinks mockingly to the ground on the other side of the washroom as I scoop more water into the wound to flush it out.

Quickly, I press a finger back into the puncture, searching for anything else that shouldn't be there. All I feel is warm, smooth muscles. My eyes burn with emotion as I take in Riall. His breaths are labored and he's still listless. Acting on instinct alone, I lean forward and seal my mouth to his cut. I suck, hard, remembering when a healer did this very thing to Yotta at the ludere when he'd been bitten by a *sablehead*. The venom had been doing damage to the tissue, and the healer insisted that they had to get it out before they could heal him, or Yotta would lose his leg.

Riall's blood tastes acidic and sour as I draw it into my mouth. It starts to burn my cheeks and tongue, and I quickly spit it out on the floor. His taste changes subtly, and

I take that as encouragement to keep going. Riall groans as I spit more mouthfuls of his blood over his shoulder. With each pull and purge, I start to detect something more nectarous buried beneath the acrid iron tainting his essence. The lines begin to look as though they're receding, but I can't tell if it's in my head or if what I'm doing is actually working.

I speed up, hope hammering my heart, as I suck and spit the poison from his body. His blood morphs into something more ambrosial with each pull from his wound, and Riall starts to wriggle beneath me. I kneel on his thighs to keep them anchored to the seat and do my best to pin his big shoulders with my hands. The horrid taste of the iron and the way it burns in my mouth grows weaker and weaker until, out of nowhere, Riall's fingers thread through my hair.

He groans as I take another deep draw from his chest. He presses my face harder against his wound, and his cock hardens. My fangs drop in my mouth when he moans again, his hips pistoning up with need as my mouth fills with his blood. I pull my lips away, spitting it out, and he turns to nuzzle me.

"What are you doing, Beasty?" he asks, his tone all gravel and rasp.

"Saving your stubborn ass," I answer huskily, which is frustrating because I mean to sound exasperated.

Relief slams into me when another resonant satisfied moan fills the air, and I notice Riall tastes perfectly clean now. Like dessert, but better. His flavors are layered and complex. He's a feast of all my favorite things mixed in a unique way that creates a mouthwatering explosion on my palate. I want to drink him dry while bathing in his essence at the same—

I shake away the cloud of lust and the image of this tub being filled with blood instead of water. My hands are trailing up Riall's chest like they have a mind of their own, and his palms are splayed wide on my ass. Astonished, I lean back and take him in. He was practically unconscious mere seconds ago, and now he's pulling my core against his very hard and very impressive dick.

I gulp and then cough, having forgotten that I didn't spit out my last mouthful of blood.

Sensation flares through me as Riall's ichor slips down my throat and warms my chest. My fangs ache and I'm suddenly rocking against him without making the conscious decision to take this from saving his life to grinding all over his cock like some beast in heat.

"Fuck, take more," Riall begs, and it's exactly what I need to snap out of my sex-hazed stupor.

I pull away despite his adorably pathetic whimpers telling me not to. His color is back. His eyes are open and bright. The deep gash now looks like a run-of-the-mill stab wound. Not willing to risk it, I take a page out of Riall's book and bite into my wrist. I hold the seeping punctures over the injury, bleeding onto him, like he once did for me.

"Beasty, your blood..." he murmurs sultrily, holding my ass more firmly as he rolls his hips up between mine.

The roughness of that satisfied exclamation settles right between my thighs. My nipples pebble, and a flurry of flutters awakens deep in my belly where Riall's blood is burning like an ember of need.

"I need to taste you," he pleads, his eyes once again closed, only this time the tremors working through him look like they're from pleasure not pain.

I look down to find that his injury is completely gone. My blood drips down the smooth plane of his hard pec as though it wasn't a festering mess mere moments ago. I stare stunned at what my blood just did for him. I've only ever seen the moon or a healer work that fast.

Wide-eyed and reeling, I watch as Riall reaches for my wrist. He pulls it slowly, carefully, to his mouth, as though he's giving me time to reclaim it. I debate doing just that, but there's an eager anticipation sparking inside of me that wants to see what will happen if he just...

Riall's long tongue snakes out, and he licks the two small wounds on my wrist. Our groans are a duet of desire as he tastes me. I swear I can feel his tongue both on my wrist and between the lips of my cunt at the same time.

"Fuck, that's good," he growls, and I agree by pressing harder against his cock and his chest. "Bite me, Beasty," he lustily orders, his fangs somehow longer as he looks at me from beneath his lashes like he wants to eat me in more ways than one.

I freeze.

Something in the back of my mind reminds me that Riall was almost just taken out by a shard of an iron dagger. He should rest...heal...recuperate. Then there's the louder part of me, the Sanguinna part, the part I haven't looked at too closely since the morning I woke up here and learned what a Sanguinna even was. That part of me wants to do very dirty, very fucked-up bloody things to this male. But I have no idea what that even entails.

Biting seems key, going by the sensual appeals so far, but I've really only ever used my fangs in defense. I don't want to hurt him.

"Hey, where'd you go?" Riall asks softly, caressing my cheek with his fingers.

His thumb brushes across the seam of my lips. Lightly he pushes the pad of his digit against the point of one of my fangs, and I gasp because it feels like he's pushing on my clit too. His grin is beaming as I stare at him in shock... and then I get pissed.

"I don't panic, Riall," I snap, and his smile drops faster than my inhibitions when it comes to these fucking Scorpions. "I don't worry, or freak out, or give a sand-covered toss when someone is sick or dying," I huff, hating the way my voice breaks slightly on the last word. "I take. I claim. I kill when I want to. Fuck when it feels good. I can't afford to be soft. I can't be weak!"

Adoring hazel eyes trace my face as Riall runs the tips of his short nails across my scalp as he threads his fingers in my knotted hair. It feels so good, so soothing, which pisses me off even more.

"You're the furthest possible thing from *weak*, Auset. I've never come across a more formidable and potent female. Your blood alone...fuck, Beasty. There isn't a frail thing about you. Worrying doesn't make you weak. Caring doesn't make you a target. Not here. Not with us, my Blood."

"It sure as shit didn't feel that way when your head was lolling back and you couldn't wake up," I argue, but it's lost some of its bite as the bastard practically rubs me, his touch trailing down my neck, my back, my arms and then rising to do it all over again. Fuck the Kings, it's helping. *"My Blood?"*

Riall's smile slinks across his face at my question.

"Yes, my Blood, it's the title used when Sanguinna find the one whose blood calls to them, sings for them, and yours is *all* I can hear right now."

I go quiet, listening as though I can hear what he's talking about, but more than hear, I feel a sonorous hum moored in my chest. I rub at it, and Riall's smirk morphs into a beaming smile.

"I'm sorry I worried you, Beasty. I wish I could say it will never happen again, but I'll never lie to you."

"You could have...I almost..."

The words *I almost lost you* sit like iron on my tongue. I can't say them out loud. I don't want to imbue them with power or tempt fate. I swallow my trepidation, hoping I never experience the taste of it again.

"I'm okay," Riall assures me. "You were here. What could ever get through you?" he challenges, speaking to my pride and ego like a fucking expert.

It's working.

"Being soft isn't bad. I for one would like to advocate for your soft parts," Riall teases as he leans forward and nips at the side of my neck. "Your tongue." The tip of his tongue flicks at my mouth. "Your breasts." He kisses my jaw. "Your ass." His hands skim slowly down my waist until he's cupping said ass. "Your perfect pussy." He sucks lightly just below my ear lobe.

I mewl softly, unable to help myself.

"Also, so there's no confusion, my Blood..." he carnally whispers in my ear. "I'm ready for you to take, to claim, to fuck me because it feels good. I want you to drink from me. Mark me all over, and then I want to do the same to you."

Riall practically purrs his words, but it starts to shift into a delicious growl that sinks into me and makes me feel eager and pliant. Then his next order sends my heart racing and adrenaline pinging through my veins.

"Now run, so I can hunt you."

51

DON'T THINK, I ONLY REACT. I GIVE IN TO A BASER instinct I don't quite understand, yet I feel completely compelled to follow. Water splashes all around as I surge out of Riall's lap and leap over him. The aggrieved grunt that sounds in my wake confirms that I might have kicked him in the sack in my effort to flee, but if he thought he could tell me to run and that I'd make it easy for him to catch me, he deserved that cheap shot, fair and square.

I skid on the slippery floor of the washroom and just barely grab the doorframe to help keep me on my feet. I can hear Riall charging out of his massive tub, and urgency slams through me to get away. I pull myself out of the bathing chamber, grateful when my bare feet find a warm rug and traction as I bolt for the door. Unbridled glee surges through me as I close the distance to the exit, and I start thinking of all the places I can hide and all the ways I can elude him. I had no idea being chased would get me this keyed up and excited. It seems I have a lot to learn about being Sanguinna.

I reach for the doorknob, practically ripping the large wood door off the hinges as I pull it open. I give no thought to the fact that I'm dripping wet and completely naked. Or that there's a prisoner in this house currently being questioned. Riall has somehow triggered this overpowering instinct in me to run, to test his worthiness, and I'm not even tempted to try to fight it.

I get one step out of the door, when an impossibly strong pair of arms wrap around my waist and yank me away from freedom. I squeal with both startled outrage and excitement as my back slams against Riall's massive chest. His hard cock digs into my ass cheeks, and I do my best to break his hold and drop my weight to throw him off balance. I manage to kick my foot hard against his knee, but all it elicits is a laugh.

A fucking laugh.

I once admitted to Eacon that I held back when I was training with the Scorpions. I lied about not wanting them to know everything I could do just in case I ever needed to use it against them. But as I throw one perfectly executed move after another at Riall, I quickly conclude that he actually has been holding back. The male is a brick wall made for battle. I'm of course not trying to maim him or get my fingers on a weapon and slice him to pieces, but I'm no slouch when it comes to grappling, and I can't get away from him for anything.

The more I fight to free myself, the more he growls with satisfaction. And the more he growls, the wetter I get. The throbbing need I'm experiencing is making it incredibly hard for me to continue to fight when I'm actually ecstatic for what's going to happen now that I'm caught.

Riall turns toward the bed across the room, and I'm airborne in the next blink, soaring through the air and onto his soft mattress with a scream that quickly morphs from thrilled to fucked when I remember I left his weapons on the bed. I crash down onto soft pillows and bedding, and thankfully nothing stabs me. I've just missed his laid out arsenal. I barely register the cache of blades before Riall is brushing them all to the ground before prowling toward me.

I don't know if I want to scold him for treating not only his weapons that way, but disrespecting Curio's unmatched craftsmanship, or if I want to swoon over the fact that Riall just chose me over his favorite blades. If the tables were turned, I might be hard-pressed to make such a hasty decision.

I make one last ditch effort to roll off the bed and flee, but Riall anticipates my every move and bounces me back onto the bed like I'm some naughty pet in need of training.

"I need you, Beasty," he practically snarls into my face, and I nip his lip hard and then suck on it.

His blood ripens in my mouth, and I moan as I swallow the few drops that the small slash offers me.

"I'm going to impale you on my cock and my fangs at the same time. Are you ready for me, my Blood?" he demands as he parts my thighs and presses his big body against me.

I run my hands up his hard pecs, over his strong shoulders, and down his rippling arms, spreading my legs as wide as I can to accommodate his big frame as I arch into him. My fangs lengthen.

"Ready—"

I barely get the word out before I smack soul-first into a wall of immaculate ecstasy. Riall thrusts inside of me deep and hard, his fangs piercing my shoulder at the exact same moment. I throw my head back and scream as an orgasm detonates. I swear Riall comes too as he swallows his first mouthful of my essence and eagerly demands more.

"I need your throat," I command breathlessly as my fangs throb and my orgasm wanes. "Give me your throat," I beg, and he drags his mouth from my shoulder and kisses me brutally. I wiggle and writhe, feasting on his mouth and tongue and the taste of my blood. It's just as good as the taste of my cum coating his kiss, and I suddenly want to drown in both.

He pulls back, panting hard, and throws his head back, offering me unfettered access to the smooth tan skin of his neck. His tendons are taut as he bares his throat. His delicious pulse beats strong and steady, calling to me, the taunting thump begging for me to lay it open and sip on the delicacies and luscious vows flowing within.

"Mark me, Blood, make me yours in every way."

Like a striking scorpion, I attack. In lightning-quick succession, I bite the front of his throat four times. Instinct guides me to only go deep enough to leave an even number of fang marks on each side of the very front of his throat. Possessive satisfaction thrums through me as I brand him, claiming him and his blood for me and only me forever. I have no idea how I know this, how I knew exactly what to do and how to do it, but I don't question the instinctual compulsion or the history and knowledge I can taste in the exchange.

Riall comes as I mark him, his encouraging moans only growing louder when I lick up the small trails of blood dripping down the front of his neck. My pussy flutters with each drop of blood that dots my tongue, and *finally* he starts to move between my thighs. His thick cock drags in and out of me tantalizingly slowly at first, his base grinding against my clit with each deep thrust. I lap at his neck just as languidly, scraping my fangs against the sensitive skin on his neck and just under his chin until he starts to piston into me harder and faster. The columns of punctures on his neck clot and stop bleeding, and I scrape my lips from my marks to his shoulder.

My heart beats slowly, even though our bodies come together more relentlessly. I can feel Riall's essence sinking into me, an even steady trickle of warmth and strength moving through my veins with each strong beat of my pulse. Our blood merges, marking and claiming from the inside out.

I feel strong.

I feel tethered.

I feel ravenous.

My fangs tear into Riall's shoulder, and his pace in my pussy turns frantic. I drink him down, slurping and moaning as his blood hums inside of me, making every part of me more sensitive. His hands squeezing my hips, my breasts, my ass, feel like they're kneading my soul too. His lips and fangs trace erotic paths across my body as he sucks and pierces me over and over again until all I am is sensation and need. Suddenly we're fucking each other in some dominant show of passion and desire. Our bodies meet and fight, our hips slam together as we bite and drink. We claw at each other, each sensation a wicked combination of overload and yet somehow still not enough.

I'm lifted from the bed and pushed up against the smooth headboard that's taller than I am as Riall fucks me even harder. We both watch, completely hypnotized, as he works in and out of my dripping cunt, my breasts bouncing wildly between us with each brutal drive of his cock. Our mouths come together in a savage clash that's more bite and suck than lips and tongue. Blood seeps from the mass of bites we decorate across each other's skin.

"More!" I snap at him, giving myself over completely to the beastly call within.

I shove away from the wall with a power I've never had before. Riall stumbles back with me clutched tightly in his arms. His dick is deep inside of me as we crash into his chair. I hear a distinct snap and tearing of fabric, and then suddenly we're falling. I'm weightless for a fraction of a second as we plummet to the floor. His strong back and ass and my knees slam down onto the rug that barely cushions our jarring drop. The tumble slams me down on top of him, shoving his cock even deeper with a slight pinch of pain that's there and gone as he reaches for my hips. I don't even pause before I'm once again riding him like the feral monster I am.

He growls his approval, his hands clamping down on my ass, encouraging me to take more, to take everything.

"That's it, fill yourself with all of me. Bounce on your Blood's cock. Take every fucking drop while you shove those pretty tits in my face."

Riall bites the top of my breast, and I'm gasping from the pleasure that surges as he does. He sucks at me, and when I throw my head back, he strikes at the front of my throat, marking me just like I marked him.

Something infinitely strong and otherworldly snaps into place between us as he brands my throat with his fangs. It's a homecoming, a uniting, a claiming of my blood and my soul. Certainty blooms in my chest and my mind as we're bound together in every way. Who he is and what he means to me is woven into the very fibers of my being now. I felt that kind of connection on a mental and emotional level with all of the Scorpions when we came together, but now I feel it in my blood with Riall in a unique and undeniable way.

I come so hard my throat feels like it constricts, trapping my exultant scream as my body locks in place. Riall is right there with me, his fangs once again in my shoulder as we're both wrapped in a heated blanket of bliss and sated completion. I'm overwhelmed by the love and gratitude I feel for this perfect and impenetrable connection. I didn't realize how badly I needed it until it was humming inside of me. So many intense emotions surge all at once, and it's hard to sort through the abundant warmth and love and light. So I don't even try. I simply feel and revel in it, sinking deeper into the beauty and security and letting it all consume me.

Riall pulls his fangs from my shoulder, lapping up the dripping blood before falling back and trying to catch his breath. I can feel his heart racing beneath my palms, and I know mine matches the hurried rhythm perfectly. His hair looks lighter to me for some reason. It seems the blood loss and the mind-blowing orgasms might be affecting my eyes. Riall smiles up at me, all smug satisfaction and radiant contentment. I grin like a fool right back, because he's home now. Curio and Tarek are too, and I've never felt so incandescently buoyant and happy. My fangs recede as though their job here is done, and I have to admit I like seeing my marks all over Riall's body.

I push my hair back and then freeze when I catch shredded fabric in my periphery. I look around, shock settling quickly in my chest as I take in the completely trashed room. I gasp and press a hand to my mouth.

"When did we break the bed?" I ask, appalled as I take in the splintered frame and shattered footboard.

Feathers coat the wreckage like we clawed our way through not only each other but through every surface in here.

"That was everything," Riall pants dreamily. "I'd read about Blood Bonds, but I never thought... That was *everything*," he repeats and laughs.

"Eh," I tease with a casual shrug.

He scowls up at me, a myriad of dark and delicious plans floating to the surface of his gleaming gaze. An irreverent smirk pulls at the corners of his mouth, and he grinds into me.

"Blood Bonds?" I question even though I can feel exactly what he just named humming in my veins.

"Sanguinna term for mates, more or less," he explains. "We're linked by blood now, so you might be able to sense things about me, how I'm feeling or where I'm located through that link. It can vary, and unfortunately it's hard to find reliable information about how it all works. I discovered plenty on how to create a bond but not a whole lot on what happens after you do."

"I got here as fast I could," Eacon announces as she shoves the door open.

There's absolutely no time to do anything before she's standing in the doorway looking around confused before her gaze lands on us.

"Oh," she chirps with surprise, her astonished gaze flitting from the shredded drapes to the splintered bed and then to the shattered chair before once again landing back on us. "Oh," she exclaims again as understanding slowly seeps in.

Eacon's cheeks flush, and her eyes grow even wider.

"Hey, Eacs," Riall greets, as though he's not cock-deep inside of me right now and *covered* in bites and blood.

I sit there like I'm daft, unsure if this is made all the more awkward by my *not* moving to get off of Riall or if uncorking his dick from my cunt in front of Eacon would take this to a whole other level of disturbing.

"This is amazing!" she coos, and thankfully she reaches for the door and tries to pull it shut. Our situation isn't helped when it falls off the hinges completely and crashes to the ground.

"Shit!" Eacon yelps, and then she turns and gives us her back, which is thoughtful, but she doesn't leave, which isn't.

"I'm so happy for you, Riall! Do your brothers know?" she asks sweetly, and I cringe as I push off of him and his cum starts to drip down my thigh.

He smiles fiendishly at me when he notices, but answers Eacon evenly.

"We all mated when we were away. Auset and I were just testing the healing properties of blood," he tells her, and I roll my eyes.

"You know she just saw us, right?" I whisper-scold him. "Healing properties of blood?" I mock.

He just shrugs, like that was the best he could come up with.

Eacon squeals with delight. "I can't wait to tell Rink. We thought for sure you all had your work cut out. Auset, I'm so thrilled. You're an incredible treasure, and I can't wait for the brothers to show you just how incredible you are every day for the rest of your life!"

Her words are kind and so sincere it makes my eyes sting a little. It's made even better by the fact that the last time I saw her she was covered in blood after ruthlessly torturing someone. Now she's welcoming me to the family like some doting mother figure who just wants her boys to settle down.

I smile.

"Thank you, Eacon. You and Rink helped me see things from a different perspective," I confess as I sneak into the washroom.

Shit, is there any part of his quarters we didn't destroy?

"Do either of you need healing?" she hedges.

I look down to see all of the blood-covered bites are already mending on their own. I turn to the mirror and inspect my body. My skin is smooth and tan like it always is—even the blood smears aren't unusual. I lift my chin and notice the two columns of four dots running up the front of my throat. The marks look old, like they've been there forever.

Tilleo was always very clear about how blade slaves couldn't have any identifying scars or marks. We were healed and sent back to suffer, time and time again. If there was an injury that blemished a blade slave in any way, they were washed from the ludere.

I run my finger down the perfect lines of healed punctures. They're sensitive, and goose bumps speckle my arms at the contact. I know somehow that they're special, that they represent the bond between me and Riall and our beastly natures.

"No healing needed," I call out, smiling when Riall sidles up behind me and wraps me in his arms.

"Very well then. I'll leave you to it. Congrats again," she calls to us, and then we both listen carefully as she moves away, her footsteps growing quieter until they disappear altogether.

"Locks," I announce as I start to clean up the mess in the washroom so that we can attend to the mess that's painted across our bodies and dripping from places. "First order of business is locks on every door in this castle. Second," I correct when I remember we have a ghost in the dungeons. "The locks are actually the second order of business. The first is finally getting some answers about why the iron-dagger-wielding fucks look like me."

"You're a regular tactician," Riall teases. "Locks and answers, it is."

"Answers and locks," I chide, smiling at his taunting smirk.

He wraps me up in a tight hug and brings his lips to my ear. "How about pussy and cock one more time before answers and locks?"

I laugh and sigh like he's just too much, but my smile brightens as his hazel gaze darkens with desire.

"Pussy and cock really should be the first order of business at all times," I agree.

"It's the natural order of things. Who are we to fight that?" he whispers conspiratorially to me.

I laugh and he hauls me up his body until I'm wrapped around his torso like the greedy beast that I am.

"There's no fighting nature," I add as our lips meet in a slow and sensual kiss.

I wouldn't now even if I could, because this is fucking perfect.

52

TAREK

ERUS GLARES AT ME, HATE AND WRATH FLOOD-ing his gaze as he fights not to swallow the whin-nip root tincture I just poured into his mouth. He jerks and struggles against his restraints and my hold, but my grip on his jaw and nose is firm. We both know it's only a matter of time before he swallows it, just like every other time I've forced him to.

His commitment to fighting the inevitable would be im-pressive if it weren't so fucking vexing. It's been four days already. Two more than I would have wagered he'd last, but we're making progress. Yesterday, we finally got his name, a feat that almost seemed to fracture the fae before he once again hardened his resolve. He'll shatter completely. He's almost there.

Judging by the abhorrence currently glowing in his silver eyes, today looks like the *fight with everything you have* day. The true warriors, the seasoned hunters, always rally. They always brawl the hardest before they break. What Verus doesn't know is that I *relish* this last battle even more than the day they finally crack. The moment when everything we want finally pours right out of someone is a thrilling experience, but there's something about going head-to-head with someone and coming out on top that feeds my fucking soul.

Verus's throat bobs and he closes his eyes in defeat before once again opening them and leveling me with a scathing glare. I let his jaw and nose go, and he sucks in deep desperate breaths. A few coughs wrack his efforts, and I scowl down at the doomed warrior as I pull the levers on the contraption he's bound to that transforms it from the flat bed it currently is into a chair.

"If you purge it, I'll scoop it back into your mouth until it goes down again, just like last time," I warn. "I'm happy to do it as many times as you need to keep it down."

Verus's lip curls with disdain. He doesn't respond, but he also doesn't retch up the solution that makes it harder for him to keep his lips closed and his secrets to himself.

"Now where were we?" I ask absently, my eyes flicking over to Curio in question as I take a seat in front of the special chair he designed just for this room. It's bolted to the stone floor and can be maneuvered into a myriad of different positions and angles, all with the pull of the levers at the back. It makes it infinitely easier to slip from one session into another without having to unbind a captive and inadvertently give them an opportunity to attack or fight while securing them again.

Verus is currently seated in the armchair option as though we're all civilized fae meeting for a chat and maybe a spot of tea.

"His hair," Curio supplies, and I nod, picking at the thread of questions we were last discussing with our captive.

We spent the first two days diving into the matter of Lord Daeral's murder. It went about as well as I expected. We gleaned very little other than what happened was some kind of lesson. Whether Lord Daeral learned that lesson or it was intended for someone else, we still don't know, but it set the tone for what Verus *thinks* we want from him.

He's confident our goal is to discover as much as we can about the massacre. He's as tight-lipped about that as he can be, so we've switched up our tactics to make him feel like he's winning, like he's outsmarting us while still saving himself from as much pain as possible. From the outside looking in, it seems as though we're attempting to soften him. That we don't want to kill him in our efforts to get the information we're *desperate* for.

Verus thinks we're now focusing on getting him talking in general. Why else would we be asking inane questions about his favorite food, why he looks the way that he does, which season of a year he likes the most, what activities he did as a child? It throws him off. We slip in the occasional massacre question to keep his focus there and to make him suspect that we're trying to trip him up for answers, but it's actually the little details about *him* that we really want.

He throws out a bread crumb or two, thinking he's stringing us along. Lies, I'm sure, but a lot can be pieced together from the simplest and most innocent untruths.

"Is your coloring from your mother's or your sire's side? Is it some kind of malady?" I ask casually, resting my ankle over my opposite knee and settling back into my chair as though I'm getting comfortable in preparation for a long day. "Do your light eyes make it difficult to see at night or during the brightest part of the day?"

Verus doesn't respond.

"Anyone ever refer to you as moon blessed?" I inquire, and this question gets me a reaction.

He glares at me as though he's fed up with my prodding, but we both know that's not it. He was surprised by the term. He responded and then realized his mistake and is now trying to bury it in anger and frustration.

I study my nails, inspecting them as though I didn't just catch every blaring detail he just gave away and once again try to recall where I saw that term. I recalled it when we met Auset at the Bidding, something about her unique coloring brought it to mind. I know I've read it somewhere, but I've searched my entire library and can't find it. I had a hunch Verus might find it familiar, and I was right, which makes the elusive text that contained the phrase all the more infuriating because I can't recall where it might be.

"What time do you usually rise to start your day?" I press.

Verus's *fuck you* mask is once again in place. Curio sets a small incubator on the far table with a small percussive thump. Verus tries not to turn his head toward it, but his eyes swiftly glance over and then away. He knows what's coming. His breaths pick up with a hint of panic before he tightens his control and forces them back to the even inhales and exhales he works hard to maintain.

I pull the dagger currently sheathed at my ankle. It's the one Auset filched from me that first night, and I debate between giving it to her as a gift or hoarding it like the prized blade it's become to me. Slowly, I begin to flip it around my fingers, expertly twisting it between my digits as though I couldn't slip and relieve myself of one of them at any moment. It could be seen as an intimidation tactic. Really, I'm just bored. We have big plans for our captive today, but Riall went overboard on breakfast, which means Auset probably won't be done eating for a bit longer.

Riall knows she's learning to pace herself, but that's warring with the instinct to provide, which his new Blood Bond is driving through him. Auset can't walk away from a single crumb left on any plate. She's feral when it comes to food, which is an adorable sight to behold, but when I think about *why* she's that way, I start to feel a little fucking feral myself.

By some miracle, Auset doesn't blame us for what happened to her anymore. I don't know if I'll ever forgive myself for it though. I've learned a priceless lesson on complacency and negligence. It's definitely changed what we allow to be done in the name of the Order of Scorpions and what we'll stand for. But the damage has been done, and there's not much we can do other than ensure it doesn't happen again and make what restitution we can when Auset is ready.

I hate the circumstances around the discovery of our mate and what she went through at the ludere. As grateful as I am that we even found her, it's a crushing blow to know that the other piece of your soul was stripped raw and irreversibly scarred by soulless monsters, and it's your fault.

I focus back on Verus and the room. Now's not the time for me to get broody, no matter how much I wish I could fix what we fucked up. I can give her Verus though, give her access to what's in his head, and that will have to do for now.

"What did you eat before you ambushed us the other night?" Curio asks as he unlatches the locks on the lid of the incubator. "What time do you usually eat dinner?"

Verus's nostrils flare in an effort to pull in more oxygen while he clamps his mouth tighter, and his lips thin into a stubborn line.

"Do you prefer a cold day or a hot one?" I chime in.

Sweat starts to bead on Verus's upper lip, and his breathing grows louder as he keeps his eyes trained on the small alcove of shadows that blanket the door and the only entrance and exit to the room.

Curio dips a hand into the incubator. "What's your favorite weapon, the one you reach for first when you're scared?"

Black swells until only a thin ring of the silver is visible in Verus's gaze. His unusual eye color is notably darker than Auset's. His has shards of gray hidden in the hue instead of the chips of pale blue and violet found in our mate's stare.

Curio turns and Verus's pale skin grows even paler.

"You remember Danes and Gilmore, right?" Curio queries as he sets two small Bolt scorpions on Verus's pale chest.

Curio moves to reset and lock the lid on the rest of the nest in the incubator and then drops into his own chair as the two small scorpions start to get comfortable. Verus tilts his chin up as though he's trying to get as far from the painful little beasts as he can. They cautiously crawl in opposite directions, Gilmore heading for Verus's shoulder while Danes skitters to the opposite armpit. Danes always picks the most painful places, a trait, sadly, none of his offspring have shown the same penchant for. I grin as I think about the tiny beast. I'm pretty sure the gifted little crawler enjoys this as much as we do.

"What's the first sound you hear when you wake in the morning?" I press as our ghost's chest starts to rise and fall faster and faster and goose bumps rise on his bare arms and chest.

Verus stays silent, but I can tell it's a struggle.

Curio smiles as he picks up a tuning fork from the table next to him. His eyes never leave Verus as he knocks the fork against the leg of his chair before lifting it up in front of him. As soon as the resonant sound begins to ring in the room, Verus tenses, but both Bolt scorpions have already seized his skin with their pincers and struck with their tails.

A low keen spills out of Verus's clenched teeth as pain from the stings works to overwhelm his senses. Bolt scorpions—aptly named for a sting that feels as though you've just been shot with the bolt of a crossbow—have the useful ability to cause maximum pain without being dangerously toxic. It makes them the perfect little helpers when it comes to this kind of work. A handful of days spent with the Bolts and the Scorchers that we breed for this exact purpose, and we usually get what we want out of someone. The Empress always joins in too, but we like to save the best for last.

Silencing the tuning fork with his hand, Curio sits back, and the bolts relax, creeping to new spots on Verus's body like they're ready and waiting for the next signal. He growls, spittle breaching the seam of his closed lips as he tries to shake the scorpions off his torso with a distressed whine that quickly morphs into a roar that rings with agony and frustration. Gilmore almost loses her hold, and Curio holds up the tuning fork in warning. Verus immediately sags against his bindings, sweat now dripping down his neck as he looks around wildly, his enraged stare now steeped in suffering.

"Be a good boy," I taunt. "Answer some questions, tell us what we want to know, and maybe, just maybe we'll let you spend some time with the moon tonight," I offer nonchalantly, and Verus's head immediately snaps in my direction. "I thought that might get your attention."

He glowers at me, but the spark of uncertainty in his eyes stokes a fire in my gut. I can practically see him thinking through everything that's been said and revealed in this room, searching for when he let that key piece of information slip. He didn't, and watching that dawn on him is the first piece in today's game, because it reminds him of her.

Curio and I discovered early on, when Verus was still in the habit of asking us a question every time we posed one to him, that he was very interested in the fourth Scorpion. The one he didn't know existed. The one who can heal by the light of the moon, just like him, it seems.

We weren't sure if the healing thing was special to Auset or if there were others who could do it. Staring into Verus's eyes right now confirms that it's not just her. The fact that he watched her do something that we suspect only he and his people can do has sparked an obsessive interest in him that we're going to use to our advantage today.

A knock at the door breaks up the tense silence, and I smile at the perfect timing. I rise to answer it, stepping out of the room and into the hallway lit by fairy light sconces spaced evenly on the walls.

"Finished with breakfast?" I tease with a sly smile, and Auset snorts.

She likes to pretend that she disapproves of my teasing Riall, but there's always a smile curving at the edges of her mouth that gives her amusement away. She can't blame us. Riall's sudden over-the-top urges to provide, protect, and preen for his new *Blood* are absolutely fair game. He's so besotted it's fucking adorable, but cooking every dish Auset has ever liked and then trying to hand feed it to her is not going to be overlooked.

The first and only time he took something from her plate and lifted it sensually to her lips, I almost pissed myself from laughing. She shut down the hand feeding so fast, offended that he would take anything from her plate even though he was trying to feed it to her and not steal it for himself. It's like his bonding instinct has forgotten who our feisty little mate is.

Auset rests a hand on Riall's chest and pets him affectionately. "It was delicious as always. I'm completely stuffed."

Riall grins but there's a lascivious tilt to it, and I just know the lucky bastard fucked her on the kitchen table to help her work off some of that big breakfast he couldn't help but make. I'll have to call dibs on her and the table for lunch.

"You ready?" I ask Auset, jutting my chin in the direction of the door.

She nods, an eager twinkle in her eye, but I can tell she's anxious too. There's a lot riding on getting Verus talking. All of us have watched Auset silently struggle with the fiery need to find answers while trying not to get her hopes up. She deserves this, and we're going to ensure she gets what she needs from this pissant.

"Ready," Riall grunts, and I'm still struck by the physical changes in him since he and Auset first drank from each other.

It's taking some getting used to.

We all researched what we could about female Sanguinna and Blood Bonds when Auset revealed she was one. There wasn't an abundance of information. It seems most of the answers disappeared when female Sanguinna did, but nothing any of us came across talked about the changes their bodies would go through after they were bonded.

Riall got taller by half a hand and filled out even more. It was like he went through some final stage of Sanguinna puberty. His hair got lighter, more ash blond than the ash brown it was before, and there's now a distinct silver ring around his pupil that fades into the hazel color he's always had. They're both faster and stronger now, although there hasn't been much time to test the full extent of that.

"Still think this is the way to go?" I ask, not really questioning Auset's plan but trying to help her feel as confident in it as she can before walking through the door.

"How fucked am I for being excited?" she asks, and I chuckle.

"Fucked up is my bread and butter, so you might be asking the wrong person," I tell her, pulling her closer until her chest is pressed against mine.

I want to untie her tunic and suck on the tight nipples I can feel against my chest through our togs. Her pupils start to dilate, and the fact that it could be from either me or what's about to go down with our captive does all kinds of salacious things for me.

"It's good to do what you're made to do," Riall assures her gently.

I cup her face before she can get too caught up in her head, and tilt her head back. I want to sample her excitement, taste the hint of desire I see floating in her eyes and tightening her perfect body. I fucking love that we're able to give her this. I was ready to scour the fucking realms and beyond to find answers for her, but somehow they fell right into our laps, like a mating present from the stars themselves.

I want to live the rest of my days doing everything I can to ensure that Auset feels exactly like she does right now. Hopeful. Elated. Loved.

I deepen the kiss just a little and then pull back, my forehead pressing to hers as I fix a glamour in place. Her eyes and hair darken until they're blacker than shadows. The skeletal mien rises to the surface of her skin as though its oil drops in water. My thura ascends and converges until she's all Scorpion on the outside. She's in a black fitted tunic and leathers, with Curio's custom blades hidden all over her body.

I'm once again astounded that we found her, that she's ours—or rather we're hers as she likes us to concede whenever we're feeling particularly possessive. I'll never stop being in awe of that, because we are, in every possible way. We're hers.

I squeeze her ass once for good measure and then give Riall his glamour.

"What no ass grab for me?" he taunts as I turn to go back inside the room.

I'm chuckling as I step through the door to find Verus intently watching. This chamber is warded, so sound doesn't travel in or out of surrounding walls, but Curio has set out two other chairs for us, and it appears that Verus is eager to discover who will be joining today's torture.

I watch him carefully as I step to the side to reveal Riall—although now he's much taller than I am, so maybe it's not much of a surprise that he's standing behind me. Verus's silver gaze dims with resigned disappointment as he takes my brother in. He must think we're once again entering the *beat it out of you* portion of his captivity.

Riall strides confidently to the seat next to Curio and plops himself down. Disappointment is quickly replaced by a flash of interest as Auset closes the door behind her and strides out of the shadows to stand behind the chair next to mine. She rests her glamoured skeletal hands on the back of the seat and stares at Verus for a second.

This is officially her show now, and I can't wait to sit back and watch her work.

We've discussed things at length, but all of us know, when it comes to extracting information from unwilling participants, things don't always go according to plan. Mostly we just want to rattle Verus and see what falls out in the process, but I love watching her take control of her fate like this.

"I wondered when you'd show up," Verus comments, and Curio raises an eyebrow at the brazenness he has despite our best efforts to wring every drop of hubris from the bastard's body.

Like the huntress she is, Auset just watches him.

Failing to get a reaction, Verus tries to match her placidity, but after a handful of minutes, Danes skitters up to his shoulder and he flinches.

When the quiet seems to grow to be too much for him, Verus asks, "Who are you?"

I don't like how he's staring at her. It's as though he's seeing a lifeline and not the threat that she is. My girl will teach him though.

Auset moves around the chair and over to the table by Curio where all of Verus's armor and weapons have been laid out. She remains silent as she runs her finger over the light gray shell of his chest plate like she's trying to find something familiar about it. Her stunning black eyes rake over the weapons as though she's both searching through them and cataloging them simultaneously. Finding what she's looking for, she reaches out and plucks the iron blade from the array.

She studies the weapon, paying careful attention to the bone hilt and the gleaming blade.

"You couldn't pay most fae to put a pebble of iron in their pocket for more than a dozen minutes," Auset observes as she walks behind the chair and out of Verus's line of sight. "And yet you carry around a blade made with the noxious metal. How long did it take you to build a tolerance?"

"Years," Verus grits out like the word is forcing its way past his lips against his will.

I grin, knowing the whinnip root is taking hold of his tongue.

"Who are you?" he demands again.

"Does it still burn you, or are you immune to even that?" she continues.

He doesn't answer.

Auset shrugs like his silence makes no difference to her and then moves in closer from behind and presses the flat of the blade to the side of his neck.

A sizzling sound starts, and the distinct smell of iron-charred flesh wafts through the room. Verus hisses and tries to move away from the blade. Auset lets him, having found the answer to her question despite his silence.

"Not immune," she observes as though she already knew this and is sweetly taunting him.

Verus clenches his jaw against the pain, his hands once again in fists as he grunts out, "Who are you?"

The shit stain clearly can't let that go.

"You fight with it, but you're not used to the bite of the blade?" she queries in that saccharine, silky, slightly taunting way of hers.

I'm intimately familiar with her candied contempt. I swallowed my fair share of it when we first met. She has an uncanny way of slicing you up with every word, judging you as lacking and beneath her, and all you want is more. It doesn't matter that she's cutting you to the quick, because she's only looking at you when she does it, and it makes you want everything she'd offer if you could only prove yourself worthy.

Auset moves to the front of Verus, and his eyes track her like she's a fresh stream in the desert. Slowly, calculatingly, Auset folds the sleeve of her tunic up until her forearm is exposed. She keeps her intense stare on Verus as she brings the flat of the iron blade to her inner arm. She stares at him with absolutely no expression on her face as the iron burns her skin and marks her as tougher than this fuck could ever hope to be.

She's a strikingly ferocious little fae.

"I've known the bite of every blade I've ever used," she declares, her voice perfectly even and casual as she finally pulls the iron from her skin. "I used to think it was more of a barbaric practice than a useful one, but I'm starting to see its merits. What do you think, Verus?"

Auset speaks his name as though she's searching for something familiar in it. Interestingly enough, Verus looks as though he's doing the same with the sound of her voice. All of us are tiptoeing around the rim of something unknown, waiting to see who will fall in first.

"Who are *you?*" she asks, parroting Verus's question.

There's a fierce and determined look in her eyes that promises she's going to get what she wants one way or another. Verus studies the iron blade in her hand, the burn on her arm, and then her face.

He clenches his teeth against the answer that's trying to crawl out of his mouth. "Verus Hathwait, second son of Chief Hathwait. Sword in the first division of the Moon's army."

He stops, panting for breath as though each word was ripped from his innards, his glare icy and filled with spite.

"*Soh thorah ruw erahda, sian hierreth vier ausooe fotil eiss,*" he demands in a language I've never heard before.

I tense as it rings around the room, falling all around

us like seedlings that have lost their guiding breeze. What shocks the ever loving shit out of me though, what knocks me across the jaw like a cheap hit, is when Auset looks him dead in the eye and then answers in the same lilting mystery tongue.

53

AUSET

I KNOW YOU'RE ONE OF US! DECLARE YOURSELF AND *your clan, or lose all honor!*" he barks at me, the words ringing around me, but there's something off about them I can't place.

It's like the pitch is wrong somehow.

"Piss on your honor. You're owed nothing! Earn the answers to those questions or shut the fuck up," I snarl back, slamming the iron dagger into the wooden arm of the chair Verus is bound to.

The blade misses his skin, but just barely.

It isn't until I hear my voice echoing off the stone walls, that I comprehend what just happened. It isn't Common that ricochets around me like some winged pest. It's a different set of strange off-key words that I hear and understand as clear as day.

I've slipped into another language without even realizing it.

It's like all the times in the ludere when I could read something on a healer's desk or scan the parchment or book that a guard was looking at. I shouldn't have been able to read anything, and yet I could, regardless of what language it was in or what realm it came from. I overheard many conversations I thought were in Common because I could understand them, only to realize later that there was something off about the words because they were a different language.

It took me longer to figure out that I could speak different languages in addition to understanding them. It happened by accident at first when a fellow blade slave was having a nightmare and talking in her sleep. I thought it was Common, but the next day when I spoke to her while we were washing up, it was in whatever native tongue she spoke.

She was washed from the ludere a handful of months after that, but I knew I had a unique ability that I needed to keep to myself.

It's as though my mind absorbs everything, reconfigures it in a way I can understand, and then lets me spit it all back out in whatever language was spoken in the first place.

Verus's silver eyes grow wide with surprise at my response, like he suspected but didn't actually *know* if I'd understand him. All too quickly, satisfaction settles in his stare like he's caught me, just like he'd hoped he would.

Fuck.

I already knew that Verus and I come from the same people. The match of his unique coloring to mine is all I really need to know. However, he didn't know that...until now. I just confirmed his suspicions, and I don't know if that's going to fuck me over or help me in getting answers from him.

Verus looks around the room and then at the Scorpions as though he's seeing things differently. I watch him try to piece together what it all means with what he just learned. His silver eyes snap back to mine, fresh desperation tinting his gaze.

"I don't know who you are exactly or why you're here with them, but one Igeeyin to another, you have to release me. My clan will offer a life debt. It's for The Cause."

I keep my face neutral as he pleads with me in a tongue I speak and understand but don't know the name of. Inside, my mind is rioting with all the clues that just came spilling out. I want to examine each and every word thoroughly right here and now, but I know that I can't. I rein in my emotions and focus on what to do.

The term *Igeeyin* stands out to me as significant, but I can't exactly ask him why. I need a new angle to make this work, to keep him talking. Maybe *The Cause*—whatever the fuck that is? It sounds vague enough and possibly big enough that I can work within its parameters. Whatever it happens to be, he thinks I should not only know it, but that it would motivate me—a perfect stranger—to help him on its behalf.

We're getting somewhere, but if I don't play this right, I have a feeling it will take a turn to nowhere fast, and there might not be any coming back from that.

"*We're here on behalf of The Cause, and yet you attacked us. I won't be tricked,*" I retort, doing my best to look incensed instead of clueless and hoping this actually works.

I turn from Verus and stride over to the chair next to Tarek. His gaze meets mine, and it's brimming with questions, but I shake my head slightly as I take a seat. In a blink, he's once again looking bored, like he understands everything going on here but has more important things to do. I want to kiss the shit out of him, out of all of them, for being so good at this subterfuge shit and for trusting me to handle things.

I settle in next to Tarek, and I fix my gaze on Verus, leveling him with a haughty look that feels appropriate to the pretend affront I'm putting on.

His face is wary as he assesses me. He doesn't know what to make of this, but that makes two of us. My claim is absurd, but he saw me heal my hand in the moonlight, and I'm speaking a language that I suspect not many fae know. I'm hoping that's enough to push what I'm saying across the line from ridiculous to plausible.

"Show me who you are," he orders again, reverting back to Common and once again tapping into whatever arrogance has convinced him that he's in any place to be dictating what happens here.

It seems Verus is a fan of going in circles.

"Prove you're worthy to know," I counter, crossing my legs and leaning back in my chair as though I'm more than happy to sit here all day making myself dizzy on this never-ending loop of sarkar shit.

Each of the Scorpions watches our exchange as though they haven't a care in the world. They're relaxed, playing with daggers absently, gazes missing nothing but not trained on any one thing that might tip the scales we're precariously balancing on. We're all lakes in the forest, still and glassy on the surface while terrifying monsters lurk in our depths ready to breach the calm to snatch our prey at any given moment.

"Would you remove these?"

Verus uses his chin to gesture to the small yellow scorpion that's lazily crawling toward the iron burn on his neck, while the other Bolt looks as though it's trying to get comfortable in his belly button. There's a hint of timidity in his question that doesn't register as authentic. Perhaps he's probing to see if a plea for mercy gets him anywhere, or maybe he's subtly saying that a little goodwill toward him would earn me some in return.

Curio looks at me, the casual unassuming tilt of his head in my direction a small gesture, but it means so much. He's transferring the power he's held in this room to me, strengthening my position in Verus's eyes and trusting me to take this where it needs to go.

Like the first time in the duke's house, when they followed without question and unwavering support, I'm struck by their steadfast and resolute devotion. I don't know what I've done to deserve it. Simply accepting them and caring about them doesn't seem like enough in comparison to the sacrosanct veneration they offer me time and time again.

I was once so worried that I would lose myself in them before I ever knew who I really was, but that worry is laughable now. I could never be buried under the weight of who they are, because they treat me like the tether that pulls *them* from the onslaught.

They lift me toward what I want instead of plucking it down and handing it over. They help me find solid ground in a world made of quicksand. I lead, they follow. I need, they give. They shift who's at the helm based on strengths, with no jealousy or competition marring the smooth transition of trust and control. They're family, a true team in every sense, and now I am too.

I've hated the thought of *belonging* to them. Spending too much time under the thumb of undeserving masters and cruel fae tainted the mere thought of feeling owned by anyone ever again. But I suddenly understand what it means to be *theirs*, and I realize that I couldn't be any safer or in more perfect hands than the loving ones they offer me.

Warmth gathers in my chest, but I place everything I'm feeling in a box and set it aside for later. I want to be somewhere safe where there are no interruptions when I wrap myself and them in these profound revelations and get lost in one another.

I give Curio a nod, and he stands up and walks over to remove the Bolt scorpions. Riall is suddenly in front of me, blocking my view. He reaches for my hand, exposing the burn on my arm that's throbbing and angry. Brow furrowed with concern, he bites into his wrist and then drips his blood all over the burn before it immediately starts looking better. Riall offers me his wrist and I take it, bringing his two puncture marks to my mouth and licking his wrist clean.

I suddenly find myself wishing I was licking other things, but I kick that thought in the throat and focus on what's important. I hate that it feels like I'm fishing for answers with untested lures. I'm not the most patient person, and this dance around for information is tedious and slow. I want what's in Verus's head, and I want it now.

Riall's bite stops bleeding. He swipes his thumb across my lip with a heated look and then pops that thumb into his mouth before returning to his seat next to Curio. My arm is completely healed; there's not even a mark. I roll down my sleeve, not wanting to give away any other secrets for free.

Curio sits down, the bolt scorpions now back in the incubator, and I level Verus with a *let's cut the shit* look. His eyes flick from me to Riall and back again as though he knows some kind of exchange just occurred but he can't pinpoint what.

"I'm done measuring cocks. You think yours is a prized piece, but we both know mine is bigger and better. Either prove that what you say is true or fucking die and stop wasting my time."

Riall snorts out a laugh before collecting himself. I can just make out Tarek's amused grin out of the corner of my eye, and Curio's chest is vibrating with silent laughter while his face is entirely blank. I have no idea how he's doing that, I'll have to ask him to teach me that trick later.

Verus's silver eyes narrow. It's like he's trying to slice me open and see all the secrets lining my insides. He's fighting not to answer, but whatever Tarek has been dosing him with is once again winning, and he sags in his chair, defeated.

"We weren't trying to kill you," he assures, looking from me to the other Scorpions and then back. "We were supposed to separate one of you from the others, capture them and then use them as bait to bring the other two heads of the Order to the negotiating table."

"When did things change?" I press, trying to keep my question vague but confident.

"Everything is changing," he admits easily. "We're getting close, and it means we need to be more aggressive. An alliance would have been smart; I just don't know why the Crescents didn't tell us about you."

The statement is open-ended, and he watches me like he's waiting for me to explain, so I mimic his resignation and huff out a deep sigh and sag back in my chair.

"I don't know," I answer truthfully as I let my eyes focus on the stacked stones that make up the wall behind him while trying to look pensive and a little lost.

I try not to hold my breath while I wait to see how he'll react to my honest but contextually *full-of-piss* confession.

"Erif was understandably upset when *he* killed his brother." Verus juts his chin in Riall's direction.

I scoff at his misplaced anger. "Did you think he was going to go peacefully?"

"We had hawx claw," he defends.

My stomach lurches at the name, and I'm suddenly yanked back to Dorsin's quarters. He was asking me questions, but I couldn't remember anything.

"Did you dose her with something?" Dorsin had asked.

"Only the hawx claw we discussed so she'd be out for the grab and transport."

The orc's jagged voice and his unforgettable stench assaults me like he's in the room with us right now. I look around, making sure that he's not, which is addled because the fucker is dead. I untether myself from the flash of memory and concentrate on Verus's mouth and what he's saying.

"Erif wasn't going to kill him, hurt him maybe, but he knew The Cause needed allies. He wouldn't have risked that even for something as personal as avenging his brother."

Erif must have been the leader.

I should probably confirm that, but instead, I'm wondering if hawx claw is commonly used in kidnappings or if it's unique to Verus's people. For some time now, I've thought that there was a family or someone left behind who cared about me. The ransom that Dorsin was hoping to collect always supported that theory, but what if I was betrayed? What if I was sold out by my own people? Where does that leave me now?

Anger and doubt start to simmer in my stomach. It feels like acid is trying to climb my insides. I force myself to prioritize the conversation at hand and not the possibility that there may not be any loving, open arms at the end of this trail. I may only find whoever started me on this fucked-up path in the first place.

Is that enough for me?

To know?

To risk the scars something like that will leave behind when I already have more than enough disfiguring my soul?

Verus shakes his head and levels me with an accusatory glower. "If you hadn't attacked, everything would have gone according to plan."

"I thought you were rogue."

"Igeeyin don't go rogue," he snaps back, thoroughly offended.

I laugh, unable to stop myself. I don't know who the Igeeyin are, but if this fool really thinks betrayal is impossible, he's a dumb shit. My existence might prove him wrong if my sudden suspicions are right.

I lean forward in my chair, done with playing subdued and patient. "I understand that staring down a member of the Order of Scorpions is terrifying, and that's probably why you missed it; however, *I* recall very clearly Erif offering only two choices"—I hold up two fingers like he's a daft cria who needs the visual—"a quick death or a brutal one. That's it. I acted because *you* piss stains gave me no choice."

Red blooms in his cheeks, and fury banks in his eyes. "Take off your glamour, or we're done here. This doesn't make any sense. You should know better than to doubt the clans, to question our vow," he snarls, pressing against his restraints so hard that the tendons in his neck strain and a vicious vein rises on his forehead.

I watch him for a beat, debating whether or not we have enough or if I should push for more. His murderous look calms to a scowl, and I want to slap the pompous look right off his face. I turn to Tarek and then stand up, moving toward the dark entryway by the door. Tarek follows, silently blocking anyone else from seeing while he leans in and pulls back his thura.

My heart races as I stand there slowly being exposed bit by bit. Tarek's powerful body protects me at the moment, but he'll have to step away, and I'll have no choice but to move out of the shadows. I don't know what will happen then, how Verus will react when he sees me.

Will he recognize me?

Will he know what happened?

Will he tell me if he does?

I swallow past the lump forming in my throat, hating how vulnerable I feel right now. It's one thing to be like this with the Scorpions, but Verus hasn't earned this. I remind myself that I have. It's not about him, even though it feels like everything is riding on whatever is about to happen. This is about me finally seeing once and for all what happens when I strip away the glamour and show the fae who looks like me who I am.

My stomach is a riot of knots.

Tarek grabs my hand, squeezing it once to tell me he's done. I hold his firm hand tightly, not ready for him to move. I look up into his glamoured black eyes, searching them for something to anchor me, to remind me that no matter what, this is going to be okay. He lifts our hands between us and sets my palm on his chest and his on mine. He doesn't say a word as we stand there. Slowly, our hearts begin to beat in unison. The steady rhythm is calming, and I'm able to match my breaths to his, stealing a little of his assured strength.

I nod to Tarek, letting him know I'm ready. I've been waiting for this since I saw the ghost leaping from rooftop to rooftop, since the cloaked figures pulled back their hoods and revealed themselves. It's time to see if Verus can tell me what exists beyond the blank wall in my mind. With one more squeeze of my hand, Tarek backs away.

My silver eyes fix on Verus as I start to move out of the shadows of the entryway. I take one step and Verus gasps. Another determined step and his eyes grow wide. He reels back and shakes his head like he doesn't understand as I move closer.

"How...you're...how are you here?"

His question is trailed by croaks of astonishment as he struggles harder against the bonds holding him down.

"Is this some kind of test?" he snarls, looking wildly from me to the other Scorpions.

Their uninterested miens have all been abandoned. They watch with rapt attention every move Verus makes and listen closely to every stunned word that spills out of his mouth.

He knows who I am.

I open my mouth to say something, but I have no idea how to frame all that I'm burning to discover. I have two surging questions sitting on the tip of my tongue, and I don't know which one is more important. How do I choose between *who am I* and *where do I come from?* Both feel vital, but there are split paths to getting Verus to answer either, and I know I can only choose one.

Fairy light illuminates me as I finally step from the dim alcove into the room. Verus looks as though everything he thought was right is now somehow wrong. His face crumples with confusion. His mouth drops open and flails as he struggles to wrap his mouth around what to say. And then it comes...on the softest of whispers...one word riding the current of a distressed exhale as his silver eyes search mine for answers.

"Princess?"

54

Princess?

I stare at Verus, *my* mouth now flapping around as I try to grasp the ludicrous thing that just came plopping out of him like some overgrown swamp toad in search of a lazy meal.

Princess?

"How?" he pleads, the word eerily haunted as though none of what's happening can be real.

The game ends. My ability to strategize or maneuver my way to the answers I want becomes a thorny hedge maze I have no hope of traversing. I can't think ten steps ahead when I'm thunderstruck and rooted to the floor, unable to take even one stride forward.

"What did you just say?" I demand, unable to stop myself because it's just so insane.

Doubt and mystification move through his features like a tidal wave as he eyes me more critically. His assessing silver gaze flits over my hair and my eyes like he's confirming what's in front of him, but when his measuring stare falls on my freckles, on the constellation of sun spots that speckle my nose and upper cheeks, he pauses.

I see the moment that another realization dawns in Verus's eyes. I wish more than anything that I knew what it was, because his face crumples in sympathetic horror, and his pupils blow out so big and so fast that they drown even the smallest hint of silver in his now alarmed gaze.

I step closer to him, menace radiating from every pore. "Who the fuck am I?"

"You're dead," he answers hauntingly, and I rear back as though he just landed a hit. "We...we looked for you, but you died before—"

"Who am I!" I shout at him, closing the distance so I can tear the truth out of him with my bare hands.

He shakes his head, terror and torment in each jerky move, and then suddenly they're gone and all that's left is steely resignation. He whispers something I can't hear over the fury pounding in my head, and then out of nowhere, the iron dagger I left lodged in the arm of the chair, is lifted by some invisible force. It hovers in the air for a beat before it suddenly goes flying.

I barely have time to react as strong arms wrap around me and pull me back. Powerful, thick, muscular bodies move to protect me, but it's not *me* the blade is aiming for.

I watch with impotent horror as the iron blade sinks deep into Verus's throat. He lurches forward with shock, and blood blooms violently around the hilt of the dagger, pouring down his throat and chest like a river that's broken its dam.

"No!" I scream as I struggle to break free of the Scorpions holding me back. "Who am I? Where do I come from?" I snarl as Verus's lids droop and his body sags.

His mouth moves as though the whinnip root is working even during death, but there's no sound, and I can't tell what he's saying.

"You fucking coward!" I screech at the dying fae, who would rather kill himself than tell me the truth, than help me.

I fight against the Scorpions, needing to break free, but they pin me between them despite my efforts.

"You will rot," I vow to Verus as I'm forced to witness his life bleeding away in steady streams down his torso and onto the floor. "I will hunt your fucking clan and make them pay for this!" I seethe, but Verus's body hunches forward, the only thing keeping him from falling out of the contraption altogether is the bindings that are still secured tightly around him.

"What the fuck?" I snap at the Scorpions, pushing them away more easily now that the damage is done and the bastard's dead. "I could have stopped it," I yell at them. "I could have tried to heal him," I argue, but three angry stares are having none of my shit.

"He was an impel, Auset. Their thura allows them to move objects with nothing more than a thought. They're dangerous until they're dead. It wasn't worth the fucking risk," Curio contends.

"We're lucky that wasn't worse," Tarek observes as he assesses Verus's dead body and the table off to the side where his weapons have been laid out since we began questioning him. "He could have cut us down at any moment. Judging by the force he used to end his own life, he wasn't a weak impel either."

"No wonder the fuck was so arrogant," Curio scoffs. "We would have never seen that kind of power coming until it was too late."

Riall shakes his head as he scans the macabre scene. "You didn't sense his thura?"

"No," Tarek admits. "But it's because I'm a daft fuck. I didn't sense any thura from Auset either when we first met. I should have realized that he might have the same ability to cloak it that she does. It didn't even cross my mind until now. Fuck, that was close!" he barks as he runs his fingers through his knotted hair, loosing dark black strands around his face as he goes.

"Shit. I'm sorry, none of this went how I thought it would. You three make this look way easier than it is," I confess with an angry huff.

I'm reeling with fury. I know this wasn't their fault, technically it's mine. But I'm pissed.

So much went wrong, and I don't know if we have enough to go on. Pulling a dagger from my leathers, I stride over to Verus and cut his wrist. I swoop a finger through the small amount of blood that wells there and stride back to Riall.

"Taste this. Maybe it will give us a clue."

He wraps his lush lips around my finger and sucks off the blood. I'm too upset to feel turned on by it, although an outlet for all the pent up rage I'm feeling right now isn't the worst idea.

Riall tilts his head in thought as he swallows Verus's blood.

I collect my own sample, careful to avoid anything that could be tainted by iron from the dagger still lodged in his throat. I shove my finger in my mouth, and a little zing sparks through me. It's on a smaller scale from what I've experienced drinking from Gartox, and nothing compared to how I feel when I drink from Riall.

"There's a foundation in the blood that's somewhat similar," Riall observes, his eyes far away as he formulates his response. "I picture a harvest moon on a crisp night. Something piney with a hint of rich soil. It's like a misty forest is where he's spent most of his time, and the notes of it are steeped in his essence. You have that cool night under a full moon too, Beasty, but layered on top of that, I taste the dry heat of a three quarter moon rising over shadowy sand dunes. You have a sweeter flavor too, like honey made from moonflowers and night-blooming jasmine. There's a hint of salt mixed in with your sweetness. A sharp little tang that amplifies the flavor even more."

I stare at Riall, my eyebrows almost to my hairline with shock.

"You can get all of that from *my* blood?" I ask, astounded.

I smack my tongue against the roof of my mouth as

though that will activate all the things he just found in Verus's small sample, but all I can really identify is that I like Riall's blood better than whatever was flowing in Verus's veins.

"I only feel a little power surge," I confess, feeling slightly disappointed. "Where's all the moon stuff? And how do you even know what a *three quarter moon rising over shadowy sand dunes* tastes like?"

He chuckles and reaches out to play with a strand of my hair. I bat his hand away, too frustrated to find him cute.

"I've been drinking longer than you have, Beasty. The blood speaks to me differently after all these years than it did when I was young. You'll get there. I'll help you."

"Can you taste thura?" I question, wondering if there are more uses for this ability than I realized.

"I can taste power levels—which fae are stronger, things like that—but I can't tell what kind of thura someone has simply by drinking from them."

I nod, but my mind is back on what happened, as renewed anger and disappointment settle through me. I need to fight something. I need to move and react and work through what the fuck just happened.

"Training room," I snap out as I move for the door.

Let the corpse rot. We'll deal with it tomorrow, but right now I need to hit something before I implode.

"For what?" Riall demands.

"So I can put you on your ass for stepping in like that."

"Good, then I can put you on your ass for putting yourself at risk," he calls to me, but I'm already out the door and stomping up the stairs.

Fucking Scorpions.

MY STAFF COMES DOWN HARD ON RIALL'S, AND HE grins as the hit vibrates up his arms. I knew I felt stronger after we bonded, but this is incredible. I look down at my hands in awe. I've already broken two bow staffs, this is my third, and I can see it starting to splinter. Riall swings for me, and I flip back to avoid his staff despite the annoying fact that he's softening his hits, and his attacks are annoyingly lazy.

I charge him, sliding on the ground to go at his legs, but he vaults himself over me and backs away.

"Come on, Riall, I thought you were going to put me on my ass?" I taunt, frustrated with the *chase the Scorpion* game he's playing.

Tarek chuckles from the bench he's commandeered on the far wall, but his focus is on the several sheets of parchment he's laid out next to him, each covered in notes trying to piece together everything we know.

"Tell me again what he said after you both switched out of Common?" Tarek asks, his ice-blue eyes flitting from one scrawled detail to the next, deep in thought.

I notice Riall is looking down at his hands as though there's something about them that's perplexing him. I ignore the strange way he's examining his palms and try to recall Verus's exact words.

"He said, 'One Igeeyin to another, you have to release me. My clan will offer a life debt. It's for The Cause.'"

"I'm linking the Moon's army and The Cause. I don't know that they're connected, but it seems more likely than not, given everything he said," Tarek announces absently, and I turn back to Riall.

"I think you're right about Igeeyin being a designation for a type of fae versus a title," I agree, picking up what we were talking about before.

Riall starts to circle me, and my stomach dips with excitement.

"It makes sense with the way we look," I note. "I've never met a fae who looks like me. Then again, I don't get around much. But you three haven't either, and Hatus certainly never came across any ghosts before that night in Lord Daeral's stables."

I get tired of waiting for Riall to engage, so I charge him. It's almost as though he's distracted, because he doesn't lift his bow to deflect, and I clip him hard on the shoulder.

I huff out an irritated breath.

"Seriously, what's going on? You were looking right at me that time; why aren't you defending yourself? Why are you letting me kick your ass?"

Riall throws his head back and growls. "I'm trying, I swear I am, but I can't seem to hurt you."

"I'm aware. That's the problem," I snark.

"No, I mean I *physically* can't," he explains, once again looking down at his arms as though he doesn't control them anymore.

My brow furrows with confusion.

"I'm trying to spar like we normally do, but every time I go for a hit, it's as though my muscles don't want to cooperate. Instead of looking for ways to push you or beat you, I'm trying to help you beat me," he explains with exasperation.

"But why?" I drop the end of my staff to the mat and lean on it as I study him.

"I think it's the Blood Bond. It won't let me hurt you because it goes against every instinct I have to protect you and keep you safe."

My face scrunches up with distaste. "Can we fix it?"

Riall takes one look at me and laughs. "I'm not broken," he defends.

"Tell that to my need to work off some aggression," I counter.

"I'd be happy to find some other way to help you, Beasty." He wags his eyebrows suggestively and offers me his half-cocked sex smirk.

"Not until your *blood* lets you fight me as hard as you fuck me," I contend, and Riall groans his dissatisfaction and stomps over to Tarek's bench.

"Curio? Tarek?"

Tarek waves my invitation away, his eyes never leaving his notes.

Curio's eyes dip down my body and languidly rake back up. "You going to let me fuck you as hard as I fight you, Moonling?"

I snort. "Only if you win."

"Mmmm," he hums, but he doesn't rise from his bench.

"We know the Igeeyin weren't interested in killing Hatus. His rantings about ghosts and what they did fell in line with Verus's confessions about the murders being a lesson and sending some kind of message. However, the Igeeyin *were* keen to discover who Hatus was talking to. They wanted to know who was listening to his story. Hence the tail that followed Hatus and the Vulpi back to the Dawn Court and then spied on our conversation.

"I should send a missive to Enay, letting her know to be cautious of any possible attempts to bring them in on some kind of a *negotiation*. I have no idea what the fuck these fae would want to talk about or why they think we'd negotiate. We'd just slaughter them," Tarek frustratedly murmurs as he crosses something off on one of the sheets of parchment.

"Do you think these Igeeyin are trying to become an Order and this is some stupid way to secure a supportive vote?" Curio asks Tarek.

"I suppose it's possible, although it's an asinine plan. But something about the way he spoke to Auset about The Cause, makes me think that there's more to it than appealing to the Orders for a seat at the table."

Curio nods his head contemplatively, and Riall points at something that's written on Tarek's parchment.

"It could be a nickname," Riall offers as he continues to read over Tarek's shoulder. "Princess, I mean. We're all taking it literally, but that might not be the case."

Tarek looks up and considers him, his features contemplative. "That's worth considering. I've looked up the bloodlines, but there are no females born to any of the high courts. Everything we've learned is pointing to the Night Court, but King Korven never married after he lost Queen Akiruh. They didn't produce any children before she died, which probably has to do with the infertile rumors that surround him, hence the reason he's sired no bastards."

"Could she be from somewhere outside of the four realms?" Riall counters.

"There are only two outliers that are monarchies," Tarek explains. "One is ruled by a high priestess with no heirs. And the other a queen with several daughters and sons. If one had gone missing, they would have looked for her. It wouldn't have been something they kept quiet."

"Maybe she wasn't missing though. Verus said she was dead. Isn't it likely that's what her family thought too?" Curio points out.

I take a deep breath and shake out the nerves now tingling in my limbs. I can't wrap my mind around any of this; it's like we're talking about someone else's life. I hoped that maybe something Verus said or some clue that we gathered would trigger a memory or a connection, but I'm still just as lost, just as blank as I was before. All this talk of royals and princesses and high courts is getting under my skin, because each option sounds more illogical than the next. Or maybe I just want them to sound wrong, because there's zero chance that who I am now could ever fit into any of those worlds.

I have *some* answers, or maybe they're more clues than actual answers. I just never anticipated how much more confusing all of this could get. I thought a blank black wall of nothing was hard enough, but I have more questions and confusion now than I did before, a feat which seemed impossible, and yet here I am boiling over with frustration.

I stretch my neck to one side and then the other, twirling my staff around me with anxious energy.

"But where's the order to hunt the perpetrator down? If a high value fae had been murdered—even if it was kept quiet publicly—the royal houses would still be working behind the scenes to punish whoever did it. If for no other reason than to ensure it never happened again, they'd hunt, and it would be vicious," Tarek argues. "If that kind of pursuit was occurring, even outside of the four courts, the Orders would know about it. One of us would have been hired to assist."

"Maybe it has something to do with the clans? These Igeeyin are playing by a different set of rules. Maybe their hierarchy has these stupid titles," I offer.

The room grows quiet as each of us considers too many questions and not enough answers. I think through my list of questions that I was saving for later.

"Is hawx claw common?" I ask, feeling suddenly tense.

"It grows all over and has several different uses. Not all of them are nefarious," Riall explains, and I nod, unsure if I feel relief about that or disappointed that another theory has met a dead end.

"I think we should leave for Sagor Coast first thing. It's the last place Lord Daeral visited before he was killed. Other clues from Verus lead to the Night Court in general. We should start there and see if there's anything to find," Tarek declares.

He looks at each of us for our agreement. I shrug, willing to do whatever they think makes the most sense, because I don't have a clue. When Tarek started writing everything down, I quickly realized that we had more pieces of the puzzle than I thought we did. The only problem is that none of us has any idea how it all fits together.

I wish I was more help, but I feel torn and unsure about what we might be walking into. I don't want my Scorpions to get hurt, especially not in the pursuit of something that could cause me more trouble or damage. On the other hand, if by some miracle, I do have loved ones waiting for me, I don't know how I would deal with that either. It was hard to trust the Scorpions, but in the end, there was no denying that we fit together perfectly. It might not be like that with anyone else. I'm violent and broken. The shards of who I am aren't easy to navigate, and I have a tendency to cut anyone who tries. How that fits in any kind of family dynamic, I don't know.

What if they expect me to be different?
What if they don't like what I had to become to survive?
Why do I care?

I feel jittery once again. Maybe I can call Eacon and she'll come fight with me.

"Are you going to involve the Vulpi?" Curio asks as both Tarek and Riall stand.

"They may have their own scouts at the coast, following up the connection to Daeral, but I think it's best to keep as low a profile as we can. I'm going to start making arrangements," Tarek declares as he grabs all the pages of parchment and distractedly leaves.

"Since I'm useless here, I'll go sort out lunch." Riall winks at me as he strides out, and I can't help but feel slightly abandoned, which is asinine because both Tarek and Riall left to do things that will help. I want to punch myself at this point for being all over the place with my emotions. I feel like a raw wound in need of tending, and yet everything hurts and I don't want anyone to touch it.

I want answers, but I don't. I care, yet I question if any

of this is worth it. I'm sure the Scorpions have actual work to do. Proper hunts that pay. Not this nonsense of chasing ghosts figuratively and now literally. I feel bad for dragging them into my mess but grateful that I'm not trying to figure it all out on my own.

Fuck, I need to fight. It's the only thing that I'll be able to make sense of right now.

"How do I call Eacon?" I ask Curio as he rises from the bench and moves closer.

I don't miss the smooth way that he moves, like he's stalking prey, and a little thrill works its way down my stomach as he closes the distance.

"Do you need healing?" he teases, his hickory-brown eyes filled with humor and tracing over me as though he's searching for some hidden wound or injury.

"No, I need to hunt."

"Ahhh, you need to hunt? Or you need to feel in control?"

I roll my eyes and huff out a sigh. "One in the same, *oh wise one*," I snark.

"But are they?" he challenges as he ties his hair back, knotting it tightly behind his head.

Riall's hair is now the same color as the light streaks in the front of Curio's mane. I tilt my head as I study that, and Curio smiles a crooked, devious grin that makes my insides start flip-flopping around.

"Okay, Moonling, you can *hunt* me, but I have a few ground rules."

I'm slightly taken aback by his offer. I've sparred with all of the Scorpions, but Curio and I have never gone toe-to-toe like this. I've always worked with the other two when it comes to training.

"I thought this wasn't your thing? Riall always—"

"Riall craves the violence more than I do. Plus, he's a better teacher. I'm more than capable of giving you what you need right now, Moonling. But if you're not interested..." Curio steps to the side, but I immediately move to block him.

"No! It's not that," I rush to reassure him. "I'm just surprised. You don't normally sign up for this sort of thing."

Curio shrugs, that crooked smile back on his face. "Maybe I need to exert a little *control* myself."

"So what are your ground rules?" I ask instead of focusing on the way he's saying one thing when I think he's really talking about something else.

I'm game for all of it though, my adrenaline already spiking as my heart rate picks up and the restless energy I always feel right before a bout wakes up my muscles and my mind.

Curio's roguish energy grows serious. "No weapons. Open-handed hits only and solely to the torso. Head and below the waist is off limits. This isn't a brawl. I'm not going to beat on you, and you're not going to beat on me. This is about strategy and control, and that's it."

"Grappling? Takedowns?" I counter.

"Fair game if you want. Sweeps but no kicks. You can use your weight and momentum against me for tackling and grappling, but that means I can do the same. Agreed?"

"Agreed," I answer easily, my exuberant anticipation hiking with each breath I take.

This will be different from when Riall and I go at it, but I'm eager for the challenge. It's exactly what I need right now.

"Oh, and one more thing," Curio calls as he walks back to the bench and strips his shirt off. "We'll be doing this naked."

55

IPULL THE HOOD OF MY HEAVY CLOAK FORWARD, hiding my face as much as I can while burrowing into the fur lining, seeking warmth. The wind's frigid fingers try to wrestle it back, and I fight against the cloying grip as I scan our surroundings. The town of Krieger is about as inviting as the last four towns we've stayed in on our painfully slow trek up north. I didn't think I'd actually miss the southern part of the Sagor Coast with their penchant for charred food and their objection to any form of seasoning, but I might trade their never-ending gloomy rain over the glacial winds and the frosty lands of the northern coastline.

At least the food's better up here. I thought I might need to cut out my own tongue to save the rest of my mouth from melting the first time I shoveled in some northern fare. For fear of offending the innkeeper, I kept my blades sheathed and swallowed it down against my better judgment. Eventually my mouth went numb from the heavy spice they put on *everything*, and I finished my meal, immediately adding it to my list of fucked-up things I've survived in life. I wasn't prepared for the way it revisited me later.

I would question how I still have mates, but they weren't immune to the stew's gifts either. It was a terrifying time for all. I don't know if we're closer for it now or blocking it all out, but valuable lessons were learned. Our bowels and mouths have adjusted well enough to the bowls of fire and pain. And having spent some time in the gelid wintery weather, I understand much better why the food needs to scorch you from the inside out.

My stomach rumbles as I wait with Riall and Curio outside while Tarek secures us rooms at the only inn this provincial town has. It's not a public house with a running kitchen unfortunately, which is why we're waiting for Tarek, because food and an opportunity to listen to the locals swap stories is the next order of business.

Twilight teases the horizon, painting the town in thick sweeps of light purple and blue. The brightest stars are already winking in the sky as though in competition with one another for our admiration. The icy temperature feels like it's dipping lower with every second that passes, and I nuzzle deeper into my furs.

The inn is on the edge of the main square, which is located in the middle of the town itself. A large fountain topped by a statue takes up the center of the cobbled square, but I can't tell who the statue is under the blurring blanket of fresh powder that must have stopped dumping from the sky right before we got here—thank the moon for small miracles. If Krieger is anything like the last few towns we've watched, the statue is probably Queen Akiruh. There seems to be a lot of love for the late queen, or maybe there used to be and things like statues and artwork aren't updated often.

"I'm freezing my sack off. What's taking him so long?" Riall grumbles, wrapping his cloak tighter around him with a disgruntled huff that has white vapor puffing out of his mouth and disappearing into the cold night air. He's like a fog dragon, not that there's such a thing, but I picture him as one all the same.

"Eh. As long as your cock still works, I think Auset will manage," Curio counters, and I can't help but smile.

He's not wrong.

Riall slaps a gloved hand against Curio's chest as he laughs. Then he seems to think better about exposing his covered limbs to the elements and snatches his arm back into the warmth of his fur lining and body heat. The black of his cloak is stark against the pure white of the snow. Gleaming onyx clasps in the shape of small scorpions keep our coverings secured, and I don't know where they found a beast with fur as thick and deep black as what's keeping each of us warm right now, but I'm grateful for its death.

I worried the scorpion accessories might be too much of a dead giveaway as to who we are, but Riall assured me that it's quite common for fae in the realms to wear an Order's symbol. It's like inviting that Order to watch over you as you go about your day. Apparently, there's quite a devout Scorpion following that invokes the Order's protection, as though my mates are more god than fae.

I smile as I think about how the other blade slaves used to talk about the Scorpions. I suppose *god* wasn't a far stretch, with the way others recounted their feats and successes. Their skill was the talk of the ludere and their death count unmatched by any other Order to ever exist.

I'll happily take *god* over *princess*.

The Kings know, I'm far more suited to one than the other, although both are a ridiculous reach I shouldn't waste time thinking about. I've tried not to ponder it too much since we started this hunt. All it does is make me confused and anxious, and I don't see the point in worrying over things that are out of my control. I learned that hard lesson in the ludere, and the realms have hammered home the importance of it once more.

My own foggy puffs trail out of my mouth as I sigh and turn back to watch the inn door. I debate asking if I can shadow walk home and return in the morning when it's hopefully warmer, but I know I'm just being silly and missing the feel of something that's familiar and ours. I'm tired of staying in inns, alehouses, and taverns. It's been a month and a half since we left and started this arduous trek up a coastline that was far bigger than I ever imagined. We're no closer to finding anything, but we're no further either, so there's that, I suppose.

The door to the inn squeaks open, and out walks Tarek in all of his divine glory. My mouth waters at the sight of him, despite the new glamour he's wearing that alters his hair and eyes. We've abandoned the skeletal glamour we've always worn when leaving the castle for a hunt, choosing anonymity and the ability to blend instead. We look like ourselves but tweaked slightly. My face and freckles are on display but my long thick tresses are currently a chestnut hue, and my eyes are cider brown. The Scorpions are their typical gorgeous selves, but their hair and eyes are a different hue. We mix it up with each town and village we come across.

"What took so long?" Riall gripes, and my stomach punctuates the question with a loud, unhappy groan.

Each of them looks down at the offended grumble and then back up at my face, which is thankfully hidden within the hood of my cloak. Why they aren't wearing theirs is beyond me; my face feels like it could freeze right off with only a couple seconds of exposure.

"The keeper insisted on giving me a personal tour of the entire property, including an extensive one of her rooms. What she was hoping would happen on the new settee she just upholstered, I don't want to think about too hard."

Curio barks out a laugh while Tarek shudders and pulls me to him. I smile, but I eye the inn with interest. Seeing that, Tarek chuckles, the deep sound reverberating through me as it tumbles from my chest down my body until it stops deliciously in my cunt.

"Should I educate her on the error of her ways now or later?" I ask absently, glaring at the jostling curtain at the front window where the eager innkeeper is most certainly getting an eyeful.

"Pretty sure a town this small would notice if their only inn minder went missing," Curio teases.

I roll my eyes. "I'm not going to kill her. I'm just going to make her listen to me fuck the three of you *very* loudly all night and all day until she learns to make better decisions with her life. A life that could be very short and very painful if she's not careful."

I turn to the window and point at it so she knows that I know she's looking. There's a jolt of movement, and the curtain instantly flutters shut. The Scorpions laugh, plumes of white pouring out of their mouths as though even the icy air wants a taste of their mirth.

"She's far too elderly to be of any concern, princess," Tarek teases, and I growl at the use of his new favorite nickname.

He defends his fuckery by saying it's to help me adjust to the idea of it, but all I want to do is punch him in the dick whenever it slips out of his luscious lips. What's worse is that it *does* help on some level, but not for the reasons he thinks. It's not about adjusting because, true or not, that will never happen. It's hearing them say it so casually, like it's no big deal, *that's* what does something for me. They make it clear in the teasing dismissal of the title that, at the end of the day, I'm still me, and they're still them, and *princess* or not, it changes nothing between us.

"She's old?" I ask, surprised as I turn from the window and back to them.

"Very," Tarek confirms with a cheeky grin.

I consider this new information for a moment and then shrug. "Good for her then, I guess."

Riall brays a laugh so loud it makes me jump. "So, what? No 'fucking until she learns her lesson' now?" he asks as he wipes laugh tears from his eyes.

"We can still give her a show, but it'd be more *something to remember us by* and less *don't make me cut you*."

Tarek shakes his head as though he doesn't know what to do with me, but I see the smirk he's wearing.

"Brothers, I think we created a monster," he declares with faux solemnity.

The other two snicker.

I give a derisive snort. "I was already a monster; you just showed me how to embrace it."

"Awww, Beasty!" Riall coos, picking me up and twirling me around. "That's the sweetest thing anyone's ever said to me!"

His exaggerated fervor is contagious, and I can't help but laugh.

"Feed me before I take it all back," I command through my giggles.

"You heard the little monster," Riall announces as he sets me on my feet.

Tarek steals me and tucks me into his side, and we start walking. "Marret said the tavern is this way."

"Her name is Marret," Riall confirms, his grin wide with glee. "Even her name is old. I haven't met a Marret in ages."

We start down one of the spoke-offshoots of the wagon-wheel-shaped town, and I take in the shops we pass as we go. Some are already closed for the night, while others are getting ready to. Thankfully, I no longer find crowds and cities as intimidating or overwhelming as I did before.

There's a comforting predictability to the hustle and bustle of fae going about their business with single-minded focus. All that matters is where they need to go and why, while everything else around them whizzes past, unimportant and unworthy of notice.

I survey the darkening snow-covered street we're on. There are only a few cloaked figures with their heads down as they shoulder through sporadic bursts of wind, in a hurry to get somewhere warmer. A sign for The Nocked Arrow squeaks forward and then back, pushed around by a bullying, frigid breeze that kicks snow up in the air and shoves it in our face. Bright orange fairy light illuminates the large, frosted windows on each side of the towering front entrance, and a wall of welcoming heat embraces us as we step inside. Riall has to wrestle the wind for the door, and it closes with a loud crack when he prevails. A dozen or so faces turn curiously in our direction as we step down into the main part of the tavern.

A short, ragged-looking barman stares at us as he sets four tankards on the long bar counter as though anticipating our thirst. There's an interesting tension in the air, a layer of caution I can feel tingling against my skin, as the patrons watch us choose a small round table from the available options. The stiff silence isn't completely unwelcoming, but it feels as though it wouldn't take much to tilt things in that direction.

"Not keen on strangers, it seems," Curio mumbles for our ears only while he unclasps his cloak and pulls it off.

I shove my hood back, and the firelit warmth of the room caresses my chilled cheeks. The fae still surveying us take one look at me and unexpectedly relax. Shoulders slouch and bodies turn back to their tables, as drinks, conversations, and companions are once again the focus of all of the tavern-goers. Just like that, our presence here is dismissed, and I look around at the other patrons, bewildered by the immediate change.

Were they worried we'd be trouble but now they're not simply because I'm here?

I pull off my cloak completely and drape it over the chair next to Curio's.

"That was interesting," Tarek observes as he takes a seat.

"I think I'm offended that they only see you three as a threat," I quip.

Riall chuckles and rests his thick arm on the back of my chair. "That'll be their downfall, Beasty. They'll never see you coming until it's too late."

I smile and spot an older woman with a tray of drinks headed in our direction. She gives me a beaming smile, one that dims slightly as it's turned on the Scorpions and Riall's hand draped behind me.

"I've got three frothing steins of our best," she declares as she sets the heavy mugs down on the table. "Aego sent this over just for you," she explains as she sets down a smaller glass in front of me filled with a bright purple liquid.

I don't much like ale, so instead of questioning the offering, I nod and pull the glass closer.

"I like this color," she compliments, gesturing to my hair. "No Lutyn today?" she asks casually, her smile once again bright, but there's a cheeky twinkle that wasn't there before.

I have no idea what Lutyn is, so I shake my head. "No, but thank you for this," I offer, raising my glass to my lips and taking a deep pull. It's sweet and potent, and I know already I'll be pissed out of my head in no time if I drink too much.

"What's on offer for food?" Tarek asks, and the lady's warm brown eyes cool a degree as she turns to him to answer.

I've grown accustomed to a very different kind of reaction to the Scorpions than the one this fae is bestowing. When they're out in public looking like normal fae, there's a certain amount of appreciation or interest thrown their way. This barmaid, however, looks jaded and concerned, like she's seen too much in life to be fooled by a pretty face and an impressive physique.

She's distinctly older than us, but with fae, it's difficult to gauge age as we mature later and age slower than other species. This barmaid has lines etched around her mouth and her eyes like she scowls and laughs in equal measure. Her light brown hair is pulled back to her nape and plaited down her back in a no frills, no nonsense fashion. There's a hardness to her that isn't surprising given the harsh weather here, her age, and the fact that she works in a tavern.

"We have a stag salmi with crusty bread, or bulo filets with winter vegetables."

We all order the salmi, which seems to reassure her for some reason, and she darts off, disappearing through a set of double doors behind the bar, probably headed out to lock up the town's daughters. I chuckle to myself, and Curio reaches over and plucks my cup away. He sniffs the purple contents and then sips cautiously. His eyebrows fly up in surprise, and he coughs, slapping his chest, as he sets the glass back down.

"That tastes like nectar and burns like fire whiskey," he croaks as he clears his throat.

I laugh. "A few more sips, and it might as well be hawx claw for all I'll remember tomorrow."

Curio passes the potent elixir to Tarek and then Curio, who are both just as surprised by the strange combination of sweet and searing. I jerk my chin in the direction of the portrait I just noticed hanging above the fireplace. It's an oil painting of Queen Akiruh. I search for anything on the walls celebrating the king, but there's nothing.

"Strange that the northerners have her but no Korven," Curio observes absently, glancing around the room once more like he expects a problem to walk out of the shadows at any moment.

"S'cause, the king is unly the king because of *her*," a lanky fae slurs as he labors to push out of his nearby booth and amble over to our table.

A trail of spilled ale wets the worn floor as he gestures around wildly with his tankard. We all go stiff as he stumbles into our table and then seems to find his feet. His hair is gray with age, his face creased and haggard. The fae's togs hang off his body like he's either wearing someone else's or he's shrunk quite a bit since he bought them.

"They want us to forget, but ice holds onna all of the secretses. *We* remember. Stee remembers," he sputters, tapping on his head with a finger before lifting his mug to his mouth and drinking deeply.

He starts to lean precariously, and Riall reaches out and straightens him so he doesn't fall over.

"Remember what?" Tarek asks evenly, his arms crossed over his chest.

He looks relaxed, but I know he has sheathed daggers sewn into the seams of his tunic down his ribs.

"That t'was the Nalroras that had it all. Every single piece of dark and light befur Isona wus betrayed by Galayas and her mates." Stee belches loudly and hits his chest once before another more demure burp is forced out.

The name Galayas rings with familiarity, but I can't place where I've heard it before.

"Therrr wus no realms, no high farten courts, just the Nalroras, an sheez gunna take it back. Aren'chya?" Stee mutters, his glazed gaze landing on me. "They thought theys could burn up tha truth, blacken books and history, an that'd be that, but we tell tha stories, we keep tha truth alive."

He lifts his almost empty stein in a toast and then drains the dregs. He shakes the empty mug as though confused as to where all the ale has gone, harrumphing sulkily when it doesn't magically fill back up. Tarek hands him his own full tankard.

"Thas kin' o you, sir. Yous a good male, butchya'd have to be to be goin aroun with ours, now wouldn'chya. Gotta lock 'em in, my Moon. We're gonna need all tha help we can get. Becuz we're comin' for 'em, ain't we?"

Again Stee toasts me, his smile wobbling like he's not sure if he's wearing it right, so he adjusts it until it fits like he thinks it should.

"Get away from here, Stee, or Aego will boot you for the night," the barmaid barks as she strides toward our table with a tray full of food. "You know not to be harassing your betters," she scolds the drunk man, who looks like he's on the verge of tipping over again.

"He's fine," I assure her, perfectly happy to listen to the male ramble away, because that's exactly what we're here to do, watch and listen for any clues.

We've been working our way up the coast, listening and following anything that may be a lead. The drunken nonsense that just slipped out of Stee's semi-functioning mouth is more intriguing than anything we've come across so far.

"You're too kind, but you've got enough to deal with without having your supper disturbed on top of it," she assures me, and she shoos Stee away with her tray after she sets our meals in front of us.

My brow furrows as she leaves, and I look over at the Scorpions. "Does she mean you three?" I ask, perplexed. "Or do you think that was a general observation? Do I give the appearance of someone who has enough to deal with?"

Curio and Tarek chuckle as they dig into their stew.

"Maybe Marret got word out that we were coming," Riall teases, and I laugh. "We'll be the talk of the town by sun up."

I scoop a heaping spoonful of the salmi in my mouth and hum at the delicious flavors that explode across my tongue, but my eyes are fixed on Stee, who's trying to sit on a stool at the bar counter and having a hard time of it.

"Was he talking about what I think he was?" I whisper between bites, my eyes quickly scanning our surroundings to make sure no other drunkards are listening too closely. "Have you heard of the Nalrora name before?"

Tarek shakes his head and pulls a chunk of bread from the intact loaf at the center of the table. "It doesn't sound familiar, but I'll look into it. If what he's saying is true, then that could answer what the Igeeyin are doing and why they need allies."

"You think there's a faction that wants to overthrow the crowns?" Curio asks so quietly it's just shy of a whisper, his eyes darting around cautiously. "They'd be mad to challenge the kings."

"No one said it was wise, but keep in mind the source—he can't even mount a stool."

We all look over just in time to see Stee fall on his ass.

Tarek shakes his head and turns back to his meal. "Like I said, worth looking into because who knows what's relevant and what's not at this point, but I wouldn't wager much on the drunken theory just yet."

"Could that be the princess link?" Curio questions. "Some offshoot of a bloodline that people think should still be in power, but isn't. A claim like that could easily rally support."

"Verus referred to *The Cause*. Doesn't exactly sound like a knitting circle, that's for sure," Riall points out.

"The queen's nephew Leyev is the heir, correct?" I ask, trying to recall what they told me about the Night Court when we first started trekking through it. "Maybe the fight is against him and not the realms as a whole. Maybe they don't think he should inherit the crown because there's another candidate."

"I suppose it's possible, but the courts have treaties in place. They're supposed to back each other up in the event of civil unrest or some other viable threat," Tarek counters.

Curio snorts and eyes Tarek. "Technically that's correct, but we all know they'd turn on each other in a minute if they thought it was in their own best interest."

"Fair point," Tarek concedes.

"Who would we back in a war? Hypothetically speaking of course," Riall asks, and both Curio and Tarek snort.

"It depends on who's trying to kill each other," Tarek jokes, and Riall gives an amused huff before he fills his mouth with a heaping spoonful of salmi.

"Let them all burn," I grumble softly into my stew.

A slow smile stretches across Curio's face as he watches me.

"What?" I demand innocently. "They're happy to allow their realms to fall to ruin under the thumbs of fae like Tilleo and Dorsin and all the others who profit off their royal apathy. Orders police the realms but only for the right price. Most fae are too busy simply trying to survive to even attempt to do anything about any of it. If someone wants to fuck things up, I'm for it."

"And if that someone's worse?" Tarek challenges.

I shrug. "What's worse than what we have now?"

"War," Riall answers evenly.

"Maybe to some..." I agree, a trickle of anger working through me and sharpening my words. "But too many of us have been shoved through the cracks of this society, and we're already at war. The three of you are the most powerful Order in all of the realms, and even you know what it is to battle for food, safety, and survival. Pretty sure more fae than not can say the same. They're all kindling just waiting for a spark."

The tall door to the tavern crashes open. Every head in the place snaps in the direction of the loud noise and the howling wind that's working hard to rush past the three fig-ures that are now standing in the entryway. Goose bumps rise on my arms, and my heart leaps to a startled cadence. Alarm jolts through me as I take in the thick cloaks of the three fae. Their light gray cloaks I would recognize anywhere because the fairy light sparkles off the hems like glittering stars have been sewn into the edges.

As though our musings conjured them from the mist, the Igeeyin walk purposefully into the tavern.

Three hoods move as though they're searching for something, each one turning slowly with careful assessment until our table is in view. I can feel their eyes on us from deep within their hoods. A warning blares in my mind, and adrenaline slams into me like a battering ram as the three figures turn toward us and start to walk over.

56

RIALL SQUEEZES MY LEG IN WARNING WHEN I casually drop my hand to reach for one of the daggers sheathed at my thigh. I glance from the approaching Igeeyin to Riall and then follow his gaze to the rest of the tavern patrons. None of them are watching the cloaked figures close in on us. They've all gone back to their tankards and discussions as though the presence of these three arrivals is nothing worth paying attention to.

A chill runs down my spine.

The odds that we've stumbled upon the same town and tavern as a random group of Igeeyin are lower than the chances that they'll be walking out of here alive if they cause us any trouble.

Have they been following us somehow?

I consider the townsfolk once more. The eerie lack of response or wariness from them toward these *strangers* is a warning that thrums against my skin. It's possible the Igeeyin were hunting us the same way we've been hunting them, but I have a sinking suspicion this is something else. We've been working our way up from coastal town to coastal town. We didn't know where to start or where it would end, but we hoped to stumble upon something that would help us make sense of what we already knew.

Our hunt has been quiet up to this point. It hasn't yielded more answers than we've already collected, and I didn't realize how much I'd grown used to finding nothing and moving on to the next town, expecting much of the same. However, the fae here seem to know these Igeeyin and are clearly comfortable in their presence as though it's a common occurrence. The way they reacted to us versus the lack of any kind of reaction to these cloaked figures tells me that the town of Krieger is either where the Igeeyin live or close enough to it that they're a familiar sight to the locals.

I ache with the need to do something, to demand to know what is going on, but Riall's warning is clear. Both Tarek and Curio have gone back to eating as though the approaching envoy is as insignificant to them as they are to everyone else here. I'm the only one still watching as the figure at the front of the trio pulls her hood back.

I expect moonbeam-colored hair and pale skin, but instead, the fae reveals a dark flowing mane, skin the color of raw sienna, and rich brown eyes. Her confident gaze narrows as she strides closer, shaking her head as though she's disappointed in something. She doesn't look overly hostile or reach for a weapon, like I'm itching to do. She appears annoyed, which is an odd reaction to have in this situation. It's as though she was expecting something from us and we didn't deliver.

I keep my breaths even and will my racing heart to calm. We've been scouring the coast for answers. The fact that they've just waltzed in as though they've been expecting us is both worrisome and suspiciously promising. I realize I'm glaring at the fae as she closes the distance. She doesn't seem bothered by this reaction in the slightest, but I settle back in my chair, and adopt the same careful mask that the other Scorpions have slipped in place. I now look unbothered, but really I'm screaming inside in both alarm and eager anticipation.

"Are you *trying* to piss off Faline?" the beautiful fae asks as she draws even with our table. "I get that you and Lutyn like to blow off steam at her expense, but do it on someone else's watch. I'm not getting demoted so you can fuck some strangers who happen to be passing through. Smarten up and stick to the Phase like the rest of us do."

"Beva!" one of the cloaked figures behind her hisses, the sound a chiming feminine censure.

"And who are you?" Curio asks as he lifts his ale to his mouth and takes a sip.

"I'm *her* problem, not yours." She gestures to me. "I suggest you keep it that way," she snips at him.

"Beva!" the fae behind warns again, her bright voice a little too silvery to be taken seriously.

My scowl returns as I take in the high-handed fae. Curio's eyebrow twitches up with amusement, but I can tell he's also trying to figure out what the fuck is going on. Beva turns her attention back to me.

"Careful," I warn the overconfident stranger, not appreciating the disrespect and dismissal she's showing him let alone me.

She's either oblivious and doesn't know who she just gave her back to or she's addled and has a death wish. Either way, I find myself wanting to watch her piss in her light-gray leathers as she realizes the mistake she's made. I have no clue why she's talking to me like she knows me or treating me like some petulant greenling in need of a solid scolding. One way or another, she's now on a collision course with one of my blades.

"No, really, who are you?" I demand, and she rolls her eyes before leveling me with an annoyed glower.

"Please, your glamour isn't fooling anyone here. Does Lutyn even try anymore or did you insist on keeping your face to lure these three in?"

She gestures to the Scorpions, looking at each of them as though they're some foul stain she just found on her cloak.

"It's okay, we didn't mean to cause any trouble," Tarek interjects charmingly, cutting off my confused retort.

My bewildered scowl snaps from Beva to him. He eyes the three Igeeyin inquisitively, and I can tell he's formulating a plan, although to them, he probably just looks flirty. His gaze flicks over to me, and I can see the coaxing in his eyes to follow his lead.

"If you have to go," he tells me pointedly, the word *go* extra silky as it slides out of his mouth, "we won't hold it against you." Tarek winks at me, the gesture saucy but loaded with meaning.

My heart starts revolting in my chest as what he intends sinks in. Unease sours the stew in my stomach, and my mind whirs. He wants me to play along with whatever is happening here. To either walk willingly into whatever trap is being set or take advantage of the providence that has these three Igeeyin somehow thinking I'm someone else. It makes absolutely no sense, and yet here are three Igeeyin strangers staring at me intently.

Does my glamour make me look like someone else they know?

But how could that be, this is **my** *face?*

My thoughts drift to Verus and how he had recognized me too, but his reaction was very different from what I'm getting from Beva and the two cloaked figures guarding her back. Verus was shocked and then horrified when he saw me. Hatus had described the Igeeyin as ghosts, but Verus looked at me like *I* was the haunting specter. Beva looks inconvenienced by my presence and pissed that I'm still sitting here instead of doing whatever it is that she thinks I need to do.

What in the crowns are they playing at?

Stalling for time, I kick out the empty chair next to our pile of cloaks. "Why don't you have a seat for a bit. Grab a drink. Take a load off," I offer, a hint of bite in my tone that I hope saps her of some of this unwarranted attitude.

One of the fae at Beva's back steps forward as though they're going to take me up on my offer and plop down, but Beva's hand shoots out, smacking the cloaked mystery figure in the chest. They stop in their tracks immediately, and I swear I catch a small, irritated sigh.

"Nice try, but I'm not Lutyn, Auset. Let's go before any-one else notices you're gone and the Crescents converge."

Air freezes in my lungs.

Chaos rings in my ears.

I fist my hands where they rest on my thighs to keep from shaking.

How in the fuck does she know my name?

Turmoil sits on my tongue like a spoonful of salt. There's no spitting it out or trying to save myself from the sharp taste. Neither can I swallow the bitter mouthful or drown it in the flavor of something else. All I can do is suf-fer through the briny burn as spans of horrifying scenarios hammer at my mind as I try to make sense of what's going on right now.

This Beva, whoever she is, recognizes me somehow. She knows my name. She wants to take me with her because she's responsible for me on some level. Her entire de-meanor reminds me of a guard, but that... Shock swarms me as something clicks into place.

Princess?

Verus's voice whispers in my mind, and I see a flash of the horrified look on his face before his voice grows haunted.

You're dead.

Rage roils in my gut as I look from Beva to the Scorpi-ons.

Fuck the Kings, could it really be true? Am I really a fucking princess? Did someone plot to get rid of me and then...take my place?

A storm grows in my chest as astonishment and anger flash through me, and the thunder of my pulse rumbles in my ears.

Is that what all of this is about? Some other fae is using my name and wearing my face, and no one has been the wiser...or have they?

I swallow down a hysterical laugh that tries to bubble up my throat. Of all the possibilities that have plagued me since Verus used his thura to shove a dagger into his own throat, I never considered this. Maybe no one ever looked for me because they didn't know I'd been taken. If that's true, then who's been pretending to be me all this time?

Immediately, I want to take Beva and her little contingent hostage. I want to bar the doors to this tavern and paint it in blood until everyone explains what in the fucked-up realms is going on here. I breathe evenly through my rage and try to think past the haze of violence that sings to me like a siren, encouraging me to make everyone in this room pay for all the ways I've been wronged.

I know I can't.

What happened with Verus taught me a valuable lesson in understanding that force isn't always the best option, but it's incredibly difficult to keep my head on straight and my fury hidden under a mask of insouciance and mild annoyance. I don't need force when the answer is staring me in the face, tapping her foot impatiently as she waits for me to fall in line at her command. There's a small part of me that thinks it's a bad idea to follow this Beva wherever it is she wants to lead, but that's drowned out by the overwhelming reality that *this* is an opportunity. One that probably won't present itself again, which means I can't pass it up. Especially not when we've been hunting for answers or some kind of sign that we're on the right track for so long.

This sign couldn't be any brighter if it were the sun itself.

Whatever this is, we're not going to get a second chance at it. If I fuck it up, I could lose all hope of ever figuring all of this out. Right now they think I'm someone else, someone they're willing to escort right to the heart of everything I want to know. Their secrets and the accompanying answers are carefully hidden somewhere, and if I'm smart about this, I can get these three to show me where. I was hoping for one clue, one lead that pointed us in the right direction. It seems destiny had other plans because it just hand delivered a whole heap of possibility right in our laps. Now I just need to figure out how to keep myself in check while this unfolds.

As though he can sense my inner struggle, Riall leans closer. "Don't worry, Beasty," he assures me as he pointedly runs two fingers down the bond marks on his throat. They're hidden behind the smooth skin of his glamour, but I know they're there. "No hard feelings if you can't stay. Maybe we'll run into each other again. Stranger things have happened."

A flash of them escaping through the window in Dorsin's office and leaving me behind accosts me. It's quickly replaced by the moment fate once again dropped them at my feet when they stepped out of the carriage to attend the Bidding. I'm blitzed by everything we've been through and overcome to get to where we are right now, and I know, no matter what, that they have my back.

I'm not alone.

I can do this.

I can pretend to be whoever these fae think I am, or spring whatever trap is lying in wait. The Scorpions will come for me, and together we'll find the truth and cut down anyone or anything that stands in our way.

"I know I'll look forward to running into you again," Riall finishes, his cocksure smirk coaxing out a small grin of my own.

Beva snorts and mumbles something under her breath about Riall's flirting, but I'm too busy pulling strength and support from the encouragement blazing in the Scorpions' eyes. I fortify my defenses and my resolve through their unwavering trust and conviction. I blow out a deep anxious breath, but it sounds more like a disgruntled huff as I stand up, finally giving in to Beva's command that it's time to go.

Without a word, I grab my cloak from the pile and pull it on.

"Where'd you get this shit?" Beva asks as she eyes the black wool and fur.

"Mind your fucking tone," I snap at her before I can stop myself.

Shit. This fae makes it hard to not want to deck her.

I know I need to play this right, *be* whoever it is they think I am, but I'm not going to tolerate anyone shitting on my Scorpions for any reason. I love my cloak. I was in awe when Tarek draped it over my shoulders. Beva can keep her unwelcome thoughts to herself, before I rethink following her and decide to gut her instead.

Beva, surprisingly, acts cowed by my rebuke. I pull the hood over my head, grateful for the shadow it now drapes over my face and the way it smothers the small, relieved sigh I let loose. Somehow my snapped warning hasn't made them suspicious. It makes me wonder about the person they think I am and how she typically interacts with these guards. It seems my irritation isn't anything new. Then again, if they're as demeaning to her as this Beva has been to me, a person is bound to snap eventually.

I try to calm my frustration and apprehension by running my palms over the daggers sheathed at my waist. I wish I had put armor on and had my entire arsenal strapped to me. I never anticipated something like this happening though, and I hate that my black tunic and leathers suddenly seem inadequate for the protection I might need tonight. I have several daggers strapped to my waist and thighs, but I feel alarmingly naked and vulnerable. I have no choice but to make do though. At least all of the weapons I do have are now hidden under my cloak. It gives the illusion of security even if it's not the case. In the event that I do need to make a move, they won't see it coming, and that helps to compose and settle me somewhat.

I sneak one last look at my mates before walking away from them. They appear unruffled and relaxed. Riall is finishing his meal like nothing's happening. He even reaches over and steals my food as though it shouldn't go to waste.

Such a shit.

I tense when the three gray cloaks surround me as we move closer to the exit. Beva takes the lead, and the two silent Igeeyin take up position behind me. I tighten my hand around a dagger, just in case. I do my best to expel all the tension and apprehension coursing through me and concentrate, but it's difficult.

"Thanks for sending word, Aego," Beva calls to the barkeep as she strides confidently to the front door, and I follow.

I snap my head in the direction of the fae who apparently ratted the other me out, and he blanches. *Good.*

Snow has once again started to fall, and the wind shrieks wildly as it streaks down the street and squeezes between the shops as though it's trying to get away. A fresh blanket of white covers the road and shop fronts, and it crunches under our feet as we leave the warmth of the tavern. I hope the flakes don't fall fast enough to cover any footprints that the Scorpions might need to follow me wherever it is we're going.

I'm guided silently down the street, and I track every shadow in range on the off chance I need to make a break for one. Hopefully, shadow walking isn't a common thura among these fae.

Beva's hood is once again pulled up and protecting her from the cold, and I'm curious why she doesn't have the same unusual hair color and eyes as the others that were sent after the Scorpions. I assumed all Igeeyin looked like me and Verus, but maybe not.

"So you have the town watching me?" I question evenly, wanting to discreetly collect what helpful information I can and hoping it's not a mistake.

"Everyone knows Lutyn is a bad influence, but at least he's one of our own. Where'd you even find those fae? Some roving mercenary group?" Beva snarks. "Of course Aego and Hinnet would have their concerns."

"Do we not need allies?" I challenge, flinging what Verus said about the Igeeyin at these guards and hoping it sticks.

One of the fae behind me titters, and Beva shakes her head with exasperation. "You think *that's* what the

Crescents had in mind when they declared that? Fuck, Auset, they looked like they'd enjoy ripping your head off, fucking it, and then using it for a piss pot until they found some new gullible girl's skull to replace yours."

I scoff.

If only she knew who she's talking to.

"I thought they were quite beguiling?" one of the cloaks behind me dares to admit, her voice deeper than the one who previously hissed at Beva inside.

"You would, Tayim," Beva calls over her shoulder as we approach the tree line of the Caleran forest.

The large woodland embraces the town of Krieger between it and the shore of the Eritas Sea. We specifically chose towns to investigate based on Riall's observation about Verus's blood tasting like he was from some misty forest. That, and the clue about where Lord Daeral traveled before he was cut down. It was a long shot at best, but Tarek was right. There was something here worth finding.

"You're no bigger than one of their thighs, Auset. What did you think you were going to do if all three of them aligned against you?" Beva demands sharply.

"I could think of a few things one could do with all three of them," the fae with the silvery voice teases.

I smile at the indignant huff that flies out of Beva, and fight the urge to punch the flirty fae in the throat. I'm on edge and ruffled, a combination that's making me feel jittery and anxious. This entire situation is disturbing and digging up all kinds of alarming new questions and emotions. I know at some point all of this is going to go to shit. They're going to realize that they've made a mistake, and I need to be ready when it happens.

Carefully, I watch the path that Beva is picking out as we pass into the trees. Long shadows from the thin trunks stretch like ghastly fingers across the smooth sparkling snow. Some animal hoots into the night, but the forest is silent other than the crunching of our boots on the carpet of snow as we walk deeper into the striated shadows.

The forest appears unusually barren under the shroud of falling snow. The trees extend as far as I can see, but they're all the same, and it makes nature look more uniform than I'm used to. I don't know how long we walk, but it doesn't feel like much time passes before the flat forest begins to slope. Large rocky outcrops creep closer to our path, and then we round a ridge, and I try not to stop in my tracks.

Nestled in the concave seam of two huge hills is a village. There's a large house that appears more functional than grand as it overlooks many smaller houses that trickle downhill like steps on a staircase. At the base of it all are two long, unpretentious buildings that immediately make me think of barracks. There's enough cleared land around them that a large amount of fae could gather and train.

I hold my breath as I wait for any hint of recognition to trickle through me.

It doesn't come.

Flickering torches fight against the falling snow, illuminating patrols that guard the edges of the village both below and above. Warm light spills from many house windows, and if I stare at it all long enough, it blurs to become a sea of stars against the hillside.

I follow my escorts down what must be a worn path under the growing layer of snow. As we draw closer to the stacked, hillside village, I notice stairs that lead up through the dappling of houses until they stop at the highest point in the village, the larger manor. I have a strong sense that this is where they're taking me.

Stealthily I try to appraise the strengths and weaknesses of wherever we are. Cloaked guards either holding torches or lanterns walk the perimeter lazily as though it's more chore than necessity. I count only a dozen of them below and another dozen and a half on the ridge above the manor. No one stops us as we stalk across the training grounds, pass the barracks, and start up the stairs. Just like in town, the weather has chased everyone inside, which makes it difficult to gauge how many fae call this place home. It certainly isn't the small group of fae with the unusual colored hair and eyes that we thought it might be.

I stay alert as we ascend. My chest feels as though it's full of rocks, and my heart is chiseling through them one by one as I take it all in. I still have no idea how I'm even here right now. Nothing looks familiar or stokes any wayward memories or flashes of recognition. It's all as strange and foreign to me as I was when I first woke up in a cage. I climb stair after stair, fully expecting groups of guards to charge toward me from between the houses any moment now. They'd no doubt laugh hysterically as they tackled me to the ground, unable to hold in how hilarious it is that I fell for their trap. But the night remains quiet all around us, our path to the large house is clear, and I grow more and more anxious and tense with each step.

I want my secrets unlocked, I want to see past the blank wall in my mind, but as I take in the size of this place, I start to wonder what other secrets are hidden behind the wood doors and stone walls. The few fae who are outside on patrol all wear the same light gray cloaks. It confirms that they're either Igeeyin or connected to them, but it doesn't afford me an opportunity to see if anyone else possesses my unique coloring.

We reach the top of the steep winding stairway, and I thank my conditioning that I'm not breathing too heavily after the harsh incline. Huffing my way to the top would probably be a dead giveaway. Anyone *from* here would be used to climbing these hills. Instead of continuing on toward the front double doors of the manor, I'm guided to the side of the large house. It's hard to tell what color it is, but it's made from stone as though it was designed to blend in with the rock and greenery of the hill at its back. The village is obvious at night, with the lit up houses and torch-bearing patrols, but I suspect during the day, that this stronghold blends into the scenery around it very effectively.

As we get closer to the side entrance Beva is aiming for, we suddenly pass through an invisible barrier that makes me tingle all over.

Warning bells chime in my head when I realize we just walked through a ward I couldn't detect at all beforehand. I hold my breath, but nothing happens to me, and no one else reacts in any way, which means whatever just happened is normal. I immediately want to make sure I can still shadow walk and then pull a weapon and try to use it, just in case the ward did something to me I don't know about yet. Instead, I grit my teeth and keep my mouth shut and my palms blade-free as I follow Beva through a wide arched door.

By some unfathomable miracle, I've made it this far, but I know better than to let that lull me into a false sense of calm and security. I'm all too familiar with how quickly things can go to shit. My mind wanders to the Scorpions. Are they somewhere back in the forest silently tracking our every step? Are they watching the village now? Or did they have to stay back at the tavern for a bit in order to keep the barkeep and townsfolk from being even more suspicious than they already were?

"Tayim, go inform the commander that there might be a group of mercenaries staying in town. We'll need to keep an eye on them until they leave," Beva orders, and just as quietly as she has been the entire time she's been behind me, Tayim slinks off.

"Vit, grab supper and then come relieve me from the Moon's quarters. I want someone outside her door for the rest of the night."

Beva's use of the moon as a title gives me pause. Verus said he was a sword in the first division of the Moon's army. If me or imposter me is the Moon, then does that mean all of this is mine? I study Beva as she pulls her hood back and starts down a hallway that leads to a back set of stairs. If I'm in charge, then why does this guard feel as though she can order me around? Beva mentioned back at the tavern something about the Crescents converging as though that was a threat. Could that be my family?

A strand of pale hair falls into my face as we ascend the staircase. Surprised, I hold my breath as I study it carefully. Tarek's glamour made my hair a chestnut brown, but it's back to my moon-kissed color, which means the ward outside must have stripped me of Tarek's thura.

Shit.

"At least you're learning to accept when you've been beaten," Beva grumbles, pulling my attention back to her as we hike another flight of stairs. "You put up far less of a fight than last time. *Moon* or not, you should listen to your betters."

I loose a derisive huff. I was just worrying about what happens if she sees me with my glamour removed. However, her scathing tone assuages my concern. I'm alone with this insolent Igeeyin guard, and she's quickly outgrowing any need I might have of her. I bide my time and keep my hood secured over my face, but Beva's contentious manner just sealed her fate.

"You speak to me like I'm a child. Does that make you reckless or daft?" I ask the guard, hoping it will coax a reaction out of her that helps me understand better what's going on here.

If I'm some *Moon* to these people, some princess or revered figure, then why is Beva such a cunt to me?

She chuckles humorlessly at my question, once again unfazed by the warning edge in my tone. "You know what's at stake, Auset, and yet you continue to do things like this." She waves an arm at me and the black cloak I'm still hidden within. "There's no escaping the role you will play in all of this, no matter how you try to rebel. Faline knows what's best, and it's time you fall in line."

I shake my head, but she doesn't see it as she leads me down an arched corridor where we pass two other offshoots of hallways and a handful of closed-up rooms. She stops in front of a grand door at the end of the hall while I try to sort through what it is imposter me is supposed to fall in line with. The door in front of us is tall and wide and surprisingly a work of art. Scenes have been carved into it, but I'm not given any time to study what's been etched into the grain before Beva is pushing it open and confidently striding through.

"Beva? What the fuck do you think you're doing?" a commanding familiar voice snaps.

Beva freezes, her head snapping in the direction of the fae that rises from the garnet-colored settee to our right. Indignant fury gleams in the Igeeyin female's stare as she glares at the guard who just barged into her quarters. Her hair is long, but not as long as mine. It's the strange combination of not quite white or gray or pale blue. Her skin is a creamy alabaster I once had too, and hard silver eyes flit from Beva to me before abruptly filling with confusion.

Shock and triumph roar in my veins as I pull my hood back with one hand to reveal a face that's almost an exact match to the fae standing in front of the sofa. With my other hand, I pluck a dagger from my waist and slink in behind Beva. Before she can stop gaping or close her shocked mouth, I shove a dagger through the side of Beva's throat. I pull her back against me and bring my lips to the guard's ear.

"Turns out you're both reckless *and* daft," I whisper to her as she chokes on her own blood. "If only someone had taught you to never turn your back on a Scorpion."

I shove Beva's body away from me and kick shut the large door at my back before I turn to deal with the fae that's stolen my face.

"Who are you?" she demands imperiously, a long knife now gripped in her shaky hand as she takes me in. Her eyes grow more and more stunned the longer she looks.

My pulse no longer has separate beats. Now it's one steady thrum of adrenaline, retribution, and wrath as I stalk carefully closer.

"Funny you should ask that," I taunt as I pull off my cloak entirely. "I'm here to find out."

57

E LEAP FOR EACH OTHER AT EXACTLY THE same time, and it surprises us both. It seems the *imposter princess* has had some training. She swipes her knife at me, but I dodge the attack and crack her in the jaw with my fist. She nails me in the thigh with a hard knee and swings for me again. I duck under her arm and then shove a push dagger I pull from my thigh into the meat of her shoulder. She cries out in pain, but what shocks me is the burning sting that just exploded in my own shoulder. I go still, stunned and confused. Her blood seeps around the edges of my blade, but it feels like *I* was the one who was just stabbed. I look down at my own shoulder, expecting to find a knife, but there's nothing there.

Taking advantage of my momentary distraction, the imposter drags her dagger across my forearm. I hiss as blood blooms from the gash. She gasps and suddenly grabs her arm as though she was the one who was cut, but her arm is smooth and unmarred; there's no wound there.

Baffled and pissed, I tap into my extra strength—courtesy of my Blood Bond with Riall—and I sink a fist into her gut. She drops her knife and staggers back.

"What the fuck is going on?" I snarl, my shoulder throbbing as though I've been stabbed when I haven't.

I pull at the neck of my tunic, looking for a wound that I somehow missed getting, but there's nothing there. Puzzlement pricks my mind like needles, and when my gaze lands on her bleeding shoulder, I realize that somehow I'm feeling her wound like it's my own. Rage engulfs me, and I tighten my grip on my dagger.

"What did you do to me?" I seethe.

Was it the ward? Did it protect her somehow? Why am I feeling what's happening to her like it's happening to me too?

She looks at me with pure shock, but the unexpected relief and sorrow I see there too gives me pause.

"It's you," she hauntingly whispers, her eyes—my eyes—welling with tears. "I...I can't believe it's actually you."

Her arms fall limp at her sides as though every ounce of fight just drained out of her.

"Who are you?" I demand, entirely unsettled by the strange way she's looking at me. "Why do you have my face?" I snap, shaking off the phantom pain in my shoulder and filling my empty hand with a dagger so I'm ready.

I wipe the blood from my forearm on my tunic and glare at her.

She looks puzzled. "You don't know?"

I scowl harder. "Would I be wasting my time asking if I did?"

"Right," she concedes. "I'm Auset," she offers, and rage rings in my head as I step threateningly closer. "Hear me out," she pleads, bringing her hands up defensively and scrambling back. "I swear that I am, I'm Neith Auset Korven Nalrora. Princess of the Night and Winter Court and rightful sovereign to all four realms."

This time, I stagger back as the weight of that declaration bears down on me like a rock slide. I run my gaze over her face and then take the rest of her in.

"Am...I...are *we*...twins?" I ask, my tongue stumbling over the words like they're craters in a path I'm struggling to traverse.

"No," Neith answers solemnly. "I have *your* face, and you have *my* name, but that's it. That's how they planned it."

"*They* who? " I demand, reeling. "Planned *what*?"

I've waited and yearned for the answers trickling out of her mouth, but now that I'm cupping them in my hands, I feel more lost than found. I don't understand what's going on. I thought I had a grasp of what happened to me, of who I was, but I couldn't be more wrong.

"It's complicated..."

She presses her palm to her bleeding shoulder and winces. Pulling her hand away, she looks at the crimson covering her hand and then grabs the bottom of her dress and presses it against the weeping wound.

"So simplify it," I growl, some of my shock fading as I start to lose what little patience I have left.

"I will, I'm just letting you know that there's history you need to know in order to understand. You really don't remember anything?" she presses, her silver eyes curious with a small glimmer of hope hidden within.

"I woke up six and a half years ago in a cage. That's my first memory."

Neith cringes and pulls in a deep breath. "Should we sit?" she asks, gesturing to the settee.

I give her a pointed look. "And let you pull a crossbow from under a chair and shoot me with it? You're fine where you are."

"Auset, I know you've been through a lot and you have no reason to trust me, but I would never hurt you. You saved my life...many times."

My brow furrows with frustrating bewilderment. *Saved her life?* I search her face, my eyes begging for it to unlock the void in my mind. The problem is it's my face, so of course it's familiar, but none of this makes any more sense than it did before I walked into this room.

"You still can't sit," I tell her, trying not to fidget at the emotion swelling in her gaze.

A small smile tilts her lips, and she snorts an amused laugh. "Fair enough. Can we at least move closer to the window so the moon can fix us?" she counters, gesturing to her shoulder and then the cut on my arm.

"Fine. But if you make me chase you out a window, I

don't care how bad it might hurt me too, I'll make you regret it," I warn.

We both slowly, cautiously move closer to a swath of moonlight that's streaming through a lofty pane. Her quarters are comfortable. A large bed, dressers and wardrobes probably filled with the finest togs, and a small desk where she does whatever it is that princesses do. The room is pleasant, warmed by a fire, with a sofa and some chairs to the side of the door. Deep reds and dusky pinks are the colors of choice around the space. It's entirely too soft and too frilly for my liking.

"What do I even call you?" I snip. "We can't both be Auset."

"Most people call me Moon, the Moon, my Moon. It's an Igeeyin thing, the highest place of honor in a clan."

She drops her dress from her shoulder and tugs at the neck so she can inspect her healing stab wound. I take in my arm, the cut there nothing more than a faint red line now.

I eye her coldly. "Yeah, I'm not going to do that."

"Then, Neith, I guess. It's technically my name even if no one has ever used it."

"Fine, Neith, get on with it, I don't have all night."

She sighs and runs her fingers through her hair, pulling at the roots a little as though it helps to pull the words from wherever they're buried.

"I don't even know where to start. There's so much to know, but I'll do the best I can," Neith offers weakly, and the blood that was trickling from her shoulder tapers before stopping as the moonlight works its magic. "Before the realms were split into half and then eventually the four

courts, it was one land. A land ruled by the Nalrora bloodline. It was a line of queens. Only female heirs were ever pro-
duced. Eligible male fae married into the matriarchy, and
the lands prospered and the people thrived. Then a family
of brothers and their mate decided they wanted more than
they were entitled to, so they set out to take it, starting with
snuffing out the Nalrora line completely, which started the
war that broke the land in half. Only they didn't get every
Nalrora like they thought they did. My great-great-great-
grandmother survived. She was a baby at the time, but she
was smuggled to safety and then raised in hiding. Through
her, the line continued."

Neith pauses, watching me as though she's making sure
I'm following. She nods once when I don't ask any questions and continues.

"We lost more than just lives when we were forced to run.
We lost texts and scrolls and proof of our existence, our history. However, as far back as any Nalrora can recall, the line
has been faithfully served and protected by a blessed group
of fae known as the Igeeyin. Lore tells a story of a Nalrora
ancestor saving the life of an Igeeyin elder, who then swore
an oath of loyalty and protection in return. That might
just be a story mothers tell their children to help them fall
asleep, but the point is, our people have been connected to
each other for as far back as our histories show."

Our people.

The two words swirl in my mind, unable to settle because I don't know how they fit anywhere inside of me just
yet.

"Millennia passed, Galayas was betrayed by her mates,
and the realms split from two to four. The purge of my

line from the realms as well as the ancient wars faded in the minds of too many fae. It was as though the Nalroras never existed, which was exactly how the old kings wanted it. Some of them never even told their heirs about how they won their crowns, as was the case for my father. The old kings died and all truth of who they really were and what they did was rewritten with a much kinder, deceitful lens.

"That is, until my father saw my mother walking down a road while he was touring his lands. He pursued her, not knowing who she was or the danger he was putting her in by doing so. They fell in love, and when she finally trusted him enough to tell him everything, he convinced her that the hunt for her blood had been long forgotten and she would be safe. She wasn't."

Neith looks down at her hands as though she needs something to ground her. She takes a few steps back and sits on the sill at the base of the window. It's so strange to see her speak and move; it's like looking in a mirror and yet not.

"They kept her pregnancy a close secret. There had already been two assassination attempts at that point from heirs to the old kings who knew the claim and the threat that the Nalrora line could pose. My parents knew they'd need to take drastic measures to protect us, but the third attempt on her life was successful. I was taken from my mother's dying body and hidden, which is where you come in," she tells me with a weary sigh.

Nervous anticipation consumes me, and I fill my lungs with a deep breath in preparation for where this story is going. All I've ever had was a wall of nothing, a void of all-consuming darkness where everything that happened before the ludere should be but isn't. I thought I'd feel more eager when this time came, more relieved when I finally found the answers I've been looking for. But the way Neith is staring at me, the remorse and regret bathing her features, fills me with dread. I'm clearly *not* long lost royalty, she is, so what does that leave me?

"To protect me, my father gave me to the remaining Igeeyin to be hidden away. Just like with the Nalroras, there weren't many of the moon blessed left. They had been killed right alongside the charges they were trying to protect from being hunted. Their numbers were slower to recover, as not every child born to an Igeeyin mother is blessed by the moon," Neith explains, motioning to her hair and then her eyes.

"Unavoidably, there were fae who knew about my mother's pregnancy, who knew about me. My father tried to tie up every loose end he could find, but it was impossible to quell every whisper or rumor. So the Igeeyin put safeguards in place. *You* are one of those safeguards," she tells me, her tone grave and her eyes apologetic.

My body and limbs feel heavy all of a sudden. It's as though the truth is settling over me, but instead of it being light and freeing, it's weighing me down and pinning me in place whether I like it or not. My heart is racing, and my throat is tight with trepidation. I want to run, but I know there's no escaping this.

"They tethered us somehow. I was never given specifics, no matter how much I demanded to know, probably because the Igeeyin who did it are dead and no one understands exactly what thura was used to link us. I didn't even know about any of it until after you'd been taken, and I..."

She trails off and then clears her throat as though she's swallowing a mouthful of guilt.

Anger and befuddlement wreak havoc on my mind and emotions. I'm struggling to keep everything contained, and we've barely scratched the surface of whatever the fuck is going on. I flip one of the daggers in my hand, twirling the hilt and the blade between my fingers. I submit to the urge to move instead of screaming and raging like I want to right now.

Neith's tone grows sharper with frustration and her silver eyes—my eyes—fill with contrition.

"The Igeeyin knew it was only a matter of time before someone came hunting for me, so they created a decoy."

She looks at me pointedly, and my stomach drops.

"The link they created between us was designed to protect me. I got your ability to heal from the moon, your features, and your coloring, which helped keep me hidden. Faline, who is the First Crescent and Igeeyin leader, gave you my name. We were moved to different corners of the realm and kept apart from each other. They raised us like we were the same person. We had the same face, used the same name, were given the same comforts and education as was befitting a royal, but there was more to it than that. Our link did other things too."

Her voice cracks and her gaze drops from mine as though she can't bear to look me in the eye anymore.

"*You* were a safeguard against *my* being taken...or killed. More than simply creating a decoy, our link was supposed to help you find me if I ever went missing. If I was taken and hurt..." She pauses, her eyes far away. "If I was hurt, if my life were in jeopardy, I could siphon your life force in order to survive."

I suck in a sharp breath as though she just kicked me in the chest. Horrific understanding dawns on me, and I stare at her completely stunned and gutted.

"And if *I* was taken? If I was hurt or killed?" I croak, needing her to confirm what I already feel slicing through the last remnants of my hope.

Neith's eyes well with tears, but she straightens her spine as though calling on some deep reserve of strength. "If *you* were taken, your role as a decoy would be fulfilled, and *I* would be moved and hidden more securely..."

Silence fills the room as I stare blankly, understanding raking my insides as new slashes are gouged into my soul.

"You would be made safer, and I would be sacrificed," I finish for her, seeing the truth of it in her eyes even though she saves me having to hear it fall from her lips. "You can pull from my life force, but I can't pull from yours, can I?"

"No, you can't," she confirms. "It only works from you to me."

I look down at my body as though it's betrayed me. It wasn't enough that they took my face, my name, my entire fucking existence, now my soul, my life, isn't mine either? She can rip it from me whenever *she* needs it? Agonizing anger crawls through me. Misery is a mire that's slowly pulling me under, and I know if it does, I'll never get free.

"So what the fuck is this?" I rasp hollowly as I drag a blade across my forearm, slicing it open.

Neith gasps in pain, her hand snapping to cover a wound that doesn't exist on her arm. Her skin is intact, her blood safe in her veins, while mine drips to the floor as the moonlight works to stitch my skin together and staunch the flow.

She rubs the sting from her arm. "*That*, I think, was an accident. From what they told me, nothing about our bond was supposed to work both ways. No one knew I could feel your pain until after you were taken. I wondered if you could feel mine too, but I never knew. You can, can't you?"

I don't answer, I just glare. Inside, my mind is racing as I recall the phantom pains I've ignored or written off. The ludere was brutal, the training was nonstop. They regularly healed us, but it was easy to dismiss the unexplainable flashes I would get from time to time in an arm or leg. I thought it was nothing more than residual pain, maybe a deep bruise or sprain that the healers missed. But it was her.

A fist tightens around my heart until I feel like it will stop beating at any moment. I want to empty everything out of me, including the tether that's robbed me of so much and promises to keep taking more. My eyes sting as rancor and desolation fight their way out of me.

"They thought I was sick or that maybe someone had tried to poison me. No one knew why I was suddenly having these unexplainable agonizing episodes. They whipped you a lot in the beginning, didn't they? Beat you constantly until you couldn't move, couldn't even cough up the blood drowning your lungs?" she asks, a knowing ache in her voice, in her tormented stare.

Her words come back to me in an avalanche of comprehension. Her comment about what I've gone through and that I can trust her. It didn't register when she'd said it, that it could be more than some soothing platitude that people offer so your pain doesn't make them too uncomfortable. Something that allows them to collect all the fucked-up things that happened to you in a neat little box that looks less horrific and intimidating.

Auset, I know you've been through a lot...

Tears well in my eyes. "You could feel it?" I ask hoarsely. "What they were doing to me all this time...you knew?"

Neith nods once, and the wretched heartache that's been pooling in her gaze finally spills out with a sob.

A tear slips down my face. I let it fall. Let it spill down my cheek and plummet off my chin to crash to the ground, cast off and alone, just like I've been since the moment I woke up in a cage.

The Scorpions and I were all so wrong. There *was* a princess, only I'm not her. I'm just the decoy. A sacrifice my people were willing to make. I'm the forfeit, the offering needed so she could live because the blood in her veins was more important than the blood in mine.

All the questions I had before tonight about family, the Igeeyin, about whether anyone looked for me or held out hope that someday I might find my way back...all of it turns to bitter acid on my tongue. I shake my head, devastated, as loss swarms me like buzzing insects I try to bat away but can't escape.

None of it matters.

All this time searching and wondering just to find out that I *never* mattered. They threw me away. Whoever my parents or my people are, they handed over their baby and decided my worth would forever be tied to a princess's survival. I was nothing. A contingency plan. Raised to die for a cause, one way or another, because all of it mattered more than *me*.

The void I've been hoping to understand pulls what's left of me into its depths because there's nothing else to fill it. No hope. No roots. No kin. Nothing. My chest and throat grow tight, and I struggle to breathe through the anguish. The abrading grief of finally knowing how little I mattered and how much I've suffered because of it scrapes me raw.

"The Igeeyin looked for you when you disappeared," Neith continues as she wipes trails of sorrow from her cheeks. "There wasn't a trace. There was no sign of you. No ransom like Faline expected. No hint of who had taken you or why. The Crescents thought you were dead. I was moved here. The village was fortified. New plans were laid out, and then we realized what the bouts of pain actually were. I begged them to look for you again. When I realized that I was feeling pain because you were, I pleaded with them to find you, to rescue you."

My vacuous gaze snaps to hers, and rage slowly trickles in. "Rescue *me*, or rescue *you* from feeling what was happening to me?" I accuse, venom dripping from every word.

"To rescue *you*, Auset. I never knew about you until guards were bursting into my room and yanking me out of bed, demanding that we leave because it wasn't safe. The Crescents were so frazzled that they were discussing things like they forgot I was there. I trusted the Igeeyin. When they said they couldn't find you, I believed them. When they figured out a way to numb the link, to keep me from suffering the way you were, I was grateful."

She shakes her head, disappointment and frustration etched in her face.

"I was stupid. It took me time to start seeing things for what they were, to really pay attention to what was going on here. They didn't want to find you, Auset. You were alive. It didn't matter that you were suffering; all that mattered was that their *backup plan* was still in place. The Crescents started getting more aggressive with their intentions and actions. They annihilated a whole clan who'd been loyal because Lord Daeral questioned Faline one time. I didn't know until Lutyn and I overheard two guards bragging about it. My eyes are open now, and I'm trying to figure out how to fix everything that Faline and the Crescents are destroying. She has a stranglehold on the Igeeyin, and I'm trying to peel her fingers from their throats without getting them or me killed."

"So you're not planning a war?" I challenge, as I finally place all of the clues together.

"They are," she confesses. "I'm not."

"And exactly how does that wor—"

I'm interrupted when the door to her room flies open. I spin as alarm kickstarts my heart.

"Princess, you sneak!" a strong blond male accuses as he walks in. "Tayim just told me you went into town without me. I'm hurt."

The male looks up from the bottle of spirits he's holding in one hand and the two glasses clutched in the other. His bright green eyes level me with an admonishing look, one that loses its chastising bite because of the cheeky smile that accompanies it.

"I heard you were found drinking with three devastatingly handsome fae. Tell me everything…"

Confusion suddenly crumples his face as his eyes dart over my shoulder.

"What the fu—"

Alarm discharges in his stare, and he drops the bottle and the glasses. Crystal and glass shatter and scatter across the floor. The scent of wine wafts through the room as his shaky, fumbling hands reach for the sword sheathed at his hip. He shouts for the Moon to run, but his eyes dart between the two of us like he's suddenly unsure which of us *is* the Moon. His panicked commands dull to a muffled murmur as I cock my arm, dagger in hand, ready to silence him.

"Auset, Lutyn, no!" Neith shouts. "He won't hurt you, Auset. I vow it, please no."

She rushes forward either to try to stop me or intercept the blade I've already sent soaring through the air. At the last moment, I adjusted my aim, and the knife sinks into the fae's wrist before he has half of his sword pulled out. He yelps in pain, and Neith tries to go to him. I step into her path, not willing to give her an opportunity to escape. Out of nowhere, a thunderous, rhythmic boom fills the air. It's like someone is beating on the sky itself, and I fight the urge to cover my ears as the eardrum-shattering beats vibrate through me.

"Shit," Neith snaps, and she dashes to the window, searching for something.

The cacophonous beat of a drum grows even louder, and I look around trying to figure out where the deafening sound is coming from.

"What is that?" I shout, my strong voice barely audible above the booming din.

"The perimeter has been breached. That's the alarm. We're under attack."

She continues to look out the window, wincing with every frantic beat of the alarm as she tries to spot who's attacking the village below.

I don't need to look. I know exactly what's happening.

The Scorpions are here.

Without warning, pain lances through my flank. Neith cries out and doubles over, and I look down, shocked to see the head of a bolt sticking out of my side. I whirl and find a guard in light gray armor struggling to reload her weapon.

Fuck. I knew someone was going to nail me with a crossbow.

I snarl and press a hand to my wound and then immediately decide against that as the embedded bolt moves, and I'm forced to swallow the cry of pain that wants to tear out of me.

"Vit, stop right this instant," Neith growls as she presses her hand to a wound she doesn't have.

The guard isn't at all interested in listening to her princess, and she fits another bolt in place.

Piss on the Kings, I need more than daggers if I'm going to fight off guards.

Desperate and out of options, I grab Neith and hold her in front of me. Thankfully, she doesn't struggle or demand to know what I'm doing, she simply gasps a shocked breath and goes with it. In other circumstances, I might respect her on some level for that, but I was just shot with an arrow, and I'm feeling too pissed to credit her for any amount of bravery.

The insubordinate guard freezes as I lift a dagger to the princess's throat. Neith shudders as the metal makes contact with her skin, but she continues to keep silent and makes no attempt to get away or disarm me. I can't tell if she's trying to help me or simply biding her time.

Or perhaps she's in as much agony as I am right now, and staying upright is all the challenge she can handle.

Warm blood trickles down my hip to my leg, but there's nothing I can do about it until the bolt is pulled free. I shut the pain out as much as possible and concentrate on getting to wherever my Scorpions are.

"I want you to back out of the room and down the hall very slowly," I order the guard, just now noticing that there are more armored fae clogging the corridor behind her. They look as though they're trying to get past the bottleneck that Vit has created by stopping in the entryway, but she just stands there, oblivious to her own obstruction.

These fae can't be serious. They really think they can take on the four realms when they can't even execute an effective counterattack in their own fucking village?

"Move!" I bark when she only stares at me instead of retreating.

Vit and the guards behind her glare with seething hatred as they're forced to withdraw or risk me slicing their *Moon's* throat. I advance until Neith and I draw even with Lutyn. He's still on the ground, cradling his hand and watching on in shock.

"Get up," I order, motioning for him to walk ahead of me and Neith.

With a grunt and a pained wince, Lutyn pushes up from the ground. Quickly, I reach out and yank the dagger from his wrist before he can so much as flinch back to stop me.

I'm going to need every weapon I can get my hands on.

"Piss and balls!" he cries out as he stumbles away from me, shielding his arm as though he expects me to try to take the entire limb next. "I didn't realize it was you," Lutyn declares apologetically as he looks from Neith to me, his gaze intense. "You surprised me and I reacted, but I won't hurt you, Auset."

Ignoring his assurances, I tighten my hold on the princess. "How many people know about me?" I growl as Lutyn starts to back out of her quarters.

We follow him out.

"Us"—she gestures to Lutyn and then back to herself—"the Crescents, and possibly some of the guards who were sent out to look for you when you first went missing."

"Great," I grumble as I cautiously advance. "How are you the Moon if no one listens to you?" I snap at her acerbically.

"I've been asking myself that same question for a while now," she admits as we step forward, claiming the ground that Lutyn and the armored guards cede as they continue to back up.

My teeth and jaw are clenched hard against the pain, and each foot forward feels as though I'm grabbing the arrow and jostling it around. Neith is faring worse. She's panting as though her lungs won't expand enough to pull in a proper breath. Sweat beads on her brow, and it's starting to drip down the back of her neck.

If she's been feeling everything I have since I was taken, she should know that this is nothing.

"They never taught you how to cope with the pain?" I ask as we reach the part of the corridor that I passed earlier, which has two hallways that split off from this one.

There's a half a dozen guards who are backing away from me and their Moon, just as I've ordered them to, but I didn't get a chance to count how many were sent to protect Neith in the first place. The hallways that split off would be the perfect place to try to ambush me. Thankfully, Lutyn is between us and the guards, and according to him, he's an ally.

"Lutyn," I call out, and his wary green gaze snaps to me. "Make sure they're clear," I command, jutting my chin in the direction of hallways up ahead.

He nods and moves to check them, still cradling his arm as he goes. I almost feel bad for stabbing him...almost. The guards who have now retreated to the opposite end of the narrow corridor watch me with pure loathing. Clearly, they have no idea what's going on here, or maybe they do. I'm just the sacrifice after all—how dare I threaten their Moon.

Lutyn crosses in front of us, moving from one offshoot to the other. I realize that he doesn't look at me the way the guards do. He studies me and Neith as though we've featured in all his favorite childhood stories and now here we are in the flesh. There's a hint of awe mixed in with the heaps of determination floating in his green eyes. It makes me wonder what they've talked about, and if he and the princess are telling the truth when she says she won't hurt me.

"No," Neith mumbles, and at first I think she's telling Lutyn not to do as he was told, but then I realize she's answering my question. "When they made the connection that it was your pain I was feeling, they figured out how to numb the link between us. I haven't felt you since then."

I scoff, the sound soaked in resentment. "Wouldn't want their *Moon* to suffer, would they?"

"If it makes you feel better, I'm suffering plenty now," she mutters back.

"Why is that?" I press, suddenly perplexed. "If you couldn't feel me before, how can you now?"

A small shudder moves through her as we wait for Lutyn to finish checking for any traps. Warmth trickles down my calf, and I can feel blood start to drip inside my boot.

"I don't know. Maybe it's because we're together? Like I said, no one has been able to explain how this connection works."

"The hallways are empty," Lutyn declares, and I eye him suspiciously for a beat.

"I'll slit her throat without a second thought if you're lying," I warn, and he winces, his eyes darting to the dagger as though he can *will* it from doing any damage.

An image of Verus using his thura to do exactly that flashes in my mind, and I tighten my grip on my blade. Neith shakes her head almost imperceptibly, and Lutyn relaxes. He should know I'm bluffing anyway. If what Neith says is true, I can't slit her throat even if I want to. It will only kill me to keep her alive, but I don't point that out.

"I'm telling you the truth, the way is clear," he assures me. He pushes his long blond hair over his shoulder as though it's a nervous habit. "They won't risk the Moon for anything. There are many loyal Igeeyin who will do exactly as you say as long as you don't hurt her."

Oddly, his words sound more like guidance than appeasement. I cant my head as I study him and then Neith. It's obvious they care about each other and that they're up to something, but I don't know what. Alarmed voices reach us from the floor below, and I realize that the booming cadence of the warning drums has stopped. Their echo still pounds in my skull, but I try to listen past that to the alarmed cries and the sound of bodies running around in preparation for an attack.

The corridor ends in a wide set of stairs to the left and the guards have already started to slowly back down them. Their eyes are intense and focused, but they don't hesitate to give me the space my blade against their princess's neck demands. These stairs aren't the ones Beva brought me up, and I realize I'm turned around, not that it matters. The guards probably think they're herding me somehow. Leading a desperate fae right where they want her. But I'm not trying to escape. I'm trying to make myself easier for the Scorpions to find.

The grand flight of steps descends to a large foyer. It's buzzing with activity and barked commands, but it all grinds to a halt when the fae below notice the retreating guards.

Gasps and shocked cries ring out when Neith and I come into view. Hushed orders are spit out, and a few armored fae go scampering off. I suspect it's to collect whoever is in charge here, because as much as they treasure their Moon and what Neith represents, she's obviously not the one in control here. She's a figurehead, a pawn in someone else's grab for the realms, and I'm dying to discover exactly who that is.

I vigilantly descend the stairs, angling Neith and myself until our backs are to the rail that butts up against a stone wall. I scan my surroundings, steadily watching for anyone who might try to sneak closer both from below and from the floor above. The collection of onlookers in the foyer starts to back up as the guards spill down to blend with them. I spot the perfect place to take a stand as Neith and I step closer to the ground.

No one tries to stop us. No one says a word. They watch with horror and tears in their eyes, gasps of confusion and shock peppering the night as they take us in. I don't know how many of them see past the threat to their princess and take in the similarities between us, but enough fae notice that an astounded murmur starts to move through the small crowd.

I stalk toward the spot that covers my back with a wall. I instruct Lutyn to extinguish the fairy light sconces behind me. He looks confused by the request, but he listens, not even trying to move against me when he has the opportunity and the advantage of being outside of my line of sight. When the sconces are dark, he stops and stands within arm's reach of Neith but not close enough to pose a threat to me.

Definitely up to something.

There's a silent communication that's happening between them, an ability born from spending a lot of time together and being close. The Scorpions used to do the same—I'm in on it now that I know them—but in the beginning, I could identify it was happening, but I had no idea what was being said. I have the same sense now as I watch Lutyn and Neith eye each other pointedly.

Several robed figures start to push their way through the crowd, and I take a deep fortifying breath, ignoring the way the wound in my abdomen throbs and the drops of blood that start to dapple the floor. My heart is surprisingly steady, even though my mind feels like a jumbled mess of fury, hurt, and outrage. I want to go home and nurse my wounds both inside and out and never think about the Igeeyin, or princesses, or the rightful heirs to any of the corrupt useless kingdoms again. I also want to raze this fucking village to the ground and bleed out everyone in it. I'm undecided on which option feels more pressing and vital.

"What is the meaning of this?" a honeyed voice commands as a robed figure pushes to the front, her dark gray eyes shrewd and her lips pursed with vexation.

I'd wager everything I have—as little as it may be—that this is Faline.

There's a flash of shock on her face that's there and gone as fast as a lightning strike when she takes in the scene. She masterfully schools her features and squares her shoulders as though that's enough to intimidate me. Her bright white hair is cropped close to her head, and several other robed figures take up position at her side but angled slightly back as though they don't want to impose on this female's authority.

I'm unimpressed.

"You want to rule the realms, and yet you can't deduce what's happening here." I tsk and shake my head with exaggerated disappointment. "Not a promising start."

The leader's eyes narrow ever so slightly before she once again blanks her reaction. Her heavy robe sparkles in the remaining fairy light that illuminates the foyer, and there is an intricate pattern of knotted lines that decorate the neck, sleeves, and hem of the garment. I thought the princess's dress was nice, but it's rags compared to what this female is draped in. It reminds me of Tilleo and how he flaunted his riches and power in subtle and not so subtle ways.

"We do not *wish* to rule the realms. They are the Moon's by right. We are simply helping *her* recover what was stolen. It is the dying wish of every Nalrora that's come before her," the female smoothly replies.

I chuckle, the sound hollow and jaded. "You don't actually think I'll believe that, do you?"

Neith presses back against me until she feels the sharp point of the bolt still embedded in my side. She stills, and I swallow down a hiss as she presses against my wound. It's almost as though subconsciously she's trying to get as far as she can from the robed leader.

"I don't much care what you believe or not. What do you want?" the leader clips in return.

"Your name, to start. Eventually your lifeless body at my feet, but I'm in no rush."

She laughs and looks pointedly around at the guards and gathered fae. "I'm Faline, First Crescent of the Moon and the Igeeyin ruler. I think you'll find you're outnumbered, Auset, and that we're more than up to the task of dealing with your little tantrum."

Shocked mumbles ripple through the crowd as my name leaves Faline's imperious mouth. She shifts slightly from one foot to the other, the subtle fidget the only indication that she feels the weight of the many eyes that bear down on her, questions blazing in their depths. I don't miss how Faline's calculating gaze shifts to how Neith is pressing her hands against her stomach.

The air behind me shifts. It's as though it thickens as the temperature of the shadows behind me grows cooler. The Igeeyin leader eyes me with scorn, but no one seems to notice what I've noticed. A slow smile stretches across my face, and I relax a little.

"Oh, did I forget to mention," I taunt as I feel my Scorpions step out from the shadows behind me. "I'm not alone."

The Scorpions spill from the dark depths like wraiths born from the shadows and dripping doom. They converge around me, comforting hands glancing across my back as they take up position at my side. Satisfaction surges through me when I see the Scorpions are shrouded in their skeletal glamour. Every inch of them is covered in armor and weapons. They look like wrath incarnate, and they're here for me. Their tender touches and their powerful presence wrap me up in strength and fortify me in all the ways I desperately need right now.

I've been scraped raw by brutal truths, eroded by the ache I feel in the depths of who I am. Instead of being made whole by the answers I've yearned for, I've been flayed by them. But now the Scorpions are here. And though their presence doesn't cleanse the anguish banding around me, it does remind me that I am more than these fucking Igeeyin ever thought I could be. I'm not a princess, but I'm sure as fuck not a decoy or a sacrifice either. I'm a survivor. A disciple of death. A purveyor of pain. I'm a Scorpion, the best of the fucking best, and it's time to show these moon-blessed bastards exactly what that means.

Faline's eyes go wide, and she starts to sputter objections about wards and how this is impossible. I survey the crowd of fae, taking in the robed leaders and guards dotted among them. Their fate is cradled in my hands, and I think it's fitting that I repay the *kindness* they've shown me all these years. I glower at Faline, uninterested in anything else she could say to me. It will all be justifications and excuses, and I've had enough of that shit to last a lifetime. I tilt my head and offer the First Crescent and ruler of the Igeeyin a menacing smile before I turn to the Scorpions and order...

"Kill them all."

58

ERRIFIED SCREAMS AND PANICKED SCREECH-ing ricochet off the stone walls as Igeeyin scramble to escape. The Scorpions don't question my command. They don't even send an inquisitive glance my way as they pull weapons from their body and fan out. Chaos explodes everywhere, and I move to join my mates in the mayhem, but Neith stops me.

"Auset, no!" she pleads, and a hot slice of pain cuts across my throat as she spins in my hold and presses a knife to my neck.

Looks like the princess has a few tricks up her sleeve after all.

Blood beads at the nick she just gave herself, and my

own throat throbs as though the injury is shared between us. I bark out a laugh, which seems to surprise her, and she watches me warily, clearly not expecting that reaction. I can't help it. We're standing here threatening to kill each other when we know we'd be hurting ourselves if we even tried.

Pain is the only thing that's kept me company all these years.

I'm certain I'd survive whatever happened if we went head-to-head, but I don't think Neith could say the same. If there wasn't the caveat that her lifeforce can feed off mine, I'd test my theory right now.

"There are good people here, Auset," she snaps at me, bringing my focus back to the foyer and the fight raging within. "You can't just slaughter them because you're pissed."

"Can't I?"

"How can you be such a monster?" she snarls. "What is wrong with you?"

I press my knife harder to her throat, ignoring the stinging twinge I feel at the front of my own. "Not a fucking thing, *princess*," I growl right back. "I'm exactly who all of you abandoned me to become."

"Fine!" she concedes as she throws her hands up with panicked exasperation. "But take it out on the ones who wronged you. Hunt them until their blood paints the entire village red. I'll help you, but there are innocent people here. Fae like you once were. They don't deserve what you're condemning them to, and you know it. Gut everyone who looks at you sideways, tear the culpable limb from bloody limb, but leave the rest alone!"

Her admonition swirls in my mind, the sound of metal on metal clanging through the foyer as the Igeeyin engage the Scorpions. I watch my mates move with lethal precision, cutting down every guard who tries to stop them. I marvel at the brutal beauty of it all while trying to sort through the need for pain and the call for vengeance that's singing in my blood. I weigh it against Neith's petition on behalf of the innocent.

She's right.

I hate it because all I want is for them to hurt and suffer the way I have for ages, but I'm not like the ones who've tried to ruin me. I don't sacrifice the innocent to slake my own gluttonous savagery. I am a monster, but I won't be *that* kind of monster.

I growl with frustration and narrow my gaze at Neith. "And how am I supposed to know who's guilty or innocent here?"

Relief washes over her at my question. She presses her hand against her chest, her gaze adamant. "I'll help you. I know."

"And why would I trust *you*?"

"Because they are my people, Auset, and whether you want to accept it or not, you are too."

I scowl as her declaration falls to the floor between us. "You're not even strong enough to lead them. You're letting yourself be played by powers more clever and conniving than you, and it's going to get all of *your* people killed. You might draw it out, thinking you're saving them, when really you're delaying the inevitable. But if you keep going like this, it *will* end on a bloody battlefield with the kings passing you around until you beg for them to kill you too."

"I know that," she yells at me. "I've been planning and waiting for the right time."

"There is no right time! Are you daft or just a coward?"

"Fuck you, Auset! You don't know anything about me! You want to know why you can trust me?" she snarls, the rage in her eyes now matching mine perfectly. "You want to see why you're safe with me? Because I could have done *this* the moment you walked through my door, but I didn't!"

Neith drops the knife in her hands as though it's useless and in the way. She lifts her arms, the crescendo of panicked yelps and scared screams rising with her movement. In a snap, as though every fae fighting in the room has been lassoed around their waist, an invisible force yanks them all back and slams them against the walls. I stare open-mouthed and aghast as my Scorpions are left standing in the middle of the room, their heads wheeling around as they try to make sense of what just happened. Blood drips from their blades as they spin and search until their black eyes fall on me and Neith.

"What the fuck?" Bones demands as he gestures with a sword to the Igeeyin who are all plastered to the walls and unable to move.

My startled stare bounces from the completely incapacitated fighters to Neith. "How...how are you doing that?" I ask, bewildered.

"It's why they wanted the Nalrora line destroyed," she whispers, her soft declaration tainted with loss. "Our thura allows us to control anything with a mere thought."

I blanch at that, unable to tear my eyes from the monster I now see lurking within the princess. With a simple thought, she pulled every one of their strings at the same time, like they were nothing more than marionettes and hers was the hand that would make them dance.

"Are you at all related to a Verus Hathwait?" I ask cautiously as I recall the way he moved a knife without touching it, just to shove it deep in his throat.

"The impel?" she asks, her tone light and curious as though she's not currently holding an entire room full of fae captive by their puppet strings. "I'm not an impel, Auset," she assures me, and I feel a warm trickle of relief fill me before she douses it in ice. "I'm infinitely stronger than an impel. They can only move objects. I can control anything and everything I want."

I'm tempted to rip her heart out, just to be sure she never tries to pull my strings simply because she wants to, but the fact that she left the Scorpions untouched, that she has that much control of her terrifying gift, it gives me pause.

"If you could do *that* this whole time, then why in the stars have you let these piss heads order you around and disrespect you? Beva should have had her neck snapped a long time ago with the way she spoke to you," I point out.

"Like I said, it took time for me to realize that everything going on here wasn't what I thought it was. They raised me." She motions toward the robed figures that are now plastered against the stone wall. "I swallowed down the rhetoric because that's all I was ever fed. When they wouldn't listen about you, even though you were one of them. When I saw the lengths that they would go to, and understood who they would sacrifice in the name of *The Cause*, I started to question everything. People I knew to be family suddenly looked like fanatics to me, but this was all I've ever known, and I had nowhere to go. I was safer here under the watch of some of the loyal Igeeyin than I was outside of our wards. I didn't know what to do."

With a flick of her wrist, the people pressed against the walls are split into two groups. I stare in awe at a power I don't understand, controlled by a princess who's wearing my face and pleading for my mercy. She could have fucked me up at any moment; the fact that she didn't doesn't make me trust her, but it does help me to see that just like me, she's been wronged in all of this too.

"They're the guilty," she announces, pointing to the group that's closest to us. "There are a few others I'll round up from the village, but that's it, Auset, I swear."

I look over at the condemned. Rage-filled stares meet my perusal, and their lips move as though they're screaming threats and expletives, but nothing spills from their enraged mouths. Their features are pinched as they try to access thura and weapons to fight back, but they can't lift a finger from the stone no matter how hard it looks like some of them are trying.

"So why now? Why fight today?" I press as the Scorpions move to surround me.

"Because I can't let you kill everyone," she answers simply. "And you're right, I haven't been strong enough to lead, but it doesn't mean I can't change that. I've been waiting for an opportunity, and I decided that you're it."

I realize suddenly that Neith is allowing me to continue to hold a dagger to her throat. In all the shock and astonishment, I didn't realize that I was still threatening her and she was content to pretend she couldn't snap me like a twig in less than a blink. I drop my hand and step back, hitting a large body behind me. I would normally revel in the welcome contact, but the strong body at my back just pushed the bolt deeper into my side.

Neith and I both hiss and fold over.

"What the fuck, Moonling?" Skull demands as he instantly drops to his knees to inspect the wound.

Bones already has his bleeding wrist held in front of my face, and Scorpius angles himself in front of me, his swords still drawn as though he'll more than happily deal with any threats that may come our way.

"What's wrong with your...twin?" he asks hesitantly as he eyes Neith like he can't decide if she's a bug that needs squashing or someone who might matter to me. "What did we miss?"

A ridiculous, slightly frantic, but mostly hysterical giggle works its way out of my mouth. I squeeze my eyes shut as I try to rein in my frenetic emotions.

"I want blood on my blades first. Then we can get this arrow out of me, find some moonlight, and I'll fill you in on everything."

"Fine, at least drink; it will help with the pain," Bones insists, and I latch onto his wrist immediately, not needing to be told twice.

"You're Sanguinna?" Neith asks as she watches, astonished.

"Who are you again?" Curio counters as he tries to block me and Bones from her view.

Relief washes over her face at the same time it warms through me. Our pain dulls to a more manageable degree, and I take one more pull from Bones's wrist before I kiss it gently and step away.

"Are you Sanguinna?" I ask Neith, watching warily as Lutyn moves to stand sentinel at her back.

"No. There are others in the village who are, but I'm not. It just made me wonder about the tether—maybe it's possible because of that part of you."

"Tether?" Bones demands with a snarl.

He tries to step around me as though he's decided that Neith *is* a bug that needs to be squished, and I press a hand to his chest to stop him. Lutyn tenses and reaches toward the sword at his hip. I roll my eyes at both of them. Neith still has this entire room of fae mashed against the walls, and there isn't anything anyone can do about it. *Why* Lutyn thinks she needs defending, and what Bones thinks he's going to do against that kind of thura, is laughable.

"Can you separate the leaders from the others?" I ask Neith. I'm pretty sure they're all the fae dressed in the fancy robes, but just in case one of them has a preference for more casual togs, I don't want to miss including them.

Five robed Igeeyin come flying from the group of *guilty* fae, and Neith arranges them in a circle so that they're standing shoulder to shoulder near us. I consider the other collection of condemned fae who are still clustered by the far wall and then focus on the Scorpions.

"You can kill them."

"Any preferences on how, my love?" Scorpius queries, his black eyes luring me in until I feel like I'm drowning in all kinds of dark and delicious things.

"Would you mind if I did it?" Neith asks.

"Seriously, who are you?" Curio questions again.

"You want to kill them?" I question her, surprised.

"I need to, but if you want them to suffer..."

I look over at them, some of them crying and pleading now that the leaders have been separated from them and they know there's no one to protect them from the Moon's wrath. Others continue to scream and threaten. Whatever Neith is doing to them though steals the sounds they should be making. I shrug and turn back to her.

"By all means," I offer.

I flinch at the sudden sound of necks breaking at once. The shocking crack reverberates around the room, and a shiver climbs up my spine as dozens of bodies fall into one large heap.

Neith looks resigned and resolute as she turns and gives the condemned her back. Silently she makes it clear to everyone else in the room who's watching, that the guilty are unworthy of any more attention or regard.

I bark out another shocked laugh, stunned by the powerful display.

And she called me *the monster.*

"Well done," I offer, impressed and suddenly thankful that she can't do that to me without fucking herself up too.

The Scorpions watch our exchange, questions scorching in their gazes, and I silently beg them to wait a little longer for the answers they've hunted just as hard as I have to find. With the group of guilty fae now dead, all that's left are the innocents that Neith fought to protect, and the condemned leaders of the Igeeyin, the Crescents, that she so kindly separated from all of the others. I walk around the circle of power-hungry Igeeyin. They're still stuck shoulder to shoulder and silently shouting things at me as I pass. I have no doubt that the Scorpions will have fun questioning them. I stop when I find Faline in the circle.

I study her face, take in the ire and condemnation blazing in her dark gray eyes. I think about everything Neith told me, about the greed and cruelty, about the Crescents' ruthlessness. I think of all the questions that still float in my mind about who my parents are, if they're alive, do I have a clan? I could ask Faline. I could demand every one of her secrets, cut them out of her if I was so inclined, but fuck her and fuck them. If *my people* are still alive, they can rot right alongside this cunt. I've found my family. I have my clan, and they wouldn't sell me out or hand me over for anything in this forsaken fucking world.

Faline's eyes snap from me to Neith, and she begins to silently snarl at her.

"What's that, Faline? I didn't hear you," Neith taunts, but then she must get curious about the poison spilling out of the First Crescent's mouth, because suddenly Faline's caustic voice rings out through the foyer.

"I should have killed you when I had the chance, you useless waste of power. How fucking dare you move against me. If Dorsin hadn't botched up the ransom your father was supposed to pay, you'd be a cold corpse already. You were given everything, and still you refused to give us *anything* in return. You were too spineless to take back what was stolen. Your ancestors would be ashamed. The only reason I kept you alive was because we needed the king's coin to reclaim the realms. You should be rotting in the ground!"

Spittle flies from Faline's mouth as her face contorts with rage. Her vicious glare snaps back to me.

"And so should you!" she shrieks like a deranged banshee.

Faline's voice cuts out just as suddenly as it started, and I turn to find Neith seething. Her expression matches mine perfectly. Cold rage hardens through me as I turn my attention back to Faline. When Neith explained how the Igeeyin leaders used me as a decoy, that there were fae out there hunting her, I figured that was the reason *I* was taken. I thought Dorsin must have somehow learned about the princess and taken me, the decoy, by mistake. What Faline just spewed disintegrated all of that, her words like pure acid eating away at the lies and exposing the truth.

"Botched the ransom or botched the kidnapping?" Neith demands of Faline, her tone flat and dangerous.

Faline flattens her lips as though she's refusing to say another word, but Neith must do something to her, because she suddenly looks as though she's been seized by agony. We watch her as silence spills out of her gaping mouth and tears start to spill down her cheeks.

"There's plenty more where that came from, so stop wasting my time," Neith orders her. "This Dorsin, did he botch the kidnapping or the ransom?"

Faline's eyes are filled with fiery fury, but she starts to speak and Neith turns her voice back on. "He thought he had the true Korven-Nalrora heir because I told him that he did. But I'm not stupid, I would never trust a leech like that with a powerful bargaining chip."

She winces as though she expects more pain to pour down her throat any moment, but when it doesn't happen, she grows more virulent.

"I needed to get rid of you, but I couldn't do that while the failsafe was still alive, and I knew I'd only get one chance at it, or the Igeeyin would figure it out and take my head," she snarls as her eyes drift to me and then back to Neith's. "The flesh dealer was supposed to ransom the little cunt to your father, he would never have known the difference. I even told Dorsin where he could find evidence to prove that the king had an heir. But something went wrong. He didn't get me the money we needed. He didn't slit her throat in front of your father like he was supposed to. Which meant I had to keep *you* alive."

Pieces flash together so fast that I can't focus on what they are, only the picture they create as they fit side by side. Dorsin was supposed to kill me, but not before he squeezed every coin he could out of King Korven. Faline was going to kill Neith as soon as I was dealt with, but something got in the way. She may not know what fucked up her plan, but I do.

I look over at the Scorpions, and I can see the same understanding dawning in their eyes.

They were what got in the way.

I thought it was all fate just fucking with us, but it was connected. It was all part of the same web, but we couldn't see the silken threads past the spiders that sat on them. The Order of Scorpions were hired to hunt Dorsin because he'd stolen documents from an Elix. Faline just said that she told him where to get *proof* that King Korven had a secret heir. He stole that proof from the Elix, probably took her apprentice too to cover his tracks. The Scorpions slit his throat for it and then returned the proof and the suspected perpetrator back to their rightful owner.

I'd laugh at the chains of fate that bind all of us together, but I feel too fucking hollow. The Scorpions abandoned me to my fate that night, but in a strange way, they also probably saved me. I take in Neith, who looks as though she's ready to raze the realms to the ground. I don't know if I want to help her or get out of her way.

"What are you going to do with her?" she asks, the unbridled fury and power in her voice causing the hair on the back of my neck to rise in warning.

I look from her to the First Crescent of the Igeeyin. Faline is once again screaming silently at us, but I don't care to hear another fucked-up word from her mouth. I know everything I care to know. If there are any secrets left, they can die with her. I let the greed and malevolence soaked in her gaze and dripping from her silently snarled words stoke my rage and call to the monster within.

I look back at Neith. "I'm going to make her suffer for all of it," I answer, menace and venom all that exists in me and in the vow.

I turn back to Faline, whose mouth is suddenly shut either by her choice or Neith's. Her glare is scathing and vitriolic. I offer her a cruel smile and step closer to her.

"Tilleo didn't like his blade slaves to have scars. Did you know that?" I ask Faline, even though I know she can't answer. "He liked our skin smooth and unmarked, liked that it made us look untried, untested, easier to underestimate. His healers were proficient," I explain as I reach for her robe, knife in hand, and start cutting it off. "I would be covered in scars if it weren't for the thura that mended me over and over and over again. Sometimes they'd heal me three or four times in one day, just to have to do it again because I was a particular favorite of the masters."

The luxurious fabric of Faline's robe falls to the ground to reveal an equally regal looking dress beneath. I start to slice through it too, the tearing sound oddly satisfying as the rich fabric becomes nothing more than scraps.

"Of course, you can't see proof of any of that now, but I remember."

I press closer to her until we're almost nose to nose.

"I remember every lash, every punch, every kick, every weapon that has ever pierced my skin. I know exactly where the marks should be, where they flayed me, ripped off my nails, sold me to be used, all because they could. You won't see any of that written across here," I tell her as I lift my arm and run my hand over its smooth surface. "But it was carved in here." I press my palm to my chest, just over my heart.

Her imperious gaze narrows, and I run the tip of my dagger across her jaw. She flinches at the sting of it. I laugh at her weakness and bend down slowly and painfully to search her robes for the iron dagger I know has to be there. I find it and Scorpius helps me stand. I smile at the First Crescent, the leader of the Igeeyin, the cunt who didn't care what happened to me, and then I show her the monster she helped create.

"I'm going to write my story in your fucking skin," I growl. "Let's see if you can survive what I endured. Ready?"

Her eyes grow wide with fear. She screams as I press the iron blade to her back, but the sound is lost to the powerful control of Neith's thura.

"Perfect," I viciously praise. "I screamed until no sound came out too. Now, let's start with how I woke up in a cage and learned that iron burns."

I DON'T THINK I HAVE FIRE THURA," I HUFF DISAPPOINT-edly as I try again to follow Tarek's meticulous instructions on how to produce a flame with my fingers.

His chest is pressed against my back, and his arms hold mine as he guides me through the familiar pattern of movement that I've been trying to perfect the entire time it's taken Curio and Riall to build the large pyre in front of us. I still can't make even the tiniest spark.

"We can keep working on it," he encourages as he nuzzles my neck.

I snort but press into his show of affection.

"I can admit defeat. As much as I'd like to be able to light things on fire at will, I don't think it's in my destiny."

"It's probably for the better; you're deadly enough as it is," Curio teases as he grabs a body from the pile that was brought up here and hefts it onto the platform of stacked logs and kindling.

I give up on my failed fire attempt and move to help pile bodies onto the pyre. The last of the guilty Igeeyin the Scorpions have been questioning bled out this morning, and it's time to clean up the mess and get as far away from this place as we can. Neith has been adamant that we're welcome to stay or visit whenever we'd like, but I'm certain the surviving Igeeyin will be happy to see our backs and hope to never lay eyes on our faces again.

I feel the same way.

Neith has made an effort to introduce me to several nice Igeeyin families, fae who weren't involved in what happened to me. They were eager to please their Moon and show me a different side of the people I come from. I tried to look past what I've been through, to bond with people who look like I do, and learn what I can about the history that shaped these people, but the connection isn't there. Maybe it was before I was taken, but the fae I am today was forged in the fighting pits of Tilleo's ludere, and none of these people, no matter how kind or welcoming they try to be, can understand who I am now because of that.

Even Neith, who experienced some of the pain I did while I was trapped as a blade slave, doesn't get it, but I wouldn't expect that she would. They helped her numb the pain, made it possible for her to escape the echo of what was being done to me. She was able to hold onto the softer parts of her soul because the nightmare was never hers, it was mine. I was the only one who had to learn how to survive it.

Curio grabs the feet of a male from the heap, I grab his hands, and together we carry the body and then swing it up on the ever-growing stack.

"I still can't believe we had the answers sitting right in our palms, but we were too focused on the hunt to see any of it," Riall grumps.

The Scorpions have been beating themselves up since Faline's confession when we finally put all the pieces of the puzzle together. I think they're waiting for me to blame them for all of this, but the person truly responsible is dead, and I can't find it in me to be mad at the Scorpions for something that was out of their control. I made peace with what happened between us before the First Crescent implicated herself in all of it, and I don't need to dredge anything back up. I won't give the cunt the power to fuck with my happiness now like she fucked with my life then.

"I still can't believe I did it to myself," I counter on a grumble as we walk back to the mound of bodies we've been adding to over the past few sun cycles.

"Your memory?" Tarek asks as he works alongside us.

"Yeah," I sigh. "I thought eventually we'd question one of them and they'd say the rest were liars, that someone *did* mess with my head when I was taken. Then every single one of them confirmed over and over again that I must have activated a failsafe."

I scoff and hear in my mind the words spoken over and over again from the mouths of doomed Igeeyin. *You would have done it to protect the princess. To guard the Igeeyin's secrets, which is why the contingency existed in the first place. You did exactly what you were trained to do!* I shake my head and resist the urge to kick one of the dead pricks responsible for this mess.

"Why the fuck would I shred my own mind?" I ask, knowing full well there isn't an answer that will satisfy me. "How could I have followed so blindly and been so weak?"

When I was first told that's what happened, I knew it was a lie. It had to be. It didn't sound like me at all. I would have fought. I would have found a way to protect myself. But whoever I was then died when I was taken, and try as I might, I don't understand much about who that girl must have been. Neith and Lutyn have spoken with me at length about the indoctrination they experienced, about how I would have been raised with it too. They explained that I could have easily believed that what was expected of me was an honor, that The Cause was worthy of such a sacrifice. But it still frustrates me beyond reason.

Could I really have been that daft? I just followed the orders of a bunch of zealots without question? It's fucking addled.

"You're probably not going to be able to reconcile the girl who did that with who you are now, Beasty. You're going to drive yourself mad trying to make sense of that. What's the point of being pissed at a ghost?"

I let loose a resigned exhale and nod. I know he's right, but I can't let it go yet.

"Any news on the blood-link front?" I ask, needing to change the subject.

Riall huffs out his own resigned sigh. "I've looked through every text the Igeeyin have, and pulled what I could from our own library, but I haven't found anything that would explain what they did or how. It has to be linked to the Sanguinna in you. I'm almost positive it's some kind of perversion of a Blood Bond and a uniquely powerful thura. However, even if we can figure out what thura is at play here, Sanguinna bonds are only broken through death."

"So we're tied together and that's that," I interject.

"I'll keep hunting for answers, but for now it's looking like that's the case," Riall agrees.

I shrug. "I don't loathe her. I suppose that should be somewhat comforting."

"I'll count that as progress," Neith declares as she walks up behind me, a cheeky twinkle in her silver gaze.

"There's an ebb and flow to it. I wouldn't get too excited," I snark, and her smile blooms.

"She's an acquired taste, there's no denying that," Lutyn agrees, and Neith slaps his stomach with an affronted gasp.

"Don't make me pull you apart limb from limb," she teases him, and this time *I* smile.

"You're such a monster," I purr at her, and she rolls her eyes.

"Anyone else coming?" Curio asks as the last of the bodies is thrown into place.

Neith shakes her head and glances mournfully down at her village. The fae that she fought for are reeling from everything that happened and everything they learned afterward. It's going to take time and a lot of work to fix what the corrupt few fucked up. She seems up for the task though. Better her than me. Although anything will be an improvement on Faline and her fanatics.

The sun is starting to set, and the hills beyond glow and preen under its warm watch. Pinks and purples streak the sky. There's a small line of red slashing through the colors in one place, like someone took a dagger to the blue and made it bleed. Tarek flicks his hand at the pyre, and a strong flame flies from his palm to the wood, catching with a powerful woosh. Flames quickly consume the guilty, and I spit on the blossoming pyre for good measure, cursing the dead as they're scorched to ash.

I walk away. Finally done with all of it. Those who deserved to suffer, did. I finally have the answers I've always wanted, and all that's left is to put it all behind me and never look back again. Neith follows me, and we both sit in companionable silence as we stare down at the village that's nestled between two towering hills below.

"What now?" I ask, unsure if the question is for her or for me.

She sighs, and in that moment I feel just as tired as she sounds.

"I don't know, stop hiding maybe. Try to right what wrongs I can."

I look over at her, a hollow laugh slipping out of my mouth. "You're going to cause trouble for me, aren't you?" I accuse with a cocked eyebrow, but there's no real bite in my tone. "That's quite audacious for someone who's wearing my face and tied to my life," I point out. "Still bound and determined to take on the kings after all this?"

Her smile is small, but the fire in her gaze is blazing. "Fuck the kings, they can rot for all I care. I don't want to rule, but I also don't want to stand by and watch fae suffer. I don't know where those two things collide or how they balance. I guess we'll find out."

Surprisingly, I understand exactly what she means. When I first left the ludere, I wanted to purge the realms of masters, suffering, the powerful preying on the weak. Then I realized just how pervasive and impossible something like that was. It felt hopeless and unobtainable, and then I hunted with Eacon for the first time. It was only one injustice satisfied, but one was something. It was infinitely better than nothing, and it got me thinking. Maybe all any of us can do is offer justice when we can. We can attempt to right the wrongs that fall into our path. Nothing more, nothing less.

"For what it's worth, I'm sorry for what was done to you, Auset. I wish I could reclaim what I really look like and who I am, and then give you back your face...and your life. I would if I could," Neith offers, her gaze fervent and genuine.

I nod solemnly as I look out over the rolling hills and the thick forest. "I'm keeping your name," I announce. "It doesn't make us even or anything; I just thought you should know since no one can remember what mine used to be."

"I think you've more than earned it," she agrees as a grin slowly spreads across her face. "Suits you better than it ever suited me anyway."

We're both quiet as we watch the sun dip lower in the sky.

"Can I count on you, if I need help or anything?" she asks simply.

I shrug. "It'll depend on what it is, and if I'm busy washing my hair or napping, you know, the important things."

"Naturally," she replies with a smooth chuckle. "Same," she proffers, and then she turns to me. "I suppose this is goodbye, Auset."

We stare at each other, faces so similar and yet so different. Two lives tied together against their will. Time will tell what's to come of that. Maybe it's for the better, or maybe it's just another fucked-up thing to happen that no one can do anything about.

"I hope the moon watches over you and you find everything you deserve in this life." Her voice cracks, but she quickly clears her throat and straightens her spine.

My eyes flit over to where the Scorpions are talking to Lutyn. I smile as I watch them for a moment, and then I look back at Neith.

"I already have," I admit, and her smile morphs from sad to radiant.

She wipes at a tear that slips down her cheek and nods approvingly. "I'm glad."

I grin back at her and then collect myself. "Toughen up, princess," I playfully chastise, and she huffs out a laugh and shakes her head at my antics. "I guess if you need anything, stab yourself or something," I tell her as I move toward the Scorpions. "That can be our signal," I call back over my shoulder.

"Or we could just send a missive," she suggests alternatively.

"Where would be the fun in that?"

"You're a monster," Neith teases with a laugh.

"Says the bigger monster," I goad, and then I step into Curio's open arms and burrow into his chest.

"Ready to go home?" he mumbles against the top of my head as he wraps me up in a strong embrace.

A warm glow fills me at the thought, and I hug Curio even tighter as my gaze finds Tarek and Riall. "Home sounds perfect."

59

S TUNNED, I READ THE NOTE AGAIN IN DISBELIEF.

Auset,

It's high time you had a room of your own. We made some adjustments to the furniture that was ordered for you. We hope you like it. Welcome to the family, Little Scorpion.

Love,

Eacon and Rink

I look up from the parchment and stare open-mouthed at the most beautiful room I've ever seen. A gargantuan four-poster bed takes up most of the space, and it's easily big enough to fit me and the Scorpions and probably half of a village. Gauzy delicate fabric curtains hang on each side of the bed, and I can picture how cozy it will be to close ourselves off from the world and get lost in the sheets and each other whenever we want.

A gorgeous giant star chart is hung on one wall, with a pretty vanity set beneath it. I skim my fingertips delicately over the combs and brushes that have been laid out for me. A wardrobe takes up the entirety of the opposite wall. When I open it, I find a place for my togs and rinds, but I squeal with excitement when I see that there's also a section for my armor and racks for my weapons.

A large hearth is nestled between two towering windows that look out on rocky cliffs and crashing waves. A couple of oversized chairs sit in front of the hearth, and I laugh when I realize they're the same style and color as the one Riall and I broke in his room. Thick colorful rugs overlap on the floor, and all my favorite colors of the sunset are splashed here and there across the stunning room. It's feminine and practical, warm and cozy. It's perfect in every possible way, and it's all mine.

I swallow the lump in my throat and blink away the stinging emotion in my eyes. After everything that's happened and everything I've learned over the past two months that we've been away, I didn't realize how badly I needed *this* until now. The room grows blurry as my eyes fill with tears. I don't know if I'm overwhelmed by the loving generosity or finally in a place where it's safe for me to break under the weight of everything I've been carrying, but it comes pouring out of me, and there's not a thing I can do to stop it.

I give in to the overwhelming feelings of grief and sorrow as strong arms wrap around me. I'm set in a lap as hands rub down my back, my hair, my arms. Soothing words are whispered to me as I finally let go of the pain and the hurt so that the love and support can begin to trickle in. I don't know how long I break for or how long it takes for the tears to stop and the cracks to slowly fill and harden.

Gentle hands begin to strip me out of my cloak and togs and undergarments. I'm lifted and carried into a gorgeous bathing chamber that's bright and beautiful. A tub, somehow bigger than the colossal one in Riall's washroom, is already filled with steaming water and two of my mates. Bubbles envelop me as I'm set carefully in the water. I look up at Tarek's gorgeous face, his ice-blue eyes filled with warmth and adoration as he begins to strip out of his clothes.

"A girl could get used to this," I tell them, my voice rough from all of the emotion that spilled out.

"A girl *should* get used to this," Tarek insists, and three fiendish grins are aimed my way as I move to the middle of the tub.

I watch hungrily as Tarek slips into the water with us, his delicious cock dipping beneath the steam and bubbles as Riall tilts my head back and starts to wet my hair. It's beyond easy to relax into their ministrations. Curio begins to wash my hair, and Tarek soaps up a cloth and slowly rubs it over every inch of my body. They touch and stroke until the last dregs of my distress and desolation disappear. The remaining holes in my soul are filled, and the broken parts of me that I thought would be forever shattered fuse together using all the love and acceptance they endlessly pour into me.

"Is it over?" I ask weakly.

"What?" Riall queries. "Our taking care of you? Or all the horrible shit you just went through?"

I snort out a laugh that sounds empty and sad. "The horrible shit," I answer.

"As *over* as anything that fucked up can be," Curio assures. He cups my face, his thumb rubbing comforting swipes across my cheek as I lean into his touch.

"I wish I could kill her every day for the rest of my life. It still wouldn't be enough, but maybe I could feel better about all of this somehow. She broke too fast."

I think about Eacon saying the same thing about the fae from the ship who killed Yaren. I should talk to her; she'd probably have some good advice about all of this.

"We can't bring her back for you, but we can find an endless number of deserving fae for you to kill every day if that helps," Tarek offers.

I look at him, expecting a cheeky twinkle in his eye, but I quickly realize that he's completely serious. His earnest offer warms me in all the places that feel cold and barren right now. I reach my hand out to him, and he threads his fingers with mine. He lifts my knuckles to his lips, kissing each of them like they're precious.

"It's hard," I admit, my voice cracking from the overpowering adoration I feel right now, and Riall pulls me into his lap and runs his big hand down my hair. "I think about how horrible and fucked up everything has been, how unfair it all was and what it's done to me. Then I look at you three and realize that there would have been no path to *you* if I hadn't gone through that. I just wish the pain of it all didn't still linger," I admit as I consider each of them.

They're so breathtakingly stunning and perfect for me in every way it's hard to fathom that they're mine, but they are.

"I don't know if the hurting or the grief ever really stops or if we just get better at living with it. In the end, I did find you, I found this, and it's more than I ever dared to hope for."

I gesture to all of us as tears well in my eyes. I embrace the vulnerability of bearing my soul, because I know it's safe with them, that it always will be no matter what.

"I'm just so fucking happy you found me. That you saw me, really saw *me*, and knew I needed you."

Curio leans forward and kisses away each tear that spills down my face. Tarek presses closer and tilts my chin until I'm staring into his snowflake-blue eyes.

"You might have needed us, Auset, but we needed you too."

"And we always will, Beasty," Riall adds. "You're not alone. The fucked-up shit is behind us."

"We've got you now. You've got us. Nothing will ever fuck with that or with you again. You hear me, Moonling? It's all love, laughter, and happiness from here on," Curio vows.

My chest is suddenly lighter, their truths and vows unlatching the heavy hurt that's been bound around me for too long. It slips away like a buoy that's lost its anchor and will soon be lost to the sea.

"Love, laughter, and happiness?" I question, my smile growing with each word.

"The trifecta," Curio doubles down.

"With some hunting and killing mixed in, of course," I tease darkly, and Riall growls his approval and drops his lips to my shoulder as his arms tighten around my waist.

Curio rolls his eyes and plants a quick kiss on my lips. "Obviously, that was the *happiness* part of the plan. Get with it, little moonbeam."

He moves to sit back, and I splash him as he does. He gives me a menacing look, and I grin even wider.

Tarek nips gently at my neck, and I feel it all the way down my body until it flutters and settles between my thighs. "We'll give you anything you need, love. You say the word and it's yours," he purrs in my ear.

"Anything?" I ask breathily.

I fidget against Riall and he adjusts how I'm sitting on him until his hard cock is pressed against the seam of my cheeks.

"Anything," Riall confirms, the vow a rumbling growl in my other ear.

"Good," I pant as I spread my legs and grind down against him.

I grab Tarek's hand, which is still holding mine, and press it against my breast.

"I need you, all of you," I demand with conviction as I stare into Curio's eyes.

Every part of me is thrumming with hunger and craving more than their gentle touches and warm adoration.

"I don't know if I heard you correctly. Would you mind repeating that?" Tarek teases, his lips skimming the edge of my jaw in a tantalizing taunt that makes me want to sit down on his dick immediately.

I whimper and goose bumps covetously climb up my arms in an effort to get closer to his sinfully delicious mouth. I turn to him.

"I need you to fuck me, claim me, make me yours."

I squeeze my thighs together desperate for friction... desperate for them.

"Mmmm, and where do you want us to fuck you, Moonling?" Curio groans as he moves closer. He dips his head, and my nipples grow even harder when he opens his mouth and sucks on my neck.

"Everywhere," I mewl, needing more but loving the way they play my body, plucking and strumming until every part of me is humming in perfect harmony.

"We're going to *need* you to be more specific, Beasty," Riall rumbles as he nuzzles my hair and grinds his thick dick against me.

"My pussy, my ass, my mouth. I need each of you filling me up, and if you don't hurry the fuck up—"

I don't get to finish my impatient warning. I'm thrown over Curio's shoulder as he climbs out of the tub. Tarek does his best to dry me off as they stride into my gorgeous room, and I'm tossed on my bed.

"Are we feeling impatient, my Blood?" Riall asks me as he prowls across the massive bed and claims my mouth.

His kiss is wild and savage, and I give him riotous and feral right back. Our tongues wind and tease, and I feel his fangs lengthen as he pulls away. I chase his lips, but he chuckles wickedly as he sucks a nipple deep into the warm heat of his mouth. Rough, callused hands rub up my inner thighs, and I run the tip of my tongue over the sharp point of my fangs as I look down just as Curio's fingers dip into my folds. Need blazes in his hickory gaze as he hums appreciatively.

"You're so wet for us, aren't you, Moonling?" he asks, his tone laced with desire. "Your pussy is dripping. Here, feel it."

Curio grabs my hand and slowly guides it down my body. Riall runs the tips of his fangs across my nipple, and I moan at the incredible sensations they're coaxing out of me. Curio wraps his large hand around mine and then dips both of our fingers through my wet lips and teases my entrance with both of our hands. He watches ravenously as he slowly presses my finger and his into my soaked cunt, working my pussy with both of our digits before he bends down and sucks our fingers clean.

"Fuck, you taste good."

I moan as he presses two of my fingers back inside of me, his guiding hand setting the pace for how I fuck myself. I moan and writhe as he forces me to go faster and faster, and then Tarek spreads my pussy with one hand and starts to circle my clit with the other.

"Watch, love," he orders silkily. "Watch us play with this cunt. Watch us get it ready to be fucked," he growls as he spreads me wide.

"Play with me harder, you all feel so fucking good." I encourage with a groan, and they chuckle darkly.

There's a decadent menace in the rumbling sound that makes me eager for play time to be over so they can bend me over their cocks and fuck me into oblivion. Curio adds his finger with mine, and I throw my head back as my orgasm starts to build. Tarek leans down and wraps his lips around my clit, sucking hard, and I come, writhing and screaming each of their names.

Curio and I both pull our fingers from my cunt as I ride out my release, and just as soon as I come down, Tarek replaces them with his. He dips into my soaked pussy and drags my desire back to my ass. Aftershocks of pleasure twitch through me as he starts to loosen me up before sinking a sopping finger into my ass.

"Are you ready for us," Riall whispers huskily as he drags his fangs across my shoulder.

I whimper and whine with need as Tarek sinks another finger deep inside of me.

"That's right, Auset, you need that, don't you," he grunts as he fingers my ass faster and firmer.

"Please," I beg. "Now, I need you now."

Tarek pulls his fingers from my body, and Riall lifts me off the bed and sets me on top of him.

"Give me that ass," he commands, and Curio presses my back into Riall's chest as he spreads my thighs wide.

Riall lines up and slowly his thick tip breaches the tight ring of my ass. I relax as he languidly works himself deeper. Tarek strokes himself as he watches Riall start to pump into me, loosening me up until he's working in and out smoothly. I moan my appreciation as he starts to fuck me the way I need. Deep and hard, his hips slapping against my cheeks as I bounce on his perfect fucking cock.

"More," I demand, reaching for both Curio and Tarek.

Curio climbs up my body and kisses me mindless, his deft fingers tweaking my breasts as Tarek moves between my thighs.

"Do you want me in your tight, wet, sweet little pussy, Auset?" Tarek demands, and I clench down so hard Riall groans.

"Our mate very much wants you to fuck that perfect pussy," Riall confirms, and he reaches around to my front and starts slowly stroking my clit.

"Are you feeling empty, my love? Need us to fill you up?"

"I *need* you in my fucking cunt, Tarek, please," I half beg, half order.

"Fuck, you're perfect," Curio purrs, and he watches as his brother starts to sink into me.

Riall goes still as Tarek presses in. He grabs my hips and sinks as deep as he can go, and I moan wantonly with approval.

"Wrap your lips around me, Moonling," Curio orders.

He fists himself in front of my face, desire weeping from his tip. I lean forward and lick it up, grabbing him at the base and feeding him into my mouth. I groan in ecstasy around Curio's cock as all of my Scorpions finally settle into my body. Another orgasm immediately starts to build as I dig my fingers into Curio's ass so that he's fucking my face the way I like. Both Tarek and Riall start to match his rhythm, and I'm lost to the hedonistic thrill of being fucked in every possible way. Each of them fills me, and they feel so good it drives me to the brink of madness as they fuck me right into another orgasm that sputters from my throat in staccato bursts as Curio fucks my mouth.

"I'm close," Riall announces, and his big hands squeeze my breasts as his lips find my shoulder.

Wicked anticipation lights me up as Curio calls out, "I'm trying to hold out, but, shit, it's too good. I'm fucking close."

"You take us all so perfectly, my Blood. You feel so fucking good," Riall hums against my shoulder.

His thrusts get wilder, and then his fangs punch deliciously into my shoulder as he fills my ass with his cum. He snarls his release as he drinks me down, each strong suck on my shoulder forcing me to clench around him and Tarek. He bites me again, and it has me fracturing into tiny pieces of pleasure that disperse in a flash and then snap back to my core in a fierce, overwhelming orgasm that rocks me to my soul.

Curio shouts and thrusts deep in my mouth, and I swallow his release as Tarek starts to fuck me harder and faster. Curio buries himself in my throat, and I hum with satisfaction as he stares down at me as though I'm worthy of worship. Slowly he starts to pull out of my mouth, and I lick him clean as he mumbles incoherent praise and then flops to his side. He's breathing hard, but he has that dreamy look in his hickory eyes that tells me he's sated and happy. He pushes sweaty strands of his long hair out of his face and watches Tarek piston into me. Riall pulls his lips from my shoulders and nips my earlobe, his fingers now tugging my nipples in perfect rhythm to Tarek's thrusts.

"We're yours, my Blood," he whispers in my ear as Tarek presses my knees back so he can take me at a deeper angle. I cry out as he hits a sweet spot inside of me, and pleasure rises inside of me like a temple built to honor and exalt them.

"Yes," I shout. "You're mine," I claim loudly, and just as Tarek buries himself as deep inside of me as he can, I scream, "And I'm yours," as another orgasm detonates through me, shattering me in all the best ways.

"Yes, you fucking are," Tarek agrees as he snarls his release and then collapses down on top of me and Riall.

I grunt from his weight, and Riall laughs, which makes the two cocks still inside of me vibrate with mirth. I moan at the flicker of pleasure it sends skating through my body and lie back against Riall's hard chest as I try to catch my breath. Both my mind and my body float in a pool of undiluted euphoria that I never want to climb out of.

"You're incredible. So fucking exquisite," Tarek huffs as he pulls out of me and rolls to the side not occupied by Curio's languid body.

Riall repositions me to the side and slips out of my ass. The telltale warmth of both his and Tarek's cum starting to drip out of me has me releasing a sated sigh. I relax into the pillowy bed and soak in the bliss. I gasp in surprise and look down when Curio's hand presses between my thighs. He starts rubbing his brothers' cum into me, the glint in his eyes dark and lecherous.

"Just keeping you ready, Moonling," he tells me, his tone dripping with delicious promise. "None of us are even close to being done with you."

"Good," I chirp happily. "Because I'm never going to be done with any of you."

I take in each of them, emotion swelling in my chest at how grateful I am that they fought for me. That they didn't give up when I tried to push them away, when I told them I'd never be theirs, that I wouldn't stay. They knew what I didn't, that I was their everything, and they were destined to be mine.

There are no more mysteries or secrets between us. No more walls or reservations. I know who I am now, and it's not because I discovered the truth about my past and how I got here. It's because three Scorpions looked right into my soul and loved everything they saw...and then they taught me to love it too.

We are the dealers of death that creep from the shadows.

We are the owners of each other's destinies.

We are the Order of Scorpions, and our reign begins now.

EPILOGUE

ILLEO," I WHISPER INTO THE MASTER'S EAR.

He twitches but doesn't wake. I smile up at the Scorpions as I press my scorpion tail dagger harder against his throat. For someone who trains assassins, he's not very vigilant. I scan the dark room and take in the opulence and riches. Being back here makes my skin crawl. Standing this close to Tilleo has all my instincts ringing in alarm, but I'm not a blade slave anymore, and I know the Scorpions won't let anything happen to me. I stare down at the master, his bedding nice enough to feed a poor fae family for months. I once coveted the luxury Tilleo filled the Scorpion's tent with when they came for the Bidding. Now, I just want to watch it all burn.

"Tilleo," I call louder, and this time his lids fly open and he sputters with confusion.

Carob-colored eyes meet mine, and I see fear and confusion pooling there until a hint of recognition trickles in.

"Auset?" he croaks, his voice rough with sleep and bewilderment. "What's the meaning of this?" he demands as he tries to sit up.

I relish the moment he realizes that sharp steel is pressed against his throat. Wild eyes snap from me to the Scorpions, and the flash of relief he feels at seeing my mates disappears when he takes in the seething looks aimed his way.

"Wh-what's happening?" he stammers, and the distinct smell of piss wafts through the room.

"We're having a Bidding," I announce gleefully, pulling the dagger from his neck and moving to stand with my Scorpions.

"I don't have blade slaves ready for another Bidding. You told me not to procure anymore," he argues, perplexed but growing annoyed.

"The Bidding isn't for any slaves, silly," I jeer with a saccharine smile. "It's for you."

He looks from me back to the Scorpions. "I'm your humble servant. I've served you faithfully," he challenges, his cheeks growing ruddy with anger.

"No, you served yourself faithfully and fucking lied to us," Scorpius snaps, and Tilleo flinches back from the venom in his tone.

"You violated the sanctum set in place to protect the Orders," Skull adds, his glare caustic.

"And you hurt our mate," Riall growls menacingly.

"Your mate?" Tilleo demands. "Who..."

His panicked gaze lands on me, and understanding dawns. His gaze narrows and his nostrils flare with anger.

"Don't you dare look at her like that," Tarek seethes, and goose bumps crawl up my arm from the cold warning in his tone.

Tilleo instantly drops his eyes and sputters several apologies. Riall hands me the togs we just collected from the barracks. I toss the deep blue silky fabric at Tilleo, followed by the chain belt that was designed to finish the look.

"Get dressed. We don't want to keep the others waiting," I chirp at him.

He doesn't look up at me, but his face crumples with appalled indignation. He pushes his limp hair from his face but doesn't reach for the dress or move to get up so that he can put it on like he's been told to do. I drop the sweetness from my tone and step forward, a malevolent gleam in my gaze.

"Put it on, or *I'll* put it on you, minus your cock and your sword hand, and I promise you're going to want to keep your sword hand for what's coming next."

His enraged stare once again bounces from me to the Scorpions, and he throws his blankets back and starts to dress. He grunts and growls as he pulls the ridiculous dress over his portly frame, turning back to us as though silently demanding if we're satisfied with his obvious humiliation.

Not even close.

"Don't forget the belt, *master*," I mock, gesturing at the metal coat of arms that will sit over his putrid cock to help keep the strips of fabric in place.

Tilleo clips it around him, his belly hanging over the delicate chain, and he crosses his arms over his chest.

"Now walk, you piece of shit," Tarek barks at him, and the master jumps with fright at the loud bellow.

Riall and Curio take turns kicking the tyrannical bastard through the corridors and down the stairs. By the time we step out of the manor into the dry desert heat, Tilleo has lost his hoity air. He looks around like a starved desert rat, hoping a scrap of salvation will be right around the corner, but all that's waiting for him is a strong dose of everything he's dished out to every blade slave who's passed in and out of the ludere doors.

"Is everyone out of the house?" I ask Tarek.

"I triple-checked, it's clear. Eacon already jumped them to the house we set up near her orphanage. Rink's girls are going to get them cleaned up and fed while we finish up here."

I nod and look back at the colossal manor house, trying not to think about all the unspeakable horrors that so many endured inside its walls. The ludere could fit inside this monstrosity a hundred times over. It was just another symbol of how powerful Tilleo was and how weak we were in comparison.

Well, fuck that.

I take a deep breath and, with one hand, execute the motion that I've been practicing every day. I open my palm at the end, hoping against hope that there will be a tiny flame glowing in the middle of it, but just like every other time, it's just my hand.

"Fuck," I snip, throwing my hands up in exasperation. "I swear you're getting off on my failure," I accuse Tarek, glaring at the smile he's doing a shit job of trying to hide.

"I would never," he defends, and my glare turns seething.

"I knew it! You are!" I point an accusatory finger at him and then shove him when he starts to laugh.

"You just look so fucking cute when you're trying to do it. I can't help myself. Your face gets all scrunched up, and you get an adorable little line here." He runs his finger between my eyebrows, and I playfully swat his hand away.

"There aren't any gestures, are there?" I demand with faux betrayal. "You totally made them up, didn't you?"

Tarek doesn't say anything, but he doesn't have to—his fiendish smile says it all. I shake my head, shock and amused outrage etched across my face. But the fucker's smile is so damn contagious I can't keep from catching one too. He pulls me to him and kisses me silly.

"You're going to pay for that," I warn against his lips.

"Looking forward to it," he taunts as he nips my bottom lip.

"Fine," I concede. "*You* burn it down then."

"With pleasure," he rumbles deliciously, and then without the fucking gesture I've been practicing for ages, he launches flames at Tilleo's manor until several catch and start to grow.

I give the palatial building my back and follow after Riall and Curio as they shove a stumbling Tilleo across the sands toward the ludere, which is nestled in the shadows of the tall wall that surrounds the stronghold. Familiar stars twinkle above me, the moon and her subjects granting me their favor as I walk beneath their gleaming gaze. The smell of sun-kissed sand beckons to me like an old friend, and

I take a moment to remember the faces of the slaves who never made it out of these walls.

I step onto the familiar stone of the ludere steps, taking it all in with new eyes. It's going to die tonight, and the realms will be better for it. Riall shoves Tilleo into the line of masters, healers, and guards we've already collected, each of them draped in the finery they forced the blade slaves to wear. Wilik eyes me contemptuously, her hair freshly shorn and the arm that's now missing a hand clutched firmly to her chest. I ignore the rage and fury aimed at me as I join Rink and Eacon on the stacked seats the masters lazed on while they bet against slaves or beat them out of boredom.

"Everything go okay with jumping the slaves out of here?" I ask Eacon, and she gives me a warm smile.

"Everything went smoothly. We can start trying to locate family or figuring out where they want to settle in a couple of days," she assures me, grabbing my hand and giving it a firm squeeze.

"Thank you, both of you, it means a lot," I offer.

Rink pulls me in for a quick hug. "Look atchya gettin' better with tha touchin' already," she coos at me. "An' no thanks be needed; thas what family's for, Little Scorpion."

My throat grows tight as she lets me go, her smile proud and beaming as I step away. I turn back to the pits and step on top of a riser. I wait until every healer, master and guard is glowering expectantly at me. I look each of them in the eye, cursing them silently as I go.

"Welcome to the last Bidding any of you will attend," I announce, spreading my arms out and gesturing with exaggerated pomp. "You will fight to the death. The last fae standing will be shown mercy. If you refuse to fight, my mates and I will *happily* show you the error of your ways. I have a new flail to break in."

Excitedly I pull the new weapon from my hip. The spiked ball drops, the chain attaching it to the handle pulling taut and making the vicious ball jerk around before it settles. I glance over at Curio and fix him with a wide, loving smile. He gifted it to me this morning, the perfect present for what we're here to do today. I'm giddy as shit to break it in. I turn back to the masters, guards, and healers, the smile on my face making them fidget with fear.

"So please, some of you refuse. I've never used one before, and it will probably take a couple of you to help me get the hang of it," I explain merrily. "You have one minute to pick your weapon and start after I say go," I order, the saccharine smile dropping away as vengeance and retribution take its place.

I take in the faces of the evil cunts who tried to break me, and those who stood by and let them. I drink down their fear and revel in their wrath as I look down on their weak, festering souls and ready myself to right the wrongs they've gouged into this world. Every single one of them will answer for their crimes, and then their dishonor will die with them when we burn this place to the ground.

"Go!" I shout, my voice ringing off the curved walls of the ludere, growing louder as though all the dead and scarred, who suffered at the hands of these cruel fae, are right here with me, demanding their penance.

I sit down next to Rink and Eacon, the Scorpions positioned around us protectively, and watch as justice finally claims what was always rightfully hers, one screaming splendid death at a time.

IVY ASHER is addicted to chai, swearing, and laughing a lot—but not in a creepy, laughing alone kind of way. She loves the snow, books, and her family of two humans, and three fur-babies. She has worlds and characters just floating around in her head, and she's lucky enough to be surrounded by amazing people who support that kind of crazy.

Join Ivy Asher's Reader Group and follow her on Instagram and TikTok for updates on your favorite series and upcoming releases!

WWW.IVYASHER.COM

@ivy.asher

@IvyAsherBooks

@ivy.asher